THE TRADING SOCIETY

SOCIETY

A Novel

By

Eric Martin

To my two families...

To the family closest to my heart, related by blood, bonded by hopes and dreams never shattered, always there with love and encouragement when I needed you.

To my 'family' of friends at Fleet Feet Sports in Chicago. You welcomed me back into the fold when I was at the lowest point of my life and allowed me once more to pursue my dreams.

Interlude

Never in the nineteen years of her young life had Samantha Grayson known the experience, or felt the chilling, desolate sensation, of being completely helpless.

Blessed of limitless self-confidence, the natural gift of graceful poise garnered for Samantha admission to the prestigious, and highly selective, Randall School of Journalism and Communications at Great Northern University, helped her earn a coveted reputation as the top reporter at *The Daily Northern*, the campus newspaper. Always in control of events swirling relentlessly about her, able to overcome any obstacle or navigate whatever tempestuous situation life placed squarely in the path towards a bright, shining future.

Now that unbridled confidence betrayed her. Samantha believed in her ability to handle the lead obtained earlier that afternoon; an anxious freshman seeking her assistance locating a roommate she'd last seen the previous afternoon in the dorm room they shared.

The innocent assumption proved horribly wrong.

Helpless...

The darkness of the cramped closet where Samantha lay on her side, broken only by a sliver of pale light seeping underneath the pencil-thin crack at the bottom of the door, smothered her in a suffocating grasp like the tentacles of an octopus. The bare wood floor, cold and hard against her body, induced a tremulous shiver as if suddenly caught outside in a biting winter wind, sent unending waves of goose bumps prickling the tender skin of her arms and legs.

Helpless...

The meager light enough to illuminate the horrifying magnitude of her peril. Samantha could barely move, bound excruciatingly tight with white cotton rope. Hands pulled behind her back, bonds cutting deep into her wrists producing a warm, numbing sensation deadening her fingers. An intricate network of rope wound about her torso, twisted around her limbs like the pressing coils of a python, bands of cord looped above and below her breasts, arms pinned uselessly to her sides, holding her slender form in an obscene lover's embrace. Samantha peered down; with shamed dismay saw her white silk blouse torn, folds of shimmering fabric pulled aside, revealing the black satin bra with a floral print worn underneath.

Helpless...

Her ankles tied, black skirt pushed up with more white rope, in stark contrast to the black microfiber tights sheathing her legs, cinched taut about her knees and thighs. A million aches vibrated ceaselessly through her body in a constant, steady thrum of pain. The stringent bondage secure and unyielding, every knot positioned out of reach of straining fingers, chances of escape reduced to the faintest of elusive hopes.

Helpless...

Samantha couldn't scream, not that it mattered, no one able to hear her plaintive cries. The cloth wadding jammed deep in her mouth, held firmly in place by a thick strip of soft white cotton knotted behind her head, fabric pulled cruelly back between her lips, muffled completely any sound she uttered, rendering useless her pleas for help. Samantha tried to suppress, but to no avail, the shiver of fear coursing through her with the crackling intensity of an electric current.

Helpless...

She heard footsteps approach her cramped cell, head lifting at the sound. Unsettling questions rattled around her mind like a handful of coins shaken in an empty glass jar. *What now? What is he going to do with me? How much time do I have left?* Each possible answer, along with violent visions accompanying every outcome, threatened to shatter into tiny shards a psyche already teetering on the edge of uncontrollable panic.

Tousled strands of auburn hair fell over brown eyes wide and moist with suffocating dread. *He can't let me go, not with what I know,* a rising tide of terror crept through her thoughts like the relentless march of vines crawling up a wall. *He has to do something with me. But what?* Samantha sobbed, chest aching with every ragged breath.

She understood exactly what her captor had to do.

Get rid of me.

Samantha struggled to rise from the floor, groaning with strenuous effort to heave her bound body into a kneeling position in the confined space, then slumping against the corner as the simple effort exhausted her stamina, drained her will. Wished she possessed a mystical gift, a sacred talisman, to turn back time, replay the day from the start and return to the safe, secure environs of the Great Northern campus, be with her cherished friends and the young man she loved with heart and soul. Wished she never chased the lead bringing her to this now uncertain fate.

The door opened and Samantha whined, blinked as bright light pierced her eyes with the sharpness of a dagger. The gauzy glow outlined the slim figure looming over her in the doorway; one Samantha only knew as a nameless captor now holding in his hands her precious life. "Are we having fun yet?" His tone deceptively soothing, yet oozed with cunning sarcasm. "It's only begun."

Samantha Grayson moaned in fearful protest, chest heaving as her breathing quickened, a fresh surge of adrenaline infused with fear injected in her veins by his terrifying presence, flowed through her body with the unleashed fury of a raging river. *What have I gotten myself into?* Worse still, she didn't fully comprehend the reason why she held captive, bound and gagged, locked in a closet, or the fate of the missing girl she set off in search of earlier that afternoon.

There was one more thing Samantha Grayson didn't know.

How am I going to get out of this?

Part One

Before...

Chapter 1

Samantha Elise Grayson was on deadline. As fingers deftly tapped out the words on her laptop she peeked at the clock in the newsroom of *The Daily Northern*, the student newspaper of Great Northern University. Had ten minutes to finish her latest assignment, an update on construction of the Tomlinson Lakeshore Student Residences scheduled to open at the start of the next scholastic year. The story wouldn't appear in the print edition or be up on the paper's website until the next day but the deadline in this instance self-imposed. Almost time for lunch and the rumble of hunger in her stomach a friendly reminder. She brushed away the auburn hair falling over her brown eyes, intent gaze shifting between her notepad and the computer screen where with each keystroke the story came to life. "Aaron, how many column inches do I have for this?"

"Fourteen inches. Six on page one, rest on page four." Aaron Dinehart, the News Editor of *The Daily Northern*, helpfully replied from his desk across the newsroom. "You've got nine minutes, Sam."

"I thought I was going to be rushed," Samantha purred; Aaron the only person on campus calling her Sam, to everyone else it was Samantha. She didn't mind, his easy North Carolina country-boy drawl made 'Sam' sound so sugary-sweet.

"So this project will be done on time?" Aaron watched her fingers dance nimbly across the keyboard. If Samantha had pursued music instead of journalism, she might've found acclaim as an accomplished concert pianist.

"For once." In the text Samantha inserted a quote from the Director of Student Housing. "The project manager says it should be completed two weeks ahead of schedule. That's more than enough time to be ready for students to move in next fall."

"On budget?"

"Ten million over," Samantha saw Aaron roll his eyes. "Total cost of two hundred thirty-five million." The alumni benefactor of the complex, already called Tomlinson Village by students, made his considerable fortune in computer software, his gift covering the entire cost of the project including inevitable construction overruns.

Aaron checked the clock again. "Eight minutes."

"Done!" The declaration triumphant as Samantha typed the final sentence, eyes scanning the text for obvious spelling or grammatical errors before wirelessly sending the document to the editing queue. "With seven minutes to spare."

"Not bad, fifty-three minutes exactly," Aaron complimented on how long it took Samantha to finish the story after arriving at the top of the hour. "Have a lunch date?" Aaron leaned his lanky six-foot-two frame back in the chair, hands behind his head. Now he had something to edit before his next class. Not that the article needed much tinkering, Samantha accurate as well as quick. Couldn't say the same for the latest batch, save for one, of wide-eyed freshman reporters, Aaron consuming several cans of Red Bull this evening editing well-meaning efforts.

"I think you know him." Samantha brightened, sliding her laptop into her brown nylon Timbuk2 messenger bag, slinging it across her body.

"He's a lucky guy," Aaron considered her lunchtime companion fortunate to have snared the attention of the lithe auburn-haired beauty. "Tell him I said howdy. Had a great game against Missouri. That was a hell of a pass to D'Artagnan Wellington in the end zone."

Samantha waved, heading towards the door. "I'll let him know." She made her way downstairs and walked through bustling Howell Student Commons, home for the offices of *The Daily Northern*, to emerge outside moments into the warm sunshine of a late summer day. She dropped the sunglasses perched atop her head down over her eyes, heading east towards Lakeside Dining Pavilion. Classes letting out before the noon hour, sidewalks transformed into a shifting microcosm of students and faculty heading to their next class, back to their dorms or, like Samantha, to lunch. The mass of humanity an army of ants marching to the next hill along the network of walkways through campus. Samantha kept alert threading her way through the milling crowds, some utilizing bikes, scooters and skateboards shaving a few minutes off their travels to the next destination. Even with classes in session for three weeks it wasn't difficult for Samantha to pick out the freshmen amidst the masses. Tended to travel in packs of familiar faces they knew from their dorms and classes, upperclassmen referred to them as 'newbie herds,' from place to place or had faces creased with confused puzzlement figuring where they were headed next. Samantha sympathized with them; a year earlier she was one of those overwhelmed freshmen, a country girl awed by her new surroundings and at times as hopelessly flustered.

She passed Main Green, the perfectly manicured expanse of Kentucky bluegrass in front of Cooper Main, the imposing Collegiate Gothic administration building constructed of Indiana limestone. In the middle of the green lawn stood Founder's Rock, a slab of granite rising seven feet into the air, resting on the spot eons prior to the school's founding, left behind by receding glaciers of the last Ice Age. Tradition, no one knew exactly when it started, dictated for student organizations, Greek houses, residential halls and varsity athletic teams to paint Founder's Rock as a sign of devotion to Great Northern. This week the women's soccer team, in advance of their Big Ten Conference opener against highly ranked Wisconsin, laid claim to the massive boulder. Samantha only guessing at the layers of paint coating Founder's Rock from decades of painting.

Both Main Green and Founder's Rock guarded by a monument to the founder of the university, Charles W. Cooper, a leading merchant and philanthropist of early Chicago who championed 'the foundation of a great northern university' on the shores of Lake Michigan and bestowing the school its unique name. His dream found a permanent home in Evanslawn north of Chicago, at the school's founding in 1850 a small rural hamlet, now a diverse and vibrant suburb bordering the Second City. The stern, bearded visage cast in bronze, one hand grasping the lapel of his coat, gazed forever impassively on the prestigious institution his tireless efforts brought to fruition and nurtured to greatness.

With a minute to spare Samantha reached Lakeside, waiting by the front door. From inside her shoulder bag she heard the melodic chime of her Apple iPhone, alerting her to a text message. She pulled out the smartphone, checked the screen. ***bhind u.*** As she read the sparse message, Samantha felt a soft, moist sensation brush the side of her neck. She closed her eyes, giggled happily as a tingling warmth raced through her body, a pair of strong arms wrapped gently around her waist. "Hello there," Samantha turned to look into the striking blue eyes of Tyler McManaway. All through high school at Canandaigua Academy back home in Upstate New York Samantha dreamed of going out with the starting quarterback of the football team. Her hopeful fantasy never happened then, that quarterback had a girlfriend, a cheerleader no less, and Samantha left to wait until college for the wistful daydream to become a pleasant reality.

"How was your morning?" Tyler kept his arms circled around her waist, despite his strength the embrace tender. If a movie director sought to cast for the role of a football hero he couldn't do any better than Tyler Ian McManaway, six-two with broad shoulders, narrow waist and taut, compact muscles Samantha felt whenever he held her close. His clear complexion, square jaw with cleft chin, crystal-clear sky blue eyes confident and self-assured and reddish blonde hair prompted her Mom-when Samantha first introduced Tyler to her parents during Homecoming Weekend the previous fall-to whisper in Samantha's ear he reminded her of a young Robert Redford. Samantha whispered back under her breath she thought Tyler resembled more of a young Brad Pitt.

"The usual," Samantha confessed, lifting her sunglasses. "Classes then off to the paper to finish the story on Tomlinson Village. And you?"

"Just as usual as yours, had the early morning conditioning session over at McIllhenny," Tyler conceded, early meant up at five in the morning to work out at the sparkling new multi-million dollar McIllhenny Family Athletic Training Center, "then off to class." Tyler not only athletically gifted but whip-smart intelligent, majoring in computer engineering and architecture, intrigued more in deciphering how the video game operated rather than completing the final level to vanquish the ultimate foe. "Hungry?"

"That's why I'm here." Samantha edged up on her toes, she stood eight inches shorter than Tyler, to kiss him. Tyler flashed a devastatingly dashing smile of perfect white teeth; Samantha wanting to melt in his arms right there like ice cream left out in the midday sun. "Aaron says hello, loved the touchdown throw you made to D'Artagnan."

"I aim to please," and on that play his accuracy unerring, "tell him I appreciate the compliment." Tyler led the Huskies of Great Northern to a 34-15 upset of sixteenth-ranked Missouri, the newest member of the Southeastern Conference following the latest round of musical-chair conference realignment, at Faurot Field in Columbia the previous Saturday. Great Northern, for decades the perennial doormat of the Big Ten and mockingly derided as "Not-So-Great Northern," found their football fortunes dramatically altered by a magical championship season and trip to the Rose Bowl almost two decades earlier. Now the Huskies no longer considered a joke, a competitive force in a Big Ten soon to count fourteen members in the conference's two divisions.

No other player in the Great Northern starting lineup competed under a more glaring spotlight of attention focused on them by devoted fans and the round-the-clock news cycle of national sports media than their starting quarterback. The top prep quarterback prospect in the nation while playing at powerhouse Wheaton Warrenville South in Chicago's western suburbs, sportswriters dubbed him 'Touchdown Tyler,' compared his football prowess to another famed son of Wheaton, the legendary Red Grange, as Tyler lead the Tigers to four consecutive state titles and in the process amassed volumes of passing records and a treasure trove of awards. Tyler the bona-fide five star blue-chip prospect every major college football program coveted, the once in a lifetime recruit high-profile teams craved to seal their national championship dreams, courted by coaches from across the nation during the lengthy recruiting process with a fervor bordering on the obsessive fanaticism of zealots seeking a Messiah to take them to the promised land. In the end, a choice made before a national television audience, Tyler decided to remain close to home and committed to Great Northern, becoming the keystone centerpiece of a stellar recruiting class an ESPN analyst christened 'The Best and The Brightest.'

"Let's see how good I am against North Carolina." The next opponent in the highly anticipated home opener at Warren Field following road victories against Bowling Green and Missouri to start the season, raising hopes for a Big Ten title and a possible berth in the Rose Bowl or the Bowl Championship Series. The Tar Heels slid into the number sixteen ranking vacated by Missouri in the Associated Press poll following their loss to the Huskies. Even with all his natural talent and skill Tyler possessed a quiet humility, a trait inherited from hard-working parents to keep his ego in check, grounded in the wake of fantastic success and blinding adulation. "We're probably keeping the others waiting," he motioned to the entrance.

"My hunger alarm went off a half-hour ago." Samantha reluctantly broke the embrace. Tyler took her hand, their fingers entwining, the reassuring touch again igniting a warm, satisfying tingling. As they entered Lakeside Samantha reflected on Aaron's comment about Tyler being the lucky guy.

Samantha smiled pleasantly. *Maybe I'm the lucky girl.*

If Tyler McManaway had known of Aaron Dinehart's opinion regarding his good fortune attracting the affections of Samantha Grayson, he would've agreed wholeheartedly with the sentiment. Some of his childhood friends questioned the choice of Great Northern over football factories far more glamorous lusting for his cannon arm and pinpoint accuracy. He gazed over at Samantha, looked into the sparkling, soft brown eyes highlighting the enchanting round face framed by flowing waves of brilliant auburn hair cascading over her shoulders and down her back. The body-hugging magenta cotton top and tight blue jeans accentuated the swell of her firm breasts and the curve of the slender hips. Samantha Grayson was a gorgeous young woman, but the beauty hardly superficial. Samantha maintained undeniable confidence in her writing talents, possessed an inner grace and passion for justice making journalism a natural choice for her future endeavors. Her stunning, gleaming smile and bright disposition a ray of sunshine breaking through a heavy overcast, dissipating whatever gloom Tyler experienced following a heart-breaking defeat or a frustrating day in the classroom. *Want to know why I chose Great Northern?* Tyler returned her welcoming smile with his own. *Here's your answer.* He couldn't have known the fact when he signed his Letter of Intent, committing his future fortunes to the school, back on National Signing Day.

They entered the foyer; a food service manager scanned their student IDs, the bar code on the back containing their meal plan information. "What are you hungry for?" Tyler asked as they walked into the serving pavilion a spacious, brightly lit area divided into stations offering a myriad of cuisines from around the world to satisfy any craving.

Samantha picked up a tray. "I think it's Italian today. I'm set on some veal marsala. You?"

Tyler checked his Samsung Android smartphone. "Have to see what 'Mom' wants me to eat." The football program employed a full-time nutritionist developing diet regimens for each player, insuring they took in the proper amount of calories and nutrients to fuel their bodies through the long, taxing season. The specific meal plan for the day sent via email to each individual player; hence the nickname for the nutritionist. Tyler scanned the recommended menu, expected a follow-up text reminding him finish everything on his plate. "See you outside?"

"I'll be there," Samantha said as they parted, meeting up minutes later. Samantha had her plate of veal marsala with a side dish of linguini and marinara sauce, salad with vinaigrette dressing and two large chocolate chip cookies for she possessed a notorious sweet tooth. Tyler's plate crammed with skinless free-range chicken breasts, steamed vegetables and a salad with fat free ranch dressing. On Samantha's tray rested a copy of the day's edition of *The Daily Northern,* distributed in the dining halls at lunchtime. Tyler knew one story on the front page always topped with the byline of Samantha Grayson, Senior Staff Reporter.

"Looks good," Tyler told Samantha, filling their glasses at the drink dispenser: ice tea for Samantha and orange Gatorade for Tyler.

"I'm a hungry girl." College journalism and fighting for truth built an appetite.

The pair entered the dining area, greeted by the hum of lively conversation and music playing over the sound system, walking past massive picture windows and the breath-taking panoramic view of Lake Michigan and the shoreline south of campus. The outline of the Chicago skyline far off in the distance shimmered in the gauzy haze of a late summer afternoon like the Emerald City in *The Wizard of Oz*. They wove a path between tables until reaching their usual spot, two other people-one male, one female- already sitting at the round table upon their arrival.

The young woman, her hand casually brushing long strands of glistening raven-black hair from her face, glanced at her watch. "You're only five minutes late," she informed matter-of-factly.

Samantha sat beside Amanda McKinnon, one of her roommates from their 'four-suite' in Falmouth Hall. "We took our time," Samantha smiled slyly at Tyler.

Amanda laughed, apple-pie cheeks dimpling, amethyst eyes gleaming brightly. "You're never the first ones here." Listening to Amanda speak one hard pressed to guess she hailed from north of the border, her hometown of Missassauga a suburb southwest of Toronto. She retained little of the familiar accent in casual conversation, only slipping into 'Canuck' when excited or agitated. An animated and fun-loving spirit, Amanda was among the top women distance runners in her home country. The thousands of miles and hundreds of hours dedicated to training as the star of the cross-country and track teams lent a sleek, defined tone to the supple muscles of her legs and a six-pack of firm, taut washboard abs Samantha secretly envied.

"We had a head-start," Connor Aanonsen, sitting beside Amanda, revealed, "got out of class ten minutes early." Both majored in archeology with Connor double majoring, at Great Northern referred to as 'Double-Dogging,' in history to pursue his interest in 'forensic military archeology,' an impressive term he coined to describe digging up old battlefield sites, though he didn't need worry about pursuing that career after graduation. Connor grew up in Eden Prairie outside of Minneapolis, a suburb whose name he joked more appropriate for an adult film star, spending frigid winters of youth on the frozen ponds and ice rinks of hockey-obsessed Minnesota honing his athletic craft, slated as the starting goalie on the varsity hockey team for the upcoming season. Although the Vancouver Canucks owned his draft rights, Connor a die-hard fan of his hometown Minnesota Wild, never without the cap adorned with the green and red logo, Samantha couldn't decide if it was supposed to be a wildcat or a bear, perched on his head. He tugged off the sweat-stained cap, ran a hand through the thick mane of golden-blonde hair, scratched the beard highlighting his hardy Nordic features.

"Thanks for telling them our secret, Goalie Boy," Amanda feigned sarcasm as Tyler sat down, traded a fist bump with his roommate from their 'four-suite' in McDonough Hall, Connor the 'oddball' of the suite-a varsity athlete but not a member of the football team.

"You're welcome," Connor replied as his blue eyes, pure and clear as the waters of one of Minnesota's ten-thousand lakes, flashed with mischief, kissing Amanda on the cheek to make amends.

They too a couple, Amanda as passionate about hockey as Connor, though all Canadians passionate about their national pastime.

Samantha studied Amanda's lunch of whole-wheat linguini covered in a marinara sauce of organic tomatoes and vegetables, Italian bread, arugula salad glazed with raspberry vinaigrette dressing and an enormous bowl of honeydew, cantaloupe and pineapple. "They do make you runners eat healthy," she observed.

Amanda pointed to the chocolate chip cookies on Samantha's tray. "Fight you to the death." She too had a weakness for chocolate.

Samantha shifted the temptation away. "Not a chance."

Another couple, a young black man and woman, approached the table. "How's it going, Doctor Jones?" D'Andre Watson, the third of the four occupants of the 'four-suite' in McDonough Hall, asked Connor as he sat down, gave him, then Tyler, a customary fist-bump. Given his major the nickname considered appropriate.

"Another day searching for the Lost Ark of the Covenant," Connor deadpanned. "But I've got a good lead on the Holy Grail."

"As long as it's not a Crystal Skull," D'Andre joked. "That's a sequel they never should've made."

The young woman, tall and statuesque with flawless mocha skin and long, flowing hair the shade of brown sugar, set her tray down next to Samantha, gave her roommate a warm hug. "Hey there, girlfriend," Ashleigh Morgan said, turned to deliver an embrace identical in warmth to Amanda. "And hello, girlfriend." A friendly soul, Ashleigh bestowed welcoming hugs to her closest friends whenever she greeted them. She sat down, lifted the copy of *The Daily Northern* from her tray. "Is there a day when you don't have a story on the front page?" Though blessed with the striking face and shapely, curvaceous body of a professional model coupled with the silky, melodious voice of a pop singer, neither career path appealed to Ashleigh Bernadette Morgan despite the fact her father a well-known record producer in Atlanta. She wished to follow example of her mother, a prominent corporate attorney, and negotiate the lucrative multi-million dollar contracts for those glamorous models and wealthy rappers. That didn't prevent Ashleigh from exercising her prodigious vocal talents every Sunday morning in Kendricks Chapel as a member of the university's gospel choir.

Samantha grinned. "Somebody has to write about the off-campus parties that got busted this weekend." Evanslawn might be a college town but, as the birthplace of the Women's Christian Temperance Union, still owned the reputation as a 'dry' town. The opposing forces of 'town and gown,' conservative sobriety and wild out-of-control partying, came into clockwork conflict every year outside the boundaries of Great Northern.

D'Andre removed a black iPad from his backpack, touched the screen. "Looked at the film from the North Carolina-Ole Miss game?" He asked Tyler. "Checked out their run defense?"

Tyler glanced at the video D'Andre brought up. "I'm more focused on that pass rush and the six sacks they had." Like D'Andre, he too had an iPad provided by the Great Northern football program as the days of playbooks in bulky three ring binders and game film on videotape faded into the not-so-distant past. Carl Hamilton, the team's head coach at times called 'The Professor' in the media for his innovative ways, embraced every new technology and training philosophy to gain an advantage on the field. Whether utilizing heart rate monitors during off-season conditioning to track each player's fitness while straining through a regimen of taxing and punishing Cross-Fit exercises or issuing iPads, the latest technological marvel, to each player in an effort to achieve success in the competitive world of college football. Every week each player's tablet uploaded with game film of their upcoming opponent along with the game plan for the contest. A few players did utilize the iPads for other pursuits, playing a game of Angry Birds or Words with Friends when not studying game film.

"That's because Ole Miss' offensive line is a set of turnstiles," D'Andre remarked. "I see a run defense that over-pursues. If the Rebs had a decent running attack, someone with the speed to cut back they might've kept it close. I'm going to have a good game this Saturday." D'Andre started at tailback for the Huskies, like Tyler a heavily recruited high school All-American from Huntington Beach, California who excelled at perennial prep powerhouse Mater Dei. Many considered D'Andre a signed, sealed and delivered recruit for a high-octane Pac-12 team, powerhouse offensive machines USC and Oregon battled to the wire for his services. Yet the prospect of starting as a freshman, instead of sitting a year or two on rosters already deep with upperclassmen, and the superior Lawson School of Business at Great Northern lured him away from the sunshine of the West Coast to the wide-open prairie of the Midwest. "I'll get a hundred against that defense."

"You're pretty confident," Connor observed.

"Have to be when you carry the mail twenty times a game." At an even six feet and two hundred pounds, upper body chiseled as if carved from marble by a magnificent Renaissance sculptor and legs charged with the energetic horsepower of a racecar engine, D'Andre able to power the ball between the tackles or break it outside, sprinting down the sidelines with lightning speed. "I want to be in the Top Twenty-Five next week, not slumming in the 'also receiving votes' crowd."

"What's our 'topic of discussion' for today?" Connor asked.

D'Andre waved his hand. "The whole gang isn't here yet." Over time the friends discovered conversation on the travails of classes and usual college gossip grew tiresome, D'Andre conceiving the idea of a daily topic to spice up their lunchtime discussion, deciding on a subject typically holding some pop culture relevance. A self-confessed comic book fan-boy, D'Andre able to channel his inner geek to explain the latest X-Men storyline with the same fervent attention to minute detail as he could the economic significance of the Laffer Curve. Politics and religion two topics he assiduously avoided, those subjects only produced intense argument rather than friendly debate.

A soft voice called out. "Sorry we're late," Lauryn Callahan apologized. "My anatomy professor," in this instance animal anatomy as Lauryn majored in veterinary sciences, "doesn't believe hungry students need to eat."

"I waited for her," Albert 'Fiji' Fatuamala added, walking alongside Lauryn, the pair couldn't be disparate in appearance. Callahan an Irish surname and Lauryn radiated every bit her Emerald Isle heritage-body slight and willowy, fair of skin with a hint of freckles on the pretty face, long hair of cinnamon and alluring emerald eyes. When speaking of Lauryn the word 'adorable' seemed a common theme. Fiji towered over the tiny redhead by a foot and a half, his chest and arms broad as the trunk of a California redwood and strong as tempered steel. His skin tanned a deep bronze from a youth spent under the blazing South Pacific sun and his hair, cropped close to his scalp, black as a chunk of Pennsylvania anthracite coal.

But in temperament the two meshed perfectly, their personalities synchronized. Samantha thought Lauryn the gentlest of souls; moments when she was shy and quiet, yet other times playful and joyous, kind and considerate to her friends and kinder still to creatures of the four-legged kind. Fiji, like Tyler and D'Andre, a starter on the football team and their roommate in McDonough Hall, a defensive end and lynchpin of the defense. His primary goal to find a way to the opposing team's quarterback by the most direct route in the shortest time and in the worse mood possible to inflict the maximum degree of chaos on the opponent's offensive designs. Yet Fiji held not a shred of malice towards his foes, assisting the ball carrier to their feet after planting them forcefully into the turf, offering a compliment as he helped them up. A philosophy major Fiji a man of few words as the reserved, stoic character nurtured an inner serenity and quiet spirituality at odds with the powerful, massive frame and the violent game at which he excelled. At times, when the friends were together, Fiji blended into the background until he made his presence known with a comment brief, yet utterly profound.

As the pair sat down, Ashleigh rising to hug Lauryn, those at the table had an identical thought. *When are you two going to get serious?* The two inseparable, studying and spending hours together yet when either pressed on the subject dodging the attraction between them apparent to everyone else, only admitting to being friends.

D'Andre shifted the iPad towards Fiji. "Take a look at this."

Fiji didn't bother looking. "They over-pursue on run defense." He received the peculiar moniker during the first week of training camp freshman year. An upperclassman insisted Albert from the island of Fiji when he'd been raised in American Samoa, the birthplace of many outstanding college and professional football players. The upperclassman's gaffe became such a joke everyone on the team started calling Albert 'Fiji' and the nickname stuck.

"How'd you know?" D'Andre amazed. "You're a defensive line guy."

Fiji shrugged the massive shoulders. "Saw it on the ESPN highlights Sunday morning. You should watch. You might learn something." Tyler and Connor suppressed amused laughter.

"We'll see who has the last laugh Saturday after I run for that hundred yards," D'Andre cautioned.

Ashleigh whispered to Amanda. "Boys will be boys."

"I heard that," D'Andre shot back.

"Everyone's here," Connor pointed out. "What's the topic?"

D'Andre looked at Ashleigh. "You ready to tweet?" Ashleigh nodded; their daily topic sent into cyberspace on Twitter with the hashtag #lunchtimetopic to other acquaintances, expanding the participants in the circle of conversation. "Who's the coolest Green Lantern: Hal Jordan, John Stewart, Kyle Raynor or Guy Gardner?"

Amanda snorted as Ashleigh tapped on her smartphone. "Fanboy topic."

"Last time we did who you want to be stranded with on a desert island," D'Andre said. "Found out more than we needed to about your fetish for Hugh Jackman."

"And how is that a bad thing?" Amanda batted not-so-innocent eyelashes.

D'Andre pointed his fork at Connor. "Aren't you worried about your girlfriend's secret sexual fantasies, Doctor Jones?"

"She puts up with my Carrie Underwood fantasies." Then Connor answered D'Andre's challenge. "Guy Gardner, he's the badass of the Green Lantern Corps. He'd be the enforcer on my hockey team. You?"

"John Stewart," D'Andre replied. "Always have to go with the brother. On the *Justice League* animated series when I was a kid he had a thing going with Hawkgirl, a superhero chick from another world with wings coming out of her back. Now that's cool, a brother getting a piece of that action."

"He gets my vote too," Ashleigh, as much a fan-girl as D'Andre a fan-boy, added watching replies roll in on her Twitter account. The pair planning to dress as Nick Fury and Storm from the X-Men for Falmouth Hall's Halloween formal. "But not because he's getting it on with an alien bird girl."

"Hal Jordan," Tyler said. "Always go with the classic."

"What about you, Fiji?" D'Andre said.

Fiji thought for a moment. "I agree with Tyler. It has to be Hal Jordan. He's the first and the best. Everyone else is an imitation, a variation on the same theme."

"I have a question." Samantha rested her elbows on the table, chin propped in her hand. "Why does Earth need four Green Lanterns? Wouldn't one suffice to handle marauding super-villains and invading alien hordes?"

"It's more than Earth, its Sector 2184, it's a whole bunch of planets they have to protect," D'Andre explained. "Besides, Earth is special. That's why Earth needs four Green Lanterns."

"Who most closely resembles Hugh Jackman?" Amanda piped up.

"I figured that's how you'd decide," D'Andre smirked. "I believe your choice is Kyle Raynor."

"He gets my vote," Amanda replied.

"Mine too," Lauryn chimed in, having no idea what anyone talking about.

"Hey gang," Ashleigh fixed her eyes on her smartphone. "Someone just confused John Stewart, Green Lantern with Jon Stewart, host of *The Daily Show*."

Tyler stopped his fork in mid-air, mouth open for his next bite. "Did anyone get the image of Jon Stewart in a skin-tight Green Lantern outfit?" Everyone nodded in agreement and started laughing.

Samantha smiled at the flow of conversation, drank the last of her ice tea. "Have to get a refill." She walked to the drink dispenser and refilled her glass, heading back to where her friends continued discussing the merits of each Green Lantern. Halfway to the table she spied a copy of the *Chicago Tribune* left by a previous diner, a headline in bold type caught her eye. '*As If They Vanished From the Face of the Earth.*' The secondary headline underneath in smaller type read: *A Year Later No Trace of Five Missing Women in California*. Underneath the headlines a row of photographs lined up of five smiling, vibrant, and still missing, young women. The faces stared silently at Samantha, lives forever frozen in time, a brief chill sweeping over her as the faces reminded Samantha of the cherished roommates back at the table, pursuing their dreams at Great Northern University, sharing hopes and aspirations as only the closest of friends able to do.

Samantha stopped, scanned the article. The five women, two of them roommates at UCLA, vanished over the span of a single weekend in the Los Angeles area. She remembered the news reports from California the previous year, at the time following the story in disjointed snippets as matters closer to her heart and new campus home occupied the first few frenetic weeks of freshman year, caused her head to spin like the carousel at an amusement park. Adjusting to a strenuous academic regimen, making acquaintances of those now considered intimate companions, breaking in as a rookie reporter at *The Daily Northern*, following a presidential campaign with a historical result and, most important of all, falling deeply in love with Tyler McManaway.

They still haven't found them? The story proved a tempting flame and Samantha, her journalistic interest piqued, the moth relentlessly attracted to the light. On impulse, she tucked the paper under her arm, couldn't fathom the compulsion for her actions. She returned to the table, tucked the paper into her shoulder bag on rejoining her friends. Perhaps there a connection to Great Northern University she might focus on, an angle to pursue, someone on campus who knew one of the missing women.

Maybe there was story here for Samantha Grayson to write.

Chapter 2

For Marcus Cowle everything in his life revolved around business and the singular matter of making money, obscene amounts of wealth other men with similar aspirations only imagined of acquiring in fanciful, hopeful daydreams.

His tireless work took him across America and to the far corners of the globe, wherever he travelled to ply his craft the results proved profitable. But his spectacular success and cunning acumen never profiled on the pages of *The Wall Street Journal* or featured on CNBC, not receiving a single boo-yah from money maven Jim Cramer, his visage never gracing the cover of *Business Week*. He lived a life not of notoriety but of anonymity, yet the lack of acclaim bothered him not at all; he preferred this state of affairs, wearing the invisible cloak of ambiguity. The glaring spotlight of fame proving more a detriment instead of an advantage given the high-stakes nature of the trade where he forged his fortune.

Now his latest venture, a proposal offered on a moment's notice from a valuable client, brought him to the remote southwest corner of New Mexico, an arid moonscape of rocks and scrub brush abutting the border with Mexico. The trip, in the black Ford Econoline cargo van parked beside him, from the nearest town of any size to the pre-determined point took two bone-rattling hours over worn, rutted trails more suitable for horses and cattle than a motorized vehicle, and that stretch only the final segment of a protracted journey from the original destination in Texas. The experience unpleasant for Cowle and Sterner, the trusted associate standing next to him, a towering, imposing giant of a man with the ferocious disposition of a rabid wolf hunting for prey. The sojourn lengthy, taxing body and spirit, yet Cowle assumed the trip didn't agree with the contents inside the van awaiting their new owner. Cowle willing to accept temporary aches and discomfort in return for the ample compensation of his services, his not a traditional profession with forty hour work week. Neither were the rewards.

Cowle thankful the sun finally slipping below the horizon, dusk settling over the arid, sparse desert landscape from the east, the unbearable dry heat of the afternoon reminded Cowle of a baking kiln. Upon arriving at the location two hours earlier, waiting under the blistering Southwest sun, Cowle kept the air conditioning running, maintaining for them and the product in the van a bare measure of comfort. The air cooling rapidly now, little moisture to hold the daytime heat, the setting sun painting the dusty ground in muted streaks of orange, red and purple.

He leaned against the van, glanced at Sterner holding night vision goggles up to his eyes, observing the terrain. Cowle checked his watch; not yet time for the rendezvous. The pair waited in silence, Sterner scanning the horizon to their south, vigilance never relaxing for a moment, as night encroached on the fading light of day. Standing next to the hulking Sterner, Marcus Cowle projected the aura of a mild-mannered milquetoast-slight of body with high cheekbones, pale gray eyes and close-cropped blond hair-the meek accountant or the ninety-eight pound weakling from the Charles Atlas ads of old who got sand kicked in his face by the Sterner-type bully. The lean physique proved deceptive; Cowle as dangerous as his more visibly forbidding companion.

Stars began glimmering in the darkness above until the sky filled with thousands of luminescent pinpoints. Cowle gazed into the darkening sky, understood this a moment for thoughts philosophical, to ponder his insignificant standing in the universe and the nature of God. *And it's all bullshit*, Cowle smiled wryly; had no time for such sanctimonious musings. His only concerns of the here and now, the impending business transaction further expanding his wealth.

The satellite phone stuffed in his jacket, this remote corner of the desert far removed from any reliable cell phone service, vibrated. He removed the device, glanced at the screen, smiled in expectation. "They're near," he informed Sterner.

"Right," his companion grunted, eyes glued to the goggles, vision trained to the south. A minute later, he pointed. "Over there."

Cowle checked his watch as three sets of headlights sliced through the night, powerful engines shattering the silence. "Right on time," reassured by his client the Border Patrol preoccupied elsewhere this evening, not in position to interfere with the exchange. Sterner eased the goggles from his eyes, slung the M4 carbine off his shoulder, in his meaty hands held the weapon at the ready.

A trio of black Hummer H3s screeched to a stop, surrounding the van, angry swirls of dust stirred up from the desert by the screeching tires. From each vehicle men dressed in black fatigues, identities hidden by balaclavas over their heads and toting an arsenal of automatic weaponry, exited with brisk military precision marking them as members of the Zetas, the most feared drug cartel in Mexico. Cowle nonplussed by the fearsome display, understood the caution exhibited by his valuable client.

From the Hummer nearest them, once the masked men formed a perimeter around the four vehicles, a man in his late forties with a trim, athletic build stepped from the front seat. Unlike his underlings a mask didn't conceal the man's darkly handsome features reminding Cowle of the fictional character Don Diego, armed only with a nine-millimeter automatic pistol strapped to his waist. He stepped forward, hand extended in friendship, a broad smile spreading across his face. "Marcus, my friend, it is good to see you!"

Cowle vigorously shook the hand offered in greeting, the man pulling him close, slapping him on the back. "It is good to see you, Commander Omega." The man, once a decorated colonel in the Mexican military, headed the fight against the drug cartels until discovering being a drug lord far more lucrative than his paltry government salary, switching sides when recalling an old maxim. *If you can't beat them, join them.*

Commander Omega released Cowle's hand. "How is business?"

Cowle grinned. "I've been busy, and busy is good. I can't complain. The economy hasn't hurt demand for my particular offerings."

"Nor has it affected demand for mine," both men laughed at their assessments while Sterner and Commander Omega's bodyguards stood silent as stone, each warily observing the other.

"I didn't think you'd go through the previous order so quickly." A shipment delivered six months earlier; Omega didn't have the reputation of being hard on his merchandise.

Omega shook his head. "This isn't for me. I'm still enjoying the product you provided last time. I'm not as...rough as some of your clients." Cowle knew Omega spoke of one profitable client. "This is for my son. It's his twenty-first birthday. I wish to present him with something special."

"Then let us proceed." Cowle motioned to Sterner, who stepped to the van, grasped the handle on the hatch, sliding back the door as Cowle retrieved a small, powerful LED flashlight from his jacket. As the door rumbled open Cowle shined the light into the cargo hold to reveal the contents locked within. The glaring light illuminated two female forms-both with long hair, one a brunette, the other a redhead-lying on a mattress inside the compartment. The pair barely moved as the intricate webbing of rope bound the pair fast, muffled whimpers the only sound passing through layers of silver duct tape wrapped around their heads, sealed cloth jammed inside their mouths. Eyes widened in terror, shuddering at the realization something horrible taking place and they were the objects at the center of that something horrible.

Omega turned to Cowle. "I only asked for one," he said matter-of-factly, motioning to the brunette with an beatific face and brown eyes now huge as silver dollars, wearing a skimpy white tank top and a pair of baby blue cotton panties, at the statement the girl squealing through her gag.

"Her roommate," Cowle pointed to the redhead with girl-next-door features, dressed in a red short-sleeve top and denim jeans torn at the knee, tears from azure-blue eyes trickling down her cheeks, "picked the wrong time to return from the library." Less than twenty-four hours earlier the pair students at Texas Tech University, sharing an off-campus apartment in Lubbock. If the redhead arrived at the apartment five minutes later, she wouldn't be sharing her friend's peril. Now their futures darkly clouded, descending into a never-ending nightmare neither able to imagine a day earlier. "Consider this a buy one, get one free deal."

Omega laughed at the jest. "I must compensate you for your troubles." He nodded to one of his men. The guard leaned into the Hummer behind Omega, pulled out a laptop computer he set on the hood of the vehicle. Omega opened the laptop, dragging his fingertip over the scanner to unlock the computer. Moments later the drug lord utilized a secure satellite uplink to transfer funds into several accounts in financial safe havens across the world-the Cayman Islands, Bahamas and Switzerland for this transaction-where the prodigious proceeds generated by Cowle's enterprise hidden from prying eyes.

Cowle peered over Omega's shoulder; smiled at the monetary amount of eight figures funneled into the selected accounts. *Not a bad haul for three days' work.* "You are far too generous, Commander." Cowle knew a portion of the substantial reward destined for his Patron, the man sharing in the success of the protégé he brought into the service of The Trading Society.

"Senor Cowle, I have no problem showing generosity to a man of your talents, especially one so adept at fulfilling a last-minute request," Omega replied.

"The customer's always right," Cowle offered the well-known mantra.

"I always take care of my friends," Omega completed the transaction, closed the computer, handing it to his underling who placed it back inside the Hummer.

"I think it's time for you to take possession of your new property," Cowle noted as the pair walked to the van. The two young women huddled close, quivering in hopeless fear at their approach. Omega leaned inside the hold, brushed his fingers across the cheek of the brunette. Kristi was her name, Cowle remembered, the redhead Meghan, though he no longer cared about either their names or their unsure fates, only product sold to his client for a handsome price. *Business is business,* and a profitable one at the moment.

Kristi, already surrendering to the inevitable and crying softly, squirmed to avoid Omega's touch but the bonds held her secure. "You caught my son's attention last spring when on spring break in Cabo San Lucas," Omega coolly informed the more endowed of the two captives, explained the reason for her abduction and of her luckless friend. He cupped her chin in his hand, turned her face towards him, staring into the brown eyes with the vicious cunning of a man capable of brutal violence who didn't lose sleep reflecting on his many sins. "Whatever my son desires, my son will have."

Omega stepped back, pivoting to face his armed cadre. With a wave of his wrist, he motioned at two guards closest him, then to the van and the captives inside. The guards understood the silent command, shouldering their M-16s, hurrying to comply. They reached within the van, grabbing for the helpless pair, roughly dragging them out into the cold night. The two girls struggled in their tight grasp, carried to the nearest Hummer, muffled screams erupting from behind the gags. The redhead Meghan losing control, realizing now all hope lost, body twisting wildly, bucking furiously against the hold of her captor, bound legs kicking wildly in the air.

"Good-bye ladies, it's been a pleasure making your acquaintance," Cowle couldn't resist the jibe, calling out as the bound and gagged duo callously shoved into the rear of the Hummer, the hatch slammed shut. The pleasure produced several million dollars for his coffers. "A shame it couldn't have been longer."

Omega chuckled, slapped Cowle on the back, pleased by the turn of events. "Where are you headed now, my friend?"

"I'm in the Midwest," Cowle cagily replied. "For the time being." Exactly how long depended on when he heard from his most treasured client, received his particular request for product.

Omega offered his hand as his men stepped into the Hummers. "May God go with you, keep you safe." Cowle didn't believe in The Almighty, only in his own talents and capabilities. Didn't care about his reward or punishment in the afterlife; he'd rather have the reward now and deal with the punishment later. "I will be in touch when I need new merchandise."

"You know how to reach me." Only a select few did, Cowle preferred this arrangement. "Tell your son to enjoy his presents. With my compliments."

"I will, my friend." Omega stepped into the Hummer containing his new possessions. The three Hummers drove off, within moments disappearing into the darkness, headed south back into Mexico.

Cowle waited a minute before pointing the flashlight to the northeast, clicking it off and on three times. In the distance an engine roared to life. Two minutes later a black Cadillac Escalade eased up beside the van and Lang, his second associate, shorter than Sterner yet with the diamond-hard body of a mixed martial artist and the lethal skills to match the taut, coiled-spring physique, exited the SUV. Like Sterner armed with an M-4 carbine, his weapon outfitted with a night scope, Lang observing the exchange concealed both by distance and darkness as an insurance policy. Although Commander Omega a valuable client, Cowle careful to take precautions of his own. *Just in case…*

"The transaction is complete," Cowle told his apprentices. From the van Sterner removed two duffel bags with their clothes and equipment, followed by a third duffel bag containing rope, cloth and tape; materials securing and silencing their prisoners, loading the bags into the Escalade. He left behind the backpack and cell phone Meghan had with her when returning to the apartment to interrupt, much to her terrible misfortune, her friend's kidnapping. Lang took two plastic gasoline containers from the Escalade, pouring the flammable contents inside the rear compartment, once the cans empty tossed those in the van. As Lang finished his work Sterner removed the license plates, the tags had magnetic backing, from the van to reveal the real license plates of the vehicle stolen from a construction company outside of Lubbock and used to transport their luckless victims to the rendezvous.

Cowle pulled out a pack of matches. He lit one match, touched it to the book igniting the remainder, created an impromptu torch. With an underhand twitch of the wrist Cowle pitched the burning matchbook into the van. The blazing matchbook and gasoline fumes interacted, in a blinding fireball flash and a hot, roaring WHOOSH the interior instantly consumed by a rush of flames. Cowle and his associates watched as the roiling inferno obliterated the evidence. "I'd like to stay for the marshmallow roast, but we do have a long trip ahead of us." The three slipped into the Escalade and drove off, back towards what passed for civilization in the wide-open spaces of New Mexico, leaving the van a lone burning beacon of reddish-orange light against the obsidian landscape.

Albuquerque to the north beckoned, at a small airport outside the city waited a private corporate jet for the next leg of their journey, compliments of the organization employing Cowle and his assistants, a necessary convenience considering the equipment in their possession. One couldn't pass through a TSA checkpoint with this gear and not expect a few pointed questions. Their temporary home and current base of operations the destination at the end of the long flight.

Cowle began to whistle a tune. *Sweet Home, Chicago...*

What's going on? The update status box on Samantha Grayson's Facebook page prompted.

Samantha pondered the request, preparing to post an answer for the world, or at least for her three hundred and sixty-one friends on the social networking site, to read when she heard the knock on the open door of her suite. "You hungry?" Allison Mayne, one of her friends from the 'four-suite' across the hall on the third floor of Falmouth Hall, asked. "You know Tuesday night is pizza night in three-eleven."

Going to have pizza with my friends across the hall, Samantha typed, hit the post icon, and the updated status appeared seconds later on her Facebook page beside her Timeline avatar; a picture of her and Tyler McManaway hugging each other on Warren Field following Great Northern's stunning upset of sixth-ranked Boise State the year before.

Allison peered about the 'four-suite,' so named for the layout accommodating four students in three rooms-two bedrooms connected to a central living room with a small kitchenette and breakfast bar. "You the only one here?"

"It's just me tonight," Samantha nodded. "Ashleigh and D'Andre went to a presentation for their marketing seminar. Amanda and Connor are at an archeology lecture at the Field Museum in Chicago. Lauryn and Fiji are studying at the Starbucks in Howell Commons. They'll probably stop by Philosopher's Grove after that."

Allison cocked her head; Samantha knew the question before she asked. "When will those two realize there's something between them? At least Lauryn isn't a figment of someone's imagination." Samantha didn't have a ready answer. "Where's Tyler?"

"He and some teammates are over at Warren Field, paying a visit to 'The Kennel.'" That the name for the tent city established outside the football stadium by adventurous students in the days prior to each home game; those populating the impromptu settlement guaranteed seats closest to the action in the student section, appropriately named 'The Dog Pound,' come kickoff Saturday afternoon.

"Natalie and I are making an appearance there tomorrow night with the rest of the squad. Put on a show for all the happy campers." Allison a varsity cheerleader, her petite body appeared as delicate as a flower, but belied the strength and flexibility of a top-flight gymnast able to withstand the rigors and immense risk of being propelled twenty feet into the air and performing a double twisting back flip in mid-flight, trusting her partner to catch her on the way down. "I wonder how the parents feel paying that sixty thousand dollar tuition while their kid camps out in a parking lot." The enchanting vision of attractiveness expected of a comely college cheerleader, Allison had an appealing beauty with dark blonde hair, sienna brown eyes and sparkling smile but as a criminal science major she exhibited a quiet cynicism and rapier sharp wit she wasn't afraid to unsheathe and brandish at the appropriate time on an unsuspecting opponent.

"Probably the same as the parents whose kids stay in their rooms all day playing Call of Duty or Farmville instead of going to class," Samantha shut down her laptop.

"Dad would kill me if that's how I spent my time," Allison admitted. Her father a no-nonsense retired Seattle police detective, the only parent in her life after her mother died from breast cancer when she was ten. The tragic loss tore a deep scar on her young soul, forced upon Allison an early maturity and made her the driving force on campus promoting awareness of the deadly disease, during the month of October the color pink always a part of her wardrobe.

"You want a bottle of wine?" Samantha asked.

Allison smiled. "Why do you think we're inviting you?" Back home in the picturesque Finger Lakes region of upstate New York, nestled on the western shoreline of Seneca Lake, her parents owned Grayson Farms Winery, one of many small estate wineries dotting the bucolic countryside. This meant Samantha-even though she wasn't yet of legal age-had access to a steady supply of wine from the family vineyards, insured an invitation to every social get-together on the third floor of Falmouth Hall. Even the hall director and the resident assistants stopped by for a bottle to share with that someone special.

"And I thought it was for my witty conversational skills," Samantha replied good-naturedly. "Dry or sweet?" She prompted Allison for her preference.

"You know I'd love that merlot." Allison possessed an affinity for dry wines. "But remember who my roommates are? They like the sweet stuff."

Samantha opened the refrigerator. "Symphony or Sonata?" The semi-sweet wines produced by Grayson Farms named after musical terms.

"Sonata is the red?" Allison asked.

Samantha cleared her throat. "Sonata is a semi-sweet red with mellow hints of berries and apricot. It's a perfect wine to pair with pasta or casual fare such as pizza. Symphony is a semi-sweet white with crisp tones of apple and honeydew for a satisfying finish. This refreshing wine is perfect for sipping on the deck during a summer afternoon or pairing with seafood or poultry."

Allison nodded, impressed. "Nicely done."

"Dad says once I'm legal I'll do wine tastings for guests." For now Samantha worked as a hostess at the café on the grounds of the winery over the summer or when home on break. "If journalism doesn't work out I'll have something to fall back on."

"Nice to know you'll have a job in this crappy economy," Allison agreed. "Since we're having pizza I think Sonata will do." Samantha removed a chilled bottle from the refrigerator. "Don't worry about glasses, we have those." Samantha opened the flatware drawer on the breakfast bar for her wine key to open the bottle, followed Allison across the hall.

"The liquid refreshment is here!" Natalie DiLaurenzo announced, setting her Kindle Fire tablet on the coffee table. A varsity cheerleader like her roommate Natalie's bright, effervescent and perpetually optimistic personality meshed perfectly with the responsibility of firing up the student body from the sidelines during athletic contests. The same height as Allison, except for chestnut-brown hair and bright turquoise eyes, many mistook them for sisters. "What did you bring?"

"Sonata," Samantha placed the bottle on the table beside three pizza boxes and two Styrofoam containers as Allison walked to the kitchenette.

"My favorite. A red goes well with pizza from DiLaurenzo's." Every Tuesday evening pizzas and boxes of appetizers from the DiLaurenzo's in downtown Evanslawn delivered without charge to the residents of three-eleven Falmouth Hall. Being the only child of the owners of the local restaurant chain had its distinct privileges; the original DiLaurenzo's located in Natalie's hometown of Homewood in the suburbs south of Chicago.

"Are we waiting for Selena to get back?" The question from Sara Chang, sitting on the couch next to Natalie. With shoulder-length black hair and dark expressive eyes, Samantha confident Sara's picture listed beside the entry for 'multitasking' in the dictionary. A pre-med major with a Dean's List GPA, Sara commuted between the Evanslawn campus and classes at Great Northern Medical Center in downtown Chicago. If that didn't occupy most of her waking hours Sara also a member of the women's golf team, played violin in the university orchestra and volunteered at a homeless shelter. Samantha wondered, with the many demands on her time, how much sleep, if any, Sara squeezed in at night.

"She sent me a text," Allison said, holding five wine glasses in her hands. "The bus just returned to campus and she's on her way. Said to start without her."

"Did they win?" Sara inquired. Selena Espinoza, their fourth roommate and a forward on the women's soccer team, had a match against Wisconsin, the preseason favorite for the Big Ten title, in Madison earlier that afternoon.

Allison set the glasses on the table, heading back to the kitchenette for plates. "They lost in overtime, three to two."

"She'll be bummed," Sara frowned.

"I'm sure a glass of wine and pizza will cheer her up," Natalie added as Samantha flipped out the miniature knife blade from the wine key, cutting away the foil from the neck of the bottle. She inserted the screw, called a worm, into the cork, began turning it clockwise. Once the screw inserted all the way, Samantha positioned the bottle opener on the other end along the lip of the bottle, using the leverage to ease the cork out from the bottle, the action completed in less than thirty seconds.

"You're handy with that," Sara remarked on Samantha's skill as she and Natalie opened the boxes of pizza and appetizers.

Samantha twisted the cork off the worm, closing the wine key. "You get plenty of practice when you grow up at a winery."

Allison set down five small blue porcelain plates. "Dig in before it gets cold." Samantha studied her choices-one pizza with cheese, one with pepperoni and the third with sausage and mushroom. Samantha chose two slices, one cheese and one pepperoni, before pouring wine into the glasses for her friends.

"Do you have a bottle of Sonata you could spare?" Natalie placed a slice of pepperoni pizza and two mozzarella sticks on her plate.

"Sure. Mom and Dad will be out for Parent's Weekend in a few weeks, they'll replenish my supply then," Samantha answered. "Have a date coming up?"

"Perhaps," was her coy answer. "Actually I've been raving to Dad how fantastic the wine is. He wants to try a bottle. He might serve it in our restaurants."

"Maybe you'll get a sales commission," Allison pointed out.

"That'd be nice," Samantha acknowledged, though she never worried about having money to cover expenses. "I'll get you a bottle after our study break."

"I love the art on the labels," Natalie added. "I think they're cute." Each label featured a different depiction of a greyhound by local artists in the Finger Lakes. Samantha's mother a vocal advocate of rescuing greyhounds following their racing days and six retired hounds-lean of body, regal of bearing, fleet of foot and gentle of heart-found their 'forever homes' at Grayson Farms. The hounds demonstrated a talent at stealing the attention of visitors to the winery, leaning against their legs waiting for a scratch or dozing in the afternoon sunlight on the floor of the tasting room.

Samantha frowned. "I miss my hounds." Especially the greyhound she considered her own, an inquisitive and friendly four-year old female named Stormy, a small, beautiful girl with a luminescent black coat broken by a heart-shaped patch of white on her breast. Natalie about to bite into her pizza when her iPhone chimed the Great Northern fight song, putting down the plate to check the screen.

"Who is it?" Sara bit into her slice of pizza.

"Bryce," Natalie answered with a glowing smile, bolting from the couch and scurrying into the bedroom she shared with Allison for privacy. Samantha heard Natalie seeing a junior named Bryce Fielding, his father a Great Northern alumnus and United States Senator from Colorado with aspirations for the highest office in the land. Samantha glanced at Allison, noticed the surreptitious roll of the eyes as her friend slipped away to take the call. Sensed something about Natalie's new beau didn't sit well with Allison, as the daughter of a police detective a good judge of character. The reporter's instincts in Samantha dying to know what troubled Allison, but this wasn't the time or place to pry with Natalie in the next room.

"Hey gang," the weary voice of Selena Espinoza called out. Still wearing her blue and white Nike warm-up suit, she dropped the duffel bag emblazoned with the giant swoosh logo to the floor, slumped down on the couch next to Sara. She ran her hands through long obsidian hair, brown eyes brimming with disappointment, and sighed.

"Bad day at the office?" Allison offered in sympathy.

"You know what the worst sound in soccer is?" Selena raised her hands, held them six inches apart. "Clank. I missed the winning goal in overtime by that much."

"That hurts," Samantha agreed.

"Here's your comfort food." Allison placed a slice of sausage and mushroom pizza, Selena's favorite, on a plate, handing it to her despondent friend, then gave her a glass of wine. "Drown your sorrows. I don't think your coach will mind."

"Sonata?" Selena glanced at Samantha, who nodded. "This will drown them real good." Her coach wouldn't mind, not that he'd even know in the first place. She took a sip, closed her eyes, smiled. "Where's Natalie?"

Allison pointed to the bedroom. "Bryce." Selena raised her eyebrows; Samantha suspected the friends shared identical sentiments regarding one Bryce Fielding.

Natalie stepped out of the bedroom. "Okay, I'm back," she sat down, said to Selena. "Sorry about the game."

Selena raised her glass. "Already over it, bring on Michigan State." Off the soccer pitch, where the focus centered on her sport and nothing else, Selena a fun-loving California girl and adventuresome free spirit, enjoyed surfing the blue waters of the Pacific Ocean when back home in Long Beach.

"That's the spirit," Allison encouraged, lifting her glass. "To best friends and good times." Five wine glasses clinked together.

Samantha thought of something, looked at Selena. "Can I ask you a question?"

"Can I answer with a 'no comment'?" Selena sipped her wine. "Or should I drink some more wine before I say anything?" She kidded. "What is it?"

"Last year about this time, in Los Angeles, do you remember five women who went missing?"

"That's a pleasant topic for conversation," Allison deadpanned with a straight face.

"I was here when all that happened, busy with soccer and classes," Selena recalled, "but my parents called me every night reminding me to be careful."

"Even though that was down in LA I got the same phone calls from my parents," Sara, who came from San Francisco, added. "They were pretty freaked out."

"My parents really got over-protective when I went home for Thanksgiving break," Selena continued. "Actually, they were paranoid. It was still in the news. I couldn't go anywhere without calling or texting them every thirty minutes to let them know I was okay. I understood why they were worried. They both grew up in the late seventies when the Hillside Stranglers were around." The mention of the notorious serial killers fired an unsettling shiver down her spine. "Guess those girls going missing brought back bad memories, wanted me to be safe."

"Must've done wonders for your social life," Allison remarked.

"You think?" Selena's reply brought laughter from her friends.

"Did the police have any ideas what happened?" Samantha probed further.

Selena thought for a moment. "There were rumors someone was copying the Hillside Strangler. But they never found any bodies. A few of my friends told me rumors Mexican drug cartels were crossing the border to kidnap women." Selena shuddered, didn't ponder why the drug gangs wished to snatch five young women, an unsavory image swiftly shoved to the far corners of her mind.

"Was there any connection between them?" Samantha pressed.

"Other than the fact they were all young, attractive and disappeared within days of each other." Then Selena remembered. "There were reports they might've met with a casting director for a proposed TV reality series."

"Was he a suspect?"

"He might have been," Selena said, "if he hadn't vanished around the same time as those women. I think his home burned down or something, I can't remember."

"Why the morbid interest?" Natalie bit into her pizza. "We could talk about other things."

"Like when Fiji and Lauryn will admit they're a couple," Allison added.

"Sorry," Samantha felt selfish forcing the macabre subject on her friends, drank some wine. "Saw an article about it in the *Chicago Tribune*. Might be a story, use it as a cautionary piece to those freshmen of the dangers being away from home for the first time."

"Like the freshmen with their fake IDs getting into the clubs down in Chicago?" Natalie sipped from her glass.

Allison snorted; shot her friend a scolding glance. "Like you're the one who should be talking?"

"Who? Me? A fake ID?" Natalie's beautiful face feigned innocence. "Besides I'm a sophomore. Just don't tell my parents."

"If you get busted you won't have to worry about me telling your parents," Allison warned.

Samantha interrupted the exchange. "Made me think if anything like that happened to Amanda, Lauryn or Ashleigh, or if any of us vanished without a trace. Here one day, gone the next, no one knowing what happened. I know I'd be an emotional wreck." The thought, momentary and fleeting, sobering for those gathered. "Sorry if I'm bringing you down, I didn't mean too," Samantha apologized after a moment of silent reflection.

"No need to say you're sorry," Allison lifted her glass again. "And let's hope that never happens to any of us." Five glasses clinked together once more in agreement.

Chapter 3

There were times, between assignments involving the capture and sale of young women to those awash in wealth and intoxicated by their omnipotent supremacy over others less powerful, when Marcus Cowle agreed wholeheartedly with a lyric penned by Tom Petty. The waiting was the hardest part. Didn't know the wait for his next, and most lucrative, consignment wouldn't be long in coming.

Cowle and his associates returned to Chicago after a comfortable overnight flight from New Mexico following the successful delivery to Commander Omega, earning a well-earned rest on the luxurious corporate jet provided through a non-existent shell company created to serve the particular purposes of The Trading Society. The private hanger at DuPage County Airport, far removed from Chicago in the western suburbs, let the trio unload their equipment undisturbed by curious eyes. From there they drove an hour east on North Avenue into the heart of Chicago where they resumed a charade of normalcy until the next order placed and their unique skills utilized to the benefit of their bank accounts and the detriment of those unfortunate ones selected as targets.

Wherever Marcus Cowle established his base of operation he was never Marcus Cowle. Here in Chicago his identity that of Marcus Evans, a professional photographer with sterling resume of work for publications of the highest eminence, an identity appropriated from one in no position to prevent the deception. In the year since his arrival in Chicago after years 'overseas' he quickly established a thriving photography studio located in the first-floor of a brownstone three-flat in the up and coming Logan Square neighborhood. To the community he was another in the vanguard of urban pioneers taking a chance on an area once down on its luck, sailing into uncharted waters, spurring the initial wave of gentrification and higher property values eventually shoving aside the current blue-collar residents possessing neither the capital nor political connections to hold back the tide. Cowle accustomed to such masquerades, deep in his soul a chameleon, a confidence man effortlessly absorbing each new identity- a television-casting director, music producer, event promoter or college professor-as one puts on a fresh set of clothes at the start of a new day. The sublime talent provided him easy access to the product, women young and attractive, his moneyed clientele preferred, blending seamlessly into the surroundings to ease any doubts from his prospective targets, a necessity given his work in the shadowy world of human trafficking. His current turn as a professional photographer with a globetrotting past, not an anonymous 'man with a camera,' no different. In his line of work one couldn't put a sign declaring 'White Slaver' over the front door or hand out business cards reading 'Human Trafficker.'

Marcus Evans Photography, with huge poster-board portraits of happy families and smiling toddlers prominently displayed in the bay windows, occupied the first floor converted storefront, once a grocery store serving the working-class neighborhood up through the sixties. But this business, a front for his true intentions, but a portion of his current 'profession.' Cowle, with the resume of 'Marcus Evans' in hand, finagled a position with a prominent local social website chronicling the vibrant nightlife of the Chicago club scene, snapping pictures of the young, fashionable and beautiful participants partaking in the after-hours milieu. Insinuating himself on prime hunting ground for his prey, the fox allowed unlimited access through the front door of the hen house to select his plunder. As a fixture on the scene Cowle flaunted his suitable bona-fide to potential victims. When the time came, and his lucrative client deciding the time ripe for another consignment, Cowle employing his position to lull the defenses of the chosen targets, weave a web of deceit and lure them into a trap from which there lay no avenue of escape.

On the second floor of the three-flat Cowle kept his apartment, the third floor home for his apprentices, Sterner and Lang. When not lounging about in the rooms where they stored a cache of automatic weapons and surveillance equipment, the pair spent their nights working as bouncers at the local nightclubs, employment suiting perfectly their imposing frames and aggressive personalities. The 'day jobs,' as they jokingly referred to their work, in turn assisted Cowle in his efforts; the pair evaluating the 'talent' frequenting the hottest nightspots, passing information to their employer. With this resource and his own legwork, Cowle compiled a lengthy list of prospective targets from which to cull the appropriate product once he received the order from his valued client. When the time came to procure the consignment Cowle and his associates accomplishing the task with swift, brutal efficiency snatching and delivering the product-women young, beautiful and, once in their grasp, totally helpless-before anyone had a hint of what was occurring. Once their work completed the trio pulling up stakes, obliterating their history in the city and after a deserved vacation to savor their wealth, moving to a new city with fertile hunting grounds, creating immaculate new identities to again commence the process. A single phone call all Cowle required to set the operation in motion.

The call arrived the very afternoon of their return from New Mexico.

Cowle had barely set down his duffel bag when his smartphone vibrated, recognized the overseas number on the screen, sensed his heart rate increase slightly on answering, the weariness from the trip dissipating instantly, excitement percolating within his veins. *The hunt begins anew.* "Sheik Rahim, it is good to hear from you," he answered simply.

"Marcus, my friend, I hope you are well." The voice on the phone, speaking from the other side of the world, clipped and precise with a hint of an English accent the mark of fine education and impeccable tastes. That his appetites cost young women their freedom, and eventually their lives, didn't bother Cowle. His only concern the money received for providing his client with these living, breathing sexual toys.

"I am doing well," Cowle replied, "I can't complain how life is treating me." Especially with the profitable delivery to Commander Omega.

"I am ready for the next consignment," the voice headed straight to the point, no need for useless small talk. "I hope you are in position to provide the necessary product?"

"There won't be a problem." Cowle calculated in his head for a moment. Prior to developing the concept of delivering product in bulk Cowle acquired the merchandise a single piece at a time. His client's appetites outpaced the supply he able to provide, strained the logistics of the delivery system, Rahim demanding far more items to satisfy ravenous, bloody cravings. The consignment system slowed the rate of consumption, but this last shipment of five pieces lasted a little more than a year, Sheik Rahim again consuming merchandise at a far more rapid rate. *He's rough on his playthings*. A detail to consider in future shipments; tweak the collection process further to keep up with his client's need for a steady supply of merchandise, while at the same time not risking exposure of his operations.

"How are you enjoying Chicago?" Sheik Rahim asked.

"It's a lovely city, I believe you'll enjoy the fruits of my labor here," Cowle knew his client understood the euphemism.

"Excellent," his client replied. "There will be a change in plans with this order. I will be arriving in Chicago on Sunday. I have business in the city on Monday and will depart early Tuesday morning." The unexpected wrinkle took Cowle by surprise; Rahim dispatched underlings tasked with taking possession of the consignment. "I wish to personally accept delivery of this shipment."

"I see," Cowle pondered the turn of events. An unforeseen complication but Cowle believed in his skills to manage the unexpected demand as compensation for his efforts. With past deliveries, Cowle handed over the merchandise to Rahim's people hours after abducting the final victim. This time he'd need to keep them quiet and tucked away in storage far longer, for the first victims likely indisposed for almost two days, until the exchange of their lives for millions of dollars. The delay heightened the chance someone might realize they were missing, report the fact to the police. A risky proposition sitting around with a quintet of abducted women, Cowle preferred a swift transfer of the items, then departing with his newfound riches for a distant locale while the trail left behind grew rapidly cold.

"You will have the product for me by that time?" Rahim asked. Cowle sensed the challenge to his proficiency, a challenge he was prepared to accept.

"The time window is...abbreviated," Cowle admitted, usually given two weeks between notification and delivery to select his targets and strike. Now forced to choose and acquire his prey in a matter of five days. *No rest for the wicked.* "But I will provide whatever you desire. You will not be disappointed."

"Excellent," Rahim said. "The prior shipment impressed me. They pleased me right to very end." Cowle understood the end in this case meant exactly that: death horrible and brutal.

"I'm sure you'll find satisfaction with the next consignment." The victims never described as women or even as human beings, only product and consignments, a commodity sold and consumed, eventually disposed like common refuse in graves unmarked.

"I will contact you when I arrive in Chicago," Rahim said, "I hope you'll have favorable news."

"I'm confident the report will be to your liking," Cowle answered, with that the call ended. Cowle went upstairs to the third floor apartment, rousing his apprentices from their slumber. Once awake Cowle announced simply.

"Gentlemen, we have work to do."

Samantha sat down at her desk in the offices of *The Daily Northern*, removing from her Timbuk 2 messenger bag the copy of the *Chicago Tribune* with the article detailing the five missing young women in Southern California, placing it beside her. Since the gathering in three-eleven Falmouth Samantha tried, but failed, to push aside the sordid story and focus on other matters more important to a college sophomore journalism major with the starting quarterback of the football team for a boyfriend. But the story hovered at the edges of her mind, images of five women lost forever and the poignant stories of lives cut short and dreams never realized clung onto her thoughts, resonated in her conscience. In her gloomiest musings the faces in the paper transformed to those of her friends, and at times Samantha imagined her own face among those of the missing.

Samantha called up Google on her computer screen, in the dialog box typed the words: *Five Missing Women Los Angeles*. In an instant the search engine returned a list of results, some thirty-thousand based on the key search words entered. She scanned the first page of results; one entry from the *Los Angeles Times* immediately captured her attention. *In Case Of Missing Women Chilling Similarities From Across the Country*. The headline surprised Samantha. *There are more than those five?* Samantha felt her stomach roil with unease. She clicked on the link, seconds later scanning the article and facts presented both troubling and terrifying.

Three other instances from across the country over the past five years bore striking parallels to the case in Los Angeles, multiple young women vanishing into thin air over a short period of time, seventy-two hours at the most, with no bodies found or any trace discovered of the fate that had befallen the missing. The first case in Boston as three women, one a student at Boston College and another from Northeastern University, disappeared. Then eighteen months later four young women going missing in the Denver area. Fifteen months passed when another four vanished in Atlanta, two of them attending Georgia Tech. Then a little over a year later the five women in southern California, two of them roommates at UCLA, became the latest victims. *Victims of what?* Samantha wondered. Two details unnerved Samantha; the interval between the string of disappearances growing shorter and the number of women there one moment and gone the next gradually increasing with each instance.

She delved further into the article, read speculation from a former FBI agent, an expert profiler in the field of behavioral sciences, of a highly skilled serial killer, described the possible suspect as an 'apex predator' with the ability to move across the country without hindrance to ply his twisted trade. He even speculated the authorities dealing with more than one subject, perhaps a team of serial killers. But if this the case where rested the remains of the many victims? Why didn't they find at least a single body? On this point the expert could offer no explanation.

Each case possessed another disquieting similarity. Some of the missing had contact with a subject vanishing around the same time of their own disappearances: a college instructor in Boston; a concert promoter in Denver; a nightclub promoter in Atlanta and a casting director in Los Angeles. With each of these occurrences the subjects' residence or place of employment destroyed by arson, obliterating whatever evidence within connecting the person in question to the one responsible for the disappearances. Or if that person might be the very killer sought by the authorities.

Samantha tried quelling the nauseous rumble deep in her stomach, only this time it wasn't hunger filling her with unease. Lauryn was from Arvada, a suburb outside of Denver, and Ashleigh called Atlanta home. Were her friends aware of the horror once so near to them? How close had either of her friends come to falling prey to the monster hunting young women to satiate whatever demented, violent fantasies darkened the passages of his mind.

"Hey Sam?" So engrossed in the article Samantha jumped at the sound of Aaron Dinehart's voice. Samantha closed the browser window, swung about in her chair, regaining her composure.

"Sorry about that," Aaron apologized.

"It's okay, I was reading something. Just took me by surprise," Samantha smiled weakly, unsettled by her discovery, then she brightened. "What did you want?"

"What are you doing Monday morning?' Aaron asked. "You think you can cover a big event?"

Samantha thought for a moment. "I think I can get out of classes, don't have any tests." She could get notes from her classmates, but the request aroused her curiosity. "So what's up?"

"Benton Fielding, United States Senator from Colorado, is giving a speech at Cockrell Auditorium," Aaron explained. "Speculation is he might drop a few hints as to his political future."

"You think he is going to announce that he's..." Samantha started to say.

"Like I said, its speculation," Aaron insisted. "He's giving a speech at his alma mater and some heavy hitters will be in attendance." Two of those 'heavy hitters' the insanely wealthy brothers, stalwart champions of free enterprise and staunch conservative causes, whose family name graced the auditorium and other buildings on campus. "Maybe he is and it's a big story, maybe he isn't and it's a run-of-the-mill policy speech. Either way I want my best reporter there to cover it."

Samantha leaned forward. "Why don't you take it?" If a story possessed the possibility of being a *big* story, the editors claimed the assignment to reap the glory of the byline and journalistic accolades.

Aaron cleared his throat, pulled up a chair, sat down. "There's a conflict of interest here."

"What?" Samantha startled, raised an eyebrow.

"Freshman year Bryce Fielding, Senator Fielding's son, was my roommate."

"Let me guess," Samantha surmised, "you two didn't get along and play nice." She knew Aaron's political leanings, likely a clash of beliefs with the son of a conservative politician.

"That's...putting it mildly," a self-conscious smile spread on Aaron's face. "The discussions between us were, I'll admit, heated at times."

"You stand your ground in an argument," Samantha complimented.

"There's one other thing," Aaron lowered his voice.

"What?" Now Aaron had Samantha's full attention.

"Last year, I was mentor for Natalie DiLaurenzo." Every freshman assigned a sophomore by the university to assist with the transition to college life.

Samantha giggled. "The plot thickens."

"She's nice, she's smart," Aaron confessed, Samantha astonished by the awkward expression of deep feelings for Natalie.

"She's pretty," Samantha added helpfully.

"I'm aware of that." Everyone noticed Natalie's beauty.

"So why didn't you ask her out last year?"

"I was her mentor, not supposed to be hitting on her." Aaron shrugged. "I didn't think it was appropriate then. I was going to ask her out at the start of this year but..."

"Bryce beat you to it," Samantha arrived at the assumption. "Did Bryce know your feelings for Natalie?"

Aaron nodded. "He did." A pause. "At least I think he did."

Samantha's jaw dropped in shock. "So Bryce swept in and snatched her away?" Aaron arched an eyebrow at the comment, agreeing with the observation. "That's so immature! That's crap you pull in high school!" Samantha's angry reply tinged with indignation.

"You know what they say about love and war. All is fair."

"Not in this case." Not when close friends involved. Samantha placed a comforting hand on Aaron's leg. "I think Natalie is missing out on a wonderful person," she told him. "You don't want to cover this speech because you're afraid you'll let it get personal."

"Best way to keep from going there is to not go there in the first place." Aaron knew other things about Bryce Fielding, serious matters coloring his views, details he couldn't reveal to Samantha. "I shouldn't do the story if I can't be impartial. That's why I want you there. You're my Lois Lane, the best reporter I've got on staff."

Samantha smiled shyly at the compliment. "I'll do my best, be objective and open-minded."

Aaron pointed at her. "You'll have to dress respectable for this one," he warned. "No blue jeans and a t-shirt, professional business attire."

"I don't mind." In the back of her mind Samantha already piecing together a perfect outfit, understated, yet sophisticated for an ambitious and talented college journalist.

Aaron noticed the glimmer in her eyes. "Thinking what Tyler will say when he sees you?"

Samantha couldn't lie. "Of course."

"I'll give the weekend police roundup to another reporter so you can rest up for Monday." There a promising freshman reporter displaying many of the same traits making Samantha his most dependable writer; she deserved a chance to shine and prove her worth. He stood up, flashing Samantha an astute smile, a sly wink. "Give Tyler a thrill," he walked back to his desk.

"I fully intend too."

"Stop by the office Sunday afternoon. I'll have the press credentials for you," Aaron told her.

"Great," Samantha turned back to her computer, anticipating the response from Tyler when he caught a glimpse of what she planned to wear Monday. She reopened the browser window, clicking on Yahoo for a quick check of the news before heading to her next class. Samantha gasped quietly, brown eyes widening, stunned by the item at the top of the page.

Search Continues For Missing Texas Tech Students.

Chapter 4

The key to success is in the preparation. Without it the only guarantee is failure.

The nugget of wisdom Cowle took to heart each day never passed the lips of a smug and arrogant Wall Street billionaire possessing no true idea of the concept. Men whose lone talent attaining fantastic wealth consisted of stepping on the backs of subordinates, making decisions with the same percentage of success a trained monkey might experience flinging darts at a board, gaming the established system to exploit loopholes for their benefit and the detriment of the unwashed masses. The observation came from his mentor, once a Collector like himself, now holding the status of his Patron in the sinister association named The Trading Society, enjoying luxurious surroundings of a sprawling, well-guarded villa in the south of France befitting his lofty stature. The man took Cowle under his wing as his Apprentice, trained him in the dark arts of hunting and capturing young women for sale to those smug and arrogant billionaires and manipulative politicians for whom rules and laws existed only to be twisted and broken for their own obscene profit and acquisition of limitless power.

Cowle relished the process of preparation, a trait setting him apart from his peers in The Trading Society, saw the effort put forth as part of the grand scheme. Some Collectors willing to cultivate vulnerable targets, runaways and prostitutes, victims no one noticed as missing or even cared had vanished. Although profitable there proved no challenge to hunt such easy pickings, required no display of skill and acumen. Cowle dealt with clients of a prominent stature with refined tastes, men such as Commander Omega and Sheik Rahm demanding quality merchandise of a higher grade. To obtain this fine product required precision and thoroughness in preparation.

The prospective targets subdued at the studio, lured there through subterfuge, once inside and their defenses lowered by the disarming charm of his professional photographer alter ego the trap sprung and their fates sealed. Yet Cowle understood the risk of storing so much product in the brownstone three-flat in Logan Square, faced too great a chance someone in the densely populated neighborhood stumbling upon their undertaking, even though the victims effectively neutralized and silenced following their abduction. Had to store his captives in a secure location both forbidding and intimidating, out-of-the-way in the midst of the big city, a place inducing the deepest fear in the hearts of his unlucky hostages, smothering their souls in a despairing dread. Any number of abandoned buildings throughout Chicago fit the bill, but many of those structures didn't offer the level of security he desired.

When Cowle first arrived in Chicago to establish his operation a quick perusal of properties on the market uncovered a fair-sized manufacturing site three miles southwest of the Logan Square brownstone, the firm going out of business and the complex falling into foreclosure. The structure perfectly suited his needs, guarded by a sturdy chain-link fence, exuded a threatening aura with expansive, menacing spaces filled with discarded equipment and smaller rooms, once offices for managers, perfect to confine and isolate his captives to heighten their helplessness, instill the sense their situation hopeless and reinforce the fact they were under his control. The hideout located in an industrialized area ravaged by global competition, many of the nearby buildings and warehouses abandoned husks of their former selves; few inquisitive souls around to worry about, railroad tracks to the north formed an additional buffer. Cowle, with proceeds from the Los Angeles consignment, made a fire-sale offer to an agent all too happy to unload a white-elephant property from a portfolio whose value decimated by the dismal economy. Cowle let the property lay fallow, though he paid the property taxes and utility bills, waiting for the time when he put the building to a use the original owners never conceived.

Transporting the luckless captives from the studio to the abandoned factory found a simpler solution. Cowle purchased, again on his arrival in Chicago, a black Ford Econoline 350 van parked in the garage attached to the back of the three-flat, keeping the residents of nearby buildings from witnessing his victims bundled into the van for the brief trip to their temporary confinement. Cowle intended, within reason, to make accommodations at the factory comfortable for his guests, no matter how short their stay, directing Sterner and Lang to purchase five mattresses at a local bedding store. This one of the few allowances, save for food and water along with access to a bathroom to relieve and clean themselves, Cowle willing to provide his merchandise during their captivity. Cowle still a businessman, even if his trade proved illicit and he needed to keep costs down and the profit margin high.

Protecting his investment the only area Cowle loath to cut corners, required proper materials to properly secure the merchandise during storage, a bad business practice letting product escape. For Sterner and Lang, grousing in good nature at being his errand boys, this entailed a trip to a Home Depot on North Avenue west of the Chicago River to purchase an ample supply of rope, cotton shop rags and duct tape. The pair then crossed the river to a shopping complex on the western edge of Lincoln Park where at a Bed, Bath and Beyond they bought several sets of cotton jersey bed sheets to be cut into strips. The purchases offering enough material to thoroughly bind and gag the five unfortunate women destined as their latest victims. The ill-fated guests kept bound and gagged for much of their time as hostages, the central element to Cowle's strategy of handling product, desired to crush the spirit of his captives, establish the fact he controlled their lives, decided when they ate or slept, reinforce they nothing more than goods for sale and never to again know of choice or freedom. At times he used handcuffs and plastic zip-ties to accomplish the same goal with efficiency and utility but rope, simple as it was, possessed an esoteric intimacy for his nefarious purposes, a brutal elegance when constructed into an inescapable prison about the female form. The captives left struggling against the unyielding bondage, fighting ropes expertly tied, seeking unreachable knots in a misguided belief they could loosen the bonds and escape, in the end tiring from useless exertions, limited to the barest of physical movement and the slightest of vocal protestations. The captives eventually overwhelmed with terror as an awful realization of the totality of their plight finally dawned, shattering the will to resist, surrendering to a dismal fate and thus made compliant and easier to handle for shipment.

Sterner and Lang headed to the factory, working on the interior, setting up a network of small video cameras inside the rooms serving as temporary cells for their captives. Wiring the surveillance system to a central location letting the pair observe their prisoners to insure, when the captives allowed respite from the bonds to eat and relieve themselves, that they didn't try anything unwise, attempt to escape their predicament. A similar surveillance system in place at the brownstone in Logan Square, but this network focused on the world beyond the residence. Able to monitor whomever walking or driving by their base of operations and if someone, in particular those involved with matters of law and order, watching them. A room in the factory and at the studio established with a set of scanners tracking the movements of the police. The intelligence gleaned so far assured Cowle the authorities had no idea of the evil taking root in the midst of their city or the fact five young women soon to vanish from the neighborhoods they swore to protect.

For other contingencies Cowle also prepared, leaving no angle exposed. Once the victims within the walls of the studio their link to the outside world impeded by a powerful cell-phone signal blocker installed in the building. After the prey subdued Cowle using those same smartphones to gain access to every facet of their social media, deleting any mention of him or his studio from their digital footprint. Erasing the trail the police might follow to the doorstep of Marcus Evans Photography, or at the least delaying the police long enough until the exchange with Sheik Rahim completed and the five packages transported to a new home in the Persian Gulf while Cowle and his assistants off to hard-earned rest and relaxation. Took the precaution to register the phone number for his own smartphone, the number on his business cards and website, to a fictional name at a post-office box address, another rabbit hole leading nowhere. When those on the hunt finally picked up the trail they'd find the brownstone and Marcus Evans Photography, as well as the vacant factory, existed no more, the structures incinerated, any evidence left behind eradicated.

While his two associates carried out the menial grunt work Cowle addressed the matter, important in this business of human trafficking, of selecting the merchandise for his prominent client. Sheik Rahim particular regarding the type of product he desired: young, in their twenties, preferred college students, intelligent, beautiful creatures with long hair. Something in Sheik Rahim's past, a previous experience traumatic or disturbing Cowle never bothered to delve into, wasn't his business to divine the demons raging within his customers, imprinted so powerful an image on the man's psyche where he paid Cowle obscene amounts of money to abduct women, then transport the victims to his homeland where he inflicted the hideous tortures and trials his demented mind conjured until the last bit of air escaped his captives' lungs and the light of life dimmed in their eyes. Then the process started over again, at another time in another city. In a peculiar way Cowle not far removed from a serial killer; seamlessly floating about the masses seeking perfect victims to fulfill his clients' heinous fantasies, though Cowle differed from those blood-thirsting murderers as money and profit solely drove his motives. To others, those who paid for his services, he left the dirty work of sexual violence and killing.

On his laptop computer Cowle constructed a database of potential victims numbering close to one hundred, each woman crossing his path over the past year. Many he encountered during his weekend jaunts chronicling Chicago's nightlife for the social website, others through a meeting of happenstance. His guise of professional photographer permitted him ample opportunity to approach targets catching his eye, trolling the masses seeking those fitting the profile of the product Rahim desired. His easy, conversational manner and reassuring appearance breaching their defenses, exploiting their vulnerability, his flattery and compliments grooming his prey, dropping their guard to let him collect every morsel of pertinent information he analyzed to select the right items. Each potential piece of merchandise logged into his hard drive with an accompanying picture and detailing the intricacies of their lives and revealing every possible weakness in a dossier worthy of the most secret of intelligence agencies.

In making his selections he consulted other parameters. Those not in steady relationships with the opposite sex, a boyfriend wishing to act as a protective escort to a photo session at a photographer's studio, made the final cut. He narrowed the list of prospective targets to a manageable twenty-five to choose four pieces of the five-item consignment, began making phone calls to set up appointments with the names on his list. Cowle understood he'd experience setbacks, some of the chosen begging off, having other plans for the weekend or not interested in modeling, never realizing their good fortune turning down his entreaty. Of the original twenty-five he selected twelve agreed to meet with him, Cowle believed his chances favorable to find the first four components of the shipment, set up photo sessions concluding in a most unexpected fashion for his chosen prey. Then he made phone calls to those legitimate clients scheduled for appointments, apologizing profusely that he'd received a last minute assignment from *National Geographic,* needed to travel overseas right away, offering to make good on the work when he returned. The people responding on the other end unaware he'd never again set foot again in Chicago, this the last they'd hear from or of the man called Marcus Evans.

As for the fifth and final piece of merchandise Cowle willing to let capricious fate select the last victim, a special offering serving as a virgin sacrifice for the bloody altar of his profitable client. On Saturday night he'd troll the club scene of Chicago one last time, searching for prey beautiful and naïve, achingly innocent of the world around her, taken with his charm, beguiled by his compliments. A susceptible young woman much too eager and enthusiastic to experience the dream of a professional model, all too blind to the danger of talking to a stranger, lured into the trap Marcus Cowle set in the confines of the studio, on ground of his choosing, in a blink snatched from all she knew and condemned to a nightmarish end. Cowle understood this action posed a risk, but without risk there couldn't be reward.

Cowle, an avid student of history, found it apt to employ his twisted skills in Chicago. In the city's sordid past there was a man very much like Cowle, though his aims different from his own, with whom he shared a blood kinship. It was the time of the 1893 World's Fair, the Columbian Exposition, a halcyon period when the world travelled to the city by Lake Michigan to visit 'The White City,' sprouting from the fallow ground of Jackson Park as rows of prairie corn shoot skyward after a soaking rain, an alabaster fairyland bathed in the amazing new phenomenon of electric light. Millions stared at gigantic buildings, the largest they'd ever seen, designed by the architectural giants of the age, men of vision with prominent names-Burnham, Sullivan, Post and Hunt-strolling on grounds sculpted by the landscape genius Frederick Law Olmstead. The dream city beckoned the luminaries of the era to congregate on the grounds as attendees marveled at the technological wonders of the coming century, gawking wide-eyed at the monstrous steel contraption, the Ferris Wheel, looming over the Midway.

But there resided the darkness of evil in the shadow of the shining White City, undetected until far too late, in a building at 63rd and Wallace in Englewood referred to as 'the castle,' a structure like the brownstone housing Marcus Evans Photography. There a man seemingly benign and harmless, as with Marcus Cowle blessed with gifts of persuasion and guile, established a hotel for guests arriving in Chicago to visit the marvelous White City. Some guests found the hotel a strange, curious collection of rooms, a layout confusing and puzzling, heard unusual noises in the dead of night. Other guests, young women away from home and on their own for the first time in their lives, flush with freedom and independence in the big, brutish and nasty city, never seen or heard from again as if a misty fog blew in off the cold waters of Lake Michigan to swallow them whole, leaving not a trace. Only long after the Fair concluded, when detectives searched for the missing and the trail lead to the property at 63rd and Wallace, did the pieces of the conundrum fit together. A twisted portrait of the hotel's seemingly kindly proprietor, a man with the respectable name of Henry Holmes but actually an alias cloaking a mundane identity of Mudgett, emerged as a calculating, cold-blooded murderer finding erotic thrill snuffing the lives of his prey, perhaps the first documented serial killer in America with a tally of victims never fully accounted. For his crimes the notorious Holmes paid with his life, secrets going with him to the Hell many thought richly deserved for his heinous actions.

A part of the story remained untold, a chapter undiscovered by the authorities. There existed victims who didn't perish by Holmes' vicious hand, instead spirited alive, yet helpless, from his lodgings. Agents from The Trading Society, as active in the past as in the present, uncovering the bloody scheme and, in exchange for keeping in confidence his twisted deeds, demanded tribute in the form of young women. With Holmes assistance Collectors from The Trading Society snatched unsuspecting victims from their rooms, hustled struggling bundles into the back of a wagon, transporting them into the night to the wealthy men of the age, guardians to immense power, who paid handsomely for human merchandise to do with as they pleased.

Soon after arriving in Chicago to establish his own 'castle' in Logan Square Cowle made pilgrimage to the corner of 63rd and Wallace to honor the memory, the spot where Holmes' castle once stood. The plot now occupied by the ordinary edifice of a United States Post Office, hardly a suitable tribute to Holmes' notoriety, no visible monument to the evil residing there more than a century earlier. After the next weekend another address to assume its own sinister significance, a new chapter written in the sordid lore of the Second City. The address of 2371 North Campbell Street, where a three-flat brownstone in Logan Square once stood, forever known as the place where five young women last seen alive before vanishing without a trace.

"What are your plans this weekend?"

Detective Devin Carson glanced over at his partner, Detective Dawson Hilliard, everyone called him 'Dawes,' sitting at his desk in the Detectives Bureau of Chicago Police Headquarters at 31st and Wentworth. "The usual this time of year," was his reply.

"Why did I bother asking?" Hilliard grunted. The answer always the same when autumn rolled around and the weather cooled, leaves changing color. Hilliard hoped this year different, a change of heart, Carson coming to terms with his past. Apparently that wouldn't be the case. *Again*.

Carson raised an eyebrow. "How long have we been partners?"

Hilliard nodded in agreement, should've known better. "It's like we're married." Both men single and by choice; one wished it so and the other for reasons dictated by his tragic past.

"Then you should know the answer," Carson replied. As with every weekend in the fall he'd be far away, isolated and distant from the realm of football, both college and professional, that once dominated his world. Though their personalities cut from bolts of different cloth, the two detectives worked as partners for years and where friction might exist there was none, the pair operating smoothly in tandem to make an effective team.

A product of refined, upscale tastes of the North Shore, Devin Carson found an upbringing in the midst of steadfast conservative values and sheltered environs of Winnetka; received an excellent education and earned a stellar athletic reputation at New Trier High School, one of the elite high schools in Illinois and the nation. His looks superbly All-American: tall and muscular, nary an ounce of fat on his robust build. His jaw set square, dark brown hair cropped short and amber eyes projected a serious, no-nonsense demeanor lending definition to his methods and attitude. He wasted no time getting the job done, at times impulsive when patience a more prudent strategy, a trait tending to rub the wrong way those not his close colleagues. When others spoke of Carson they mentioned the 'what might have been' in his life. How fate played a cruel trick on one destined for fame and fortune, only to find his future find a different outcome following a tragic occurrence in his past, the deep emotional scars Carson never allowed to heal.

Rough around the edges is how many judged the appearance of Dawson Hilliard. Where Carson grew up in upper-class stability, Hilliard lived a hardscrabble, rambunctious youth in the alleys and side streets of Chicago's Bucktown prior to its transformation into an urban haven for refined young professionals and artists. As sturdily built as his partner, though his frame a touch leaner and the dark, short hair and beard always seemed a bit scraggly as if Hilliard took immeasurable pride waking up every day to peer in the mirror at his unkempt appearance and deciding it wholly acceptable. His upper body and arms a Chinese tapestry of tattoos and body art, the significance of many of the images gracing his skin only Hilliard able to explain if allowed time to pontificate. An unabashed liberal majoring in literature and fine arts in college, Hilliard steered a path hard left on the political spectrum, believed in the benefits of diversity where fellow associates veered right or spouted opinions, dubious and questionable and at times downright racist, concerning particular ethnic groups residing in the city. While other peers drowned the stress and strain of the job in rivers of liquor Hilliard followed the strictest abstinence, lips never once touching alcohol. Those who found his methods strange knew better than to call him out, taut body and sharp mind able to handle any challenge verbal and physical.

"Gentlemen," Captain Andrew Hardaway approached their desks, their commander known to Chicago years before a decorated career in the department, a star on the basketball court for the Fighting Illini of the University of Illinois where on the downstate Champaign campus his All-American exploits were legendary.

"Cap'n, what's the latest on the talks between the city and the dispatchers at the 911 Call Center?" Hilliard inquired. The contract between the city and the responders at the city's Emergency Operations and Communication Center set to expire at midnight on Sunday.

"Both sides are talking," Hardaway said, "so that's good. But if they walk out expect a tough time until they decide to come back to work."

"Amateur hour," Hilliard snorted, "at least the deadline isn't tonight." Hilliard did most of the talking for the pair, Carson stoically silent. "Might've made for an exciting weekend, and I mean in a sarcastic sense."

"If they were going out tonight you'd be working this weekend," Hardaway pointed out, his manner direct and straightforward, words kept to the minimum.

"Who does Mount Carmel play this weekend?" Hilliard asked. Gawain and Geraint, the twin sons of Andrew Hardaway, both bona-fide five-star recruits in their senior year at the private South Side Catholic institution, the most highly sought recruits to play for the Caravan since Donovan McNabb starred for the prep powerhouse in the nineties. The two, playing on both sides of the ball, had the city's sports media abuzz with speculation which college football program lucky enough to snare the services of the pair, or if they split up and headed to different schools. The twins generating the same heated interest as Tyler McManaway, 'Touchdown Tyler,' had two years earlier before his decision to cast his lot with the resurgent Huskies of Great Northern University.

"Rivalry game against Saint Rita," Hardaway noted, the other private Catholic high school on Chicago's South Side, the Mustangs' football tradition as long and proud as that of Mount Carmel. "Media is already calling it the 'Game of the Year.'"

"Might make the trip down from the North Side." Hilliard added. The team Hilliard followed with a passion, the Chicago Cubs, suffering through yet another dismal year in confines less than friendly and another year, more than a century now as the very definition of futility, without a World Series. "How does the recruiting go?"

"I'll be on a first name basis with the head coach from every major college football program by the time this is all over," Hardaway noted, adding. "And this can't be over soon enough."

"Who are the favorites?"

"They still have to decide where they're taking their visits," NCAA rules allowed five on-campus visits. "They know I want them to attend a school with strong academics," Hardaway remarked, not concerned with his sons' educational standing, both at the top of their class with exemplary grade point averages and nearly perfect SAT scores. "I know Notre Dame and Stanford rank high on their lists." He looked at Carson. "They're pretty impressed with Great Northern."

Carson cleared his throat, suddenly uncomfortable. "It's a good school."

"Think about them on the same offense with McManaway, Watson and Wellington," Hilliard observed, "they'd be tough to beat."

"Captain," Carson interrupted, "I don't think you came out here to talk football with us."

"I need both of you in my office," Hardaway said.

Now Hilliard cleared his throat. "Is there a problem?"

"Depends on your definition of a problem," Hardaway motioned for the pair to follow him.

"Always feels like I'm off to see the principal," Hilliard muttered under his breath.

Hardaway heard the comment. "I'm sure you were familiar with what that office looked like?"

"My teachers never said a word," Hilliard admitted, "pointed at the door whenever I acted up."

Hardaway got down to business. "You know this department will be occupied next April."

Hilliard snorted. "You don't happen to mean 'Summitgeddon?'" This was the name coined by a beat cop Hilliard knew describing the simultaneous international summits, a meeting of the G-20 and the World Trade Organization, now even talk of the addition of a NATO summit, taking place at McCormick Place over three days the next spring. The Feds, the FBI and Secret Service, handling security measures at the convention complex, a mile south of the Loop on the shore of Lake Michigan. The Chicago Police Department slated to deal with everything else, mainly the estimated tens of thousands of protesters and many mad as hell at the state of economic injustice and not willing to take it anymore, descending with the ferocity of a Biblical plague of locusts on the city. Add to that volatile mix the presence of leaders from the world's wealthy and powerful countries and a cocktail for trouble of epic proportions waited to be shaken and stirred. Many pundits already predicting a repeat performance of the 1968 Democratic Convention when protestors and police clashed in the streets and the whole world watched the bloody, chaotic result.

"I mean exactly that," Hardaway stopped at the door to his office. "With most of the world leaders in Chicago at that time, we still don't have an idea how many events and meetings will be taking place outside the McCormick Place security zone. So we'll be seeing colleagues from around the world coming here in the next few months to liaison with the department, get a lay of the land before the summit weekend. The Superintendent is forming a special unit to handle this matter. The two of you have been assigned to that unit, or will be when it gets up to speed."

"Wonderful," Hilliard said dryly. "This thing is months away and we're only now getting ready for the party." The rumbles among the rank and file hinted the department in no way prepared for the possibly massive complications arising from a multiple dose of global summits. The blunt, no-nonsense new Superintendent, brought in from New York by the newly elected Mayor, talking a good game of how they'd be ready for anything while in reality resources and organization already sorely lacking.

"What does that mean for us?" Carson asked.

"Starting today, I hope you don't mind being tour guides for the next few months," Hardaway turned the knob to his office door.

"The Cubs have a two-twenty game against the Nationals, we can start there," Hilliard added as Hardaway opened the door. Inside stood two men, both the same size and build as Carson and Hilliard.

"Detective Patrick Flannery, Dublin Police Department." His face projected the visage of ferocity passed down from warrior forefathers, his hair and beard the bright color a carrot, the clear blue eyes piercing and alert. "Inspector Nathanial Hampton, Scotland Yard." The slight crook in a nose broken somewhere in his life gave the man a tough, no-nonsense appearance, the brown eyes cool, expression calm, exuding an aura of one capable of handling any situation no matter how fraught with danger.

"Detectives Devin Carson and Dawson Hilliard, the four of you will be spending time together over the next few months."

Handshakes were exchanged. "Call me Dawes, everyone else does," Hilliard told them.

"First time in Chicago?" Carson asked the pair.

Both men nodded. "Hopefully our time together will be valuable preparing for these summits your Mayor has graciously allowed to be held here," Hampton said, his accent unmistakable, the Savile Row suit impeccably tailored to fit the sturdy frame.

"Would've been nice if our Mayor asked our opinion before he put us up to this," Hilliard noted. "You don't get much sun where you're from?" Hilliard asked of the pale-skinned Flannery.

"Oh, that bright yellow thing in the sky, fella?" Flannery jerked a thumb out the window at the brilliant afternoon. "My ancestors sacrificed virgins so we'd get a few days of sunshine until Saint Patrick came around and put a stop to that whole business."

"I thought he drove the snakes out of Ireland?" Hilliard asked.

"That too," Flannery conceded.

"I see we're off on the right foot," Hardaway observed. "So I will let you," nodding at Carson and Hilliard, "start showing our guests the city."

"So which part of Chicago do you want to see first?" Hilliard asked. Like the Roman god Janus every city presented two faces: one the glittering image of civic pride culled from a brochure issued by the Chamber of Commerce, the other of neighborhoods far removed from the attractions in the public eye frequented by out-of-town tourists, places they dare not step foot in even in broad daylight lest they valued their lives. Police officers never given this choice of destination, going wherever duty called them in a city of three million.

"I can see why you're unhappy with how your portfolio turned out," Marcus Cowle, cloaked in his persona as Marcus Evans, commented perusing the glossy prints lying on the table, glancing up at the petite brunette with turquoise eyes sitting across from him. The prints did no justice to her wholesome, appealing girl-next-door beauty.

"I think I got what I paid for," Emma Hayden frowned, sipping from the white chocolate mocha latte in her hand, a drink Cowle paid for, "and it wasn't much." The pair occupied a table in the middle of the Starbucks in Piper's Alley at the corner of North Avenue and Wells Street. The popular location in the Old Town neighborhood, with the distinction as one of the first in the global coffee chain to remain open twenty-four hours a day, experiencing a bustling crowd of students, moms with kids in tow and business people taking advantage of the free Wi-Fi service this late Thursday morning. Meeting at the Starbucks posed no problem for Emma, a film and drama major at Pacifica College in Chicago's Loop, time between classes spent at whichever locations she closest to, on a first-name basis with half of the baristas in the city.

"I think I can help you," Cowle dropped his bait into the water, waiting to see if lovely Emma might bite on the jiggling lure, "if you help me with a project."

"What sort of 'help' are we talking about?" Emma put down her cup, elbows resting on the table, wistfully twisting a strand of silky hair around her finger, a trait Cowle thought endearing. He first encountered Emma during a late-night foray through Chicago's nightclub scene, snapping several pictures of the seductive outfit she wore that night. As was his method Cowle made casual conversation with the attractive drama student, measuring her potential worth as an item for when good Sheik Rahim with his bottomless pocketbook placed the request for his next consignment. In his computer he logged the basic information regarding Emma in his computer, added her to the database of names, faces and personal details from which four young women chosen as winners in his deadly lottery and sent off on a long, unwilling journey to the land of his favored client. A journey none of them to ever return from.

Over time, as with all his potential targets, Cowle cultivated Emma as their paths crossed in the clubs of River North. Discovered Emma wished to embark on an acting career, needed presentable headshots and profile pictures to give to agents and casting directors, for the task enlisting the aid of a fellow student at the college. From the quality, or apparent lack of, the student better off studying something other than photography, especially if he desired to have a roof over his head and something to eat.

"I'm working on a project for an online clothing retailer, it's very trendy product," Cowle explained, a fable believable enough to convince his prey the offer genuine, tempting them into the snare he carefully set. "Their art director is looking for models, but not any models. She wants fresh faces who haven't been seen before."

"So you think I have that fresh face they're searching for?" Emma smiled; her teeth white as alabaster, perfect in alignment, a delicate hand running through mahogany tresses. "Who's it for?"

Time to pour on the flattery. "And it is a fresh and beautiful face you have," Cowle remarked, sighing, Emma smiling at the comment. "I wish I could let you know, but they want confidentiality while conducting this search."

"So if I help you out then you'll take my headshots and profile pictures?" Emma asked hopefully.

"Even better," Cowle sweetened the deal, "I'll pay you for the work on the project. You might receive more if the art director decides you're the type she wants."

Her interest stimulated. "How much would you pay me?"

"Two hundred dollars an hour?" Cowle offered gallantly. "You'd be at the studio three, four hours at the most." Emma unaware Cowle intended her stay in his presence to be far longer than that.

"But I'd still have to pay you for the pictures for my portfolio?" Emma figured part of the money going right back into Cowle's pocket.

"For helping me out," Cowle shook his head. "I'll do the portfolio for free."

"That's so sweet of you!" Emma cooed in gratitude, calculating financial numbers in her head, still a college student and money always appreciated with the economy sputtering along. "I think you have a deal," Emma beamed, shaking Cowle's hand, unknowingly sealing a deal with a devil. "When do you want to do this?"

"That's the thing, the art director wants examples of her prospective choices by Monday morning," Cowle replied, asked haltingly. "Would you be available Saturday?"

"I can make myself available." Emma's answer came without a moment of hesitation. "I don't have anything planned."

Good. How Cowle preferred it. "Bring a variety of outfits, something you'd wear when going out. Would noon work for you?" Cowle proposed.

"That'll be fine." Emma nodded, sipped her White Chocolate Mocha. "I can sleep in." Emma didn't know this to be the last peaceful sleep she'd ever experience.

Chapter 5

"Last time we're together until after the game tomorrow," Tyler McManaway commented as he and Samantha Grayson sat down at their usual table in Lakeside Dining Pavilion for lunch on Friday afternoon. This day the eight friends arrived on time, no waiting for stragglers.

"We'll be on 'Lockdown,'" D'Andre Watson used a term the players coined for the night prior to a home game. "No contact with the outside world." He, Tyler and Albert 'Fiji' Fatuamala already had overnight bags packed, after classes heading to practice for a final run-through, followed by meetings and a team dinner, then to the pep rally at Brennan Fieldhouse. After energizing students and alumni with guarantees of certain victory the team bussed to a hotel in Glenview far from the tumult and temptations of a campus caught in the throes of a football weekend.

"Think you can handle not having me around?" Tyler kissed Samantha on the cheek.

Samantha smiled. "I think I can manage." Other matters weighed on her mind this day.

"You'll have the suite all to yourself and I won't be around either," Amanda told Connor Aanonsen, spending the night away from campus with her cross-country teammates, resting up for the Great Northern Invitational the next morning. At least her competition over early and able to attend the game against North Carolina, hitting the tailgaters before kickoff. "What will you do to keep yourself occupied?"

"Nothing but online porn," Connor said with a straight face.

"So that's what you do when I'm not around?" Amanda shot him the dirtiest of looks, snickers breaking out from her friends.

"I'm sure you'll be reading your whips and chains bondage porn before bedtime," Connor replied, Amanda deep into the erotic trilogy currently at the top of the best-seller list. "After the pep rally some of the team is coming over for a pre-season viewing of *Slap Shot*."

Tyler grinned. "Old time hockey. Eddie Shore. Toe Blake." He rattled off a memorable line from the movie.

"What did we trade for these guys? A used puck bag?" Connor replied, Tyler doubling up laughing.

"How could you?" Amanda's expression turned to one of disappointment, as if not finding the pony she'd asked Santa for under the tree on Christmas morning. "I won't be there!"

"You're upset over this?" Ashleigh Morgan said, disbelieving.

"Stupid machine took my quarter, Coach," Tyler repeated another snippet of dialogue.

"Maybe they've got *Speed Racer* on TV here," Connor said, tried to keep from chortling.

"I'm Canadian, we love our hockey, and *Slap Shot* is the greatest hockey movie ever," Amanda explained. "There must be a law in Canada that says you must watch *Slap Shot* whenever it's on TV. If I change the channel and it's on, even if I catch it in the middle, I have to watch it through to the end."

Lauryn Callahan lowered her glass. "If I'm watching TV and I come across *The Shawshank Redemption*, there goes the next few hours. I can't turn it off."

"I have the same problem," Fiji agreed. He cleared his throat and in a perfect sonorous imitation of Morgan Freeman intoned. "I hope the Pacific Ocean is as blue as it is in my dreams."

"That's good," Lauryn smiled warmly at the giant Samoan.

"*Saving Private Ryan*," Tyler added, "that pulls me in every time I'm channel surfing," he paused, "or *Caddyshack*."

Samantha studied her friends, relaxed, anticipating a memorable weekend, finding comfort in each other's company. She wondered if there was a group like them at Texas Tech, close companions who enjoyed lives together, now torn apart by capricious circumstance. Agonizing for two friends gone missing, spending every moment searching for any sign the pair still counted among the living or praying at a candlelight vigil for a happy ending where the two women found unharmed. Likely left powerless bystanders to the unfolding tragedy, suffering the loss for years to come. Was the person, or persons, guilty for the cluster of disappearances across the nation also responsible for these two students vanishing without a trace?

"Let's get to more important things," Connor said. "What's our topic for today?"

"Do we need one?" D'Andre shrugged indifferently. "You're doing fine reciting movie dialogue."

"That's the appetizer before the main course," Connor replied.

"Gender neutral first names," D'Andre stated, then clarified, "ones that work for guys and girls."

"Robin." Fiji the first to respond as Ashleigh sent the topic out over Twitter on her smartphone.

"Sidney." This response from Lauryn, Samantha wanted to ask her about the four women who went missing in Denver three years earlier. Had Lauryn ever been aware of the shadowy evil lurking so close, consuming whole four innocent lives?

"Ashley," Ashleigh said, "but not the way my name is spelled. Think Ashley Wilkes in *Gone With The Wind*." Had Ashleigh known of the four young women disappearing a year after the four vanished in Denver? Ashleigh had applied to Georgia Tech where two of the victims attended school. Samantha wanted to say something, inquire what Ashleigh might remember, but her will resisted, preventing lips from uttering the words, asking questions dampening high spirits around the table.

"Jordan." Amanda said as she finished her drink.

"Need a refill?" Connor motioned to her glass.

Amanda gave him the glass. "Get me some orange or grape but none of that stupid root beer."

Connor rose from his seat. "I love a woman who can quote from *Slap Shot*."

Amanda swept black hair away from her forehead, batted her eyelashes. "You love me for more than that."

"You've got that right," Connor grinned, about to walk away when he said. "Riley. There's Riley Bannister on the hockey team and wouldn't you know he's mentoring this freshman girl whose name is Riley too."

"Peyton," Tyler added. "You know, as in Peyton Manning."

"You should've come up with that one sooner, Touchdown," D'Andre replied.

Samantha listened, head down, appetite absent, picked at the food on her plate, lost in thoughts concerning missing women. Images of posters and billboards asking for information flashed in her head. Had no idea why what caught her fleeting interest at lunch on Monday now consumed every ounce of her attention. Was it her roommates, her best friends, a reminder of those who disappeared into thin air? Could it be such a terrible thing very easily happening to any of them on the presumed safety of the Great Northern campus? *Is it that it could even happen to me?*

"Samantha? You okay?" The concern in Tyler's voice shook Samantha from her melancholy. She glanced up from her plate, surprise filling her brown eyes, noticed everyone looking at her.

"What?" Samantha hoped she didn't appear too distracted.

"You've been quiet today," Tyler told her. "This topic is right up your alley."

"Oh...um, Morgan," Samantha dredged a reply from a mind mired in quicksand, the effort not very convincing. "Sorry, have something on my mind."

"What is it?" Lauryn asked, worried.

Samantha swallowed hard. *I can't bring it up*, she thought. *I can't spoil this by asking Lauryn and Ashleigh those questions*. Everyone happy, expecting much of the weekend and the first home football game on Saturday afternoon. Still felt guilty bringing the subject up with her friends across the hall three nights earlier. Wouldn't be fair to any of them. "Um, Aaron's gave me this assignment for Monday morning. I'm covering a speech by Senator Benton Fielding at Cockrell Auditorium. It might be a big deal. Aaron says I have to dress professionally for this one."

"You know," Tyler grinned. "I've never seen you dress up to do a story."

Samantha brightened at the comment and the satisfying prospect the opportunity offered. "Since I won't make lunch on Monday because of the speech, I'll give you a preview at breakfast."

"That'll wake me up," Tyler admitted, sly mischief in his voice, moving close to Samantha, their noses brushed as he kissed her. "You know high heels turn me on."

"Get a room you two," Connor remarked on the display of affection as he returned to the table.

"So you get to listen to Bryce's dad run his mouth," Amanda accepted the glass of grape Gatorade from Connor, Samantha caught a whiff of scorn in the reply. "I hope Dad isn't an arrogant jerk like his son, but I wouldn't be surprised if it runs in the family."

"I don't know what Natalie sees in him," Lauryn added, Samantha saw Ashleigh nod in agreement. "I'm not keen on his father either, even if he is from Colorado."

"Am I missing something?" Samantha recalled the sour reaction of Allison Mayne when Bryce called Natalie during Pizza Night in three-eleven Falmouth Hall.

"You're the only one here who hasn't had the pleasure of making Bryce's acquaintance," Amanda said. "Consider yourself lucky."

"I agree with his dad on accepting personal responsibility, a thing some of my people seem to have a problem with," D'Andre added. "Don't judge the father because you don't like his son. I met him at a Young Republicans meeting, seemed an okay guy but I'll admit he's a little full of himself."

"This is why we don't talk politics at lunch, babe," Ashleigh reminded, then to Samantha. "To say he's conceited is an understatement. Talk to Allison Mayne when you get a chance, she'll tell you more."

"Well, I'm writing about his father, so I'll keep an open mind," Samantha guessed something about Bryce Fielding didn't sit well with her friends, decided to have a conversation with Allison on the matter, learn her suspicions. "I hope I do a good job on this."

"You're worried about a story?" Amanda asked in disbelief. "Who has her byline on the front page of *The Daily Northern* every day?"

Tyler took Samantha's hand, fingers caressing the sensitive fold of skin between the thumb and forefinger, sent a tingle racing through her body, a comforting gesture reminding Samantha why she loved him. "You'll do fine," Tyler reassured. They kissed again and for a moment, but only for a moment, Samantha Grayson pushed thoughts of sixteen missing women out of her mind.

*   *   *   *   *

The multitude of Starbucks dotting the Chicago landscape afforded a convenient setting for Marcus Cowle to conduct his business, another meeting with a young woman unaware of his true motives. "So how's work going, Alexandra?" Marcus Cowle politely asked the woman sitting across from him at the small round table in the location situated one street west of the LaSalle Street financial district.

Alexandra Cole glared at him over the grande iced Caramel Macchiato with a touch of cream and two sugars, another drink Cowle paid for in his scheme to lower the resistance of his prospective prey. The bitter expression not meant for Cowle but for the job he inquired about. A sales position she so fervently wished rid of, working for a superior making Simon LeGree seem like a benevolent George Bailey. But every time she considered submitting her two-week notice the issue of college loans outstanding reared their ugly head, in this case eighty-thousand dollars owed for her studies at the University of Texas in Austin.

"I'm in a good mood, don't ruin it," Alexandra warned. "My boss took the day off so the office is quiet for once."

"Sorry about that," Cowle apologized, knew exactly why he said what he did, exhibiting sympathy for his target. "I do wish things were going better for you."

"I know you're trying to be nice." Alexandra waved off the mea culpa. Fit and athletic, one inch over six feet with long legs and a body more of a California beach volleyball player than the small-town Kansas girl she was. Alexandra the tallest of his potential victims with pin-straight dark hair streaked with reddish sienna brown falling gracefully down her back, her eyes the lightest shade of beige and at twenty-seven also the oldest of the prospects he considered. Sheik Rahim preferred his merchandise younger, but Alexandra a gorgeous creature and Cowle believed his client agreeing with the wisdom of this selection when time came for introductions.

Unlike many of his other possible targets, whom Cowle established an acquaintance with through his travels on the Chicago nightclub circuit, he crossed paths with Alexandra at a wedding he was hired to shoot, the strikingly attractive bridesmaid in the wedding party. As he posed the bridal party in front of Buckingham Fountain, Cowle wondered in the depths of his perverted mind how much he'd fetch from clients if he offered the bride and attendant bridesmaids as a package deal to the highest bidder. Such flights of lurid fancy passed the time while pretending to be someone he wasn't. By the end of the evening he and Alexandra deep in discussion over drinks at the bar of the Chicago Hilton and Towers, Cowle displaying his talent for attentive listening, allowing Alexandra to spill a litany of sorrows while downing glasses of white wine. As she slowly grew inebriated, Cowle a rapt audience nursing his glass of wine, she gushed about her troubles: trapped in a dead-end job working spirit-crushing hours; terrorized by a despicable superior; fiancé cheating on her with a co-worker from his job leading to a broken engagement. For one blessed with luminescent beauty Alexandra lived a miserable, lonely existence with a social life in ruins, a job she hated and the only true friend in her world a three-year old golden retriever named Wrigley sharing her Lakeview apartment.

In her vulnerability Cowle spied an opening, exploited the weakness to insinuate himself into her life. Complimenting Alexandra on her appealing appearance, suggesting she could make a career as a professional model if the right opportunity arose. As with Emma Cowle groomed his potential quarry over time, shooting headshots and profiles free of charge, patiently listening to Alexandra vent about her lousy job and dearth of romantic prospects on the horizon. All the while letting her know he continued the search for that 'perfect opportunity,' a chance to alter her mundane reality and tell her superior, in no uncertain terms, what she could do with the horrid job.

Now time to see if Alexandra, as Emma had the day before, took the bait dangled enticingly in the water. "I think I have something which might interest you," Cowle offered.

The perfectly shaped eyebrow over her left eye rose. "What is it?"

"I'm working on a project, a catalog for an online clothing retailer, very stylish apparel," Cowle started the spiel again, commencing the performance. "The art director and president of the company are looking for new faces for the project. Not the models you already see everywhere."

"You think they might want me?" Alexandra leaned forward, brown eyes gleaming with interest.

"You're exactly what they're looking for," Cowle continued. "I can't tell you who the company is yet. They want this search to be confidential."

"When do I start?" Alexandra said. *So I can tell my boss to take this job and...*

"I showed them your portfolio but they want more samples," Cowle shook his head, "something a bit more extensive than what we've already done. They're making a decision Monday. They're looking at some other models I've recommended but I feel you might have the inside track. We'd have to shoot this weekend, I have time open Saturday afternoon if you're..."

"I'm interested," Alexandra cut him off, not wanting the chance to slip away. "Believe me, I'm interested."

"I'll pay you for your time, so you'll get paid even if you don't get the job," Cowle smiled, Alexandra hooked on the line and slowly reeling her in.

"How much?" Alexandra attempted not to appear greedy, but a substantial student loan payment lurked at the end of the month.

"Two hundred dollars an hour," Cowle told her. "The session will take three to four hours."

"I'll say it again, I'm interested," Alexandra insisted, even more so now with the money she'd receive even if the plum assignment didn't come her way.

"So Saturday afternoon it is," Cowle said. "Bring a selection of outfits, something trendy, what you'd wear on a night out." Not that Alexandra experienced many of those with the crushing hours and incessant demands of her job. "How does three sound?"

"That will work for me." Alexandra's smile for Cowle, or the man she knew as Marcus Evans, effervescent and expectant. "Gives me the morning to spend time with Wrigley and get ready."

"Excellent, I'll see you then," Cowle lifted his cup of coffee in salute.

"Thanks for all you've done," Alexandra touched Cowle's hand. He returned the gesture with a modest shrug of the shoulders, a cavalier grin. "I hope this works so I can make a career change."

Cowle' smile remained unchanged. Alexandra Cole about to start a new career, but one she never expected in the darkest depths of her imagination.

Chapter 6

In the past, when Great Northern University football a passing afterthought on a sunny autumn Saturday and students more likely to spend the day crammed in the library studying instead of filling the stands cheering an overmatched squad facing odds similar to those the Christians faced against the lions in the Coliseum of Imperial Rome, the Friday evening pep rallies proved sad, moribund affairs where the team, band and cheerleaders easily outnumbered those diehard fans in attendance.

But following a magical Rose Bowl season Great Northern football gained a newfound measure of relevance, the Huskies now meant something in the hierarchy of the Big Ten other than a guaranteed 'W' in the win column for the opposing team. A bowl game at the end of the season now expected, no longer the exception and talk of winning the Big Ten no longer thought of as a hallucinogenic college football fantasy. With the recruiting coup of the class dubbed 'The Best and The Brightest' some speculated out-loud, without being labeled absolutely insane, a national championship for the Huskies not so far-fetched a possibility.

Tyler McManaway stood off the stage at Brennan Fieldhouse as the Warren Field public address announcer, serving as the master of ceremonies, called out the starting lineup for the offensive unit. As each player's name announced they stepped on the stage, received approving cheers from the massed throng of students and alumni expecting great accomplishments from this year's squad.

"*At the flanker position, a sophomore out of Woodrow Wilson High School in Dallas, Texas, number eighty-one, D'Artagnan Wellington!*" The voice of the emcee boomed over the crowd.

"Wave to all the nice people," Tyler traded a fist-bump with his favorite targets.

"As long as they wave back." D'Artagnan enjoyed a particular football pedigree, having starred at the same high school as two previous winners of the Heisman Trophy and wearing the same number the most recent winner donned during his college days at Notre Dame. D'Artagnan did as Tyler suggested as he bounded up on the stage, greeted by a throaty roar.

"*At the fullback position, a junior from Saint Matthew's School in Auckland, New Zealand, number forty-four, Dante Clarke!*" Tyler gave a fist-bump to his 'cobber,' a stalwart Maori from the island nation south of the Land Down Under before he ascended the stairs. Dante Clarke didn't come to Evanslawn with the expectation of playing football, like Albert 'Fiji' Fatuamala at Great Northern to study philosophy. Coach Hamilton spotted him one afternoon during a rugby club match trampling over everyone in sight with relentless ferocity, convinced the young man with tree-trunks for legs to try out as a walk-on. By the conclusion of the season Clarke earned the starting position at fullback and secured a full scholarship for his efforts.

D'Andre Watson sidled up beside Tyler. "Time to meet my adoring public. You know they love me."

"They'll love you more if you get that hundred yards tomorrow like you've been yapping about all week," Tyler kidded his friend about his constant boasting.

"*At the tailback position, a sophomore from Mater Dei High School, from Huntington Beach, California, number twenty-two, D'Andre Watson!*" The announcer exclaimed, cheers erupting even before D'Andre hit the stage waving and smiling broadly to the boisterous crowd.

Now Tyler stood alone and, as the quarterback expected to lead Great Northern to the pinnacle of college football, the hopes and aspirations of students and alumni rested on his broad shoulders. Tyler used to the barrage of constant attention, the center of acclaim since his first touchdown pass in Pop Warner. The hype magnified through high school as each four-hundred yard, multiple touchdown performance and every state championship raised his notoriety another notch. Brought a Who's Who of college football head coaches from across the nation through the family living room, making their sales pitch why Tyler should come and play for his program, promising Tyler everything but the sun and moon in the process.

"And at quarterback, a sophomore from Wheaton Warrenville South High School in Wheaton, Illinois, number four, Tyler McManaway!" Tyler took a deep breath and ascended the stairs to face the pandemonium.

"There's your man," Ashleigh Morgan shouted to Samantha Grayson over the raucous cheering from the masses crowded around them and the marching band blaring the refrain of the school's fight song, each attempting to drown the other out as Tyler McManaway stepped on stage, waving to the crowd as he walked across, exchanging high-fives with fellow teammates on the offensive unit as he strode confidently to his place at the end of the line.

"And he's standing next to your man," Samantha replied as Tyler reached D'Andre Watson, the best of friends trading fist bumps. The band continued with another chorus of the fight song as the cheerleaders on stage, Allison Mayne and Natalie DiLaurenzo among them, exhorted on the gathering of the school's followers.

The master of ceremonies motioned for the crowd to quiet for the rally to proceed, introducing the main speaker for the event, a former Great Northern player now commanding one of the newest attack submarines of the United State Navy, prepared to deliver a rousing speech to team and fans on the eve of the home opener. As the players took their seats Samantha waved towards the stage, hoping Tyler saw her among the teeming throng.

Tyler did; a casual wave letting Samantha know he spotted her and, even during the pep rally and preparing for a pivotal home opener against a ranked opponent, was thinking of her.

As Tyler stepped on the stage, waving to the fans jammed into every nook of Brennan Fieldhouse he sensed the body heat generated by the multitudes filling the gymnasium floor. He flashed a self-assured, winning smile; exactly what students and alumni expected of the potential superstar, a display of confidence to the mass of humanity dressed in blue, silver and white. Their field general exhibiting his game-face, show he was ready and able to face the Tar Heels of North Carolina.

Striding in front of the line of cheerleaders, he smiled at Allison Mayne and Natalie DiLaurenzo, friends of Samantha from across the hallway in Falmouth Hall. Made his way down the line of teammates on the starting offensive unit, doling out high-fives to the beefy-legged, thick-shouldered quintet prepared to guard Tyler from the onrushing charge of the defense. Then greeting his receiving corps, those on the business end of the hoped-for many completions against the Tar Heel defensive backfield. Finally reaching the running backs who shared the backfield with him, fullback Dante Clarke and his closest comrade on and off the field, D'Andre Watson.

"Nice of you to join us tonight," D'Andre and Tyler traded fist-bumps.

"Didn't have anything on my social calendar," Tyler took his place in front of his seat, waved to an adoring crowd like a politician acknowledging the party faithful before an important address. The emcee requested the crowd to quiet before introducing the featured speaker for the rally as Tyler and his teammates sat down. As he settled into his seat, Tyler scanned the audience for one special person, found the familiar head of luxuriant auburn hair fifteen rows deep in the crowd. Samantha Grayson raised her hand to wave at him and Tyler waved back, a wide grin on his face, letting Samantha know she was in his thoughts hours before a huge game to make or break their season.

His parents and family wouldn't be attending the game, but Tyler understood their absence. Travelling to the East Coast to watch his twin brother Colin start his first game at split end for Cornell University, an academic bastion of the Ivy League, the Big Red playing Bucknell in central Pennsylvania. Tyler envied his younger brother by seventeen minutes, playing the game out of love of the sport, for the thrill and enjoyment, not because he put his signature on the bottom of a scholarship offer, expected to lead his school to the big-money nirvana of a top-tier bowl game. Colin recruited by many of the same schools pursuing Tyler, coaches promising his brother a scholarship if it convinced Tyler to join their program. In the end Colin, a free spirit bucking the status-quo, eschewed the allure of major college football, going his own way to enroll in a fine arts program at the prestigious school in Ithaca, high above the waters of New York's Cayuga Lake.

Tyler McManaway understood the trade-off, yet didn't possess any qualm about. He travelled one route while Colin treading a different road, as Robert Frost eloquently mused, less travelled. To play college football at a Big Ten school was to exist in a fish bowl resting beneath a powerful electron microscope: every action scrutinized; every decision on the field criticized or praised; every statement parsed; every intention dissected. Tyler taking the path to Great Northern a school, though an academic powerhouse, a player in the high-pressure, big business realm of college football. The game he grew up loving and at which he excelled remained a moneymaking proposition for the university and Tyler, in exchange for a scholarship, nothing more than a punch-clock employee helping the school fill its coffers through his success on the playing field. For the stands packed with paying fans in Warren Field, the money received for a bowl game appearance and all the apparel, some with his jersey number and name stitched across the back, sold in the campus bookstore Tyler and his teammates received not a cent of compensation. The education, along with free room and board, considered fair recompense for their lengthy hours on the practice field and in the classroom fulfilling their end of the contract. The 'winning-at-any-cost' mentality throughout the game brought forth a steady stream of scandal and wrongdoing, of rules skirted, money and benefits delivered under the table, and regulations flaunted as one Big Ten school in particular, once thought a paragon of doing things the right way, now grappled with repercussions from a shocking, sordid scandal unlike any other, losing their soul and sentenced to years of irrelevance because certain individuals in positions of power placed the sport of football over morality and common decency.

The radical social activist, leading the march championing the rights of the oppressed, might consider the deal Tyler signed no better than forced labor in a sweatshop. Tyler considered the matter differently. It might be an agreement benefitting one side more than the other, the case at any of the schools Tyler could've signed with, the way the system designed. But Tyler planned to use cards dealt him to his advantage. Great Northern offered an education in a field where once his playing days finished, and Tyler understood one couldn't play a game where the impacts suffered so devastating, to head down another path for the rest of his life, seek success in an arena other than one contested on a field of grass on a weekend afternoon. A life Tyler hoped to spend with the slender, auburn haired and brown-eyed beauty standing in the crowd some fifty feet away from him.

"This is the hardest part of the weekend," Samantha told Tyler, holding his hand as they walked towards the buses taking the players and coaching staff to the peaceful isolation of a suburban hotel far removed from the distracting excitement bubbling on campus.

Tyler bent over to kiss Samantha. "It's only twenty-four hours," he grinned. "Not like I'm going off to war or something."

"But you're so close," Samantha pointed out, sadness on her face, "out there on the field, yet so far away."

"Better here than on the road," Tyler answered. "At least you're seeing me in person and not on television. Besides, I'm not gone as long."

"She pines for you when you're away," Amanda McKinnon informed Tyler. "We should have a drinking game when we watch you play on TV where you drink every time Samantha says 'I miss Tyler'."

"You're the one to talk?" Samantha scowled playfully. "I'll remember that when Connor's on his first weekend road-trip and you're moping around the suite saying 'I miss my Connor Bear'."

"Connor Bear?" Connor Aanonsen glanced at a now sheepish Amanda.

"I'll take video evidence to prove it," Samantha smirked at Amanda. "And post it on YouTube." *Two can play this game...*

"Break it up, girls," Ashleigh Morgan warned before Amanda could reply. "Don't make me call a time-out for you two."

"Have to go anyway," Amanda jerked a thumb at one of the buses. "My ride is about to leave," she hugged her roommates. "See you at the start tomorrow, bright and early."

"Have a good night," Lauryn Callahan said as Amanda and Connor walked hand in hand, Amanda waving back at her friends, to the charter taking the cross-country team to their lodging for the evening.

Tyler glanced at the charters assigned for the football team, spotted an assistant coach motioning for players to board. "Looks like we're heading out," he held Samantha. "One for the road?"

"Happy to oblige," Samantha eased her arms around the broad shoulders, gave him a good-luck and goodnight kiss. "See you tomorrow after the game." Both Ashleigh and Lauryn offered farewell kisses to D'Andre Watson and Albert 'Fiji' Fatuamala, Samantha admiring how adorable tiny Lauryn looked in the strong, yet caring arms of the muscular Samoan. *When are you going to admit there's something between you?* With a reluctant, downcast frown, Samantha released Tyler and he and his friends walked over to the buses.

"Love you, babe," Tyler called out as he boarded the charter.

"Love you too," Samantha replied quietly, already felt a hole in her heart at his absence.

"Now what do we do?" Lauryn asked as they watched the buses pull away, heading off to the hotel for quiet solitude.

"Let's head home, see if anyone is around," Samantha suggested, suddenly adrift without Tyler.

"Maybe we can go out somewhere?" Lauryn asked.

Ashleigh added. "Or we can sit around the suite and mope."

Samantha nodded. "That's a possibility." The three started walking from Brennan Fieldhouse back towards campus.

"Hey! Wait up!" They heard Allison Mayne, stopped and turned to see her and Natalie DiLaurenzo approaching, both still wearing their cheerleading uniforms. Natalie held hands with a young man the same height as Tyler but with a much thinner build. His distinct nose sharp and long, a disinterested look in his blue eyes as if meeting Natalie's friends from Falmouth Hall something he'd rather not do.

"Here comes trouble..." Samantha heard Ashleigh murmur under her breath, suspected she was about to meet Bryce Fielding. *Keep an open mind, Samantha...*

"Heading back to the dorm?" Allison asked, Natalie and her boyfriend trailing steps behind.

"With our guys gone until tomorrow," Lauryn said, "we have to figure out something to keep us occupied for the evening."

"Mind if I join you?" Allison wondered.

"Why not?" Ashleigh offered. "The more the merrier."

"Hey, how're you doing?" Natalie arrived with an obviously unwilling boyfriend in tow.

"Nice job up there tonight." As she spoke Samantha studied the young man with surreptitious care.

"We do our best to get everyone excited for the weekend," Natalie smiled.

"Don't you ever get scared being thrown in the air?" Lauryn asked.

Allison crossed her arms, seemed uncomfortable in the presence of Natalie's boyfriend. "It's not something you do if you're afraid of heights." This wasn't a problem for Allison and her fearless nature. "As long as someone's there to catch me on the way down."

"Samantha, I don't think you two have met," Natalie motioned to the young man at her side.

The young man with brown hair grudgingly extended his hand. "Bryce Fielding."

"Samantha Grayson." *At last we meet.* Samantha accepted the handshake, found it cordial and cold.

"Samantha lives across the hall in Falmouth," Natalie informed Bryce, the stony expression a sign he wanted to be somewhere else right then. "She works at *The Daily Northern*. She's the best reporter there."

Bryce nodded, Samantha quickly put off by his aloof manner, the haughty air of arrogance. *What could Natalie possibly see in him?* Samantha smiled at Bryce, her tone friendly and polite. "I'm covering your father's speech Monday at Cockrell Hall. I'm looking forward to hearing what he has to say."

"As long as you don't do a hatchet job on him like all the other media types." The reply, curt and sharp, delivered without a trace of tact, took Samantha by surprise.

"Excuse me?" Samantha cleared her throat, from the corner of her eye spotted Allison stiffen, pursing her lips tightly as if expecting what Bryce said.

"It seems the media can't keep their political views out of their coverage when it comes to my father," Bryce plunged the knife, "they have a problem leaving their liberal bias at the door," and twisted it into Samantha's back.

So you want to play rough now? Samantha stood straight. "I consider myself to be a fair-minded reporter. I'll write what he says in the speech on Monday and nothing more," Samantha not backing down from the outrageous charge. "I won't make any judgment one way or the other regarding his speech." Samantha crossed her arms, eyes unwavering under the icy blue-eyed gaze of Bryce Fielding. "I think I'm able to be more than impartial."

"That's what they all say, seems to be the party-line among you journalist hacks," Bryce shot back. "You preach how fair you are then go and take your pot-shots anyway, rip him for what he stands for. I know it's because you don't agree with the values he stands for. For the America he believes in." Bryce stared at Samantha. "I don't expect you to be any different from the rest," he allowed the last accusation to sink in.

Samantha raised her eyebrows, a sharp retort she'd regret poised on her lips when Natalie interjected. "I'm sure Samantha will do a great job Monday and she'll be more than fair," the comment arriving not a moment too soon as Samantha sensed her blood rapidly boiling, biting her tongue to hold back from expressing true feelings regarding Bryce Fielding. *Don't go questioning my objectivity. And while you're at it take your conservative bias and shove it up...*

"Do you want to join us tonight?" Lauryn asked, sought to play peacemaker.

"Sorry, we can't." On her face Natalie plastered a fake smile, defusing the tense encounter between college journalist and son of a conservative senator with presidential aspirations. "Bryce and I are heading into Chicago." Allison knew exactly where. "I'm going over to his frat house to change."

"Have a nice night out," Ashleigh said; Samantha heard the condescending sarcasm dripping from each word.

"Get back early," Allison reminded Natalie. "We have to be at Cooper Main for our first appearance at eight sharp. Coach doesn't want any of us being late." *Or hung-over.*

"Don't worry, I won't stay out too long," Natalie reassured Allison.

"Be safe, okay?" Allison hugged Natalie as they parted, received no farewell from Bryce tugging impatiently at Natalie's hand, hurriedly stalking off into the night. The four friends left behind stood silent, Samantha's ego smoldering like glowing embers in a dying campfire from the brief, yet contentious, introduction.

"Well, that escalated quickly," Allison broke the awkward silence. "So you finally got to meet Bryce Fielding. Pleasant fellow now, isn't he?"

"If you're trying to be friendly with Ann Coulter," Samantha growled. "Or Michelle Malkin."

"Did Bryce give you the verbal middle finger there?" Ashleigh amazed by the conceited display.

"I don't think you deserved that," Lauryn added in disgust. "You were polite. You didn't say a bad word about his father."

"I see why you want to hang with us, girlfriend," Ashleigh told Allison. "I wouldn't want to spend a second with that jerk."

"I'd rather be with people I like," Allison replied. "Besides, I don't have a fake ID to get into where they're going."

"You okay, Samantha?" Lauryn sensed the anger simmering underneath.

"I'm fine. He's a jerk, that doesn't mean his father is." Samantha stared at the back of Bryce Fielding as his figure shrank in the distance. She needed to have that talk with Allison Mayne to discuss her feelings, and suspicions, regarding the boyfriend of Natalie DiLaurenzo.

"Can we talk?" Samantha poked her head into the suite where Allison Mayne changed out of her cheerleading outfit into denim shorts and a long sleeve gray knit top. The four deciding to head to Greystone's, a popular restaurant in downtown Evanslawn, for a late-evening meal.

"I think so," Allison stood before the mirror, with her hand fluffing up the dark blonde mane. She turned to Samantha and smiled, but the expression sarcastic, accompanied an acerbic statement. "Isn't Bryce such a pleasant person?" She paused. "If they need a picture to go with the definition of asshole in the dictionary he'd be a perfect example."

"That's what I wanted to ask you." Samantha glanced about the suite for any sign of Allison's other roommates, Selena Espinosa and Sara Chang. "We're the only ones here?"

"Selena is out with her soccer teammates. They're over at Cooper's," another popular Evanslawn restaurant, "for dinner, then going to the movies after that, it's a team-building thing. Sara is in

Bloomington," the home of fellow Big Ten member Indiana, "for a golf tournament. We both know where Natalie is. So I think we can talk."

Samantha leaned against the wall. "What is it about Bryce that rubs you the wrong way?"

"I think you got a taste." Allison turned to face Samantha, hands on her hips. "He's a self-centered, pompous blowhole who runs his mouth and doesn't care who he pisses off." Allison sighed; disappointed her friend involved with one so narcissistic. "It's a long list if you have time."

"I think I do." Samantha nodded to her suite. "Ashleigh and Lauryn are still getting ready."

Allison motioned to the couch and they sat down. "This is between us for now, okay?"

"Strictly confidential," Samantha leaned forward. "What's the story?"

"Sorry about that up close and personal sample of Bryce's winning personality," Allison apologized. "Had a feeling he'd go there. Takes exception to what others think of his father, believes if you're against what his father stands for it's some sort of personal attack."

"I can accept standing up for family, there's nothing wrong with that." Samantha shrugged. "But the way he went about it that I have a problem with."

"There's no middle ground with Bryce, you're either with him or against him, friend or enemy," Allison agreed. "I'm no tree-hugger with my politics but I've gotten into some intense arguments over issues on which we don't agree."

"Aaron Dinehart said the same thing," Samantha admitted.

"He's the guy I wish Natalie was seeing," Allison rubbed her eyes. "He's the nicest person in the world and I think that's the problem."

"How so?"

"For one who defends the wholesome family values his father stands for Bryce is quite the bad boy." Allison bit her lip. "He's always out drinking, even without Natalie tagging along." Allison sighed again. "I think that's the attraction for Natalie. I don't know who I'm more upset with, Bryce for being the insensitive jerk or Natalie falling for him instead of someone kind and considerate like Aaron."

"Maybe after tonight," Samantha offered, "she'll see him for what he really is."

"That won't happen," Allison replied. "When he goes off on me or one of our friends because they disagree with his father, I always think that's the tipping point when Natalie will question what she sees in him." Allison shook her head in recollection. "Bryce and Selena had a royal smack-down fight over immigration, by the end they were shouting and screaming at each other. I saw Natalie was about to burst into tears, thought that was it between them." Allison shook her head. "But Bryce knows when he crosses that line with Natalie, starts up with the flattery, takes her out to dinner or the clubs. He throws money around, buys her clothes or jewelry, does whatever it takes to stay on her good side."

"So where does he get the money?" Samantha probed. "From his family?"

"I don't think it all comes from his father," Allison conceded, Benton Fielding accumulating a fortune on Wall Street as a venture capitalist before entering politics. "I think he has his own source of income." Allison lowered her voice. "At times he'll go off to make phone calls, doesn't want Natalie or any of us around. Then there's nights he goes out by himself, doesn't tell Natalie where he's going."

"Any ideas?" The perceptive antennae of a journalist twitched in speculation.

"Not off the top of my head," Allison confessed. "Three guesses where Natalie got the fake ID she's using and the first two don't count."

"Are you sure?" Samantha understood the serious allegation against the son of a possible presidential contender.

"I can't say for certain," Allison hedged. "But soon after they got serious last spring and started going out she showed me the fake ID. I asked where she got it. She wouldn't tell me but I knew Bryce had something to do with it. Looks like the real deal and she hasn't gotten busted yet."

"She wouldn't tell you?" Samantha sat there pondering Bryce Fielding, now a far more complex figure than a son fiercely protective of his politically powerful father, contradictions unexplored existed in his character. Samantha about to ask a follow-up question when Lauryn Callahan popped her head through the door.

"Ashleigh and I wondered where you went," Lauryn said. "We're ready to go."

"Okay." A pang of hunger rumbled in Samantha's stomach. "Allison and I were talking about something."

"Bryce?" No fooling Lauryn about their subject of conversation.

"We were," Samantha admitted.

"There's one good thing about him," Lauryn commented brightly.

"What's that?" Allison had to know what redeeming quality the redhead saw in Bryce Fielding.

"He's not here." On this point Allison and Samantha agreed.

"Having a good time?" Bryce Fielding asked Natalie DiLaurenzo, leaning close so she could hear him over the throbbing dance music reverberating through the club, named Buzz Thrill in Chicago's vibrant River North neighborhood, the pair patronized this evening.

Natalie barely heard him over the din, but nodded. "I am," she nursed the appletini in her hand, trying not to imbibe too heavily this evening knowing she'd be up early the next morning, had to be perky and charming fulfilling the many appearances as a member of the varsity cheerleading squad during a home football weekend. A drowsy, hung-over cheerleader with dark circles under her eyes not looked upon too kindly.

"I have to go make a call," Bryce told her, "I'll be right back."

"Okay, but can we head back to campus soon?" Natalie asked. "Have to get some sleep so I'm good for tomorrow."

"I'll only be a minute," Bryce left Natalie sitting at the bar, weaving his way through the shifting throng until he stood in the rear of the club near the restrooms. He punched up a number not listed in the contacts on his Apple iPhone.

"Yes?" A voice answered with a heavy, slurring Slavic accent; Bryce only knew the speaker as The Russian. The man, a heavy smoker, coughed.

"I'm looking for my usual action on this weekend's games," Bryce didn't engage with small talk.

"Last weekend was profitable for you," The Russian observed, coughing again.

"Let's keep the hot streak going," Bryce replied. "I'll place five on each one," that meant five hundred dollars on each selection. "I'll take Florida State to cover against Miami. Michigan and the points over Notre Dame. I want the over on LSU and Georgia. I'll take the Rams to cover against the Bears and the Patriots and the points over the Dolphins."

"Very well, good selections." The Russian commented as if taking down an order at a restaurant.

"What's the latest line on the Great Northern game?"

A pause as another cough rumbled from deep in The Russian's lungs. "Great Northern is favored by two, the over/under is fifty," Bryce found it incongruous listening to The Russian rattle off a betting line like a Vegas bookie in his thick accent.

"Twenty on North Carolina to cover and ten on the under," Bryce told him, twenty in this case two thousand dollars and ten a thousand, placing three thousand dollars on the outcome.

"You're betting against Great Northern this week." Bryce picked the upset over Missouri a week earlier and won big.

"They can't pull back-to-back upsets," Bryce explained matter-of-factly, no place in the realm of sports betting for the sentimentality of school loyalty. "North Carolina will be ready for them."

"Of course," The Russian acknowledged simply.

Bryce proceeded to his second business transaction with The Russian. "I have some more customers interested in your greeting cards." The code word Bryce used for the fake IDs. In the course of his sports betting with The Russian Bryce discovered the goldmine, funneling customers from campus their way and earning for himself a slice of the action. He scored fake IDs for a group of freshmen at the start of the year, one cute little thing whose father an influential player on Wall Street and a fervent supporter of his father's political ambitions. Bryce already had his sights focused on the pretty freshman, ready to move on to her when he tired of Natalie.

"Very well then, I appreciate you patronizing my other business venture," The Russian said. "It has been beneficial for both of us. Good luck this weekend."

Like you want me to have good luck, was Bryce's silent, cynical reflection ending the call, *doesn't do shit for your bottom line*. He walked back to the bar where Natalie patiently waited his return.

"Finished your call?" Natalie asked over the music. Bryce nodded. "Who were you talking to?"

"A friend," Bryce lied. *A Russian friend I do business with*. "You ready to head back?"

"I am," Natalie finished her cocktail, collecting her handbag, sliding off the barstool. "Can I tell you something?"

Bryce cocked his head. The look in her blue eyes a warning something troubled her. He didn't like drama, Bryce preferred his girlfriends compliant but Natalie possessed an independent streak he found difficult to control at times. "What's up?"

"I think you were rude to Samantha after the pep rally," Natalie told him, disappointment and anger mixing in her voice. "She didn't deserve what you said and she didn't deserve the tone either."

So that's it, Bryce realized, better to douse the fire right away. "Sorry, I didn't mean to be harsh," his tone apologetic, contrite, an act to soothe Natalie's fury. "You know how I am with the media, how they treat my dad. How they jump all over what he says and twist it around. Give him crap for what he believes in. I overreacted," Bryce shrugged, "guess I'm a little sensitive."

"Samantha is my friend." Natalie shot him an accusatory stare, not satisfied with the excuse. "She's doing her job. She'll be fair with whatever she writes about your father's speech."

"All right, I'm sure she'll do a good job. I'm sorry how I acted earlier, I was a jerk," Bryce knew Natalie desired a show of remorse. He leaned over, kissed her, hands caressing her hips. "Are we good?"

Natalie sighed, after a moment smiled at him. "Okay." The mea culpa did the trick. "But if Samantha is at my parents' tailgater tomorrow I think you should apologize to her."

"I will." Bryce Fielding swallowed his ego. *As long as I get something in return, baby*. Bryce eyed Natalie's body, continued rubbing her hips. He had needs of his own to address.

Chapter 7

Detective Devin Carson raised the pint of Smithwick ale in his hand. "God bless America."

"God save The Queen," Detective Nathaniel Hampton lifted his pint of Guinness.

Detective Patrick Flannery joined the toast with his pint of Guinness. "Ireland Forever."

A pint of whole milk, clenched in the hand of Detective Dawson Hilliard, the final glass raised. "Fifty-four forty or fight." The glasses clinked together.

"Teetotaler?" Hampton asked Hilliard.

"Never had the taste and never will," Hilliard took a drink, winding up with the coating of white on his beard. He set the glass down, rested his arms on the bar. "Like the ad says, it does a body good."

"You're in for a wild time if he's hitting the chocolate stuff," Carson joked.

"If it's strawberry," Hilliard warned, "lock up your daughters."

"Don't impress me as a straight arrow," Hampton motioned to the gallery of tattoos inked on Hilliard's forearms.

"Looks can be deceiving," Hilliard grinned devilishly. "By the way, where'd you get the crooked nose?"

"Did a little bare knuckles fighting when I was younger lad," Hampton drank his Guinness. He judged Yank pubs by the way they poured a pint and this establishment, The Kensington Arms, rated rather highly in his estimation. "A few times the other bloke's fist found my nose before my fist found his jaw."

"And he found the floor," Hilliard raised his pint of milk to him.

"Usually face first," Hampton said flatly, a sign a person not to be trifled with lightly.

"So," Flannery put down his pint, already downed half of the coffee-colored beverage so popular in his home country, directing his question to Hilliard. "Being a cop run in your family?"

"The first cop responding to the report of a fire at Mrs. O'Leary's barn that night in 1871 was a Hilliard," he answered. "We all know how that turned out for Chicago. Let's say I was expected to pursue the family business. What about the two of you?"

"I wanted to go to university and study fine arts," Flannery noted, an incompatible fact considering the Irishman's fierce appearance. "I was in a boys' choir when I was a wee lad."

"I guess you didn't sing soprano," Carson joked.

"Only if I got a swift kick in the jewels," Flannery rifled back.

"I don't see you giving tours at the Art Institute," Hilliard took a swig of milk, draining the glass.

The bartender knew Carson and Hilliard as regulars, walked over, placed her hand on the bar and smiled at Hilliard. "Refill?"

"Make it skim," Hilliard winked, "have to watch my weight." He turned to Hampton. "What about you?"

"Hard to avoid when your father is Inspector General at Scotland Yard and my grandfather once ran the place." Hampton sipped his Guinness, taking his time savoring the stout.

"Sounds like you didn't have a choice," Carson observed, dreading when the same question posed to him by his peers from across the pond. *They deserve to know why*, though the reason a painful reminder of a loss he still refused to completely accept.

"Oh my Pop let me get the wildness out of my system before I became a cop," Hampton acknowledged. "That's the reason I fought, seeking a thrill, sowing my oats you Yanks might say. Then one day I was over it and joined the force."

"We all grow out of our youthful indiscretions," Hilliard commented.

"I get the sense," Hampton turned to Carson, noticed his hesitation joining the conversation, "being a cop isn't what you originally had in mind."

"No, it wasn't." Carson stared into his glass, swirled the contents around to form a mini-whirlpool. The time had come to rip away the scabs from festering wounds and expose them for all to see. "The family I'm from being a cop doesn't rank high at all on the list of future professions." The careers pursued by his family typically found in corner offices of skyscraper towers lining LaSalle Street in the Loop.

"Don't mind me asking," this from Flannery. "What made you decide to become a cop. Something personal?"

"I don't mind you asking." They deserved to know, for the next few months they were partners, brothers. Even if the explanation brought back pain he quietly suffered every day and night. "And you could say that it was personal."

The four remained silent until Hilliard broke the silence. "Devin here should've been playing on Sunday afternoons, earning outrageous sums of money for catching a football." A pause. "Maybe waiting for the Hall of Fame in Canton to cast that handsome face of his in bronze."

"The two of us go way back," Carson pointed at his partner. "Before being partners."

"We tried to kill each other in the first round of the state high school football playoffs," Hilliard added a memory of youthful days. "I played for Lane Tech, he played for New Trier. We didn't particularly like each other that November afternoon."

"Remember who won," Carson reminded him, "and went on to win the state championship."

"You might've won and took the state title," Hilliard tipped his glass of milk. "But who made you hurt like hell during and after that game."

"You might've played American football professionally?" To Hampton the only football he followed the English Premier League and the FA Cup. "What happened?"

"I was recruited by Great Northern up in Evanslawn, played tight end," Carson lifted his glass, drank down more his Smithwick's ale.

Hampton nodded. "My niece is starting her first semester there, her name's Caitlin. She's on scholarship with their women's soccer team. Works out nicely. I spend a few months here, get to see her play. Going up there Sunday to catch their match, she's doesn't know I'm in the States yet. Give her a pleasant surprise."

"Keep an eye on her," Hilliard cautioned, "make sure she isn't using a fake ID to get into the bars here in the city." Someone producing fake IDs practically impossible to detect, becoming a problem in the hub of Chicago's nightlife and at the same time gaining the interest of Homeland Security.

"She's too serious for that sort of rubbish," Hampton snorted. "Sorry for the interruption."

"No problem." Carson raised his hand. "I played for Great Northern, getting a degree in business for what came after I got done playing. I had a girlfriend, Tracie. We'd been seeing each other since freshman year in high school. She was lovely, she was gentle, and she never said a bad word to anyone. Everyone who knew Tracie thought the world of her. She was special and she was mine. We had plans for after college, when I was in the pros and she was teaching. That's what she wanted to do. She was fantastic with children, they adored her. She'd have been a great mother." Carson closed his eyes, remembered the serene face, the soulful brown eyes. "She was the best thing in my life."

"What happened?" Hampton suspected something terrible snuffed out what was once the shining light in Devin Carson's life.

"She was at the University of Colorado out in Boulder while I was at Great Northern," Carson lowered his head. "One morning she left her apartment, walking to campus for classes." The next sentence hurting like a knife plunged into his chest, piercing his heart, a wound never healing. "She never got there, never showed up. No one ever saw her again."

Flannery cursed. "Christ, fella, I'm sorry."

"Sorry, mate," Hampton wished he hadn't broached the subject.

Carson waved off the apologies. "It was during spring football practice. Her parents left me a message on my voicemail. I got it when I returned from studying at the library." He stared into the half-empty pint glass. "I stood there in my room, the phone in my hand, couldn't move, couldn't speak. I never felt so helpless, so useless in all my life. I kept thinking how I should've been there for her. How I should've done something to protect her. The one time in her life she needed me and I wasn't there for her. Maybe if I'd been..." His voice trailed off, the flood of memories dammed up in his conscious every so often allowed to rush unrestrained, wiping out everything standing in its path.

"Everyone in that position thinks that way, mate. Believe it'd have been different if they'd been there." Hampton rubbed his chin. "I've done my share of missing person cases." They all had. "They're the worst thing. All the questions you never find answers for. We've all been there. Don't beat yourself up over it."

"I flew out to Colorado the next morning," Carson continued. "The next few weeks were a blur, spent most of it helping with the search. It's all mountains and forests around Boulder, a lot of ground to cover. Kept thinking she was out there somewhere in that wilderness, held by a lunatic in a secluded cabin, how she was praying for me to find her, to rescue her. I tried being strong for her parents, they were devastated, Tracie was their only child, but all the while I was tearing up inside."

"Without a trace?" Flannery drank from his pint glass.

"Nothing at all." Carson glanced at his reflection in the mirror behind the bar; saw the redness in his eyes. He warned himself: *Don't break down, be strong*. "Into thin air. No one saw a thing except a white van in the area where she was last seen. No reason why someone would've taken her. Nothing was left behind. They didn't even know where on the way to campus she was taken." He exhaled deeply. "Haven't found anything of her since then."

"Any ideas what may have happened?" This from Flannery. "Who might've taken her?"

"There was speculation some whack-job right-wing militia survivalists in the mountains took her," Carson offered one of the few tangible theories concerning the disappearance of Tracie Weatherly. "Then there's always the possible serial killer travelling through the area, searching for a target of opportunity. Maybe Tracie happened to be at that wrong place at that wrong time." A sharp throbbing bloomed behind his eyes, rubbing thumb and index finger on the bridge of his nose to dispel the ache.

"Has to be tough," Hampton sympathized.

"I was out there the entire summer, right up until training camp in August," Carson continued, recalling dark days. "I came back to Evanslawn and I no longer had the passion, didn't have the desire, to play football. Without Tracie in my life, knowing she was gone and I could never replace her, I couldn't bring myself to play. Some said I should play in her memory. They didn't understand that wasn't going to bring her back."

"So you walked away?" Hampton observed.

"The coaching staff and my teammates knew the hell I was going through. Great Northern let me keep my scholarship, considered it a hardship case. My Dad could've paid for tuition with the change in his pocket. Some people weren't so forgiving," Carson drank the last of the amber ale in his pint glass. "Used another word for what I did." A word starting with the letter Q.

"Bollocks to that," Hampton snorted.

"Bloomin' idiots." Flannery added, offended. "I'll bet none of those bloody fools ever went through anything like you did, fella."

Hilliard lifted his glass to salute Flannery's remark, taking a liking to their new, yet temporary, colleagues. "My sentiments exactly."

"So where did you go from there?" Flannery asked.

"Went to the Registrar's Office, changed my major from business to criminal sciences, loaded up on credit hours to graduate as quickly as possible," Carson dragged his finger over the rim of the empty pint glass. The bartender glanced at Carson, checking if he wanted a refill, but he motioned her away. "You know when you're a kid? One day you want to be a fireman, the next day you want to be a cop..."

"I wanted to be an astronaut when I was a kid," Hilliard said, "or the guy at the carnival sideshow who wrestled the bear."

"My money is on the bear," Carson smirked.

"Bear doesn't stand a chance," Hilliard replied, rubbed his chin with a knowing grin.

Hampton drained the last of his Guinness, motioned to the bartender for another. Hilliard pointed at himself that this round on him. "So after school you became a cop."

"That's when we," Carson jerked a thumb at his partner, "wound up in the same cadet class."

"I wasn't exactly thrilled to see you either." Hilliard answered, turned to Flannery and Hampton. "I knew what he'd gone through, the millions he walked away from. I let bygones be bygones and now we're partners."

"Kinda' noticed that," Flannery emptied his pint of stout, motioned for a refill, again Hilliard nodding he was paying for this one too. Flannery glanced at Hilliard. "You married?"

"No one will have me," Hilliard answered. "Except for a mutt I rescued from the shelter."

Hampton rested his elbows on the bar. "You're still trying to find out what happened?" More of a statement than a question.

"I'll keep at it until I know the truth," Carson stared straight ahead. "Until I find out where Tracie is, bring her home, give her family peace." His comment an acknowledgment he no longer considered Tracie Weatherly among the living. "A year after she disappeared her father died of a heart attack, some said it was of a broken heart. That he was as much a victim as Tracie."

Hampton drank from his fresh pint. "Hell of a world we live in."

Carson turned to Hampton, a fire in his eyes. "If I'm working a missing person case, I'm not a pleasant person to be around. I will do everything to bring that person home. Don't know if you've heard this over in Europe but there've been these string of disappearances across the country, clusters of women vanishing over a short period of time, nothing found of them." *Just like Tracie...*

"I have." Flannery took his fresh pint of Guinness from the bartender, smiled at her, admiring the lovely fiery-haired lass. "The time between these things is gettin' shorter. Looks like whoever's doing it moves around without a problem."

"I've been following the case, keeping up on the leads, what the police and FBI know," Carson's voice took a strident tone. "I know what to look for if this monster decides to come here. I won't let it happen here."

"You think there's a connection to your Tracie going missing," Hampton commented.

"Maybe there is, maybe there isn't." Carson stared at his glass. "Sorry, this is a bad time of year," Carson apologized. "Football is how Tracie and I met in high school. I was the star of the team, she was the cheerleader on the sidelines. Colorado offered me a scholarship, I wonder if I'd gone there instead would I have been there that day for her? Stopped whoever it was who took her? If it would all be different now?" He took a deep breath. "I can't watch a college football game, don't even try to read about it, too many memories, too many reminders. So tomorrow I'll drive up to my parent's cabin in Lake Geneva and spend the weekend without any television."

"That's why he won't go back to Great Northern when they ask him to attend a reunion of the teams he played on," Hilliard explained.

"I keep thinking of all the 'last times' Tracie and I had together." Memories rolled through Carson's mind like a movie, though a film without a happy conclusion. "The last time I saw her. The last time I spoke to her. The last time I kissed her." *The last time we made love.* "I don't want anyone else to go through the hell that I did."

"None of us do." Hilliard rested his elbows on the bar. "That's why we do what we do."

"At times I wonder if it's enough." Carson rotated the pint glass in his hand, as empty as his life since the day Tracie Weatherly disappeared. "At times I wonder if it even matters."

"I hope you don't mind the short notice asking if you can do this, but I'm on a tight deadline," Marcus Cowle told the two women sitting across from him in a booth at the nightclub named DeLuxxe, "the art director for this internet catalog wants to have prospective models to decide between by this Monday." His request directed to one of the pair in particular, Isabella DiBenedetto, a senior at Saint Vincent University in Chicago's Lincoln Park neighborhood. Though he didn't show it Cowle anxious about this meeting, hoped the young woman accepted his proposition. Experiencing an unusual string of bad luck, several possible targets turning him down over the phone and a promising prospect he met with earlier in the afternoon declining his offer, heading to Ann Arbor at the last minute with a friend acquiring tickets to the Michigan-Notre Dame football game. Needed three more women fill the order for Sheik Rahim, time no longer his ally but a persistent adversary.

"How much does it pay?" Isabella asked. A social work major at the Catholic university nestled among the priciest real estate in Chicago, she had graceful waves of dark hair shimmering in the light and expressive dark chocolate eyes, a body gifted with curves in all the appropriate places. Her skin the slightest shade of olive and a face glowing with sultry Mediterranean features made some mistake her heritage as Hispanic, though her nose a touch large yet attractive in an appealing sort of way. Their paths, as with Emma Hayden, crossed at another nightclub in the chic and fashionable River North neighborhood. Cowle took her photo, offered a compliment on the outfit she wore that night and engaged in pleasant, unthreatening conversation while measuring her value as a potential item for the shipment. Unlike most of his prospective prey, Cowle worked with Isabella on a legitimate project earlier in the summer so she was familiar, and comfortable, with the studio in Logan Square, possessed few qualms going there for a session. She wouldn't suspect anything, and the trap triggered, until it was too late.

"Two hundred dollars an hour," Cowle again rattled his spiel like a door-to-door salesman hawking encyclopedias. "I figure the entire session will take three to four hours. If they decide you're the one they're looking for the pay will be substantially higher."

"Sounds reasonable," Isabella sipped from the martini Cowle bought for her and Gabriella Taylor, her friend and roommate, an engineering student at Saint Vincent University. This the first time Cowle met Isabella's friend, in the dim lighting of the club's interior couldn't get a good sense of her appearance, if she might be the type Sheik Rahim preferred. She wore glasses with rectangular-shaped frames, presented a scholarly air. Cowle pondered if he'd need to deal with Isabella's roommate if she posed a complication to the acquisition. *Not the first time...*

"I'm glad you like it," Cowle confident the money offered a suitable lure to snare his victims in his web. College students always needed money, especially in an economy sputtering along and job prospects once they graduated not very promising.

Isabella reached a quick decision. "Count me in," came her reply. Cowle smiled; *jackpot, three down, two to go.* "Do you need anyone else for this project?" Isabella asked.

"I might." Cowle shrugged, noncommittal, a suspicion Isabella about to make his quandary regarding Gabriella moot, cutting down the number of items needed by one. "Who do you have in mind?"

Isabella motioned to her roommate. "I think she's sitting right next to me."

Gabriella, who had spoken barely a word as Cowle and Isabella discussed the proposed photo shoot, stared at Isabella in startled disbelief. "Me?"

"Yes." Isabella looked intently at Gabriella. "You."

"I'm not the model type, Bella," Gabriella answered; Cowle heard awkward shyness in her voice.

"Briella, move over here," Isabella pointed to a spot in the booth where the light from above cast the brightest glow. Her companion shifted underneath the light, Cowle gaining his first good look at the young woman, pleased with what he observed despite the glasses. A comely, feminine face highlighted by glittering hazel green eyes behind the spectacles and golden blonde hair, bangs dropping down over her forehead, the color of ripened wheat ready for harvest. She wore a baby-blue camisole tank top trimmed in lace, the plunging neckline accentuating a satisfying cleavage. "One more thing, let's lose the 'Nerd Girl' glasses." Isabella plucked the eyewear from her friend's face and Gabriella looked over at Cowle, a timid smile creasing her oval face.

Perfect, she's the kind Sheik Rahim prefers. Cowle pleased with the unexpected find; appreciative of Isabella's helpful suggestion. *Thanks for doing the heavy lifting.* "I think you're correct, Isabella. I think she's perfect, a fresh face nobody's seen before." *Two birds, one stone.* All Cowle needed was to convince Gabriella to accompany Isabella to the studio and the trap awaiting them there.

"I can't do this, Bella." Gabriella shook her head. "I'm not a model."

"The art director isn't looking for models," Cowle cooed with reassurance. "She's looking for someone new. I agree with Isabella, you're the type they're looking for."

Doubt clouded Gabriella's lovely face, turned to her friend, sought her affirmation. "Briella, you're a beautiful girl," Isabella encouraged. "You can do this."

"I don't know…" Gabriella started to say, about to decline the offer.

"Six hundred to eight hundred dollars for three to four hours of work?" Isabella reiterated. "How easy is that? Don't you want that kind of money?"

"Yes, but…"

"How much do to you make working twenty hours a week in the computer lab? Two hundred dollars after taxes?" Isabella explained the numbers. "You'll get triple that doing this for Marcus!"

"You think I can do this?" Gabriella still not convinced.

"Try it once, sometimes you have to take a risk," Isabella replied, handing Gabriella back her glasses. "You might find out you like it. Get some extra spending money too."

Gabriella took a deep breath, closed her eyes, thinking, deciding. A few seconds later her eyes opened and she answered. "Okay, Bella, I'll do it." Exactly the answer Cowle wished to hear.

"Excellent, I'm looking forward to working with both of you," Cowle pleased with the outcome. Four pieces of Sheik Rahim's consignment now secured, only one piece remained to be secured. Tomorrow night Cowle trolling the nightlife scene of Chicago, searching for an innocent young woman sure to capture the imagination of his favorite client. *The sacrificial virgin.* "Can you come to the studio around one on Sunday?"

Isabella glanced at Gabriella, answered as her friend nodded. "That'll work for us."

"Excellent," Cowle said. "I need you to bring different outfits for the session, things you'd wear to the clubs."

"We can do that too," Isabella nudged Gabriella. "You excited?"

"I think so, Bella." Gabriella smiled self-consciously, Cowle smiling back at the duo. Not only did Isabella DiBenedetto doom herself to a life of captivity, hideous torture and eventual death, her act of generosity sealed an identical and likewise horrible fate for her best friend.

Chapter 8

If it hadn't been the Saturday of a home football game, and their best friend competing in a cross-country race that morning, shutting off the alarm on her iPhone the last thing Samantha Grayson sought to do. Saturday mornings set aside for sleeping in after a long week of classes, resting after working late nights at the *Daily Northern*, but not on this day. *Things to do and places to be,* Samantha groaned, leaned over the edge of her loft reaching for the phone resting on her dresser, softly chiming Beethoven's *Fur Elise*, her finger brushing the screen. *Don't hit the snooze button, you have to get going,* mind bleary from slumber as the screen flashed to life. Samantha touched the prompt, quieted the alarm, a blissful silence settling over the room. She stared up at the whitewashed ceiling, took several deep breaths, letting her thoughts drift aimlessly before anticipation of the day ahead roused Samantha from the her lethargy.

Samantha heard Lauryn Callahan stirring in the loft across from her, checked the time on the phone, six-fifteen in the morning, sky beginning to brighten with the orange and red hues of the approaching dawn. "What time is Amanda's race?" Samantha tossed back the covers, eased down from the loft to the floor.

Lauryn yawned, rubbing the drowsy residue of sleep from emerald eyes. "Her race is at nine. We have to meet Connor at eight-fifteen for our ride." The racecourse laid out at the Cook County Forest Preserve west of campus and Connor Aanonsen, Amanda's boyfriend, providing transportation.

"You do know what's good about today?" Ashleigh Morgan came over from the room she shared with Amanda McKinnon, a room she had to herself the previous night.

Samantha gazed at her flannel pajama bottoms and oversized white Nike football jersey with a number four in dark blue on the front and McMANAWAY splayed across the shoulders on the back, smiled as she slipped feet into furry pink bunny slippers. "We don't have to get dressed to go to breakfast." Every home football Saturday the residents of Falmouth Hall gathered in the main lobby, still dressed in sleepwear and slippers, before trooping en masse to Lakeside Dining Pavilion.

"Too bad we can't go to the game like this," Lauryn added wistfully.

Energized and relaxed from a peaceful night's sleep, showered and dressed in her blue and white Nike warm-up suit with her uniform underneath, Amanda McKinnon already wide-awake for two hours before her friends stirred back at Falmouth Hall. She consumed her customary breakfast of fruit and yogurt prior to a big race, a meal loaded with carbohydrates to fuel the body yet nothing heavy to upset the stomach so close to competition. With her teammates gathered around her, Amanda sat on the floor of the hotel lobby stretching the strong, yet slender legs she hoped carried her to victory this glorious September morning.

Amanda eased her right foot in towards her waist, keeping the left leg straight, and slowly leaned forward, feeling the gradual pull in her hamstring. She closed her eyes, listening to the steady thrum of soothing New Age music through the earbuds of her iPod, the dulcet tones calmed the soul, breathing softly as she visualized each incline and drop, every twist and turn of the three-mile course. In her mind's eye Amanda always in the lead, surging away from her pursuers on route to triumph.

She reversed the stretch, left foot in towards her waist, right leg straight, leaned forward until her forehead brushed against her knee. Amanda thought then of her boyfriend, Connor Aanonsen, and a pleasant smile illuminated her face. *Too bad he isn't here*, she mused. *Always gets turned on when I'm stretching*. Not that the feeling wasn't mutual, Connor possessed the flexibility of a cat, when in the crease defending the net able to contort his body one way, then in a split-second bending in the opposite direction to deflect a shot on goal. The pair took yoga classes together, admiring the other's flexibility and aroused by the sexual stimulation such supple contortions encouraged.

"Hey, Gazelle," Haley Ryan, the senior captain of the squad, interrupted Amanda's brief reverie, the nickname a play on her middle name, Giselle, and her swift, effortless running form. "The bus is here to take us to the course." Amanda opened her eyes, the willowy brown-haired senior from San Diego motioning to the hotel entrance where the charter bus idled outside.

Amanda got out of her stretch, stood up, picking up her duffel bag from the floor. "It's a beautiful day," she commented brightly. "Let's go for a run." Saw on Haley's wrist the rubber bracelet in the yellow and baby blue colors of UCLA, never without the talisman worn in memory of a close high school friend who attended the school and disappeared a year earlier, never seen or heard from since.

Twenty-seven across; native of SC neighbor, seven letters.

Well that one's easy. Tyler McManaway dragged his finger across the iPad to highlight the entry on the crossword puzzle he worked on, occupying his mind while eating breakfast at the team hotel. Found crossword puzzles helped him to focus, a trait picked up from his father, an architect with an eye for detail. Tyler's earliest memory of his father was of him lying on the couch every evening with the crossword from the Sunday *New York Times*. Tyler had yet to reach that level of proficiency, using the virtual keyboard to type in *tarheel*.

"You ready for today, Tyler?" The familiar drawling voice of Head Coach Carl Hamilton, or 'Coach Carl' as the players called him, asked.

"I'm set," came Tyler's straightforward reply. Hamilton a bright, wily coach with an energetic personality, at thirty-six still young for the position, in his second head coaching job after taking Miami of Ohio of the Mid-American Conference to back-to-back eleven win seasons and bowl victories. Hamilton blessed with a charismatic personality, proved a useful attribute on the recruiting trail persuading high school superstars to play for Great Northern and not more glamorous programs. His looks were strikingly handsome: tall, blond, blue eyes and a smooth yet rugged face caused even Samantha Grayson to remark Hamilton 'a hottie' for a football coach. The sports pundits speculating on how long Hamilton lasted at Great Northern before departing for a program with far greener pastures. Tyler placed his bet squarely on Hamilton staying until the elite recruiting class he brought to Evanslawn either graduated or attained the loftiest of goals in a national championship.

"Crossword puzzle?" Hamilton asked, seeing what was on the screen of Tyler's iPad.

"I think I've watched more than enough film for this week," Tyler said, familiar with every detail and scheme of the North Carolina defense. "This keeps my mind sharp, keeps me loose."

"I'll take that as a good sign," Hamilton pointed to the answer for twenty-seven across.

In the kitchen of his darkened apartment Marcus Cowle sat with a cup of coffee in his hand, gazing out the window as the sun rose over a city beginning to awaken from slumber this Saturday morning. The radio tuned to WFMT, the classical radio station in Chicago, the volume low. He closed his eyes, sipped hot coffee black and strong. In his mind went over the schedule for the day, Emma Hayden arriving first for her session at noon, followed by Alexandra Cole three hours later. When she arrived Alexandra unaware Emma a subdued, silenced package locked in a closet and soon joining her as a permanent guest of their hospitality.

From above he heard thumping sounds, footsteps on the floor, a muttered curse. Cowle smirked at the noise. *About time the boys woke up*, he smirked. While he'd been grooming two of his victims for their Sunday appointment, his associates partaking of sinful pleasures on their final 'free' night in Chicago. Cowle wondered how much Sterner and Lang paid to indulge in pleasures of the flesh and if the experience worth the expenditure.

Cowle sat at the table, drinking his coffee, like any businessman worth his weight going over a mental checklist to insure this operation a success and in the process reaping obscene profits. Approached the task of abducting five young women, selling them overseas, with the detached focus of a banker foreclosing on a home and throwing the family out into the street in the middle of a blizzard. There wasn't much difference between the two actions; everything boiled down to a simple dictum, maximize the profit. He heard someone coming down the steps, glanced over his shoulder. Sterner stumbled into the kitchen, dressed in a pair of boxer shorts, rubbing his eyes. He said nothing, yawned as he grabbed a cup from the counter and filled it with coffee.

"What time did we roll in last night?" Cowle offered a jibe. "I do hope we had a good time?"

"You're my boss, not my father," Sterner growled, dumping four spoons of sugar, followed by a generous pouring of cream, into the cup. Lang, wearing sweatpants and bare-chested, joined his comrade in the kitchen, took a cup from the counter as Sterner handed him the pot.

"We had a damn good time," Lang remarked, pouring his cup, like Cowle drank his coffee unadulterated.

"We got our money's worth," Sterner grinned. "You missed out on the fun."

"I still had work to do, gentlemen." Cowle pictured the debauchery, his associates' sexual desires rather crude. "Perhaps you'll enlighten me with the sordid details when we're finished," Cowle reminded them of their purpose in Chicago. "You're able to complete your jobs today?"

"Don't worry," Lang drank from his cup. "For what the Arab pays us, we'll get the job done." That the chore involved assisting in the abduction of five women, holding them prisoner, terrorizing the unfortunate captives during their captivity, then handing them over to an owner who'd eventually end their lives didn't bother either man as long as they were paid for their work.

I can't believe I have to go in to work! On a Saturday morning!

Alexandra Cole growled, slinging her attaché bag over her shoulder as she stepped from her Lakeview apartment, locking the door behind her. Bad enough going to work on a Saturday morning, time she should've spent relaxing from a long week at work, enjoy a run on the lakefront with her dog, then unwinding with a coffee at Starbucks. That the demand made at the absolute last minute aggravated her sensibilities, the boss who took the day off calling with a demand disguised as a thinly-veiled request as Alexandra leaving for the weekend, forced to live her own Bill Lundberg moment. *Ah, I'm going to need to have you come in on Saturday…* That she had to dress as if it a regular business day only added insult to a wounded ego. If they wanted her to waste a Saturday at the office, they'd at least have the decency to let her wear something comfortable, blue jeans and running shoes, instead of a business pantsuit and heels.

God, I hate my job. Melancholy seeped through her pores as Alexandra hurried downstairs, depression only deepened as she stepped outside and saw how gorgeous the day turned out. She waved to the landlord working in the courtyard garden, a phony smile plastered on her face. She headed to her blue Ford Fusion parked down the street, passing people out enjoying activities far more pleasurable than work this Saturday morning. *Not little old me*, Alexandra thought sourly, wished she among those taking in the brilliant late summer day, *I have to go slave away in the salt mines.*

The appointment with Marcus Evans for the photo shoot the single bright spot in her dreary day. Alexandra liked Marcus, a charming man with a sympathetic ear, took an interest in the drama of her life, thankful for his offer. Perhaps the opportunity opening the door to a new life, a career she found fulfilling and not the menial, mind-numbing drudgery she dreaded waking to face anew each dawn.

Marcus Cowle made his way about the studio, whiling away the time until his first guest of the day arrived for her rendezvous with a cruel destiny. With meticulous care he adjusted lights, positioned the white background drapery. Understood the setting a charade but the masquerade needed to be convincing, continuing until the moment his targets taken down, began their lives first as his prisoners, then handed over to their new owner as sexual toys for what remained of now abbreviated lives.

One final detail to address before his first victim arrived, the lithe and appealing Emma Hayden, her appointment with a fate she never imagined. Cowle walked to the refrigerator against the wall, removed the six-pack of bottled water chilling inside. The bottles shrink-wrapped in plastic but the bottom of each container exposed, flipping the bottles over on the counter to rest the package on their tops. From a drawer he removed a small hole punch, a bottle of clear liquid and syringe, a tube of plastic adhesive. Cowle took the hole punch, in the bottom of the first bottle poked an opening large enough for the tip of the syringe to pass through.

He whistled Beethoven's Seventh Symphony as he toiled, taking the syringe and the bottle of clear liquid, a powerful designer-drug sedative rendering a person unconscious within minutes. He stuck the syringe in the bottle, pulled back on the plunger, liquid filling the syringe. Stuck the needle through the tiny hole in the bottom of the water bottle, injected enough of the drug to incapacitate his victims, leave them helpless to his will. Took the tube of plastic adhesive, dabbed a small drop over the hole to seal it, letting the glue dry. Since the cap remained unbroken his prey unaware the contents tampered with until too late, rendered out cold and vulnerable for Cowle and his associates to tightly package and quiet for storage.

Wash, rinse, repeat. Cowle followed an identical procedure with the remaining bottles. Once the glue dried on the final bottle he lifted the six-pack of bottled water, gave the package a thorough shake, placing the water into the refrigerator. The bright lights of the studio emitting a fair amount of radiant heat, his prey growing thirsty under the glare. He'd graciously offer them water from the refrigerator, the unbroken cap lulling their defenses, suspecting nothing wrong. They'd drink from the bottle and...*game over.* Unless the intended targets didn't drink the water he offered. *Always have a Plan B.* Cowle then resorting to more direct, and terribly painful and brutal, methods of subjugation. Either way the young women with appointments over the next two days didn't stand a chance against Cowle and his associates, ending as it had so many times before, kidnapped and sold as merchandise to a man with designs dark, violent and deadly.

Cowle heard the back door open, heavy footfalls on the floor as his two associates returned from the abandoned factory soon temporary lodging for five unfortunate guests. "Is everything ready?"

"We're all set, bring them on," Sterner the first to enter, followed by Lang.

"Relax, gentlemen," Cowle checked his watch. "All we have to do now is wait." *Soon, very soon.*

Amanda McKinnon took the last of her warm-up sprints as the start of her race approached, limber legs turning over effortlessly as she ran across the glade. The stride-out lasted only a hundred meters before Amanda stopped, turned around, jogging back to the starting line. Her head down, amethyst eyes fixed on the green grass beneath her blue and silver Nike spikes, listened to her breathing slacken, grow calm as a pond on a tranquil dawn. This her first big test of the season, facing a field stacked with talented athletes including the top two runners in the nation. The desire burning within Amanda to succeed, already in peak condition this early in the season, to win on her home course in front of her friends fueled her desire and stoked the furnace of competitive spirit. She breathed evenly, adjusted the number 101 pinned beneath blue and silver lettering reading GREAT NORTHERN across the chest of the form-hugging white spandex tank top.

"Good luck, Amanda!" Lifting her head at the sound of three familiar voices calling her name in unison, spotted her roommates and best friends near the start line waving at her, tiny Lauryn Callahan bouncing up and down in excited anticipation. Gave them a nonchalant wave, an unruffled smile, maintaining a cool composure while fighting down churning waves of anxiety sloshing about in her stomach.

A second shout followed, loud and recognizable. "Run like hell, Amanda!" Connor Aanonsen's voice boomed over the crowd. "I love you, babe!"

"I love you too..." Amanda muttered, face flushing red from momentary embarrassment. *Wait until your first game this season.* But her boyfriend's exhortation did the trick, nerves tormenting her psyche instantly settled, now relaxed and collected as she reached the start line, slid into line beside her teammates.

"Connor loves you," Haley Ryan told Amanda with a teasing smile.

Amanda grinned. "I know."

Amanda shook her legs and arms, bouncing on the balls of her feet, staying loose before the three-mile journey. She stared straight ahead and exhaled, vision narrowing on what lay directly ahead of her, the green grass and white line marking the path to a destination where victory awaited. She eased into a ready position, setting her body, blocked out teammates and competitors tensed and crouched beside her, the starter off to her right giving final instructions, lifting the starter's pistol towards the blue sky, his finger placing pressure on the trigger.

At the start of every race Amanda McKinnon invoked an inspirational citation to spur her to excellence, a passage from literature or a quote from an admired athlete fitting with her buoyant, self-assured personality and aggressive, go-for-broke running style. Her choice for this day a quote from William Shakespeare's *Julius Caesar*.

"Now bid me run and I will strive with things impossible," Amanda whispered, then held her breath, waited.

A millisecond later the report from the pistol echoed through the air and Amanda McKinnon leapt forward, sprinting to the lead of the pack of humanity breaking from the start, a stampeding herd thundering across the grass. Amanda running and doing what she loved most in the world, soul filled with unbridled freedom, hoping this day she did strive with things impossible.

Chapter 9

"You're so hot when you're sweaty," Connor Aanonsen whispered to Amanda McKinnon, embracing her tightly, yet gently, in his arms. Four minutes earlier Amanda crossed the finish line, arms outstretched in triumph, face glowing in satisfaction sprinting past her two closest competitors in the home stretch to win in the women's title at the Great Northern Invitational, shattering the course record with the effort. Connor the first of her friends to reach her in the finishing corral, waited impatiently as she congratulated her fellow runners and teammates before taking his cue to move in and sweep the slender, but deceptively powerful, body up in his arms.

"I know what else turns you on," Amanda grinned as Connor kissed her forehead damp with salty perspiration.

"Those bun-hugger shorts do it every time," Connor added, a roguish smile on his face, speaking of the tight blue spandex running shorts Amanda wore, hands dropping down, placed firmly on her rear.

"Hey! There are kids around!" Amanda yelped, warned of the high-school runners preparing for their contest observing, and finding gleeful entertainment in, the obvious display of affection.

Connor kissed her again. "They already know about the birds and the bees, babe."

"That's our Gazelle! She's awesome!" Ashleigh Morgan rushed up, followed by Samantha Grayson and Lauryn Callahan. Connor stepped aside so Amanda could celebrate with her friends, received a congratulatory hug from Ashleigh. He couldn't be the only one having all the fun.

"You looked fantastic!" Samantha gave Amanda a warm embrace, Lauryn next to wrap her arms around Amanda's shoulders.

"Couldn't have done it without my cheering section," Amanda gasped, still catching her breath from her feat. "Did you get the finish?"

"Every second of it," Ashleigh held up her smartphone; the device recording the thrilling climax, handing the phone to Amanda as they crowded around to watch the replay.

"Looked like you were shot out of a cannon, babe," Connor remarked as on the video Amanda charged past two runners-one from Wisconsin and the other from Villanova, both among the best in the nation-down the final stretch. Timing her move to catch the pair by surprise, taking and holding the lead with a hundred yards to go before the pair able to react and respond to her maneuver.

"It looked so easy," Lauryn commented. "When you run you float over the ground."

"I make it look easy, but it's not." *I beat the two girls who're favored to win the NCAA championship.* Amanda replayed the video, marveled at her effortless stride, graceful and formidable, as she forged ahead of her competition, arrived at a breathtaking revelation watching herself cross the finish line. *I'm as good as they are, if only for today.* She'd face the runner from Wisconsin at an invitational in Madison and then at the Big Ten Championships, a rematch with the girl from Villanova to wait until the end of the season at the NCAA Championships in Louisville. Amanda to find out then if she was as good, or even better, than her competition on the most important stage of her life. "Did you...?" She started to ask Ashleigh.

"Already posted on Facebook and Twitter, Gazelle," Ashleigh told her. "Your parents back in Toronto should know you won by now."

"Speak of the devil," Connor remarked, holding onto Amanda's phone during the race. The ringtone fit both her personality and heritage, a snippet of the bawdy 'Blame Canada' anthem from the *South Park* movie. Amanda took the phone and stepped away, relating good news with bubbling excitement to parents already aware of her stunning achievement.

Ashleigh sidled up to Connor. "Nice job there groping her butt," she whispered.

"Can't help it," Connor grinned, knew he'd been caught. "Those shorts make her..."

Ashleigh cut him off. "I get the picture, you pervert."

"And proud of it too," Connor couldn't wipe the huge smile from his face.

Ashleigh nudged Samantha, said quietly so Amanda couldn't hear. "Do you think you can get away from *The Daily Northern* for a few hours Monday evening?"

"Probably, should be finished with the Fielding speech story," Samantha replied. "What's up?"

"Let's take Amanda out for dinner, celebrate her victory."

"Have an idea where to take her?" Samantha asked.

"Price is no object. I have an American Express gold card and I know how to use it," Ashleigh joked. "There's this Italian place down in River North in Chicago everyone's talking about."

"Toscana?" Samantha asked and Ashleigh nodded. "The one with the head chef who won last season's *Top Chef*?" The popular cooking competition show on Food Network. "I've heard the food is to die for but a meal there costs a mortgage payment."

"Like I said, I have a gold card," Ashleigh smiled. "This is on me."

"Did you tell Lauryn?" Samantha asked.

"She's occupied. She found a dog to pet." Ashleigh pointed over to their redheaded friend crouched next to a spectator's golden retriever, vigorously rubbing the thick shiny coat, receiving a wagging tail of gratitude and a slew of wet kisses on her face. Lauryn a passionate lover of man's four-legged best friend, stopped to pet every dog she came across even if the owner a complete stranger. Her love of dogs the reason she majored in veterinary sciences, owned three back home in Colorado: Sugar, a yellow lab; Pepper, a Bernese mountain dog and Cinnamon, a golden retriever whose pictures adorned her desk and the screen savers of both her laptop and smartphone. Watching Lauryn cavort with the playful canine made Samantha yearn for the affection of her greyhounds back at Grayson Farms Winery, missing most of all Stormy, the small, inquisitive girl with shiny black coat likely spending the morning greeting visitors to the tasting room.

"When do we tell Amanda?"

"Let me make the reservations first," Ashleigh answered, "but I think tomorrow night."

"Don't they have a three month waiting list for reservations?" Samantha questioned.

"Not only do I have a gold card, but I have an in for reservations," Ashleigh said, Samantha cocking her head at the statement. "The owners want to open a location in Atlanta and Mom's law firm is representing them. I'll have Mom call them and..."

"We're good to go," Samantha completed the sentence. "Nicely played, Ashleigh Morgan."

Amanda bounded back to the group, her face beaming, hugged Ashleigh. "Thanks for posting the video. They watched before calling. They say hello, looking forward to coming out for Parents' Weekend next month and taking us out to dinner."

"What do we do now?" Connor checked his watch.

"I have to do my warm-down jog and stretch," Amanda tugged the elastic band holding her hair in a ponytail, hand shaking out long raven tresses damp and stringy from sweat. "Then I get my hardware at the awards ceremony after which I'm free to head to Warren Field and hit some tailgate parties before the game. I figure it'll be another hour or so."

"We'll have time to hit the DiLaurenzo tailgate," Samantha said. Owning a restaurant chain meant Natalie DiLaurenzo's parents laid out an impressive spread outside of the stadium.

"Let me guess," Connor said to Amanda, "you're wearing the medal the rest of the day?"

"It's a thing with runners," she explained, eyes bright with joy. "Isn't it the same with you hockey players spending a day with the Stanley Cup."

Connor hugged her. "Show off."

"Admit it." Amanda threw her arms around his shoulders, exchanged a fervent kiss. "You love my exhibitionist ways." Samantha smiled as she watched, for the first time in days darker musings lurking in the corners of her mind, of women never seen again, receded from her thoughts as a tide ebbs out to sea. Yet Samantha knew all tides returned eventually.

"Nice to be done with work for the day," Amanda McKinnon noted as they walked among the tailgate parties in full swing around Warren Field. Hazy clouds of charcoal smoke hung lazily against the sapphire blue sky as the succulent, juicy aroma of hot dogs and hamburgers cooking on grills drifted through the late morning air. "Thanks for letting me stop by McIllhenny to clean up."

"Are you saying we'd regret standing next to you during the game?" Ashleigh Morgan observed.

"You would've noticed," Amanda remarked as they wove a path through impromptu touch football games and others partaking of the particularly Midwestern game called Cornhole, "after I stood sweating in the sun for a few hours."

Connor Aanonsen put his arm around Amanda's shoulders, nose sniffing the scent of lavender in the sable hair, the hint of cocoa butter from the sunscreen slathered on her smooth skin. "I love the smell of freshly showered runner."

Amanda sighed, her skin tingling as his nose buried in her hair. "Keep going..."

Lauryn Callahan shook her head. "You two are pretty frisky today."

"Winning makes me very frisky," Amanda happily replied.

"When she wins, I win too," Connor kissed Amanda, drew from his girlfriend an eruption of joyous schoolgirl giggling.

"Don't start rolling on the ground ripping each other's clothes off," Ashleigh remarked dryly.

Amanda raised an eyebrow, sending a subtle message to Connor. "We'll save that for tonight."

"You're the ones who should be getting a room," Samantha Grayson added under her breath.

Ashleigh pointed off to their right at the silver helium balloon floating in the sky above a converted charter bus, both emblazoned with the red, green and white logo of the DiLaurenzo's restaurant chain. "There it is."

"About time," Amanda took Connor's hand. "I need to put some fuel in the tank after all that work this morning." The enticing smell of pizza baking inside the portable wood-burning ovens Matthew and Patricia DiLaurenzo, the owners of the well-known Chicago dining chain, hooked up to the back of the charter bus and hauled six times a year to a spot outside Warren Field, greeted the four friends. They wound their way through gathered revelers milling around the bus, found Natalie's parents holding court underneath a canopy extending from the side of the bus.

Patricia DiLaurenzo noticed the glimmering gold medallion on the ribbon of blue, silver and white dangling from Amanda's neck. "Someone did pretty good for herself this morning!" She gave Amanda, one of Natalie's close friends in Falmouth Hall, a welcoming embrace.

"A trinket for finishing my run through the woods before everybody else," Amanda innocently played down the accomplishment.

"Going to wear it all day?" Matthew DiLaurenzo asked.

Amanda fingered the medal reverently as one worships a lost holy relic. "Anything wrong with taking pride in one's achievements?"

Connor came up to the four roommates, passing out red plastic Solo cups. "It's not a tailgate without your red Solo cup." Though the DiLaurenzo's put on one of the more expansive tailgate parties, it was one of the few not serving alcohol. The four loaded up on the fare spread out on the tables, drank lemonade and soda, filling their stomachs in preparation of the long afternoon ahead cheering on the Great Northern football team.

"Pizza at a tailgate, not something you have every day." Amanda bit into a slice of veggie pizza.

"Are any of us complaining?" Samantha licked teriyaki sauce from barbequed chicken wings off her fingers.

"Heads up, everyone," Lauryn warned under her breath. "Here comes trouble looking for an encore performance." Samantha turned to see Natalie DiLaurenzo and Allison Mayne, dressed in their cheerleading outfits, blue and white ribbons in their hair, approaching the tailgater, Bryce Fielding walking by Natalie's side. Samantha bit her lip, the hot anger from the previous evening again bubbling to the surface.

"Down girl," Ashleigh warned, knew Samantha still stung by Bryce's comments.

'Mom! Dad!' Natalie rushed into the arms of her parents. Samantha noticed Bryce stood back, waiting, as daughter and parents hugged. Allison received her own affectionate welcome from Matthew and Patricia who considered Natalie's roommate a second daughter.

"How's it been this morning?" Patricia asked.

"Fantastic," Natalie smiled with a sigh, wished to spend more time with her parents, enjoy the tailgate party with her friends but the schedule tight. "A quick stop before we head over to the Alumni Tent for a performance, then we head into the stadium to get ready for the game."

Allison put an arm around Natalie's shoulders. "Our work as cheerleaders is never done."

"Good morning, nice to see you," Bryce finally stepped forward, greeted Matthew and Patricia apprehensively; Samantha noted the uneasiness in his manner. The arrogance from the previous night tempered in the presence of Natalie's parents.

"Glad you could come by, Bryce," Matthew replied evenly and Samantha quickly surmised their coolness towards Bryce, for reasons known only to them not pleased with their daughter's choice of an intimate acquaintance.

"Samantha," Natalie motioned Samantha to join her and Bryce away from the others. "Bryce has something to say to you."

"What's up?" Samantha plastered a gracious smile on her face, burying tumultuous emotions and ego bruised from unfair accusations Bryce Fielding directed towards her the previous evening.

Bryce cleared his throat, Samantha suspecting whatever he about to say not of his own will. "I want to apologize for last night," he started his act of contrition, "I shouldn't have said what I did, you didn't deserve that. I was way out of line."

Yeah, you were out of line. Samantha crossed her arms, nodding in agreement, said nothing yet guessed the amount of arm-twisting Natalie employed on Bryce to force the apology.

"I know you'll do a good job covering my father's speech on Monday. I'm looking forward to reading what you write in *The Daily Northern*," Bryce continued, head down, eyes focused on the ground. "I'm sorry I was a little...outspoken last night, it was uncalled for."

A little outspoken? Samantha knew by his tone what Bryce said neither genuine nor honest, only offering the olive branch to stay on Natalie's good side. But this wasn't time or place to refuse the gesture, no matter how disingenuous it might be. "So, are we good?" Bryce hoped the act of false humility enough to satisfy Samantha.

Make him squirm for a moment. Samantha stared quietly at Bryce, left him twisting under her unyielding gaze, she sensed him growing nervous at her silence. "Apology accepted," Samantha said finally and Bryce relaxed. Samantha couldn't resist a clever dig with her next comment. "But I hope what I write will be fair enough for your liking, since I do have that liberal bias."

"Fine by me," Bryce swallowed his pride as Natalie stood by his side, holding an invisible leash reining him in, unable to respond to the verbal prod as he might've wished.

"Samantha! We're heading to the McDonough Hall tailgater!" Amanda waved to gain her attention.

"Have to get moving," Samantha told Natalie, ignoring Bryce. "Have a good game."

Natalie hugged Samantha. "I'll do my best."

Samantha headed over to rejoin her friends. "Lauryn and Ashleigh filled me and Connor in on what happened between you and Bryce the Bigmouth last night," Amanda said.

"Was that an apology from Bryce?" Ashleigh noticed the uncomfortable body language as he spoke to Samantha.

Samantha brushed auburn bangs from her eyes. "What you witnessed was a mea culpa."

"I think someone wasn't happy with Bryce and convinced him to apologize," Lauryn agreed.

"I could tell Natalie was yanking his chain," Connor added. Samantha watched as Natalie and Bryce walked away, for now the score even between them.

"Now if only someone will convince Natalie to dump his sorry ass," Amanda commented as they headed to the next tailgater.

"Venti double latte, please," Emma Hayden ordered at the cash register, handing the green-aproned barista her gold Starbucks card with a remaining balance of five dollars and seventy-two cents. The Starbucks, at one of Chicago's notorious six-way intersections at Milwaukee, Damen and North Avenues in Wicker Park, humming with brisk business this late September Saturday morning. Every table and seat occupied by a wide-ranging collection of young urban professionals, college students and young mothers with children in strollers starting their weekend with a cup of coffee or some other drink laced heavily with caffeine.

The barista handed her the drink. Emma handed her a Citibank Visa card. "Can you put fifty dollars on the card, please?" She asked of the barista. The amount she added, with all the coffee she drank, at least getting her through the next week.

The barista ran the transaction through. "Have anything planned for today?"

Emma replied with a cheerful smile, signing the charge slip. "Have an appointment with a photographer, getting some head shots for my portfolio." Emma took her coffee and departed the bustling coffee shop, heading for her car parked on Damen. No one in the Starbucks knew they were to be the last to see Emma Hayden.

Tyler McManaway stepped off the team bus into the expectant throng of fans and students parting for the Great Northern players as the Red Sea had for Moses and the Israelites fleeing Pharaoh and his charioteers. Tyler hoisted the overnight bag over his shoulder, striding forward cutting a splendid figure in a grey suit and electric blue silk tie. Rather than wearing baggy warm-up suits, Coach Carl wanted his players to exhibit sartorial flair with their game-day arrival at the stadium, display a touch of sophisticated class to the waiting fans. Tyler didn't mind the dress code, instilling a sense of heading to work, ready to take care of business in his corner office of Kentucky bluegrass inside Warren Field. Tyler accepted good luck handshakes, slapped outstretched palms offering well wishes from alumni and kids lining the route to the home team locker room, hearing the cheers and shouts of encouragement filling the air. He glanced at D'Andre Watson, his friend affecting an air of nonchalant poise with sunglasses on his face, head bobbing to the music on his iPod fed through the Doctor Dre Beats headphones covering his ears, listening to a specifically selected playlist getting him 'gigged up' for the upcoming contest.

The players filed through the team entrance, heading down the wide hallway towards the dressing room. As each player entered they surrendered their iPad to the team managers. Over the course of the next day the game plan and video for the North Carolina game deleted and material for the next week's game at Minnesota loaded on the tablets.

The immaculate blue carpet with the white and silver block N in the center greeted Tyler as he walked inside, each locker a mirror image of the others, a stool with the Husky logo set before each cubicle. Tyler strode to his locker; fingered the cobalt blue jersey with the number four in white trimmed with silver hanging in the locker. His helmet polished to a glossy sheen, shimmered in the light. Football cleats adorned with the Nike swoosh shined to an immaculate gleam.

"Let's do this," D'Andre said in a low voice, "time to put on the super suit." Tyler silently nodded in agreement, dropped his overnight bag to the floor, tugging loose the knot of his tie, ready to don the modern-day high-tech armor of plastic and foam like a medieval knight preparing for a jousting match against the dreaded Black Knight.

Game time.

Wow, a parking space! Emma Hayden thought gleefully, pulling up near the three-flat brownstone where Marcus Evans Photography occupied the first floor. The Logan Square neighborhood not as bad for parking as Wicker Park, where Emma wasted fifteen minutes finding a legal space for her stop at Starbucks, spent another five minutes squeezing the sunshine yellow Chevrolet Impala into a gap only a few inches bigger than the car. At least this space offered more room, Emma easily backing in. She switched off the ignition, checking her makeup in the rearview mirror, running a hand through thick mahogany brown hair. *He'll let me freshen up before we start shooting*, but Emma knew first impressions important in the modeling business.

She slipped the strap of her purse over her shoulder, stepped out of the driver's seat and opened the back door. With a grunt she hauled out an overnight bag about to burst with outfits brought for her session and a backpack with makeup and accessories. Hadn't been able to decide on what she wanted to wear, the solution to bring whatever fit in the bag. Emma heaved the heavy overnight bag over one shoulder, then the backpack over the shoulder from which her purse dangled, for a second teetering precariously to maintain her balance underneath the awkward weight. She headed across the street, smiling in expectation of great things as sun bathed her face with warmth.

Emma had no idea this sunlight the last she'd ever know.

On the closed circuit surveillance monitor Marcus Cowle watched Emma Hayden park her bright yellow Chevy Impala across from the brownstone, exit the car with her baggage and walk towards the building. Cowle glanced over his shoulder at Sterner and Lang, raised an eyebrow and both men silently nodded, the pair disposing of the car after they dealt with the girl in a cruelly efficient fashion.

"Time to earn our pay," Cowle told them, switched on the device to jam the signal from her cell phone. They heard the doorbell ring from out front and Cowle left his associates sitting before the bank of surveillance screens, closed the door where they'd stay concealed until their services required. The doorbell rang a second time as Cowle walked through the waiting room to the door, took a deep breath as he grasped the doorknob, a transformation descending over him. Now he was Marcus Evans, professional photographer, and Emma Hayden, film and drama major at Pacifica College, his client. The relationship to continue until the moment she took the poisoned bait and Marcus Cowle, human trafficker, emerged from hiding to make young Emma the first of five helpless captives with a price stamped upon their lovely heads.

Cowle opened the door for Emma; standing on the stoop with an effervescent smile spread across her face, dressed in black yoga pants and a simple blue knit top, a black leather jacket worn over that with Adidas running shoes on her feet. Emma had an affinity for jewelry with necklaces draped around her neck, rings on every finger and golden hoop earrings dangling from her earlobes. Marcus Cowle smiled pleasantly at his unsuspecting guest, showed no trace of the monster concealed within. "Emma! Great to see you! Come on in, please."

"Thanks," Emma stepped inside, "these bags are starting to get heavy." Cowle closed the door behind her. With that simple action Emma Hayden sealed her doom.

Chapter 10

"Looking very good, Emma," Marcus Cowle snapped another picture of Emma Hayden as she posed for her first set under the bright lights of the studio. After a ten-minute deliberation over the many outfits she brought to the studio Cowle suggested they start with something simple and straightforward. Emma retreated to the dressing room to change and freshen up her makeup, stepping out twenty minutes later in a unpretentious form-fitting black skirt and body-hugging short-sleeve turquoise knit top, adding black hosiery and high heel pumps adding three inches to her sixty-two inches of height.

"Now place your hands on your hips," Emma did as instructed, "and lean a little forward." Emma leaned. "That's too much, back a little." Emma raised herself up an inch and Marcus Cowle raised his hand. "Perfect. Give me a big smile."

"Like this?" Emma asked, lips spreading in a gorgeous smile of glistening teeth, mahogany hair pouring over the willowy shoulders.

"Just like that," Cowle lifted the camera, started shooting, moving about Emma as he clicked off exposures, getting her from every angle. Experienced a brief pang of remorse, a shame such a beautiful young thing as Emma destined to be ravaged and destroyed. The feeling of regret lasted but a fleeting second, if Cowle wished to receive the substantial compensation for his labor from his generous benefactor lovely young creatures such as Emma needed to be sacrificed upon his altar of his greed.

"Turn your head slightly to the right." Cowle prompted his unknowing prey once he shot enough pictures of the previous position. "I want a little less smile and a little more pout on that sweet face," Cowle realizing such platitudes lowered the defenses of his prey.

Emma smiled at the compliment, her expression switching in an instant to one of subdued sensuality. "Is this what you want?"

Cowle gave her an OK signal. "Excellent, that's what I want." He snapped off several more exposures. The pictures taken during these sessions with Emma and the four other women slated for sale to Sheik Rahim permanent reminders of the exquisite items he selected for the consignment.

"Any plans for tonight?" Cowle asked, seemingly innocent small talk. Had to know if she planned to meet anyone, if required to take necessary precautions.

Emma shook her head. "I might go out with some friends, but I haven't decided yet. Give them a call when I'm done here and see what they're doing." She frowned. "You know I broke up a few weeks ago with that guy I was seeing, the one who played bass in a band," Cowle, through ongoing communication with Emma, already aware of a possible complication averted. "I'm not quite ready to hit the scene again."

"Give yourself time to breathe," Cowle advised, "Get your bearings." He motioned. "Now place your left hand on your hip, let the other arm hang free, turn your head to the right and give me that pretty smile again."

Emma changed the position as directed. "This good?"

Cowle smiled. "Perfect, you're a natural." Emma trying to keep from blinking as the synchronized flash from camera and strobe lights exploded in her eyes with every click.

"I know there's someone out there for me," Emma released pent up emotions. The break-up without any acrimony, but disappointed things hadn't worked out as she hoped. "Someone who's, you know, a soul-mate, not perfect but someone who cares about me." She sighed. "Why is it so hard to find Prince Charming?" Or at least a close acquaintance of his who was available.

Cowle lowered the camera. "If love was easy there'd be no need for divorce lawyers."

"You have a point." Emma giggled, her cheeks dimpling, Cowle thought the expression precious. *Such a shame you have to die.* But her demise enriched his bottom line. "I think I have enough pictures of you in that outfit. Want to take a break before you change for the next set?"

"That works for me." Emma nodded, thirsty from exposure to the hot lights. "Do you have anything to drink?"

Why in fact I do, pretty Emma. "I have some bottled water, will that do?"

"It will if it's cold." Emma sat on the couch as Cowle walked to the refrigerator. As he opened the door Emma removed her smartphone from her purse, checked the screen and frowned. "You have terrible reception here. I don't have a signal." She dropped the phone back into her bag.

I don't want you to have a signal. "It's been like that the past week, comes and goes," Cowle removed one of the doctored bottles from the refrigerator. "You'd think reception would be better in the city." Cowle walked over and handed Emma the water bottle as she rose from the couch. "Have any plans after graduation?"

"Thank you." Emma accepted the bottle, a smile of gratitude on the lovely face, twisting the cap. "I'm applying to Great Northern. I'm hoping to get accepted into their graduate school for theater and performing arts." The cap made a cracking sound as the seal broken, Emma lifting the bottle to her lips, took a long drink to slake her thirst never suspecting the water laced with a powerful sedative. Cowle noted the time on the clock, with her petite stature estimating how long until Emma rendered unconscious and at his mercy. *Not long at all.*

"I've heard Great Northern is an excellent school," Cowle added helpfully.

"They have a fantastic program," Emma took another drink, unaware the casual action sealing her fate. "The campus is beautiful and Evanslawn is a nice town. I'll probably move up there if I get accepted."

"When will you find out?" Cowle watched Emma, waiting for the first sign the drug taking effect on her system.

"Not until the spring." Despite drinking a quarter of the bottle's contents Emma's mouth still dry, felt a strange tingling sensation traversing her legs.

"What if you don't get accepted?" Cowle glanced at the clock, one minute elapsing since Emma first drank from the bottle.

"If it doesn't work out," Emma took another drink, forehead creasing, puzzled by a sudden buzzing in her ears, blinking as vision blurred, tried to focus, "I might move to New York or Los Angeles for a few years, try to break into the business there."

"No plans on staying in Chicago?" Cowle saw Emma rubbing her temple, shaking her head, the sedative swiftly breaking down her body's defenses.

"I'd like to but..." Emma started to answer, about to say how all the best opportunities were on the coasts when she suddenly stopped, hands trembling as she placed the water bottle down on the table by the couch. She breathed heavily, found it difficult maintaining her balance. "It's...kind of...warm in here," Emma stuttered, staring at Cowle.

Cowle said nothing, watched her closely. *It will be all over for you soon, Emma.* He smiled at her.

What's going on? At that moment Emma Hayden, though she didn't understand exactly why, experienced a sudden fear fill her body. *What's happening to me? Am I sick? What's...wrong with me?* Emma swallowed, grew dizzy and faint, eyelids fluttering like the wings of a robin in flight as the room started to spin about her with the breakneck velocity of a crazy thrill ride at an amusement park. "I...don't think...I feel..."

"Feel what?" Cowle asked. The malicious glint in his gray eyes frightened the confused girl, realizing much too late something wrong and she faced a terrible danger. Emma tried to answer, lips quivering, never completed her statement, a question asking *why* never spoken as turquoise blue eyes rolled into the back of her head at the same moment her legs gave out, a marionette with the wires holding her upright cut, collapsing to the floor in a lifeless heap without uttering a sound.

Cowle studied impassively the crumpled form lying at his feet, glanced back at the clock. *Two minutes...about how long I thought it would take.* Emma only drank a third of the tampered bottle, but the liquid spiked with enough sedative to leave her helpless. Cowle crouched beside Emma, touching her neck to check for a pulse, make sure she hadn't ingested too much sedative to induce harm. Didn't want one of his precious parcels expiring prior to delivery.

"I have someone here requiring your unique type of service, gentlemen." Cowle called to the rear of the first floor where his associates waited in hidden silence for this signal. Two sets of footsteps approached, Sterner and Lang entering the studio, Lang lugging an olive green duffel bag over his shoulder. "Emma, I'd like you to meet my associates, Mister Sterner and Mister Lang," he told the motionless body at his feet. "You'll be well acquainted with them by the time we bid you a fond farewell."

"Cute little thing," Sterner studied the unconscious woman, powerless to prevent the two from carrying out their assigned duties. "How long?"

"Two minutes," Cowle said. "Time to dispense your particular hospitality."

Lang placed the duffel on the floor, unzipped the top, removed a coil of white cotton rope and tossed it to Sterner. "You get the top," took a second coil from the duffel. "I'll take the bottom."

"Thanks buddy," Sterner leered at Emma, easing the unresisting body into a sitting position, looping rope around her wrists. "I get to check out," motioned to her firm breasts, "the merchandise."

"Pervert," Lang wrapped rope around Emma's ankles, cinching tight the knot.

"Look who's talking," Sterner snorted. "You're letting me do her so you get the next one."

"I'm not stupid, buddy." Lang had spied a picture of Alexandra Cole, the next victim slated to experience their skill at restraint, and lusted to feel the assets that chick possessed. "I know prime talent."

"And you can thank the one who selects this exceptional talent for you to enjoy?" Cowle grinned at the banter between his apprentices. Sterner trussed Emma's upper body, pausing to squeeze her breasts, copping his lecherous feel, then deftly weaving a secure webbing of rope like a spider spinning a cocoon about her prey, arms pinned fast against her sides. Lang moved up to bind her knees and thighs, finding opportunity to stroke nylon-sheathed legs. The pair acting with the brazen audacity of delinquent kids in a candy store stuffing their pockets full of penny candy, treating the crime of kidnapping as a spirited lark. Within minutes Emma Hayden tightly bound on the floor. Lang removed a pad of cloth and a long strip of cotton cloth from the duffel, handed the material to Sterner. "Make sure little Emma stays quiet," Cowle told them.

"Don't want you warning our next guest what's in store for her," Sterner informed the unresponsive Emma, head lolling forward, hair dropping listlessly over her face. Forced the cloth pad between unresisting lips and back into her mouth, wrapping the cloth strip several times around her head to hold the stuffing in place, checked the long mahogany hair not tangled in the knot. Lang handed a second strip of white cloth to Sterner, tied the fabric over her closed eyes. "All packaged up." Sterner eased the bound, gagged and blindfolded body to the floor and the pair stood to admire their handiwork.

"One down, four to go," Lang smacked his hands together as if dispersing dust following a hard physical job completed.

Cowle stepped up, lifted the camera, snapped off photos of their captive. *I would rather remember you this way, Emma.* "Put Emma in one of the guest rooms in back," Cowle told Sterner. "You two need to dispose of her car before Alexandra arrives for her session."

Sterner crouched down, slid a meaty arm underneath Emma's legs, the other supporting her back, heaved the limp, bound form up from the floor, a slight moan escaping the gagged mouth. "Hope you don't have a problem with cramped spaces, little lady."

"Does it matter if she does?" Cowle asked. Emma had far larger problems to worry about now.

"She'll be out for a few hours," Sterner entered the studio after depositing Emma Hayden-bundled up into a tightly bound, gagged and blindfolded package-inside one of the two small closets towards the back of the first floor space.

Cowle checked the clock. Had time before their next victim, Alexandra Cole, arrived at the studio to experience the same fate as adorable Emma. "We might be able to knock off a little early."

"First round is on me," Lang joked, though that wouldn't be the case, each of them still had work this evening. While Cowle trolled the nightclub scene for their final victim Sterner and Lang left at the empty factory babysitting the first two acquisitions, insuring the stay for their unwilling guests a slice of uncompromising hell. Neither man had any complaint regarding those responsibilities of the job.

Cowle retrieved Emma's purse, dug through the contents for her smartphone. The age of digital communication connected people around the globe with an instantaneous ease their ancestors might consider ripped from the pages of a science fiction pulp novel, though the marvels of science did little to improve how people continued to interact, despite the advances no improvement found in that sphere, the masses remaining ignorant and self-centered. But the electronic interactions left an trail of data bytes his predecessors in The Trading Society never had to deal with. He flipped open his laptop, launched a software program designed by an intelligence like his darkly committed to evil, though pursuing a far different set of goals. The devious mind behind the program, a young computer genius from Germany enamored with the teachings of Karl Marx and Che Guevara, utilized a complex code the law enforcement agencies of the world had yet to crack to wreak untold mayhem on the mainframes of multinational corporations and government entities to promote his message of global anarchy and revolution. Cowle didn't possess such lofty goals of world disintegration, simply employed the software to cover his tracks, make difficult the work of those tasked to discover the fate of the young woman now tied and locked away in the rear of the studio.

Cowle plugged a USB cord into the phone, the other end into the laptop, ran the software program. In a blink of an eye the program quickly broke the password for Emma's phone, the portal safeguarding the contents within breached as easily as a castle door shattered by the battering ram of a barbarian horde. Cowle instantly gained access to everything-email accounts, social media sites-that existed in the virtual world Emma Hayden inhabited. The software performed a swift search for any mention of Marcus Evans or Marcus Evans Photography in her electronic missives. Cowle scanned through the webpages Emma visited, the emails sent and received, the online postings to Twitter and Facebook. Saw a friend on Twitter asking if she wanted to go out that night. *Sorry, Emma has other plans now.* Cowle assumed the identity of his captive, stating she didn't feel good, deciding to stay in for the evening. Cowle deleted emails exchanged between them, though he understood the data never truly disappeared, remained on a server in a network somewhere in the digital netherworld. But by deleting the emails the police wasting precious time on the internet reconstructing his victims' footprints, tracking down the electronic bits and pieces floating in the transparent cloud of data. The time the police spent stitching together the trail in the digital realm allowed Cowle breathing space to collect and sell his product, then slip away with his proceeds.

Done erasing the electronic trail Cowle went to work on the phone itself, knew the device contained technology recording where Emma had been. He disabled the GPS locator application used to locate a lost or stolen phone, the police forced to fall back on tracking where the device pinged the nearest cell phone tower. By the time they initiated that action and received the information from the cellular service provider Emma, along with the other women joining her in this latest consignment, on their final journey to a place of unremitting horror halfway around the world.

Cowle finished his work with the smartphone, unplugged the device, tossed it to Sterner who caught the phone in mid-air. "You have an appropriate place where you'll leave Emma's vehicle and phone?"

"Sure do." Sterner stuck the smartphone in his pocket. "A wonderful neighborhood where we won't have to worry about anything happening to that car." Cowle quite sure Sterner lying through his teeth.

"Never thought we'd get here," Samantha Grayson noted as they reached their seats across from the fifteen yard line at the north end of Warren Field, squeezing past fellow students milling about in 'The Dog Pound' quivering with a concoction of anxious excitement and anticipation for kickoff of the first home game of the season. Everyone in the student section-save those deciding to paint their bodies blue or decked out in outlandish costumes-attired in the bright blue and white tie-dyed t-shirts distributed by Student Government who declared a 'Blue Crush' for the home opener. The front of the shirt read *Great Northern Football: Fear the Huskies*. The back of the shirt said *Don't Worry About the Bark. Our Bite is Worse.*

"How are you holding up?" Ashleigh Morgan asked Amanda McKinnon, around her neck still wearing the gold medal from the Great Northern Invitational, receiving congratulations for her accomplishment from friends in the stands.

"I'm wearing my compression socks," the pink knee socks assisting with post-race recovery, "and I have my Gatorade." She lifted the plastic bottle of yellow liquid. "I'm good."

Connor Aanonsen nudged Amanda as the crowd grew silent, motioning to the field where the Great Northern Marching Band lined up in formation at midfield. "Hey, it's time for the National Anthem," he told her, removing his sweat-stained Minnesota Wild cap. As the crowds quieted waiting for the band to start playing, everyone in the stands knew kickoff between the Huskies of Great Northern University and the Tar Heels from the University of North Carolina only minutes away.

Sterner stepped out from the brownstone, with singular focus walked across the street to the bright yellow Chevy Impala that Emma Hayden, imprisoned inside the studio and now condemned to her fate, had driven to the studio earlier that afternoon.

A simple rule dictated Sterner's actions as he headed towards the parked car. If one acted suspiciously, with guarded movements or shifting glances, onlookers always thought the person engaged in activities questionable or illegal and either called the authorities or remembered the person when the police came poking around searching for information. If one acted with purpose, appeared like they knew what they were doing and blended in with the scenery, then witnesses tended to disregard what they saw. *Look like you own the place.* So Sterner acted as if he, and not a petite college girl, owned the yellow Impala. He reached the car, moved to the back fender, bending down to inspect underneath, to a passer-by checking the undercarriage for a leak of some sort. As he did his hand slipped beneath his sweater, extracted an Illinois license plate with a non-existent tag number. The back of the plate magnetized, Sterner slapping it over the Minnesota tag. He moved to the front of the Impala, repeated the performance while executing the same maneuver, a show of examining the front of the car while attaching a second magnetized license plate.

Sterner came to driver's side and stepped inside, cursing under his breath as he adjusted the seat, set for Emma's small stature, to accommodate his bulky frame. He despised compact cars, thought the vehicles only designed for midgets and eco-freaks, preferred a brawny SUV with an engine amply fed by fuel-injected horsepower. He adjusted the mirrors as the black Ford Econoline van pulled up behind him, the license plate on the van covered by a thin film, the number unreadable to traffic cameras. Lang stopped the van, waited for Sterner to exit the parking space.

The walkie-talkie Sterner removed from the pocket of his sweater crackled. "You there?"

Sterner keyed the device. "Talk to me."

"Where do we dump this one?" Lang asked.

"South Side," Sterner had a specific area in mind. "Lovely place. It'll get stripped within days, if not sooner."

"Lead on, MacDuff," Lang answered as Sterner drove away, the black van trailing close behind the yellow Chevrolet whose owner lay incapacitated inside the studio on North Campbell Street.

"I've been hearing talk this week," Great Northern Football Head Coach Carl Hamilton stood in the middle of the locker room, players gathered about him down on one knee. He didn't shout, maintained an even, business-like tone in his easy Missouri drawl, "that you think we should be ranked in the Top 25. That you don't like being listed as a team also receiving votes."

Tyler glanced at D'Andre, who nodded. *Yeah, I'm the one he's talking about.*

"The only way we break into the Top 25 is by proving we belong there, not by running our mouths. To get respect you have to earn respect, you don't get it by talking. We took a big step when we went to Missouri," where Hamilton played quarterback his college career and started his coaching career as a graduate assistant, "and beat them in their house, spoiled their opener." Low murmurs of agreement greeted the observation. "North Carolina wants to come here today and beat us in our house. They want to spoil our home opener in front of our fans like we did down at Missouri. Are we going to let them do that?" Now came murmurs of disagreement, players calling 'no' and 'no way' out loud.

Hamilton pointed to Tyler. "Will you lead us to victory today?"

"Yes sir, I will," Tyler didn't back down from the challenge.

Another finger pointed, to D'Andre kneeling next to Tyler. "Are you going to run for that hundred yards you've been telling everyone this week?"

D'Andre flashed at cocky smile. "I'll run for that and more if that's what it takes."

"If we want respect, we have to earn respect," Coach Carl repeated, motioned for the players to their feet, now raising his voice, shouting. "We stand alone together!" He recited a line of dialogue from the mini-series *Band of Brothers,* had a personal connection to the story, an uncle serving in the 101st Airborne during World War II who stood freezing yet unyieldingly resolute during the siege of Bastogne when he and his brothers-in-arms surrounded by the Nazis. During pre-season camp he made his players watch the mini-series in the evenings after two-a-day practices so they learned of the teamwork and sacrifice shown by that greatest generation, standing together against overwhelming odds, hoped the lesson translated to the playing field of this generation.

"CURRAHEE!" The team shouted in unison, fists thrust into the air, the Native American word for the phrase, the rallying cry for those brave men of the 101st Airborne.

Hamilton pointed to the door. "Sixty minutes at a hundred percent and we will triumph, that's all it takes."

Teammates surged towards the door, keyed up by the pep talk, a staccato beat of slamming fists against shoulder pads, hands slapping together, players anxious to step out on the field and, after two weeks on the road, play before their fans, family, and fellow students, hear cheers directed towards and not against them. Tyler glanced at D'Andre and Albert 'Fiji' Fatuamala, saw both his friends ready to go. Tyler slid his helmet down on his head. *Sixty minutes at one hundred percent*, the equation asked by his coach seemed amazingly simple, yet in practice a most difficult endeavor. A sign hung above the door to the team's dressing room, next to a rock from the Bastogne battlefield cemented into the wall. An exhortation each player touched on exiting before tramping down the tunnel towards the field and sixty-thousand expectant spectators. *Challenge Yesterday. Challenge History. Win Today.*

As Tyler passed through the door he reached up, tapped the 'Rock of Bastogne' and the sign in succession. The time arriving again for Tyler McManaway to see if he could meet the challenge.

Chapter 11

"Damn, damn, damn!" Alexandra Cole muttered angrily under her breath leaving the Loop building where she worked. *A perfect way to waste a beautiful Saturday*, she thought darkly, *working like a slave in a galley*. She glanced at her phone, growled in dismay, running late for her photo session with Marcus Evans. For a moment she considered cancelling the appointment, tired and frustrated with her job, go back home and curl up on the couch with a cup of hot chocolate and Wrigley, her beloved golden retriever. *No, you can't do that*. Alexandra dismissed the thought as quickly it entered her mind. Sick and tired of her dead-end career, the grinding drudgery, suffering the dual indignities of being underappreciated and underpaid despite her well-meaning best efforts, the long hours not helping a non-existent social life. Had college loans to pay off and if she could break into modeling, even if a part-time proposition, so much the better. Alexandra wanted something more out of her life than winding up a cog in a corporate machine, replaced when worn down and obsolete. *I have to start taking control of my life*. She brought up the number on her phone, Marcus Evans answered on the second ring.

"Alexandra, how are you today?" his voice pleasant, instantly made her feel better.

"I'm running late," Alexandra hoped the admission didn't upset the photographer, knew they appreciated punctuality. "I'm sorry. My company made me come in to work today at the last minute. I'm just getting out now."

"I completely understand," was the cheery reply, Alexandra sighed in relief. "When do you think you'll get here?"

Alexandra checked the time, thinking what she needed to do. "I have to return to my apartment for the outfits I'm going to wear. And I have to take my dog for a walk, his bladder is probably about to burst if I don't." She silently prayed the time she then offered acceptable. "I should get there around four. I hope that isn't too late."

"That'll be fine, I don't have anything else scheduled," Marcus reassured her, Alexandra appreciative of his sympathy, wished her boss showed a fraction of the same compassion. "Don't rush, take your time and get here when you can."

"I'll see you then, and thank you," Alexandra headed to the garage where she parked her Ford Fusion, had no idea in the back of the studio of Marcus Evans Photography, locked in a dark closet lay the secured, silenced, unconscious Emma Hayden. Alexandra Cole, so grateful for his generosity, didn't realize the photographer she trusted so implicitly planned for her a similar predicament.

The blinding light at the end of the tunnel leading to the turf of Warren Field beckoned the Great Northern University Huskies football team. They marched forward as one, arms linked together, cleats clicking a staccato rhythm on the cement surface. Heard the rising, enthusiastic roar from the crowd waiting for their grand entrance. Deep in his gut Tyler experienced a sensation not far removed from a prizefighter heading to the ring at Madison Square Garden for a championship bout.

The team reached the end of the tunnel, halting as the rumbling cheers reached a noisy crescendo matching the shriek of a jet taking off from a runway at O'Hare International Airport, the squad waiting for the signal from Coach Carl to take the field, players bouncing up and down with energy bottled up and ready to be released. The marching band formed a passage for the team's entrance and lined up at the goal line, ahead of the players waiting in the tunnel, the cheerleading squad stood ready to lead the team onto the field. Tyler spotted Allison Mayne and Natalie DiLaurenzo glancing back over their shoulders, waiting for the sign to go. Beside the cheerleaders waited Cooper VIII, a four-year old purebred Siberian Husky and the team's mascot, straining at the leash of his student keeper, barking and yelping, as anxiously excited as his human counterparts. Tyler watched Coach Carl standing ahead of them, hand raised to hold them back waiting for the right moment, when the pandemonium reached its apex, to lead them onto the turf. Tyler closed his eyes, said a quick prayer, hoped for luck. *Let's do this...*

"Gentlemen, let's own this field!" Coach Carl dropped his hand and the mass of blue, white and silver surged from the tunnel, running down the corridor formed by the marching band now breaking into the school's fight song. The crowd erupted into a deafening, ear-splitting roar filling the bowl of Warren Field. The wave of humanity flowed across the grass as the student keeper let go of Cooper VIII's leash, the dog hurtling down the field, behind the canine mascot cheerleaders rushed forward at a dead sprint steps ahead of the Great Northern players, male cheerleaders hoisting enormous flags spelling out H-U-S-K-I-E-S as they lead the team out on the field.

In the stands Samantha Grayson found it difficult to focus on one specific detail, vision jumping between the riot of color and movement battling for her attention at the same instant. The school's Siberian Husky mascot hurtling across midfield as if pulling a pack sled across the frigid tundra of Alaska. The cheerleaders ahead of the players, the vanguard escorting the team on the field, for a moment Samantha hoping neither Natalie DiLaurenzo or Allison Mayne tripped and fell in front of the onrushing throng. The wave of blue, white and silver poured from the tunnel and across the lush emerald green turf of Warren Field, triumphant notes of the school's fight song filling the air, the brilliant September sunlight gleaming off helmets of cobalt blue.

In the middle of the pack of players entering the stadium Samantha saw the one she cared for the most, the number four on his jersey, as Tyler McManaway jogged to the sidelines. She felt a nudge from Ashleigh Morgan. "Don't our men look fine in those football pants, make their asses..."

Connor Aanonsen interrupted, shouting above the din. "So I'm the pervert?"

"We're admiring our men from afar," Ashleigh replied. "You were doing a hands-on inspection of Gazelle's rear-end suspension." At the retort Amanda McKinnon doubled up with laughter.

"I think you have a point about the football pants, Ashleigh," Lauryn spoke up, a smile on her face watching Albert 'Fiji' Fatuamala stride on to the field.

Connor turned to Amanda. "You think I'm sexy when I'm in my goalie pads?"

Amanda rubbed his cheek, kissed him, wrapped her arms tightly around his waist. "You look like the big teddy bear I snuggled with when I was a kid," she cooed with the delight of a first-grade schoolgirl. "You're my cuddly Connor Bear!"

Samantha, Ashleigh and Lauryn turned to the pair, shouted in unison. "Get a room!"

On the field Tyler McManaway gathered his teammates around him, bellowing at the top of his lungs, accepting his role as leader of the team. "You heard what Coach Carl said! Let's own this field! Let's own this game! Let's own that team on the other side! This is our house and those guys are trespassing!" He pointed to the North Carolina players in uniforms of white smartly trimmed with Carolina blue gathered on the opposite side of the field. "We stand alone together! CURRAHEE!"

The players crowding on Tyler responded in a guttural response. "CURRAHEE!"

Senior Brendan Quinn, one of the team captains and the starting center on the offensive line trotted over, out at midfield for the coin toss. "We've got the ball first."

Tyler took a deep breath, secured his chinstrap as the kick return squad took the field, the public address system blaring the thumping bass line of 'Seven Nation Army' by The White Stripes, students in the stands bouncing and chanting in unison to the beat as Quentin Kennedy and D'Artagnan Wellington jogged to the goal line to take the kick. Albert 'Fiji' Fatuamala stepped up to Tyler, a huge hand patting his shoulder pads, Tyler hoped those hands found their way to the Tar Heels quarterback. "Ready to let North Carolina know who 'Touchdown Tyler' is?"

D'Andre Watson stood on the other side of his friend. "Ready to roll?"

Tyler glanced at D'Andre. "Ready to run for that hundred?"

D'Andre grinned, buckled his chinstrap. "You know I am."

Tyler nodded. "Let's own these guys."

Quentin Kennedy fielded the kick at the Great Northern four-yard line, the North Carolina kicker under orders to keep the ball away from the explosive D'Artagnan Wellington who already tallied return scores against their first two opponents. The strategy didn't work quite as designed, 'Q' Kennedy threading and shifting his way through the coverage to the Great Northern thirty-seven yard line, gave the offense excellent field position to start the game. Tyler jogged on the field, stepped into the huddle. "Okay, let's welcome our guests from down South to friendly Evanslawn."

The first play simple, D'Andre taking a handoff from Tyler, running off right tackle for seven yards, the offensive line carving out a huge hole. On second and three Tyler rolled to his left, hit tight end Casey Ellerbie cutting across the middle for a pickup of eight and the Huskies initial first down of the game, eliciting a full-throated 'Husky Howl' from the student section, the ball across midfield to the North Carolina forty-eight.

Tyler glanced to the sideline for the next play, the method of sending in the play on the same level as transmitting a message via a top-secret superpower code, the three backup quarterbacks each performing a role in the deception. Coach Carl consulted the play chart listing all the scenarios and corresponding formations, selected one, then covered his mouth with the card as he relayed the call to the three backups. Wendell Carlton initiated a series of complex hand signals while Breckin Moore held up a giant piece of green poster-board and Ian Worley held up a second poster board with a meme of four unrelated pictures, the images changing for each play. For this call the series of four memes were a lion prowling the African grassland, late-night talk show host David Letterman, the Grand Canyon and cartoon character Magilla Gorilla.

Tyler studied the boards, from spending time on computers since he was young developed the ability to instantly assimilate information. *Green, David Letterman, on three.* After deciphering the three disparate signals-each week the pattern changed so no opponent able to pick up on the system-Tyler flipped up the panel on the wristband on his left wrist, on it an identical, yet miniaturized, version of the play chart held by Coach Carl. He found the corresponding formation, stepped back into the huddle, called the play and the count. "Rip Delta 22 Slash 84 on three." The play a fake into the line by D'Andre Watson turning quickly into a bubble-screen toss out to Quentin Kennedy in the flat. The play worked to perfection, Kennedy using his blockers to juke his way through the defense for thirteen yards and another first down at the North Carolina thirty-five.

D'Andre Watson gained four yards on the next play, taking the ball down to the Tar Heel thirty-one. An incomplete pass resulted on second down, Tyler's first misfire of the day, the ball thrown behind D.B. Bailey who cut to the outside when Tyler thought him heading towards the middle. The first third down play of the day another pass, this one complete to Michael Haindelhaven at the twenty-five yard line, as he stepped out of bounds for another first down.

Tyler peered over to the sidelines. Coach Carl holding up the play chart in front of his mouth, relaying the call to the trio of backup quarterbacks. Wendell Carlton went through another set of hand signals, Breckin Moore holding up an orange poster-board and Ian Worley a poster-board with four new pictures: cartoon character Scooby Doo, President Abraham Lincoln, the Chicago Cubs logo and a litter of black Labrador retriever puppies. *Orange, puppies, on three, got it.* Tyler stepped into the huddle, again consulted his wristband. The key to the code the color card, told Tyler which of the pictures to focus on, Carlton's gestures told him the count. "Whirlwind Zorro Gatling Blue 81 on three." The team broke huddle, approached the line.

Tyler crouched under center before stepping back into a shotgun formation for the first time, the crowds in the stands roaring as Great Northern drove closer to the Tar Heel goal line for a score on the opening drive. Four receivers lined up in the formation with D.B. Bailey split wide to the left and D'Artagnan Wellington wide right, Quentin Kennedy lined up in the slot to the left and Michael Haindelhaven set in the right slot, D'Andre the lone back with Tyler in the backfield. Kennedy turned, went in motion towards the right side of the formation, the defensive back covering him shadowing the move from across the line. Tyler smiled, the three receivers on the right side of the formation to cause a slight traffic jam to allow his primary target to break loose.

Tyler called out the signals, on three the ball snapped back into his waiting hands. He faked a quick handoff to D'Andre, freezing the linebackers in place for an instant. To Tyler's right the convergence of three receivers in the same area caused a brief moment of confusion for the defensive coverage as Haindelhaven cut out to the sideline and down the field and Wellington back towards the inside of the field, Kennedy adding further deception crossing behind Wellington, running into the space between Wellington and Haindelhaven. The defensive backs in coverage hesitating, trying not run into each other. The time Wellington needed to slip down the seam and get open.

Tyler saw Wellington cutting to the inside, breaking into the open at the twenty. Tyler planted his feet as a Tar Heel pass rusher charged from his left, putting pressure on him, stopped in his tracks by D'Andre staying in the backfield to block after the fake, giving up his body to protect his quarterback and friend. Tyler cocked his arm behind his head, in a fluid motion fired it forward, releasing the ball from his hand. The ball, in a tight spiral, travelled inches above the outstretched hands of the defenders, aiming for a point a few steps ahead of his receiver, estimating the trajectory of ball and receiver to meet at the same place at an exact moment.

The Trading Society

The football and the hands of the receiver made contact at the thirteen-yard line, Wellington never breaking stride as he gathered the throw into his grasp, defensive back covering Wellington trying desperately to close the gap on him. The stands erupted at the reception, the roar increasing to a climax as Wellington outsprinted his defender into the end zone for the Great Northern touchdown.

Tyler watched from the pocket, protection shielding him from the rush long enough to get the pass off, as Wellington made the catch and ran in for the score. As the throngs cheered the touchdown Tyler started down the field to join the celebration, pumping his fist in satisfaction watching Wellington and Kennedy leap and body-bump in the end zone. "That's how to start off our first home game," D'Andre shouted, trading a forearm smash with Tyler as they ran towards the end zone.

An urban wasteland of trash-filled empty lots and boarded-up foreclosed homes, a few teetering on the verge of collapse, plundered of anything of value and left like skeletal carcasses in the desert stripped of every shred of meat by a flock of vultures, lined the street of the Englewood neighborhood. How many secret clients of Marcus Cowle and the other Collectors of The Trading Society responsible for this rampant decay neither Sterner nor Lang knew or cared. But whoever accountable their actions effective degrading and denigrating an entire segment of the populace, shunting them further to the outer margins of society and ever closer to the edge of oblivion.

Sterner walked along the rear of the car, removed the magnetic plate covering the car's license plate, strode up to the front bumper and did the same. Lang, driving the black Ford van, eased up beside the yellow Chevrolet Impala, Sterner quickly jumping in on the passenger side. "What's the over/under until the locals take care of the car?" Lang asked his partner.

Sterner pondered the proposition; a glance out the window at the desolation cemented his answer. "I'll give it less than an hour until someone checks the car out. You know they'll take the phone first, smash the window to get it." Sterner left the iPhone exposed on the passenger seat. "That'll give the cops something to chase whenever this chick is reported missing." Sending the police on a quixotic hunt in a dead-end direction away from the vacant factory on the city's northwest side. Lang listening to the Great Northern-North Carolina game on WGN as Sterner got in the van. In their opinion fall the best season for sports with college and pro football in full swing, the two betting whenever possible transforming financial windfalls from kidnapping young women into further riches, here in Chicago placing their wagers through a man called The Russian.

"What's the score?" Sterner asked.

"Great Northern's up 7-0, but Carolina's driving," Lang informed him. "Crap." North Carolina scored, their running back plunging in from the two to cap a seven-minute, eighty-nine yard drive. The extra point tied the game.

"They give any other scores?" Sterner stared out the window as they drove from the god-forsaken urban hellhole reminding him of similar shell-blasted hellholes on the other side of the world. Sterner had money riding on the Florida State-Miami game.

"Not yet," Lang shook his head. "Wonder what the mood is down in Lubbock this weekend?" The city home to Texas Tech University where earlier that week the pair and their employer visited plying their evil trade, student body missing two students now property of a brutal Mexican drug lord.

"Gee, ain't that a shame." The souls of Christopher Sterner and Curtis Lang devoid of any shred of remorse, empty of pity for the victims they abducted as acolytes of Marcus Cowle and The Trading

Society. The pair a 'Mutt and Jeff' combination, Sterner towering and broad in stature, physically imposing where Lang short and compact, a coiled spring of tension, sudden and explosive in his violence. Both men merciless and coldblooded, proficient in arts lethal and deadly, presented an intimidating front to those unlucky to cross their path, many of them the unfortunate women they aided Marcus Cowle in abducting and selling to moneyed, omnipotent entities. To the duo their victims only represented fabulous sums of money, their boss generous in compensation for their adept assistance.

The route the pair travelled to personify the hired muscle of a human trafficking operation a circuitous one, never suspecting this curious circumstance when meeting as fresh faced recruits in the United States Army. Both products of broken homes and families with whom they no longer desired contact, enduring troubled childhoods where they depended on their own wits and abilities to survive the turmoil. Through this shared experience the two bonded easily, found a brotherly kinship missing in their past, progressing up the military structure acquiring skills they soon found lucrative in pursuing criminal activities the upper echelon might find troubling to line their pockets with money.

The pair served in the invasion of Iraq, despite their faults doing their part to liberate the country from the iron-fist rule of Saddam Hussein. Whatever pride they might've felt freeing the country from the grip of tyranny soon faded at the realization the locals not keen on wanting the Americans to stick around once the dictator toppled from power. The lack of gratitude, seeing comrades killed by those they freed, lit a fire of resentment in the pair and they, now in an intelligence-gathering role for their unit, lashed out at adversaries real and imagined with increasing brutality, reaching a point where they hovered on the edge of court-martial for the cruelty of their deeds.

That fate avoided when they were surreptitiously discharged from service and quickly hired as 'consultants' for a private contractor with connections to the Administration in power in Washington, handling security matters in the Byzantine maze of chaotic post-war Iraq. They soon found their duties not about guarding corporate bigwigs but 'collecting' and 'extracting' intelligence concerning insurgent activity from the locals, passing the bits and scraps on to the military for them to deal with. As contractors allowed free reign to take whatever action, as vicious and callous if need be, deemed necessary to get the job done in the name of security for the American presence in Iraq.

To accomplish this they snatched whatever Iraqi civilians connected to the insurgents, mainly family members, spiriting them to an isolated location to employ enhanced interrogation tactics, a plain-sounding euphemism for painful, excruciating torture to extricate information from their captives. In the shadows they did their work until one interrogation spiraled out of control and a detainee died in their custody. Then they discovered the expired prisoner related to an influential cleric whose support the Americans badly needed if the country ever to emerge from the chaos of insurrection. The incident might've disappeared in the fog of the occupation, but one with knowledge of the incident suffered an attack of conscience and passed the story to the media.

A senior manager tipped the pair off the Feds about to arrest them for their actions in an effort to placate the Iraqis, portray Sterner and Lang as loose cannons, scapegoats for those at higher levels calling the shots, taking the fall for carrying out orders issued by others beyond the reach of punishment. They slipped out of the country, with their finely honed skills a simple exercise, and faded into a seamy, untidy reality as soldiers-for-hire peddling their deadly skills to the highest bidder in flashpoint guerilla wars, small yet brutal, dotting the globe.

The money they received decent but the atmosphere not conducive with death a constant workplace hazard. One day, as they sat in a bombed-out school inhaling the stench of rotting corpses pervading the hot air of a war-torn African nation, Marcus Cowle appeared like a wraith from the searing haze and announced he was in the market for men with their particular skill-set, wished to offer a business proposition. The idea of an organization Cowle called The Trading Society, dealing in human merchandise generating millions from those willing to pay for living product, seemed far-fetched. But Sterner and Lang made inquiries to underworld connections they'd come acquainted with during their time as mercenaries, confirming the existence of the shadowy group and validity of Cowle's proposal.

Why not? Their current prospects didn't appear all too rosy, Sterner and Lang deciding to take the slight man up on the offer. Discovered their employer, with his whisper-thin build and nondescript appearance of a corporate account, soft-spoken and erudite, as ruthless and cruel as they could be on their best days. Never exhibiting the slightest hint of sympathy for the women he snatched and shipped off to despicable fates. The money earned from this enterprise far more lucrative than any payment a local warlord or guerilla leader could provide, found practicing skills of capture and restraint on young, beautiful women instead of Iraqi men a state of affairs far more agreeable. Whenever they kidnapped another target the pair experienced a dark sensual thrill, the scent of fear from their prey trapped in their inescapable captivity concocted an intoxicating drink from which the two heavily imbibed.

Now they anticipated the biggest payday of their nascent careers with The Trading Society, the Arab known as Sheik Rahim, and the demons of sexually violent appetites raging within the man, required nourishment once more. Sterner and Lang doing their part to satisfy his appetite, receiving a handsome reward for serving five women on a platter for their wealthy benefactor to feast on.

Tyler McManaway leaned into the huddle, glanced at the wristband after deciphering the code of the meme and signals-*blue, the Death Star, on two*-communicated from the sideline. "Tango Split 22 Blue Squadron on two," he told teammates circled around him. Said to D'Andre Watson. "Time to show them what you've got."

"Show time," D'Andre replied. The play a run to the right side of the formation, if executed perfectly putting the talents of the running back from Huntington Beach on full display for those in the stands and watching on the ESPN national telecast. Hands clapped together and the huddle broke, the players moving up to the line.

In the backfield D'Andre lined up in an I-formation behind fullback Dante Clark. Standing with a slight lean forward, hands resting on his thigh pads, D'Andre studied the defensive front, observing the linebackers dancing up and down the line. D'Andre never focused on where he was going to run the ball, never tipped which direction the play to go. The call a classic, no-frills ground game play, designed to sweep around the right end. Left guard pulling out and heading down the line, adding force to the point of attack, designed to use D'Andre's speed to break containment, gain big yards once around the end.

Tyler crouched behind center, called out the signals. On two Brendan Quinn snapped the ball into his hands and the linemen, offensive and defensive, engaged. Immense bodies moving, shifting and colliding as left guard N'dokowe N'derena stepped out and charged down the line to the right. Tyler eased out from center, ball held out in his left hand; D'Andre moved to meet Tyler, arms formed to cradle the hand-off against his chest like a swaddling newborn. The ball slid effortlessly into his arms,

D'Andre secured his grip, heading to the right with N'derena and Clarke leading him towards the hole when a most peculiar sensation occurred.

For one gifted with blinding speed every time D'Andre carried the ball and knew he was about to break a big play, time and space seemed to decelerate to the point of nothingness, his vision sharpened to the clarity of an expensive high-definition television. He observed each clump of earth chewed from the turf by churning Nike football cleats, the spray of sweat shaken loose from skin by physical contact. The movements of the players about him reduced to a super-slow motion video shot by NFL Films, all D'Andre needed to hear was the stentorian voice of John Faccenda in his head. *Moving relentlessly like a train rumbling down the side of a mountain without any brakes...*

The Tar Heel defense reacting with respect to his speed, moving to cut off the sideline, stringing out the play to force him out of bounds. As they'd done against Ole Miss they were *over-pursuing,* as D'Andre studied on game film replayed on his iPad hundreds of times this week. From the corner of his eye saw tight end Casey Ellerbie seal off the linebacker, open the slightest gap back to the *inside,* towards the middle of the field. *Go where they don't expect you to go.* D'Andre planted his right foot, changed direction in a blink, cutting back against the grain, accelerating through a hole no more than two feet in width and already closing around him, catching the bulk of the North Carolina defense shifting the wrong way, altering the angle of attack. Plunged through the gap made by Ellerbie, crossed the thirty.

The strong safety sprinted back from the sideline, had the best angle to take D'Andre down, diving for his feet, D'Andre accelerating to avoid the lunging move. The safety unable to wrap his arms around the running back, D'Andre shaking off the attempted tackle, sprinted into the wide-open space of the middle of the field, in quick succession crossed the twenty-five, then the twenty. D'Artagnan Wellington blocked the last defender with a chance of stopping D'Andre, the Tar Heel defender unable to disengage from the receiver as D'Andre sprinted past, covered the final fifteen yards untouched. As he crossed the goal line time, space and all around him: the cheering crowds; the teammates rushing to congratulate him; the band playing the fight song and cheerleaders jumping in celebration of the score once more resumed a normal velocity. D'Andre tossed the ball to the nearest official, traded a jumping body bump first with Wellington, then with Ellerbie who threw the pivotal block to spring him loose, before Tyler ran up and the pair exchanged a celebratory fist-bump.

"On the way to that one hundred yards," Tyler said as they jogged to the sidelines, the Great Northern fans ecstatic at the play.

"O' ye of little faith." In his skills, D'Andre possessed faith and more, though he still had yards to gain before reaching his coveted mark.

"Watson around the right end. Cuts back inside, he's down to the thirty! He breaks a tackle! Has open field in front of him! Twenty-five, twenty! Wellington blocking in front of him! Fifteen! Ten! Five! D'Andre Watson in for the score! Touchdown, Great Northern! And the Huskies take the lead at 13-7!" The announcer on WGN breathlessly called the play putting Great Northern back in front.

"Nice play," Lang turned off the radio, parking the van in the garage, "too bad we couldn't have seen it."

"We can catch the replay," Sterner got out of the van. "Come on, we're running late and have more work to do." One more young woman to visit Marcus Evans Photography this day and later that afternoon departing the building in a fashion she never expected, with another vehicle disposed on a desolate street somewhere in Chicago.

They entered the brownstone, Cowle waiting for them. "You can relax, gentlemen," he told them. "Alexandra is running a little late this afternoon."

"Good." Sterner smiled at Lang. "We can watch some football."

Chapter 12

"What do you think?" Tyler McManaway asked Head Coach Carl Hamilton as they stood on the sidelines after calling time-out. Great Northern held a 14-7 lead over North Carolina with six minutes left in the first half, facing a crucial fourth and one at the Tar Heel thirty-three. "Fish or cut bait?"

Coach Carl crossed his arms. "Cut bait means a fifty-one yard field goal. Into the wind." A wind blowing fifteen miles an hour and their kicker, senior Martin DeRosa, accurate from close in but lacked the leg strength for an attempt this far out. The kicking game a glaring weakness for Great Northern, lucky not to have been exposed this far into the season.

"Or we can fish and see if they take the bait." Tyler accepted a Gatorade squeeze bottle from a student manager, shot a stream of orange liquid into his mouth. "Game film doesn't lie. That freshman cornerback on the left side of the formation likes to crowd the line on short-yardage situations. Leaves the flat wide open." The coaching staff uncovered the tendency in the opposing player, a highly-recruited freshman, on two separate four-and-short situations in the game against Ole Miss the previous weekend, then formulating a specific play taking advantage of the weakness. Football, like chess, a game of strategy where one discovered tendencies in the opponent and took steps to exploit them.

"Jumbo Lightning?" Hamilton cocked his head; understood what Tyler proposed, pleased he thought the same way.

"No better place to try it," Tyler said. "Fourth and short, if it doesn't work they have the ball on their thirty-three. It's the same spot if we miss the field goal."

Coach Carl grinned. "You make the call at the line if it's Dive or Sprint." He turned to an assistant. "Get Fiji over here." A moment later Albert 'Fiji' Fatuamala, who already tallied a sack of the Tar Heel quarterback on the afternoon, causing his typical mayhem along the line of scrimmage, joined the conference of head coach, quarterback and offensive unit.

"Want to try that play we've been running in practice?" Tyler asked.

"It's a change of pace," Fiji agreed simply, slid on his helmet.

"If it's Dive, make a big hole for me to run through, Jumbo," D'Andre Watson told him.

"Jumbo Lightning, Tyler makes the call at the line, go on two," Hamilton informed the offensive unit, the sideline huddle broke and the players trotted back on the field.

"And now for something completely different," Connor Aanonsen commented as the Great Northern offense lined up to go for it on fourth and one. The crowd buzzed at the sight of one player from the defense, massive and imposing, wearing number ninety-seven taking his assigned place in the formation.

"Fiji's never played offense before," Samantha Grayson added as Albert 'Fiji' Fatuamala lined up in the fullback position, replacing Dante Clarke, with D'Andre Watson set behind Fiji.

"Using him like 'Refrigerator' Perry," Ashleigh Morgan invoked the name of the defensive lineman of the 1985 Super Bowl champion Chicago Bears employed in a similar role. Lauryn Callahan said nothing, but Samantha noticed her fingers now tightly crossed.

Tyler came up to the line, slid the mouth guard between his teeth, easing his hands under center. Performed a quick study of the Tar Heels defense, a unit primed to stop the play and not yield the single yard the Huskies needed for the first down, force a turnover on downs. The front four crowding the line, the three linebackers and the strong safety filling the gaps, presenting an eight-man front. The cornerback on the right side of their formation, an experienced junior, covered D'Artagnan Wellington tight, respecting his talent. Tyler expected that. He turned to his right.

The cornerback on the left side of the defense, a highly recruited freshman heralded for his raw speed, covering Michael Haindelhaven, the five-eleven split-end with the number ninety, unusual for a receiver, on his jersey. The corner taking the bait, as Tyler noted from game film studied on his iPad. Unlike his counterpart across the formation, the defender dismissive of the receiver he assigned to cover, his attention centered on the presence of Fiji lined up at fullback, the 'Jumbo' part of the play. Michael Haindelhaven a high-school sprint champion from Virginia nicknamed 'White Lightning' and the play called Jumbo Lightning for a reason as the freshman corner about to discover to his detriment.

"Blue!" That the cue the play Sprint and not Dive, the rest padding. "Zorro! Eighteen! Zorro! Hut, hut!" Brendan Quinn snapped the ball back into Tyler's hands, pivoting away from center, the ball fake crucial to sell the play, the North Carolina defense assuming the play designed to gain the first-down yardage. Fiji rushed past Tyler, charging towards the line, D'Andre following close behind his massive blocker. Tyler held the ball out slightly, offered the impression of handing off to D'Andre. As they passed, D'Andre closed his arms together tight, acting like he had the ball. As Fiji tore a hole into the line of scrimmage, knocking back both a defensive tackle and linebacker, D'Andre plunged into the line, diving for what would've been first down yardage. Tyler tucked the ball back on his hip, body shielding the ball from view.

The cornerback the target of the intended play bit on the fake, inexperience readily apparent as he fell for the deception, reacted as the Great Northern coaching staff expected, diving into the line to stop the rush leaving Haindelhaven, who made a slight feint inside as if blocking in support of the play, then releasing downfield into the open. Tyler took three steps back, spun about, planting his feet, the defense now realizing the handoff into the line a fake and an excellent one at that, catching them unprepared. *You'd better make this pass good*, Tyler thought, made the call at the line, depended on him to complete a perfect toss. He lofted the throw into the air, the arcing pass falling softly into the hands of Michael Haindelhaven at the twenty, never breaking stride making the catch. The free safety, who drifted over to help the other cornerback covering Wellington, correctly read the play's intent at the last moment, running back towards the other sideline to prevent Haindelhaven from scoring. The speed of the sophomore split-end too telling, outsprinting the defender to the end zone to unleash a pandemonium only a two-touchdown lead over a ranked opponent could produce.

"Okay Wrigley, you be a good boy for Mommy," Alexandra Cole told the golden retriever staring at her with sad brown eyes and forlorn expression knowing his Mommy about to leave again after coming home, taking him for a quick walk around the block. "I'll be back in a few hours," she reassured her best friend, at times seemed the only friend, in the world. A ten-week old puppy all floppy ears, soft downy coat and shambling legs when rescued from a shelter, Wrigley in turn displayed his everlasting affection rescuing Alexandra from the darkness of depression. "We'll spend time together when I get back, my pretty boy." *Why do I need a man in my life*, Alexandra mused, *I have a dog*.

Wrigley understood, trotted to his bed in the living room, plopping down on the cushion, resting his head over the edge. The woebegone expression he gave Alexandra almost made her break down, consider bringing Wrigley along with her to the studio. Then she thought better of the notion, pushing the limits of the good will Marcus Evans bestowed her. He understood the reason for being late for the appointment, but probably not keen on having a dog, even one as well behaved as Wrigley, in the studio while they were shooting.

"Come on, don't let them score, got money on this game," Lang muttered at the television as North Carolina drove towards the Great Northern end zone late in the first half. The Tar Heels faced a second and seven at the Huskies' twenty-seven yard line with a minute left in the second quarter.

"Who'd you take?" Sterner asked his compatriot.

"Great Northern," Lang said. "I think they have another upset in them." North Carolina snapped the ball, a pitch to the running back sprinting to get around the left end. He didn't get very far, stuffed at the line of scrimmage by defensive end Albert Fatuamala, shrugging off the double-team block of the tight end and left tackle to reach the back, effortlessly wrenching him to the ground as one shakes rain from an umbrella.

"That kid's a beast." Sterner pointed at number ninety-seven, offering a hand to the running back he squashed into the turf, helped him to his feet. "He'll make a mint playing on Sundays in a few years."

"I could take him," Lang replied confidently.

"Sure you could," Sterner didn't believe his friend's boast. "The kid's a beast, man."

"Won't make what we will for our work this weekend," Marcus Cowle observed the contest with passing interest, whiling the time until Alexandra Cole arrived for her delayed session, only postponing the inevitable. Cowle believed college good for one thing, affording him and the Collectors of The Trading Society with product-delectably beautiful young women-to snatch and sell to wealthy clients.

North Carolina faced third and seven, time running down in the half. The Tar Heel quarterback dropped back to pass, searching for an open receiver downfield. Albert Fatuamala blew past the left tackle, placed a meaty hand on the quarterback's shoulder pads, dragging him to the turf as a lion pulls down an antelope on the grasslands of Africa.

"Down he goes!" Lang shouted. North Carolina lost seven yards on the play, faced a long field goal attempt to salvage three points from the drive.

"Keep it down," Cowle cautioned. "You might wake our guest."

Sterner snorted. "I'm sure she's still in dreamland."

"Reminds me," Cowle said. "I should see that she's comfortable." He walked down the hall, leaving the pair to their diversions. He reached the first of the two closets, pressing his ear against the door, heard soft moaning from inside. He opened the door, light from the hallway pouring into the confined space to illuminate the imprisoned occupant. Their hostage did remain a resident of dreamland as Sterner suggested, still senseless as the sedative continued to course its way through her system. Cowle stood quietly in the doorway, gazed down at his defenseless captive, studying the petite and restrained form of Emma Hayden, an entertainment he preferred to a contest between muscle-bound oafs. Emma sat nestled in the corner her head, gagged and blindfolded with thick bands of white cloth, rested against the wall. His eyes trailed down the body wrapped tightly in coils of rope, spent minutes watching her chest, breasts ensnared in the webbing of bondage, moving up and down with each shallow breath. He crouched beside her bound form, checked the bindings around her wrists and ankles, taking the opportunity to slowly trail his fingers along legs shrouded in black pantyhose. Something about the female form so securely restrained, and utterly helpless, Cowle found beguiling and mesmerizing, fascinated by the hypnotic sexual allure of her plight. *And to think I get paid for this.*

"Emma, if I weren't an honorable businessman you'd be in deep trouble now," Cowle told the unmoving form, stroking her cheek with the back of his hand, fingers playing with silky strands of mahogany hair, a whimpering groan escaping the gagged lips. He and his associates very easily having their way with so vulnerable a captive, taking advantage of her defenselessness in horribly violent ways. That wasn't good business practice though, paid to capture and process the merchandise for the clients, not sample the product for their own gratification. The sordid pleasures of the flesh left to those paying Cowle for services not many others able to provide. In the eyes of Marcus Cowle Emma no longer a person, the girl reduced to a meal ticket, a product for sale, a single component to a multi-million dollar business deal with his most generous client. He stood, closed the door as Emma stirred from the drugged stupor, head moving slightly as her senses finally started clearing of the drug-induced fog.

He hoped Emma didn't make too much noise when Alexandra Cole arrived to join her.

Thought I'd never find a space! The third time around the block finally proved the charm for Alexandra Cole in her quest for parking near Marcus Evans Photography. Luck provided a spot large enough, and not near a fire hydrant, across from the brownstone at 2371 North Campbell Street where the studio occupied the first floor. She backed the dark blue Ford Fusion into the spot, shut off the engine, grabbing the overnight bag from the seat next to her. She checked her makeup in the rearview mirror, hoping Marcus allowed her time to freshen up prior to the first set.

Alexandra closed her eyes, forgot about work and her terrible boss. "Let's do this and start a new life, girl." Satisfied with her appearance Alexandra stepped from the car, walked across the street to the brownstone.

"I thought she'd never find a space," Marcus Cowle remarked dryly from inside the building, watching Alexandra drive around the block three times in search of parking. Not upset with her tardy arrival, wasn't in any hurry to finish his work this day. His next victim about to enter his lair, her fate inevitably decided once she did, not leaving the premises of her own volition, but with Emma Hayden as an unwilling passengers in the back of the cargo van.

He heard the front door bell chime; clicking on the cell phone signal jammer, insuring Alexandra no longer had contact with the outside world. "Time for our second appointment of the afternoon," Cowle told Sterner and Lang, waiting in the back room until needed. For Alexandra the afternoon about to stretch into a very long and torturous night.

Chapter 13

"So far, so good," Samantha Grayson remarked as the teams headed off the field at half time. North Carolina driving towards the Great Northern end zone in the final minutes but came up short, forced to kick a field goal, trimming the lead to 21-10 in favor of Great Northern.

"Now for our halftime entertainment," Connor Aanonsen intoned with gravitas as the Great Northern Marching Band took the field. For years, when Great Northern football less than great and at times downright abysmal, the entertainingly inventive halftime shows performed by the marching band the lone reason students attended the game, at least through half-time when they departed afterwards to avoid witnessing the ritual second-half slaughter of undermanned squads. Now the action during the game as entertaining as the imaginative shows contrived by the band. With the eleven-point lead against the Tar Heels the students of the 'Dog Pound' relaxed, resting strained vocal chords in preparation for the second half.

"What show are they doing?" Lauryn Callahan watched as props pushed on the field, band members scurrying into position for the first number.

"Music from Pixar movies," Amanda McKinnon said, the cutting-edge computer animation studio known for the successful *Toy Story* and *Cars* franchises.

"The guy playing Frozone during the fight scene from *The Incredibles*," Connor said, "lives below me in McDonough."

"Mister Incredible is in my Media and Society class," Samantha added.

"You know what D'Andre's favorite line from that movie is?" Ashleigh said. "Honey, where's my super suit?"

"He sure is wearing that super suit today." Samantha sat down; thankful for the break as she'd been standing, as with the rest of the students, throughout the first half, her legs sore and tired. She adjusted her sunglasses, at ease with her friends and at this moment all was right with her world. "Let's sit back and enjoy the show."

"Thirty minutes, let's keep it up," Tyler McManaway wove his way through the Great Northern locker room, slapping hands and shoulder pads of his comrades on the offensive unit, pumping up their spirits. "Another thirty minutes and we're still perfect." He glanced over at Albert 'Fiji' Fatuamala, leaning his massive frame against his cubicle, eyes closed deep in meditation, a calm harbor amidst the swirling excitement. Tyler shook his head in admiring disbelief. *To each his own….*

Tyler approached D'Andre Watson. "Nice job so far," exchanged a handshake with his friend.

"Seventy-four yards down, twenty-six to go," D'Andre reminded Tyler of his weeklong claim, thirty-five of those yards coming on a single explosive play. "I think that hundred is in the bag. Let's see how close I get to doubling that."

"You know they'll make adjustments," Tyler warned.

"Let them," D'Andre shook his head. "Whatever they do, it won't work."

"Connor is right," Tyler noted. "You are one confident son of a bitch."

"That's why they gave me a scholarship." A wide grin spread over D'Andre's face. "Self-confidence is part of the job description." The same held true for Tyler as quarterback and team leader.

*   *   *   *   *

"Alexandra! You made it!" Marcus Cowle welcomed Alexandra; her entrance into the studio unknowingly sealed her fate of sexual slavery and a hideous, lonely death on the far side of the world. Soon she'd join pretty little Emma Hayden in hopeless captivity.

"I'm sorry for being late," Alexandra brushed dark hair from her brown eyes. "I know photographers hate it when models are late. My boss made me come in today at the last minute to work," she repeated the apology given earlier over the phone.

"I completely understand," Marcus Cowle soothed the jangled nerves, wanted Alexandra calm, defenses lulled so when time came to subjugate her the affair proved uncomplicated.

"You don't know how much this means to me," Alexandra continued, walking through the reception area. "I really want to dump this job, I hate it so much. I think today might've been the last straw. Maybe I can make it as a model, make more money, pay off those loans I took to get through school."

"Let's see what I can do," Cowle studied her attire with a discerning eye. "Why don't we start with what you're wearing?" The dark blue business pantsuit, white top and heels a perfect ensemble, Cowle already picturing Alexandra bound, silenced and powerless in the outfit.

"They made me come in on a Saturday and insisted I dress as if it were during the week," her tone bitter like sour milk. Had considered changing into something more comfortable to come to the studio but didn't have the time.

"I think it actually worked out for both of us. You can use the dressing room to freshen up," Cowle pointed to the open door down the hall. "We'll start when you're ready."

Alexandra smiled, her apprehension receding in the photographer's reassuring presence. "I'll only be a few minutes." She went down the hall to the room, after closing the door Alexandra removed the makeup bag, placed it on the counter, pulling her clothes from the bag, hanging them on hooks on the opposite wall, checking none of the apparel wrinkled. She turned to the mirror, opening her makeup bag, removing a tube of lipstick, a muted dark red shade, gliding the tip across full lips.

What's that? She heard a far-off thumping noise through the walls, pausing for a moment listening before starting on her eye shadow and liner, searched for the source of the sound, then shook her head, didn't think anymore of it, the brownstone an older structure, attention shifting back to the mirror.

Probably mice. She had no idea what made the sound not a rodent.

The audible gasp, followed by a groan, rose in unison from the throat of every Great Northern fan as the pass over the middle from Tyler McManaway to slot receiver D.B. Bailey tipped by a Tar Heel linebacker into the receptive hands of the lunging free safety at the North Carolina thirty-one yard line, snuffing the Huskies drive midway through the third quarter. The safety didn't get far with his newfound prize, brought down at the thirty-four by tight end Casey Ellerbie. The Tar Heel sidelines and small contingent of fans in the southwest corner of Warren Field erupted at the change of fortunes, sensed the shift of momentum in their favor.

"That's not good," Ashleigh checked the scoreboard. North Carolina scored on their first drive of the second half to narrow the score to 21-17. Now the Tar Heels had a perfect chance to take the lead.

Samantha grimaced as Tyler stalked off the field, tugged angrily at his chinstrap. "He's not happy," Amanda observed.

"Don't think he saw that linebacker until after he threw it," Connor added. Samantha remained silent, even from this far distance saw Tyler's disgust at what transpired. She and the rest of the Great Northern fans hoped this not a harbinger darkening their prospects of victory.

"Didn't see that linebacker until the ball left my hand," Tyler McManaway apologized to Coach Carl, yanking the helmet off upon reaching the sidelines, admitting the mistake. "That's on me."

"Watch for that next time," Hamilton cautioned, didn't have a reputation for yelling when mistakes made, believed players understood when they committed a miscue and screaming that obvious fact at him wouldn't improve the situation. He'd point out to Tyler during film sessions how he locked onto Bailey from the start of the play instead of going through his progressions. Even the most talented of quarterbacks made mistakes, though Tyler's rare. "We'll get it back, stay focused. We're still moving the ball."

Tyler nodded at his coach's statement, jogged to the defense huddled around the assistant defensive coordinator, found Albert 'Fiji' Fatuamala. "Get it back for me." He slapped his friend on the back, shouted in his ear. "Have to make up for that screw-up."

"Don't worry," Fiji reassured him, "I'll take care of it." Fiji and the defense trotting onto the field as Tyler paced the sidelines licking the temporary wound to his ego.

Fiji moved to the line of scrimmage as the stadium waited for the sideline official to indicate ESPN coverage returned from commercial break following the change of possession. He lowered his head, channeled inner thoughts, centered his energy on a singular purpose. *Get to the quarterback, get the ball back.* The shrill whistle signaling the resumption of play filled the air and Fiji took a deep breath, opened his eyes as if emerging from a psychic trance. The North Carolina offense broke their huddle, moved up to the line. Fiji dropped down into a three-point stance, lifted his head. Eyes locked on those of the North Carolina left tackle, the number seventy-four on white jersey stained with grass and sweat; the player assigned the important task of protecting the quarterback's blind side in pass protection. The player not in the down position, hands resting on tree-trunk thighs, a tipoff the Tar Heels taking advantage of the turnover and seeking to pass on first down.

Fiji's dark eyes never left those of the tackle; saw the furtive glance to the right, then looking back at Fiji, measuring him up, trying to guess the move Fiji might employ to break through the line to reach the quarterback. Already this day the battle between the two turning into a toe-to-toe epic, a titanic struggle for supremacy on each snap of the ball. Fiji's strategy straightforward and simple: *Use your speed, rush him, get him off balance, go around him.* He kept his three-point stance, eyes never leaving the left tackle, listening to the cadence of the Tar Heel quarterback, Colton Colquitt, as he called the signals. Fiji crouched, coiled to strike, a wolf in the deep woods waiting to spring forward and take down his prey.

The ball snapped on the third 'Hut' and Fiji lunged across the line, the left tackle backpedaling with hands raised to fend off his charge. As the quarterback dropped back Fiji rushed ahead, big right hand making contact with the tackle's chest, forcing his girth backward, the jab sending the tackle slightly off balance, wasn't as set in his stance as on previous plays. Fiji sensed the left tackle expected him to move to the inside, able to find assistance from the left guard neutralizing his attack. Pivoting on his foot Fiji spun to the outside, for one so large he twisted gracefully like Fred Astaire twirling around Grace Kelly on the ballroom floor, catching the left tackle moving in the other direction, out of position to stop Fiji getting around him save for grabbing his jersey and drawing a holding penalty. The left tackled swiped harmlessly at Fiji as he blew past, a rocket heading into orbit, dark eyes locked on the number eight in Carolina blue on the back of the quarterback's jersey, sitting in the pocket unaware of the defensive end's onrushing presence.

Colton Colquitt, holding the ball by his waist, waiting for his receivers to get open downfield, only became aware of Albert Fatuamala when the full force of his three-hundred twenty-five pounds crashed into the small of his back, slamming him face-first to the ground. With his right hand Fiji swatted at the ball, forced it loose from Colquitt's grip, the ball sent tumbling and bobbling along the turf, the Great Northern crowd yelling at the sack, screaming at the sight of the loose football spinning like a top along the grass. Linebacker Tyrone Hemmings leapt for the bouncing ball, falling on it at the North Carolina twenty-eight, with a single play effectively extinguishing whatever momentum North Carolina thought gained from the interception.

Fiji watched as Hemmings recovered the ball, carefully lifting his frame off the quarterback he mashed into the ground, offered a hand to the fallen North Carolina signal caller. "You okay?" Colquitt accepted the extended hand, Fiji pulling him up, patted him on the shoulder. "Didn't mean to hit you so hard."

"I'm cool." Colquitt answered, body felt like Wil E. Coyote after having a piano dropped on him, the expression on his face speaking volumes. *Why are you apologizing to me?* If anyone needed to apologize it was the tackle allowing Fiji to blow past him for the sack, causing the fumble to stop the drive before it even started.

As his defense celebrated the turnover on the field, Coach Carl glanced at Tyler McManaway after checking the play chart in his hands. "Want to go for the jugular?"

"Let's get this over with," Tyler answered with a grin, Coach Carl giving him the play. "That was quick," Tyler complimented Fiji as their paths crossed, teammates congratulating Fiji on the sack and forced fumble.

"Told you I'd take care of it," Fiji slapped Tyler's outstretched hand. "See what you can do."

Tyler buckled his chinstrap. "I'll see what I can manage." He leaned into huddle, already had the play from Coach Carl, no need to check for a meme from the sideline. "Tango Vector 81 on two," Tyler told his offense, used the other name for the formation. "Dagger in the Heart."

The offense broke huddle, jogged to the line, getting set. Tyler crouched under Brendan Quinn, the center calling out the blocking scheme to the offensive line, pointing with one hand to his line-mates who to block, his other meaty hand grasping the ball, ready to snap it back on Tyler's signal. The formation was trips to the right with two receivers-D'Artagnan Wellington out wide and Quentin Kennedy lined up in the slot-on the right side, Michael Haindelhaven out to the left. Tyler watched the linebackers, the strong safety crowding the line, coming with the blitz, an aggressive call by their defensive coordinator. Tyler called signals, on two Quinn fired the ball up into his waiting hands.

Tyler dropped back from the line, saw the strong side linebacker and strong safety coming through the gaps. The linebacker picked up by left tackle Dieter Baumann while fullback Dante Clarke filled the other gap, halted the charging strong safety in his tracks. D'Andre remained in the backfield with Tyler, ready to pick up any other defenders coming on the blitz.

Just a few seconds, Tyler thought, spotting D'Artagnan Wellington in full-out sprint down the right sideline, the defensive back burned earlier in the game right with him. Tyler waited until the last possible second under duress of the pass rush, arm rearing back, launching a high-arching throw towards the corner of the end zone, targeting a spot where only Wellington could catch the pass over his outside shoulder. *Nothing but a simple matter of geometry and physics,* Tyler thought. The ball reached the apex of its journey, dropping down from the sky like an artillery shell screaming towards impact. Wellington's speed gave him a step of separation on the defensive back as he crossed the five, head turned back to locate the ball descending out of the blue towards him, estimating the space between him, the sidelines and the corner of the end zone. As the pair crossed the goal line the defensive back tried timing his leap, lunging into the air, hand outstretched to bat the ball away.

The ball thrown perfectly, dropping to the outside and into Wellington's hands, giving the defensive back no chance at a deflection. Hands of the receiver catching the ball over his shoulder, Wellington dragging his feet once...twice...three times before stepping out of bounds. The official's arms shot into the air to signal the score, no need for a replay on this touchdown.

"A twenty-eight yard pass from number four Tyler McManaway to number eighty-one D'Artagnan Wellington for the Great Northern touchdown!" The public address announcer shouted over the cacophony of cheering fans and outbreak of joyous mayhem sweeping over 'The Dog Pound' where the student body exploded in celebration with one person in particular more thrilled than the rest. Samantha Grayson leapt into the arms of her friends, screaming at the top of her lungs in unbridled ecstasy at the performance of Tyler McManaway.

"I think Tyler just made up for that interception," Connor Aanonsen commented. Samantha couldn't have said it any better.

"All right, tilt your head a little to the left," Marcus Cowle coaxed, Alexandra Cole doing as directed. "Put your left hand on your hip." Alexandra complied with the request. "Perfect." Cowle snapped off several shots.

"How am I doing?" Cowle sensed underneath the polished veneer of a career woman laid an excess of doubt and dearth of self-confidence; Alexandra seemed to crave his constant stream of encouragement and affirmation.

"Outstanding, you're a very lovely lady, Alexandra," Cowle complimented, made his prey feel comfortable, have nothing to fear from him until it was too late.

"You know how to make a girl feel appreciated," Alexandra replied, brown eyes glimmering.

"The job's easier when you're relaxed," Cowle told her. "Turn your body to the left. Put both hands on your hips and look straight ahead into the camera. I want a look that tells me you don't take any crap from anyone."

"Not even my boss?" Alexandra turned serious, Cowle thought the frown exuded a passionate sensuality. *Sheik Rahim will like her...*

"Especially your boss," Cowle clicked off a few shots. "Now I want a big smile, a happy face."

Alexandra's smile widened, eyes sparkling, Cowle noted the perfect white teeth. "Big enough?"

"Absolutely dazzling," Cowle gave her thumbs up, took a few more exposures. "Need to take a break? Then change into another outfit?"

"Why don't I change first," Alexandra shrugged, smiled mischievously. "I have something I brought that I think you'll like."

"I'd like to see what you have in mind." Cowle could wait, no one else stopping by the studio the rest of the day to interrupt them. *Just you, me, my associates and Emma.* "I have bottled water if you're thirsty."

"That's sweet of you," Alexandra replied. "It gets warm under those lights."

"Go change into your next outfit," Cowle told her. "I'll be waiting." Alexandra hurried to the dressing room as Cowle removed the second of the doctored bottles of water from the refrigerator. He didn't open the bottle, would leave that to Alexandra, doing nothing to raise her suspicions. Disappointed she decided to change, wanting her to stay in the dark blue pantsuit, found the outfit appealing, enticed by the image of a confident businesswoman helplessly bound. Fifteen minutes passed before he heard the click of high heels against the wooden floor, nodded pleasantly as she entered the studio, whistled in appreciation at the sight.

"What do you think?" Alexandra spun about, now wearing a form-fitting black mock turtleneck and gray miniskirt, black tights and knee-high leather boots, a wide black belt with burnished gold buckle cinched about her waist. A pair of gold necklaces contrasted perfectly with the stretchy black fabric, dark brown hair spilling gently down over her shoulders.

"I like it." Cowle commented, admitting the outfit far more stimulating than the pantsuit she wore to the studio. "I think the art director will like it too."

"That's the whole idea." Alexandra explained with the shiest of smiles, Cowle noticed she taking an interest in him, or an interest in his alter ego. *What she doesn't know will definitely hurt her.* "Let me see if I have any messages," Alexandra retrieved the smartphone from her purse. "Don't have any signal," she stated matter-of-factly, checking the screen. Her service carrier AT&T and it seemed everyone who used the provider complained about signal reception.

"It's been sporadic all week," Cowle confirmed what she saw on the screen, only he knew the truth of the signal jammer installed in the building, preventing communication with the outside world, Alexandra unaware she already his prisoner.

Cowle motioned to the couch. "When are you telling your employer you've had enough?" He handed Alexandra the cold bottle of water as they sat down. Alexandra took the bottle, cracked open the cap, took a long drink never suspecting the liquid tampered. *Perfect.* Cowle looked at the clock, noted the time, based on her height expected the effects of the sedative to take longer with Alexandra than the much smaller Emma.

"If this works out," Alexandra took another drink, surprised at her thirst, "it'll be very soon." She'd enjoy the moment she handed in her two-week notice. "I appreciate what you've done for me."

"You're welcome." Cowle smiled graciously, playing to the last the role of mentor and friend. "I enjoy helping people I like." *Or women I get a good price for.*

"Thanks for giving me this chance when they're others available," Alexandra poured out heartfelt sentiments, took a drink from the bottle, wiped her head, started feeling light-headed, brushed off the peculiar sensation to excited anticipation.

"What if the art director decides you're not the type she wants?" Cowle watched Alexandra closely, looking for signs the sedative doing its surreptitious work, noted her brown eyes beginning to show a glassy haze.

"There's always Plan B." Alexandra struggled to focus her vision. Didn't think she was that tired after working at the office on a Saturday morning. "I've been talking to friends who work at non-profit charity organizations. The pay isn't as good, but that's not a point. I want a job where I'll make a difference." She shrugged. "Maybe I'll go back to school."

"That's admirable of you," Cowle peered over Alexandra's shoulder at the clock on the wall while she reflexively took another drink from the bottle. *Two minutes...should be soon*.

Alexandra shook her head, blinking her eyes as the room swayed and blurred, hand moving up to her temple, experiencing a sudden, stinging pain. "Anything wrong?" Cowle reached for the bottle, took it from her shaking hand, placing it on the end table.

"I...don't feel...right," Alexandra's speech slurring as if intoxicated. A flush of warmth overwhelmed her as, with great effort struggling on wobbly legs, she rose from the couch. She realized then, with a sick feeling deep in her stomach, what was happening. She faced Cowle, her head rocked by a pounding drumbeat, a powerful surge of overwhelming fear at the recognition of betrayal, how she blundered into a devious trap. "What was...?"

"In the water?" Cowle finished the sentence for Alexandra, the smile once pleasant now evil, eyes hungry with desire. "Something to help you...relax."

What have you done to me? I trusted you! The brown eyes widened in terror as Alexandra turned drunkenly, no control over her limbs. She lurched towards the front of the studio, took three steps towards the reception area and the door leading to freedom, had to escape, flee the predator in her midst. She staggered to the left, fought to maintain her balance as the room spun wildly. At that moment the sedative took full effect, shutting down her nervous system, everything going black, sending her spiraling deep down a twisting slide into a swallowing darkness. In a heap she collapsed on the floor, her only cry a weak, gasping whimper no more than a puff of air escaping a balloon. Cowle rose from the couch, crouched over the motionless form. He rolled Alexandra on her back, checked her pulse, his prey out cold, noted the time on the clock. *A little sooner than I thought*.

"Have another one for you, gentlemen," Cowle called, heard Sterner and Lang moving, interrupting their viewing of college football. A minute later his compatriots entered the studio. "Three minutes this time," Cowle remarked, a minute longer than it took for Emma to succumb to the drug.

"We always show up when there's a pretty girl to be tied up," Lang joked.

"*What's Up Tiger Lily*," Cowle appreciated the reference. "Woody Allen."

"Let's do this quick," Sterner studied the unconscious woman. "Get back to the game," though again relegated to listening on the radio as they disposed of her car.

"I'll take care of what's up top this time," Lang reminded Sterner, dropped the duffel bag crammed with rope beside the insensate Alexandra, breathing shallow as the sedative kept her comatose, powerless to prevent her incapacitation, coils of rope removed from the duffle and the pair efficiently set about to neutralize their victim. Within ten minutes Alexandra Cole inescapably bound, gagged and blindfolded in the same fashion as Emma Hayden secured hours earlier, now waiting fearfully for her fate back in her closet cell.

As Sterner and Lang attended to their second capture of the day, Cowle fetched the smartphone from where Alexandra set it down. He plugged the device into his laptop and in seconds, as with the smartphone of their first victim, passwords cracked allowing Cowle access to Alexandra's email and social media accounts. Erasing any digital reference to Marcus Evans or to Marcus Evans Photography, most of the communication consisting of emails exchanged, wiped clean from the digital footprint Alexandra left behind. The inner workings of the smartphone scrambled like eggs in a frying pan for

Sunday brunch, the police left to trace a digital trail gone cold long after Alexandra and her luckless companions shipped to a place far from Chicago.

"Where are you folks from?" Garrett Grayson asked the young couple sitting at the bar of polished oak, pouring a sample of Grayson Farms Rhapsody into their glasses. He could tell, from the way they held hands and gazed into each other's eyes, the pair hopelessly in love.

"Chicago," the man's name was Tom, wearing jeans and blue polo top, had the lean build of a triathlete with brown hair and brown eyes. "We're," he motioned to Brianna, the young woman to his right, a lissome Irish beauty with red hair and green eyes, "on our honeymoon. Brianna has family in Rochester. They suggested we spend it here in the Finger Lakes."

"I remember our honeymoon like it was yesterday," Melanie Grayson said, pouring samples of wine for a party of six seated down from the couple, dark brown eyes flashing with passion. Even in her forties the former Melanie Barrett maintained the slender shape, those same genes passed on to their lovely daughter, she had in college when first encountering the love of her life.

"Isn't every day here a honeymoon?" Garrett replied with a rakish grin. Twenty years had passed since the winery on the western shore of Seneca Lake in upstate New York's fertile Eden of clear lakes and rolling drumlins opened for business, growing over the decades to encompass more than the winery. The tasting room housed in a converted barn on the property, built at the same time as the late nineteenth-century Victorian mansion serving both as home for their family and a bed and breakfast inn. The interior of the barn gutted and redesigned with vaulted ceilings and stained glass windows to offer visitors a comfortable, rustic atmosphere.

"Love your accent," Brianna commented.

"When you're from Australia you're sort of born with it," Garrett replied, a solid man of average height, muscles hardened and skin bronzed from the daily physical toil required to run an estate winery. His blue eyes burned with sharp intelligence and easy charm. The brown hair cropped short and rough beard denoted a man comfortable working the soil, though that hadn't always been the case. "No matter where you end up you never quite get rid of it."

"That accent is what first attracted me," Melanie told those gathered at the bar, playfully placing a kiss on his cheek while walking behind him to get another bottle from the wine cooler. Their marriage approaching twenty-five years, the story of how they came together the tale of a whirlwind romance in London, a dashing young naval officer assigned to the Australian Embassy and a beautiful dark-haired American college student from Cornell University spending a year studying in Europe falling hopelessly in love. At least that is what they told everyone, including their daughter and only child Samantha. No one needed to know the complicated truth not the stuff of fairy-tale romances but torn instead from a Brothers Grimm nightmare.

"I love your dogs," Brianna added. Another draw for guests to Grayson Farms Winery as two of their six greyhounds, rescued at the end of their racing days and finding forever homes on the grounds of the winery, lounged about on the floor of the tasting room this afternoon, ready to greet visitors. This day the duty fell upon Rocky, a seven-year-old brindle male and Stormy, a four-year-old female with soft, gleaming coat black as a moonless night broken by the heart-shaped patch of white on her chest. Friendly and inquisitive, Stormy quickly became their daughter's favorite when brought home from the kennel, sharing Samantha's bedroom before she headed off to Chicago to pursue future aspirations at Great Northern University.

"They're the sweetest hounds," Melanie never called them dogs, hounds sounded far more appropriate for the sleek, swift greys, one of the oldest breeds known to man. When she was young her family among the first in Upstate New York to rescue the breed. With her the tradition continued and the greyhounds, creatures lean yet docile, now an integral part of winery's identity with labels featuring depictions of the regal canines rendered by local artists. Every summer the winery hosted a gathering of greys and their owners to promote the noble cause of adoption. "They're very friendly."

"I thought they'd be more active?" Tom noted, both hounds dozing on their beds, basking in sunshine beaming through the windows.

"In spurts, they're more sprinters, not long distance runners," Garrett explained. "Unless they see a squirrel, then they're a bundle of energy."

The door from the outside opened and another group of visitors entered the tasting room. "Welcome to Grayson Farms," Garret said as the group stepped inside. As if taking a director's cue on a movie set, knowing it time to display abundant charm in a star turn, Stormy rose from her bed, first stretching backwards as if bowing, then forwards as taut muscles trembled. She glanced over her shoulder at Rocky, who lifted his head. *I've got this one,* she seemed to tell him. The obsidian beauty trotted across the floor, toenails clicking against the wood, understood this her reason for being at Grayson Farms, coming up to lean against the leg of an older woman with white hair, looking up with brown eyes soulful and sympathetic.

"Aren't you a pretty girl," the woman stroked Stormy's shimmering coat. "You're so soft too."

"Scratch behind her front leg and you'll have a friend for life," Garrett advised.

Tom motioned to the television above the bar, on the screen a college football game. "You have the Great Northern game on? Brianna and I graduated from there."

"Our daughter Samantha goes there," Melanie told them. "She's a sophomore. She loves it there, loves Chicago."

"It's a great city to be in," this comment from Brianna. "What's she majoring in?"

"She's in the Randall School of Journalism and Communications," Melanie replied.

"That's a good program to be in," Tom acknowledged. "I graduated from Lawson School of Business, have a degree in finance."

Garrett pointed to the screen. "That fellow wearing number four," saying it as Tyler McManaway dropped back to pass, withstanding the North Carolina rush to rifle a completion over the middle to a sliding Michael Haindelhaven for another Great Northern first down, "happens to be our daughter's boyfriend."

"He's the best quarterback Great Northern has ever had," Tom grinned. "I'm glad we were able to get him away from everyone else."

"I think your daughter's lucky," Brianna added. "I hear he's the nicest person."

"Tyler's a wonderful young man," Melanie agreed, finished the wine tasting with her guests, ready to welcome the next batch of visitors who entered the tasting room.

"I can't get him to stop calling me 'sir' when we're visiting Samantha," Garrett grinned. On the television Tyler scrambling after his pass protection broke down, turning what should've been a loss of yardage into an eleven-yard gain and another first down. "I think he'll make a great son-in-law." *If it comes to that*, Garrett knew circumstances might prevent the possibility. The newlyweds finished their samples of Rhapsody, Garrett proceeded with the tasting, checked the wines on the list they had marked. "So, you," he motioned to Tom, "want to try the Pinot Noir and you," motioning to Brianna, "want to sample the Vintner's Reserve Merlot..."

Tyler McManaway faded back into the pocket, eyes scanning the field from left to right, going through his progressions, checking each of his receivers as they ran their routes downfield, at the same time sensing the proximity of the pass rush exerted by the North Carolina defense. D'Artagnan Wellington, his primary receiver on the deep route, covered by both the cornerback and free safety, couldn't force the pass between the tight coverage. D. B. Bailey, the second option on the intermediate route across the middle, also covered. Michael Haindelhaven had the freshman left corner who'd been burned twice this afternoon tight on him, not wishing a third strike against him. A linebacker draped over tight end Casey Ellerbie. He listened, heard the peculiar deep-throated grunting of left tackle Dieter Baumann, the sophomore from Germany nicknamed 'The Berlin Wall,' getting closer as he fended off the North Carolina defensive end, saw the weak side linebacker charging through the gap. Tyler realized time for action running out and his options rapidly diminishing.

Safety valve, final option, Tyler decided, glancing to his left where in the flat D'Andre Watson drifted after releasing from the backfield. As the linebacker bore down on him Tyler lofted a toss, a bit wobbly as he was back on his heels, towards D'Andre. A split second later the defender slammed into him, impact of two hundred and thirty pounds lifting his body from his feet, driving him down hard on the turf, couldn't see if D'Andre caught the pass, nothing in his vision but the pristine blue sky above him. Yet the cheering of the crowd, rising and growing, told him something good resulting from the throw.

D'Andre's eyes locked on the ball arcing towards him, relaxing his hands, catching it in full stride, shifting the ball to rest securely in the crook of his left arm. Once again his vision widened, viewing the entire field, action around him slowing, knew he again about to break a big play. A wide-open expanse of manicured Kentucky bluegrass beckoned D'Andre, sprinting down the field, easily picking up the first down. The pass routes of the receivers pulling the defensive backs down towards the end zone, opening up the gap.

D'Artagnan Wellington, coming back towards Tyler to get open, now turned to tie up the defensive back covering him, switching from target to blocker as D'Andre approached in full stride. D'Andre moved to the right, peripheral vision caught sight of a linebacker bearing down on him from that direction. D'Andre stopped dead in his tracks as the linebacker lunged at him, the momentum of the defender carried him past D'Andre, his arms flailing wildly, grasping out at him. A millisecond later D'Andre shifted his feet, pirouetting away from the linebacker to resume his charge without missing a beat, defender stumbling out of the play. *That's a highlight for the ESPN College Game Day crew.* D'Andre cut to the right against the grain, sprinted into the middle of the field. At the audacious maneuver the roar of the crowd rose to that of a rock concert audience as the main act took the stage, sensing D'Andre on his way to another score.

He crossed the twenty, then the fifteen as D.B. Bailey and Michael Haindelhaven blocked for him, engaging the Tar Heel defenders who had them in coverage, preventing them from getting a shot at D'Andre. Sprinted past the ten, one last defender closing on him from behind, the cornerback Wellington blocked. At D'Andre's churning legs he made a final, desperate lunge but his attempt clutched nothing but air, landed flat on his chest as D'Andre scampered across the goal line for the score.

The band started the fight song as D'Andre stepped into the end zone and the referee's arms shot into the air to signal the touchdown, cheerleaders jumping in elation with this final nail hammered into North Carolina's coffin. D'Andre flipped the ball to the closest official, turning to face his onrushing teammates. D'Artagnan Wellington the first one to reach him and the two leapt in the air, bumping bodies together, repeated the move with D.B. Bailey and Michael Haindelhaven. Tyler pushed himself up from the turf, ran downfield as the play ended, reaching D'Andre as he ran towards the sidelines, they too leapt in the air and bumped together. Tyler didn't know if the celebratory move even had a name.

"I think that'll do it," D'Andre slapped Tyler's hand, both receiving warm handshakes from Coach Carl as they stepped off the field.

"I think you're right." Tyler checked the clock, eight minutes left in the game and, with the extra point, Great Northern making it a three-score lead at 35-17. With the way the defense was performing Tyler didn't expect the Tar Heels to score three times in the time remaining.

"Such a nice package you are, Alexandra, you wear ropes quite well." Marcus Cowle admired the handiwork of his apprentices, complimenting the securely bound, unconscious form of Alexandra Cole resting on the cold wood of the studio floor, blind and mute from bands of white cloth over the eyes and between her lips. *The way I like them...and the way my clients like them too,* he mused, watching the rise and fall of her chest constrained by the winding of rope. "You wanted a career change," Cowle taunted a silent captive unable to respond. "I hope you don't mind the travel involved." Her destination early Tuesday morning the Middle East alongside four other women, Cowle and his men paid handsomely for delivery to their new owner. Though Cowle starting to wish he could make the exchange sooner.

"She's a fine piece of ass," Sterner leaned down, checked the ropes one more time, taking advantage to grope soft flesh, admired her body. "Tits aren't bad either."

"Why don't we make this a set?" Cowle motioned Sterner to the back. "Go fetch our other guest," the similarly indisposed Emma Hayden. "I believe she should be awake," and thoroughly terrified with her situation, "by now."

"Double the fun?" Lang asked. Sterner headed to the closet where Emma, defenseless and fearing for her life, imprisoned.

"I do think you have a future as a model," Cowle informed the motionless Alexandra, picked up his camera, clicking off shots of his hostage. "Though I don't think this is was what you originally had in mind."

Cowle heard a muffled squeal of frightened protest. "Come on, baby. You still have work to do," Sterner informed Emma. "But I don't think you're going to get paid for this." Sterner returned with the bound form slung casually over his shoulder as if toting a sailor's sea bag, ready to amble up the gangway for an overseas cruise. Emma's mahogany hair hung down over her head, tied legs kicking at empty air, squirming against the firm grip. "She's a feisty little bitch," Emma growling at the statement. "I don't think she likes this new gig."

"I don't think she'll like this new assignment either," Cowle remarked coolly. Sterner easily swung the body from his shoulder down to the floor. Emma whined through the thick cloth gag, lying on the floor next to the immobilized Alexandra. Emma curled up defensively, blindfolded head moving about listening to the three as they talked, attempting to decipher the peril so close by but unable to see. *What are you going to do with me?*

"Nice pair we've got," Lang nodded. "I'm sure the Arab will get his money's worth from these two." Emma moaned at the callous remark. *What do you mean by that?*

"This isn't even the complete set," Sterner leaned over, cupped Emma's chin in his huge palm. She snorted in disgust, pulled away from him, chest heaving with each panicked breath.

"Your playtime is over, gentlemen," Cowle admired his initial prizes of the weekend, one awake and struggling furiously, the other drifting in a hazy netherworld. "You do have a car to dispose of."

Sterner grunted. Work was work. "Get to miss the fun."

"Don't worry, you'll have time this weekend to play with our new acquaintances," Cowle reminded his companions. Sterner and Lang departed to perform the same procedure with Alexandra Cole's Ford Fusion as they'd done with the Chevy Impala of Emma Hayden now parked and waiting to be plundered and ravaged on a deserted street in Englewood. Cowle heard the door close, alone with his prisoners.

"Let's spend some quality time together now, shall we, pretty little Emma?" He crouched next to Emma and her head swung about, blindfold robbing her of sight, only her hearing left to sense the nearness of the deadly predator into whose cunning trap she unwittingly fell. He reached out, with the back of his hand stroked the perfectly supple cheek. Emma froze, whimpering past the cloth filling her mouth. *What's going on? What are you going to do with me? Don't hurt me. Please, just let me go.* Emma asked her captor in muffled pleas of mercy.

"Don't worry Emma," his gaze trailed down her trim legs to the high heels on her dainty feet, back to her chest, round breasts poking through the rope, appreciating her tightly trussed form. Smelled the musky scent of fear, her dread of what to happen next. "We'll finish taking those pictures for your portfolio now. Hope you don't mind sharing the studio with another model."

Cowle stood, raised the camera to his eye, focused on the bound, gagged and blindfolded pair at his feet. "Now why don't you give me that lovely smile, Emma?" He taunted, starting to shoot. *Souvenirs,* he rationalized, *a memento to remember you by.* Cowle clicked off exposure after exposure, the moaning whimpers from Emma the only other sound in the studio, no need coaxing a position from his subjects. Collecting souvenirs a trait he did share with serial killers but the compulsions far dissimilar. Serial killers acted out of selfish deviancy, sacrificed victims to sexual bloodlust while Cowle prayed at the altar of profit, pursued the almighty dollar with laser-point efficiency. *I don't kill my prey, I just sell them.* As he watched the struggling Emma Hayden and the inert Alexandra Cole through the viewfinder, Cowle thought that simple distinction made all the difference.

Chapter 14

If Tyler McManaway preferred one offensive formation to the hundreds in the Great Northern playbook the one simply named Victory, called with the game in hand and the clock ticking off the final seconds, was that play. He viewed the scoreboard in the north end zone as he walked to the line, the clock within twenty seconds of zero and, more importantly, displaying a score reading Great Northern 38, North Carolina 17. Tyler placed his hands underneath center, behind him Dante Clarke and D'Andre Watson up close behind him. The Tar Heel defense crowded the line, but the intensity half-hearted, knew they were beaten. "TEN…NINE…EIGHT!" The crowd shouted in unison, counting down as the clock wound down towards zero. Tyler called a quick single hut and Brendan Quinn snapped the ball back into his hands.

"SEVEN…SIX…FIVE!" The crowd chanted as Tyler took a step back, knelt down on one knee as the North Carolina defense attempted to break through the line, the finishing touch to a successful, hard-earned win. Tyler flipped the ball to the referee, turned to embrace D'Andre.

"FOUR…THREE…TWO…ONE!" A tremendous cheer erupted from the stands once the game clock showed zeroes across and the game went final. *"The final score this afternoon at Warren Field North Carolina 17, your Huskies of Great Northern University 38!"* The public address announcer made official what everyone knew as a second roar emerged from the crowd.

"That's the ballgame, we are still undefeated and tomorrow we have got to be in the Top 25," D'Andre hooted, slapping Tyler on the shoulder.

"If the voters agree," Tyler shook hands with the North Carolina defensive linemen who tried their best to make his afternoon unpleasant. After two convincing upsets over ranked opponents how could the voters not rank them among the nation's best?

"I think we'll be number eighteen," D'Andre guessed. "Four touchdowns for you today." Going along with three hundred and twenty-nine yards through the air.

"One hundred and thirty-nine yards for you," Tyler removed his helmet, grasping D'Andre's outstretched hand, "and two scores. You backed up that talk." The pair threaded their way through the milling mass of players, offering handshakes, congratulating opponents on a hard-fought game. Head Coach Carl Hamilton, after receiving the customary Gatorade bath with a minute left, met the North Carolina coach at mid-field to exchange post-game pleasantries. Minutes earlier where players fought as fierce competitors the interactions now far more cordial.

"A fine offensive output for today," D'Andre agreed. "Think Mark May on ESPN will take back that pick he made?" On the network's Thursday night game between Cincinnati and Virginia the college football analyst, and former Pitt and Washington Redskins star, predicting the Tar Heels 'too fast and too good' for the Huskies to defeat.

"Lou Holtz said we'd win," Tyler replied.

Albert 'Fiji' Fatuamala, after exchanging handshakes with Colton Colquitt, the North Carolina quarterback he harassed all afternoon, approached his friends, grasped D'Andre's hand and slapped Tyler on the shoulder. "Nice game," all he said, Fiji never one for many words.

"Not too shabby either," Tyler complimented. "Three sacks and that forced fumble. I don't think their quarterback ever wants to see you across the line of scrimmage again."

"He won't," Fiji noted succinctly, "they're not on our schedule next year."

D'Andre motioned to the north end of the field, where the student section stood for the entire contest, joining the rest of the team headed in that direction, the Great Northern marching band forming up on the far sideline for the post game performance. "Let's show our appreciation to our fans," and for three fans in particular.

"Nice neighborhood," Lang commented on the West Side North Lawndale neighborhood as Sterner hopped into the van. The street a carbon-copy of the one in Englewood where they dumped the Chevy Impala of Emma Hayden, pockmarked by weed-choked vacant lots and boarded-up houses, run-down apartment blocks destined in due time to become their own empty voids. As he'd done with the Hayden girl's car he left Alexandra Cole's Ford Fusion unlocked, phone resting on the front seats as a glowing beacon of opportunity to the local criminal element.

"Works for us," Sterner said, "gets rid of the evidence, sends the police on a chase for some punk-ass kid who grabs the phone." He heard the post-game report on the radio following the Great Northern-North Carolina game. "What was the final?"

"Great Northern 38-17." Lang smiled. "I think I won me some money."

"Like either of us will be hurting for cash in a few days," Sterner replied. Neither man cared their expected wealth meant innocent lives taken and sacrificed. *Eat or be eaten…*

The smartphone in Bryce Fielding's pocket vibrated even before the final seconds ticked off the clock, notifying him of a text message. "Damn," Bryce muttered, fake smile plastered on his face while everyone around him celebrating the victory, probably the only student on the Great Northern campus not pleased with the outcome. He glanced at the screen, read a brief message from The Russian. *Sorry about the losses. Hope your luck is better tomorrow.*

Bryce shook his head; the bastard did posses a dry sense of humor. On his picks Bryce taking a cold bath; not only had Great Northern won and hit the over, Notre Dame upset Michigan in Ann Arbor and Miami obliterated Florida State, the only parley coming through his bet on the LSU-Georgia game. The message meant one thing: *pay up soon or bad things will happen.* No need to reply, Bryce stuffed the phone back into his pocket, had action on the Sunday NFL slate to hopefully recover from Saturday's financial bloodletting, perhaps break even for the weekend. If that didn't pan out Bryce knew he was welcome at a high-stakes, backroom poker game where he might recoup his losses and pay off The Russian. At least he could look forward to a night in Chicago with Natalie and his friends, bringing along the cute, yet naïve, little freshman he had his eye on. By the end of the evening one of his companions sure to ease his sorrows over losing big money this afternoon.

"Now that's a convincing win!" Connor Aanonsen exchanged a high-five with Amanda McKinnon.

"Going to be a happy campus tonight." In her head Samantha Grayson estimated how many parties campus Public Safety and the Evanslawn police swooping in to raid this evening. No need to worry about spending tomorrow afternoon writing that story, Aaron Dinehart giving her a well-deserved day off as reward for covering the Monday morning speech by Senator Fielding.

"You know what this means," Lauryn Callahan said, students around them cheering as the team approached 'The Dog Pound' in the north end of Warren Field, helmets raised in salute to a boisterous student body thrilling in the victory and the glow of an undefeated record.

"We get our men back," Ashleigh Morgan hugged Lauryn, "and they'll be in a good mood!"

The band played the first notes of the school's alma mater, "Hail Thee, Great Northern," and the students in the stands and players on the field draped arms over those next to them, swaying back and forth singing the words. Samantha's vision focused on Tyler McManaway, her quarterback hero standing in the front echelon of players, arms over the shoulders of D'Andre Watson and Albert 'Fiji' Fatuamala. Soon they'd be together, his presence making everything right again in her world.

"Take the scenic route back?" Marcus Cowle heard the door from the garage open, his accomplices entering the studio. He peered down at his prisoners, reveling in their shared terror. Alexandra Cole finally stirring from her sedated stupor, brain no longer clouded by the powerful narcotic, panicked discovering the enormity of her dire predicament. Trembling against the bondage tightly grasping her limbs, mewling softly through the gag muffling every sound. The blindfolded head whipped about at the sound of footsteps approaching, wondering their significance, petrified what might happen next and fearing her time left among the living trickling rapidly away and resigned to a possibly violent demise.

"Those neighborhoods aren't very picturesque," Lang replied.

"Unless you enjoy shitholes," Sterner gazed at the helpless pair huddled on the floor. "So our second guest decided to wake up?"

"I believe Alexandra wishes she hadn't." Cowle crouched by Alexandra, brought the camera up, snapped off a close-up shot of her gagged and blindfolded face, despite the cloth over her eyes and between her lips recorded the impression of damp fear on her face. *Perfect.*

"Having fun?" Sterner remarked dryly.

"What do you think? Work should be fun," Cowle placed the camera in the bag on the table. "Had to pass the time until you returned. Not going to squander," he waved at his bound captives, "such an opportunity."

"Not like you won't have another one tomorrow," Lang noted, having their fun with three new victims, the final one yet to be chosen.

"I think our guests are ready for the trip to their accommodations for the evening." The comment brought muffled screams from Emma and Alexandra. Spirited away to an unknown location, feared this declaration sealed their doom, might not live to see another day. His apprentices stepped over to the debilitated duo, Sterner lifting Alexandra from the floor, standing her on bound feet before heaving her over his shoulder. Lang scooped up the petite Emma, one arm underneath her knees, the other around her back, grasping the body in his arms as if the bundled hostage a bride carried over the threshold. Cowle had gathered up the clothes and overnight bags the women brought with them. "Let's move along, gentlemen. We're keeping our guests waiting. Have to get them settled in for the night."

Sterner laughed. "I'm sure they'll love our hospitality," he patted Alexandra's hip, a Norse plunderer lugging living booty from a raid, Alexandra squealing in protest. "It's a real five-star place." They strode through the first floor to the rear of the building, into the attached garage where the black van, parked beside the white Lexus Cowle drove about the city, awaited the human cargo. In hopeless futility Alexandra and Emma struggled against the hold of their captors, starting an unwilling journey where neither knew, yet feared, the final destination. Sterner and Lang carted the squirming, moaning parcels to the side of the van, Cowle opening the sliding door for them, tossed the overnight bags in first, his associates unceremoniously dumping the hostages on the cold metal floor. "Enjoy the ride," Sterner said before slamming the door shut, then cautioned, "might get a little bumpy." Minutes later the black van, with the white Lexus following behind, exited the garage behind the brownstone, headed down the narrow alley towards Fullerton Avenue.

Lang turned the radio on, with the Great Northern game concluded he switched to one of Chicago's sports-talk radio stations, WSCR, to listen to the Chicago White Sox-Baltimore Orioles broadcast, the whimpering cries of Emma Hayden and Alexandra Cole, experiencing every bump and dip in the road through the metal surface, drowned out by the voices of announcers Ed Farmer and Darrin Jackson calling the action. "Think our passengers are comfortable back there?" Sterner asked.

Lang peered through metal grating separating the cargo bay from the driver's compartment, observed the two women tightly tied and rolling on the floor, suffering through the trip, thick cloth gags lips stifling cries for help to the world outside the thin aluminum walls of the van. "Define 'comfortable' for me?" Lang asked.

"I'd take that as a no," Sterner checked the side mirror; saw Cowle in the white Lexus behind them. Sterner drove carefully, didn't speed, observed every traffic rule, coming to a complete stop at every intersection, no running of red lights or trying to beat the yellow, the epitome of a law-abiding safe driver. Had no desire to be stopped by the police with the human, and helpless, packages loaded in the van. The trip between Marcus Evans Photography and the abandoned factory where their captives kept until delivery to Sheik Rahim took only twenty minutes, but Sterner and Lang confident the journey seemed an eternity for their reluctant passengers

Lang pressed the remote on the dashboard, the front gate guarding their imposing red brick fortress trundled open, the van and Lexus driving inside the compound. Lang waited until both vehicles inside the fenced-in area, and the gate closed behind them, before pressing a second button on the remote. The door on the loading bay lifting to allow them entrance into their lair, a dungeon for five women unfortunate to end up their prisoners. Once the door up Sterner drove inside, followed by Cowle in the Lexus. Sterner parked the van, switched off the radio just as the White Sox scored the first run of the game. The pair exited as Cowle parked next to the van, got out. "You drive like an old lady," Cowle commented with wry sarcasm.

"You want the cops to pull me over? Find out what we're hauling here?" Sterner asked.

Cowle thought for a moment, then smiled. "Drive like an old lady then." He motioned to the van, listened to muted crying from human contents inside. "Let's get our guests settled in," he told them. "Have to explain the rules for their stay."

"I always like this part." Lang slid open the van door, bound forms of Emma and Alexandra reacting to the grinding sound of metal, gagged and blindfolded heads lifting from the floor. Alexandra lay still while Emma shifted away from the sound, quaking in fear yet only able to slide along the floor to the opposite side of the compartment.

"Did we enjoy the trip?" Cowle inquired politely as Sterner dragged Alexandra from the cargo hold, the woman screaming through her gag as he tossed her body over his shoulder. "Sorry we couldn't allow you to enjoy the sights along the way," he needled his captives as Lang leaned inside, collecting a squirming Emma in his arms. "Now let's get you checked in," Cowle noted with the feigned civility of a concierge manning the front desk of a hotel, associates in his wake bearing the struggling hostages as they exited the loading bay. Wound their way through the silent, cavernous complex until reaching the room Cowle set up to indoctrinate his acquisitions on their new, uncertain reality as product destined for sale and shipment overseas.

Cowle flicked a switch on the wall and two sets of high-powered lamps came to life, illuminating the center of the sparse, empty room of bare concrete walls and floor, the confines brought to mind an interrogation chamber of a secret police organization in a third world hellhole. *That's exactly what I want them to think*, Cowle smiled as Sterner and Lang deposited their human bundles in the center of the room, heaving them up to their knees.

"Please maintain that position, ladies," Cowle insisted coldly. "Don't move an inch, not a muscle." Emma and Alexandra froze at the terse command, fearing possible retribution if they wavered in the slightest, agonizing discomfort swiftly induced by the weight of bound bodies resting on their knees against the unforgiving surface. Heard Alexandra emit a pathetic wail of pain through the gag, Cowle pleased with the sound. *Good, I like them scared.* Over their heads Sterner and Lang donned black balaclavas, only their cruel eyes seen by the captives through the single opening. The pair stepped behind the women, Sterner by Alexandra and Lang next to Emma. Cowle let his blindfolded captives wait for several minutes, letting their terror grow and fester with each passing second. Hearing the last vestige of physical awareness left them, able to hear movement as chests heaved with unnerved, frightened gasps, but unable to see the peril they knew lurked close. Once Cowle confident their psyches fragile and unsteady, he nodded to Sterner and Lang to remove the blindfolds from their captives.

Both women blinked at the brilliant white light searing eyes shrouded for so long in darkness, blinking to focus on their stark surroundings. Sterner placed a heavy hand on Alexandra's shoulder. Startled, her head swung about, a muffled shriek of terror through the gag at the sight of the masked visage looming above her echoing through the room. Emma didn't move, body shaking as Lang reached out, cupped her chin, forcing her to look at him, her only reaction a subdued whimper. Cowle smiled, his captives off-balance, under his complete control, wishing they'd been kept blindfolded upon viewing the foreboding interior, comprehending the grim situation. Cowle stood before his property, temporary as they may be, blocking the light, the two staring wide-eyed in horror at the man they believed a friend. "Emma," Cowle studied the trembling form of Emma, then at Alexandra, brown eyes panicky, filled with lingering disbelief at her betrayal, "Alexandra. Welcome to your home for the next few days." Their heads turned to the other, unsure by the meaning of the statement.

"Allow me to explain why you are here and why I have you," he waved at the bondage imprisoning them, "like this." Cowle placed his hands behind his back. "My name isn't Marcus Evans, it never was, my name is Marcus Cowle. By now I assume you also realize I'm not a professional photographer, though both of you far too gullible to see though my masquerade." Emma's expression changed then as the fear in her turquoise eyes replaced by a flash of anger, a whine of indignation. Cowle's lips curled upward in a slight grin. *Well, little Emma does has some fight left in her; Sheik Rahim will enjoy ridding her of so troublesome a trait.*

"I am a simple businessman, an entrepreneur," Cowle told them; the faces of his captives creased with confusion, afraid of what sort of business Marcus Cowle plied. Why it meant their abduction, kneeling bound and gagged in a Spartan room at an unknown location under the glare of blinding lights. Cowle paced before them, his eyes locked on theirs, holding their frightened gaze as they hung on each word. "I provide merchandise for certain interested parties, extremely wealthy parties, around the world." Cowle paused to let the words sink in. "Whatever they want, they receive. Price is no object to those I deal with. They wish to have precious, pretty things to do with at their pleasure."

"I deal in young, beautiful women such as yourselves." Emma and Alexandra stared at each other, with his pronouncement sickly suspecting their fate but didn't wish to believe. His next sentence confirmed the worst fears, neither of them to see home or family again. "Simply put, I collect and sell women like you." Cowle leaned over to stroke Alexandra's cheek, the smile on his face brittle and ravenous. Alexandra shaking against the ropes, staring transfixed in horror at Cowle. "You are the first pieces of the next consignment for my most generous client." The pair moaned in despair as Cowle continued, showing not a hint of sympathy. "You'll be staying here, consider these your accommodations, for the next few days while I and my associates," Cowle motioned to Sterner and Lang, taking their cue, roughly grabbing the women, forcing again to look at frightful masked faces, ratcheting up the fear settling deep in their stomachs, "secure the remainder of the shipment and await the arrival of your new owner to complete the transaction and arrange transit to your new home."

Cowle brushed the mahogany hair from Emma's blue eyes, damp with terror and hatred. "I hope you enjoy travel, it'll be a long trip. You're going to a place quite far from here." Both whimpered in utter, defeated desperation, understanding this only a way station on the journey, no return once they reached the ultimate destination. Cowle gazed at Alexandra, flashed a wicked, evil smile. "I know you wanted a new career, Alexandra. I do hope you enjoy this opportunity." Alexandra lowered her head, sobbed. "Might not be what you expected."

"We won't keep you tied like this the entire time," Cowle went on. "I'm a businessman, not a beast. We'll allow you occasional respite so you can rest, regain your strength. We'll feed you, though the menu is limited, and allow you use of the facilities. We have the clothes you brought for our photo sessions, let you change into something fresh. I wish to ensure my merchandise is in a presentable condition for my client when he arrives to take possession of you."

Cowle stopped pacing, stood in front of the pair, feet spread apart, hands on his hips in a gesture of superiority, time to lay down the most important rule. "There is one thing I must stress while you're our guests." He paused for effect. "You don't want to do anything stupid. By that I mean trying to escape or fighting back against me or my assistants," he warned in the stern tone of an eighteenth-century schoolmaster. "You don't want to do anything unwise. I don't want to damage the merchandise, but if you decide to be stubborn or act foolishly, I think my client will understand if there are a few dents and scratches in the product. My associates here," he motioned to Sterner and Lang standing nearby, silent and threatening, "are quite capable inflicting pain on those who don't do as they're told." He waited a moment, saw Emma shift slightly, trying to ease the pressure on her knees, whining at the fiery pain burning her tendons. "Do you understand what I'm telling you?"

To this grave admonition Emma and Alexandra nodded meekly, their resistance, if there'd been any to begin with, cowed and shattered. "Excellent," Cowle smiled warmly, "I'm pleased you view the matter my way. I'll let my associates see you are settled in. They'll check in on you tonight to make sure you're…comfortable." Heard Lang snicker at the statement, seeing more to the discomfort and agony of their vulnerable captives.

"Let's get you to your rooms, ladies." Sterner lifted Alexandra from the floor, the bound hostage screaming as he tossed her over his shoulder, long hair dropping towards the floor as Lang heaved Emma on his shoulder. Lang patted Emma on her hip, brought forth an indignant wail from the helpless girl. "I know you can't wait to see your rooms, ladies," Sterner goaded the hostages.

As his apprentices hauled their struggling parcels to the cells where they'd spend a long, harrowing night, Cowle entered the room where they set up the monitors for the closed-circuit cameras to observe the captives around the clock, watched Sterner and Lang deposit Alexandra and Emma in their respective cells, dumping them on the mattresses. From down the hall heard the forceful threats from his henchmen, reinforcing the warning Cowle had given them. *No funny stuff or you'll really have a bad night.*

Sterner and Lang joined Cowle as he viewed his captives on the monitors. 'I think they got the message," Sterner informed Cowle, tugging off the balaclava. "Don't think they'll be much trouble at all."

"I didn't think so," Cowle agreed, "but please make life difficult for them. The sooner we break their spirit," like a wildcat in a snare Emma resisting her situation, tugging and straining against her bonds, screaming through the gag while Alexandra, sobbing and crying, lay unmoving on the mattress in her cell, "the better. Make it tough, scare the crap out them."

"We can do tough. We like scaring the crap out of chicks like them," Sterner reassured.

"We'll have fun." Lang, grinning like a hyena, found his orders agreeable.

"Then I bid you farewell for the evening," Cowle said, leaving his apprentices to wreak psychological havoc on their prisoners. "I'm off to find that special one for Sheik Rahim." A victim innocent and unsuspecting of her intended fate, a virgin sacrifice offered to satisfy their benefactor's hunger for flesh.

"Heading to the clubs?" Lang asked, familiar hunting grounds Cowle trolled for victims.

"Perhaps later tonight," Cowle told him, "I'm heading to Evanslawn, have some street festival going on, I'm sure plenty of Big Ten college coeds out and about." He smiled. "Maybe I'll get lucky."

Chapter 15

"Nice to see you again," Tyler McManaway wrapped his arms around Samantha Grayson, placed a long anticipated kiss on the soft lips, embracing among the milling post-game throng outside the home locker room of Warren Field.

"You weren't even gone for twenty-four hours," Samantha giggled, repeated what Tyler told her the night before, the lingering kiss igniting a reassuring tingling arcing through her lithe body.

Tyler kissed her again, in an even better mood learning Cornell had beaten Bucknell, his twin brother Colin catching the game-winning touchdown pass. "That's still too long."

"Didn't you tell me it wasn't like you were going off to war?" Samantha said skeptically.

Tyler gave Samantha the drop-dead smile, her heart skipping a beat. "I lied."

"Now we get our twenty-four hours of freedom," D'Andre Watson collected Ashleigh Morgan in his arms. "Coach Carl gave us marching orders, doesn't want any four in the morning phone calls." That call, when received by the head coach of a major college football program, usually a portent of misbehavior by one or more of his players.

"You're mine for the next day, no watching game film," Ashleigh kissed D'Andre. "We have to celebrate this hundred yard game of yours."

"Told you I'd do it," D'Andre said, "but did anyone believe me?"

"Everyone believed you," Albert 'Fiji' Fatuamala gently draped a chiseled arm over the slender shoulders of Lauryn Callahan. "But you had to let everyone know to find validation for your actions."

D'Andre wagged a finger at Fiji. "Don't give me that philosophical mumbo-jumbo."

Tyler saw the gold medal dangling around Amanda McKinnon's neck, her expression one of serene satisfaction. "Looks like somebody else had a good day."

"Wore it all day?" Fiji noted.

"I couldn't take it off," Amanda fingered the medal. "It's so bright and shiny."

"So we're good to go?" Lauryn asked.

"Let's make like a hockey team and skate off the ice," Connor Aanonsen remarked.

D'Andre nudged Tyler in the shoulder, whispered under his breath. "Can't be like Steve McQueen and make our great escape yet," he motioned to a party of older men and women, many sporting the school's blue, white and silver colors, approaching. "Big time supporter of the athletic program coming this way, it'd be in bad taste to slip away without saying hello."

"Gentlemen, that was as fine a game I have seen in years here at Great Northern," Caleb 'Cal' McIllhenny congratulated the three football stars. The passage of years softened muscles once firm and lean, added pounds and girth to the six-three frame and whitened the shock of hair once dark and wavy when he'd been a three-sport legend at Great Northern, lettering in football, basketball and baseball during the sixties. After a stint in the Marines and serving a tour in Vietnam leading an infantry platoon, McIllhenny returned to his native Texas to grow his business from a hardscrabble sprout of a start-up into the energy conglomerate McIllhenny Energy, the sturdy billion dollar corporation spanning the globe. A fervent supporter of Great Northern McIllhenny, like Nike founder Phil Knight and oilman T. Boone Pickens had done at their respective alma maters of Oregon and Oklahoma State, donated a three hundred million dollar gift to improve the university's athletic facilities in an effort to bring the sports programs to par with their formidable competition in the Big Ten, keeping pace in an ongoing athletic arms race. His dream to place Great Northern on the same lofty footing with other institutions, specifically Notre Dame and Stanford, combining excellence in the classroom and on the playing field. Sparkling new state-of-the-art facilities, surrounding the McIllhenny Family Athletic Training Center, sprouting up on the newly designated McIllhenny Athletic Campus. At the completion of the season Warren Field undergoing a major renovation to add a Field Turf playing surface, a Jumbotron scoreboard, twenty-thousand seats and luxury suites to the stadium, improvements a tempting enticement to every highly sought high-school athlete Great Northern now recruited.

Tyler stepped forward, shook the extended hand. "Glad you enjoyed the game."

"I knew there'd come days like this when you fellows made the commitment to Great Northern," McIllhenny shook hands with D'Andre and Fiji, his down-home manner matched that of a kindly country grandfather. "D'Andre, you had a hell of a game running the ball and Albert," he didn't use the nickname bestowed by his teammates, "I don't think that quarterback ever wants to cross paths with you again. Hell, I don't think he wants you in the same time zone."

"It was a team effort," Fiji replied modestly, "everyone did their job."

"Can't wait until you show the Big Ten what you can do," McIllhenny said, chest puffed out proud as a father handing out cigars on the arrival of his first-born.

"We'll start next week against the Golden Gophers," D'Andre added. The first two games in conference against lower-lights Minnesota and Indiana, offered a chance to go undefeated before the first conference test against Iowa, ranked eleventh in the nation going into the weekend.

"I know you can't wait to start your season." McIllhenny turned to Connor. "What do you think about that new arena you'll be playing in?"

"Sir, I'm counting down the days until I'm in net for our first game there." Connor nodded in appreciation, the varsity hockey program receiving a major upgrade with the completion of the Thomas C. Travener Ice Arena, named in honor of a classmate of McIllhenny's who served in Vietnam but never returned. Prior to the arena's construction the hockey team played at the Allstate Arena in suburban

Rosemont far from campus. The Huskies christening their new home with a contest against defending national champion Boston College. "That palace is the reason I came here."

"Glad to hear that," he glanced at Amanda beside Connor, nodded at the medal she wore with pride. "I heard you did one fine job this morning, Amanda McKinnon." Samantha recognized the benefactor playing the room, showering attention on every scholarship athlete present.

"Didn't do too badly," Amanda batted her eyelashes, made an obvious understatement.

"Wish I could've made it out there to watch you win, Amanda. I've heard great things about you," McIllhenny complimented. "I had a prior engagement on campus, pressing the flesh to raise money for the university." He leaned over to Amanda, lowered his voice but everyone could still hear. "Hell, would've liked to have found a way out of that shindig to watch you run, those damn things get boring sometimes."

"I understand, Mister McIllhenny," Amanda replied.

"Call me Cal, only people who work for me call me Mister McIllhenny." He informed her, a mischievous sparkle in the blue eyes. "You wore that shiny trinket all day, didn't you?"

"Couldn't help it," Amanda touched the medal, smiling broadly. "I'm such a show-off."

"I hope you bring back some more hardware from the NCAA Championships," Cal said.

"That's the plan," Amanda agreed.

McIllhenny looked at Samantha. "You're Samantha Grayson, aren't you?" No secret she and Tyler an item on campus, yet Samantha taken by surprise a donor with the stature of Cal McIllhenny aware of the fact. "Every day I check *The Daily Northern* website and I see your name on a story. You're a busy young lady, I like your work."

"Thank you," Samantha taken back by the compliment, tried to remain professional and stay impartial. "There's always something on campus keeping me busy."

"A reporter like you has to be covering that speech by Senator Fielding on Monday morning," McIllhenny said, a touch of flattery in his statement.

"I'll be there in the front row," Samantha nodded. "I'm looking forward to it."

"If you need a reaction," McIllhenny told her, "track me down afterwards. I'll be more than happy to share my thoughts." Samantha surprised by the unexpected show of candor. "Now I don't want to keep you from celebrating this victory. Have a good evening and stay safe." With that McIllhenny and his entourage moved on to congratulate other players emerging from the locker room.

"You heard the man," Connor grinned. "Now we can make like a hockey team and skate."

"You got a shout out there," Lauryn smiled at Samantha.

"That's my girl." Tyler wrapped an arm over Samantha's shoulders, pulled her close. "You don't have to be an athlete to get attention around here." Tyler saw D'Andre checking the palm of his hand. "What're you doing?"

"Making sure ol' Cal didn't slip a hundred into my hand when he pressed the flesh," D'Andre answered. "Don't want any trouble from the NCAA."

"Flying solo again?" Ashleigh Morgan asked Allison Mayne.

"Whatever gave you that idea?" Allison replied, voice hoarse from a day spent cheering on the sidelines. Brushed dark blonde hair from her eyes, opening the door to her suite as Ashleigh watched from their suite across the hall. "Natalie and Bryce are off to the bright lights of the big city, so I won't be seeing Natalie until the wee hours of the morning."

"Have any plans?" Lauryn Callahan asked, she and Amanda McKinnon joined Ashleigh.

"Like you said," Allison replied, "flying solo."

"Want to join the formation?" Amanda offered. "We're off to Summer's End Fest downtown with the guys."

"Do I have time to slip out of the work clothes?" Allison meant her cheerleading outfit.

"Take your time," Ashleigh said. "The guys are back at their dorm. D'Andre and Fiji had to drop off their bags and change."

"Where's Samantha?" Allison noticed there were three, and not four, of the residents of three-twelve Falmouth Hall.

"She's already changed and gone, went with Tyler into Chicago," Amanda told her, "watching the fireworks down at Navy Pier."

"And make a few of their own." A sly smile flashed across Lauryn's sweetly adorable face.

Amanda raised an eyebrow. "Wow, you with the witty comeback." *When will you and Fiji starting making some fireworks of your own?* She so badly wanted to ask Lauryn.

"Well, it's true," Lauryn defended her opinion.

"There's more to Chicago than clubs and bars," Allison wished her friend and roommate someday recognized this fact.

"This is why I enjoy what I do for a living." Lang divided his attention between two closed circuit television monitors, keeping tabs on Emma Hayden and Alexandra Cole. Their prisoners separated and alone in adjoining rooms, able to hear the other's muted cries, cloth cleave gags replaced with thick silver duct tape wrapped around their heads sealing silencing waddling within their mouths. Alexandra immobilized in a wooden chair, bound with hundreds of feet of rope melding her to the seat while in her cell Emma struggled on the mattress, ankles pulled up and tied to her wrists to limit her movements. No need for them to remain blindfolded, Lang watched frightened eyes darting about, absorbing the darkly ominous, severe atmosphere of the abandoned factory.

"Sure beats the old nine to five job," Sterner remarked, his eyes intent on the book in his meaty hands. "Pay's not too shabby either."

"Especially once the Arab gets his hands on them." Lang chuckled at his partner's comment, peering over to the laptop next to him streaming video from ESPN of the weekend's marquee college football game, mighty USC facing national champion Alabama in Tuscaloosa. Still had work left before receiving payment, three additional parcels yet to be acquired for the full consignment, a detail completed by tomorrow afternoon. Then a day spent babysitting the packages until the Arab showed up with their money, passing the time until then terrorizing the unfortunate captives, preparing them for tortures and agonies far worse at the whim of their new owner. The delay in delivery the lone potential hitch in the operation, usually handing over the shipment hours after the final victim abducted. Lang thought it no big deal, though he suspected Cowle growing apprehensive sitting on product for so long. He didn't mind, gave him and Sterner more time to play with the merchandise. *And the fun never stops.*

Lang checked the laptop, crimson clad Alabama driving for a score to break the 14-14 tie, switching his attention back to the monitors. Alexandra long ago surrendering to her bondage, head dropped to her chest, crying uncontrollably while Emma rolled about from side to side, continuing to fight her hopeless predicament, anguished cries angry yet despairing. "I didn't think Emma was the feisty type," he remarked, "I thought Alexandra would be the fighter, gave up pretty quick."

"Appearances can be deceiving," Sterner noted simply.

"What're you reading?" Lang asked his partner.

"Dickens," Sterner said. "*Tale of Two Cities*." He flipped a page of the thick tome.

Lang snorted. "That's the sort of long-hair crap they forced me to read in high school."

"It's called a classic," Sterner retorted. "Better than the crap you read. Does that one guy have a book out every other Tuesday?" The snide aside directed at a popular thriller author churning out a new release hitting the shelves, and the best-seller list, with clockwork regularity.

"Only takes me a day or two get through his stuff, and I can relate to some of the plots," especially the villains populating the tales. Lang observed Emma haul her bound body into a kneeling position, throwing her head back, letting loose a pathetic wail for help, but no one around for blocks to hear the plaintive screams. "You've been reading that for a month and you're only half-way through."

"Classic literature is to be savored," Sterner replied, "not devoured."

Lang cocked his head. "You're starting to sound like Cowle," he said. "Wonder what that guy studied in college." Lang assumed Cowle attended a prestigious university like Great Northern, surprised they'd worked for Cowle as his apprentices for years yet knew little about his past, the man never opening up, revealing his origins, declining to even tell them where he grew up, or how one cultured and refined turned into a cold, vicious trader in the lives of women.

"He's a businessman," Sterner's eyes never left the printed page. "So my guess is he studied at one of those big-time MBA schools."

Lang leaned back in his chair, appreciating the performance the helpless Emma putting forth for him, a rapt audience of one. "You ever want to move up to what Cowle does? Become a Collector? Run our own operation?"

"Not really." Sterner turned another page, didn't lift his head. "Cowle has to deal with all the logistics, finding the product. I wouldn't want that headache. I have no problem with my position," being well-paid muscle and protection, "the pay is good. Can't bitch about the benefits either."

"No, I can't complain either," Lang admitted. He checked the laptop, the Crimson Tide running back plunging in from the three to break the deadlock. "Think we should check on our guests again? It's your turn this time."

"Why not? Have to keep the girls entertained." The irregular pattern of torment, hostages never knowing when their captors would come to molest and taunt them, keeping their nerves frayed. Sterner folded the corner of the page, placed the book down, taking the black balaclava and tugging it over his head, adjusting the opening so only his eyes showed. The concealment heightening the experience of unbridled fear for their captives once he appeared in their midst.

"Have fun," Lang told Sterner as he left the room.

"I will," Sterner answered casually. "Don't know if I can say the same for them." He headed down the corridor. On the monitors Lang saw Alexandra lift her head, Emma halt her struggles once they heard the footsteps approach. He heard the muffled shriek from Alexandra as he watched Sterner step into her cell on the monitor.

Lang divided his attention between the football game on the laptop and the drama unfolding on the video monitors, captives once more threatened and intimidated by the hulking, masked figure invading their space, cries of terror echoing through the cavernous expanse of the vacant factory going unanswered. He'd get his chance to play with them later, for now the show on the monitors better than anything else, even a matchup between the top college football programs in the nation.

"This is the way to spend an evening," D'Andre Watson commented, walking in the company of his friends, holding tightly the hand of Ashleigh Morgan. "Who has the betting line on how many off-campus parties get busted tonight?"

"What about the festivities over on Greek Row?" This observation from Amanda McKinnon. Greek Row the name of the street where Great Northern's fraternities and sororities stood, no doubt the police presence there conspicuous following the home victory.

"Why do you think we're here," Allison Mayne said, "instead of there?" The 'here' in question Summer's End Fest on the streets of downtown Evanslawn. Off in the distance, back towards the Great Northern campus, the wail of a police siren drifted through the air. "That was quick."

"Not even ten." D'Andre checked the time. "Should've put a betting line on when the first party gets busted too."

"The boys in blue aren't wasting any time," Connor Aanonsen added.

"Like the lady said," D'Andre pointed at Allison. "Why we're here and not there. I don't want to be the reason for an early morning phone call to Coach Carl and be riding the bench next week."

"So let's enjoy the evening," Allison added. For the next hour the group browsed exhibitor booths displaying crafts and art, taking a break by the main stage to listen to a folk-rock band comprised of students from Great Northern's Hamlin School of Music and Performance, Connor had class with the drummer of the ensemble inexplicably named "Wedge Antilles And The Rebel Alliance." After listening to a few numbers they resumed their trek through the festival, D'Andre and Albert 'Fiji' Fatuamala stopping to sign autographs or pose for photos with fans and alumni who remained in Evanslawn following the afternoon contest, still the center of attention away from the playing field.

Connor saw Amanda yawn; stretch her arms. "Is my Gazelle finally running out of steam?"

"I think I hit the wall and it's hitting back," Amanda covered her mouth, stifled a second yawn. "I've been up since before the crack of dawn."

"Want to head back?" Connor kissed her forehead.

"I think so." Amanda swept her hands through her raven hair, shook out the luminous tresses. "I'm calling it a night if you all don't mind, this girl is pooped."

"You look it," Lauryn Callahan hugged Amanda. "Get some rest."

"Sorry to bail on you, but the fuel tank is empty," Amanda said, Connor draping an arm over her shoulders as the pair turned towards campus.

"How much you want to bet they'll have the door to our room closed and are making out when we get back?" Ashleigh offered once the pair out of earshot.

"I'm not crazy enough to take that action," Allison replied.

"Hey babe," Ashleigh turned to D'Andre. "There's an exhibitor I want to check out, had some necklaces that caught my eye. See if there's anything I might want to buy before he closes shop."

D'Andre kissed Ashleigh on the cheek. "Knock yourself out, babe." He pointed to the stage. "We'll go and listen to the band."

Ashleigh headed over to the tent and the jewelry attracting her attention, nodding pleasantly at the exhibitor as she perused the wares. As she fingered a necklace of gold interlaid with jade stones, she heard a clicking sound, blinked at the flash of light bathing her face. Knew the sound of a camera, raised her head to see a thin man with blond hair standing to her right, camera up to his eye and pointed at her. *Terrific. I attract them like bees to Winnie the Pooh's honey pot.* Ashleigh sighed, smiled coolly as the photographer lowered his camera. From accompanying her father through the social circles of entertainment Ashleigh encountered both true professionals and those playing the game, her sixth sense instantly discerning this 'professional' nothing but a player. The same went for talent scouts and promoters who heard her sing, flashing glossy business cards and claiming they had the connections to make Ashleigh the next big pop star, unaware that's what her father did for a living and advised his daughter against pursuing. No need for Ashleigh Morgan to tread the route of *American Idol* to find success, her destiny at Great Northern University with a path marked through the law school.

The photographer about to speak, delve into his pitch, when Ashleigh raised her hand, palm facing out at him. "I know what you're going to say. I have the look, I should be a model."

"I was going to say…" the photographer started, taken off guard by Ashleigh's brusque reply, "that you're a very lovely young women and…"

"Thank you." Ashleigh cut off his response, nodded politely, arms crossed over her chest. "Then you were about to tell me how I should be a model and you'll help me make it in the business, right?"

"Well…" the photographer began to say, Ashleigh guessed he not used to so blunt a reaction. Ashleigh shivered, didn't know why but the guy seemed creepy, hiding a darker motive for taking her picture and engaging in conversation.

"You aren't the first man with a camera, and likely not the last, to snap my picture and try to sweet talk me with the glamour and glitz of the modeling life," Ashleigh explained, getting to her point. "I go to Great Northern, one of the top colleges in the nation. They don't accept anyone. I'm majoring in business and pre-law, going to law school after this so when I graduate I'll be the one sitting across the table from you negotiating the contract for my client, not the one in front of the camera wearing next to nothing and trying to be sexy."

"I was trying to be nice," the photographer said, his voice now frosty like a January morning; Ashleigh picked up indignant anger lacing the tone. "I thought you might have an interest."

"Well, I don't," Ashleigh told him, spotted Allison Mayne two booths over, admiring a set of wood carvings, Ashleigh overcome by a sudden urge to get away from this man, something about him, the gray eyes now boring into her, troubling and made her uncomfortable. "Now if you'll excuse me." Ashleigh brushed by the man, headed towards Allison.

"Who was that?" Allison asked as Ashleigh came up to her, witnessed the exchange and took note of the photographer's unpleasant expression.

"Some photographer giving me the spiel how I should be a model." Ashleigh explained as they headed back to their friends sitting at a table listening to the music from the stage. "I've heard it all before. It's not going to happen." Ashleigh quickly pushed the encounter out of her mind, breathing a sigh of relief as the distance between her and the photographer grew until he was nothing but an unpleasant memory.

Ashleigh couldn't have known how correct her suspicions had been. Unaware the man accosting her not a professional photographer, but a dangerous hunter hiding a deadly purpose. Marcus Cowle seethed at the harsh treatment heaped on him, eyes flaring with hatred watching her walk away. *Bitch needs to be taught a lesson*, Cowle thought, wished there a way to administer appropriate punishment within the shuttered factory on Chicago's West Side where two women held as his captives and aware of the dark secret hidden beneath the surface.

Chapter 16

As they drove down Lake Shore Drive towards downtown Chicago Samantha Grayson lowered the front window of Tyler McManaway's Nissan Xterra, the languid warm breeze of a late September evening rushed though her auburn hair. She closed her eyes, settling into the front seat, and relaxed. *This is bliss*. She opened her eyes, looked over at Tyler in the driver's seat, smiling with contentment as a flawless day melted into a perfect evening. She listened to the Ben Folds song on the CD player, the piano melody soothing her spirit. "Enjoying the ride?" Tyler kept an eye on the traffic, wary of drivers more focused talking or texting on their smartphones than on the road.

"Enjoying the driver more than the drive," Samantha reached over, rested her hand on his thigh.

"Don't distract the driver," Tyler glanced at her. "You know distracted driving is the leading cause of automobile accidents," he cautioned, sounding like his father. "When we get downtown you can distract me to your heart's content."

"You mean I have to wait?" Samantha eased her hand away, cooed in mock disappointment.

"You want to explain to the police officer how frisky you were when they're filling out the accident report?" Tyler warned.

"Okay, I'll wait." Samantha slumped in the seat, a playful pout on her face, made a show of innocently biting her lower lip. "Then I'm distracting you all I want."

"I won't have a problem with that," Tyler replied and they laughed, his presence comforting her soul. Samantha turned back to the glittering skyline of nighttime Chicago, the buildings rising and falling against the night sky like the diamond encrusted points on a tiara. Every second the perspective changed as they neared the center of the city, towers once far off in the distance grew larger until looming over them with the imposing grandeur of a mountain range. Tyler slowed to make the sharp left hand curve at Oak Street, Lake Shore Drive the barrier separating the popular lakefront beach from the ritzy towers of the Gold Coast and the Magnificent Mile, Samantha peering up at the distinctive twin antenna spires of the John Hancock Building pointed heavenward. She shifted her gaze east, out over the tranquil waters of Lake Michigan teeming with illuminated sailboats and motor cruisers, dwarfed the by larger dinner cruise ships among them. Even at this hour the lakefront bike path jammed with runners and cyclists or people out for a walk taking in the pleasant evening. Samantha sucked in the mild air, the lake reminding her of the ocean, as a single thought blossomed in her mind.

I love this city…I love Chicago. This is where I should be. This is where I want to be.

She reflected on where she might've gone to college, during her senior year at Canandaigua Academy received scholarships from many universities with outstanding journalism programs, considered how different her life could've turned out if she'd gone somewhere else. Syracuse and

Cornell University, where her mother went to college, too close to home. Although she loved her parents dearly, Samantha wished to explore new surroundings and those schools far too familiar. Columbia University in New York City offered desired new environs with the constant bustle and excitement of Manhattan, far enough from home to feel like she was away at school, yet close enough if she yearned to taste the comforts of family. Yet the city too overwhelming, induced within Samantha a perception of sensory overload, the sheer density of everything and everyone crammed onto the thin strip of island produced a sensation of claustrophobia. Left with the opinion she'd love to visit, but didn't want to live there. USC promised an exciting, yet laid-back, atmosphere under brilliant blue skies and bright sunshine of southern California, the glitz and glamour of the entertainment world beckoning beyond the campus an added stimulation. But USC too far away, too many miles and time zones separating her from her parents. A dark thought clouded her reverie; if she'd decided on USC might she be one of the five women who disappeared a year earlier? Her smiling face staring out silently from missing posters as passersby took pity on her unfortunate fate? *The flight of a butterfly...*

Samantha banished the morose musing, for this night with Tyler desired only happiness. The Xterra crossed over the Chicago River, Samantha looked west down the river at the canyon formed by the buildings rising along each bank, towards the glittering spire of the Trump Tower rising above the bend at Wabash Avenue, past the Spanish baroque splendor of the Wrigley Building awash in floodlights. They took the sweeping right hand turn to enter Grant Park, considered the front lawn of downtown Chicago, Samantha catching a glimpse of the Frank Gehry designed Pritzker Pavilion amphitheater at Millennium Park above the trees, polished stainless steel gleaming under the city lights. The row of buildings along Michigan Avenue at the western boundary of Grant Park park stood like an escarpment along the edge of an ocean, reminding Samantha of the Cliffs of Dover towering above the English Channel.

"Enjoying the view?" Tyler never let his eyes leave the road.

"Never get tired of it." Samantha placed her hand out the window, flow of air tickling the skin.

Great Northern the last school she visited, parents accompanying her on the trip the week before Thanksgiving, had business in Chicago. They knew indecision raged in their daughter's mind, weighing the advantages of each school as she made this final visit, hoping one tiny detail separated one school from the others and sealed the choice. Her trip encouraging, the campus nestled on the picturesque shore of Lake Michigan, Evanslawn a lively and intimate suburb. The academics excellent, Samantha impressed with the course offerings at the Randall School of Journalism and Communications and the opportunity to work at the award-winning student newspaper, *The Daily Northern*. Still, nothing tipped the balance for Samantha to select the prestigious Big Ten school over the competition. The next day she spent the day with her parents taking in the sights of Chicago and where Samantha seemed small and insignificant amidst the hyperactive neon canyons of New York or far away from the familiar in Los Angeles, she suddenly felt at ease walking the streets of Chicago. Samantha amazed by the welcoming friendliness of the people, distinguished a vibrant energy and excitement that didn't overpower, marveled at the contrast between the openness of the prairie to the west and the endless expanse of the lake to the east. Those few hours spent in the Second City cemented the decision, Great Northern University the dream school Samantha wanted to attend and, after nervously waiting out the application process, joyfully accepted the full scholarship upon its offering the following spring.

Samantha recalled the first date with Tyler, discovering the attraction between them, as he turned the Xterra onto Jackson, heading towards the Loop. They'd become acquainted in Freshman

Composition class, Tyler gallantly offering to show her the city. On a Saturday morning when the football team had an off date from the schedule Tyler picked her up at her room in Cockrell Hall. They drove into Chicago as dawn broke over the city, the streets deserted and quiet, escorting Samantha on a personal tour of the city he called home. Having gained an interest in architecture from his architect father, Tyler pointed out buildings designed by Daniel Burnham and Louis Sullivan, took her to where their groundbreaking mastery no longer existed, using his smartphone to call up images from the internet of wondrous structures and fascinating towers once standing there but now faded into history. Tyler offered a bit of advice as they strolled along silent avenues. 'Look up.' Samantha did as instructed, amazed at the intricate ornament crafted into the edifices many never noticed in their daily travels, their eyes fixed on the ground or straight ahead, never looking up to discover the magical, delicate splendors of craftsmanship hidden within the exteriors.

Brunch at a quaint restaurant in Lincoln Park was followed by a cup of coffee at a Starbucks in Old Town, then off to explore quirky shops in the Wicker Park and Bucktown neighborhoods northwest of downtown. The whirlwind day stretched through the afternoon and into the evening to encompass a visit to the Lincoln Park Zoo, taking in a German festival in the Lincoln Square neighborhood, walking around Wrigley Field and culminating with a visit to Navy Pier and riding the Ferris Wheel. Their long adventure concluded with Tyler and Samantha barefoot on the sand of North Avenue Beach, Samantha held in his strong arms watching the moonrise over the lake, the skyline glimmering to their west like an earthbound constellation of stars. That day Samantha Grayson fell hopelessly in love with Tyler McManaway, forever thankful of her decision to attend Great Northern where she found not only a city to love and explore but someone special who cared so deeply for her.

Tyler turned onto Columbus Drive, eased the Xterra to the curb. "Have to feed the meter. Don't want to get a ticket." Tyler went to an automated kiosk along the sidewalk where he dipped his credit card. Several years earlier the city leased the parking rights to a private company and rates skyrocketed accordingly, Chicago still had a sordid reputation as the 'City on the Take,' a long litany of corruption and backroom deals. The owners of the company purchasing the rights and those politically connected few who arranged the agreement coming out handsomely at the expense of those shelling out money to park their vehicles. The kiosk spat out a slip of paper noting the time his parking expired. Tyler walked to the Xterra, opened the passenger side door, placed the paper on the dashboard. He checked his watch, saw they had time. "Come on," Tyler offered his hand to Samantha, the lovers strolling into Grant Park.

After a short walk they reached Buckingham Fountain, the water arcing and cascading through the air, sound of the crashing spray combined with the hum of traffic on Michigan Avenue for a soothing real-life white noise. Every few seconds the lights of the fountain changed, bathing the monument in luminescent shades of soft colors. Samantha noted the presence of other couples gathered around the landmark with the same idea this warm late-summer evening. A BOOM echoed off in the distance and Samantha swiveled about in Tyler's arms as the fireworks display from Navy Pier commenced. She nestled into his embrace, let him hold her tight, treasured the security of his touch. She watched the expanding blossoms of radiant color exploding against the blue-black sky, lights of the tourist attraction glistening like the tail of a comet into the dark waters of the lake.

Tyler leaned close. "What's wrong?" He whispered in her ear.

"What do you mean?" Samantha knew what he meant, pivoting to face him.

"You weren't your usual self Friday at lunch." Samantha grimaced at the observation. "I don't think you're worried about this speech Monday. You've never doubted yourself on a story, I know you too well. Something's bothering that beautiful head of yours." Tyler paused. "Got an instructor who's giving you trouble?"

Samantha shook off the question. "No, classes are fine."

Tyler remained silent for a moment before asking. "Is it something about us?"

Oh God! How could I let him think that! "No! It's nothing like that!" Samantha swallowed, mortified her moping lead Tyler to consider this unlikely possibility. She reached up, stroked his cheek, gazed longingly into dashing blue eyes she found comforting. The light breeze ruffled his blonde hair. "Tyler, I love you and nothing in the world will change that."

"What is it?" Tyler rubbed her shoulders, his fingers sensing tension in her muscles. "Something has you upset. This isn't like you. Whatever it is I want to help."

Samantha stared over his shoulder at the lights of the city, sighed, unsure how to express what troubled her. She needed to tell him, couldn't keep what tormented her this past week bottled inside; perhaps talking with Tyler, the one she loved with all her heart, soothing the lingering anxiety. Samantha took solace Tyler willing to listen, offering reassurance with a gentle embrace.

"What if I were gone?" Samantha finally asked Tyler. "What would you do?"

"If you were gone?" The question caught Tyler off-guard, an eyebrow raised in puzzlement, uncertain tone in the voice out of character for Samantha. "Like you left school?"

Samantha shook her head, prayed she might phrase the question so not to upset him. "What if I were gone? Like no longer here?" She rested her head against his chest, listened to the steady beat of his strong heart. "What if I were here one minute and gone the next and you didn't know what happened to me?"

Tyler gazed into the alluring brown eyes, saw the love for him whenever he looked into those eyes. Now the same eyes that enchanted him clouded with distress, Tyler slowly realizing, as a sickening knot formed deep in the pit of his stomach, what Samantha tried telling him. "Like you...disappeared? If someone took you?" Found difficult to speak the words, couldn't imagine, even conceive, the thought of Samantha being *gone*, vanishing from his life without a trace. That someone might consider harming one so beautiful and compassionate, so precious to him, a possibility too horrible to contemplate.

"Is that what you're saying?" Samantha nodded silently, didn't say another word, buried her head into his chest, sought comfort in his presence. "Samantha," Tyler whispered, stroked the lush reddish-brown hair hair. Never seen Samantha this seemingly off-balance, so unsure. "What's wrong?" Samantha didn't reply, Tyler not about to compel an answer until she was ready.

A minute passed before Samantha, done soaking up the affection of his loving embrace, gave voice to her apprehension. "Monday at lunch, when I went to refill my glass, I passed a table with a *Chicago Tribune* on it. There was a story on the page that caught my eye, stopped to read it."

"What was it about?" Tyler kissed Samantha lightly on the forehead.

"A year ago, there were these five women, about our age, who disappeared in Los Angeles," Samantha explained, soothed by the sound of water cascading from Buckingham Fountain. "They all vanished over a weekend. The police don't know what happened to them, never found any trace of them."

Tyler thought what his life entailed the previous year, didn't recall the story in the news as other, more immediate, matters occupied his attention. Immediately thrust on the field when fifth-year starter Tanner Broyles and backup Wendell Carlton both lost for the season during the opening game against Florida State. Tyler forced into the starting role, facing a baptism of fire against a killer schedule instead of taking a redshirt year standing safely on the sidelines beside Coach Carl, holding a clipboard and learning the offense, preparing to take over the next season. *No wonder I don't remember this.* At that time another thing gaining his attention, a special person entering his life, changing it for the better: Samantha Grayson.

Samantha continued, once started didn't wish to stop until all her anxieties expressed. "I picked up the paper, I don't know why. Thought there might be a connection to Great Northern. Maybe it's how those women in the pictures, the ones who went missing, remind me of Amanda, Lauryn and Ashleigh. Made me think what I would do, how I'd feel if one of them disappeared."

Now Tyler made the connection, understood her subdued spirit on Friday afternoon. "Or how I, and your friends and family, would feel if it were you who went missing."

"There's more." Samantha blinked, her eyes misting, with the sleeve of her top wiped at damp eyes. "I did some research and I came up with some things that don't feel right."

"What?" Tyler asked.

"This isn't the first time this has happened," Samantha told him. "There's been a series of disappearances like these in cities across the country, going back a few years. Started in Boston, then Denver and Atlanta, finally in Los Angeles. Women going missing over a few days, no trace of them turning up. The police and FBI think it might be a serial killer…"

"You wanted to ask Lauryn and Ashleigh, didn't you?" From memory Tyler pieced together their time at lunch on Friday, the reason for Samantha's withdrawn mood now clear while the rest of them upbeat. "Ask them what they knew."

Samantha nodded again. "I wanted to, but I couldn't. Everyone was having a good time. I didn't want to spoil it. I had pizza with Allison Mayne and her roommates on Tuesday and I asked Selena Espinosa, she's from Los Angeles, about it and I felt I ruined the good mood they were in."

"We would've understood," Tyler explained.

"This is why I've been a little wound up." Samantha let Tyler's presence calm her fears. "The time between these disappearances is getting shorter. I think it's going to happen again soon, somewhere." *Hopefully not here…*

Tyler placed his hand gently under her chin, lifting her head to look into the passionate brown eyes, offered Samantha a pledge of reassurance, praying the oath he spoke never needing to be fulfilled. "I will never let anything happen to you. I will always be there to protect you. I will do everything to find you and I will never, ever, let anyone hurt you."

"Promise?" Samantha edged up on her toes, kissed her hero.

Tyler smiled the perfect, relaxed smile of immaculate white teeth melting her soul. "Promise." Silently they stood in each other's arms beside Buckingham Fountain under the night sky as fireworks exploded in a universe of color over Lake Michigan. Nothing more needed to be discussed between the young lovers.

She's the one.

Marcus Cowle knew he'd found the special offering for Sheik Rahim the moment she started talking to him while standing at the bar in the exclusive nightclub Vibe in Chicago's River North, a favorite trolling ground for his purposes, where he made his initial contact with Emma Hayden, now his helpless prisoner at the abandoned factory. The bubbling excitement in the singsong voice, the naïve manner in her response to his entreaty regarding an interest in modeling only betrayed her carefree innocence, suspecting she wasn't of legal age to be in this establishment in the first place. *Her mistake,* he thought, *Sheik Rahim will enjoy her.*

"Presley, that's such a lovely name," he complimented his prospective target, flattery a weapon he wielded with adroit perfection.

"Thank you, that's very sweet of you." The girl to whom he directed the comment dressed in a dark burgundy sleeveless silk mini-dress with matching high heels, her smile bright, yet had a fetchingly delicious overbite. Despite the makeup the comely face, reminiscent of a Renaissance Madonna, slightly flushed from alcohol. A willowy, delicate creature with long, silken brown hair the color of caramel and big brown eyes Cowle guessed she stood a petite five-two without the heels, the same height as unfortunate Emma. Cowle smiled, he'd experience little difficulty subduing this girl.

"How did your parents come up with the name?" Cowle inquired.

"My parents are big Elvis Presley fans," Presley Harding explained. "My dad named his business Graceland Capital because he's such an Elvis fan. It's a private equity firm on Wall Street. You should see all the memorabilia my parents have collected, fills up two rooms of our home."

"Let me guess, if you were born a boy..." Cowle started to say.

Presley nodded. "I would've been named Elvis," she grimaced at what might've been. "But instead I came out like this," she spread her arms out wide, Cowle admiring the supple curves of her breasts and hips. "Neither of them keen on naming me Lisa Marie or Priscilla. So they thought it over and decided to name me Presley."

"I think they made a fine choice," Cowle groomed her with fawning attentiveness; right then desired this pretty babe in the woods as the final victim of this kidnapping spree. "It's a beautiful name for a very beautiful young woman."

"Thank you again," her eyes glowed as she answered; unaware she fell further under the spell of deceit Cowle cast over her. "So you think I could be a model?"

"You have the look, I'm confident you'd go far," Cowle said over the throbbing dance music. Being truthful in this respect, Presley Harding an attractive young woman. "You already have a memorable name."

Presley smiled, sipped her cocktail, Cowle knew then he had her. This encounter proceeding more smoothly than in Evanslawn with the black bitch who mouthed off at him, the words about him being 'a man with a camera' still bruised the ego. *I am so much more than that,* Cowle grinned, *so much more.* A shame he couldn't show the uppity black girl his true colors, an experience Cowle sure to enjoy, though much to that missed target's regret.

"You know how to make a girl feel appreciated," Presley replied, her smile continuing to glow.

"I have a project I'm working on, an online catalog for a clothing company." Cowle laid the bait, jiggling the lure, seeing if she'd bite. "They specifically requested models that haven't been in the public eye. A fresh face." He paused. "I think you fit the bill perfectly. Would you be free tomorrow afternoon or early evening?"

"Me?" Presley taken aback, flattered. "You think they'd want me?" Cowle nodded. "What do I have to do?"

"I'd have to get approval from their artistic director," Cowle explained. "So I need to take a portfolio of you to show them. You'd need to bring some outfits with you, something you wear to place like this. It'll only take three or four hours," Presley having no idea the session lasting the rest of her soon-to-be short life, ending with a quite violent demise, "and I'll pay you two hundred dollars an hour for your trouble. Would you be interested?"

"Would I be interested?" Presley repeated excitedly. Cowle heard gears in her cute head turning over the monetary figure, with her reply the adorable smile shining brightly. "I think I am."

"Here's my card. Can I get your number? I'll give you a call tomorrow morning to set a time," Cowle handed Presley a business card. "Is that all right with you?"

"That will work," Presley said, "do you have another card and a pen?" Cowle gave her a second card and a pen, Presley scribbling her cell phone number on the back. "Can I tell you a little secret?" Presley handed the card back to Cowle.

"I think I can keep it," Cowle told her.

Presley leaned close so no one able to hear. "I'm not supposed to be here," she revealed.

"Is that so?" Cowle grinned. *Tell me something I didn't already figure out.*

"I'm only eighteen," Presley told him, didn't know Cowle already assumed her tender age.

"How did you get in?" Cowle wondered. His interest piqued how a girl barely out of high school gained entrance to the trendy club so effortlessly, slipping past wary bouncers checking ID's at the door.

"I'm a freshman at Great Northern. I have a friend there whose father, he's a US senator, is friends with my father. He knows where to get fake IDs, they're real good ones, look like the real thing. He got me one and I've been using it since school started. No one checking has suspected it's a fake." Presley impressed with her good fortune yet unaware her premature entry into Chicago nightlife dooming her to a horrendous fate.

"Sounds like you got lucky," Cowle complimented Presley.

A dark-haired young woman, about the same height as his prey, called from across the room, waving at her. "Presley! Presley! We're leaving!"

"I'll be right there, Natalie!" Presley shouted back, setting her empty cocktail glass on the bar, collecting her handbag. "Call me tomorrow. I'm looking forward to working with you!"

"I'm looking forward to working with you too," Cowle watched Presley weave her way through the crowded floor, admired the sway of her hips in the skimpy dress. *In more ways than you think, pretty little Presley.* The girl Presley met with attractive, unfortunate he couldn't have made her acquaintance as well. *Get another matched set for Sheik Rahim.*

Presley Harding approached Natalie DiLaurenzo. "Who was that you were talking to?" Natalie studied the reedy man with blond hair standing at the bar, the camera draped around his neck. All evening Natalie uneasy having the pretty freshman again tagging along with Bryce and his friends, but Bryce insisted Presley accompany them on this excursion, reassuring Natalie that everything would be fine. Natalie didn't believe his assessment, keeping an eye on Presley all night, the girl a tad too wide-eyed innocent and trusting, life for the freshman before Great Northern seemed a sheltered affair, taking advantage being on her own for the first time. Natalie had done a good job watching Presley until entering Vibe, the two then separated in the crowd.

120

"Just someone I met," Presley replied carefully, "taking photos for a social website. Liked what I was wearing." Presley thought it wise not to tell Natalie of the modeling offer from the man she only knew as Marcus Evans. At least not until she achieved stardom as a model.

"So how was Chicago?" Lauryn Callahan asked Samantha Grayson while sitting down on the couch in their suite in Falmouth Hall. Albert 'Fiji' Fatuamala sitting beside Lauryn as Tyler McManaway squeezed in alongside Samantha on the loveseat. Tyler and Samantha arriving back from their trip into the city as the others returned from Summer's End Fest followed by a stop at the Chipotle in Howell Commons for a late-night bite to eat.

"We were at Buckingham Fountain," Samantha smiled, "watched the fireworks at Navy Pier. Had a quiet dinner at a restaurant on Michigan Avenue."

"Nice way to spend the evening," Ashleigh Morgan commented, sliding down on the floor as D'Andre Watson pulled up a chair and sat down behind her, Ashleigh resting her back against the powerful legs that ran for one hundred and thirty-nine yards earlier that afternoon. Allison Mayne sat cross-legged on the floor, leaning her back against the couch.

"It was nice." Samantha took and gently stroked the back of Tyler's hand, leaned over to kiss the love of her life. Relaxed after revealing to Tyler what troubled her, confidence again flowing freely; ready once more to take on the world. *I can handle myself.* "This girl doesn't need much to be impressed."

"Thank you very much," Tyler kissed Samantha, listened to her delicious giggle. "Where are Amanda and Connor?"

"They came back early," Lauryn pointed to the closed door of Amanda and Ashleigh's bedroom. "Amanda started to get tired. She had a long day."

"Hasn't it been a long day for all of us?" Allison noted.

"But it was a damn good day," D'Andre leaned over, kissed Ashleigh on the forehead.

"Good day for everyone, honey," Ashleigh dispelled her earlier encounter with the photographer, yet something nagged at her mind, unsettled by the man's attitude. *Not like I'll ever run into him again*, Ashleigh reminded herself.

From behind the closed door to the bedroom where Amanda McKinnon and Connor Aanonsen were they heard the yelp of a high-pitched female voice. Tyler called out. "So who was saying Samantha and I should get a room?"

A muffled reply, the voice Amanda's, came from behind the door. "It's not what you think!" A moment later the door opened, Amanda and Connor stepping into the common room. Connor dressed though barefoot, Amanda wearing a white spandex sports bra and running shorts. Didn't appear the duo involved in activities of a sexual nature, though Amanda's raven hair disheveled about her head. "Connor was working on me with my Trigger Point roller, found a nice little knot in my soleus." Amanda eased herself down the floor, crossed her legs.

"Call me Mister Magic Fingers." Connor wiggled his digits, sitting next to Amanda, arm eased around her slender shoulders.

"And that's what she said," Tyler kidded, Samantha punching him playfully in the arm.

"Isn't it time for the glass of Grayson Farms victory wine?" Ashleigh reminded Samantha.

Samantha stood up, stretched. "I think it's time to celebrate." Went behind the breakfast bar where she kept the wine her parents brought from the family winery. "Is the merlot okay for those who like their wine dry? Symphony for those with a sweeter tooth?" There were nods of agreement at her question. "Okay, who wants the merlot?"

"Give me a glass, Samantha," D'Andre said as Samantha counted raised hands, assuming the rest wanted the sweeter Symphony, a bottle of the semi-sweet white wine chilling in the refrigerator.

"My roomies aren't here," Allison added, "so I'll have the merlot."

Tyler got up from the couch, joined Samantha at the breakfast bar. "Let me help." As Samantha skillfully wielded her wine key to strip the foil caps and uncork the bottles Tyler took wine glasses from the cupboard. Samantha filled the glasses halfway with Tyler distributing the wine. Samantha filled the two glasses for her and Tyler with merlot, rejoining friends gathered about the center of the room.

"Since we're drinking your wine you should have the honors," Fiji told Samantha, his glass filled with the sweeter Symphony.

Samantha lifted her glass, smiled at her friends and the one to whom she gave her heart, those around which her world revolved. "To a fantastic weekend and the best friends in the world, I wouldn't trade anything for any of you." As the glasses clinked together Samantha hoped nothing in the world ever shattered the intimate bonds.

Chapter 17

I didn't realize it was that late! Presley Harding grimaced, turning the key to her room in the silent second-floor corridor of Cockrell Hall, hearing the loud click as she pushed the door open, quietly entered the room. She slipped off her high heels; the coolness of the floor against bare feet made her shiver, closing the door behind her. She tiptoed across the room, reached underneath her loft, switched on the lamp to get undressed, hoping the light didn't wake her roommate. She glanced under the loft on the other side of the room, in the pale illumination saw the pile of open books on the desk and frowned, peered up at the form huddled under the covers of the bed.

Don't tell me you spent the whole night studying? Presley asked silently of the unresponsive form of Riley Bradford while unzipping the back of the burgundy silk mini-dress, eased it from her shoulders, let it drop to the floor, nose wrinkling catching a whiff of stale beer embedded in the fabric, someone at the last bar they hit spilling his pint on her dress. *That's going to the dry cleaners.* Going out to the clubs did mean dealing with other people's mishaps winding up on her clothes.

Down to her black bra and panties, shaking slightly from the cool air circulating through the room, Presley moved quietly to her dresser, opened the top drawer for a grey cotton Victoria's Secret nightshirt. She unhooked the back of her bra, shrugged the lingerie off, let it drop to the floor before slipping the nightshirt over her head, draping over her sleek body. She looked again at her roommate's desk with the thick texts of organic chemistry, biology and anatomy piled high, and sighed. Riley Bradford was pre-med, Presley understood the major meant long hours of studying and admired her roommate's commitment. *But does it mean studying all the time?* Riley never allowed herself a moment's respite from an already grueling academic regimen. Even at the football game that afternoon, when she should've been excited watching a thrilling win over North Carolina, Riley fretted endlessly how she was wasting time, should be studying, preparing for classes and tests in the coming week. Riley even spent the morning before the game studying at the library instead of accompanying Presley and the girls from their section to the tailgate parties around Warren Field. Presley didn't bother asking if Riley wanted to head into the city, not that it mattered, Riley unwilling to take advantage of her connection with Bryce Fielding to secure a fake ID and gain entrance into usually forbidden clubs beckoning underneath the bright lights of downtown Chicago. A shame for Riley a pretty girl, the same height as Presley with long, shiny strawberry blonde hair and charming blue eyes. But her head so stuck in her books, already anxious about her grades barely a month into freshmen year she never noticed the guys checking her out as she hurried across the quad to her next class or the library.

For the first time in her life Presley was on her own, away from the protective shadows her parents cast over her every action and decision. The sense of freedom, the ability to do what she wanted, proving an exhilarating breath of liberation. She adored her parents, thought the world of them, but until the moment they flew back to New York on their private jet four weeks earlier they orchestrated every waking minute of her life and Presley found the well-meaning attention suffocating. Everything they did for Presley, from enrolling her in the finest private girls' school in Manhattan to deciding what major, business and finance, she should pursue at Great Northern done in the name of ensuring her future success in the rarefied air of the financial world and social circles within which they dwelled. Her parents didn't yet understand what they wanted for Presley and what she secretly desired might drastically differ. *I don't want to study business, I want to study art. I want to write, I want to create. I don't want to work on Wall Street.* That the domain of her father, creating from nothing one of the most powerful private equity firms in America. Her father thrived in the pressure-cooker world of risk and cutthroat capitalism Presley knew, even with all the preparation Great Northern might provide, her bubbly personality ill-suited for mortal combat in such an arena. But she couldn't tell her parents the future they'd already decided for her had no appeal.

Presley climbed into her loft, slid under the covers, tugging them up to her chin, lying in the bed pondering the circumstances of the evening, reflecting on the fortuitous encounter with the professional photographer Marcus Evans. She hoped he called tomorrow, that she received a chance to garner the assignment for the online retailer. Maybe this out-of-the blue opportunity the trigger she needed to make her parents to change their minds, allow Presley to pursue her dreams, not project theirs upon her. The thought of modeling enticing and the extra money in her pocket, money she earned instead of drawing from the account her parents established, a taste of liberty she'd never known living in the well-appointed home on the Upper East Side or the mansion in the Hamptons on Long Island.

Presley glanced to the loft where Riley slept, felt sorry for her roommate. Presley soon pledging one of the sororities at Great Northern, already invited to visit several houses for rush week by sororities coveting a freshman with her rarified pedigree, after initiation moving out of Cockrell Hall and into a house on Greek Row. *It's what Mom and Dad want*, Presley silently told Riley. Her mother especially dissatisfied she'd been matched with a girl who lived in the suburbs north of Detroit with parents many rungs down on the social ladder. During Freshman Orientation Presley overheard her mother whispering to her father about talking to the Office of Student Housing, changing her room assignment to pair her with someone closer to her social standing.

If only you wanted to have some fun, Presley told the slumbering Riley, *if you wanted to live a little instead of burying your head in a book all day!* Riley told Presley of the hopes of her family, both parents working two jobs to pay what her partial scholarship to Great Northern didn't cover, how she couldn't fail, needed to work killing hours to succeed. Riley a nice and thoughtful girl, but how could they develop a friendship when all Riley did was study from the crack of dawn to the stroke of midnight?

Presley yawned, eyelids growing heavy, and drifted off to sleep, dreaming of stardom.

"How are things on the Western Front?" Cowle entered the room where his assistants monitored the initial parcels of this latest order for Sheik Rahim through the surveillance system.

"As the title says, all quiet," Sterner yawned. Lang sprawled on a cot snoring, sleeping as Sterner stood watch over the two precious commodities waiting to be sold at market like bushels of wheat.

"And our guests?"

Sterner pointed at the screens. After hours in confining bondage, the only respite the brief moments between arduous, taxing positions insured to chip away the defiant spirit left in their bodies, Emma Hayden and Alexandra Cole finally released from the suffering of ropes and gags, but not entirely free. Locked in their separate cells, wrists secured before them with handcuffs. Exhausted from the strenuous bondage and the unpredictable sessions of terror orchestrated by their keepers, tormented by the uncertainty of their immediate future the hostages dozed fitfully on the mattresses provided them. "Quiet as lambs," he said. "Let them loose about an hour ago to visit the ladies room. Don't want them having any accidents."

"Let them rest," Cowle agreed. "They'll have another long day tomorrow." The luckless duo joined by an equally unfortunate trio by the end of the day to complete the consignment.

"Did you find what you were looking for?" By now Lang heard the conversation, stirred from his slumber, rolling off the cot, stretching as he stood.

"I believe we hit pay-dirt," Cowle swung the digital camera around so they could see the preview screen. Cowle scrolled through the images of their final target.

"She's a cute one." Sterner nodded his approval. "The Arab will have fun with her."

"Her name is Presley Harding," Cowle explained.

"Where do they come up with these names?" Sterner asked.

Cowle grinned. "Her parents are Elvis Presley fans. Father runs Graceland Capital, one of those big private equity firms on Wall Street."

"That guy's a player," Sterner grunted. "We could get a nice ransom for a chick like her."

"We're not in the ransom business," Cowle reminded. "We're in the selling business."

Lang shrugged. "At least they didn't cop out and name her Lisa Marie or Priscilla."

"She's a student at Great Northern. Should never have been there in the first place but she had a fake ID. Seems a trusting little soul, swallowed my story without hesitation. I'll call her tomorrow to confirm our session for the afternoon." Cowle almost certain Presley to show up blissfully believing in a chance for sudden fame, only to be violently disabused of such fanciful notions.

Sterner laughed. "She'll regret using that fake ID."

"Her mistake," Cowle said, "is our financial gain."

"We like financial gain," this from Lang. "The Arab will enjoy this shipment."

"I'm heading back to the studio, get some sleep," Cowle informed his men. Had to ready the studio for the sessions on Sunday. Did have a fallback position, albeit risky, if Presley backed out at the last minute. *Snatch and grab.* "You'll be able to manage here?"

"Are you kidding?" Lang pointed at the monitors. "With our Sleeping Beauties here?"

"Feed them in the morning." Cowle yawned, fatigue whittling away his endurance, turned towards the door.

"Nice to see you care about their well-being," Sterner replied.

Cowle reached the door. "I care for them until we hand them over to Sheik Rahim and we receive payment for our services." Then his concern for the five women destined for a fate worse than any nightmare imaginable over and done with.

What if I were gone? Like no longer here. What if I were here one minute and gone the next and you didn't know what happened to me? As he stared at the ceiling of his room in McDonough Hall, the question Samantha Grayson posed earlier that evening as they stood by Buckingham Fountain while fireworks burst in the sky above Navy Pier burned a hole in the mind of Tyler McManaway, preventing him the rejuvenating effects of peaceful slumber. Afraid if he closed his eyes to sleep the question might induce horrid nocturnal visions of the one he dearly treasured threatened by dangers of a mortal sort. The story of the missing women in Los Angeles, and the link to other disappearances across the country, rattled the nerves of his girlfriend, normally so poised and unperturbed by events. Incidents so unsettling they forced Samantha to seek reassurance from Tyler a similar fate, snatching her from those she loved, didn't befall her.

What would I do? Tyler asked the silence. He recalled his answer, a brave and stridently confident statement invoked as he gazed into the brown eyes placing in him the utmost trust. *I will never let anything happen to you, I will always be there to protect you. I will do everything to find you and I will never let anyone hurt you.* Then why did his declaration feel hollow and meaningless? Why did the promise, simple, direct and from the heart, seem a guarantee he couldn't fulfill?

I can't watch her twenty-four hours a day. How he wished he could, but the demands placed on him as the starting quarterback of a Big Ten football program, and one of the top players in the nation, pulled him in a hundred different directions to fully devote his undivided attention to Samantha's well-being. His class load only added to his responsibilities, computer engineering not the easiest of majors for a football player to balance with hours dedicated to practice, and his commitment to the safety of Samantha Grayson grew more daunting. What if by some horrible chance Samantha did disappear, as she said there one minute and gone the next, what exactly *would* he do? With the uncertainty of her absence weighing on his shoulders how could he ever concentrate on football, on playing a *game*? Would he even want to continue playing after so devastating a loss? Hadn't there been a Great Northern player around the time of the magical Rose Bowl season who suffered a similar tragedy, walked away from the game? *Would I do the same under those circumstances?*

Tyler sat up in bed, rubbed his temple, head aching considering the possibilities, couldn't fall asleep with troubling thoughts tugging relentlessly at his conscience. He dropped down from his loft, sat at his desk, flipped open his laptop. He glanced over his shoulder to the loft where Albert 'Fiji' Fatuamala slept soundly, didn't wish to wake his friend this early in the morning. Tyler launched the Firefox web browser, logged into his personal Gmail account, several of his teammates from Wheaton Warrenville South played football at colleges across the country, kept in touch during the season. The first email came from his parents, couldn't yet grasp the simplicity of sending a quick 140-character missive over Twitter, settling instead for an involved, detailed account of Cornell's victory over the Bucknell Bison and his twin brother Colin's heroics on the game's final drive. After leaving the stadium they caught the second half of the Great Northern game at a Buffalo Wild Wings restaurant close to the Bucknell campus. *Guess the McManaway family had a good day*, his father wrote, Tyler smiling at the statement.

The next email from Russell Millen, 'Big Russ' one of his protectors on the offensive line in high school, now on scholarship with the Red Raiders of Texas Tech in the Big 12. Had an easy game against Colorado State, winning in a 56-12 rout, but what Tyler read next from his former teammate stopped his heart in mid-beat. *Don't know if you saw this on the news, but the campus is on edge down here. No one is in the mood to celebrate winning a football game. Two juniors disappeared from their apartment off-campus Monday night. No one knows where they went or what happened to them. The police think something bad happened. My girlfriend had a class with one of the girls who went missing. She's pretty upset, afraid whoever took them might still be around. There was a moment of silence for them before kickoff, could've heard a pin drop in the stadium. They have a big search planned for tomorrow and Coach is having the team go out and help. I hope we find those girls safe, but I've got a bad feeling that won't happen.*

Tyler stared at the passage for minutes, thought of Samantha, the disappearances in Los Angeles, and the other incidents which might be linked in one disturbing panorama. His world revolved around playing football, suddenly felt that world terribly selfish and self-centered. His mind went back to what Samantha asked of him.

What if I were gone?

He read the email his friend sent him again. Samantha still here in his life, but two young women at Texas Tech had vanished into nothingness.

What if I were here one minute and gone the next and you didn't know what happened to me?

Tyler rubbed his eyes, shook his head, didn't want to ever consider the possibility of Samantha being...*gone*. There remained emails to be read and answered from other acquaintances but Tyler unable to continue. The message from his friend, and what Samantha asked of him, a reminder a real world full of evil people doing terrible things existed beyond the turf of Warren Field and the comfortable domain of college football. He logged out of his email, clicked on the Google homepage. Couldn't go fall back to sleep, not with what he knew.

He typed the words *Los Angeles Missing Women* into the search box and, as Samantha had done days earlier in the offices of *The Daily Northern*, started his own research into the tragic topic. As his stomach turned and head hurt reading stories of terrible loss and never-ending sadness, each link dragging him further down a rabbit hole of terror, he began to fear for the safety of Samantha Grayson. So engrossed was Tyler as he scrolled down the screen scanning the text, clicking link after link to delve deeper into the dark, disturbing story he hadn't noticed Fiji laying awake in his loft. He rolled over on his side, observed Tyler sitting at his laptop, from his vantage point able to see what his friend studied intently on the screen. Fiji said nothing, watching Tyler read and knew his friend's heart troubled.

Chapter 18

The rancid odor of stale beer hanging listlessly in the air the first thing Riley Bradford noticed as she clicked off the alarm, trying not to disturb her roommate. Not that it mattered; Presley Harding barely stirred, slumbered through the buzzing of the alarm. *Wonder what time she got in last night?* Riley thought, never heard her roommate enter their room. Had to have been late, probably sometime in the early morning. Lying on the floor she spotted the burgundy mini-dress, instantly knew where the smell originated. *I guess she had a good time.* Riley frowned, threw back the covers, slid down from her loft. She glanced over at Presley's loft; saw the lump underneath the covers shift slightly, a low moan escaping the barely moving form. Riley shook her head, Presley dead to the world sleeping off her latest hangover.

Riley sighed as she started to get dressed, the expectation of meeting her new roommate and establishing a friendship to guide each other through the tumult of their first year at a prestigious Big Ten school, to have a shoulder to lean on, faded quickly following Freshman Orientation. Riley suspected Presley's parents not thrilled the roommate of their well-to-do daughter from a blue-collar household in Troy, Michigan, a suburb in the shadow of the devastated urban moonscape once called Detroit. Presley grew up in a mansion where she found want of nothing, enjoyed closets overflowing with stylish clothes, drove a shiny new Lexus, all she desired provided by parents successful in the world of high finance. Riley did many times without, clothes bought at Target and Wal-Mart, no car at her disposal to go where she wanted, both parents working two jobs enduring back-breaking hours scraping up enough to make ends meet, pay what the partial scholarship from Great Northern and financial aid didn't cover. Riley shook her head again. Presley Harding had it all; tuition and expenses paid for in full by parents flush with Wall Street wealth, never to know the crushing weight of student debt awaiting Riley at the end of her schooling. But Presley seemed more interested in partying instead studying, the reason Riley there, to earn her pre-med degree and gain acceptance to Great Northern's Weinberg School of Medicine.

It wasn't that Presley a bad person or treated Riley with disrespect born of privilege; Riley truly wanted to like her roommate, deep-down Presley Harding a kind, considerate, if a bit too trusting, young soul with a good heart. Perhaps her roommate's flippant attitude towards school irked Riley's own sensibilities of hard work and effort, constructing an unbreakable, invisible barrier between them too difficult to overcome. Riley had yet to see Presley open a book in the weeks since classes started where they were her constant companions morning, noon and late into the night. She wondered the reaction of Presley's parents when their daughter suffered failing grades in her business classes. *There might be the problem,* Riley thought, a major in finance from the Lawson School of Business the last thing Presley wanted to pursue at Great Northern. Presley confessed to Riley she'd rather study fine arts or writing, but admitted her parents wouldn't allow her the freedom to chase those dreams. The late night carousing to sample Chicago's nightlife, Riley now believed, nothing more than a subconscious act of outright rebellion against her parents, a protest of a life already predetermined. The fake ID Presley acquired a ticket of passage into a world Riley not ready to experience until she reached legal age, feared the wrath and disappointment from disciplined, yet loving, parents if caught committing that illegal act. Whenever Presley skipped out to join her upperclassmen friends, one the son of a prominent politician inviting her into the partying-into-the-wee-hours circle, Riley prayed she returned safely to Cockrell Hall. Understood amid the bright lights and excitement lurked danger, people with less than noble intentions far too willing to take advantage of an innocent such as Presley on her own for the first time.

"Hey, Presley?" Riley called out. "I'm heading to breakfast at Lakeside, you want to come?"

The heap under the covers shifted. A murmuring voice from underneath the comforter answered. "Kind of tired. I'll eat later."

"Okay, see you then," Riley muttered, leaving the room alone, an occurrence fairly common between the roommates.

"You're the best part about going to church," D'Andre Watson informed Ashleigh Morgan as the party of eight friends sat down for brunch at Lakeshore Dining Pavilion following the religious service at Kendricks Chapel. "You have the voice of an angel, makes me want to sit there the entire day and be holy." Ashleigh sang in the campus gospel choir, a featured soloist during the service.

"You'll sit there until noon when the pro football games come on," Ashleigh replied, her dark eyes gleaming, leaning close to D'Andre, rubbed noses together in an obvious Public Display of Affection. "Then you're out of there."

"On the seventh day God rested, but only after he created the NFL so he'd have something to watch with a beer and a bowl of popcorn and his feet up on the ottoman after that long week creating the universe," D'Andre kidded.

Amanda McKinnon glanced over at Samantha Grayson, sipping her glass of orange juice. "You're in a better mood today than Friday at lunch."

"I had a great time last night with someone who loves me," Samantha smiled at Tyler McManaway, who returned her gesture with a grin. "I have the day off from *The Daily Northern*, so I don't have to pester Public Safety and the Evanslawn police department for the juicy details regarding the parties they busted last night." The detail an unforeseen, yet appreciated, benefit from covering the speech by Senator Benton Fielding at Cockrell Auditorium.

Connor Aanonsen pointed at the English muffins on Amanda's plate. "Butter your muffins?"

"You did that last night," Amanda said with a straight face.

"After he checked for freshness," Samantha teased.

"Toasted them too." Amanda winked at Samantha. "Well played, Samantha Grayson."

Connor ignored the dig, shoveled a forkful of eggs into his mouth, chewing as he spoke. "I heard from Riley Bannister the party patrols were quite busy last night."

"How many?" Lauryn Callahan asked.

"He said Public Safety broke up four parties on Greek Row and the Evanslawn cops busted a huge party on Central Avenue. Might be a record number of citations for underage drinking."

"You get to miss all the excitement," Amanda told Samantha.

"I'm so heart-broken," was Samantha's answer, the look on her face said otherwise.

Tyler yawned, rubbed his eyes, D'Andre pointed his fork at his friend. "Looks like someone didn't get his beauty sleep last night."

Tyler drank some orange juice before he answering, his reply a white lie. "I was looking at the highlights from the Minnesota game. Getting a head start on next week." Their next opponent the Golden Gophers of the University of Minnesota in the Big Ten opener, a squad suffering through a disastrous start to the season and winless in three games.

"Dude, Minnesota lost to an FCS school at home!" D'Andre's expression one of disbelief. "I don't think we need to be too concerned when we go to Minneapolis and hang another loss on them."

Albert 'Fiji' Fatuamala shook his head. "I think Tyler's right. Can't take them too lightly." Didn't let on he knew what Tyler really looking at on his computer during those early hours.

"They lost to a FCS school," D'Andre repeated. "They won't be a problem. We'll be playing the walk-ons by the fourth quarter!"

Samantha perceived the redness in Tyler's eyes, tilted her head at him. *Are you okay*?

Tyler offered a weak smile. *I'm fine, just tired*. For a moment Samantha didn't think he'd been up watching highlights of the next team on the schedule.

"Hope you don't mind the golden arches," Sterner, the balaclava concealing his identity, dropped white paper bags before Emma Hayden and Alexandra Cole. The pair reunited since first brought, helplessly bound and gagged bundles in the back of a van, to the grimly cavernous factory. Sterner dragged Alexandra from her dank cell to join Emma, wrists handcuffed in front of them, the pair sitting on the mattress and huddling close, a meager comfort gleaned from the other's presence. "Promised to feed you while you're our guests," Sterner said. To the best of their ability the pair used restrained hands to open the sacks and remove the contents.

"That's so thoughtful of you," Emma remarked sarcastically, fingers peeling away the yellow wrapping around the lukewarm breakfast sandwich. "I hate Egg McMuffins," she grunted distastefully, studying the sandwich. Alexandra remained quiet, head bowed as she ate, spirit already crushed from the ordeal.

"Sorry honey," Sterner told her gruffly, "you don't get a choice. I couldn't take you through the drive-through." He pointed at the fast-food meal. "Eat up, that's it until tonight."

Emma glared at Sterner, a flame of resistance not yet extinguished alight in her turquoise eyes. "I guess the clerk wouldn't understand my order with cloth jammed in my mouth." She took a bite, no matter how frightened Emma understood she had to maintain her strength for whatever horrors lay ahead.

Sterner gave a wickedly malicious laugh. "Sharp tongue there, honey," he admitted, then warned, "I don't think your new owner will appreciate that mouth."

"If someone's buying me then he's getting the whole package," Emma snarled back.

Sterner nodded; figured Emma not to last long as property of The Arab, but her survival once sold to Sheik Rahim none of his concern, only keeping them in storage until the exchange. "Enjoy your meal, ladies. Once you're done we'll let you wash up, change into some clean clothes," the overnight bags with the outfits brought for the bogus photo shoots. "Have a long day ahead of you, I hope you're rested. My partner and I have some fun activities planned for you." Alexandra and Emma shivered with a rush of fear as Sterner departed, locking the door behind him, trying not to imagine the sick, twisted notions passing for fun in their minds of their captors.

"We aren't getting out this." Alexandra said in a voice quietly tinged with surrender, already giving up hope of rescue, any chance of seeing her family or beloved dog, left alone in her apartment, again. For that statement Emma could offer no reply.

"What time do we have to be there?" Gabriella Taylor asked Isabella DiBenedetto as they entered their Lincoln Park apartment near Saint Vincent University. Returning from a Sunday brunch of down-home southern cooking and Bloody Mary's at Stanley's Kitchen and Tap on the six-way intersection of Armitage, Lincoln and Sedgwick.

"For an engineer you have a short memory," Isabella DiBenedetto scolded. "The session is set for one." She checked the time on her smartphone. "We have time to pack before we have to leave."

The glimmer of doubt again blossomed in Gabriella's hazel eyes. "You really think I can do this?"

Isabella sighed. After four years in the big city her friend remained a shy, introverted small town Iowa girl. "If I didn't think so I wouldn't have dragged you along to meet Marcus."

"Are you sure?" Gabriella asked.

Isabella heaved an overnight bag from her closet, threw it on the bed. "I'm sure. You saw Marcus' reaction when I took off your glasses?"

Gabriella nodded slightly. "Do you think he was being nice?"

"Of course not," Isabella put her hands on Gabriella's arms, turned her to face the reflection in the mirror. "You have to stop selling yourself short, Briella, thinking you're an ugly duckling."

"Really?" Gabriella still didn't believe the advice, staring at her image, not seeing what Isabella and others did. "I don't know if I have the sort of clothes Marcus wants me to wear for this. Don't think I have what he'd consider...sexy."

Isabella released her friend, moving to her closet, started selecting outfits for the appointment. "I can help you with that," Isabella said, "you don't need fancy designer stuff. You can be sexy in what you wear every day."

"Blue jeans and t-shirts?" For an engineering major Gabriella didn't spend time worrying about her appearance, clothes chosen more for comfort than style.

"Especially blue jeans and t-shirts, guys love that look," Isabella switched on her iPod sitting in the docking station; hit the play button and the electronic beats of English techno-pop group The Postal Service filled the room. "Guys think smart girls are sexy. Those 'Nerd Girl' glasses are sexy." Though Isabella believed Gabriella should get contacts to highlight her hazel eyes.

"I never thought of being smart as sexy," Gabriella hauled a bag from the closet.

"Wait until they see the pictures," Isabella added, "they're going to see the smartest, sexiest girl on campus." What Marcus Evans paying them for the shoot, whether or not they scored the job from the online retailer, wasn't a bad incentive either.

The chime of the smartphone resting on the dresser underneath her loft broke the spell of blissful sleep draped softly over Presley Harding. *God! Who's calling me this morning?* She thought angrily, reaching clumsily for the phone. Her head ached with a steady drumbeat of pain, eyes burned from the combination of cigarette smoke and one too many appletinis from the late night of club hopping in Chicago. *Can't you just let me get some sleep?* She grabbed the phone, peered through bleary eyes at the number displayed on the screen. The lethargy evaporated as she recognized the caller, replaced by excited anticipation, running her hand through long caramel brown hair tousled by a serious case of bedhead. "Hello?"

"Good morning, Presley!" The cheerful voice of Marcus Evans greeted her, no sign he suffered any ill effects from his night on the town. "I hope you remember me from last night?"

"Yes!" She answered with too much enthusiasm, calmed down. "It's good to hear from you."

"So are we just waking up?" Marcus asked, a playful scolding in his tone. "What time did we make it back to Great Northern?"

"Yes, I'm just getting up." Presley replied sheepishly, understood he was being polite, not offended by the statement. "It was more like this morning. I think around three, I can't remember."

"Well," Marcus paused, Presley hoped he'd say what she wanted to hear, "are you still interested in a session later this afternoon?"

Presley closed her eyes, smiled in satisfaction, her reply immediate. "I'd be very interested."

"Could you come around four or so?" Marcus requested. "It'll only take a few hours, you'll be back on campus before it's too late. I'll pay you two hundred an hour for your time."

Presley sighed in exhilaration. "I can be there at four." Though she never needed to worry about spending money, her parents a steady source of funds, the payday to come in handy. Had her eye on some hot outfits at the high-end fashion shops lining Chicago's Magnificent Mile.

"Bring what you'd wear to the clubs," Marcus informed; Presley immediately had one outfit in mind. "If I know what the art director wants, I think you'll be doing more modeling work in the future."

"I hope so too." Presley replied.

"Can you let me know what you'll be driving so I can keep an eye out for you."

For a brief moment Presley thought the request unusual, then brushed aside any doubts. The thrilling prospect of a new opportunity, and a source of spending money, overcame any suspicion. "It's a blue Lexus, my favorite color." The luxury sedan a graduation present from her parents.

"So I'll expect you around four," Marcus continued. "If you think you're going to be late or have to cancel," Presley knew either likelihood not going to happen, "please call to let me know."

"I'll see you then." Presley turned off the phone, sitting up in her bed contemplating the commitment. For several minutes the smile didn't fade from her face, brown eyes sparkling with elation. *Do I let Riley know what I'm doing? Where I'm going?* A second later she decided against that, Riley the serious no-nonsense type, likely distrustful of the offer, might attempt to talk her from going through with the appointment. Presley thought of some way to pack her outfits and makeup, slipping out of the room without Riley noticing. *Maybe she'll head to the library to study*, Presley assumed. *That's where she spends most of her time anyway.* Presley easily slipping away unnoticed, driving into Chicago for her meeting with Marcus Evans without her roommate even knowing she was gone.

Chapter 19

"What's bothering you?" Samantha Grayson asked Tyler McManaway as they strolled across the Great Northern campus towards Brighton Field where the women's soccer team, and their friend Selena Espinosa, about to play the Spartans of Michigan State. Tyler silent for most of the walk, as the two held hands, lost in a haze of worried brooding.

Tyler smiled. "Nothing," he said absently. Samantha knew his thoughts occupied and not, as he said during brunch, about an upcoming game against an outmatched opponent.

"Pants on fire," Samantha scolded. Tyler stopped, turned to face her. "It's about last night, isn't it?" Samantha saw the blue eyes betrayed his uneasiness. "I threw you for a loop with what I said?"

"A little," Tyler stopped, refocused. "No, a lot."

"How much is a lot?" Samantha slipped her arms around his waist, let him pull her close, as always found the embrace comforting.

"I couldn't sleep last night," Tyler admitted. "That's why I seemed out of it this morning."

"Sorry, I didn't mean..."

"It's not your fault," Tyler caressed her cheek. "I couldn't stop thinking about what you told me and what I promised."

"I believe you," Samantha replied. "I know you'll be there if I need you."

"I went online last night," Tyler confessed. "Looked up what you told me. It's pretty scary stuff, the police and the FBI don't have a clue what's going on. These women are there one minute and gone the next." Tyler swallowed, closed his eyes. "They've found nothing of any of them."

Samantha reached up, stroked Tyler's blonde hair. "It's not the best late night reading material."

"But there's more," Tyler said. 'I got an email from a former teammate in high school. He's on scholarship at Texas Tech and..."

"About the two girls who're missing down there?" Tyler cocked his head. "I saw it on Yahoo Thursday, after Aaron gave me the assignment to cover the Senator Fielding speech. That and researching the other disappearances didn't help my usually sunny disposition."

"They disappeared from their apartment," Tyler said. "The police have no idea where they are, who took them. They're just gone." He ran his hand through Samantha's thick tresses of reddish-brown and copper, lowered his head until their foreheads touched. "I worry that..."

"Something might happen to me?" More of a statement and less of a question.

"It's more than that." Tyler bit his lip. "I made a promise to keep you safe, but with who I am, the quarterback of the football team and what I deal with every day, everyone wanting a piece of me, I can't be there to protect you around the clock." He paused. "I'm afraid there'll come a time when you really need me and..."

Samantha arched an eyebrow. "You don't think I can take of myself?"

"I didn't mean that." His tone awkward, regretting the remark.

"I know all this has me upset and worried, but I'm not some delicate, defenseless girl." Samantha placed a hand on Tyler's firm chest, confidence returning after expressing concerns to Tyler the previous evening. "I'm the daughter of an Australian naval officer." For a fleeting moment she reflected on how her parents met in London, the beautiful American student studying abroad and the dashing naval attaché at the Australian Embassy. How romantic their courtship must've been the autumn they met. Samantha owned a unique dual citizenship, born in Melbourne. "He's a tough customer, doesn't shy away from a scrap, I have his genes. He taught me self-defense, how to fight back, use anything as a weapon. If by chance you're not there, and somebody even thinks of trying to take me or do something to me, I'll be able to handle myself." Samantha noticed the uncertainty glisten in Tyler's blue eyes. "You don't believe me?"

"As my Russian geometry teacher in high school used to tell me, prove it," Tyler replied.

Samantha broke their embrace, stepped back. "Time for a little demonstration."

"Be gentle with me," Tyler raised his hands, cautioning. "You don't want to hurt me and have to explain to Coach Carl and Husky Nation I'm out for the season because you demonstrated your martial arts skills on me."

Samantha placed her hands on her hips, an expression of playful scorn on the lovely face. "So I'm the fragile little thing?"

"You're not on scholarship and starting at quarterback next week," Tyler said.

"Okay, I'll be gentle," Samantha smirked at Tyler. "Don't want to *hurt* you." She turned her back to him. "I want you to come up from behind, put your arm around my throat like you're grabbing me."

Tyler hesitated, noticing students out on the quad enjoying the late summer afternoon, lounging in the sun or throwing about a Frisbee through the air. "Hold it, people might think..."

"God, you worry too much!" Samantha exclaimed, calling out to those around. "No problem here, just a little demonstration!"

Tyler took a deep breath. "I hope no one takes a picture and sends it to *Deadspin*." The prominent online sports commentary site a chronicle of all things good and bad in the sporting world, in his mind pictured a lurid headline. With exaggerated caution he wrapped his arm, forearm nudging up against her neck, barely touching under her chin. "Is this okay?"

"Perfect." Samantha brought her hands up, grasped Tyler's arm. "Ready for the show?"

"Slow-motion, if you please," Tyler warned. "So what do you do?"

"An attacker would've more pressure on my neck, trying to choke me," Samantha pointed out, understood Tyler being gentle with her. "I'd let my body relax, become dead weight," she slumped slightly, Tyler adjusting his grip to hold her up, "so you'd have to use your strength and transfer your weight to maintain your balance and keep me upright."

"That's step one," Tyler conceded. "What's step two?"

"While you're concentrating on keeping me from falling to the ground," Samantha smiled evilly, "My heel is on a collision course with the most vulnerable part of the male anatomy." She slowly brought her right leg up, back of her heel sliding between Tyler's legs, stopping inches removed from a very sensitive area.

"I appreciate your not going any further," Tyler admitted, letting out a low whistle. "I see your point. The boys downstairs appreciate your concern."

"We might need them someday," Samantha giggled. "But if this was real and, as you say in football going full speed, you'd be in a world of hurt." Tyler cleared his throat, understood perfectly her meaning. "Wouldn't be too focused on keeping your arm around my throat," Samantha's right hand let go of his arm, dropped to his side, "so I can inflict some more damage." She slowly edged her elbow into his ribcage, initiating the slightest contact. "Not only are you hurting between the legs I've also taken the air out of your lungs."

"Anything else?" Tyler guessing if he were an attacker he'd be lying on the ground writhing in agony. In reply Samantha took her left hand, twisted Tyler's wrist, swiveling around out of his hold to face him. "Watch it there, I need that next Saturday."

"Don't worry, I'll be careful," Samantha reassured, continuing with the demonstration. "I can hit you in the face," Samantha explained, closed fist heading towards his jaw. "Or go for the eyes with these," she flashed her long fingernails, "you can't hurt me if you can't see me." Samantha released his hand. "Or I can break away and run like hell. As Dad says 'fight, then flight'."

Tyler relaxed, straightened himself, took a deep breath. "Don't think anyone will be chasing you while holding on to the family jewels."

"That's the idea. Dad told me to stay calm, think it through, then react, don't panic," Samantha explained, easing his lingering apprehension. "Dad says anything can be a weapon. I have a canister of mace in my shoulder bag and if I'm walking alone on campus at night I have my keys out and in my hand." She removed the set of keys from her pocket, inserting them into her palm, fist closing so two sharp points stuck out between her fingers. "Instant weapon, no one can hurt me after I jab this in their eye."

"Okay, you can take care of yourself," Tyler nodded, convinced, but only to a point, gathered his girlfriend in an affectionate embrace. "Doesn't mean I'm not going to worry any less about you, Samantha Grayson." Tyler kissed her. "Or that I won't keep the promise I made."

"I know," Samantha said. She didn't expect anything less.

"That'll hold them for a while," Sterner entered the room where Lang stood watch over the closed circuit video screen observing their unwilling guests. The two captives kept in one cell, Sterner leaving left pair bound tightly to chairs facing each other, fear and terror shared between the captives watching the other struggle against the secure bindings. Lang listened to their muffled cries from down the hall, *music to the ears*, through the cloth tied in her mouth Emma calling them nasty names. Later that evening Alexandra and Emma to welcome the company of three additional hapless guests, no longer any vacancy at the inn. *We'll have more fun too...*

Sterner tugged off the balaclava, ran his hand through sweat-matted hair. "Wish I didn't have to wear this damn thing," he groused. "They won't be around to pick us out of a police lineup."

"You know it keeps them scared," Lang replied, "and scared chicks are easier to control."

"They know they ain't getting out of this." Sterner motioned at the bound and gagged women straining against the expertly tied ropes. "You can handle them while I'm gone?"

For questioning his abilities Lang flipped his partner the middle finger. "I'll change things up for them after awhile, put them through their paces." Nowhere approaching the tortures The Arab planned for them.

"See you later," Sterner grunted. "We'll have three more packages for storage when I get back." Sterner departed the abandoned factory complex in the black Ford van, on his way out checking the surroundings to see if anyone, most important of all the police, observing the building. Confident no one about interested in the factory or the highly illegal activities occurring within, Sterner drove to the studio in Logan Square. The trip, from door to door, taking fifteen minutes on streets light of traffic this Sunday morning.

Cowle heard him enter. "How are our guests faring?" He asked, drinking a cup of black coffee, checking the studio on its last day of business, ready to entertain his final three clients.

"Emma and Alexandra are sharing some quiet time," Sterner reflected on the image of the pair bound facing the other. "We gave them breakfast. Let them clean up and change their clothes."

"Any problems?" Not that Cowle expect any.

Sterner grinned. "They understand the mess they're in, but that little Emma has some fight still left in her." He checked his watch. "The first two are coming soon?"

"Should be here within the hour," Cowle sensed the pride of satisfaction welling inside in chest. Everything so far going exactly to plan, the consignment secured by the evening, imprisoned at the abandoned factory. Yet even so close to apparent success a nagging doubt nibbled at his confidence.

Troubled by the fact he now forced to hold the hostages in captivity for more than a day, dictated by Sheik Rahim's insistence of personally accepting this delivery instead of handing over the product to his underlings' hours after the last victim taken. *Let's hope this doesn't screw up a good thing.* Unforeseen complications which might occur due to the delay a sticking point of concern. *Anything can happen.* Cowle had to prepare for any possible contingency, even the police poking around asking questions.

"I'll need your assistance on this one," Cowle said, thoughts returning to the immediate task. Cowle couldn't expect both women to ingest the drugged water at the same time. They had methods, quick and violent, of subduing prey that didn't drink the water.

Isabella DiBenedetto eased the silver Nissan Altima into the open parking space one building down from Marcus Evans Photography. "Lucky on the first time," Gabriella Taylor complimented her friend's good fortune at finding a parking space in the Logan Square neighborhood.

Isabella checked the clock on the dashboard. "Five minutes early," she added. "I'm sure Marcus will be happy."

"Really? That big a deal?" Gabriella wondered.

"Oh God, yes it is," Isabella replied, not the first time she worked with Marcus Evans. "Professional photographers hate it when models are late or flake out and don't show. They hate it more if you don't call to let them know." She checked her makeup in the rearview mirror, understood first impressions at every session always the most lasting. "You nervous, Briella?"

"A little bit, Bella," Gabriella admitted truthfully, a knot of anxiety tying up her stomach. "I've never done this. Like you said, I'm a Nerd Girl. What if I look like a dork in all these pictures?"

"You'll do fine," with her hand Isabella fluffed up her blue-black hair, reassuring her friend as Gabriella swung the rearview mirror about to check her makeup. "Let me tell you something, you may be a Nerd Girl who'll graduate summa cum laude, but there are guys on campus who've told me they think you're the hottest Nerd Girl around."

"I had no idea." Gabriella said, a hint of surprise brightened her face.

Isabella touched Gabriella's shoulder. "If you pulled your head away from your laptop and spent more time being sociable you'd notice that."

"So what are you doing with your money?" Gabriella changed the subject.

Isabella smirked ruefully, the windfall already spoken for and not pleased with where it going. "I have a few credit card balances," she said, "my parents told me I have to pay down. You?"

Gabriella pondered the possibilities, didn't have any exorbitant bills other than her student loans. "Maybe I'll update the wardrobe," she remarked, reaching for the overnight bag in the back seat. The outfits she brought, in her opinion, not the most appealing. "Since you're telling me the guys think I'm such a hot Nerd Girl, maybe this Nerd Girl needs something sexy to wear the next time we go out."

"Now you're seeing the light, I'll even help pick them out," Isabella retrieved her bag from the back. "Let's go make some money, Briella," she said as they exited the Altima, walked down to Marcus Evans Photography, unaware they'd leave later that day in a different mode of transportation and in the company of another sharing their terrible fate.

Time for the Act Three. On the video feed from the external surveillance cameras Marcus Cowle watched Isabella DiBenedetto and Gabriella Taylor exit the silver Nissan sedan, approach the front of the studio. "Time to welcome the next contestants," he joked to Sterner, leaving him waiting silently in the back room, heading to the reception area. He reached the door on the second chime of the bell. Cowle took a second to compose himself, closed his eyes, sucked in a deep breath. *Now.* He opened the door, ready to welcome the young women inside, again becoming Marcus Evans, professional photographer, the act as effortless as turning the page of a book.

"Isabella! Gabriella!" He smiled at the duo, instantly putting the pair at ease, pleased with the melodic flow of his greeting. "It's so good to see you! And a little early I see." The women entered, Cowle closing the door behind them, neither woman realizing a trap now sprung.

"You two make a wonderful pair," Marcus Cowle informed Isabella and Gabriella as they stood underneath the bright lights of the studio seventy minutes later.

"Don't they say things come better in pairs?" Isabella offered, wearing a black miniskirt and red silk tank top, candy-apple red platform high heels on her feet.

"I have to say you two are the best I've seen yet." Cowle flattered the duo, defenses lowered by his playful banter. "And you're quite a beautiful one," he smiled at Gabriella dressed in a white long-sleeve sweater dress, black leather belt cinched about her waist, wearing knee-high black patent leather boots. The attractiveness lying underneath the bookish glasses, now removed from her face, readily apparent. At his statement Gabriella shyly smiled.

"Isn't this fun?" Isabella asked her friend. "Like I told you it would be?"

"I didn't think I'd be able to do this," Gabriella admitted, posing for the second set of the day. Exhibited an endearing awkwardness at the start of the first session, but with encouragement from Isabella and Cowle's soothing coaxing Gabriella relaxed, her movements grew more natural. Cowle had Gabriella look at the first set, downloading the pictures from the camera to his laptop, to see her own stunning beauty for herself. *Is that really me?* Cowle noted the reaction, Gabriella's eyes widening in wonderment.

Too bad your first job will be your last, Cowle silently lamented, a mourning swiftly erased by thoughts of profits reaped from her sale. "Now I want you to stand back to back," Cowle motioned with his hand as the two positioned themselves at his direction. "And lean forward, Isabella put your left hand on your thigh and Gabriella put your hands on your hips. Look straight at the camera and I want sexy, sensual expressions."

"Think you can do sexy, Briella?" Isabella pushed midnight black hair away from her eyes.

Gabriella grinned. "I think I can do sexy now, Bella," throwing back the thick mane of golden blonde hair, expression transforming into a suggestive, come-hither pout.

"I think you do sexy quite well, Gabriella," Cowle lifted the camera, shot off several exposures. "Now stay back to back but stand straight up, cross your arms across your chest. Keep that expression on those pretty faces, sexy and sensual, okay?"

The pair did as directed. "How's this?" Isabella said.

"Wonderful, just what I want to see," Cowle clicked off several more shots.

Gabriella giggled, with her hand pantomiming a gun. "If we had one more we could do a Charlie's Angels pose." *Too bad we couldn't wait for Presley to show up*, Cowle thought at the mischievous remark, a quite enticing possibility, never taking down three targets at once. But unwilling to risk such an action, too great a chance one might slip from their grasp, alert the authorities. By the time Presley arrived the pair standing before him incapacitated, silenced, and locked up in the rear of the studio.

"Can you do some pictures with Gabriella?" Isabella motioned to her friend. "I need a break."

"I don't see why not," Cowle answered.

"Time for you to shine," Isabella smiled at Gabriella, then asked Cowle. "Do you have anything to drink?"

Cowle pointed to the refrigerator by the wall. "I have some water in there. Help yourself."

"Those lights are hot." Isabella walked to the refrigerator, looked back at Gabriella. "You need one, Briella?"

Gabriella waved her off. "I'm fine for now, Bella."

"Gabriella, face me and put your hands on your hips," Cowle told Gabriella, from the corner of his eye observing Isabella as she opened the refrigerator, removed one of the four remaining tampered water bottles. Didn't immediately open the bottle, standing off to the side, a playful smile on her face watching her friend spread her wings.

"Is this good?" Gabriella assumed the pose.

"Spread the right leg out a little further, an inch or so," Cowle prompted, Gabriella shifting the right foot forward until Cowle held up his hand. "Perfect." He snapped off several pictures. Time for small talk, keep the conversation going, lulling them in the presence of looming peril. "What are your plans after graduation?"

"Grad school, what else?" The initial reply came from Isabella. She twisted the cap on the bottle, the crackling sound as the seal broken, didn't take a drink. *Please, hurry up; I don't have all day here*, Cowle silently pleaded to his prey.

"Same here," Gabriella chimed in. "Maybe Stanford or Cal Tech. Looking at Great Northern too."

"All of them are good schools," Cowle offered in agreement.

"Put off the real world for as long as we can," Isabella kidded, finally drinking from the bottle, Cowle checking the time, estimating how long until the sedative disabled his victim. Once Isabella rendered unconscious Gabriella subdued through a more direct method, the pair then never needing again to worry about the real world.

"Okay, Gabriella, move your body to the left, keep the right hand on your hip, let your left hand drop to your side, turn your head to face me like your looking over your shoulder," Cowle prompted Gabriella as Isabella sat down on the couch, took out her phone. She shook her head checking the screen, drinking more water as she did.

"I don't know if it's my provider or the reception, but I have no signal," Isabella said, couldn't focus on the screen, suddenly felt warm and light-headed, her mouth dry as cotton despite drinking the water. *Must be from standing under those lights*, she reasoned, wiped her forehead, took another drink of water, didn't realize this was the source of her discomfort, the reflexive action sealing her fate.

"Been like that the past few days," Cowle watched as the drug started taking effect, attention turning back to a visibly concerned Gabriella. "Now move your body..."

Gabriella interrupted him, saw her friend slump over, drop her phone to the floor. "Isabella, are you all right?"

"I don't...know," Isabella said, words stumbling over her lips, slurring her speech, "I don't...feel so good." She blinked, the room seemed to tilt forty-five degrees, her final thought a realization something not right. She tried standing up from the couch but her legs gave out, dark eyes rolling back into her head, with a gasp pitching forward, hand going limp, water bottle falling to the floor, contents dribbling out in a puddle on the hardwood as Isabella collapsed beside the couch.

"ISABELLA!" Gabriella cried out, rushing past Cowle to her fallen friend. Cowle reached into his pocket, keyed the remote locking the front door, both girls trapped, their final avenue of escape sealed. *No way out.*

Gabriella knelt down next to Isabella, checked her pulse, found it weak. "Isabella? Isabella! Are you okay? What's wrong?" The lack of response frightened Gabriella, uncertainty clouding her hazel-green eyes. "Isabella, say something, please!" She pleaded to the unmoving form, turned to Cowle. "We have to call an ambulance," she told him, panic rising in her voice, "something's wrong with her!"

"Nothing's wrong with her," Cowle replied coldly, "and there's no need to call an ambulance."

The change of tone, a moment earlier pleasant and kind now brittle and threatening, suddenly terrified Gabriella. A knob turned in her mind and she realized the man she thought as Marcus Evans wasn't who he seemed. She heard footsteps, heavy boots against the floor, another person in the studio, a recognition coming far too late she, and the unconscious Isabella, faced terrible danger. "What's going on here?" Gabriella heard a trembling fear, a disquieting sound, in her question.

"Let's just say," Cowle said with an evil, crooked grin unsettling Gabriella as he stood over her, "your friend here," nodded at the unconscious Isabella "has placed you in considerable danger." In the doorway leading to the back emerged a huge man, a hostile and intimidating presence, studio lights reflecting off his bald head, Gabriella knew she'd have no chance fighting off this hulking brute, outnumbered, quickly overpowered. Her mind raced, putting things together, eyes darting to the spilled water bottle on the floor. *The water, something in the water,* she understood now the snare entangling them, *it must've been drugged.* Gabriella looked at Isabella lying motionless on the floor, whimpered in regret. *I'm sorry.* Fighting back the terror of her situation, a wave of overwhelming remorse washed over Gabriella, forced to make a terrible choice, the worst decision in her young life, but the only one possibly saving their lives, even if it meant leaving her friend behind.

I have to get out of here.

Gabriella sprung to her feet, sprinting past Cowle who made no attempt to prevent her from fleeing, running from the studio into the reception area. A surge of hope burst forth in Gabriella as she sprinted to the front entrance, beyond the door the outside world and freedom from the threat, escaping their grasp to find help for Isabella before any harm came of her. Never occurred to Gabriella her apparent flight from danger seemed too easy. She lunged at the door, took hold and twisted the knob, yanked on the handle. The door locked, wouldn't yield an inch. "No, no, no, no!" Gabriella screamed at the discovery, sobbing in frustration, defeat sweeping her over the precipice into a bottomless abyss of terror, heard footsteps approaching from behind, getting closer. She prayed someone on the street heard her cry. "Somebody help me! Please!" The salvation which a moment earlier appeared so close at hand now brutally deprived.

"Leaving so soon, Gabriella?" Cowle taunted his quarry as he and his henchman entered, found Gabriella tugging on a door refusing to budge, crying hysterically at the realization she the cowering rabbit cornered by wolves, no escape for the hunted from the cunning hunters. "Your session isn't over yet." She faced her tormentors, back against the door, hazel-green eyes growing big seeing something in the hand of the burly henchman, not a gun but an object resembling a television remote.

"Please…don't do this…please…" Gabriella begged, knew her pitiful pleading useless.

Cowle gave an emotionless direction to Sterner. "You may fire when ready, Gridley."

Sterner lifted the stun gun, with a nonchalant indifference aimed at Gabriella's midsection, pressed the trigger. Two darts, with wires leading back to the stun gun, shot out from the device, the sharp barbs piercing the fabric of her dress, lodging in her skin. Gabriella flinched from the impact, screamed in agony, the pain sharp as if bitten by a vicious animal. A second later volts surged through her vulnerable body, in a blink frying her nervous system to a smoldering crisp. In the millisecond before she blacked out a childhood memory flashed in Gabriella's mind, touching an electrified fence on her uncle's farm in Iowa, the shock like putting her finger in an electrical socket, sobbing uncontrollably from the pain. This relentless surge racing through her body made that shock insignificant, every lightning bolt unleashed from a powerful thunderhead converging on where she stood, the blinding explosion of white light immediately obliterated everything around her, replaced by an impenetrable darkness swiftly shrouding a devastated consciousness.

Cowle smiled impassively, watched Gabriella writhe uncontrollably, the electric surge rippling like a tidal wave through her, limbs and muscles tightened and clenched, then just as quickly falling limp. A piteous gasp of defeat her only cry as she collapsed to the floor, crumpling by the door where safety lay so near on the other side now quite distant. *Close doesn't count, Gabriella.* Sterner went to the helpless girl, checked her pulse. "She's still with us," Sterner said, heaving Gabriella up from the floor, head rolling back, hair the color of honey hanging down, arms dangling listlessly.

"Good," Cowle motioned to the studio where Isabella lay. "Let's get them packaged and stored away." Sterner, cradling the inert form in his arms, followed Cowle. "Have to prepare for our final appointment." Only one more piece of merchandise remained to complete the consignment, the innocent girl from Great Northern University, Presley Harding.

Chapter 20

Revenge. That is all that matters. Nothing more and nothing less.

The notion, a singular purpose for his existence, burned as hot in the soul of Sheik Abdullah al-Aziz Rahim as the midafternoon sun high in the cloudless Midwestern sky baking the tarmac outside the private hanger at O'Hare International Airport as he stepped down from the Gulfstream V jet. He buttoned his suit coat, striding purposefully to the waiting limousine, a cohort of security following in his wake. For years that fire burned blazing in his heart, kept aflame and never extinguished thanks to a constant infusion of fuel provided him by the human trafficker Marcus Cowle, stoking the endless conflagration raging within.

For one with the modest title of Senior Trade Representative for the Persian Gulf nation of Daharan, a country whose wealth and influence in world affairs far exceed its minuscule, postage-stamp size not much larger than the municipality where is his jet had landed, his security detail numbered twelve large and strong men; all suitably armed and aptly skilled in physical combat, loyal only to him, a member of the ruling family. The zealous devotion to their charge forged by an intimate knowledge of his darkest secrets, willing to protect him, and in turn the reputation of Daharan, at any cost to prevent exposure of the bloodthirsty monster hiding beneath the veneer of a cultured diplomat and the price paid in human life, of defenseless young women served like platters of food at a sumptuous feast, keeping the beast fed and satisfied.

Rahim slipped into the rear passenger compartment of the limo, driven by one of his detail from the Daharan Embassy in Washington. One of his detail got into the front seat with the driver, three others joining their master in the passenger compartment. The remainder of his detail loaded the luggage into the trunk of the limo, then split up in two black Audi S8 sedans also driven from the embassy in the American capital by members of his detail. A third sedan left at the hanger for the pilots to drive to their hotel near the airport, waiting there until the return trip once Rahim done with his business and collected his goods from Marcus Cowle. The limo, with one Audi in front and the second tailing close behind, sped away from the hanger, within minutes blended into traffic on the Kennedy Expressway heading to downtown Chicago. An escort from the local law enforcement authorities typically accompanied Rahim when travelling, but given the true purpose of his visit on this occasion the symbolic protection dispensed with. Once in the city center Rahim and his party staying at the Chicago Hilton and Towers, occupying the impressive Conrad Hilton Suite, accommodations compliments of the wealthy American capitalists, the Cockrell brothers, with whom his country did much business. The next morning Rahim their invited guest for a speech given by Senator Benton Fielding on the campus of Great Northern University.

Rahim glanced out the window, watched the neighborhoods of northwest Chicago pass in a blur as the three-car train travelled at an even speed along the superhighway, on both sides faster traffic zipping around and past them. Through the tinted windows of the limo he observed with disdain the assumed superiority of the Americans-the affluence of cars and houses, illusions of wealth purchased on credit-and sensed the arrogance, their belief in a vaunted *exceptionalism* brought about by delusions of nationalistic grandeur. *If it were not for my country, tiny Daharan, you would have none of this*, Rahim quietly sneered. *You would be helpless, pathetic, powerless.* As vulnerable as the five women to accompany him home, a trip for them from which no return ever possible. His country home to their Fifth Fleet, guarding the strategically vulnerable Persian Gulf and Straits of Hormuz from the ambitions of radical Iran, allowing free flow of precious black oil from the Middle East to eventually become the gasoline filling the tanks of their vehicles. To sustain their extravagant lifestyle, their Potemkin illusion of world dominance, this nation of expressed Christian moral virtues entered into compacts with hidden costs they never did fully comprehend. Did they truly understand the price in human lives paid for their dependence on countries like Daharan and people like him?

The traffic slowed as the Kennedy merged with the Edens Expressway, funneling traffic in from the north suburbs, cars and trucks jockeying for position as two streams of vehicles became one. In the distance through the afternoon haze Rahim caught a glimpse of downtown Chicago, shimmering in the sunlight. The city skyline much transformed from the first time his eyes set sight on the vista, new gleaming towers of steel and glass reaching for the heavens, the panorama evolving from years earlier when he arrived to study at the University of Chicago in Hyde Park and the encounter forever altering his life.

To his fellow graduate students Sheik Rahim the handsome, enigmatic scion of a ruling family from a Persian Gulf emirate rich with oil and flush with influence the viscous substance black as midnight engendered from nations dependent on the fuel to power their prosperity. None knew of his darker side, the service with his country's secret police, stamping out dissent with ruthless efficiency and brutal expediency, of callous indifference to the suffering of his countrymen and women as he tortured them into submission, of sexual pleasure derived from inflicting horrible pain. A simple dictum guided his life: *Fear is power and power is fear.* For one young woman, a fellow student of stunning beauty and intelligence who made his acquaintance, lacking suspicion of the demon lurking inside waiting to be unleashed, of his capacity for ghastly violence, the encounter to bring about her own eventual demise by his hand and horrible suffering for countless others in her wake.

The young woman assumed the relationship nothing more than friendship, unaware Rahim viewed the matter differently, wished to make this beauty his own, willing to do anything to act on those desires. When she graduated and moved to Washington, lobbying on the behalf of environmental causes, he followed, taking a position of trade representative in his country's embassy. He continued his pursuit of the woman, who grew increasingly frightened at the ardor of his attention, yet unable to stop him for Rahim connected to the conduits of power in America, cultivated influential friends from both sides of the political spectrum. She sought protection from Rahim, found solace in the arms of a friend from her undergraduate years at the University of Michigan, now working as an attorney with the Department of Justice, a relationship blossoming into love and engagement for marriage.

Rahim discovered the relationship and his obsession with the young woman exploded into murderous rage. In his eyes this betrayal couldn't stand, the woman spurning him for another, considered her act the ultimate transgression and for that she must pay the ultimate penalty. How dare she rebuff his desires, how dare she exercise...*freedom*? His arrogance flared, anger burning, believed the woman his property, a thing to be used and not shared with anyone. If he couldn't have her for his own, then no one would. The perceived slight avenged, even if the vengeance drenched in blood and unleashed with violence, the woman paying with her life for a sin to which she wholly oblivious.

To carry out the insidious plan he devised Rahim sought the aid of his most trusted bodyguard, snatch the woman he once desired and now wished to destroy, assassinate the man she depended on for safety. Weeks of surveillance followed, tracking her every movement before striking, one evening the pair breaking into the isolated country home the two shared, ambushed the woman as she returned from work, subduing her, killed her fiancé as he entered, unaware to the danger and never having a chance to fight back. Rahim made sure the woman saw his final breath as the light in his eyes faded and died, let her realize all was lost and her life, in time, also forfeit. Taken from the home along with her fiancé's body, loaded on one of his country's diplomatic jets, spirited away to his private compound a half a world away. The body of the man who loved and swore to protect her dumped somewhere over the dark expanse of the Atlantic Ocean and never recovered. In the media the disappearance of the attractive, successful couple proved a mystery without resolution, generated vapid speculation and whispered rumors. As the public pondered the fate of the missing the young woman suffered cruelly at Rahim's hand, enduring weeks in a private hell, viciously abused and horrendously violated until she breathed her last and suffered no more.

With her agonizing death Rahim thought the matter finished, the perceived crime against his manhood avenged, until he realized he couldn't erase the memory of her from his mind, in the face of every young American woman he saw the woman who rejected his attention. Their flaunted independence appalled him to no end; didn't realize their place one of subservience. In thoughts repressed he replayed the torture and pain he wrought on his victim, veering deeper into a fantasy world where the women he quietly noticed every day, so decadent in their liberty, took the place of the woman he murdered. The visions couldn't slake his thirst to redress what he believed a continuing stain on his honor, Rahim deciding to act on his impulses and commenced a descent down a slippery slope of madness.

He consulted with three trusted members of his security detail, one the associate who assisted him in the abduction of the woman and the murder of her fiancé. As a son of the ruling family his protection paramount, his desires satisfied, none of them questioned what Rahim proposed though understood the dire implications if the audacious plot exposed. At Rahim's direction the trio hunted down and snatched by ruthless force young women to gratify the twisted fantasies simmering and boiling in Rahim's mind, captives spirited away on a diplomatic jet to a fate where the only outcome could be a brutal, violent death.

The events of September 11th might've brought a halt to his atrocious spree; Rahim couldn't risk his people caught abducting American women to feed his deviant pleasures. The fallout from such a revelation endangering the relationship between the Western world and his country dependent on their money and protection against the forces of Islamic radicalism, a partnership already on shaky, unsettled ground following the attacks in New York and Washington. The solution evaded him and Rahim resigned never to nourish the hunger of revenge burning inside with the sacrifice of human life until, during a visit to the estate of a cousin, he found in the subterranean dungeon of his mansion captive young women from Western Europe, unwilling toys utilized solely for his sexual pleasure. He asked his cousin how he had come to possess the women. The relative gleefully related the existence of an organization lurking in the shadows of society, kidnapping and trading in female flesh, a group simply called The Trading Society. With this discovery Rahim uncovered a resolution to his quandary, a proxy to execute his bidding and grandly compensate for their services.

Through surreptitious intermediaries and cautious back-channel inquiries Rahim investigated The Trading Society, the possibility of using them to accomplish his aims. He soon found in Marcus Cowle-an erudite and intelligent individual, soft-spoken, seemingly harmless but vicious and merciless, a heart hard as stone and cold as ice-the man with the necessary skills to achieve his objectives. They met in a tiny, discreet Paris café, discussing the matter of abducting women, transporting them to his country in the blasé manner people talked about the weather. The sterile, bland language of the business world dominated the conversation with words like product, merchandise and deliveries employed as euphemisms regarding the cruel criminal acts of kidnapping and human trafficking. Negotiations hammered out between the two, Cowle a clear-eyed bargainer who understood the gravity of Rahim's proposal, demanded for his troubles ample compensation. Before setting the final price for his services Rahim challenged Cowle to prove his worth.

Cowle returned to America and procured the first item, arranging the transfer to his cadre of bodyguards shipping the victim on a diplomatic Gulfstream jet to his compound in Daharan, within a week of their meeting. Rahim duly impressed with the swift alacrity of Cowle's response, agreeing to the proposed fee for his services and the pipeline to satiate his hunger for vengeance, quenched with the blood of young American women, began to flow once more unabated.

The current moved slowly at first. A 'consignment,' as Cowle referred to the hostage he procured, handed over to Rahim's contacts in America every few months, transported to Daharan for Rahim to inflict his sick desires for brutality on the helpless captive. But as soon as the spigot turned on, Rahim found difficult restraining the demented cravings, requiring more victims to satisfy the urges, more blood to slake the unquenchable thirst. The accelerating pace of demand taxed Cowle, even his capabilities had limits, and he approached Rahim with a proposition to acquire the product Rahim sought in 'bulk' quantities, multiple victims delivered at one time to his people, allowing Rahim a supply of flesh to spread his violence out over time. Of course like any able entrepreneur Cowle requested a hike in his compensation to expand his operation, adding two apprentices to assist in his endeavors. The first 'bulk consignment' of three hostages taken in Boston, Rahim pleased with the results, thought this might curb his appetite, but the belief proved mistaken and only served to further accelerate the cycle. The three spirited from Boston lasted him a year and a half, the four snatched from Denver over a year and the four taken in Atlanta survived only weeks past a full year.

The five snatched from Los Angeles, an increase in the consignment that should've placated Rahim for far longer, didn't last out the year, his sadistic blood-thirst increasing exponentially with the number of victims provided. Now he demanded more, and in a shorter period of time, to feed the craving lust for blood ravaging him, the need for this consignment from Chicago. One he'd take delivery of personally, brought about by the confluence of Cowle's decision to set up in the Midwestern city and the invitation from the Cockrell brothers to attend the speech by Senator Fielding at their alma mater. He understood his presence to take possession of the order carried immeasurable risk, but with anxious excitement Rahim wished to witness the raw fear of his new property from the moment they understood he owned them, able to do whatever he pleased with their bodies and controlled the means of their exit from the mortal world.

Even if he were found out, what could the Americans do? They were powerless to punish him even if they wished. He possessed diplomatic immunity, bulletproof as the Americans might say. Besides, the Americans based their Fifth Fleet, so pivotal to guarding their strategic and economic interests in the Persian Gulf, in his homeland. If by some chance his activity in America uncovered, how he plundered their land for young women to assuage his hunger for sexual savagery, they couldn't move against him without losing the home for their powerful fleet, especially at a time when Iran flexed their military muscle, rattled sabers perhaps forged of nuclear materials.

Rahim nodded to Saleh, the most trusted of his bodyguards and with him since the beginning, a silent, humorless, bald and bullet-headed man with square shoulders. A pitiless functionary capable of eliminating any complication without compunction, the man Rahim trusted to dispose of the merchandise once he finished extracting all he desired, finishing with their very lives, from his defenseless captives. Saleh removed a smartphone from his jacket, handing the device to Rahim. Now that he was in Chicago checking on the progress of Marcus Cowle securing the consignment for delivery and shipment back to Daharan on early Tuesday morning.

The phone rang as Marcus Cowle tightened the final knot on the webbing of rope pinning the arms of Isabella DiBenedetto to her sides. Hadn't yet gagged or blindfolded the girl, easing the lifeless body to the floor before reaching for his smartphone, no need to address the matter now, for a few hours more the sedative keeping poor Isabella dead to the world. He noticed the number, had expected the call at some point this afternoon.

"Sheik Rahim, my friend," Cowle answered pleasantly. "I presume you are in Chicago?"

"I landed ten minutes ago," Rahim replied, voice colored by the crisp English accent.

"I hope your trip was uneventful?" Cowle inquired politely.

"So far," Rahim said, "though I'm looking forward to the trip home with my merchandise." He paused. "How is your progress in securing the consignment?"

"I already have two pieces in storage," Cowle referred to Emma Hayden and Alexandra Cole, prisoners at the vacant factory on the West Side. He peered down at Isabella DiBenedetto, out cold and lying bound at his feet. "We just acquired the third and fourth items of your order."

"Excellent," Rahim pleased. "And the final piece?"

"She'll be arriving shortly," Cowle remarked. "The entire consignment will be processed and ready for shipment this evening." Cowle paused, had to say what weighed on his mind. "I do wish we could complete this transaction tonight rather than waiting until your departure on Tuesday."

"Is there a problem?" Rahim asked. "I'm sorry if my schedule dictates the necessity."

Cowle cleared his throat. "In the past I've handed over the consignment to your people hours after I secured the final parcel. By the time the police begin to suspect something is amiss we, and your product, are far away and untouchable. I don't like this delay with the transfer," Cowle needed to reinforce the point, of the risk the delay presented. "It allows far too much time for someone to figure these women are missing, gives someone the opportunity to start looking for them. Increases the chances of something going *wrong*. Even with all the precautions I take to cover my trail there's a chance someone will stumble on our operation. This delay is that opportunity. I don't need to remind you of the damage discovery will cause to your country and to The Trading Society."

"Marcus, my friend, I value your...input into this matter," Cowle heard the condescending tone in the answer. Rahim might be his most profitable client, but the man possessed the tendency to be an arrogant son of a bitch if so desired. "I have come to respect your talents over the years. I do not feel you have anything to fear with this delay. If you are not...confident in your skills and capabilities, I know there are other Collectors in The Trading Society who'd value my business. I don't think they would have any complaint with how I wish to take delivery of the product."

Bastard. Cowle grimaced at the dig, knew of competitors within The Trading Society who envied his relationship with Sheik Rahim and secretly yearned for the proceeds earned from his dealings, waiting like vultures perched in trees to swoop in on the carcass if he faltered. "I only wished to make known my reservations regarding this consignment," Cowle back-stepped from the earlier statement. "I do believe the exchange will go as planned without complications. I also believe after this consignment we need to discuss the process of this operation going forward."

"As you wish, my friend," Rahim said, unperturbed by Cowle's strident warning. "I hope you didn't take offense with what I just said."

You'd better believe I took offense, Cowle kept silent the rebuke. *I'm the one doing the heavy lifting here, my ass is the one on the line.* "None taken, my friend. The consignment will be ready for your departure."

"Excellent," Rahim said.

"I'll contact you tomorrow with the location of the exchange, a precaution since we're dealing with this delay," Cowle added, had this advantage over his client. He held the treasured captives and Rahim didn't know where.

"I understand your desire for caution," Rahim acknowledged, "one never knows who might be listening. I patiently await your call." Cowle switched off the phone, placed it on the table, attention turning back to Isabella. Sterner finished with Gabriella, now a secured, silenced and blind package, lifting her still form in his thick arms from the floor.

"Stash her in the back. I'll finish with Isabella." Sterner carried Gabriella down the hall to the closets where their captives temporarily kept until moved to the factory. Cowle knelt behind Isabella, propped her up against his knee. He reached into the duffel bag, removed a thick red cloth pad and two long strips of white cloth. Isabella's mouth yielded easily to the cloth wad shoved past her lips, the first strip of thick cotton wound around her head three times, wedging the stuffing further back in her mouth to create an effective sound-muffling gag he knotted tightly at the nape of her neck. Took the second strip of white cloth, folded the fabric wide enough to obstruct her vision, dropped it over closed eyes, tightening the blindfold behind her head.

"Pretty girls never know the danger they're in until it's far too late, so naïve you ladies tend to be sometimes," Cowle cooed to his defenseless prisoner. All of them so blithely trusting until the last moment when the masquerade ended, overcome with stunned awareness at the betrayal. Cowle heaved the bound Isabella DiBenedetto into his arms, carried her down the hallway. The door to the other closet still open and saw the tied, silenced form of Gabriella Taylor slumped in the corner, head resting against the wall, grinned in satisfaction at the sight. *Money in the bank.* He deposited his roped parcel into the second closet, gingerly easing Isabella to the floor, gagged and blindfolded head drooping to the side. He closed the door, made a final check of the restrained Gabriella and shut the door to her cramped cell. *Four down and one to go.*

Cowle heard the television from the back as he entered the studio where their handbags lay. "*And the Bears take over after the fumble recovery at the Rams forty-six yard line with Chicago leading thirteen to six...*" He allowed Sterner his entertainment, for now his work done, understood his apprentice placed money on the game, Cowle able to complete the next phase of the operation on his own. Isabella's Samsung smartphone rested on the floor where she dropped it, rummaging through Gabriella's bag for her Apple iPhone. He started up the software on the laptop, proceeded to destroy any pertinent information contained on their phones, in the process erasing every detail and mention regarding the photography studio bearing his fictitious name the pair left on the internet. Once done Marcus Cowle sat down on the couch, eased his head back, closing his eyes to refocus his energy. Waiting for the final piece of merchandise to arrive, innocent and captivating Presley Harding, and complete the consignment for Sheik Rahim. Hoped nothing unforeseen occurred during the lengthy interval between this final capture and the transfer to Sheik Rahim of the parcels, that nothing interfered to keep him from the millions received for this delivery.

Chapter 21

"Heading to the library?" Presley Harding asked as Riley Bradford shoved textbooks and Dell laptop into her shoulder bag. She nervously glanced at the clock, cutting it close to have enough time to get packed and ready, drive into Chicago for her appointment at Marcus Evans Photography. *Come on, Riley!* She silently prodded her roommate. *Hurry up and get out of here!*

"I have a monster of an organic chemistry test tomorrow afternoon," Riley nodded. "And I have a ten-page essay for my English Lit class due on Tuesday. Plus an anatomy test on Thursday. I have lots of studying to do. It's going to be a late night."

"What floor will you be on?" Presley offered, smiling. "I might be over later to join you."

Really, I didn't think you knew where the library was? But you know where the nightclubs are. Riley incredulous at Presley's comment, yet swallowed the biting reply, settled for an answer far more civil. "I'll be on the third floor, near the multimedia center."

"Okay," Presley smiled. "Maybe I'll see you later this evening."

I wouldn't bet on that. Was Riley's silent, sarcastic reflection, but again she held her tongue. "Great, I'll see you there." Riley left the room, closing the door behind her.

Presley waited for a minute, praying Riley hadn't forgotten something and on her way back to the room. She peeked out the window, their room above the main entrance to Cockrell Hall, saw Riley exit, heading off to the library. *I thought she'd never leave!* A relieved sigh escaped Presley's lungs, springing up from the couch, hurrying to the closet for an overnight bag. Had an idea of the outfits she wanted to bring to the photo shoot, ripping them from the hangers. She checked the clock again, now smiled, able to make the appointment but couldn't waste a minute. Presley stuffed into her bag the sexy, tempting clothes she wore to the clubs that Marcus Evans requested, along with heels and boots to go with the outfits. She moved to the medicine cabinet over the sink, gathering up tubes of lipstick, eye shadow and eyeliner, hurriedly cramming the items into her makeup bag. No need to worry about nail polish, her fingernails already done in a shade called Captivating Coral. Brushes and combs followed and she zipped the bag shut, tossing it into the larger bag.

She checked her phone, directions to the studio already programmed into the device, didn't need the business card Marcus gave her, leaving it on the dresser. Presley quivered with nervous anticipation, breaths coming out short and rapid. *Calm down, girl*, she closed her eyes. *This is going to work out fine.* She opened her eyes, looked in the mirror, smiled at her reflection, ran a hand through caramel brown hair spilling over her shoulders, checking the blue jeans and tank top with horizontal stripes of blue and white she wore.

"All right, Presley, let's do this," she said to her image, "and get out of this place." Heaving her overnight bag over one shoulder, slung her purse across the other. She left the room, maneuvered between other residents in the hallway, heard sounds of music and conversation as she passed. Said not a word to anyone of where she headed or whom she was meeting and no one asked of her destination. She'd be back at Great Northern in a few hours before anyone even knew she'd been gone.

"Sounds like I'm missing the fun today," Samantha Grayson told Aaron Dinehart, sitting down in the chair beside his desk in the bustling offices of *The Daily Northern*.

"You picked a great day to have off." Though it had been Aaron who gave her the Sunday respite. "Local law enforcement was busy on the party beat last night," Aaron explained, eyes focused on the laptop screen as he edited an article. "There are some unhappy campers on Greek Row today. And from what I've heard the bust on the northwest side of Evanslawn will set a record for the number of citations issued for underage drinking." He looked at Samantha. "I hope you're not upset missing the action?"

"Not at all," Samantha said with a blissful smile. "I enjoyed a gorgeous Sunday afternoon with Tyler instead of cooped up here getting the runaround from Great Northern Pubic Safety and the Evanslawn Police Department."

"And how'd we spend the day off?" Aaron asked.

"Tyler and I went to morning service over at Kendricks Chapel, had brunch with the usual suspects," that meant with her roommates and friends. "Tyler and I walked around campus before heading to the women's soccer game. Just came from there."

"They win?" Aaron inquired.

"They did, 3-2." Her smile grew brighter. "Selena Espinosa had the game-winning goal in the eighty-eighth minute, made her fans," the residents of rooms across from each other on the third floor of Falmouth Hall, "very happy."

"You're here because Tyler is..."

Samantha finished the sentence. "Back at work for next week's game." Then she reminded him. "I need the credentials for the speech tomorrow at Cockrell Auditorium."

Aaron stopped typing, opened the top drawer of his desk, removed a blue, white and silver Great Northern lanyard with the plastic press credential attached. "Make sure your *Daily Northern* press identification and student ID are on there too. Get reaction from the audience. I know President Welland and some members of the Board of Trustees will be attending, as well as a whole gaggle of faculty members. Don't forget to talk to the protesters outside of the event, I'm getting hints there may be as many protesters outside the speech as there are people inside the auditorium. I think you can work at least three, maybe even four, stories out of this."

"So Tuesday's edition of *The Daily Northern* will be a Samantha Grayson production," Samantha accepted the lanyard, attaching her press and student IDs back at her room. "Where am I sitting?"

"I pulled a few strings with the Office of University Communications to get you a front row seat in the press section," Aaron informed her. "You'll be with those heavy mainstream media hitters."

Samantha cocked her head. "Now I understand why you wanted me to dress up for this."

"That's right, Sam. Need to look professional," Aaron took a break from editing, leaning his lanky form back in his chair. "Have something nice picked out?"

"Yes I do," Samantha replied. "Very professional, I'll blend in with all the media types. You'll see tomorrow evening when we go over the stories." Aaron had a big test tomorrow afternoon, wouldn't be in the office until late in the day when Samantha with her friends enjoying dinner in the city.

"Will it drive Tyler wild?" Aaron asked.

"What do you think?" Samantha admitted. "I'm giving him a preview at breakfast."

"You have anything planned for when you're done here for the night?" Aaron smiled.

"I think we'll spend some quality time after I get back from dinner in Chicago with the roomies to celebrate Amanda's win on Saturday and go over the stories with you," Samantha told him, brown eyes sparkling with anticipation. "How's my replacement on the party beat doing?"

"She's doing just fine," Aaron motioned to a desk across the newsroom where a freshman with shoulder-length sienna brown hair typed away on her laptop, blue eyes fixed on the screen. "She's eager, enthusiastic, types like a speed-demon without any errors to boot. Reminds me of a certain starry-eyed freshman from last year."

"Thanks." Samantha knew that reporter Aaron spoke of and blushed at the flattering comparison. "So I'll have competition?"

Aaron grinned, jealousy a trait absent from Samantha's good-natured personality. "Your competition is an absolute sweetheart. Have you've met Lily Rosenberg yet?" Aaron asked as Samantha shook her head. The two watched as Lily stopped typing, reached for the cup of Starbucks iced coffee beside her, almost knocking it over, at the last second righting the drink before it spilled the contents across the keyboard.

Aaron sighed. "That's the fourth time she's almost done that today."

Samantha stifled a giggle. "We can't all be perfect."

"Then I wouldn't have a job," Aaron joked, then told her. "I'd like to have you work with Lily. You can be her guardian angel, how I was for you last year."

"You were the best angel this wide-eyed freshman ever had," Samantha acknowledged, touching Aaron's hand, remembered his support after she uncovered the scandal forcing a change at the very top of the university's administration. "You were there when I needed you, stood by me when no one else believed I could do the job."

Aaron flashed an aw-shucks country boy grin, Samantha thought of Aaron as the protective big brother she never had. "You did the heavy lifting. All I did was watch your back."

"I hope I can be as good a mentor to Lily as you were for me," Samantha said, then remembered what she wanted to discuss with Aaron. "Since I'm doing a favor for you covering this speech, could you let me work on something for the paper?"

Aaron leaned forward. "What is it?"

"Have you been following these series of disappearances over the past few years?" Samantha asked. "They've happened across the country with three, four, five women vanishing almost at the same time?"

"There was something down in Atlanta about two years back, that's my neck of the woods." Aaron rubbed his chin. "Last year, about now, didn't that happen in California?"

"Los Angeles, five women over one weekend," Samantha informed him. "Two of the missing were roommates at UCLA."

"What do you want to do with it?" Aaron attempted to fathom the angle of the story.

Samantha shrugged. "Find people on campus with connections to the missing, work the human interest aspect. Talk to Public Safety and the Evanslawn police and use anecdotes to put together a piece of cautionary advice for those freshmen away from home for the first time, the importance of being aware of their surroundings and taking precautions?"

"That'll work," Aaron agreed, a somber thought entering his head. "I know the editor of the student paper at Texas Tech. Bad things going on down there. Had two girls go missing last week, vanished from their off-campus apartment."

"Read about that online," Samantha said soberly. "Makes you think..."

"Yeah, it does," Aaron agreed. "How much time do you think you'll need?"

Samantha thought through her schedule. "About a week, maybe two if I get enough material?"

"Sounds good," Aaron noted. "Now get out of here, enjoy the rest of the evening. Do me proud tomorrow," Aaron called out as Samantha stood up, walked to the door, "show them why you're my best reporter."

Samantha twirled around, waving to him. "Do you expect anything less from me?"

"That twenty-four hours of freedom was fun while it lasted," D'Andre Watson sighed, sinking into his seat in the McIllhenny Family Athletic Training Center auditorium, waiting for the first team meeting of the week in preparation of the road trip to Minneapolis and the Big Ten season opener against winless Minnesota in TCF Bank Stadium.

"Wasn't exactly twenty-four hours," Albert 'Fiji' Fatuamala pointed out.

"More like twenty-two hours," Tyler McManaway sat beside D'Andre as Fiji sat next to Tyler.

"Please tell me again you're not worried about a team that lost by twenty-four to South Dakota State," D'Andre pleaded with Tyler. "Minnesota got run off the field, at home no less, by a FCS school! They didn't make a first down until the third quarter and only scored on an interception return!"

"I'm not worried," Tyler admitted, other unspoken matters the cause for concern. Even with Samantha's assurances of her ability to defend herself his urge to protect her still burned brightly. "I'm taking our next opponent seriously, even if they got blown out by a FCS school."

D'Andre shook his head dismissively. "All I'm saying is this will be the shortest team meeting in history," he said. "We'll be out of here in time to watch *Family Guy* and *American Dad*."

Conrad Purvis, one of Tyler's stalwart guardian on the offensive line, heard D'Andre's comment. "All right! Giggty-giggty!" Imitated the exaggeratedly jawed and notoriously lecherous Quagmire character from *Family Guy* as those in the auditorium broke up laughing. The door to the right at the front of the auditorium opened and Head Coach Carl Hamilton entered, followed by his staff, the conversation and fooling around quickly subsiding.

"I hope everyone enjoyed their day of freedom," Coach Carl stood before his players, arms akimbo, murmurs and nods of agreement greeted the comment. "Thank you for allowing me and my wife and family a good night's sleep, no phone calls at four in the morning." This brought a ripple of self-conscious laughter, no players getting into trouble when many other students had found themselves on the wrong side of the law. "And I'd like to congratulate you on being ranked eighteenth in the Associated Press poll and nineteenth in the *USA Today* coaches' poll after Saturday's win." The news elicited a surge of whooping and applause, their back-to-back victories over ranked opponents Missouri and North Carolina gaining notice from the national media.

Coach Carl raised his hand to quiet them. "I think there's a group of players in a meeting room at Minnesota licking their wounds right now, their head coach telling them they have an opportunity to beat a ranked opponent at home in their Big Ten opener."

D'Andre covered his mouth, leaned over to Tyler. "Ain't gonna happen."

"What was that, D'Andre?" Coach Carl asked.

D'Andre straightened in his seat, cleared his throat, Tyler suppressing a chuckle. "Telling Tyler here we have to be ready for Minnesota. They could upset us."

"Sure you were," Casey Ellerbie kiddingly mocked the star running back, prompting another round of laughter from a loose and confident team.

Coach Carl raised his hand, the room quieted once more. "D'Andre is right. We have to be ready for them. We have to prepare as thoroughly and be as focused for a Minnesota team who haven't won a game as we did for Missouri and North Carolina. If we don't prepare, if we aren't focused, we'll be leaving the field with our heads down and our tails between our asses." He motioned to the student

149

manager operating the multimedia equipment, lights in the auditorium dimmed. "Fun time is over. Let's get to work."

"He got you there," Tyler muttered to D'Andre.

"He did," D'Andre acknowledged, activating his iPad. "But like Coach Carl said, let's get to work."

Presley Harding gently nudged the blue Lexus sedan into the space between a red Mini Cooper and a silver Nissan Altima, careful not to hit either car as she parked. The particular maneuver not her strongest suit, failing the first try for her license after brushing against a car on her test. After a minute or so of backing the car in, then backing out, and backing in again Presley finally wedged the Lexus between the vehicles. Presley rested her hands on the steering wheel, sat for a moment with eyes closed and head down. *Be calm, don't be nervous, don't act like...a college freshman*, she reminded herself, beating down butterflies of anxiety fluttering around her stomach. She opened her eyes, made a quick check of her makeup in the mirror. *Let's do this.* Presley grabbed her purse and overnight bag from the seat beside her, exiting the Lexus, walking up to the studio and rang the bell. She waited, tapping her foot on the ground as currents of excitement and apprehension swept through her, until a minute later the door opened and the smiling face of Marcus Evans greeted her.

"Presley! It's good to see you!" Marcus welcomed her with effusive grace. "You're right on time too! Have any trouble finding the place?"

"None at all. I Googled the directions," Presley stepped inside, Marcus closing the door behind her. "Can we get started?"

"You're quite eager," Marcus chuckled good-naturedly. "Have to take care of the legal stuff first. It's not all glamour. You have to fill out a model release." Presley blushed, embarrassed by the show of youthful impatience. "Do you have your identification with you," he inquired, "and not the one you use to get into the clubs."

"Yes, I have a real one," Presley grinned sheepishly, knew Marcus had her. *I wouldn't have this chance if I didn't have that fake ID*. She removed the New York State driver's license showing she was eighteen from her purse. Marcus handed her a clipboard with a form to complete.

"Have a seat while I make a copy for my records," Marcus said as Presley sat down, filling out the form while the photographer stepped back into the studio, heard the hum of a copy machine as he copied the identification. "Are you done?" Marcus stepped back into the front room as Presley finished with the form, handed the clipboard back to him.

"I think I have everything," Presley said as Marcus checked the form.

Marcus nodded. "You have all the T's crossed and I's dotted." He took the form, stapled the copy of her license to the paper, handed the card back to Presley. He asked a seemingly innocuous question. "Did you tell anyone you were doing this?"

Presley shook her head. "No, I want everyone to be surprised when I become famous."

"I'm sure they will be quite surprised." Marcus smiled at Presley, unaware of the true meaning of his expression and the evil lurking behind congenial eyes.

"Now can we get started?" Presley asked, expectation rising once more.

Marcus laughed, seemingly impressed by her enthusiasm. "Now we can." Looked over what Presley wore, the white and blue striped tank top and blue jeans, sandals on her feet. "You can take your bag and set up in the dressing room down the hall. I think that outfit will do nicely for a first set."

"I guess so…" Presley answered, disappointed, expecting to start with a more daring outfit.

"Don't worry. You'll have a chance to wear what you brought." He motioned towards the studio, Presley following excitedly without hesitation, an innocent lamb unwittingly led to her own slaughter.

"Has Amanda returned yet?" Samantha entered her suite in Falmouth Hall after the visit to *The Daily Northern*. Found Ashleigh Morgan and Lauryn Callahan plopped on the couch in the common room studying.

"She texted me ten minutes ago," Ashleigh said. "She's on her way, saying goodbye to Connor at McDonough."

"Hope they don't get distracted," Samantha sat beside Lauryn, friends giggling at the comment, knew the sort of 'distraction' she implied. "Did you make the reservations?"

"We're good to go," Ashleigh gave her a thumbs up. "Told you I had an inside track."

"I read a review online," Lauryn put her book down. "I think Amanda's in for a treat."

"She's deserves it after winning Saturday," Samantha pointed out.

"That's because our Gazelle beat the best in the nation," Ashleigh added proudly.

Samantha removed her laptop from her shoulder bag. "So if she wins a national championship where do we take her to celebrate?"

"You ever heard of Alinea?" Ashleigh had a ready answer. "Down in Lincoln Park?"

"One of the most expensive restaurants in America," Samantha said.

"If she wins it all," Ashleigh nodded, "that's where we're taking Gazelle for her victory dinner."

"I hope your parents know your gold card is getting a workout," Lauryn warned.

Amanda entered the suite, wearing a Nike top proclaiming 'Fast, Fierce and Fearless' on the front. "I'm back from an afternoon of doing nothing and enjoying every wonderful second," she announced, slipped off her backpack, tossed her body down into the love seat across from her friends.

"What are you doing tomorrow night, Gazelle?" Ashleigh asked innocently.

"Other than studying with Connor for a test in my Comparative Cultures and Societies class on Wednesday," Amanda replied, *among other things*. Realized her friends had something to tell her. "What's up?"

"How about a Girls Night Out in the city," Samantha kicked off her Brooks running shoes, legs tucked up underneath her on the couch. "A victory dinner to celebrate your win?"

Amanda pondered the offer. How could she possibly refuse a free dinner? "Oh darn, means I'll have to skip out on training table."

"I know you're so heartbroken," Lauryn added.

"Don't count on it. So where are we going?" Amanda inquired.

"A little Italian place in Chicago," Ashleigh paused, allowed the drama to grow. "Toscana."

"Their head chef won last season's *Top Chef*, right?" Amanda's mouth opened wide in surprise. "It's next to impossible to get a reservation and insanely expensive," Amanda shocked by their generosity.

"I took care of the reservation," Ashleigh informed her friend. "I'm taking care of the tab too."

"Your Mom knows you're picking up the bill?" Amanda wondered.

"How do you think I got the reservations on such short notice?" Ashleigh dark eyes glowed. "She's representing the owners for their location opening in Atlanta. She won't be surprised when the statement comes in the mail next month."

"Nice," Amanda taken back by the gesture. "What time are the reservations?"

"Seven," Ashleigh said. "Enough time for dinner, a little girl talk between us, then get back to campus for whatever else you have planned."

Amanda leapt from the loveseat, bounding over to hug her roommates on the couch. "You're the best friends this Canadian girl can ever have!"

"You won the race," Samantha told her. "You deserve the reward."

"If this is what I can look forward to I'm wining every race this year," Amanda dropped back on the loveseat once done displaying her heartfelt appreciation.

"Is Connor treating you for your win?" Lauryn sipped from her Diet Coke.

"Where he wants to celebrate," Amanda grinned, "we're waiting until the season is over."

Samantha puzzled by the admission. "Where does he want to take you?"

"You heard of a place in Chicago called Kuma's Corner?" Amanda asked.

Lauryn nodded. "I went there with my study group from organic chemistry last year. They have these delicious hamburgers, but they're huge and the macaroni and cheese is to die for. Because the portions are so big you end up taking food home."

"Connor is calling it my 'Night of Sin' after I'm done eating healthy for cross-country season," Amanda added. "I'll satisfy my inner carnivore and savor with passionate abandon every calorie of fat."

"Then you and Connor will do other things with passionate abandon," Samantha kidded.

The four broke into laughter. "That too," Amanda admitted, though Samantha knew there may be similar moments of such romantic abandon between her and Tyler after she returned from dinner and finished her work at *The Daily Northern*. Something Samantha looking forward to after a long day.

Gabriella Taylor stirred from the vivid nightmare. A session for a modeling job in a photography studio, her friend Isabella passing out from a drugged drink, trying to escape, finding the door locked, trapped by men with intentions of grievous harm, a burst of excruciating pain surging through her body then darkness. Her eyes fluttered open; vision greeted by a continuing darkness, confused for a moment, sensed pressure of something soft against her eyelids. Realized she hadn't slept through a terrifying dream, troubling visions one able to awaken from. A sick feeling exploded deep in her stomach, caught up in something far more terrible than an unsettling vision, living a nightmare in real time and uncertain how much longer she had left to live.

She attempted to move, tried to scream. Discovered limbs melded in place by ropes wound tight, cutting harshly into her flesh. Pathetic cries for help muffled by cloth jammed into her mouth, struggled to keep from choking on the wadding silencing her. Couldn't see with cloth bound over her eyes. She could only feel and hear, body resting against a wall, moved her legs, heard her feet bump against another wall. *Where am I?* The space about her cramped and confined.

Gabriella furiously worked through the torrent of fear threatening to drown her, trying not to panic, questions in her mind crashed against each other like colored balls knocked about on a barroom pool table. *What's going on here? Why are they doing this to us? Where's Isabella? What have they done with her?* Was she also bound and gagged, completely helpless? Who was Marcus Evans? Had he, and the burly man who attacked her, harmed Isabella, committed unspeakable acts on her friend? What, and Gabriella petrified by the horrendous possibilities, did they want with them? What were they going to do with them? She used the only physical sense her captivity allowed, listened to voices outside her prison. One she recognized, that of the photographer Marcus Evans, voice pleasant and accommodating, concealing the truth of his evil nature. Heard a second voice, higher-pitched with a sweet singsong quality, bright and excited and very oblivious she stood in the presence of a predator.

Oh God, alarm burst in Gabriella's chest, heart plummeting, *another girl! I have to warn her!* Gabriella Taylor banged bound booted feet against the wall of the constricted chamber, cried out through the fabric between her lips, had to alert this woman of the danger she unknowingly faced before it was too late.

The first set of photos with Marcus Evans had lasted thirty minutes, Presley Harding awkward at first, tried acting natural and poised while posing under the glaring, hot lights, failing miserably in the initial attempts, movements stiff and uncoordinated. Her initial assessment of her performance brutally frank. *God, I suck at this! I feel like a total dork!* Presley raged, disappointed with her earnest efforts, wondering if she even possessed the talent to be a model, if her desire nothing more than a misguided fantasy. Only when the photographer encouraged her to relax, offering helpful suggestions and honest compliments, did Presley grow more at ease, the results improving with each exposure. After they finished Marcus let her examine the first set of pictures downloaded to his laptop, flattered by his comments how attractive she was, reassurance she was doing fine. Then sent her off to the dressing room to change into a new outfit for the second set.

Presley admired her reflection in the full-length mirror, smiling with pleased satisfaction at her appearance and choice of attire. *Wait until he gets a look at me in this*, Presley thought of the photographer waiting back in the studio, preparing for the next set. *You want sexy? I'll show you sexy.* She changed from jeans and tank top into a form fitting long-sleeve paisley print top with plunging neckline and sleeves flared at the cuff, Presley knew the garment accentuated the cleavage and swell of her breasts. *Well isn't that what they want in advertising? Sex sells.* She wore a mini skirt and high-heeled thigh-high boots, both of a gray suede material, even pulled on fawn-colored tights to compliment her shapely legs.

What was that? Presley heard a bumping sound as she arranged necklaces about her neck, from one dangled a silver crucifix a gift from a beloved grandmother, passing away when she was eight. She listened, heard nothing, shrugging off the noise. She checked her makeup, adding a touch more turquoise and violet to her eye shadow, highlighting the doe-brown eyes, freshening up her eyelashes, stroked lip-gloss over her lips, under the lights emitting a gleaming shine.

Why do I need to go to college anyway? Presley mused, running a brush through her tresses, fluffing up the caramel brown hair to heighten the suggestive appearance. *Why can't I make it as a model?* She knew her parents, both Great Northern graduates, wanted her to pursue a degree in business, disappointed if she decided to leave school to chase dreams of which they didn't approve. But this was her life; she should do what she wanted, what made her happy. Daydreams of glamour and travelling the world as a model, rather than sitting bored to death in a classroom studying a subject she had no interest, filled her mind. Wasn't college a time of discovery? Perhaps a degree and humdrum career in the financial world wasn't what Presley Harding envisioned for her life.

I have to get a picture of this, Presley thought, reached for her smartphone, *and post it on Instagram.* She raised the phone, pointed it at her reflection in the full-length mirror, placed a hand on one hip, tilted her head to the side and smiled as she clicked the button, a bright flash filling the room as she snapped her own picture. About to connect to the internet and upload the image when she noticed she didn't have a signal. *Well, that kind of sucks*, she snorted, put the phone down on the counter. *Relax.* Presley took a deep breath; exhaled while she checked her appearance one final time, content with the results. *Time to rock this look*, she told the reflection staring back from the mirror, stepped from the dressing room.

Presley froze in the hallway. *What was that?* Again heard the unusual thumping sounds, a chill suddenly tingling down her spine. Now the noise sounded like *moaning*. She stood and listened, tried to locate the origin of the sound, spotted two closets down from the dressing room towards the rear of the building. The noise coming from that direction. Presley swallowed, curiosity aroused, silently made her way to the first closet. Pressed an ear against the door, heard nothing. Cautiously stepped up to the second door, leaned against it and listened. Heard movement inside, and a muffled whimpering a sound only possible from a human being.

Someone was inside the closet.

Instead of turning and running as fast as her feet could carry her from the studio to safety, as instinct should've dictated in the presence of apparent danger, Presley Harding reached for the doorknob, turned it, swinging the door open to see what lay inside. Presley gasped at the disturbing sight greeting her. "Oh my God!" Hand covering her mouth at the discovery of the young woman sitting on the floor. About the same age as Presley with honey blonde hair, wearing a white sweater dress and black boots. What stunned Presley was her body wrapped in what seemed hundreds of feet of rope, securing tightly her limbs, cloth bound over her eyes and between her lips. The girl whined through the gag at the sound of Presley's voice, straining against the ropes holding her, the unintelligible groans Presley able to decipher as a plea for help.

"Don't worry, I'll get you loose!" Presley crouched down, hands fumbling for the knots, free the unknown victim from her bondage. Her mind spun as if a top skidding on the floor, suddenly confused, absolutely frightened. What was going on? Who was this girl? Why was she hidden in the closet bound, gagged and blindfolded? If Marcus Evans did this to her, then who was Marcus Evans? Why had he done this to the girl? Did he plan an identical fate for Presley as well? Was this modeling job nothing but a trap to subdue her and do…?

The possibilities, every one of them bad and dancing in her head with the maniacal glee of skeletons rising to life in a graveyard on Halloween night, terrified Presley Harding, understood now her trusting nature placed her in a dangerous situation, the unknown peril threatening her life. *What am I doing?* Presley panicked, realized her well-meaning but misguided actions, trying to free the girl, the wrong thing to do, made a horrendous decision to insure continued survival. *I have to get out of here!* She started to stand, ready to flee the studio, get help for the hostage helpless at her feet. She heard the creak of a footfall against the wooden floor behind her, horror sweeping her as comprehension of her predicament arrived a moment too late to save her. A thick, muscular arm grabbed Presley, pinning her arms to her sides, lifting the tiny body from the floor, legs kicking at the air. Before a scream for help escaped her lips a massive hand clamped down over her mouth, stifling her cry. She twisted her head, eyes widening seeing not the face of Marcus Evans but of another man, a giant in size, bald with a scraggly goatee, offering a callous, intimidating grin. Powerful arms squeezed her torso, forcing oxygen from her lungs; left sucking air through her nose, the snorting made Presley sound like a wild animal trapped in snare.

"Find something, Presley?" She heard the voice of Marcus Evans, stepping out from behind the monstrous man holding her firmly with no chance for escape, nodding down at the bound girl squirming in the closet. The friendly glow in his eyes had vanished, replaced by something menacing and far more malevolent. Presley trembled in fear, whimpered, understood how foolish she'd been to trust a man she only met the night before, allowing whimsical dreams to cloud her judgment, for a single immature mistake perhaps paying with her life. "You know what they say about curiosity and cats?" Cowle told her. "Not good for the life expectancy of the feline."

Marcus produced a syringe containing a clear liquid. "I think you need to relax," his polite, soothing tone only adding to her fear. "Time for a brief nap, little Presley," Marcus cooed soothingly. Presley struggled furiously in the grip of her immense captor, frightened cries silenced by the hand pressed over her mouth, as he approached. "Keep a hold on her," Marcus ordered the henchman restraining the writhing young woman.

"She's not going anywhere," the man noted coldly, "aren't you now, little angel?" Presley mewled in distress; never able to muster the strength to break his grasp. *Please don't hurt me! Please let me go!* Presley's brown eyes, damp with panic, implored of her captors.

"This will only hurt for a moment," Marcus raised the syringe, Presley yelping in muffled anguish as the needle plunged deep into her arm. *I hate needles.* A breathtakingly warm, bewildering sensation flooded her body as he pressed down the plunger, injecting into her bloodstream whatever horrid substance filled the syringe.

"Pleasant dreams, Presley," Marcus whispered as the sedative took effect within seconds. *I don't want it to end like this! This can't happen to me!* Presley tried to resist, twisting and writhing against the forearm pressed against her midsection, but her efforts subsided quickly as the drug attacked her senses, limbs weakening, going lifeless and dead. She struggled to keep her eyes open, eyelids fluttering, fought against darkness nibbling away at the corners of her vision, a black haze encroaching further each time she closed her eyes. *No, don't pass out! Stay awake! Don't pass out!* Her frantic panting, coming in short snorts through flaring nostrils, slowed as her nervous system started to shut down. *I want to go home. I...want...to...go home.* Defenses finally overwhelmed by nothingness, eyelids flittering like the wings of a bird before closing one final time, slumped heavily in the arms of her captor.

"She's done," Sterner told Marcus Cowle, the injection of sedative taking moments to incapacitate Presley as opposed to the minutes if ingested through the tampered water bottle.

Cowle grinned. "Take her in the other room. Package her up nice and tight." He checked the clothes his final parcel wore. "Too bad you were so inquisitive, Presley. Would've liked to have gotten a few pictures of you in that outfit." Shrugged, still had the opportunity, though not the type of images Presley might've expected.

Sterner lugged the motionless body to the studio. "You almost got some help," Marcus Cowle taunted the bound form of Gabriella Taylor, moaning in defeat at a drama she couldn't see but heard as the chance for freedom, possibly her last, dashed against the shoals of despair. "But almost doesn't count." Cowle closed the door. "Don't worry. We'll be on our way soon." Gabriella whined as she heard the door shut, locked inside her prison once more. She feared where her captor wished to take her, Isabella and this unknown girl and, once they arrived there, what he intended for them.

Chapter 22

The throbbing in Presley Harding's head matched the constant vibration rumbling through her body, a muddled mind attempting to comprehend through a dissipating fog the connection between the differing sensations. The sudden jolt, and sharp pain in her right shoulder, immediately shocked her to awareness. Presley opened her eyes and saw nothing. *What's going on?* Felt something soft pressed firmly against her eyes, sealed in a shroud of darkness.

Then she remembered. *The girl tied up in the closet...*

Presley swallowed, realized something wedged deep behind her teeth, tightness at the corners of her mouth, pulling at her lips to hold the padding in place. Out of reflex she screamed, the action producing nothing but a low, pitiful moan. She tried to move, fear injecting a potent dose of adrenaline into already aching muscles, willing arms to reach up, hands to tear away from her face the blindfold and gag. Found her body immobile, imprisoned by ropes strictly bound about her, slumped in despair at the implication of the hopeless situation. *Oh God, I've been kidnapped!* Presley whimpered, understood the vibration from an engine, cold metal brushing her skin. In the back of a van transported to an unknown destination she didn't want to reach and an uncertain fate she didn't wish to experience. Presley shuddered, remembered overhearing a conversation between her parents about the lagging economy with so many out of work and struggling to survive, strident protests of class-warfare directed against the wealthy earning their reward in the world of finance, expressing anxious trepidation radicals taking out their rage by targeting their only child, their precious Presley, for harm. Was she the powerless pawn in a battle between the classes? She heard the girl from the closet whimpering next to her, moved her legs over to nudge the body. Presley heard another voice, it too muffled and shrill with fright, startled by the added presence. *There are three of us? What do they want with us?* Presley resisted the surge of panic heightening the fear this predicament something far more terrible than a kidnapping for ransom or political motive.

"Enjoying the ride, ladies?" The voice of the man who grabbed her in the studio while Marcus Evans, if that was even his real name, injected her with the powerful drug. Muffled cries all he received in reply from his helpless passengers. "Sorry about the ride, complain to the city about the potholes."

I didn't tell anyone where I was going! No one knows where I am! Presley rested her head against the metal surface, chest aching with each painful breath, shuddering at the possibility her life might not last much longer, tried to keep from crying. *No one knows I'm in trouble!* Now Presley wished she'd told Riley Bradford of her plans. But she didn't and for that simple, selfish oversight, Presley realized she might pay the ultimate price with her young life.

Lang waited as the door to the loading bay rumbled upwards, the black Ford cargo van waiting to enter with Cowle's white Lexus idling behind. Once the door fully elevated the vehicles drove inside and parked, drivers stepping out. "We have the full shipment now?" Lang asked as Cowle and Sterner exited the vehicles.

"All packaged for storage until we hand them over to our generous client Tuesday morning." Cowle content with the accomplishment yet remained apprehensive with the delay in delivery. If this exchange like those in the past, the transfer of product to Rahim's people already, or about to, occur following the final abduction. This time, due to Sheik Rahim's impertinent insistence to receive his precious product in person, Cowle forced to hold on to the consignment for more than a day, Rahim's arrogance inviting disaster and a chance of unwanted discovery. The sooner the consignment out of his hands, and the millions in payment in his hands, the better.

"Go down without a hitch?" Lang asked.

"One of the first guests decided to wake up while Presley was in the dressing room," Cowle explained. "Presley's curiosity got the best of her. She received a very unpleasant surprise." And now shared the fate of Gabriella Taylor and Isabella DiBenedetto, the three bound, gagged and blindfolded in the back of the van, muted cries emanating from the cargo hold. "Any problems here?"

"Everything's fine," Lang reported. "I like playing babysitter," thought of the two women already bound and gagged in the cells, "I had the chance to mess with their heads."

"And they're...?" Cowle inquired.

"The way you like them," Lang smirked. "I know you'll have fun with them while we're off doing the dirty work dumping their cars," he jerked a thumb at the van and the helpless occupants within.

"Before you depart we need to establish ground rules for our new arrivals," Cowle stated plainly, motioning to the van.

"Showtime." Sterner joked; found he enjoyed this part of the job.

The three walked to the van, Cowle heaving back the sliding door, the rumble of the panel startling the captives inside, screaming through the gags, blindfolded heads swinging in the direction of the sudden sound. "End of the line, ladies," Cowle briskly informed his hostages. "I hope you enjoy your accommodations as much as you did the ride." No escape for the bound forms from hands lustily grabbing them, dragging the struggling bodies out of the van.

Sterner flung Gabriella Taylor over his shoulder, tied legs bucking. "She's a feisty one like little Emma."

Lang cupped the chin of Isabella DiBenedetto, examined the gagged and blindfolded face, listened to her pleading whimpers, checking other attributes. *What's not to like?* Tossed her body over his shoulder. "You have an eye for good stuff," he complimented his employer.

Cowle reached for Presley Harding, trying desperately to slide away, evade his grasp. "Our client doesn't pay us for poor quality," Cowle explained, "he wants only the best. That is what I," he corrected to give credit where due, "what we give him."

"I ain't got any complaint with what The Arab pays," Sterner tightened his hold on the resisting Gabriella, patted her rear. "Relax, you're not going anywhere."

"Come on, Presley," Cowle grabbed Presley by the shoulders, roughly hauling her out. Through the cloth in her mouth she screamed, felt her body lifted over Cowle's shoulder, fighting her captor the entire time, scared and bewildered by the circumstances of her abduction. "Time for you to join your new friends, you'll be together for a long time." Cowle motioned for his accomplices, and the bound forms they carried, to follow him, headed to the room Lang now jokingly dubbed 'The Welcome Center' to orient the newest captives. The freestanding lamps cast brilliant light on the center of the room, setting their hostages on the floor, forcing them to kneel, the burning pain on their kneecaps quickly unbearable.

"Please remain in that position, ladies," Cowle commanded his newest acquisitions, walking around the captives as they fearfully waited, exerting omnipotent control over his hapless guests. Observed their heads, blindfolds robbing them of precious awareness, swivel back and forth listening to his footsteps, only hearing left to make sense of the terrifying situation, chests heaving with each tortured breath. Sterner and Lang tugged balaclavas over their heads, joined Cowle behind the line of captives.

Cowle undid the blindfold around Presley's head as Lang and Sterner did the same with Gabriella and Isabella, let cloth strips drop to the floor. The blinding light stabbing at their eyes as if staring directly into a blinding sun disoriented their senses, blinking to focus as Cowle stepped in front of them. "I hope we had a pleasant trip, ladies?" He asked in a solicitous, yet mocking, tone. The three prisoners moaned sharing furtive, frightened glances between them and at the threatening presence of the masked apprentices looming over them. "I'll take that as a yes," Cowle smiled in delight. "By the way, and I'm sure you're wondering by now, the name's not Marcus Evans. It's Marcus Cowle." He paused. "I do hope you'll remember that where you're going."

The bound captives gazed at Cowle, anxious eyes wide over the gags silencing the protests. "Where are my manners?" He asked in cavalier fashion. 'Presley,' he nodded at the powerless Presley Harding, a whimper at the acknowledgement, "I think you already know Gabriella," he waved at the girl Presley encountered tied and hidden in the closet, "and this is her roommate Isabella." He stepped up to the dark-haired woman, dark brown eyes watering, tears trickling down her cheeks as Cowle stroked strands of shimmering raven hair. "Isabella convinced Gabriella she could be a model." He nodded at Gabriella, her body shaking. "Too bad," directed a cruel smile at Presley, "you all possess such foolish dreams. The three of you trusted me. Now you've learned trust is a thing quite easily broken." Cowle cleared his throat. "There are two others, Emma and Alexandra, whom you'll meet soon enough," the revelation shocked the helpless trio. There were more captives besides the three of them? The same questions burned in their collective thoughts. *What is going on here? What do they want with us?* The possible answers none of them found particularly comforting.

Cowle noted the stunned expressions. "I'm sure you're wondering why you're here," Cowle stepped back, behind his back placed his hands, studied trembling prisoners kneeling before him, condemned supplicants awaiting a sentence of impending doom. "The reason for your present condition," he motioned to the ropes imprisoning them, "I'll put it into terms you can understand. I am in business, a very profitable business. I deal with supply and demand. There is a demand from people with a great deal of money for pretty things like you to with as they please. It is my business to meet that demand. You, my fair damsels," he smiled crookedly at his prisoners, "happen to be the supply."

The statement had the devastating effect on his hostages Cowle intended, shattering the last sliver of hope they clutched at of surviving this ordeal. Terrified glances exchanged between the three: a wail of horror from Gabriella; the whimper of shocked disbelief from Presley, her body shaking uncontrollably; Isabella lowering her head, sobbing hysterically. "You are going to be sold to my most favored client, a man paying millions to make your acquaintance. He's arriving early Tuesday morning to take delivery and compensate me richly for my services in acquiring you to fulfill his particular...pleasures. You'll have a very long trip ahead of you."

"Until that time you will be our guests." Cowle saw Isabella start to sag, resting back on her legs, nodded at Sterner who violently jerked the girl back up on her knees, a startled scream forced past the gag. "Don't worry, you won't be inconvenienced like this the entire time," Cowle acknowledged, smiling, "you'll have time to rest and eat, take care of yourselves, clean up, change clothes." Cowle paced before the line of bound women, thrilling in the power held over them, followed by the wide and petrified stares of his captive audience. *Three damsels in distress,* the image before him enthralling, a fixture in literature since Andromeda chained to the rock as a sacrifice for the Kraken. "There's one simple rule I'll impose during your stay." He stopped, glared intently at his prisoners. "I don't want any of you doing something stupid. If you're wondering what I mean, I don't want you attempting something unadvisable like trying to escape or fighting back against I or my associates here. Be foolish to commit such a transgression and the punishment will be severe. My assistants here," he waved to Sterner and Lang, "are adept at making naughty, disobedient girls suffer for their sins." The captives glanced back at the menacing thugs, shuddering at what violence the pair capable of inflicting. Cowle studied faces frozen with fear, pleased by the reaction, reveled in their horror. "Do you understand?"

The captives remained motionless until Cowle prompted once more. "You do understand?" At this his prisoners meekly nodded in capitulation. "Good, I'm pleased to see we're in agreement. My associates will take you to your accommodations. See you're settled in for the evening." Cowle nodded to his apprentices, Sterner picked Isabella up from the floor as Lang dragged Gabriella to her feet, carrying the struggling women, muted screams echoing through the empty factory, from the room, leaving Cowle and Presley alone.

"Just you and me now, little one." Presley stared up at Cowle, brown eyes disbelieving of the fate revealed, exhaling in hitching spurts, whimpering as he approached, tilting his head to examine the precious prize. Presley closed her eyes, shuddered as he caressed the caramel brown hair, wrists twisting against bonds securing them behind her back. Cowle knew a singular thought raced through the mind of the unfortunate girl. *Please don't hurt me. Please don't hurt me.* The fear she exuded an intoxicating narcotic, Cowle achieving an exhilarating high no other drug able to produce, absorbing as a sponge the terror of the frightened girl. *Yes, I do like them scared, very scared.*

Cowle bent over, whispered in her ear, breath hot on her alabaster skin. "Don't you regret using that fake ID now?" Presley's petite body wracked with uncontrollable shaking, sobbing, unable to rectify the foolish mistake placing her in mortal peril, never to see her home and family. Cowle wrapped his arms around her waist, lifting her bound form over his shoulder, a feeble whine of protest in response. Carried her from the orientation room, down the hall past four rooms where Sterner and Lang terrorized and harassed her fellow captives. Cowle walked into the next empty room, unceremoniously dumped Presley on the mattress. On instinct Presley curled up into a tight ball, knees pulled up against her chest as if the position afforded some miniscule measure of protection from her cruel captor. Tears trickled down her cheeks as Cowle crouched beside her.

Don't touch me, Presley implored. *Please don't touch me.* Cowle ignored the plea

"My associates will see to your car," Cowle said, stroking her hair. "Move it where they won't find it for days. By then you'll be off to your new home and I'll be enjoying the money from your sale." Cowle touched her cheek; Presley tried pulling away, bonds preventing anything but the barest movement. "You're an enchanting young girl, Presley. You're very beautiful, would've made a lovely model. A shame that'll never happen. But I'm confident my client will very much appreciate your company." Presley cried a plaintive wail, feared the appreciation Cowle meant.

Cowle stood up, walked away, called over his shoulder. "I'll be back to check on you, spend some time together. I still have photos to take of you. I do like that outfit." Cowle departed, left Presley crying softly, tormented by muffled screams and pleading from the other prisoners, enduring hellish torture, experiencing a shared agony. She wished to be anywhere, back at her room on the campus of Great

Northern University or home with her parents in Manhattan, instead of lying on a mattress, bound and gagged, inside a barren room of cinder block walls with stale, dusty air infiltrating her nostrils and assailing her lungs, a helpless victim awaiting sale to an unknown entity intending unspeakable acts upon her. Yet safety in the form of Great Northern University, or her home in New York, never as distant as they now seemed.

"Where did you dump the cars?" Marcus Cowle inquired upon his apprentices' return to the abandoned factory hours later.

"The Nissan is down by the Chicago River, around Pilsen," Sterner told him. "We were gentle with the Lexus, not a bad ride for a cute little chick like Presley. Left it down on the lakefront, parking lot by the Shedd Aquarium. Might make the police think she jumped in the lake, offed herself."

"Good." Cowle satisfied with their efforts, each abandoned car a dot and the police forced to spend valuable time connecting each far-off point to form a coherent picture. *By the time they do our fair damsels will be on their way to the Middle East and we'll be heading for parts unknown all the richer.* At least that the plan, the delay in the exchange continued to trouble his thoughts, growing increasingly uncomfortable with the lengthy interval between the final acquisition and delivery. "Did you pick up dinner for our guests?"

"Why God created McDonald's drive-thru, they deserve a break today." Lang couldn't resist.

Cowle smirked. "You know women worry about their figures." The captive quintet soon having issues far more grim about which to be concerned.

"Spend quality time with our guests?" Sterner asked.

"That I did," Cowle acknowledged, lifting the camera in his hand with the evidence recorded on the memory chip. "They're not getting paid for this modeling." The photos his personal souvenirs of a successful hunt in the Second City. "Our guests have earned a respite from their current condition. Get them loose, make sure they're handcuffed and feed them." Cowle paused. "They still have a long night ahead of them." Not to mention an equally long day awaiting the arrival of Sheik Rahim to finally take ownership of his latest order of flesh.

Sterner and Lang headed off to the cells, balaclavas pulled down over their heads, to free the hostages, leaving fast-food meals with them. Cowle waited until his assistants finished the task, then slowly strode down the hallway past each room, doors left open to peer inside and check on his prized merchandise as they ate with the hard, measured gaze of a warden walking the cellblock at a maximum-security prison.

Emma Hayden glared at Cowle as he passed, turquoise blue eyes burning hot with hatred. Despite the arduous ordeal, a glimmer of resistance remained afire within her soul. *You're not going to last long.* Sheik Rahim crushing such stubbornness in swift fashion once he took possession of Emma, already assuming she would be the first to perish violently by his hand. Alexandra ate quietly; body slumped in defeat, not looking up at Cowle as he passed, resigned spirit already surrendering to her fate. Gabriella's hazel eyes locked on Cowle with the dazed stare of the shell-shocked as he stood in the open doorway watching her eat. The bag of food in Isabella's cell sat untouched beside the mattress, Isabella lying on her side crying, dark eyes vacant, curled up in a fetal position. She'd regret not eating later this night when Sterner and Lang again plied on her their brutal skills of restraint.

Presley Harding, the young woman of moneyed privilege, huddled in the corner, knees tucked up to her chest, cuffed hands listlessly holding her drink. She heard him walk up to the cell, gazed at Cowle with brown eyes red from anguished tears, a forlorn, sympathetic figure melting the soul of a cold-hearted man. *If I had a soul.* Yet Cowle sensed that she too, like Emma, not yet broken in spirit, an ember of defiance glowing deep inside. "My parents will pay you anything to let me go," Presley said, the only hostage brave, or foolish enough, to speak to him. "Whatever you want, they'll pay it."

Cowle cocked his head in surprise. "I don't think you understood what I told you." He shook his head at the impetuous girl as he entered. "I'm receiving quite a payout from my client for you and the others, millions for each of you. You're worth a great deal to me. Why would I want to give that up?"

Presley swallowed hard, eyes tearing up. "My father is one of the richest men on Wall Street. He'd pay anything to get me back. He'd give you more than anything you'll get from this buyer."

"So he'd pay a ransom for your return?" Cowle heard ragged desperation in her voice, bargaining for her freedom. Presley nodded at his reply. "And how would he transfer the money without raising the interest of the authorities? Wouldn't a transaction of such considerable size raise suspicions? Or wouldn't he go straight to the police, or the FBI, once he knew I had you?"

"He wouldn't tell anyone! He wouldn't say a word!" Presley insisted, gambling on her persuasion. "My parents would only want me to come home."

"And I'm supposed to believe that," Cowle snorted in disbelief. "What about your new friends? What happens to them?" Cowle waved a hand in the direction of the other cells, the four women sharing her terrible plight. "If I do decide to let you go the others still go off to their new owner." Cowle laughed, the sharp, piercing sound unnerving the girl. "That's quite selfish of you, thinking only of yourself, getting out of this mess you made while others suffer." Watched Presley cower as he took a step closer. "But isn't it always that way for spoiled bitches like you? Getting your way while others pay the price?"

"No! He'd pay the ransom for all of us!" Presley shook her head in denial, the statement bruising. Despite her parents' wealth she wasn't that kind of person. "He'd want all of us to be free!" She paused, gulped down a breath. "Please, don't do this to us."

"Even if I did agree to this…proposition," Cowle crouched before Presley, enjoyed the game she unknowingly initiated, a contest at which the girl outmatched, destined to lose. "You and the others know who I am, what I look like. You have information regarding how I operate, about my methods, details the authorities no doubt quite keen in learning. I work for an organization that treasures secrecy. They don't like their secrets to become public knowledge. Even if I had a change of heart, which is highly unlikely, and decided to act out of common decency to spare your lives, the organization I work for wouldn't look too kindly upon such a display of…humanity."

"Please…" Presley pleaded.

"I'm a businessman, just like your Daddy," Cowle taunted, cutting her off. "I'm in this to make money. How do you think Daddy has been able to provide the good life for his little daughter? He runs a private equity fund. You do know what he does for a living, I don't think you're that clueless. Or are you? How many companies he's taken over? The people he's put out of work and out on the street without caring what happens to them? The towns and cities he's raped for profits by taking away the source of their livelihoods?" He continued to goad his captive, throwing her off balance. "We're both in business, we're in it for the money. Your Daddy and I are very much alike."

"No! Daddy isn't like that!" Presley shook her head wildly, trying not to believe him. "He's not like you! He's a good man! He cares for people! He would never…"

"I own you now," Cowle interrupted Presley, his grin cunningly malicious, froze solid her heart, understood then her hopeless gambit failed. "You're no longer Presley Harding. You're nothing but a piece of property with a hefty price tag on that sexy little body of yours, and there's someone willing to pay a price to do whatever he wishes with you." He leaned in close, cold gray eyes a drill bit boring through her spirit. "I can assure you what he does with you won't be the least bit pleasant."

Cowle leaned back on his heels, Presley lowering her head in submission, sobbing now. "I think you deserve what will happen. Being so careless to use a fake ID, falling for every word I told you about modeling. You're a trusting person, aren't you, Presley? You're what we call in my line of work 'easy pickings.' If I didn't take you, someone else with less honorable intentions would have their way with you," he mocked. "You're the dumb, gullible type, aren't you? You'd probably let some frat guy get you falling-down drunk at a party, then he'd take advantage of that cute tight ass. Let his frat buddies in on the fun." He smiled again, a deliciously wicked expression. "You're a virgin, aren't you, Presley?"

Presley raised her head, something inside snapping at the crude observation. "You fucking bastard!" Her eyes glared red with anger, the comment triggering anger exploding deep within. She didn't consider the consequences of what she did, forgetting from her earlier arrival to this hellhole his sinister admonition, acting out of shame and indignation for allowing herself to become his powerless victim. Bound hands holding the paper cup filled with liquid shot forward, propelling the fluid through the air, catching her captor unaware, drenching Cowle's face with the carbonated drink, a chunk of ice smacking him square in the right eye and causing him to flinch, provided her an opportunity. Presley dropped the cup, handcuffed hands clasped together as one, swinging at her tormentor's head, striking hard on his jaw. Cowle clutched at his face, the pain sharp and intense, falling backwards in a heap, swearing and cursing.

Presley saw her chance for freedom, springing to her feet, landing the toe of her boot into his side for good measure, running for the door and immediately bemoaning the choice of footwear made at the studio, high-heeled boots not proper footwear for fleeing from human traffickers. She stumbled, at the last second righted her balance to keep from falling face-first on the cement floor, throwing her body through the open doorway into the corridor. Her head swung about, trying to decide where to go, the large masked man coming towards her down the hall from the left, alerted by Cowle's angry shout, hurrying to his aid. Presley bolted to her right, fleeing her captors to escape this nightmare and find help for the other prisoners.

Sterner stopped at the cell to check Cowle, found him sitting on the floor rubbing his jaw, eyes burning with smoldering rage. "I'm all right," he said, angrily bit off each word. "Make sure the others are locked up. Then go after that little bitch. She won't be going anywhere." One of his prisoners always acted up, required the unique discipline delivered by his assistants, though Cowle never thought it to be Presley, assumed Emma the one to cross him and fight back. "That little bitch needs to learn a lesson." Sterner nodded, hurrying off to do as ordered, Presley Harding soon to regret angering Marcus Cowle, breaking his cardinal rule. *You're in for a long night, honey.*

Presley Harding ran for her life. In the matter she didn't have much choice.

Presley sprinted down the hall, turned left, ran down another corridor, turned left again, with each step fighting to maintain her balance in the high-heeled boots she wore. *Why did I have to wear these damn things!* A crazy thought now, but hadn't expected to be kidnapped when deciding to wear the stylish footwear. She turned yet another corner, now disoriented, a sinking sensation she already hopelessly lost in the labyrinth of corridors. *There has to be a door out of here!* Her hopes rose as she turned another corner, saw an exit at the end of the hallway. She ran up, placed bound hands on the handle and pressed down. The door locked, didn't budge. Presley stared at the door, disbelieving, again jammed down on the handle, trying without success to get the door to open, groaning in frustration. *Oh shit, this is so not happening to me!* Presley sniffed back tears, stepped away from the door; the freedom lying on the other side denied. *The loading bay*, an idea bloomed in her head, *where they brought us in here, maybe I can get out that way.* She turned around, retracing her steps. *If I knew where it was*, she thought worriedly, blindfolded when brought to this foreboding prison.

As she headed back the way she came, heading towards where she thought the loading bay might be in the vacant factory, Presley heard footsteps approaching, froze in place. *They're looking for me*. With each second the head start she gained rapidly evaporating. Outnumbered and hopelessly outmatched, three of them against her, bigger and stronger, Presley feeling like a video game character caught in a maze and chased by monsters. Presley feared the consequences if they caught her. *I don't want this to be game over*. She turned, fled from the footsteps growing closer, plunged deeper into the expanse of the abandoned complex, praying she could evade their pursuit, then work her way to the loading bay, slip out into the night and salvation. She passed through a room, noticed a large number of propane tanks resting on the floor. *What are these for?* The tanks, shiny and new, seemed out of place among the grimy, discarded machinery and barrels marked with bright orange and red stickers warning of explosive and flammable contents.

She moved deeper into the factory, corridors no longer illuminated, Presley ignoring the primordial fear of the dark, using her hands to feel along the wall, frantically searching for another door to escape this madness. She cursed the handcuffs binding her hands, couldn't fight back against her captors even if she wished. Her lungs already on fire, breathing heavily from exertion and fear, legs aching from her frenetic effort. Entered a cavernous, darkened space with a cathedral ceiling, pale moonlight seeping through the windows at the roofline cast an eerie, ghostly haze on the workspace cluttered with abandoned machinery long left dormant and rusting. *Where do I go? How do I get out of here!* Presley fought back terror ready to swallow her, tried staying calm, heard the heavy steps approaching.

They're getting closer! I have to do something! She crept through the unlit workspace, the floor littered with debris and garbage, realized her heels clicked against the cement floor, the footwear an audible beacon her pursuers homing in on to track her down. Her eyes darted about, searching for a hiding place. She squeezed her slender form into the cramped gap between two massive pieces of machinery that hadn't been operated in years, the space barely larger than her body. She edged back towards the wall, once there bending down, curling her body into a tight ball, darkness shrouding her location. *Never thought I'd be playing hide and seek for my life.* Flight no longer the immediate strategy, now resorting to concealment, waiting out her captors until they moved to another part of the empty factory in their search, giving her a chance to escape this terrible trap.

Presley peered through the gap, body trembling uncontrollably listening to the footsteps coming near where she crouched hidden. She stilled her breathing. *Stay calm, Presley, don't panic! Let them go away! Don't let them find you!* Through a space underneath the machinery, she spied a pair of black combat boots and held her breath, staring at the boots as they moved closer, then stopped by the very machine she huddled behind. She peeked through the gap, saw the larger of Cowle's two assistants, the one who accosted her at the studio, stand there for a moment, masked head moving about searching for her. *He's knows I'm near!* For a brief second Presley thought of making a run for it, fought down the impulse, knew she'd never get far. Tightly closed her eyes, prayed for deliverance. *Please God, let him go away! Please, let him go away! I want to go home!*

The footsteps resumed, moving away from her hiding place, growing fainter until she no longer heard them. Presley quietly exhaled, lungs burning from holding her breath for so long, relieved for the briefest of moments, given another slim chance to slip away from her captors. She waited another minute to be sure the hunter had departed, stood up and silently eased out from between the machinery, shuffling her feet to make little noise as possible. She stepped into the workspace, eyes squinting through the darkness, seeking any sign of her pursuers. Presley saw nothing, silence filling her ears, and that scared her. *They couldn't have given up that easily*, Presley unnerved by the stillness. *They're still looking for me, but where are they?* She could no longer wait, had to find an elusive passage to freedom. Through the gloom spotted a corridor to her right, tiptoed towards the entrance, hoping in that direction lay a route out of this ordeal.

Presley never reached the destination, only aware of the presence of another when powerful arms locked tight around her waist, lifting her feet up from the floor. She screamed in shocked surprise, legs thrashing wildly, believing she was alone, the thug hunting her proceeding on with his search. She hadn't counted on the second apprentice silently trailing in his partner's wake, mirroring his movements, or the fact he donned a set of night vision goggles easily picking out the overmatched prey in the darkness once she emerged from behind the machine she hunkered down, waiting in the shadows until Presley made herself a vulnerable target.

"Leaving so soon, Presley?" Cowle stepped up to Presley, struggling fiercely against the grip of his second associate. "Seems you forgot that little rule I told you about on your arrival."

"Let me go, you fucking bastard!" Presley screamed at him, cursing, brown eyes flaring with hatred and terror, dreading the consequences now she'd been captured once more. "LET ME GO!"

"You're a naughty girl, Presley, very disobedient," Cowle cooed his disappointment. "Such a foul mouth too. You didn't listen to me, and that's not good for you." His hand shot out, wrapped around Presley's throat and she choked, the flow of air to her lungs disrupted. The fiery anger in her eyes replaced with fear, vociferous protests reduced to a gurgle, fighting for each wheezing breath, realized only seconds separated her from death. "We have methods of dealing with girls who break the rules. You need to be taught a lesson." Presley gasped, struggles weakening, lungs scorched from lack of oxygen, coughing as the palm of his hand pressed against her windpipe. Her vision clouded, waves of obsidian emptiness washing over her, plunging closer to drowning in a shadowy, lifeless void. "I could finish you right here," Cowle sighed, exasperated. "But I really don't wish to dispose of you. I'd have to go find a piece of merchandise to replace you. It'd be a shame to waste a fine piece of ass such as yours, Presley." He stared coldly at his prisoner. "Besides, I don't want to go through the hassle."

Cowle released his hold of Presley's throat and the girl slumped weakly in her captor's arms, sucking in air, sobbing hysterically, the attempted escape a massive failure, a foolish, insolent mistake for which Presley about to pay dearly. Cowle cupped her chin, forced her to look at him. What Presley saw reflected in those cold gray eyes, a ferocious desire to make her suffer and feel pain, was absolutely terrifying.

"It's going to be a very long night for you, Presley…"

Riley Bradford stifled a yawn, stepping out of the elevator onto the second floor of Cockrell Hall, checked her watch. Almost two, the late night of studying for a week of tests at the library turned into an early morning, only leaving when the library staff shooed Riley from her desk and the doors locked behind her. She rubbed her blue eyes, bloodshot and aching from reading, staring at the glowing screen of her laptop. The venti cup of Starbucks Pike Place coffee keeping her alert as she plodded through the notes and study materials with the single-minded focus of a soldier on a twenty-mile forced march, hoped the lingering effects from the caffeine didn't keep her too wide-eyed when she tried to fall asleep and be rested for her organic chemistry test that afternoon.

She wasn't surprised by the no-show of her roommate, Presley Harding, at the library. Did Presley even study? Riley didn't believe so. Perhaps a needed change in attitude emerging after she received the first failing grades to shock Presley, or more likely alarming parents footing the bill for her education at Great Northern, into putting more effort into her studies. Now the only serious effort she put forth using her fake ID to get into the bars and clubs in Chicago. *Maybe she decided to stay in the room and study*, Riley thought, ashamed how hard she was on her roommate. Presley a kind, if flighty, soul but they came from different backgrounds, realities worlds apart. Riley was raised in a blue-collar family where every expense scrutinized and pennies saved religiously while Presley brought up in the lap of luxury, having the best of everything and never knowing what it was to do without.

Riley reached her room, opened the door, switched on the light and found the room empty, her roommate nowhere to be seen. *Figures*, Riley shrugged her shoulders as if expecting the discovery, *she went into Chicago to go clubbing*. She sighed, exasperated. Was there a night Presley didn't go into Chicago? Riley eased her backpack to the floor by her desk, didn't bother removing the books. She undressed, slipped on sleepwear of t-shirt and shorts, climbing up into her loft and tugging the sheets underneath her chin. Fell fast asleep as soon as she closed her eyes, wondering when Presley might stumble into the room after another night of partying.

Chapter 23

At the sound of the alarm the empty and undisturbed bed of Presley Harding the first thing Riley Bradford noticed upon opening her eyes. *She didn't come home last night?* Riley wondered. *Or did she already wake up?* That prospect unlikely as Presley a habitual late riser. If Presley cavorting about Chicago that her business and nothing more, Riley faced her own issues, couldn't be concerned with her roommate's desire to fritter away her life and future in search of a good time. *Wherever she is, I hope she's having fun.*

Riley jumped down from the loft, she had an organic chemistry test to worry about.

*   *   *   *   *

"You're looking very business-like today," Amanda McKinnon commented as Samantha Grayson stood before the mirror, buttoning up the shimmering white silk blouse she slipped on, covering up the black floral print satin bra cupping her firm breasts.

"Aaron warned me I had to dress up for this," Samantha finished with the last button. She stepped into the slim black pencil skirt, sliding it to her waist, pulling up zipper on the side, the hem resting two inches above her knees.

"Pantyhose?" Amanda examined the black hosiery.

"Microfiber tights," Samantha tucked the blouse into the skirt, buckling a wide black leather belt around her slender waist. "Feels softer on the skin."

"How'd you do with your makeup?" Amanda asked, Samantha turned from the mirror. "Nicely done with the eye shadow." The muted metallic bronze highlighted Samantha's sparkling brown eyes. Not that Samantha, blessed with natural girl-next-door beauty Amanda found charming, needed any additional assistance but the subdued makeup accentuated the positives. "Bare Minerals?"

"Of course," Samantha replied, then thought. "You know, Tyler's seen me dressed up before."

"He's seen you dressed up for dances and formals," Amanda offered. "Those are times he's expecting you to look fantastic, like you spent hours getting ready. This is an everyday kind of sexy. You know guys have that fantasy of making out with the hot secretary or librarian."

Samantha laughed at Amanda's remark. "Or reporter. You think Tyler's no different?"

"Trust me, he's a guy, it's all that testosterone in their system," Amanda continued, "getting dressed up all professional-like with the skirt and heels gets them hot and bothered."

"You think I'll get Tyler all excited when I see him at breakfast?"

"I'd make a bet but it's not fair since I know I'd win," Amanda said. "I think he'll like what he sees of his pretty college journalist girlfriend."

"Ever turn Connor on with your professional work attire?" Samantha wondered.

Amanda giggled. "For an archeologist our workplace attire is blue jeans and t-shirt caked with dirt." Amanda leaned against the doorway. "You know what floats his boat, I turn him on wearing a pair of spandex running tights and a sports bra."

"Don't forget those shorts," Samantha reminded her of the tight-fitting garment hugging the curves of her friend's firm posterior.

"Those too," Amanda nodded in agreement. "And my yoga pants."

"I want your opinion," Samantha reached into her closet, came out with a pair of black leather high-heel open-toe pumps and a pair of knee-high black leather boots. "What do I go with today, heels or boots?"

"Go with the heels," Amanda told her. "Too warm for boots. If it were October or November the boots would be perfect. Either way your feet will be aching by the end of the day."

"That bad?" Samantha asked as she slipped on the heels, added three inches to her height.

"High heels do horrible things to your arches and Achilles tendons, play havoc with the plantar fascia not to mention your calf muscles. High-heels are the footwear that keep podiatrists in business. That's why I wear flats unless I absolutely have to," Amanda explained as Samantha slipped on a black jacket. "Of course high heels cause the calf muscles to look firm and compact and that drives men crazy. That's why they want to see us in high heels."

"Let me see! Let me see!" Lauryn Callahan shouted gleefully bolting into the room, returning from an early breakfast at Lakeside with Ashleigh Morgan. Samantha spun about on her toes, arms spread out to give her returning friends a full view of her ensemble.

"Girlfriend, you do look like Lois Lane," Ashleigh whistled. "You're going to need some Kryptonite to hold Superman off," that Superman would be Tyler, "when he gets a look at you."

"You look fantastic," Lauryn admired Samantha's appearance. Samantha draped a gold necklace around her neck; the Irish claddagh, a symbol of interlocking hands imposed over a heart, hanging from the chain, the necklace a treasured Christmas gift from Tyler sealing their shared devotion. Golden hoop earrings and a ring with an amethyst stone once the cherished possession of a great-grandmother the only other jewelry she wore. "You'll belong with those big-time newspaper and television reporters."

Samantha hugged Lauryn. "Thanks for the compliment." She checked the contents in her Timbuk2 shoulder bag, made sure she had the press credentials, then slung it over her shoulder.

"So the reservations at Toscana for my victory dinner are at seven," Amanda reminded Samantha. "What time do we swing by *The Daily Northern* office to pick you up?"

"Does five sound good?" Samantha suggested. "Gives us time to get there if traffic is bad."

"I think that'll work," Ashleigh nodded in agreement.

Lauryn nodded. "I'm looking forward to this."

"Our Girls' Night Out," Amanda said proudly, "and all because I ran faster than everyone else."

Samantha checked her watch. "I have to meet Tyler for breakfast, then head to Cockrell Auditorium." She hugged her friends, a bright smile on her face. "Have to show Tyler he's in love with a professional journalist." She left the suite, expectantly anticipating the reaction of Tyler McManaway when he saw his girlfriend all dressed up to head to work.

Marcus Cowle gave his watch a perfunctory check, glanced at his apprentices as they strode down the corridor of the abandoned factory. "I believe it's time to check on Presley." He stated flatly. "See if she's finally learned what happens to naughty girls who break the rules in my establishment?"

"If she hasn't figured that out by now," Sterner tugged the balaclava down over his head, Lang did the same as they reached the vault with the headstrong freshman from Great Northern University left isolated inside. "She got a taste of our past work experience with enhanced interrogation methods." Periodically through the long night Sterner and Lang checked on the helpless girl, no pattern to their visits, keeping her psyche off-kilter, changing the torturous positions of her captivity to pulverize her stubborn resistance into rubble, terrorizing the stubborn hostage with a disturbing combination of their menacing presence, threatened torture and brutal bondage.

"How long has she been in this latest position?" Cowle inquired.

"About thirty minutes," Lang said. "I think she'll be a good little girl after this."

"I want to make sure." The vault protected by a heavy steel door, Sterner lifted the latch, with a grunt taxing his ropy muscles heaving open the door. From the darkness Cowle heard a pitiful whine for mercy, a sound beautiful to his ears like the melodic call of a songbird at dawn, pushed the switch and light flooded the room.

Presley Harding stood in the center of the room; her wrists and elbows bound and pulled up behind her, bonds about her wrists attached to a hook at the end of a chain. The chain passed up through a pulley in the ceiling, leading down to a crank on the wall. Her ankles and knees bound, forced to stand on her toes with all her weight supported by shoulders almost yanked from their sockets. She lifted her head, tears streaming down her cheeks in rivulets, chest heaving in fear, brown eyes glazed with hopeless anguish, a pathetic moan escaping from behind the large red ball-gag strapped in her small mouth to silence her cries, creating a throbbing, excruciating pain throughout her jaw. *Please, let me down*, Presley cried past the gag, a trickle of drool dribbling from the corner of her mouth, pleas imploring for a measure of sympathy. *Please, let me down...this hurts.*

Cowle walked up to her. "Have we learned our lesson now, Presley?" He placed a hand on the quivering cheek, wasn't ready to release his captive. "Have we learned to follow the rules?" Presley nodded frantically, agreeing to anything Cowle said to end the tortuous suffering from the endless night of pain. Cowle sighed, removed his hand, striding over to the crank. "Have you learned you're nothing but a piece of merchandise? I think you'll be a good girl for the remainder of your stay. Thing is, I'm not quite convinced yet." Presley knew what Cowle intended, eyes imploring for mercy, wildly shaking her head, muffled protests from her gagged mouth Cowle found easy to ignore.

"I want you to know you don't screw with me," Cowle scolded his prisoner, turning the crank. "I want my other guests to know that as well." Presley screamed as her arms jerked higher towards the ceiling, toes barely brushing the floor as her petite body suspended, a searing torment rippling through every muscle, shoulders on the verge of dislocation. Pathetic cries echoed through the corridors of the abandoned edifice, Cowle sure the other hostages heard every ounce of distress Presley Harding experienced to reiterate the message, if they had a problem understanding in the first place, resistance indeed futile.

"My associates and I can do very vile and despicable things to break this habit of being so uncooperative. We could have our way with you, make you hurt while we're having our fun. You'd be in no position to stop us." Presley cried out at the statement, understood the meaning. "But we don't want to spoil you for our client, I want you to remain as pure as snow, allow him the honor of taking away your chastity." Cowle studied his watch; let the seconds tick by as Presley shrieked with animalistic fury, praying fervently for the torture to end, body wracked with excruciating pain and uncontrollable sobs. Every muscle trembled, rocked by painful spasms, left her shaking helplessly as she hung like a side of beef in the center of the room. She raised her head to Sterner and Lang standing impassively off to the side, only their intimidating eyes observing her through the opening of their masks; from them she'd receive no pity or comfort. The pain becoming too unbearable, absolute and unending agony to keep her head up, let it drop towards the floor, caramel brown hair dropping down, obscuring her face.

"Will you be a good girl now, Presley?" Cowle asked softly after two minutes passed. Her head moved a fraction, a nod of total capitulation, a whimper of complete surrender. "I'm so glad we've finally come to this understanding." Cowle released the latch on the crank, lowering Presley's arms, the exhausted victim slumping weakly into Lang's grasp, eased to the floor as he unhooked the chain from her tied wrists.

"Cut her loose and put her with the others," Cowle ordered, exhibiting not a shred of remorse for the suffering girl. "She's earned a break." Lang undid the buckle of the leather strap, slipped the red ball slick with saliva from her mouth, Presley gasping greedily for air between moans as Sterner untied her limbs. The pair lifted her into a sitting position; Sterner taking a pair of handcuffs to lock her hands in front of her, hauled the unresisting girl to her feet. Presley sagged in their grip, a tiny whimper of anguish as legs wobbling like gelatin in a bowl gave out underneath her. Sterner and Lang clutched

168

Presley under the arms, dragging her to the cell where the other hostages left to dine on a lukewarm fast-food breakfast.

The sound of the door being unlocked and swung open startled the remaining captives, sitting in morose silence listening to heartrending screams of torture from down the hall. "You have a guest for breakfast," Cowle announced grandly, Sterner and Lang heaved the inert Presley inside, dumping her on the mattress where the hostages huddled.

"You bastards! What did you do to her!" Emma Hayden demanded, companions crowding around the prostrate Presley to form a protective barrier between the sobbing girl balled up on the mattress and their merciless captors.

Cowle cocked his head, surprised by the outburst. "If you don't watch that mouth, Emma, you'll find out exactly what we did to her. I don't think you'll find it pleasurable either." Emma backed down, edged towards the other captives. "Let me reassure you we didn't sample the merchandise," they cringed at his implication, "my client wouldn't approve of such actions on my part. I needed to ensure Presley understood the rules of this establishment through persuasive reinforcement." Alexandra Cole helped Presley sit up, Gabriella Taylor handing her a plastic cup of orange juice. With her assistance Presley wrapped shaking hands around the container, guided the glass to trembling lips and drank, the cool liquid soothing a throat raw from muffled screams of pain during the endless night of suffering.

"Do we understand the rules now, ladies?" Cowle asked his prisoners. There were no nods, not a word of reply, only silent, scared expressions in answer. "I will take that as a yes." Cowle and his associates backed out of the cell. "Enjoy your breakfast," he told them while shutting the door.

Alexandra stroked Presley's hair as Gabriella leaned over, gently rubbed the hands of the young woman, petite body wracked by tremors of terror. "Presley? It'll be all right, they're gone," Gabriella comforted the girl who the day before tried to save her, only to be joined together in captivity, offered a heartfelt confession. "I'm sorry I got you into this."

"It's my own fault." Presley sniffed back tears, cursing her own careless innocence, duped by Cowle's ruse. "It was going to happen anyway." *I let it happen, and nobody knows I'm here.*

"They're gone for now," Isabella DiBenedetto pulled her arms close, body shuddering not from cold but from an overwhelming fear. "But they'll be back."

"It's not all right," Emma snarled, wanting so desperately to fight back, yet in the cowering Presley saw the results for any show of resistance. *You're a braver person than I am, Presley.* "Not for any of us." Emma frustrated they couldn't fight back, totally at his mercy, the advantage Marcus Cowle held over them and willing to exploit if they contemplated a challenge to his authority.

"We're helpless," Emma said finally, "and that bastard knows it."

"Usually don't see you around these parts this time of the morning."

Tyler McManaway heard a familiar voice as he stood in front of Lakeside Dining Pavilion waiting for Samantha Grayson to arrive for breakfast. "Hey Mitts," he greeted Sean Mittersley. Like Tyler enrolled in the computer engineering program and one of Connor Aanonsen's teammates on the hockey team, a sharp-shooting center from Boston with a skating style smooth as quicksilver. Tyler typically grabbed his breakfast to go, sneaking a bite to eat between conditioning sessions at McIllhenny and his first class. "Samantha and I are having breakfast this morning."

"You don't do breakfast together," Sean replied, steel-gray eyes questioning, the same height as Tyler though broader in the shoulders to check opponents into the boards and sturdier in the thighs to power his frame down the ice with the unbridled acceleration of a locomotive on an express run. "You're more a lunchtime couple."

"Today we do breakfast," Tyler said. "She's covering that speech by Senator Fielding at Cockrell Auditorium this morning." Then he remembered. "Isn't this speech in honor of one of your relatives?"

"The Milton J. Mittersley School of Government and International Relations Speech on American Public Policy," Sean recited, his great great uncle a leading political scientist during the early part of the last century. "The university named a building after him too." Mittersley Hall housed the aforementioned discipline of study.

"You going to check it out?" Tyler asked.

"Because it's named in honor of a relative I never knew?" Sean snorted. "My politics don't jibe with the speaker they have this year." He jerked a thumb in the direction of Cockrell Auditorium. "I did pass by on my way here. The demonstrators are out in force."

"Hope there isn't any trouble," Tyler concerned for Samantha if the protests got out of hand.

Sean grinned not for Tyler but at the slender brunette walking past catching his eye, she smiled back, blushing at the attention from the varsity hockey star who resembled a young Harrison Ford; his dashing looks earned from his teammates the nickname 'Han Solo.' "With all the police and campus security they have outside the building I don't think you have anything to worry about."

"Good," Tyler satisfied with the observation, "don't want anything to happen to Samantha."

Sean glanced over Tyler's shoulder. *You're getting a special prize with your breakfast cereal today.* "Speaking of which," he motioned Tyler to turn around.

Tyler turned, saw Samantha and couldn't avert his eyes as she approached, knew right then he was staring. "Hey Tyler, Sean," Samantha wrapped her arms around Tyler's shoulders, kissed him. "Like the outfit?"

"You look great, Samantha," Sean complimented, jerked a thumb at Lakeside. "I'm going in to eat. Don't want to spoil things hanging around too long."

As Sean departed Tyler stepped back from Samantha, holding her hands, eyes trailing over her attire: the skirt and black hose, white silk blouse and black jacket, the high heels. *Yeah, it's the heels that do it, definitely the heels.* "So I get to look forward to this every day when you get a job in the media?" Tyler continued gazing wide-eyed at his girlfriend.

"You'll have a lot to look forward to," Samantha told him, the glistening smile bright as always.

Tyler pulled her close, the scent of lilac in her auburn hair and rose clinging to her skin infiltrated his nostrils, able to smell those fragrances all day and never tire of the intoxicating scents. "God, you're absolutely gorgeous," he whispered into her ear.

Samantha gave Tyler a sly glance, an eyebrow raised. "Are you undressing me with your eyes?"

Tyler frowned, blushing. "Is it that obvious?"

"Yes it is," Samantha playfully scolded him. "By the way, if you're wondering," she lowered her voice, "black floral print bra and panties."

Tyler blushed even more, cleared his throat. "You...didn't have to tell me that," Tyler stammered, surprised by her candor.

Samantha kissed him, sensed the passion burning inside. "Don't want to leave anything to your imagination." She sighed. "We have to get rolling. I have to be at Cockrell Auditorium in thirty minutes."

"That's enough time for a nice breakfast together." They walked into Lakeside, holding hands, finding pleasure in the other's company. "What about tonight? Still up for something after your night with the girls and finishing work at the paper?"

Samantha tilted her head. "You think I'm letting this outfit go to waste?" Samantha stroked his cheek. "How about the Rathskeller?" That was the student-run coffeehouse with an intimate candle-lit ambiance. "I'll send you a text when I'm at the office, I'll have an idea how long I'll be."

"Sounds like a plan," Tyler agreed, then thought. "Why don't you text me after you're done with dinner and on the way back to campus so I have time to get ready?"

"I can do that, maybe I'll send you a play-by-play of our dinner conversation too," Samantha said as the pair entered Lakeside for breakfast together. She knew she'd send him a text at some point during the day. "I need to eat something. This journalist has a long day ahead of her."

Where is Presley? Riley Bradford entered the room she shared with Presley Harding; found it exactly the way she left it earlier. Presley not asleep in her loft, no indication she returned to the room and headed to class while Riley at breakfast. Riley poked her head out into the hall, spotted Caitlin Hampton leaving her room, a fellow freshman from England who played on the woman's soccer team. "Hey Duchess Kate," someone on the floor bestowed the nickname, fitting considering her country of origin, "have you seen Presley this morning?"

"I haven't seen her since yesterday morning," the dark-haired, brown-eyed young woman who closely resembled the royal she'd been dubbed for, answered in her proper British accent.

"I heard you scored the tying goal yesterday, congratulations," Riley added politely when receiving her answer, even if it didn't help resolve the issue. "Where are you going?"

"Thank you," Caitlin replied. "I'm off to calculus," she said, nothing putting a damper on soaring spirits from the day before. Scoring against Michigan State and learning her Uncle Nathanial, an inspector at Scotland Yard, in Chicago for the next several months assisting with preparations for the global summits Chicago slated to host in the coming spring, his appearance at the game a surprise. "If we're dealing with imaginary numbers shouldn't we be allowed to make them up?" She proposed as she walked away.

"Have fun," Riley said, though knew calculus not considered fun by many, stepped back inside her room and closed the door. *Where is she?* Had Presley gone out, hooked up with someone she met at a club and spent the night somewhere? Riley pulled out her phone, fingers dancing on the keypad. *Where are u? Let me know.* She walked to Presley's closet, noticed immediately her overnight bag missing, spotting hangers empty of clothes, thought the absence peculiar. *Maybe she did go off with someone she met at a club*, Riley wondered. Presley might go out every night, but she at least exhibited the common courtesy of letting Riley know where she was going. *If she did go out, why didn't she tell me where she was going this time?* A curious, yet uncertain doubt blossomed inside Riley as she dialed Presley's cell phone. She checked the time, had to head to her first class. The call went directly into voicemail. *Hey, this is Presley. Leave a message and I'll get right back to you...*

"Hey Presley, its Riley," she spoke while leaving the room, tried not sounding too worried. "Saw you haven't been back to the room today. Want to know you're okay. Give me a call when you get this, okay?" Perhaps Presley considerate enough to realize, from the tone of Riley's voice on the message, her concern and sending a reply with her whereabouts before Riley returned from her first class of the morning.

Even with the press credentials hanging from the lanyard around her neck providing entrée and a front row seat to a policy speech brimming with gravitas by a potential presidential contender Samantha Grayson felt out of place and overwhelmed by her surroundings within Cockrell Auditorium. The business attire helped her blend in with the journalists and television reporters milling about, yet did little to assuage the sensation she still a reporter for a college newspaper and a small fish swimming in a very big pond.

She already ran a seething gauntlet of demonstrators outside of the building, activists from both sides of the political spectrum using the occasion to disseminate their views and stridently express either their disapproval or support of the invited speaker and the values he stood for. From each vociferous faction she gathered quotes to use in her stories, those she interviewed believing in the righteous certitude of their cause, heaping scorn for those in opposition of their viewpoint, at times resorting to schoolyard name-calling to make their opinion known. *This is why we don't talk politics at lunch.* The sidewalk separating the two blocs-left and right-served as a symbolic microcosm of the chasm splitting neatly in two the spectrum of politics in America, a gap growing seemingly wider with each election cycle and the infusion of billions of dollars from corporate benefactors seeking to influence the process and ensure victory for their chosen cause. Samantha wondered if this gulf between left and right, liberal and conservative, might ever be bridged for the good of the country or if the widening breach eventually ripped apart the fabric of a country founded in the name of liberty.

She glanced at the front of the auditorium; saw Bryce Fielding with his family, caught a close-up glimpse of Senator Benton Fielding of Colorado as he spoke with members of the Board of Trustees. A tall man with robust features and dark hair, a touch of stately gray flecking the temples, a photogenic image well suited for a possible presidential candidate, Fielding reminded Samantha of her own father but the similarity ended there, their politics couldn't be more diametrically opposed. Bryce spotted Samantha, made no acknowledgement of her presence, on his face a blank reaction as they made brief eye contact, Samantha wondering if his ego still bruised from Natalie compelling his apology at the DiLaurenzo tailgater for the brusque comments following the pep rally.

"Miss Grayson," a voice spoke from behind her, "you look very nice this morning."

Samantha turned to face William Wilson Welland, President of Great Northern University, in the position for six months now following his appointment to the post, a direct result of Samantha's investigation of his predecessor's malfeasance the previous year, uncovering the scandal that brought crashing down his tenure. Serving as Provost before replacing the disgraced Richard C. Russell, Welland was tall in stature with a Lincolnesque jaw and high cheekbones, his wavy hair a dark russet red. His hazel eyes warmly appraised the student journalist. Samantha had interviewed him in the course of other assignments since his elevation to the presidency, found him a fair administrator with an open-door policy towards the student body. A marked difference from the cold, manipulative man, secretive to the very end, he replaced. "Thank you very much," Samantha smiled graciously.

"So Aaron sent his best reporter for this one," Welland observed, returned the smile. His voice had an easy, congenial tone. "Don't think he could've chosen any better."

Samantha blushed. "I don't know if I'm the best reporter at *The Daily Northern*."

"I see your byline on the front page every day," Welland pointed out. "I think that counts for something."

"That means I enjoying writing and don't mind doing the work," Samantha replied. "Can I get your reaction after the speech?"

"I'd be more than welcome," Welland nodded with a hospitable smile.

"You wouldn't happen to know if Senator Fielding is going to..." Samantha started to ask regarding the political aspirations of the distinguished speaker.

"Can't help you there," Welland shook his head. "I'm as in the dark as everybody else is."

Samantha gazed about the auditorium, spotted Caleb McIllhenny near the stage. Unlike Bryce Fielding he nodded pleasantly when seeing her. McIllhenny moved towards the Cockrell brothers, Thomas and Edward, owners of Cockrell Enterprises, the multinational corporate monolith and like McIllhenny prominent benefactors to Great Northern. "Caleb McIllhenny is giving me his reaction."

"He's a good man, loves Great Northern," Welland leaned over, whispered. "I wouldn't bother with the Cockrell brothers," he cautioned. "I don't think they'd be willing to speak with you."

"I'll take that under advisement." Samantha understood the guidance. President Russell the chosen man of the Cockrell brothers at Great Northern and through him, along with their positions on the Board of Trustees, the siblings exercised a lofty degree of undue influence over university policies. Samantha heard through sources in the administration the powerful pair held no love for either her or *The Daily Northern* in the wake of her investigative reporting leading to Russell's dismissal. That a lowly freshman reporter uncovered the wrongdoing only further galled the brothers Cockrell.

"By the way, let Tyler know he had a great game Saturday," Welland told her, seemed everyone on campus knew Samantha Grayson and Tyler McManaway were an item.

Samantha smiled shyly. "I'll let him know."

"If you'll excuse me, Samantha," Welland said, "I have to speak with Senator Fielding since I'm the one introducing him. Find me after the speech, I'll give you my thoughts." The comments likely enlightening as Welland an unabashed liberal, proudly wearing those beliefs as a badge of honor.

"I appreciate it," Samantha watched President Welland head down the aisle to the front, shake hands with Senator Fielding, engaging in polite conversation with the politician and his family. Samantha resumed her way to a seat in the press section to the left of the stage. She glanced back to where Caleb McIllhenny stood with the Cockrell brothers, gathered around a man Samantha estimated in his mid-forties, about the same height as Tyler McManaway with tanned skin and handsome Arabic features, attired in a finely tailored dark suit. Samantha had no idea of the man's identity, yet assumed he held a position of importance given the hovering presence of two muscular men with no-nonsense countenances standing by his side, eyes appraising with wary attentiveness the crowd gathering in Cockrell Auditorium. Samantha knew bodyguards when she saw them.

"Your Excellency, welcome to Great Northern University," Thomas Cockrell held out a hand of greeting, welcoming Sheik Abdullah al-Aziz Rahim to the auditorium bearing the family name, "I hope you enjoy your time on the campus."

"I thank you for the gracious invitation to attend this speech." Rahim shook the extended hand, then of the other Cockrell brother, Edward, nodding cordially to the pair, the twin brothers both gray-haired and patrician, bodies and jowls grown soft from a life of immense wealth and the comforts offered by such largesse. "The school you graduated from is quite magnificent and the academic reputation of Great Northern University is well-known in my part of the world." Cockrell Enterprises engaged in several lucrative business ventures in his home country of Daharan, the reason for the brothers' fawning dotage and the offer to attend this occasion. The true reason for his acceptance had nothing to do with the business of Cockrell Enterprises or the speech by Senator Benton Fielding. Here to complete his business with Marcus Cowle, the representative of The Trading Society, in his possession retained five packages for Rahim to take with him on the trip back home.

"We appreciate your presence here today, Your Excellency," Edward Cockrell added. "I believe you'll find much of interest in Senator Fielding's speech. He is a powerful advocate for the alliance between our countries, especially at this time of heightened tensions with Iran." He leaned close, whispered. "He might well be the next President, a far better representative of our shared interests than the current occupant of the White House."

"Perhaps he will be." Rahim smiled, familiar with the vagaries of the American political system, how this politician enjoyed the support of wealthy, influential capitalists of conservative values loathing 'Madame President.' Though Rahim understood a presumed favorite one moment easily relegated to also-ran status in the blink of a twenty-four hour news cycle by an ill-spoken slip of the tongue. "He has yet to declare his intentions."

Thomas edged closer, lowered his voice. "That day might come soon enough."

"Your Excellency," Caleb McIllhenny stepped up, shook Rahim's hand, the handshake firm and polite. "Welcome to Great Northern. I hope you enjoy your time here."

"Caleb McIllhenny, it is good to see you," Rahim smiled and nodded, accepting the token of welcome. "I only wonder when your company will pursue the opportunities available in my country."

"McIllhenny Energy already has plenty of operations in that neck of the woods," Caleb replied evenly in his Texas drawl. "I don't want to stretch my resources too thin."

"If you decide otherwise," Rahim answered courteously, "my country will do whatever it can to make any venture a profitable success."

Caleb's answer diplomatic. "I'll take that under consideration." As McIllhenny replied, from the other side of the auditorium Sheik Rahim saw a flash of auburn hair in the crowd, a reminder from his past, then caught sight of a slender young woman in a dark skirt and jacket heading towards the stage. His breath stopped, dark eyes locked intently on the figure gliding effortlessly down the aisle. *It is her.* Rahim stared at the woman as she slipped into a front row seat, as if an ethereal spirit had arisen from the grave and took the human form it once possessed. An almost identical image of the woman-the hair, the face, the eyes-he ravaged and brutalized so many years ago. At that moment Rahim cursed fate, if he'd been aware of this young woman's presence in the city where Marcus Cowle held five parcels for delivery this evening he'd have instead directed the human trafficker to hunt down and capture this resurrected embodiment of his original obsession, the one driving him on his continuing murderous frenzy, and not bother with the rest. Rahim resigned to content his bloody urges with the items Cowle procured for him, pitied the pathetic women of this consignment destined to die by his hand, paying dearly for the missed opportunity to satiate his inner rage.

"Is there something wrong, Your Excellency?" Thomas Cockrell asked out of concern, noticed the startled expression creasing his face.

Rahim turned to Thomas Cockrell, shifting his gaze from the young woman with the auburn hair. "No, nothing is wrong. I thought I saw someone who looked...familiar." He shook his head, offered a melancholy smile. "I guess I was mistaken." Rahim pondered the discovery, watched the woman sitting across the auditorium, considered that perhaps all not lost. Could direct his assistants at the embassy to discreetly uncover the woman's identity, then have Cowle return to Chicago once the furor and hysteria over the disappearances quieted to hunt down this revived spirit from his past, snatch her for his twisted pleasures. Rahim pleased with the decision, for once needed to exercise patience, but to possess this woman who resembled the initial source of his homicidal fixation worth every moment he waited.

In her seat, Samantha Grayson activated the recording application on her smartphone after exchanging pleasantries with a correspondent from CNN and a reporter from the *Washington Post*, stepped forward to place the phone on the edge of the stage, settling back into the chair, checking her background notes on Senator Benton Fielding. She glanced over again to where the Cockrell brothers and Caleb McIllhenny stood, conversing with the handsome dignitary. Samantha noticed the man studying her closely and her brown eyes returned the gaze, brushed auburn hair back from her ear, smiled shyly at the man though felt slightly uncomfortable with the persistent attention. Samantha didn't yet realize at that moment she'd become the target of an obsessive and murderous predator.

The sound of silence from Presley Harding continued to trouble Riley Bradford, receiving no reply from either the text she sent or voicemail she left on her roommate's phone, as she sat through morning classes and a quick early lunch at Lakeside, though an unsettled stomach meant she only took a couple of bites of what on her plate, worried she might be sick if she ate anymore.

Returning to Cockrell Hall Riley stopped by the rooms of the Residence Director and her floor's Residence Assistant to seek their help in the matter, found both of them were out. As her anxiety increased with each passing minute without word from Presley and not knowing where to turn, Riley took the next possible step, contacted the authorities once she reached her room. The lack of answers she received from them only added to the aggravation and growing apprehension. *I have to wait twenty-four hours! Why can't they help me before then?* Riley railed silently at what she was told by Great Northern University Pubic Safety and the Evanslawn Police Department. Since it appeared Presley left of her own volition, and twenty-four hours yet to elapse since Riley last saw her roommate in Cockrell Hall, neither agency able to take an official missing persons report. The officer from the Evanslawn Police Department taking her call possessed the temerity to suggest Presley running off with a boyfriend. Riley wanted to shout back, despite the many nights Presley spent carousing the clubs in Chicago, the one thing she didn't have was a boyfriend. At least one Riley knew about.

What if she's in trouble? A surge of panic overtook Riley. What then? What if Presley needed help and no one coming to her aid? Riley checked Presley's Facebook page and Twitter account, the last status update and tweet from Sunday morning, out of the ordinary since Presley always posting on the social media sites. The last posts hinted that nothing amiss, but no indication of where she may have gone. The combined stress of worrying about her missing roommate, and the relentless approach of a massive early semester organic chemistry test, weighed heavily on Riley, not knowing what to do or where next to turn for assistance. Out of frustration Riley started searching the room. Had Presley left a note, some clue, to where she had gone? She started with Presley's desk, cluttered with papers and books, rifling through the piles searching for any scrap of paper with a phone number, a scribbled address or name to contact, found nothing to arouse her suspicions. Riley moved next to the dresser, tried not to stare at a framed picture of Presley with her parents. What if something bad had happened to Presley? What if someone hurt her? *What if....?* Riley pushed the horrible possibility from her mind. If that were the terrible case what would she tell Presley's parents? *At least I'll be able to tell them I tried to do all I could to help Presley*, but no one bothered to listen, nobody bothered to help.

What's this?

Riley picked up the business card lying on the dresser, noted the name of the business, *Marcus Evans Photography*. The address in Chicago, 2371 North Campbell Street, and by the number Riley guessed it located somewhere on the north side of the city. *Did Presley go there yesterday after I went to the library?* Was this the reason Presley seemed on edge before she left to study? Riley grabber her smartphone, dialed the number. There were two rings before the other end picked up, the sound of a typical voicemail greeting and a smooth, mellow male voice speaking. *"You have reached Marcus Evans Photography. Unfortunately no one is available to take your call at this time. Please leave your name and number and I will return your call at the earliest opportunity. Thank you for calling. Good day."*

Riley heard the beep, throat suddenly as dry as the sandy floor of a desert. "Hello...my name is...Riley Bradford," she stammered, couldn't understand her abrupt nervousness or the chill prickling her spine, "I'm calling about...my roommate, Presley Harding. I'm wondering if she might...be there or if she...was there. If you could call me at 616-555-6129 and let me know...I'd really appreciate it."

Now what do I do?

For a moment Riley considered heading into Chicago and Marcus Evans Photography, find out for herself if Presley had been there. But unlike her roommate she didn't have a car, didn't know from whom she could borrow one on such short notice. Thought about calling a cab, but the cost too high. Then there was the organic chemistry test, no way to skip out on it, a guaranteed route to certain failure in the class. Only two hours remained until the exam, not enough time for Riley to make the trip into the city and get back to campus in time to take the test.

What do I do? Riley wanted to sit in the center of the room and cry in exasperation. *Who can I turn to now?* She spotted a copy of *The Daily Northern* from the previous Friday on Presley's desk, a name on the paper caught her attention: Samantha Grayson. Every day it seemed she had a story on the front page, heard someone once remark Samantha responsible for breaking the scandal leading to the removal of the former university president. Riley tucked the business card in the pocket of her jeans, grabbed her backpack, headed for the door as a resolute rush of determination drove her forward, provided direction to her actions. Maybe Samantha Grayson able to help her find out what happened to Presley. Why it seemed as if the very Earth swallowed Presley Harding whole.

Chapter 24

"Do we have a topic for today?" Amanda McKinnon asked the usual lunchtime contingent, though absent one person this day. "Since Samantha has another engagement?" Samantha Grayson busy writing her stories at *The Daily Northern* following the speech by Senator Benton Fielding that morning.

D'Andre Watson, decider of the subject for discussion, shrugged his shoulders. "It's up to you if we have one or not since Samantha's AWOL. I've got one in mind if you want to go ahead. Or we hold off until tomorrow when she's back."

"I say we hold off," Lauryn Callahan sighed. "It's not the same without Samantha here."

I agree with that, Tyler McManaway thought, glancing where Samantha usually sat next to him, melancholy at her absence, no matter how brief, after the weighty issues discussed over the weekend.

Albert 'Fiji' Fatuamala nodded. "I'm with Lauryn."

"That's two," D'Andre pointed out. "Two more votes make it a majority."

"I say we do it tomorrow," Amanda added, glancing at Connor with a raised eyebrow.

"Well, I was going to say go for it," Connor correctly interpreted his girlfriend's expression. "But I'll put my vote in the no column."

"Then the lunchtime topic is on hiatus for today," D'Andre announced. "I guess we'll have to pass the time talking about other things."

"Did you see all the demonstrators in front of Cockrell Auditorium for the speech by Bryce's father?" Ashleigh Morgan referred to Senator Fielding. "The guy has a lot of haters, but I can see why considering what he stands for."

"That's because they don't agree with what he believes in," D'Andre replied. "People should be listening to what he has to say because the man happens to be right. Some people don't like the truth."

"Children, no politics at the table," Amanda cautioned. D'Andre and Ashleigh might be in a committed relationship, but their political beliefs-D'Andre a staunch conservative while Ashleigh a vocal liberal-the only area of contention between them. The reason politics so assiduously avoided during their lunchtime discussions. "Unless it's Canadian politics," she added, and Amanda the only one of their group who knew anything about that.

"So what do we talk about?" Lauryn asked.

"Well Tyler has a look on his face like he'll never see Samantha again," D'Andre noticed his friend's subdued demeanor.

Tyler shrugged. "Doesn't feel the same without her here." Still couldn't shake the troubled thoughts from the discussion, the revelation of her fears, with Samantha that past Saturday night.

"Are you going to be like this on the trip to Minneapolis? Dude, she'll be back tomorrow," D'Andre told him. "It's not like she's gone on an overseas assignment and won't be back for months."

"I know, she'll be here tomorrow," Tyler couldn't dispel the continued unease at Samantha's absence. Only feeling better later that evening when they were together again after Samantha returned from dinner with her roommates and finished work at *The Daily Northern*.

"Why do all politicians sound the same?" Samantha muttered under her breath, sitting in front of her laptop in the offices of *The Daily Northern*, fingers tapping out her third story for the day. Already finished with articles detailing the protests and reactions from members of the faculty and Board of Trustees, that story minus any comment from the Cockrell brothers. Now she hammered away on the biggest story of the morning, the speech by Senator Benton Fielding.

"What's that?" The question came not from Aaron Dinehart, off at class this Monday afternoon. The voice belonged to Ali Fahrajani, sitting at the group of desks and banks of computers comprising the sports department of the student newspaper. "Something on your mind that's bothering you?" The lead writer covering the football program, Ali the son of Iraqi immigrants fleeing the hell of the uprising in Basra with only their lives and the clothes they wore in the tragic and tumultuous wake of the First Gulf War, the family settling in Dearborn, a suburb outside of Detroit.

"Am I too young to be cynical?" Samantha exhaled, typing as she spoke, on a tear with the final story, had most of it written. *Might be able to work on other things this afternoon.* "Or do I expect far too much from those who represent us?"

"You can never be too young to be cynical," Ali replied to the first point. "Besides you are expecting too much from our politicians, thinking they'll act rationally with the best interests of the country in mind. Considering how they've been acting the past few years," like preschoolers fighting over who gets to play with the best toys during recess, "you should've realized that by now."

Samantha stopped typing, looked at Ali who continued pecking away on his laptop. "I got into an argument on Friday night with Bryce Fielding, Senator Fielding's son."

"I know him, nice guy," Ali paused, then expressed true feelings. "Not so much."

Samantha leaned back in her chair, the story almost finished, wanted a respite after working at breakneck speed since returning to the office, eating a sandwich at her desk purchased at the Panera downstairs in Howell Commons for lunch. "He lit into me when I told him I was covering the speech. Since I'm a member of the media said I'd interject a liberal bias in whatever I wrote. I told him I'd approach his father's speech with an open-mind."

"And...?" Ali let the question hang in the air.

Samantha sighed, a frown creasing her pretty face. "It's the same thing we've heard before, and I've only been able to vote since last year."

"Wish to elaborate?" Ali probed further.

"I'm one of those independents they talk about, the important swing voter," she reflected, "at least that's what I'm registered as. Being a journalist I don't want to be identified with one party or the other." She searched for the proper words. "I try to see both sides of the issue. We need to address health care for those who don't have it but we can't create a monstrous bureaucracy taking decisions out of our hands. We need regulation to protect workers, safeguard the environment, but we can't stifle business growth and the economy in the process, just as we need checks on the banks and the financial markets so they don't melt down like they did awhile back. As a nation we need to address social issues, but we can't throw money at a problem and hope it solves everything, there must be an acceptance of responsibility from those we're trying to help. We should have a smaller, more efficient government but at the same time those same people who want a smaller government also want it involved in our most personal decisions." Samantha shook her head. "I don't want the government in my bedroom, telling me what I can do with my body."

"I don't want them in my bedroom either," Ali deadpanned, "because it's a mess right now."

"I'm conflicted." Samantha pushed her hands through her auburn hair. "I want the people we elect to work together to solve problems. Not take an 'it's my way or the highway' approach to everything. Senator Fielding's main point boiled down to was if America follows conservative values and solutions everything will be sunshine and rainbows. I know that won't be the case because the other half of the country sees things differently. Why can't they act like adults and compromise? Do what's best for America instead of trying to earn first prize in a shit throwing contest?"

"Nice analogy there, Grayson," Ali chuckled, amused by the crude choice of words, Samantha not known as one who dropped obscenities. "Did he get on his high horse about the decline in morality?" Ali asked. "How all our problems are because we're a bunch of sex-hungry heathens who watch dirty movies and don't pray to God?" He paused. "Especially me since I worship the wrong one five times a day."

"He toned it down." Samantha replied; one of her background notes detailed far-right leaning positions on social issues of the day, a reason for the presence of many demonstrators outside Cockrell Auditorium. "I think he played to the audience." Samantha placed her elbows on the desk, chin resting in her hands. "So tell me the truth, am I being too cynical?"

"Think of the American political scene as the Michigan-Ohio State football rivalry," Ali said.

Samantha cocked her head, puzzled by the remark. "Why not Great Northern-Illinois?"

"Not a big enough rivalry for this analogy to work." Ali waved off Samantha's comment. "One party is Michigan and the other is Ohio State, substitute any political issue for their annual football game. When one side wins the other side gets pissed off, wants to win very badly the next time they play. Doesn't help when the winning side rubs it in the face of the losing team at every opportunity."

"I'm starting to see your point," Samantha admitted.

"Now why do you want to work with your hated enemy?" Ali explained. "The one you stare at across the line of scrimmage, want to knock down and grind into the mud, on every play."

"So we have a vicious cycle," Samantha added.

"Correct, my dear," Ali nodded, "one team wins, they get their way, the other team sits on the sidelines fuming watching the victory dance, promising to make the other side pay when they win. Of course you add the fans into this equation, the rooters for each team are the people voting them into office, the base of support. Then add the commentators, those yapping away on radio and television, people with big mouths and small minds like Rush Limbaugh, Sean Hannity, Breck Glendenning and Trace Kilcannon. They hate the other side as much as the players do on the field. The last thing they want is an exchange of handshakes at the conclusion of the game. They want to win at all costs."

"So it's all about winner takes all, getting your own way," Samantha theorized. "Not working for what's in the best interests of the country but for the best interests of your party or supporters."

"That's what gets them reelected over and over again and keeps the money flowing into the campaign coffers." Ali grinned. "The lovely student reporter with the starting quarterback for a boyfriend wins a prize." He pointed at Samantha. "By the way Tyler locked onto D. B. Bailey and telegraphed that interception in the third quarter."

Samantha smiled at Ali. "Your analysis is very perceptive," she complimented her colleague, turning back to her final story, checking it for errors. "You should work in the news department. I find your opinion refreshing."

"No way will that happen," Ali conceded. "I'd rather play in the sandbox of journalism." Not that covering sports solely entailed recapping games and extolling the athletic talents of the participants. One smelled plenty pungent whiffs of scandal-from a coach involved in an despicable child abuse scandal at another Big Ten school to a star linebacker falling for a fake online girlfriend-in that sandbox.

The resolve to locate her missing roommate brimming in Riley Bradford's soul when she left her room at Cockrell Hall started running dry during the brisk walk across the Great Northern campus to

Howell Commons, all but evaporated by the time she entered the student union and the third floor offices of *The Daily Northern*. Doubt began creeping into her mind, chipping away at the boulder of determination to find Presley Harding, know that she was safe, until a tiny pebble of resolution remained. What if Samantha Grayson, the reporter whose byline topped stories in every edition, wasn't there this afternoon? What if she was too busy to help search for her roommate? What if it turned out Presley did run off with a new romantic flame and didn't let anyone know, returning to campus following her fling and embarrassing Riley for the frantic show of concern?

But other 'what ifs' forced Riley on, reinforced her insistence to see this through, troubled in particular by a single 'what if.' That Presley in terrible trouble, desperately needed help as soon as possible. The unnerving likelihood propelled Riley up the stairs to the doors of *The Daily Northern* office, slowing her pace entering the reception area. Saw a sign reading EDITORIAL DEPARTMENT next to a door leading from the front, stepped into a large office space almost empty at the early afternoon hour, only two people working at the desks filling the room. At one cluster of desks a young man with darker skin and Middle-Eastern features typed away. A sign atop one desk stating: *Sports-Where News Reporters Want to Work When They Grow Up*. At a second cluster of desks sat a young woman with auburn hair dressed in a white blouse and skirt, jacket draped over the back of the chair, typing on a laptop, brown eyes intently fixed on the screen. Judging by the serious demeanor and professional attire Riley naturally assumed this was Samantha Grayson.

Riley took a deep breath, stepped up to the desk.

"Excuse me, are you Samantha Grayson?" An unsure, and nervous, female voice asked.

At the sound of her name Samantha lifted her head from the laptop where a moment earlier she typed the final sentence of the main story recapping the speech given by Senator Benton Fielding at Cockrell Auditorium. She glanced up at a sweetly adorable face with strawberry-blonde hair framing gentle azure blue eyes, the young woman petite and slight, about the same height as Lauryn Callahan. Under those bright blue eyes Samantha immediately noticed dark circles, the young woman's manner apprehensive and jittery as if her mind weighed down by matters of importance. Suspicions instantly alerted, reporter's sixth-sense heightened, yet Samantha smiled warmly at her. "Yes, that's me," Samantha said calmly, put the girl at ease, motioning to the chair beside her desk, "how can I help you?"

The girl sat down, hands clasped and twisting in her lap, Samantha noticed how tense she was, couldn't relax, foot tapping against the floor. "My name is Riley Bradford, I'm a freshman." Judging her halting, hesitant actions the admission didn't surprise Samantha. "I was hoping you could help me?"

"What is it?" Samantha turned her focus away from the completed story, didn't let on she already aware something deeply troubled Riley.

"My roommate, Presley Harding," Riley started, "I haven't seen her since yesterday afternoon."

The statement caught Samantha's full, and now undivided, attention, alarms ringing in her head. "You think she's missing?"

"I don't know," Riley swallowed, shaking her head.

"You haven't seen her since yesterday," Samantha added helpfully, keeping her voice even not to betray a blossoming trepidation. "That qualifies in my book as being missing."

Riley sighed, slumped in the chair. "I think I need to tell you some things about Presley."

Samantha nodded. "Like what?" From across the room Ali finished his work, collecting his backpack, waving to Samantha as he exited, leaving her and Riley alone in the newsroom.

"Presley has a fake ID," Samantha sensed Riley's reluctance revealing the detail. "I don't know where she got it. She's been going out with these upperclassmen since the start of the year, right after Freshman Orientation. I think one of them, his father knows her father, Presley's dad runs a big private equity firm on Wall Street, might've gotten it for her."

"Do you know any of them?" Samantha wondered if one of the group Natalie DiLaurenzo, and if Bryce Fielding the one procuring the fake ID for the missing freshman. A potential landmine loomed on the horizon, how to approach her friend and inquire about this matter, careful where she stepped without causing collateral damage to their friendship.

"No, I don't," Riley's finger twisted a strand of hair. "They're not the type of people I'd hang around with. Presley offered to get me a fake ID, but my parents would kill me if I got caught with it."

"So you think she went out with her friends last night and didn't come back?" Samantha probed further. "Did she tell you she was going out?"

"The last time I saw her she said she might come to the library and study with me, didn't tell me she was going out with them," Riley explained, "but that's what I'm assuming she did. She does tell me when she goes out with them. She wasn't in the room when I returned from the library last night, it was more like this morning, and she wasn't there when I woke up. I left a text and message on her phone, but I haven't heard anything from her. She hasn't posted on Facebook or Twitter since yesterday morning, she's always posting or tweeting." Riley bit her lip. "It's not like her to be this…quiet."

"Did you contact the authorities?" Samantha sought to hide her own growing anxieties.

"I did," Riley sighed again, this time out of frustration, "both Public Safety and the Evanslawn Police Department. They said I had to wait twenty-four hours before they could take a report." Samantha grimaced, hardly surprised by the lackadaisical attitude of law enforcement, the relationship with Great Northern students wary at best and contentious at its worst. "It did look like she took an overnight bag with her, and some of her outfits from her closet were gone. They think she might have gone out and spent the night with someone."

"Does she have a boyfriend?" Perhaps here lay the logical explanation for Presley's absence.

"No, she doesn't," Riley replied. "Not that I know of. Or that she'd have any problem finding one." Riley pulled out her smartphone, brought up a photo of the two from Freshman Orientation Weekend, showing it to Samantha. "This is Presley." Presley Harding the same height as Riley with sparkling toffee-brown eyes and long hair the color of caramel, blessed with a radiant, glowing smile. Samantha thought Riley's assumption on the mark, if her roommate sought a boyfriend she'd easily find one on the Great Northern campus.

"Is there anything else?" Samantha asked. Something about this…*wasn't right*.

"I found this on her dresser," Riley handed a business card to Samantha; it read *Marcus Evans Photography* with an address on Chicago's Northwest side in the Logan Square neighborhood. Samantha copied down the address, 2371 North Campbell Avenue, phone number and website address on a notepad beside her, handing the card back to Riley. "I don't know how long it's been on her dresser. I called the number to see if Presley had been there, or if this person knew Presley but all I got was his voicemail. I left a message, but I haven't heard back from him."

"Has Presley ever mentioned this Marcus Evans," Samantha inquired, "or that she might be working with him?"

"That card is the first I've ever heard of him," Riley acknowledged, Samantha heard the distress rising in her voice. "She hasn't said anything on Facebook or Twitter about him. I was thinking about going into the city, see if he knows her, if she'd been there. But I don't have a car and I have an organic chemistry test this afternoon. I'm pre-med and I've been studying for it all weekend. I need to do well on it." Riley looked down, kneading her hands in her lap. "Presley and I, we're not really friends but she's my roommate. I'm worried about her, I don't want anything to happen to her." Riley breathed deeply, blue eyes frightened confronting the unknown. "I'm scared."

"Let me look into this for you." Samantha brushed a stray strand of auburn hair from her eyes, touched Riley's hand to calm her. "I'll go into Chicago to see this Marcus Evans, ask if he knows Presley. She might've gotten his card when she was out with her friends at the clubs."

"If anything happened to Presley," Riley sniffed back a tear, feared the worst. "God, what will I tell her parents?"

"I'm sure everything is okay and Presley is fine," Samantha reassured the freshman, but unconvinced by her own words. "You take this test, so don't worry. I'll go check into this, maybe make a few phone calls, and I'll contact you as soon as I find something." Samantha handed her a card. "Here's my number if you need to reach me."

Riley nodded, relieved someone cared for her plight and willing to help. "You'll do that for me?"

"I will," Samantha smiled to soothe her fears. "If I suspect anything is wrong I'll contact the police right away and let them handle it."

Riley smiled, blue eyes watering, wiping at them with her sleeve. "I really appreciate what you're doing."

Samantha leaned forward, held Riley's trembling hands. "I'd do it for anyone who needs help." Right now Riley Bradford desperately needed the assistance of Samantha Grayson to find her friend. *That's why I do what I do.*

"You're having way too much fun with this," Sterner stated, observing Marcus Cowle rummaging through the overnight bags their captives brought to the fake photo sessions ending with them trapped with no hope for escape.

"You know what they say about first impressions. Want to insure the product is presentable for our client," Cowle responded curtly, laying out in separate piles the outfits he wanted each captive to wear. "Nice of Alexandra to bring another business suit." This outfit in a gunmetal gray, selecting a simple white silk top to go with it. "I hope Sheik Rahim enjoys the look as much as you do."

"Business chicks are hot," Sterner admitted.

"I like those boots Presley is wearing," Cowle commented, dropped a black mini-skirt and a purple long sleeve floral knit top on the pile for the luckless freshman from Great Northern University. "I think that'll work nicely."

Sterner nodded. "Can't disagree with you there, Boss." Cowle laid out the final outfit, this for Emma Hayden, a denim miniskirt and plain white knit top. Her leather jacket and a pair of black knee high boots the perfect complement for an ensemble befitting Emma's defiant, truculent attitude.

"That's done." Cowle walked back to the room with the video monitors recording the movement of their captives, left his phone on the table there while taking a short nap before selecting the outfits for the merchandise to wear this night for their delivery to their new owner. "I'm heading over to the studio," Cowle announced, his last trip to the Logan Square brownstone housing Marcus Evans Photography. At this time the next day nothing left of the building but a smoldering pile of blackened rubble, any evidence linking Marcus Evans to the five missing women incinerated in the explosion and ensuing conflagration. "I'll start to pack so we can load up quickly. Prepare our former residence for foreclosure tonight." He picked up his phone; noticed the red light blinking indicating a message in his voicemail. He checked the number, one he didn't recognize. He connected to voicemail and listened, expression turning grim. *This is exactly what I feared might happen with this stupid delay.*

Sterner noticed his reaction. "Something wrong?"

"We might have a complication to deal with," Cowle explained. Presley told him she didn't tell anyone of the appointment at the studio. Then he remembered: *The business card, I gave one to Presley at the club.* Cowle quickly pieced together a possible scenario, their prisoner left the card in her room and this Riley discovered it. "Presley's roommate found out where she might've gone yesterday. Let's hope she doesn't tell anyone." Cowle sighed. "I'd better get back to the studio right now, in case she, or someone else, happens to knock on the door asking questions." Cowle pointed to Sterner. "When you're done packaging the items and preparing this place for the big bang," the warehouse to suffer the same fiery fate as the Logan Square brownstone, "get over to the studio, I might need your assistance there a little sooner than I expected."

Sterner nodded. "No problem." Cowle headed to the white Lexus in the loading bay. If Riley Bradford decided to come to the studio to find her friend instead of going to the police, then he'd deal with the potential problem in a straightforward, and brutal, manner. *The things I have to do for my clients.*

Samantha Grayson watched Riley Bradford depart the *Daily Northern* office. The young freshman distraught over her roommate's absence, but from what she told Samantha about Presley Harding it apparent her roommate enjoyed life on her own for the first time a bit too vicariously. Sitting alone in the newsroom, the silence allowed Samantha the solitude to consider the situation.

She studied the information regarding Marcus Evans Photography she jotted down on the notepad. Where had Presley gained possession of a fake ID? Riley said Presley frequenting the clubs in Chicago with a group of upperclassmen, Samantha recalling the suspicions of Allison Mayne that Bryce Fielding procured a fake ID for Natalie DiLaurenzo. Riley noted the father of one of those upperclassmen also a friend of Presley's father. Might Natalie or Bryce know if Presley met up with someone while out at the clubs? Decided to spend the night with a new, and as yet unknown to Riley, boyfriend? Samantha thought better to approach Natalie, no telling what Bryce Fielding's reaction to such a pointed inquiry, didn't want to cross him again.

That avenue of investigation had to wait, the business card Riley found in their room the only tangible lead to Presley's whereabouts. Samantha opened the Internet Explorer browser on her laptop, typed in the web address, directed to a professionally designed website for the business. The featured samples of his work showed a photographer with consummate skill and flair, five-star feedback from customers brimming with satisfaction at the finished product and expertise of the owner. Samantha clicked on the biography for owner, found it odd there no picture of the man but a lengthy resume of his education, a lengthy list of professional credits for respected publications like *National Geographic* and *Time*. Samantha opened another tab on the browser, called up Google, in the search box typed in Marcus Evans Photography. The results of her search generated additional reviews of the business from Yelp, each one heaping copious praise for the photographer's ability. Found photos credited to the man from the publications listed in the bio along with a lone photo of Marcus Evans, a rugged man in his late fifties with dark hair, silver at the temples, crouching amidst a rainforest exhibiting an adventurous, devil-may-care attitude, camera dangling from his neck. She came across additional photo credits from a website named *Chicago at Night*, chronicling happenings in the city's nightclub scene. Could this be the explanation for the business card Riley found on Presley's dresser? By chance crossed paths one night at a club where Presley had been with Natalie and Bryce?

Samantha noticed an odd detail about the business in the reviews and the photo credits from the social website; it appeared Marcus Evans in the city, and his business operating at the Logan Square address, for a little under a year, shortly after the five women vanished in Los Angeles. Was this coincidence or something far more sinister to consider? A thought chilled Samantha's soul. Was this missing freshman related to the disappearances that caught her attention? *One way to find out.* Samantha brought up the *Chicago Tribune* website, clicked on the tab for the Breaking News section featuring the most immediate news items. If any young women going missing over the weekend Samantha surmised she'd find details here. A quick scan of the headlines came up empty.

God, you're being paranoid! Making a leap of faith, Samantha! She chided herself. Right away assuming something wicked transpiring to the missing girl, linking it to the cases from across the country. Perhaps Marcus Evans a legitimate businessman only connected to Presley through happenstance. But the business card the solitary lead at Samantha's disposal to track down the wayward freshman, put Riley Bradford's mind at ease. Only one way to proceed, head to Marcus Evans Photography, see if Presley had even been there and find out if any connection existed between her and the owner. The work on the stories from the Senator Fielding speech completed, only needed to review the material with Aaron Dinehart later that evening after returning from dinner with her roommates. She glanced at the clock, noted the time, planned on meeting her friends at the office around five, figured in her head how long it'd take to drive into Chicago, check out Marcus Evans Photography, then return to campus. *I have more than enough time*, Samantha estimated. Maybe by then Presley showing up on her own, bringing an end to the crisis. But if she discovered Presley hadn't been there...*might have to take a rain check on dinner.*

Should I have someone go with me? Samantha thought. The newsroom deserted, no one coming in to work on the next day's paper until later in the afternoon at the earliest, Samantha promised Riley she'd check into this right away, weighing her options. *I can handle this*, Samantha mused, *I can't be afraid of shadows*. She couldn't let the details of the disappearances she researched turn her confident, assured manner into a timid, cautious attitude. Samantha could defend herself if trouble came her way, demonstrated the proficiency to Tyler the day before. *I should let someone know where I'm going just in case*, Samantha acknowledged. *But who?*

She knew better than to text Tyler of her intentions, had class in the Wharton Computer Sciences and Technology Center, the complex a notorious black hole for cell phone reception, earned the building the nickname 'The Eleventh Circle of Hell.' After classes Tyler heading to football practice, occupying his attention the remainder of the afternoon. Samantha didn't wish to worry Tyler, not after her confession to him Saturday night. Amanda also had class, followed by cross-country practice while Ashleigh had an unfortunate habit of forgetting messages in the rapid-fire stream of texts she received and sent out over her phone.

That left one roommate, Samantha knew she'd remember the message. *Always dependable Lauryn.* She picked up her phone, typed the briefest of messages, sent it to Lauryn Callahan's phone. Once done Samantha turned off her laptop, slid the computer into the top drawer of the desk, no need for it on this trip. Over her arm slung her Timbuk2 messenger bag and left the empty offices of *The Daily Northern.*

From the corner of her eye, as she listened to her instructor's lecture, Lauryn Callahan caught the screen of her smartphone flash, kept on mute during class, an alert she received a text message; saw the communication from Samantha. Without attracting unwanted attention from a professor despising students' texting in the middle of class Lauryn reached for the phone, slid it beside her, touched the screen to read the message.

If not at office when you get there at 2371 North Campbell Avenue in Chicago. The digital communication said. Lauryn jotted the address down on her notebook, her habit to always write things down. Why was Samantha going there when she was supposed to be working on an important story, recapping a speech by a potential presidential contender? Lauryn didn't question it any further, focus returning to the lecture, hoping the professor hadn't spotted her checking the phone.

Chapter 25

Cowle entered the studio soon made a vacant shell after he and Sterner loaded their gear and Spartan possessions into the van, rigging the building for vaporization in a supernova fireball in the dead of night. A fitting distraction occupying the forces of order while he and Sheik Rahim finalized a business arrangement sending five defenseless women on a one-way sojourn towards an inevitable doom.

If it works out that way. The message left by Presley's roommate presented a potential roadblock on the path to success. Would this girl go to the police? Or come to the studio searching for her missing friend? Cowle prepared for either possibility as he began dismantling and packing equipment from their operation along with sparse personal belongings.

He placed his camera bag on a table in the studio next to his laptop computer, from the closet removed cardboard boxes, took them to the back. *Let's start to wrap things up.* If he had time later, once everything squared away, Cowle intended to download images of his prizes, eternal mementos of what he hoped soon-to-be success in Chicago, on to the laptop.

"Time to get you cleaned up and ready for your trip," Sterner, with Lang standing beside him, both wearing balaclavas to hide their identities and induce a dark aura of fear, informed his helpless charges. The quintet handcuffed, huddled tightly on the floor of the cell, backs pressed hard against the concrete wall, bunching together as if strength in numbers offered protection from their captors. "Want you all nice and pretty for your new owner."

"You ladies have a hot date," Lang added, glee in his voice, basking in the moment.

"I'm sure we do." Emma Hayden glared angrily at them, turquoise eyes drilling holes through her keepers. "What if we don't want to?" She fired back. Sterner and Lang laying bets Emma the first of this shipment to die at the homicidal whims of The Arab, the consensus she'd last two weeks at the most.

"You can get cleaned up and dressed on your own and have a little privacy," Sterner explained, "or you can be a stubborn little bitch and we'll," he nodded to his partner, "help you get ready." Let the statement sink in before adding. "And we're not the gentle type. If you have any doubts, why don't you ask your friend," he motioned to Presley Harding, cowering in their presence, scarred and reeling from the endless hours of brutal punishment for her attempt to escape, "how her night was."

Emma glanced at Presley, shuddered at the image of her suffering. "I'll go," Emma stood up.

Sterner smiled as Lang grabbed Emma by the arm, dragging her roughly from the room. "I knew you'd see it our way." He stepped out of the cell, closed the door; leaving the remaining hostages to silently dread the time they'd be forced to prepare for a trip on which none of them wished to embark.

With the afternoon hour traffic on the Kennedy Expressway mercifully light, the drive from the Great Northern campus in Evanslawn into Chicago took half the time it usually did when battling the rush-hour horde. There a chance Samantha able to make the trip, check out the lead, then return to the office of *The Daily Northern* well before meeting up with her roommates for their dinner at Toscana in the city. Though depending on what Samantha uncovered during her visit to Marcus Evans Photography regarding the whereabouts of Presley Harding, those plans might be put on hold. If Presley hadn't been at the studio Samantha already deciding her next step to contact Natalie DiLaurenzo, inquire if the freshman out club-hopping in Chicago with her and Bryce Fielding. Samantha hoped Presley turned up safe and sound before she returned to campus, not looking forward to a possibly heated confrontation with a close friend on a sensitive matter.

Samantha spotted the exit sign for Fullerton Avenue, easing her blue Ford Mustang into the exit lane, checking one final time the directions on her Garmin, kept the volume muted as the automated voice telling her when and where to turn annoyingly disconcerting. The address for Marcus Evans Photography at 2371 North Campbell Avenue less than a mile west of the Kennedy. She stopped at the bottom of the ramp, turning right on Fullerton when the light changed to green.

The stoplight at Western Avenue caught her, gave Samantha a moment to ponder her surroundings. Logan Square a neighborhood in transition, the artists who established their studios and lofts in the Wicker Park and Bucktown on the city's Northwest Side, made those once rough and tumble locales into desirable neighborhoods for the young and affluent dislodged by the very forces of gentrification they initiated, moving northwest along the Milwaukee Avenue corridor to new and fertile territory, starting the process all over again as trendy nightspots and well-reviewed restaurants sprang up like fresh flowers after a spring rain. Samantha wrote a story the previous year detailing tensions between long-time residents, along with a prevalent simmering gang problem, and the wave of newcomers pushed into their neighborhood by the rising property values of where they left.

The light changed and Samantha drove on, Campbell the first street to her left past Western, a one-way going south. She waited until traffic cleared, swung on the street. *There it is.* Samantha spotted the address for Marcus Evans Photography on the east side of the street, not far from the intersection with Fullerton, sought the closest open parking space to the three-story brownstone flat. Being the middle of the day, with people off to work, several spots vacant and Samantha pulled the Mustang to the curb, parking on the west side of the street one building down from the brownstone. She noticed the first floor of the three-flat brownstone a converted storefront, in some past incarnation offering a necessary amenity to the residents of the working-class neighborhood.

So how do I do this? Samantha considered her next move, ignoring the cloud of butterflies suddenly taking flight deep in her stomach. Did she come right out and identify herself as a reporter for *The Daily Northern* and the reason for her visit to the studio, searching for Presley Harding, last seen by her roommate a day earlier and a business card for the photographer found in her dorm room? Or did she play it coy, tell Marcus Evans she was a friend of the freshman also interested in modeling, and Presley suggested she approach him about the possibility?

If I'm going that route, at least I'm dressed for the part, Samantha thought, knew it wasn't the most ethical way to learn if Presley had been here, or if this Marcus Evans even knew Presley. Samantha glanced in the rearview mirror, checked her makeup. *Better make sure I look good in case he wants to take a few pictures.* She freshened up her eyelashes and eye shadow, gliding lips gloss across her lips. She grabbed her messenger bag, stepped out of the Mustang and started across the street, fighting down a sudden burst of anxiety as she approached the brownstone.

Samantha had no idea she was already being watched.

On the closet circuit video surveillance system Cowle caught a glimpse of the cobalt blue Ford Mustang parking outside of the building as he wiped the website for the studio from the internet, erasing the presence of Marcus Evans Photography from the electronic world, eliminating another trail for the police to follow. "What do we have here?" Cowle asked out loud, watched as the person remained inside the car. He switched to another camera; the vantage point allowed him a better view. A woman sitting in the driver's seat. Was this Presley's roommate coming to the studio looking for her companion? Once the woman stepped from the car Cowle instantly reassessed the assumption. The auburn-haired young woman, hair falling in thick waves over her shoulders, dressed too professionally for a college student, of that Cowle certain, the bearing far too poised for that of the stammering girl leaving the message on his voicemail. Was she a co-worker of Alexandra Cole? Had Alexandra told someone of the appointment on Saturday, no record left of it on the electronic data he erased? The woman crossed the street, heading directly for the front entrance of Marcus Evans Photography.

The question of who the woman was not as pertinent as addressing what seemed yet another unforeseen complication. *I should've convinced Rahim to change this stupid idea of his to take delivery personally, I wouldn't be dealing with any of this!* Cowle grimaced. *But the damn customer is always damn right.* Even if the customer happened to patronize a trafficker of human flesh. If the woman found the door locked she might suspect something amiss, return with the police. The woman, whoever she was, at least had the temerity to come alone and that to his advantage. Needed to get the woman inside the studio; handle her on his terms, violent if necessary. Cowle hit the button on the remote to unlock the front door, flipped the switch to activate the cell phone signal jammer so she couldn't call or text for help.

He hurried to the studio to lay in wait, already something of interest on the table for this woman to find. Cowle knew a good trap required a tempting piece of bait.

*   *   *   *   *

Samantha strode up to the brownstone, studied the framed pictures of smiling close-knit families and happily married couples on their wedding day with love for the other filling their eyes displayed in the bay windows. *Maybe that'll be Tyler and me someday.* The prints exhibiting the artistic flair of the studio's owner. She reached for and turned the knob, the door opened easily. Samantha took a deep breath, steadied quivering nerves as she stepped inside.

The reception room what Samantha expected of a small business: a desk, a couch and a sofa chair, a coffee table with magazines on top along with additional framed examples of the photographer's work hanging on the walls. Nothing present to stoke suspicions of Marcus Evans or any sign Presley Harding had been there. She dropped her shoulder bag on the couch, walked into the next room. Entered the studio space, noting the white backdrop and expensive lighting. There was another couch against the wall, a second Mission-style coffee table with more magazines, a plastic milk crate filled with toys beside the couch. *Something to keep the little ones occupied while getting their picture taken*, Samantha surmised.

"Hello?" Samantha finally called out. "Is anyone here?" The fact she didn't receive an answer heightened her apprehension. She stood still, listened, heard nothing. "Is there a Marcus Evans here?" Silence, a troubling sound when seemingly alone, the only reply. Her eyes shifted to a table off to the side; saw the camera resting next to a laptop computer. Samantha walked over, lifted the camera from the table to examine it, the Canon an expensive piece of equipment she expected a professional to own. She turned the camera around; though she left photography accompanying her stories to those in the graphic arts department at *The Daily Northern* she knew how to operate a digital camera, especially those storing images on memory chips with the clarity and detail of now archaic thirty-five millimeter film. *No need to develop the film to see what pictures have been taken.* She switched the camera on, scrolled through the menu to find the images recorded within. Flashing on the preview screen on the back of the camera pictures of young women in various modeling poses, all attractive and around her age. Then a single image brought a gasp from deep in her lungs, at the discovery Samantha's hand shooting up to cover mouth in shock, immediately recognizing the face from the picture Riley Bradford showed her back at *The Daily Northern*.

Presley Harding...

In the image Presley wore a white and blue striped tank top and blue jeans, a bright smile splashed across the eager face, brown eyes glowing with enthusiasm, standing in the sort of pose Samantha expected from a model though it seemed awkward in an appealing sort of way. Samantha felt her breathing quicken as she scrolled through the images. *She was here...but where is she now? Did this Marcus Evans do something to her? Where is he?* The questions bounced around in her head until an image flashed on the screen and Samantha found an answer both terrible and awful.

Oh my God...

Samantha felt her stomach lurch, fought down the sudden urge to vomit. Presley now dressed in a different outfit-miniskirt, thigh high gray boots and a long-sleeve paisley print knit top-but her position now not the pose of a potential model. Lying on the floor, appeared unconscious. Her body bound up in a brutal, confining macramé of rope, cloth wrapped around her mouth and eyes, helplessly gagged and blindfolded.

Samantha froze, back stiffening, a sixth sense alerting her something wrong. A sensation she stood in the presence of terrible danger, the longer she stayed in the studio the greater her peril. Samantha raised her head, a mirror hung on the wall before her, in the reflection spied a figure approaching silently from behind. Samantha didn't pause to think, didn't consider possible ramifications from her actions. *I can apologize later...*

She recalled the lesson of her father, *anything can be a weapon*, in her hands holding a perfect deterrent. Samantha swung around in a quick, fluid motion, bringing up the camera she grasped; saw the figure try to duck away. She aimed for the side of the head, the movement like hitting a forehand smash with a tennis racket, a natural action for Samantha who played the game in high school, earned league honors for her efforts. Striking the figure solidly above the eye, staggering him backward, heard an exclamation of pain and curse of anger as he wobbled drunkenly from the blow, falling to the floor.

Samantha didn't linger to admire her handiwork. *You have to get out of here!* The single thought compelled her forward as she dropped the camera, stepped over her fallen adversary, tried to run, remembered she wearing high heels at the moment she tripped and stumbled. *Damn high heels, now I understand what Amanda meant!* Samantha felt a hand wrap around her right ankle and pull, sending her tumbling, crashing to the floor, screaming loudly as she fell hard on the wood floor, right elbow flaring on impact. She blocked out the pain, rolled on her back as the figure, moving too quickly to focus on his physical features, lunged at her. Samantha targeted his face, struck with the open palm of her hand, hitting him squarely on the nose. The figure hesitated for a split second, writhing in pain and Samantha reared back with her right leg, kicked at him, satisfied by the howl of anguish as the point of her heel struck home, dug deep into the soft flesh of his thigh.

Scrambling to her knees, Samantha felt her attacker grab at her, arms wrapped around her upper body, pin her arms to her sides, dragging her to the ground. Her attacker strong and quick; absorbing the punishment Samantha already dealt him. *If he gets me down on the floor, I'm finished*, unable to fight off her attacker, using his size to hold her down. She growled, with a yell of fury launched her left elbow into his ribs, made contact, heard him curse again, releasing his grip, Samantha squirming free of his grasp. Her attacker reached out, grabbing at her blouse, heard fabric tear, saw a button pop off. Samantha twisted about, the instinct to live driving her actions, swinging her fist to strike where she first made contact with the camera, a solid blow landed. Saw the figure sag, drop to the floor.

I have to get out of here! Staggering to her feet Samantha decided now the time for flight over fight, done enough to hurt him, had to escape to save her life and possibly that of Presley Harding. She sprinted into the front reception room, high heels forcing her to shuffle along on the balls of her feet, heading for the front door, every step widening the distance between her and the attacker, chances increasing by the second she might survive to live another day.

Samantha grabbed the door handle, pulled it. *Locked...but how?* Panic swept over her, whimpering in dismay as she understood a grim fate now sealed. *I'm trapped.* As she yanked on a door handle that wouldn't give, Samantha heard a popping sound from behind, something sharp plunging into her back, lodging in her spine with a biting sting so intense it seemed as if she'd stepped on a hornet's nest and every angry insect lodged within attacking at the same instant. Samantha gasped, her vision blurring, staggering back from the door, hand fumbling behind her to remove the painful object. She heard a crackling noise and an excruciating flash of pain enveloped her body, a white-hot globe of light surrounded her, wiped out everything in her vision, obliterating her senses like a nuclear blast, muscles and limbs made useless, felt herself twisting, falling. In the second before her brain shut down images of those she loved: her friends, her parents, Tyler, and the sickening realization she might never see any of them again flashed through her mind. *No, it can't end like this…* The bright light faded and she plummeted into a bottomless maw enveloping her like Jonah swallowed by the whale.

Samantha never felt her body hit the floor.

"So, you're a fighter?" With the back of his hand Cowle wiped at the trickle of blood from his cut lip, staring down at the prostrate young woman sprawled on the floor. Cowle shook away cobwebs clouding his mind, she landed a few good blows but it didn't matter. He glanced at the stun gun in his hand; the woman never stood a chance. *You almost got away, but I always win in the end.*

"I like girls who put up a struggle, more of a challenge," he informed the unmoving form. The bitch landed a lucky shot with the camera, Cowle fortunate to have maintained his composure, able to trigger the front door lock and reach the stun gun, taking her down before she could escape, put a sudden end to his charade and entire illegal enterprise. He scrutinized his unconscious prey, watched her chest rise and fall on each shallow breath. Medium height, about five-five or five-six, with a perfectly round face and a shapely body. The long auburn hair splayed about her head as if floating on water. He crouched down, shifted back the fabric of the white satin blouse torn during the furious struggle, examined her firm breasts. "Not too bad, honey. You've got a nice set here," came forth his judgment. Couldn't be Presley's roommate, Cowle thought, had to be a co-worker of Alexandra Cole at the company she so deeply loathed. "One way to find out," Cowle reached for the brown nylon shoulder bag on the couch. He rummaged inside, located a lanyard with identification cards attached, expected these were the woman's corporate credentials. He checked the name, realized his mistake, events taking a quite unexpected turn.

"Samantha Grayson, Senior Staff Reporter, *The Daily Northern*, Great Northern University," Cowle read out loud. He glanced at the lifeless young woman now with a name and perhaps a purpose for coming to the studio. Riley, Presley's roommate, called earlier, left a message on his phone, Cowle piecing together a new scenario. Riley giving the business card Presley had to this student reporter to check out. *That has to be the case.* Cowle thankful Riley did that instead of going to the police, or perhaps the police rebuffed her request for assistance, a fortuitous opportunity preserving his secret, buy him a precious commodity in the form of time. *But for how long?* "You have yourself a story, Samantha," he told the defenseless girl. "Too bad it's will be your last." He snickered. "I hope you weren't planning to win a Pulitzer for this little adventure."

Now Marcus Cowle faced a more pressing issue.

"So what am I going to do with you, Samantha Grayson?" Cowle asked. The girl a fighter and strikingly beautiful; perhaps Sheik Rahim amenable to an additional piece of merchandise to this consignment, take her off his hands. *The least he could do,* Cowle thought, *I just kept your dirty little secret from being discovered.* He'd need to contact Rahim first, this not a matter to spring on him during the exchange as Rahim,, unlike Commander Omega, not one for surprises, even one as lovely as that lying at his feet.

"You might add a little extra to my bottom line," Cowle reached under Samantha's knees and behind her back, scooping the limp body up from the floor, arms dangling uselessly. "Hope you didn't have any plans for the rest of your life." Before calling his client had matters to address. Cowle carried Samantha back to the studio to immobilize and silence the unexpected guest so she caused no further trouble.

On the verge of tears Riley Bradford entered her silent room in Cockrell Hall, despite hours of study and preparation she either failed, or had come close to failing, the organic chemistry test so conspicuous in her thoughts. *God, I screwed that up!* Unable to concentrate, the equations and formulas a muddled jumble as all she could ponder was where Presley Harding might be and if she was safe.

Riley entered the room, no sign Presley returned or been there in her absence. *Damn you, Presley! Where are you!* Riley swallowed, fought down a rush of searing bile surging up from her stomach, sick from the combined stress of her friend's whereabouts and the disastrous effort on the test. She sat on the couch, rubbing her eyes to banish the throbbing behind them. She laid her head down on the pillow, wanted to rest awaiting word from Samantha Grayson of what she discovered on her visit to Marcus Evans Photography and if Presley had been there.

Riley closed her eyes, sniffed back the tears. *Just relax, Riley, just relax.* Within ten seconds she was fast asleep.

One by one Samantha's senses slowly turned back, a power grid restored block by block after a severe storm. Her hearing returned first, ears filled with the ragged sound of her breathing. Touch came next, lying on something cold and hard, puzzled by the tightness encircling her wrists and chest, about her legs. Her mouth ached, jaw sore. She heard her own moan and found it strange, muffled in some way, a steady drumbeat pounding in her temples.

What...happened?

Samantha attempted to reach up, rub her aching head, realized her arms pinned behind her. *Why can't I...?* Sight the final sense restored, eyelids fluttering open, greeted by darkness. *Where am I?* Then the memory of a desperate fight to survive flashed in her mind. Finding the camera in the studio of Marcus Evans, the photos on the preview screen of Presley Harding in peril, someone accosting her from behind, a struggle, running for the door and then...incredible pain never before experienced, a burning relentless wildfire annihilating her consciousness, plunged deep into a darkness that even now, awake and aware, continued to surround her.

Terror swept over Samantha, vision clearing, a horrified cognizance the darkness unnatural, laying on her side in a closet devoid of light except for a thin sliver of illumination seeping under the door. The constriction she sensed ropes coiled tight around her, biting deep into the skin, held motionless. Out of horrified reflex Samantha screamed. The cloth filling her mouth, held in place by the gag tied around her head, kept the cry for help left unheard except by her captor.

Samantha Grayson shuddered, a chilling recognition her life now veered down a dangerous path towards a terrible, and possibly deadly, destination.

Helpless...

Part Two

After...

Chapter 26

This is not good. Through the thick cloth gag set deep between her lips Samantha Grayson moaned, shivering in stupefied fear, bound body wriggling back into the corner of the closet. *This is bad, very bad.* Her nameless captor, was this the Marcus Evans whose name graced the storefront studio, stepped into the cramped cubicle, crouching before his luckless captive, on his face an expression of contentment examining her hopeless circumstance. He reached out, like an amorous lover the back of his hand caressing the flawless smooth skin of her cheek. Samantha wanted to jerk away from his touch yet remained still except for the frightened trembling of her body, a rabbit caught in the open under the predatory gaze of a falcon. A cold knot of terror twisted her stomach imagining every despicable act of violence this man capable of perpetrating on her in this utterly helpless condition. Samantha was, like Presley Harding in those pictures, at the uncertain mercies of the sick, twisted intentions burrowing through the mind of her captor.

She studied the man as he leaned over to check the bonds imprisoning her; he bore no resemblance to the image of Marcus Evans, the weathered face and dark hair, she found on the Internet. He wasn't a large man, his size hardly imposing, a stature and build Samantha considered slight. His features cut with angular sharpness, cheeks high and hollow, pale blonde hair cropped close to the scalp; satisfied smile thin and humorless as impassive gray eyes studied her, his face resembling a character from a Japanese anime cartoon. Samantha spotted the dark bruise under the right eye where she struck him hard with the camera. *At least I got a good shot in on the bastard*, now given her hapless state the accomplishment of no comfort.

Her captor noticed Samantha staring at the wound; the smile remained undisturbed as he touched the purplish spot, the bruise a badge of honor earned in battle against an outmatched opponent. "At least you put up a fight," he remarked casually. "They usually go down far easier than you did." The use of 'they' set off alarms in her head. Were there more victims than Presley? If so, what had this man done with them? *What have I gotten myself into?* Her captor edged forward, whispered in her ear. "I like ones who fight, it's more of a challenge. But I always win in the end." Samantha shuddered, mind whirling crazily at the statement's implication, not knowing exactly what he planned but understood those designs bode ill omens for her continued existence.

"Let's see who you are." From behind his back he produced the lanyard with her *Daily Northern* ID card, the press credentials from the Senator Fielding speech, Samantha already suspected he knew her identity, discovered the fact while she was unconscious, transformed into his powerless hostage, bound and gagged to prevent escape. With a theatrical flourish he read her name from the credentials. "Samantha Grayson," he nodded his head, "a charming name for a beautiful young woman."

He glanced at the credential, the smiling face on her staff ID card. "Senior Staff Reporter, *The Daily Northern*, Great Northern University," he announced dramatically, acting as if surprised by the fact. "I think Lois Lane has a big story here," he shot her a malicious sneer, Samantha whimpering through the gag. "Too bad Superman isn't coming to your rescue this time."

With a contemptuous nonchalance he dropped the lanyard and credentials on the floor at her bound feet. "So who else do I happen to know from Great Northern University?" Her captor asked out loud. "Her name wouldn't happen to be Presley Harding?" Samantha moaned a wordless reply of confirmation, the only answer she could offer. "Presley's a lovely young lady," the captor observing Samantha's discomfort as she struggled against the bonds, swept back the auburn hair falling over brown eyes filled with increasing trepidation, fighting to hold back a torrent of terrified sobbing. "Did you find those pictures of Presley interesting? All tied up snug and quiet, like you are now?" Samantha groaned, interesting not the word she'd use to describe the disturbing images.

"So you're here but Presley is nowhere to be found," the gray-eyed captor leaned closer, his presence let Samantha know he controlled the situation, acting as judge and possible executioner. "Now where could she be?" Samantha conflicted at the same time both wanting, and not wanting, to know the fate of the missing girl, the object of her search. "Don't you wonder what I did with Presley?" His voice dripped with sinister intent. "Or what I'm going to do with you?" The question produced a pathetic wail of fear from a thoroughly silenced Samantha. Behind her back fingers frantically groped for, but had no luck finding, the knot holding her wrists bound.

"I don't think anyone will know you're missing for a few hours," her captor continued. Samantha nodded weakly; no one knew she faced this life-threatening dilemma. All of her friends in class, only the ambiguous text sent to Lauryn Callahan. The earliest any of them realizing she was missing when her roommates went to meet her at *The Daily Northern* office to head into Chicago for Amanda's victory dinner at Toscana. By then, even if someone checked out the studio, it might be too late to save her. "That gives me enough time to take care of you."

He paused for a moment as Samantha squirmed uncomfortably in her captivity, finding obvious pleasure in her vulnerability. "For all you know, pretty Presley might already be dead." Samantha whined at the possibility, closing her eyes, shuddering at realization she might soon share an identical fate. "I could be a serial killer. Didn't you think of that when you came here? Poking around where you shouldn't have? That's not very intelligent for someone who attends a prestigious school like Great Northern. Then again, I don't think Presley was too smart either, took care of her without any problem," he laughed grimly. "You're going to wind up like her and the others." The reference to 'others' frightened Samantha, wondering how many had found themselves trapped in these dangerous straits. And if any of them were still alive.

Samantha fought back tears threatening to flow in an unrestrained cascade down her cheeks, tried remaining calm in the grasp of this monster, to be brave. He spoke the truth and it hurt, Samantha hadn't considered the likelihood Presley in horrendous peril when deciding at *The Daily Northern* to pursue this course of action, searching for the freshman on her own, without any assistance. She now thought of her decision in different terms, each word assailing a tortured ego: *stupid, dumb, foolhardy, lethal, deadly*.

"Wouldn't take much to get rid of you," her captor explained coldly. "Wouldn't take long at all." He reached forward, fingers brushing against her throat. "You're quite vulnerable like this. Could take a piece of rope, wrap it around that pretty neck, pull it a few times and no more Samantha, no more reporter snooping around in my affairs." He found gleeful enjoyment taunting the powerless Samantha. "Or I could take a plastic bag, put it over your head, tape the bottom closed. That'll cut off your air. It'll take a few minutes for you to suffocate. I can sit back, watch you struggle, enjoy the show. Tied up as you are there's no way you can fight back." Samantha squealed through the thick fabric muting her protests, brown eyes glistening with terror, resuming a useless fight against unyielding ropes as her captor continued his macabre soliloquy. Visions of such states of deadly distress, fighting hopelessly against the bondage as the last breath of life seeped from her bound body, tormented her mind.

"Of course, before I do away with you," her captor's hand slipped down to her bound legs, stroking the black microfiber tights, fingers trailing up her thighs, Samantha shaking as his touch fraught with carnal, yet violent, insinuations, sent panicked tremors rumbling through her muscles. "I'll have my fun with you. I do believe you know what I mean." Samantha understood and the horror, the fact she unable to stop him from violating her in vicious ways overwhelming. "I'm sure you'd be as enjoyable as Presley and the others." Even with threat of sexual violence hanging over her like a Sword of Damocles, Samantha heard him again mention victims other than Presley. Grew ever more convinced the unfortunate freshman a prisoner, or had already perished, at the hands of a homicidal maniac, another name added to a tragic list of murdered victims. And Samantha about to become the next name on that list.

"After I'm done with you, Samantha, I'll have to dispose of your body," he remarked with callous indifference. "I'd have to wait until dark so no one will notice. Wrap your body up in a sheet and load it in the trunk of my car. Drive out to the country, somewhere isolated, in the sticks. Wouldn't need to bury you very deep." He shrugged. "Might never find your grave out in the middle of nowhere and if they did, I don't think there'd be much left of you by then." He parted his hands. "A shame really, a beautiful young woman like you going to waste like that."

Samantha felt the trickle of a tear run down her cheek, the realization no one ever knowing her terrible final destiny, the brutal and lonely end. Not her parents back home in Upstate New York running the family winery, Grayson Farms, on the shores of tranquil Seneca Lake. Not her roommates and best friends in her life: Amanda McKinnon, Lauryn Callahan and Ashleigh Morgan. Not Tyler McManaway, her hero, the love of her young life. Not Aaron Dinehart and her fellow staff members at *The Daily Northern*. Fate forever a puzzling mystery as her body rotted away to bones in a shallow grave deep in a secluded Illinois woodland.

"That'd be a terrible thing, to rape and murder you like that." Her captor brought his hand back up to Samantha's cheek, stroked it gently, wiped at the tears streaming from her eyes, Samantha glared back in hatred and fear. "But you know what, Samantha? You're lucky. Nothing like that will happen to you." He paused. "Not yet, at least. I'm not going to have my way with you or hurt you. I won't kill you. And Presley and the others," again saying 'others,' how many victims were there beside Presley, "are still alive, though at the moment indisposed like you." He smiled, gray eyes glistening with evil. "You'll be joining them soon enough."

Samantha stared at him, brown eyes now clouded with confusion. Was her captor playing some sort of trick, a cruel joke to prolong the agony? "You see, I'm not what you think I am. Although, with where you may be going, you might wish I had finished you off anyway," he warned. *What is he talking about?* Samantha murmured in bewilderment through the gag. Was he, knowing Samantha's predicament hopeless, toying with her? He produced a smartphone from his jacket, pointing the device at her, used the camera to film her. "I need to discuss your particular situation with an interested party." Once done recording her defenseless state, the captor punched a number into the phone, Samantha wondering who waited on the other end of the call, and how they'd decide what to do with her, but knew whatever decision made meant terrible things for her continued existence.

For one familiar with countless brutal methods of heartless, pain-inducing torture, Sheik Abdullah al-Aziz Rahim considered being trapped amongst the politicians and businessmen at the reception following lunch at the Chicago Hilton and Towers an instrument of methodical torment not even he dare inflict on his most hated rival. Compelled to be cordial and conversational when his thoughts focused on the five new possessions Marcus Cowle secured for him and the one prize that for now eluded his grasp. Early tomorrow, before the sun rose over this cursed land, returning to Daharan on his diplomatic jet with his precious cargo, this time present to experience the abject terror and utter helplessness of his captives from the first moment of ownership. With such musings clouding his mind, he found difficult concentrating on the discussions eddying about him.

Listening half-heartedly to the self-serving drivel pouring from the mouth of the man representing Illinois' Ninth District in the United States Congress, Sheik Rahim nodded politely, trying to keep his gaze from fixing too intently on the man's attractive wife, a woman in her late forties and a trim physical specimen. Rahim smiled at her, but for his particular desires preferred women far younger. No doubt the wife here playing her supporting role in the stagecraft of power, a trophy to parade about, the politician presenting to gullible constituents an image of a durable, stable marriage. Rahim knew the appearance of happily wedded bliss a deceptive charade, contacts informing him the man possessed a mistress, an aide half his age working in his Washington office. *Such hypocrisy*, Rahim thought, *the way of all of their politicians*. As he listened to the man endlessly drone on Rahim couldn't dispel the vision of the young woman with auburn hair he spotted among the media gathered for Senator Fielding's speech at Cockrell Auditorium, a living reincarnation of the one who long ago spurned his advances, paid for her impertinence with her life yet in her violent passing triggered a never-ending quest to satisfy his bloodlust. Needed his people to discover her identity, then direct Marcus Cowle to hunt and subdue the woman, deliver her for his sadistic pleasure. This time, when he gained possession of the woman who so resembled the one whose life he brutally snuffed years earlier, he'd take care to insure this time the cruel suffering lasted far much longer until he at last extinguished her life.

From the corner of his eye he noted Saleh reach into his suit coat for his smartphone, check the screen, an imperceptible nod in his direction. *Cowle is calling so soon with the arrangements?* Rahim arched an eyebrow at Saleh, who nodded again in confirmation. "Will you excuse me," Rahim graciously explained to the congressman and his wife, "there is an important phone call I must take." With the courteous apology offered Sheik Rahim took leave, followed Saleh and a second bodyguard to an empty room off the reception hall to ensure privacy. Rahim and Saleh entered the room as the second bodyguard stood watch outside, preventing anyone from entering and interrupting, or overhearing, the subject of conversation.

Rahim took the phone from Saleh. "This is early to be contacting me regarding the arrangements for tonight, my friend."

"I wish that were so," Marcus Cowle replied, "but we have a complication to address."

"I see," Rahim answered coolly. "What is the nature of this problem?"

"One we needn't have worried about if the delivery hadn't been delayed at *your* request," Cowle returned, Rahim caught the snide insinuation. "Someone visited the studio searching for one of the packages. To assure this operation of ours remains a secret I had to take immediate measures. I'm calling to see if you'd be so willing to accept a sixth piece of merchandise to the consignment. Take care of this loose end for me. I'm not seeking much in compensation, but I do think you'll find this one quite fetching. She is the type who appeals to your tastes." Cowle paused. "I really don't wish to liquidate this piece of merchandise. It would be such a shameful waste."

That someone in question unfortunately stumbling on the operation a woman, Rahim rightly assumed, the only reason Cowle offered an extra parcel for the consignment. If it hadn't Cowle capable of expeditiously eliminating the problem out of hand. "In this case I need to examine the item beforehand," Rahim commented. "I hope you aren't attempting to pawn off something of poor quality."

"I understand your concern. Believe me," Cowle replied, "this one is up to your exacting standards. If she wasn't I wouldn't bother with this offer. I'm sending you a video of my guest. Don't worry, the file is encrypted." Rahim waited as the video downloaded and began to play, shocked at what he observed. *How can this be?* For a second his heart stopped studying the image of the young woman with auburn hair, brown eyes wide above the gag staring fearfully back at the lens, bound body cowering in a closet. The same woman who only hours earlier snared his attention at Cockrell Auditorium. *How could Marcus Cowle have known she is the one I wanted?* Only the capricious whims of fate explaining this happenstance, depositing the newfound object of his fervent, murderous lust into the hands of his trusted operative.

"Her name is Samantha Grayson, she's a reporter for the student newspaper at Great Northern University," Cowle intoned over the video of the girl struggling against secure bonds. Rahim enthralled with her beauty, intoxicated by her terror, provided a reason for her presence at the speech that morning. *She even shares the same first name.* "She came looking for the final piece of the shipment. Let's say she found something she didn't quite expect."

"I don't care how you have accomplished this." Rahim stared at the screen, unable to divert his gaze from the woman now known as Samantha Grayson, a woman to suffer for the sins of another who bore her given name many years earlier. Could only be the will of Allah for this to pass. "For the addition of this woman I will double what was originally decided on for the consignment."

A silent pause greeted his response; Cowle aware of the price arranged in advance for the five parcels of this shipment. "Really?" Was Cowle's surprised reply, taken back by the unexpected largesse. "I'm thankful for your...generosity in settling this matter."

"You have done for me a great service, my friend," Rahim watched, mesmerized by his object of obsession until the video ended. The picture of the helpless Samantha Grayson disappearing from the screen but burned into memory, desired to have her then, force her to submit, break her spirit. For Rahim to focus on any other matter this day, to bear the crass arrogance of his American hosts during the remainder of his stay in Chicago while waiting to take possession of his consignment, to own Samantha Grayson, posed a daunting prospect. For now he must restrain his desires, must remain a diplomat, must remain *a gentleman*. "For that I am ever grateful."

"I humbly accept your gratitude," Cowle replied. "Let us hope there are no further complications to address before the day is out and the exchange made."

"If there are, and whatever they might be, I am confident you will handle them accordingly," Rahim answered.

"I will contact you later with the location for the transfer." Cowle a cautious man despite their profitable partnership, The Trading Society an organization known for prudence when the situation called, never revealing to Rahim's people where the delivery to occur until hours prior to the rendezvous.

Rahim nodded, pleased at the blessing of good fortune, the rest of the consignment inconsequential. He'd take his pleasures with them anyway, delectable appetizers consumed before indulging in the main course. *Why waste a fine banquet when it is laid out before you?* "I will await your call." Rahim turned off the phone, turned to Saleh. "We will have an extra passenger for our trip home." An unwilling passenger fate delivered into his hands.

Samantha listened to the conversation between her captor and the person on the other end of the call. Her forehead creased in confusion. *Merchandise? Shipment? Consignment? What is he talking about?* Realization then hit Samantha with the force of a sledgehammer shattering a rock, dashing what little hope she grasped onto of escaping this peril. *Oh my God, he's a human trafficker! That's what he's done with Presley and the others! He's going to sell them! He's going to sell me!* Samantha aware of human trafficking, the vile practice of women and children sold by criminals into horrid lives of sexual slavery and sweatshop labor, but never imagining a dark evil of this appalling magnitude. Among unproven urban legends told, the tale of bands of kidnappers prowling the country abducting vulnerable, unsuspecting young women and shipping them overseas to cruel and wealthy overlords among the more far-fetched rumors circulated. Samantha laughed off so implausible a likelihood, thought it nothing but a plot contrivance on a television crime drama or Hollywood action movie, a product of overactive imaginations dealing with the tragedy of a person gone mysteriously missing. In her digging into the clusters of missing women across America this possibility of human trafficking, the deranged work of a clever serial killer seemed far more plausible, never once entered her mind. Samantha forced to face a cruel lesson the urban legend indeed an insidious reality, caught in its inescapable web, about to be sold, taken against her will to a place far from Chicago and Great Northern University and the life she once knew.

Her captor switched off the phone, looked at Samantha with a contented smile spreading across his smug face. "Never thought I'd see so tidy a payday from someone walking in off the street." He laughed maliciously. "I believe the good Sheik is quite smitten with you, Samantha."

What is going on here! Samantha screamed pitifully. *You can't do this to me! I'm a person, not something to be sold!* She pleaded futilely through the gag.

"I typically don't have philosophical conversations with the merchandise I'm about to sell. I'd rather have you seen and not heard," her captor shrugged his shoulders, one hand pushing her head down, the other reaching to tug at the knot, releasing the gag. "However, as you're a reporter, I think I'll give you the benefit of the story of a lifetime. A shame you'll never see your work in print as you're now part of the action."

Samantha felt the gag loosen, spat sodden wadding from her mouth, gasping for air, moving a jaw sore and aching from the cloth silencing her cries. Samantha raised her head, stared at her captor, brown eyes afire with what courage she could muster. "Who are you?" She demanded.

"The name on the front of the studio says Marcus Evans, an identity I acquired along the way. I'm quite good at being someone I'm not supposed to be. The real name is Marcus Cowle." His hand cupped Samantha's chin, frigid gray eyes returning Samantha's gaze. "And I, my dear, am a businessman."

"A businessman?" Samantha sneered with indignant disbelief. "You're a kidnapper, you sell women! You sell people! You're a human trafficker."

"I prefer white slaver," Cowle said with unabashed pride, "I like the sound of that better, direct and to the point. Has a certain ring to it, not as politically correct as human trafficker."

"Get your kicks tying up women?" Samantha strained against the ropes Cowle bound her with, noticed him leering at her vulnerable condition. "Enjoy your deviant jollies before you sell them off?"

"On that point, I wholeheartedly agree with your observation. You seem to know me quite well indeed," the laugh did little to ease her fear. "Such confinements make you easier to control, keeps you from causing any further trouble." Cowle grinned lecherously. "I'd say it's a perk of the profession. The female form seems accentuated with the addition of rope." He waved at her breasts, the black floral print bra exposed through the blouse ruined in the struggle, rope tightly wound about them. "Especially certain parts of the female form, you do have a fine pair there." At the lewd comment Samantha's face flushed red with embarrassment.

Samantha dreaded the answer she might receive for her next question. "Those women, the ones who've disappeared in other cities. You're the one responsible?"

"There are many more than those." The statement direct, devoid of emotion or regret for lives forever lost. "Before I convinced my client to order in bulk I snatched what he desired one at a time. Not an efficient method of supplying product in my opinion. This way far more economical, improves the profit margin, makes both of us happy." Cowle grinned devilishly. "I do have clients other than the generous Sheik, was down in Texas last week fulfilling an order for another client." Cowle sighed, mocking disappointment. "The demands of the business keep me on the move, but the compensation makes up for the hassle of travel and constant relocation."

Oh God, Samantha stunned by the revelation, *the two women from Texas Tech!* This evil far-reaching, and much larger, than a single person acting alone. How big was all this? "How could you..."

"Like I said, it's about business, nothing personal," Cowle cut Samantha off. "Each of them is worth a great deal to me. You're all product to be traded, bought and sold on the market like a bushel of wheat or a barrel of oil. Every woman I've collected over the years is money in my bank account. You and the others are the latest consignment which, thanks to your fortuitous arrival looking for pretty little Presley, will be one of my most profitable deliveries ever."

It's more than sixteen women, it's so much more. What was the total number of missing women Marcus Cowle snatched plying this despicable trade? Samantha feared the number might tally in the triple digits. "Don't you care what you've done? How much pain and suffering you've caused their families?" Thought of the emotional devastation her disappearance to wreak upon her family, to her friends, on Tyler. "They'll never know what happened to the ones they love."

"Honest answer, Samantha?" Cowle offered, and Samantha nodded. "I don't care at all what I've done. Like I said, I'm a businessman. I'll let you in on a little secret, most of the people in the business world care only about two things: money and power. They don't care if they've laid off hundreds of people to improve the bottom line or dump chemicals into the environment. They don't bother with worrying who they hurt, or the damage they wreak increasing their wealth, accumulating their power. It's all about them and no one else. They don't go to sleep each night worrying about the consequences of what they do. To survive, to thrive, they need to be cold, merciless, look out for one person and it's the one staring back at them in the mirror. That's why they're rich and powerful and everyone else isn't." Cowle continued. "I don't have a conscience, it's only a burden preventing me from achieving success. Why should I be troubled with what I do? This is about business and I have clients to please. If I don't give them what they want I don't get paid. When I satisfy their desires I get paid handsomely." He smiled. "If I don't do it someone else will."

"You sick bastard," Samantha cursed angrily through gritted teeth, shaking with rage.

"I'll take that as a compliment." Samantha disappointed if she thought Cowle insulted.

"How big is this?" Samantha didn't want to ask the question. "It has to be more than you."

"It's far bigger than you could ever imagine, Samantha. I'm not the only one engaged in this enterprise," Cowle admitted, Samantha shivered at the realization. "Let me tell you a story. You know from history slavery once was legal. You can't deny the practice helped build our nation. In fact slavery and servitude built many great nations and empires, it's been around since the dawn of mankind."

"Slavery was, and is, evil," Samantha shot back defiantly. "We fought a war to destroy it. Good people put an end to slavery."

"Such a textbook answer, but slavery still exists no matter who attempts to end to the practice, like any organism it adapts and evolves to survive in its environment," Cowle noted. "Look around today, do you see what ending slavery has done to this country? Has it solved anything? Did it really make anything better? Is everyone equal? To this day we're dealing with the ramifications, we might've been better off if we'd left the institution alone," Cowle acknowledged with a cool detachment. "But I digress from what's important, our little history lesson. You see, Samantha, there were bankers and ship-owners and crews of ships involved in the slave trade, earned their livelihoods and built fortunes on the business of human trade. Then one day, due to the misguided beliefs of self-righteous fools, their work declared illegal, banned, kicked out of their way of life. Were considered no better than criminals and now faced financial ruin."

"As they should have," Samantha retorted, shifting her body to lessen the strain on her back sitting bound in the closet.

"These men needed to find a different field in which to make their living," Cowle continued, the instructor presenting a classroom lecture to a single indisposed student. "Some moved on, left the trade behind, found respectable vocations. Others saw there still remained a demand for their particular talents. So like any good, forward-thinking capitalists they changed the business model. These like-minded gentlemen established what they called The Trading Society, albeit secret, to ply their unique type of commerce and offer a new product to a different customer base." Samantha suspected what the new product entailed, didn't need to be told by Cowle: defenseless young women.

"You're familiar with that 'one-percent' garbage those Occupy This and Occupy That do-gooders spout at their demonstrations? Being a college student hanging around those liberal types you must hear that drivel a lot?" Samantha nodded silently as Cowle plowed on with his discourse for his captive audience. "I deal with the one percent of the one percent. Our best customers, they're the ones truly running the world, they're the ones behind the curtain controlling the machinery. What drives them isn't the money, that's an ancillary benefit of their success, but the power to control everyone and influence everything that's around them. That's what they want, the power. They're the ones who decide who's elected to make the laws benefiting them. They think," Cowle paused, "they *know* they're above the laws that already exist. They manipulate the markets to their advantage so they'll have all the money, leave the dirty masses begging for morsels, fighting for the meager scraps. Start wars filling their coffers with profit while the less fortunate go off to fight and die for God and country. They control the message, manipulate the debate, silence voices of dissent. Decide who lives in comfort and who suffers in poverty and squalor. They control it all. They're the ones pulling all the levers, Samantha, and you can't do anything to stop them, they're far too powerful to defeat. All the sheep are too stupid, too willing to listen to what they want to hear, to ever realize they're being lead to the slaughter."

Cowle paused, more for dramatic effect than anything else. "Some of those people, rich and powerful, like to possess pretty young women to do whatever their hearts and minds desire, and some of those desires are very sick and demented. I allow them to do in private deeds if the public knew of would destroy their image, bring down their empires. You're a commodity for trade to them, something to be consumed, tossed aside like trash when used up. Many of them, including the man who's paying handsomely for you, like you exactly the way," he motioned at the ropes holding firm against Samantha's slender body, "you are right now." He leaned over, whispered in her ear. "For them it's all about control, about the power over life and death."

"How many have you...?" Samantha started to ask, feared the answer.

"Well, besides you and Presley there's four more ready for delivery tonight," Cowle explained. "As you might've heard, you've raised considerably the profit margin on this consignment."

Samantha lowered her head, defeated. "At least you're alive for now. I do know my client eventually tires of his playthings. His vigorous appetites are what keeps me in business. I've heard his methods for dispatch aren't particularly pleasant." Samantha felt her breathing quicken, an inevitable and ugly death awaited at the end of this tragic journey. She started once more to fight the ropes cutting harshly into her skin, straining for release. *I have to get free, I have to escape! I have to get help for Presley and the others!* She groaned as she labored, but the bonds refused to yield as she struggled, not ready to surrender, to give up hope.

"It's no use." Cowle watched Samantha battle the bondage, amused by fruitless efforts. "I tie good and tight. Had practice over the years, don't want my investments getting away."

"You'll never get away with this," all Samantha could say facing the enormity of her peril.

"How cliché, Samantha, how cliché. I expected far better from a student of such an illustrious university," Cowle disappointed the retort lacked originality. "I've gotten away with this many times before and I will get away with it again. I can't be stopped. There's no way you can escape, I'd consider your situation to be quite hopeless."

Within Samantha's soul anger flared. "You're a sick bastard! That's all you are!" She snarled at him.

"You're getting a little mouthy, Samantha," Cowle cautioned. "I don't like it when the merchandise starts talking back. I think it's about time I put an end to that." He reached into his jacket, brought forth another wad of cloth and a long strip of white cloth in his hand. He bunched up the cloth in his hand. "Be a good girl, Samantha, open that pretty mouth of yours." Samantha pressed her lips shut, twisting her head away from him. Knew she'd lose this contest in the end yet still resisted, exhibiting a paltry defiance against her captor.

"I guess we'll do this the hard way if you won't cooperate." Cowle hissed, expected the reaction, with blinding speed hand moving forward, pinching her nose shut. Samantha squealed, kept her mouth closed until lungs burned from lack of oxygen and she grew faint. As her lips parted to suck in a breath, Cowle released her nose, grabbed a fistful of hair and yanked her head back, shoving the cloth wadding in her mouth. With a deft movement the cloth strip, the fabric soft and giving, wound several times around her head, pushing the wadding further back behind her teeth, fixed firmly in place. He knotted the gag so tightly Samantha yelped in pain.

"No use trying to scream now," Cowle wagged a scolding finger at his prisoner, shoving her into the corner, Samantha whining weakly in protest. "No one will hear you." Cowle stroked Samantha's auburn tresses. "In due time you'll join Presley and the others," he informed her with the bland directness of a middle management executive delivering a termination notice to a laid-off employee. "You and your new friends are going far away. You'll never see your home, or your family or friends, ever again. It's a little excursion you'll never return from."

Cowle stood and reached for the doorknob, pulling the door closed, the cramped closet once more transformed into a dark, confined, solitary hell for Samantha. "Don't you wish you never came here in the first place, Samantha?" With the callous farewell Cowle shut the door. The inky darkness enveloped Samantha, extinguished her spirit. *Helpless.* She slumped to the floor, pulling bound legs towards her chest. She sobbed quietly knowing the wish Marcus Cowle spoke of to never come true.

So how do I play this? Cowle thought as he returned to the studio, leaving Samantha in the closet. For a moment he toyed with the idea of luring Presley Harding's roommate to the studio, then thought better of it, the move far too risky. The girl sought out Samantha's assistance after being rebuffed by the authorities, likely waiting for some bit of news regarding Presley from the now subdued reporter. How long would she be willing to wait until she suspected something wrong and went back to the police? *Unless she first calls Samantha to find out what happened to Presley*, then Cowle presented with an opportunity to compel Riley to come to the studio, take care of that solitary, dangling loose end. *Maybe another present for Sheik Rahim.* Knew he took a calculated risk allowing Presley's roommate to remain out there, a potential threat, the exercise of free market capitalism required the acceptance of a certain degree of risk.

"Let's see if anyone else knows you're here, Samantha," Cowle removed Samantha's iPhone from the shoulder bag in the front reception area, brought the device to his laptop for the unique software to pry every detail locked within. The software cracked the passcode instantaneously and Cowle discovered, much to his displeasure, a text message with the address of the studio sent to a Lauryn Callahan, noted the text received and read. He deleted it anyway, though the damage already done.

"The hits keep on coming," he cursed silently. *This is exactly what I was afraid of.* Had to expect the possibility others besides Riley Bradford, and not knowing how soon or how many it might be, coming to the studio in search of Samantha and Presley. *At least she didn't tell her to call the police.* Cowle picked up his phone, dialed a number. On the second ring Sterner answered. "Yeah?"

"How soon until you're done preparing the merchandise?" Cowle inquired.

"Presley's the last one getting cleaned up, then they'll be packaged for the Arab," he sensed urgency in his employer's voice. "What's up?"

"I need you here as soon as you're finished," Cowle said, "I'll explain when you arrive."

"I'll get there when I get there," Sterner answered, "have to place the last of the charges here in the factory."

"Make sure you bring the one for here." Cowle told him tersely, then switched off the phone wondering, due to his client's demands, what other unnecessary complications they'd be forced to handle in violent fashion.

Chapter 27

"How does your Mayor expect to handle the World Trade Organization and G-20 summits next year," Detective Patrick Flannery barely concealed the sarcasm in his voice. Contract talks between the city and the dispatchers at the city's 911 Call Center at the Office Emergency Management and Communications breaking down, the union making good their threat to walk out, not a good way to instill confidence in their guests of the city's capabilities to handle so important a world event.

"I asked that same question when they announced we were hosting the damn things," Detective Dawson 'Dawes' Hilliard told his new, yet temporary, colleague from the Dublin Police Department. "Hopefully it'll be settled by then. If not, we'll have a little problem handling this."

"Tell you this," Detective Devin Carson added, "it'll be an interesting next few days until this is cleared up. Get ready for some action." Heard response times to incoming calls-the 911 Center manned by a skeleton crew of supervisory personnel and trainees until the strike settled-growing longer by the minute and not helped by merry pranksters with bogus calls, sending police and fire crews to nonexistent emergencies, sowing mayhem in a chaotic situation.

Captain Andrew Hardaway approached their desks, holding two sheets of paper in his hand. "What are your plans right now?"

"We're about to head," Carson motioned to Nathanial Hampton of Scotland Yard and Flannery, "over to McCormick Place. Get the lay of the land since that's where the summit is taking place."

"Put it on hold for now," Hardaway told them. "I need both of you and your new partners on this." He handed one sheet of paper to Carson, the other to Hilliard. "We have two missing women," Hardaway stated the information on the sheets as Hampton and Flannery edged in. "Emma Hayden is a senior at Pacifica College and Alexandra Cole is a sales representative at McKinley and Ross in the Loop, she's never missed a day of work since she started there. Both live in Lakeview. Neither woman has been seen or heard from since Saturday. The Hayden woman's car was found in Englewood, it's been torched."

"That's not a good sign," Hampton said.

"I wouldn't say it is either," Carson said, examining the sheet.

"Why isn't Area North handling this?" Hilliard asked. "Lakeview is their stomping grounds."

"The detective who took both cases feels something isn't right here," Hardaway looked at Carson. "Thought you're the best person to handle it."

"Does he think…" Carson started to ask, stomach already turning in knots studying the photos of the missing staring at him from dispatch, reminding him of Tracie Weatherly and what he lost years earlier. Only two missing women, *for now*, but the similarities to the series of disappearances across the country the past four years troubled Carson, cases closely followed and his interest hardly a secret. Was the monster in Chicago, trolling and hunting for prey on the streets of the city? Had he already claimed two lives with the possibility of more victims out there?

"All I know is we have two missing women who appear to have vanished within hours of each other," Hardaway acknowledged. "And one of their vehicles was found abandoned on the South Side."

Hilliard snorted. "Not the place you leave your car parked overnight."

"Carson, take Flannery and check out the car," Hardaway ordered. "Hilliard, you and Hampton check out the apartments of the two women, both live in Lakeview, pretty close to each other. See if you can find anything to tell us where they went or who they might've been in contact with. The detective who received the cases is Benderson and he'll give you," Hardaway pointed at Carson, "what he knows so far about the two missing women."

"I guess this is where we earn our keep," Nathanial Hampton reached for the suit coat draped over his chair.

Carson shook his head. "You knew the honeymoon wasn't going to last."

"Well, back to work," D'Andre Watson leaned over to lace up his Nike football cleats.

"It's does feel better after a win," Tyler McManaway adjusted the red jersey with the number four over his shoulder pads, alerting the prep team defense Tyler the starting quarterback and should handle him with care. The first day of practice for the upcoming game, a contest against Minnesota in Minneapolis, not at all daunting or taxing, mostly agility and technique drills, loosening muscles and getting the kinks out following the win over North Carolina. The heavy lifting, when the coaches installed the game plan for the contest, taking place during practice on Tuesday and Wednesday.

"Everything is better after a win," Albert "Fiji" Fatuamala, the massive defensive end and companion, lifted his eyes from the book he read, *The Tao of Pooh*. "Everything is worse after a loss."

D'Andre shot him a look. "Which philosopher said that?"

"Me." Fiji pointed to his chest.

Tyler pulled his stool beside Fiji. "I have to ask you something."

"What is it?" Fiji puzzled by the request.

Tyler cleared his throat. "When are you going to get serious with Lauryn?"

"I like her." The question caught Fiji off-guard, cleared his throat. "Isn't that serious enough?"

"No, it isn't." This came from D'Andre. "Dude, the two of you are inseparable. You eat together, you study together, you go out together. You do everything together. To me that sounds like she's someone special."

Tyler added. "So tell Lauryn you love her and make it official."

"Make it official?" Fiji uncomfortable with the discussion playing out in the public square of the locker room. For one able to slash and tear through an offensive line comprised of three hundred pound behemoths with the dexterity of a jungle cat Fiji an introverted sort.

"At least then you'd know you had a real girlfriend," D'Andre kidded.

"Hey, watch it there," Fiji pointed at D'Andre, knew the college star now in the pros who'd been the target of the cruel online hoax.

"They say love conquers all, mate," Dante Clarke, the other philosopher on the squad, said from where he sat listening to the conversation.

"Even a big guy like you," D'Andre pointed at the Samoan. "Don't make us take bets on this."

"How do I go about it? Tell Lauryn..." Fiji sought their advice.

"Ask her out to dinner. Saturday after we get back from Minneapolis would work." Tyler put his hand on Fiji's shoulder pad. "Take her to a nice place, nothing fancy, just the two of you."

"Make sure it has candles," D'Andre advised. "You know, for ambiance. Good for when you want to get all romantic with the lady you love."

"Then what?" Fiji inquired.

Tyler grinned. "Sometime during dinner let her know how you feel for her," he explained. "Or you can tell her on one of your trips to Philosopher's Grove, the two of you feel comfortable there." Tyler paused. "If I know Lauryn I think she feels the same way about you."

"Really?"

D'Andre shook his head. "You're a man of few words."

"Actions always speak louder," Fiji replied. His actions on the field spoke loudest of all.

"Then start acting and tell Lauryn you care for her," Tyler told him, "so everyone will stop wondering when you and Lauryn are going to get serious."

"Speaking of serious," D'Andre changed the subject. "Ashleigh told me Samantha looked pretty fine this morning heading off to cover that speech."

"Fine? She looked fantastic." Tyler smiled, the image of Samantha from the morning a pleasant picture to occupy his mind during passing drills.

D'Andre arched an eyebrow. "High heels turn you on?"

Tyler nodded. "That, and the skirt, and the blouse, and the black hose..."

"I get the idea," D'Andre raised his hand, stopped him from going further. "Doing anything with Samantha after the girls get back from dinner?"

"Head to the Rathskeller for coffee, then sit on the deck at Howell Commons looking at the stars," Tyler stood from his stool as players started heading out to the practice field.

"Sounds like a hot date," D'Andre kidded.

Tyler shrugged his shoulders. "Anything is a hot date as long as I'm with Samantha." No need for extravagance, being with Samantha Grayson at a candlelit table or under a canopy of stars enough to satisfy him. Only had to wait until this evening to spend time with the woman he loved.

What once had been a bright sunshine yellow Chevrolet Impala now sat a charred, stripped framework of blackened metal and melted plastic, its final resting place a desolate street in the middle of the equally bleak Englewood neighborhood on Chicago's South Side. Devin Carson checked the license plates declaring Minnesota the 'Land of 10,000 Lakes.' "The car is registered to Emma Hayden, 2742 Willowbrook Lane in Edina, Minnesota," the uniformed officer from the Englewood District, Pennington his name, informed Carson and Patrick Flannery.

Carson nodded, the home address matching the information Benderson gave him over the phone on the way to the location. "The same Emma Hayden who's a student at Pacifica College."

"Any idea how long the car's been here?" Flannery asked, the thick Irish accent catching Pennington's attention though he knew better to ask where the detective from. The single-minded expression creasing Carson's face told him this not the time for small talk.

"One of the residents," getting people in the neighborhood to talk to the police on any subject a difficult task, an echo chamber of silence, "saw the car out here on Saturday afternoon."

"See anyone fitting the description of the Hayden woman?" Carson asked. A white female, five foot two and a hundred and ten pounds with long brown hair and blue eyes couldn't be missed in this area, glaringly standing out given Englewood's racial makeup.

Pennington shook his head. "She didn't see anyone, just the car." The officer paused. "Do you think she was down here to buy...?"

Carson cut him off. "None of her friends said Emma used drugs, wouldn't have a reason to be down here," he replied curtly. "For now I'll believe them until I think otherwise."

"The woman said she saw a black van pass her house with two white men inside, about ten minutes before she looked out and saw the Impala. Didn't think anything of it at the time," Pennington offered.

Here a detail for Carson to ponder. Was the black van and the men inside connected to Emma's disappearance? How many black cargo vans were there in Chicago? And without a license plate number to go on. *Too damn many.* "The gangs are slacking off if it took until this morning to get to stripping and torching the car," Carson remarked absently, motioning to the trunk.

"Haven't checked it yet," Pennington replied, "dispatch said to wait for you to get here."

Carson and Flannery walked to the rear of the car. Carson crouched down, peering under the chassis, no trace of blood on the pavement, a telltale sign a body inside the trunk. He nodded to Pennington, who leaned inside the shattered remains of the vehicle, popped the trunk latch. Carson eased up the deck lid, charred metal creaking, holding his breath at what he might find.

Nothing. *Thank God.* Carson exhaled, relieved the worst not yet realized, but no small consolation since Emma Hayden still missing, the abandoned vehicle an unsettling indication of foul play. At least he didn't have to inform a grieving family, already on their way to Chicago from Minneapolis, of their daughter's death. *But for how long?*

"What do you think?" Flannery asked him.

"I'm thinking someone dumped the car, intended the locals take care of the evidence, do their dirty work," Carson surmised, insinuating himself into the mind of his possible subject. *But why? And where is Emma?* "I'd love to talk to those men in that black van."

"Doesn't get us any closer to findin' either her or the Cole woman," Flannery acknowledged, looking about the street, dumbfounded at the blight and desolation of an area ground down to the bone by crushing poverty. Dublin had a fair share of poor neighborhoods but nothing resembling a shattered Third World war-zone.

"No, it doesn't," Carson felt his phone vibrate, pulled it out to answer. "Carson," he said, then listened. "Okay, we're on our way."

"What is it?" Flannery asked.

"They found Alexandra Cole's car," Carson said, "up in North Lawndale. If you think this is bad, up there isn't much better." Same relentless poverty and bleak hopelessness, different part of the city.

"Where's that in relation to here?"

Carson answered as they headed to their unmarked sedan. "About six miles northwest."

"Got a bad feeling about this, fella?" Flannery wondered.

"Getting worse by the minute," Carson replied. If the same party responsible for the disappearances going to far-reaching lengths to dump the cars in separate locations, places where the vehicles became easy targets for other, far more opportunistic, criminals. Already two women missing over the same weekend, were there more they didn't yet know about? Only then might Devin Carson know they faced a shadowy, unknown evil responsible for a reign of terror across the country.

"You haven't seen her since Saturday morning?" Detective Dawson 'Dawes' Hilliard questioned the landlord of the Lakeview building where Alexandra Cole rented her one-bedroom apartment.

The landlord, a balding older-aged man with a pear-shaped body narrow up top and rounder along the waist, nodded as they reached the third floor landing. The exertion induced a shortness of breath for the landlord, panting heavily ascending the stairs. "Saw her leaving that morning. I waved to her," working in the garden in courtyard, "she didn't look too happy. She's a nice kid, quiet, keeps to herself, doesn't cause any trouble, pays her rent on time. Kind of tenant you want. Looked like she was dressed for work. Damn shame, going into work on a Saturday."

"Did she say anything as she was leaving?" Detective Nathanial Hampton asked. This the first thing he said during the visit.

The landlord caught Hampton's accent. "You not from around here?" He asked in an earthy Chicago accent, the you coming out as more of a rough and tumble *youse*.

"Let's say I'm on loan from across the pond," Hampton cordial in his response, then repeated politely. "Did she say anything?"

"No." The landlord shook his head. "She waved at me, then walked to her car."

"Last you saw of her?" Hilliard said as they reached the apartment.

"That I did," the landlord started unlocking the door. "Maybe she came back that afternoon and someone else saw her. But Saturday morning was the last time I saw her." As he turned the key they heard a scratching sound from behind the door, detectives quickly pulling nine-millimeter automatic pistols from their holsters, motioning the landlord to step aside. Hilliard turned the doorknob, pushed the door open, entering the apartment with guns at the ready.

There was no danger to confront, no threat to face, only a golden retriever standing in the foyer staring up with woeful brown eyes at the detectives, whimpering in distress, pawing nervously at the floor. *Where's my Mommy?* Hilliard and Hampton moved past the dog, checking rooms for any sign of the missing occupant, found nothing. Hilliard glanced at ceramic dog bowls barren of food and water, caught the pungent whiff of urine and feces before seeing stained newspaper by the locked sliding glass door to the balcony.

Hampton peered into the bedroom as Hilliard crouched down to rub the dog's neck, checked his tag, the retriever licking his face in appreciation. "Wrigley," Hilliard noted, "good name for a dog. Better than Comiskey." Hilliard glanced about the apartment, turned back to the dog. "You wouldn't know where your Mommy might be?" Wrigley gave Hilliard a despondent look he had as much idea as Hilliard did to the whereabouts of Alexandra Cole.

"Damn, this place stinks," the landlord, standing at the odor, cursed.

Hilliard scratched the dog's ears. "Let's see you hold it for two days in a locked apartment."

The landlord shrugged. "Do I have to wait to clean this up? Until you send some crime scene guys to check this out?"

"I don't think his poop is evidence," Hilliard joked lamely, rubbing the coat of the retriever, tail wagging broadly with the newfound attention.

"Like what we found at the Hayden woman's flat." Hampton emerged from the bedroom, holstering his pistol. The two searched the apartment of Emma Hayden a half-mile north of Alexandra Cole's apartment. "Looks like she went somewhere. Empty hangers in the closet, makeup taken from the bathroom. Maybe she went on a trip, didn't tell anyone where she was going." Hampton assumed. "She wasn't too fond of her job, perhaps she decided to get away from it for a stretch."

"And leave her dog alone like this?" Hilliard shook his head, apparent to him the dog well cared for, anxious at his owner's unexplained absence. "I can tell Alexandra loves this dog. I think wherever she went she expected to return that day. If she was heading out of town or was planning on being gone longer she'd put him," he rubbed Wrigley's head, "in a dog kennel. Or at least have someone in the building look after him. Wouldn't leave him to fend for himself." Now the evidence clear Alexandra Cole indeed missing and not of her own free will.

"So we have no idea where either woman went," Hampton noted. "We know they haven't posted on their social media accounts since early Saturday afternoon." This detail gleaned from friends of the two women, in turn communicated to them by Detective Benderson. *As if they fell into a hole and never came out*, Hampton thought, the search of the apartments proving a dead end.

"Emma's last post on Twitter had her telling a friend she didn't feel like going out Saturday night," Hilliard added. "I lay even odds she didn't send that tweet."

"I'm not a betting man, but even if I were I wouldn't touch that," Hampton replied. "We don't have much to go on, mate."

"We might," Hilliard reached for the leash hanging by the front door, attached it to Wrigley's collar, "but I don't think he's able to tell us." The dog happily licked Hilliard's hand.

"You're taking him with us?" Hampton incredulous by his action.

"I don't trust Animal Care and Control." The dog lover inside Hilliard unwilling to chance leaving the dog with the agency. Their luck to find Alexandra only to learn someone at the city shelter put the dog down through a bureaucratic mistake. "Besides, he's a witness."

Cowle heard the door from the garage open, footsteps against the wooden floor. Another visitor to the studio but this one Cowle expected. "Are they settled in?" Cowle asked of the five pieces of merchandise awaiting shipment at the factory. "Ready for their trip?"

"All cleaned up," Sterner entered the room. "Nice little packages for the Arab."

"Have to help any of them get ready?" Cowle inquired.

"No," a crooked smile on his face, "we convinced them it'd be better if they took care of themselves instead of having Lang and I do it for them."

"Good," Cowle satisfied at least one thing going his way this day.

Sterner noticed the bright red welt on the side of Cowle's face. "Is that the reason you wanted me here?"

"We have another guest." Cowle brushed at the bruise where the captive in the closet struck him with the camera. "Her name is Samantha Grayson. She's a student reporter from Great Northern University. Seems Presley's roommate went and convinced Samantha to go looking for her friend."

"You want me to dump the body?" Sterner scratched his goatee. "Or do you want me to finish her off?" He pondered the quickest, most efficient method to dispatch the interloper. Capable of brutal violence, utilized the grim skills during their time in Atlanta to deal with a similar complication.

"No need for that," Cowle dismissed the offer. "I had a pleasant conversation with Sheik Rahim after I put her away for safekeeping." Cowle smiled. "He'll take her off our hands and for a handsome fee. He's doubling what he's already paying us to add her to the consignment."

Sterner let out a contented whistle. *Payday.* "Is she hot?"

"Do you think he'd spend that sort of money if she wasn't?" Cowle brought out his smartphone. Played for Sterner the video of Samantha sitting on the floor of the closet, struggling against her bondage.

Sterner nodded, his question answered. "Yeah, she's hot." *Too bad for her*. "Like I said, the Arab's got good taste in women," Sterner noted with a satisfied grin, in his head tallying the proceeds from the unexpected windfall. Already expecting a lengthy respite after delivery of this order, unlike the past when time off fleeting, heading to the next city to set up their operation. *Let the booze and whores flow like water*. "Not a bad bit of luck."

Cowle snorted. "Might've turned out differently if I hadn't taken care of our guest before she could escape." He rubbed his head, still aching from the blow Samantha dealt, exhaled in frustration. "I was afraid of something like this with the delay in delivery."

"I wouldn't sweat it," Sterner said, "been following the news today while helping our guests get ready. The dispatchers at the city's 911 call center are on strike, they got trainees handling the calls, turning into a huge clusterfuck. Even if those chicks are reported missing it'll take a while before the cops find out, by that time we'll be long gone," Sterner examined the positive. "I think we're in the clear."

"I wish I could be as optimistic but Samantha sent a text to a friend, I wasn't able to erase it in time." Cowle informed his associate. "And we have to worry about what Presley's roommate will do when she doesn't hear from Samantha. There's a chance we'll have to deal with additional problems before we dispose of this property."

"I can handle problems," Sterner nonplussed by the possibility.

"That's why I want you here now instead of later," Cowle told him. "Is the factory rigged?"

Sterner fished a small object the size of a car key fob from his pocket, tossed it to Cowle. "Press that button when we're through dealing with the Arab and twelve minutes later there'll be a hot time on the town."

"Do you have the device for here?"

"It's in the van." Sterner jerked a thumb to the garage. "This place will go up like a Roman candle on the Fourth of July."

"Excellent," Cowle pleased, "we don't want to leave a trail for the police." By the time they finished sifting through the blackened debris of both structures Sheik Rahim home with his merchandise and Cowle and his associate enjoying their proceeds in an exotic locale. "Let's pack what we need from here." The furniture and trappings of home left behind, consumed in the coming conflagration, purchasing whatever furnishings they desired in the next city they called home.

"No problem, Boss," Sterner said.

"Leave the surveillance monitors for last," Cowle told him. "I want to keep my eyes open." He suspected, though hoped the possibility didn't come to fruition, they'd have to deal with further guests before departing the address on North Campbell Street for the final time.

Chapter 28

Amanda McKinnon stood before the mirror, running a brush through raven hair damp after her shower, shaking her head and using a hand to fluff up the pin-straight tresses. Amanda usually showered at the 'Mick,' as the McIllhenny Family Athletic Training Center called by the varsity athletes, following cross-country practice, today returning to Falmouth Hall, preparing for a celebratory dinner in Chicago, a treat from her roommates for her victory. "You ready to head to *The Daily Northern* office and drag Samantha away from her computer?" Amanda asked her roommates as they finished dressing for the evening out. "I'd think Lois Lane needs a break about now."

"I'm ready," Lauryn Callahan emerged from the room she shared with Samantha Grayson.

"You look fantastic, Little Red," Amanda observed. Lauryn wore khaki pants, a light blue blouse with a black blazer, brown flats on her feet. "I think Fiji," that being Albert 'Fiji' Fatuamala, the gentle Samoan giant, "would like seeing you in that."

"Thank you, I think he would too. That's why I'm seeing him after we get back," Lauryn replied, smiling at the compliment. "I think your outfit's nice too." Amanda chose a black skirt and tights, a lightweight black merino wool cardigan sweater draped over a white camisole top trimmed in delicate lace, sensible black leather flats on her feet. Unlike Samantha no high heels for her. "Seeing Connor tonight?"

"You think I'm letting this go to waste?" A sly smile dimpled Amanda's cheeks, Lauryn understood the look in those amethyst eyes. "Besides, we still have to study for a test on Wednesday." She called out. "Ashleigh! Are you almost ready?"

"Now I am, Gazelle," Ashleigh Morgan stepped from the room she shared with Amanda, dressed in a gray linen pantsuit and black knit top, wearing black high heels. She knew what her friend about to ask. "Yes, I'm meeting D'Andre when we get back."

"You know what he's going to say about that outfit," Amanda said.

"That the pants show off my bodacious booty," Ashleigh replied with a straight face, grinning brightly as a second later the three broke into laughter.

Amanda checked her watch. "Come on, let's get going." Amanda offered to drive into Chicago since her friends picking up the tab for dinner. "I don't want to be stuck in traffic with that wonderful Italian gourmet dinner waiting for me." *Better when I'm not paying for it.*

The trio stepped into the hallway as Allison Mayne and Natalie DiLaurenzo returned from cheerleading practice. "Look at the girls all dressed up for a night on the town," Allison cooed to the well-attired threesome.

"We should've asked if you wanted to join us," Ashleigh said.

"This is Amanda's night," Natalie told her. "We'll get together some other time."

As long as Bryce doesn't tag along, Ashleigh thought. "Let's set a date when we get back."

"Off to fetch Samantha?" Allison asked.

Amanda nodded. "Have to drag Little Miss Pulitzer away from her story for a few hours."

"Have fun," Natalie said as the two groups went their separate ways.

The trio exited Falmouth Hall, headed across campus to Howell Commons, the late afternoon mild and agreeable with barely a trace of humidity in the air. Took the elevator to the third floor when they reached Howell, entered the offices of *The Daily Northern*. Two of them instantly surprised by what they found.

"So…where's Samantha?" Amanda expected to find their friend sitting at a desk typing away.

Ashleigh waved to get the attention of a young man sitting at the nearest desk. "Is Samantha Grayson here?"

The reporter lifted his head from his laptop, shook his head. "Haven't seen her all afternoon."

"Then she must be where she said she's going to be," Lauryn announced matter-of-factly.

"Come again?" Amanda shot Lauryn a puzzled look. "What are you talking about?"

"She sent me a text when I was in class this afternoon," Lauryn explained. "Good thing I wrote it down," she removed the notepad from her shoulder bag, "because it got deleted somehow." She looked at the notation on the paper. "Here it is, 2371 North Campbell Street."

"Why didn't you tell us back at the room?" Amanda wondered. "Before we came over here?"

"Because I didn't know if she would be here or there," Lauryn added. "So now that we're here and she isn't here then it's obvious she's there. So that's why I'm telling you about it now, because she's not here, she's there."

"You have a way of putting things," Ashleigh smiled at their friend's peculiar method of expressing her thoughts. At times Lauryn's comments resembled a road winding through the rolling countryside until it, after countless twists and turns, finally reached the destination.

"Let's see what's at this this address that's so important Samantha had to go there." Amanda tapped the Google app on her phone, typed the address in the search box. Her eyebrow rose in surprise at the result, informed her friends of the discovery. "Marcus Evans Photography."

Puzzlement blossomed on Ashleigh's face. "Did she ever mention this place to you?"

Amanda shook her head. "Nope," then asked Lauryn, "did Samantha give a reason why she was going there?"

"No, just sent me the address and to meet her there if she wasn't here," Lauryn replied.

"So why would she go there?" Ashleigh wondered out loud.

"We aren't getting any answers standing around here," Amanda typed a text in reply to Samantha's phone. ***Got ur message. On r way***. She motioned to the doorway of *The Daily Northern*. "I hope this little side trip doesn't make us late for our reservation."

They didn't tell any of the staff of *The Daily Northern* where they were headed.

Marcus Cowle saw the screen of Samantha Grayson's iPhone flash, the device vibrating on the table. He checked the screen, a text message from an Amanda McKinnon, another of Samantha's friends. *There are at least two of them*, on their way to the studio to meet their friend. *If only Sheik Rahim knew how close we're cutting it*, Cowle thought sourly. At least none of the disappearances yet publicized in the media, the strike by the city's emergency dispatchers providing him an unexpected advantage.

He called out to Sterner. "It seems we'll have some more guests stopping by," he informed simply. "I think we should prepare an appropriate welcome."

"I'm good with that." Sterner knew the sort of greeting Cowle intended.

"This reminds me of Toronto, traffic is just like the QEW." Amanda McKinnon spoke of the Queen Elizabeth Way in her native Ontario, grumbling while threading her Hyundai Sonata through the stop-

and-go automotive conga-line of rush hour on the Kennedy Expressway. The names of the roads might change, and in Canada speeds and distances posted in kilometers, but the frustration of navigating bumper-to-bumper traffic remained the same.

"No different from Atlanta," Ashleigh Morgan added from the back, watching scenery crawl by.

"And Denver," Lauryn Callahan sat in front alongside Amanda.

Amanda glanced at Lauryn. "What exit do I take?"

Lauryn checked her smartphone. "Fullerton Avenue," she pointed at the sign above the freeway, "it's coming up in a half-mile."

Amanda peered over her shoulder, switched on the turn signal. "Hey! I want to get off!" She shouted at a tan minivan not allowing her space to pull over. "That's what the flashing red signal on the back of the car is for, you hoser!"

Ashleigh laughed at the outburst. "Don't go Canuck on them, Gazelle."

"I won't go Canuck on them if," Amanda peered back over her shoulder again, the minivan finally relenting, giving her room, "they'd let me in!" Amanda eased the candy-apple red Hyundai into the exit lane.

"I'm sure they aren't too fond of you either," Ashleigh remarked.

"Feeling's mutual," Amanda shrugged. "We wouldn't be dealing with this if Samantha weren't at this photo studio in the first place. Any idea why she's there?" Amanda asked. "She didn't say anything about it this morning."

"Maybe she's getting racy photos for Tyler in that outfit she wore to the speech," Ashleigh offered. Seemed odd for Samantha, ever responsible and reliable, not to tell them of her plans.

Amanda tilted her head. "Can you imagine Samantha getting sexy pictures for Tyler?"

"If it's for your man, you'll do whatever it takes to get him all excited," Ashleigh replied with a seductive lilt. "Some naughty pictures might do the trick."

"Would you do it for D'Andre?" Lauryn asked.

"Perhaps," an evasive answer from Ashleigh, then added with a shrewd smile. "Hell, yeah."

"Maybe Samantha's working on a story," Lauryn proposed helpfully, "something coming up at the last minute."

"Then she should've said so when she sent that text." Amanda reached the bottom of the exit ramp, turned right to head west, lowering the visor to block the glare of a sun setting on the horizon from her amethyst eyes. "She has a one-track mind when she's working a story." Amanda paused. "Have either of you gotten the sense something's bothering Samantha?"

"You got that vibe too?" Ashleigh said. "She seemed out of it at lunch on Friday."

"She wasn't her usual upbeat self," Lauryn gave her observation. "I wonder what was troubling her. But Tyler's been a little up and down too." Lauryn hoped it wasn't what she suggested next. "Do you think Samantha and Tyler are having...?"

"No, it's not that," Amanda cut her off. "She would've told us if there was something going on between them." No visible signs of trouble in paradise between Samantha Grayson and Tyler McManaway. "But I don't think it was the reason she told us, being nervous about covering this speech today. She's worked bigger stories." One of those stories, during her freshman year, propelled Samantha from lowly rookie to star reporter at *The Daily Northern*. Amanda wondered. *Then what's bothering her? Not like her to keep us in the dark.*

"Maybe Samantha's working on something she can't tell us about," Lauryn added. "You know how she loves journalism and working at *The Daily Northern*. Doing what you love is important in life. You don't want to get stuck doing something you hate. That's bad and bad is never a good career move." Amanda and Ashleigh smiled as Lauryn spoke; wandering off on a tangent in the middle of the sentence. "But I guess you're right. I don't think Samantha and Tyler are, you know, breaking up."

"Speaking of relationships," Amanda saw her opening. "When are you and Fiji getting serious?"

"Aren't we already serious?" Lauryn blushed, pale cheeks turning red. "We spend a lot of time together." The two studied together and, when possible, dined together. A day didn't pass without them spending time by themselves. Lauryn glanced at her friends. *Maybe they're on to something.*

Ashleigh wagged a finger at Lauryn. "I think you and Fiji are beyond the 'being friends' stage."

"You two are absolutely adorable together," Amanda added. "Everyone can see how deeply you feel for each other."

"I do like him, I really like him," Lauryn finally confessed. "I feel good when I'm with him. He makes me happy."

"This is more than 'liking' him, Lauryn," Ashleigh prodded.

"He's a big teddy bear," Lauryn added with a glowing, satisfied smile.

"One that'll rip the arms off the other team's quarterback," Amanda remarked.

"So you're saying Fiji and I are in love?" Lauryn pondered Ashleigh's proposition for a moment, stared in astonishment at her friends. "But we haven't admitted it yet?"

"If it looks like love and it sounds like love, believe me, you're in love," Ashleigh counseled.

"At last the light bulb in that pretty red head of yours turned on," Amanda grinned. "And you wouldn't be an imaginary girlfriend either."

"So how do I tell him? When do I tell him?" Lauryn asked, bewilderment shining in the emerald eyes. "That I love him."

"Next time the two of you are alone, take his hand and tell him how you feel for him," was Amanda's straightforward, to-the-point suggestion. "No need for dramatics. Go to Starbuck's at Howell Commons, you always go there, get a table in a quiet corner and tell him he's the one who sets your little heart on fire."

"I think the feeling is mutual," Ashleigh agreed. "Girl, the two of you should've been serious a long time ago! Everyone's wondering when it's going to happen."

"Really?" Lauryn quietly acknowledged, considering what her friends said. Lauryn silently admitted she did care deeply for Albert 'Fiji' Fatuamala, comforted in his presence. Made her feel special, times when Lauryn able to spend every waking moment with him. *I guess that's what love is,* she thought, floating along in a dream-like trance, *and I'm in love.* Lauryn glanced down at her smartphone and the Google map with the directions, jolted back to reality. "Amanda, the turn is coming up on the left," she warned.

"Got it." Amanda slowed the Hyundai, waited for traffic from the opposite direction to pass until she had an opening, turned left onto North Campbell Street. Samantha's blue Ford Mustang parked on the west side of the street caught Amanda's immediate attention, only a few doors down from the address for Marcus Evans Photography.

"There's her car," Amanda leaned forward as they passed. Nothing seemed amiss with the vehicle but the storefront, slightly incongruous on the residential street, appeared dark. She spied an empty space five cars down from Samantha's car, eased the Hyundai into the space with a contented smile. Finding parking the only drawback of driving into Chicago.

Marcus Cowle, with Sterner standing by his side, studied the monitor as the red Hyundai Sonata slowed while passing Samantha Grayson's blue Mustang, drove further down the street to slide into the next open parking space. Smiled seeing three women inside the car, perhaps his payday to treble if Sheik Rahim amenable to delivery of additional merchandise.

"Our guests have arrived," Cowle told Sterner, picked Samantha's iPhone up from the table. "Why don't we invite them inside?" Pressed the remote to unlock the front door. He tapped out a message on the virtual keyboard, sent the text to the number Samantha sent her earlier missive. *Come into my parlor said the spider to the fly.* In this case it wasn't one fly but three young women about to be caught in this web.

"Don't worry," Sterner remarked coldly, "I think we have more than enough rope."

The ringtone on Lauryn Callahan's phone, a recording of her three dogs barking, was a reflection of her personality and what she considered important in life. She checked the screen, read the incoming text message. "It's from Samantha," she told her friends.

"What does she say?" Amanda asked.

"She says to come in," Lauryn said. "She's almost done."

"Doing what?" Ashleigh studied the storefront, couldn't express why but suddenly something about this didn't seem right, or why her suspicions now heightened.

"She doesn't say," Lauryn replied.

Amanda tilted her head. "Guess we'll find out when we go in."

"How did Samantha know we're here?" Ashleigh insistent with her question. *Why did she text us instead of calling? Why doesn't she say she'll be right out? Why does she want us to come inside?* Then came a final conclusion quite unsettling. *Why do I have a bad feeling about this?*

"Maybe she saw us drive up and park?" Lauryn offered helpfully.

Ashleigh glanced at the bay windows of the storefront; saw black cloth draped across the back of each one, wanted to reply. *How could she have seen us drive past?*

"Come on, let's go," Amanda stepped out of the car. "My victory dinner at a four-star nouveau Italian restaurant is waiting and I know you're," she pointed to Ashleigh, "itching to throw down that American Express gold card to pay the bill."

Lauryn exited the car, Ashleigh joining them after a moment's hesitation, troubled by the out of the blue text from Samantha as they arrived. The three crossed the street, walked towards Marcus Evans Photography.

Samantha was inside. But the friends didn't know Samantha not the one who sent the message.

"They've taken the bait," Cowle understood the psychology of his targets, studied the subject during his brief stint in college. They felt safe, 'Samantha' had contacted them. They'd enter unaware of danger. He switched on the cell phone signal jammer, watching with hungry eyes as they exited the vehicle, instantly recognized one of the women, statuesque and dark-skinned, crossing the street towards the studio. *Well, isn't this a pleasant surprise.*

"Let's set the trap." He motioned for Sterner to follow.

Chapter 29

An overpowering shudder ran down Ashleigh Morgan's back, dispersing throughout her body, bringing forth an involuntary shiver, as they reached the front of Marcus Evans Photography. Through the door saw the front room dark; no sign Samantha Grayson waiting for them. A sudden apprehension swept over her, an ocean wave crashing on shore, a silent warning under no circumstances should she, or her friends, go inside this building. "I think I'll wait out here," Ashleigh stopped on the sidewalk.

Amanda raised an eyebrow at her hesitation. "What's wrong?"

Ashleigh shook her head. "Something about this doesn't feel….right," was the only way to put her misgivings into words.

"We know she's inside," Lauryn said. "She sent us a text."

Amanda waved at Lauryn. "There you go."

Ashleigh placed her hands on her hips, stared at her companions. "How do we know it was Samantha who sent that?"

"God, you're being paranoid!" Amanda rolled her amethyst eyes, easily brushing aside Ashleigh's doubt. "She's probably doing something special for Tyler, we talked about on the way here." She frowned at Ashleigh. "You're the one who suggested that in the first place."

"Why didn't she tell us what she was doing?" Ashleigh stood her ground. "Why is she doing it on a day when she's working on one of her biggest stories for *The Daily Northern*?"

"Maybe she wants this to be a surprise," Amanda flicked out a finger, then flicking out a second finger, "and she might've already scheduled it for today."

"Why didn't she tell us yesterday when we told you about dinner tonight?" Ashleigh surprised at her passion pursuing the argument. Lauryn stood quietly watching her friends' quarrel, head swiveling between the two like a front row spectator at a tennis match and their words the ball volleyed over the net.

Amanda sighed, her tone condescending. "Because if she told us that defeats the purpose of it being a surprise!"

"It doesn't bother you she didn't tell us?" Ashleigh reiterated.

"Fine, she didn't tell us," Amanda admitted, spread out her arms, growing exasperated, "But it doesn't bother me enough to stand here arguing about it!" She checked her watch. "We have forty-five minutes to get to Toscana in time for the reservation. I've been looking forward to this all day! We aren't getting there any sooner standing out here wondering why Samantha's here or why she sent a text instead of calling! Let's get Samantha and get to the restaurant!"

"Amanda, you can't be so trusting in this world," Ashleigh tilted her her head, disappointed with her friend's blithe innocence. "This isn't the Great Northern campus, this is the real world and things get weird out here." Amanda's upbringing in Toronto one of private girls' schools and a life protectively sheltered by loving parents. "I might've grown up in a big mansion in a gated community, but this sister has some street sense and it's telling her something isn't right!"

"So what are you going to do?" Amanda put her hands on her hips, stared at Ashleigh. "Because I'm going inside."

"I'll come with you," Lauryn managed to say, interrupting the combative friends.

Ashleigh regarded her friends, sense of foreboding remained despite Amanda's insistence to enter the studio, unable to convince Amanda otherwise. Ashleigh took a deep breath, they'd have a lengthy heart-to-heart discussion on their return to campus after dinner. "I'm waiting outside. If you aren't out in two minutes with Samantha I'm calling someone."

"The police?" Amanda realized her friend serious.

"I might," Ashleigh said.

"Fine, wait out here," Amanda opened the door. "I'm sure we'll be back in a minute with Samantha and be on our merry way to that fabulous Italian dinner you're paying for." Amanda entered the studio, Lauryn following a step behind.

God I hope you're right, Gazelle, Ashleigh watched her friends enter, struggling to stay calm. She moved up on the stoop, peering through the slats of the venetian blinds as the pair walked through the reception room and entered the next room, disappearing from sight.

Ashleigh made a decision. *Like Hell I'm waiting for you to get back out here.* She reached for her phone, about to dial 911 and explain the situation to an emergency operator, when she noticed her phone didn't have any signal.

As they entered the reception area, closing the door behind them, Lauryn whispered to Amanda. "You were a little rough on Ashleigh."

"Don't worry about it," Amanda reassured. "You know Ashleigh, she tends to be dramatic sometimes. At dinner we'll gossip and tell stories about our men and by the time we get back to campus all will be forgotten." Wasn't the first time the close friends going toe to toe, Amanda's competitive nature rearing up, but the ability to mend fences in the wake of such squabbling a reason they remained friends. She glanced at Samantha's Timbuk2 shoulder bag on the couch. "We know Samantha's here."

Amanda saw lights from the next room, stepped up to the open doorway. "Hey Samantha, we're here!" She called. "Let's get going, I'm starving for my gourmet Italian victory dinner!" They didn't hear the melodic voice of their roommate in reply, the silence unbroken. *She knows we're here, so why isn't she answering?* "Samantha, we're here," Amanda said again, "where are you?"

The pair entered the studio space; set up with lights and a white fabric backdrop hanging down from the ceiling. The room appeared vacant, nary a sign of Samantha Grayson or the owner of the studio, whoever this Marcus Evans might be. Amanda and Lauryn scanned the room. "Samantha….it's Amanda and Lauryn….where are you?" Amanda called, voice now tinged with anxiety.

"Maybe Ashleigh was right about this…" Lauryn started to say and the two understood, but a moment too late, Ashleigh Morgan had good reason for her apprehensive misgivings.

Everything happened swiftly, so sudden neither woman given the slightest chance to defend themselves, the situation ripped out of their control. Amanda heard something from behind the backdrop, started turning to the sound when she heard Lauryn cry out in surprise. Her head swung about, saw Lauryn stumbling backward, away from the other end of backdrop, a huge figure lunging at Lauryn, towering over her. *What the hell is going on!* Shocked at the imminent threat to her petite friend, Amanda stepped towards Lauryn, a shout of warning growing deep in her lungs, when she felt fingers dig into her shoulder, acidic bile of horrified comprehension bubbled in her stomach realizing she too in danger. Amanda spun around, with tremendous force thrown back against the wall, feet stumbling, squealing in anguish from the detonation of pain between her shoulder blades on impact. Amanda gasped as the air from her lungs escaped, vision blurred, head spinning in confusion. The hand released its hold from her arm, Amanda sucked in a breath, about to scream at the top of her lungs to alert Ashleigh standing outside the studio something was terribly wrong.

The cry never passed her lips, the hand grabbing her shoulder now squeezed tightly about her throat, choking her into gurgling silence. Her vision cleared and Amanda stared, amethyst eyes gaping wide in terror, into the hollow barrel of an automatic pistol pointed at the middle of her forehead, compelled her to ignore the pain racing at breakneck speed through her spine, wheezing for breath as fingers clawed the soft flesh of her neck. A scarecrow thin, blond figure stared back at her with icy gray eyes and smiled but there nothing pleasant in the expression only a murderous, cold-hearted evil.

"I hope you don't mind, but this is how we greet unwelcome guests," The Thin One said in a flat, emotionless tone freezing Amanda's soul into a solid block of ice. Across the room Lauryn struggled feebly in the iron-vise grip of a bald man with a goatee, his girth as massive and imposing as their friend Albert Fatuamala, little Lauryn unable to break free of the crushing hold. Over Lauryn's mouth The Big One clamped a gigantic hand, silencing her, reducing cries to muffled whimpers.

Amanda swallowed, struggling for each breath, fought to stay calm, a sick sensation realizing she'd committed an error possibly fatal in nature. *Amanda, you're so stupid! Why didn't I listen to Ashleigh?* Hoped her friend carrying out her intentions of contacting the police. A dark thought overtook her, a consideration too sinister to dispel. *If they're doing this to us*, Amanda shuddered, *what have they done with Samantha?*

"Why don't you go convince their friend to join us?" The Thin One told the Big One clutching in his grasp a frantically squirming Lauryn. With the terse order The Big One dragged a still struggling Lauryn from the studio towards the front door where they left Ashleigh moments earlier.

Ashleigh stood on the stoop, facing the street, staring at the icon on her smartphone. The satellite dish scanning back and forth, informing her the device searching for a signal. *Not now!* Ashleigh railed at the phone in her hand. *I don't have time for this!*

She glanced over her shoulder into the reception area, saw no sign of her friends. Now her fears multiplied exponentially, unanswered questions piling on top of each other. What was going on here? Why was Samantha here in the first place? Why had her phone turned into useless electronic garbage when she needed to call the police? She glared at the phone, dark eyes shooting venom at the inanimate object. With an angry growl she demanded. "Why do I pay Verizon one hundred fifty dollars a month so it can crap out at a time like this?"

Ashleigh heard tapping on the door behind her. *Finally! Thank God!* Ashleigh thought, relieved, turned to see Lauryn's face behind the glass, bewildered by the fearful expression and frightened eyes. Then Ashleigh froze, seeing the gigantic man standing behind Lauryn with an arm the size of a tree trunk around her throat, a pistol jammed against her temple. The man nodded at Ashleigh and smiled, no trace of geniality in the gesture. *Come inside or your friend dies.* Ashleigh understood perfectly the silent command.

Ashleigh thought of bolting into the street for help, realized she didn't know what happened to Amanda, assumed she faced an equal, or even greater, danger inside the studio. *And Samantha…* Ashleigh arrived at a horrible realization she had no choice in the matter. If she fled, or didn't comply with the demands of Lauryn's captor, her friends doomed to death. With shaking hand Ashleigh opened door and stepped into a place she might never leave alive. The huge man backed away, pulling Lauryn with him as Ashleigh slowly entered. "Don't hurt her," Ashleigh told the hulking man. The building a trap and Ashleigh, along with her friends, now its prisoners for reasons yet unknown.

The man pointed the gun at Ashleigh. "Put your hands on top of your head," then he nudged the barrel lightly against Lauryn's head. "Nothing stupid or something unpleasant happens to your friend."

"Lauryn, are you okay?" Ashleigh, doing as ordered, asked in a trembling voice.

"I'm okay." Lauryn nodded, Ashleigh sensed her fear. "A little scared here." *You and me both, girl,* Ashleigh silently added her own assessment of Lauryn's understatement.

"Move," the man waved the gun; forcing Ashleigh towards the door leading to the studio and whatever awaited her there. Their captor a step behind, dragging Lauryn with him. Resting on the couch Ashleigh spotted Samantha's Timbuk2. Samantha was here, but Ashleigh had no idea if she was alive, dreading whatever fate befell Samantha Grayson might soon be their own.

"Get over here!" Amanda McKinnon yelped in distress as the Thin One moved the gun from her forehead over to her temple, hand releasing its hold on her throat to grasp tightly around her wrist, yanking her towards him, twisting it behind her back as a sharp stab of pain shot up her arm. He dragged Amanda to a wooden chair. "Sit down! Put your hands on your head!" He ordered brusquely, releasing her, shoving the slender frame down on the seat. Amanda acted without hesitation, the maniac holding a gun to her head and she not in a position to argue, utterly powerless to resist. *Unless I want a gaping hole in my skull.* Eyes never leaving the gun. *This is why we have gun control in Canada.* Rested trembling hands atop her head, fought to quell uncontrollable shaking produced by equal doses of panic and fear.

"What have you done with Samantha? What's going on?" Despite the dire situation, Amanda thought of her friend. Samantha somewhere in this building, no idea if her friend harmed or even if she was still alive. *Don't think that!* "Where is she?" Amanda demanded, summoning courage in the face of danger.

"You'll find out in due time," the Thin One told her. Amanda watched warily as he shuffled over to a duffel bag on the floor, nudging it with his foot over to where she sat, the pistol never shifting from the side of her head. "Don't think of doing anything stupid, wouldn't be beneficial to your continued well-being."

No kidding. Amanda swallowed hard, her mouth dry. With frightened eyes she watched as the Thin One reached into the duffel, removed several bundled coils of white cotton rope, dropped them on the floor. He took a coil of rope, moved behind the chair. Amanda realized his intentions, knew her situation grew more dire with each passing second. The Thin One jammed the pistol into the waistband of his trousers, in a fluid motion grabbed her hands from atop her head, jerked them behind the chair, binding them with the rope. Amanda whined as the cord tightened, wrists melded painfully together as her captor finished knotting the bonds.

Amanda twisted her wrists against the rope, found the binding secure, the knot far removed from probing fingers as the Thin One looped a second length of rope about her elbows. "God! That hurts!" Amanda gasped in agony as he cinched the rope until her elbows touched, shoulder blades thrust back. His movements efficient and swift, apparent he'd done this action many times previously and practiced at his craft, a familiarity that terrified Amanda. She heard noise coming from the front room. *Maybe Ashleigh got away.* The momentary glimmer of hope through the gloom evaporated, heart sinking in a morass of despair as Ashleigh staggered into the studio, hands clasped on top of her head, followed by the Big One, Lauryn a powerless prisoner in the burly arms.

"Down on the floor, ladies," the Big One released Lauryn, kneeling down on the floor, placing hands on her head without being told.

Amanda glanced at Ashleigh, tried concealing fear in her eyes. "Before you say it, you told me so and I didn't listen, my bad," Amanda grimaced, voice trembling, testing the bonds about her elbows, scowled at the throbbing ache the slight resistance caused. "Dad says when I screw up, I don't go halfway."

"Amanda, what's going on?" Ashleigh asked Amanda, dark eyes filled with distress as the Big One pushed her to her knees.

"I don't know but I think whatever it is it's very, very bad. Tell me you were able to call…" Amanda pleaded, hoping.

Ashleigh didn't let Amanda finish, face shaded with defeated sorrow. "I couldn't get a signal," she explained, voice tinged with regret. Lauryn remained silent, emerald eyes staring fearfully at the Big One looming over them.

"Cell phone reception tends to quit at the most inopportune times," the Thin One informed. A shiver ran through Ashleigh at the familiar voice.

"YOU!" Ashleigh exclaimed in shocked recognition when the Thin One peered at her from around the chair, done tying Amanda's elbows. The Thin One studied Ashleigh with a grim, pleased satisfaction as the Big One snatched the phone from her hands, tossed it on the table. He moved over to the duffel bag, removed several more coils of white cotton rope. Ashleigh and Lauryn knew, when seeing Amanda being bound, the same fate planned for them.

"Now isn't this a small world," the Thin One replied with a smirk. "Never thought our paths might cross again. It must suck to be you right now." He laughed, retrieving a long length of rope, commenced looping the rope around Amanda's upper body, winding it above and under her breasts. "You might want to take back those nasty things you said to me."

"You know this creep!" Amanda cried out in shock as the Thin One started cinching the ropes, grunted in shamed indignation as he grasped her breasts, took carnal liberties with a lewd squeeze, then resumed wrapping Amanda in a cocoon of confining cordage.

"It was Saturday night at Summer's End Fest," an angry rage flared in Ashleigh's dark eyes in spite of the uncertainty of their plight. "You and Connor had gone back to the room by then." Not to get some rest as Amanda told her friends, engaging in sexual escapades with her boyfriend. "I was looking at jewelry when this creep took my picture. Told him I wasn't interested in a modeling career before he could sweet talk me." Ashleigh feared for not only her own safety and her two friends but especially for Samantha. *Why did Samantha come here? She's not the type to fall for those sort of lies. Is Samantha even alive?* Ashleigh shoved the ugly probability aside, a horrible prospect they too might soon experience. "I didn't think this was the type of modeling this pervert was talking about."

"Let's say photography is but a diversion from my true line of business." The Thin One finished securing Amanda's upper body to the chair, the network of rope fusing her to the wooden frame, the constriction making it difficult to breathe, lungs already searing.

Fear filled Lauryn's emerald eyes. "Where's Samantha?"

"You'll find out soon enough," the Thin One replied simply, no other explanation offered.

The Big One grabbed Ashleigh's hands, jerked them behind her back. Ashleigh screamed as the Big One bound her wrists. "That hurts, you asshole!"

"You'll be hurting a lot more, baby." The Big One finished tying Ashleigh's hands, grabbed another rope, jerked Lauryn's hands behind her back to secure them. "And I'd watch that mouth," he threateningly cautioned Ashleigh. "I don't like girls who talk back."

"Where's Samantha! What have you done with her?" Amanda demanded of the Thin One, the fate of her friend overriding the terror of her own peril, ignoring the fact they were helpless and at the unknown mercies of their captors. *And this is all your fault, Amanda.*

"Like I said, you'll find out soon enough," the Thin One sternly repeated, "Aren't we impatient." Taking another length of rope, threading it around her waist, jamming hips back into the chair. The Big One finished binding Lauryn's hands, returned to Ashleigh, long lengths of rope used to entwine elbows and upper body.

"Where is she?" Amanda glared at The Thin One, fury exploding in the amethyst eyes. "You bastard! I want to know where Samantha is NOW!" She screamed an ultimatum at the Thin One.

"Where's Samantha?" Ashleigh joined the chorus. "What have you done to her?"

The Thin One stood up, sighed, stared down at Amanda with the exasperated countenance of a schoolteacher confronted by an unruly pupil. "There are times where women don't know when to shut their damn mouths."

The Big One nodded in agreement as the Thin One walked over to the duffel bag. "These two," he pointed at Amanda and Ashleigh, "are mouthy little bitches. Not like their friend who knows to keep quiet." Lauryn cringed as he jerked a thumb at her.

"I prefer a peaceful work environment," the Thin One noted, reaching into the bag, retrieved three thick pads of cloth, a roll of silver duct tape and a roll of a white elastic material.

Amanda shuddered in her bonds, lip bit in apprehension. "What are you doing...with that?" She stammered, eyeing the Thin One with trepidation, despite her wavering question knew exactly what he intended.

"What do you think, honey?" The Thin One asked, a death's head grin spreading across his face. "I want you to stay quiet." The Thin One motioned to the Big One. "Make sure she," meaning Ashleigh, "doesn't act up until I get to her." Ashleigh unable to react as the Big One pressed a meaty paw over her mouth, reduced screamed protests to muffled moans, other arm firmly about her midsection to subdue desperate struggles. Lauryn said nothing, remained motionless, staring on in shock.

"You're not putting that in my mouth." Amanda shook her head, eyes widening as he tore several strips of duct tape from the roll, stuck the ends on the table to reach them easily, wadded the cloth pad in a tight ball, approached Amanda bound to the chair. "I won't let you."

The Thin One laughed derisively. "I don't think you're in any position to stop me." Amanda pressed her lips together, the Thin One snaking his arm underneath her chin, preventing her head from moving. "You have to breathe sometime, pretty thing," he told her, fingers pinching her nostrils closed.

Amanda's eyes shot open, realized the show of resistance might bring swift death by suffocation. She held her breath until lack of oxygen ignited her lungs, vision growing hazy. She opened her mouth to suck in a breath, afforded the opportunity the Thin One sought, stuffing cloth past her teeth, forcing her mouth closed. "Don't spit it out," the Thin One warned, plastered four strips of sticky silver duct tape over her face, lips sealed shut and muting her cries. Amanda grunted angrily, screaming through the gag, glaring in hatred as the Thin One released her.

"Not done yet," the Thin One told Amanda, took the roll of elastic bandage, pushing her head down, raven hair falling away from her neck, winding the stretchy material several times around her head, elastic sticking tight against skin without any slack, pressing the adhesive to her face. Amanda cried through the layers covering her mouth, dismayed by what little sound she heard. So effective the gag no one outside the building hearing her cries for help, even if she screamed at the top of her lungs.

The Thin One turned to Ashleigh, trembling in fright yet dark eyes continuing to burn with anger. "Now it's your turn, my dear," he commented icily. "I'm going to enjoy shutting you up, bitch."

"You fucking bastard!" Ashleigh cursed when the Big One removed his hand from her face, a second before the Thin One jammed the cloth between her lips to silence any further outcry.

"Such a foul mouth on you," the Thin One scolded, slapping strips of tape over Ashleigh's lips, completing the gag with elastic tape wound four times about her head. Protests now limited to a series of inaudible grunts and whimpers.

"I'll won't talk," Lauryn pleaded feebly, emerald eyes damp. "I'll be quiet."

"I know you won't," the Thin One smiled, "but I need to make sure in case you change your mind." Lauryn quickly gagged in the same process as her friends: wadding stuffed into the mouth, strips of duct tape over her lips, elastic bandage wrapped around her head. The room grew deathly quiet save for stifled cries from the hapless women. The Thin One stood, nodded contently at the silence. "Now we can finish our work in peace," he informed the Big One, and the pair resumed the grim work of binding their captives. The Thin One bound up Amanda's legs and ankles, bound her thighs against the seat, then tugging tied ankles back underneath the chair, a length of rope linking them to the bindings around her wrists. Amanda could barely budge in the chair, any movement unleashed piercing lances of white-hot pain through muscles already shrieking in anguish from the constraint, every joint, especially her hips and thighs wedged against the seat of the chair, ached from the pressure. The Big One finished with Ashleigh, tying her legs and ankles, pushed her to the floor then turned his attention to Lauryn who until now only had her wrists tied. Amanda and Ashleigh left silent and miserable witness as the Big One subdued Lauryn with the same quick efficiency and cruelty shown them, tortured by the sobbing of their gentle friend, painfully trussed until she couldn't move. The hulking thug did demonstrate a modicum of mercy, gently easing Lauryn down next to Ashleigh once he finished with his task.

Amanda stared at her friends bound and gagged at her feet; powerless victims trapped in a waking nightmare, praying for survival, unsure the time left them, understood they might never see families and friends again and those they loved never learning what had become of them. *We're in big trouble.* Amanda thought of Connor Aanonsen, longed for him to burst through the door, vanquish these animals, spirit her from this horrible predicament, knew the wishful imaginings nothing but fantasy. *And it's my fault.* She tried not to think what these thugs had done with Samantha. *Something bad is going on here! Why did Samantha come here? What did they do with her? What are they going to do with us?*

The Thin One stroked Amanda's cheek with the feigned affection of an amorous admirer, trembling at the erotic nature of the caress. *The bastard is turned on by this!* Fearing what violent fantasies burrowed in his mind, how her thoughtless, impatient action provided him three easy victims. "I hope you're enjoying your visit," the Thin One said. "I think it is time for an introduction. Please ignore the sign out front. It's an identity of convenience. The name is Marcus Cowle," Amanda shook involuntarily, didn't know why but the banal name sounded evil. Cowle pointed to his hulking assistant. "This is my associate Sterner. We're very good at what we do."

Tell me about it, Amanda snorted through the gag, glanced at her imprisoning bonds, afraid to find out exactly what it was the pair did.

"Now you want to know what we did with your friend, Samantha?" Marcus Cowle asked, Amanda murmuring weakly in agreement, meekly nodding her head, the rope and bandages freezing her in place like an ice sculpture in the middle of a winter festival. Cowle smiled; Amanda found no warmth in the expression. "You may not like what you find out."

Somewhere deep in the troubled slumber exhaustion finally imposed on a weakened body, Samantha Grayson thought she heard someone calling her name.

Samantha....Samantha...Samantha....

Her eyes fluttered open, groaning in pain as aching muscles and joints, held securely in place by rope, rebelled against movement. *I was only dreaming.*

Samantha shook the cobwebs clinging inside her head, gazing at her bound body, heard the muffled whimper of her own voice through the gag. Awakened from unsettled dreams back into a hellish reality she would never escape.

She heard voices from the other room; certain one of her captor Marcus Cowle. A deeper voice as well. Was it the police? She froze as footsteps approached her cell, shrunk back against the corner of the closet, no idea if the person who opened the door her captor or a savior.

The door swung open, light from the hall flooding the space, a man of immense size dressed in dark military-style fatigue pants and a leather jacket over a dark t-shirt loomed over her, offered an admiring smile examining her hopeless condition, pleased at the sight of her helpless form. Her heart sank, Samantha realizing he not there to rescue her from this horror. "Hey sweetie," the large man, bald with a goatee, cooed while leering at her, "you've got company."

What's he talking about? Her brain fogged from sleep, heard muffled female voices, sounds from those gagged as thoroughly as she was now. Had Cowle brought Presley and the other hostages to the studio to wait out the time until their delivery to an owner with violent designs, taken to a land far from home?

The man effortlessly lifted her from the closet, heaved over his shoulder, Samantha emitted a peep of surprise, head dropping as long auburn hair dangled past her face, obscured her vision. She noticed pale light drifting through the windows, dusk settling over the city. *What time is it?* The man carried her towards the studio, muffled cries growing louder, sounding terribly familiar. *If it's after five...* A horrid realization struck Samantha with the impact of cars involved in a head-on collision.

Her muscular captor entered the studio, swung her from his shoulder to the floor, body striking the hard surface with a soft thud. Samantha shook hair from her brown eyes, whined in despair as they met the emerald green eyes of Lauryn Callahan staring at her in stupefied terror over a thick bandage gag wound over her mouth. In terror Samantha's head whipped about, saw Ashleigh Morgan lying next to her, Amanda McKinnon sitting in a chair in front of her, all three bound with hundreds of feet of rope and gagged so thoroughly barely a sound escaped their lips.

Oh my God, Samantha wailed in horror at the discovery of her friends' plight, *the text message! They came here for me!* Samantha now wished she added three additional words, a simple statement, to the message she sent Lauryn Callahan hours earlier telling them where to find her if she wasn't at the office of *The Daily Northern*.

Call the police.

Chapter 30

Over the tight bandage wrapped around her head, holding the cloth inside her mouth keeping her, except for muffled whimpers, all but mute, Amanda McKinnon looked down at Samantha Grayson lying on the floor. Like Amanda and her friends, Samantha immobilized with rope but silenced by a thick strip of white cloth wedged deep between her lips. Amanda saw her white silk blouse torn, exposing the black floral print satin bra she wore underneath. Had these creeps harmed Samantha? *What were they going to do with her? Had they...?* Amanda pushed aside a ugly, horrid, disgusting word of sexual degradation starting with the letter R. A more sobering thought emerged. *What are they going to do with us?* Amanda gazed into Samantha's despairing eyes, attempted to communicate a single, stupefied notion.

Samantha, what is going on here!

Samantha mewled a weak answer through the gag, struggling feebly against yards of rope coiled about her body, cutting sharply into flesh. Brown eyes betrayed apprehension for friends now sharing her terrible fate as innocent, unwilling victims.

You don't want to know.

"So what do we have here, Samantha?" Marcus Cowle sneered, bent down next to her. "These wouldn't happen to be your friends?" Samantha groaned in misery. "Coming to see what was taking you so long?" Cowle stood up. "Where are my manners?" His gaze trailed over her defenseless friends, a sly smile of gratification creeping over his face. "I've introduced myself and my friend Sterner here," the immense, glowering thug who fetched Samantha from the closet now had a name, "to your friends but I haven't made the full pleasure of their acquaintance." Sterner collected their purses and handbags, handed them to Cowle who proceed to rummage inside each until he found their identification.

"Now let's see who we have here," Cowle smiled at Samantha, fingered the Canadian passport belonging to Amanda. "Not every day I come across this." He opened the document, studied the smiling face in picture, compared that to the fear-stricken expression of the passport's owner staring at him. "Amanda McKinnon, Missassauga, Ontario, that's near Toronto, isn't it?" Amanda whimpered, prayed she might survive this ordeal to see her home once more. "I've never done business in Canada, but if you're a sample of the product I'd find there," his eyes keenly appraised the bound body, "I might have to cross the border to pursue some opportunities."

Business? Amanda whined at Samantha. *What is he talking about?*

Cowle checked the next driver's license. "Lauryn Callahan, Arvada, Colorado," he glanced at the petite redhead cruelly bound at his feet. Lauryn closed her eyes, crying, wishing to be anywhere in the world but the prison this studio had become. "That's outside of Denver. I've done business there, a charming city indeed. My client was pleased with the quality of merchandise I procured for him there."

Samantha, what's going on here! Amanda snorted, eyes darting between Samantha and the gloating Cowle, confused by his statements and dreading what it all meant.

"And, last but not least, I put a name to your face," Cowle crouched down next to Ashleigh Morgan, with a grunt she heaved bound body up from the floor into a kneeling position, eyes hot with wrath directed at her captor, growling with indignation despite the cloth shoved in her mouth, the layers of tape and bandage sealing it shut. "Ashleigh Morgan," he off read her Georgia driver's license, "Atlanta. I've been there too, about two years ago, on business as usual. My work is never done. My client enjoyed the product from there that I delivered to him." He clamped his hand on her chin, forced Ashleigh to look in his cold, gray eyes. "He liked those Southern girls," Cowle chuckled as Ashleigh screamed, muffled shriek both outraged and fearful. "I'm sure he had an enjoyable time with them." He released her chin, roughly shoving Ashleigh to the floor beside Samantha and Lauryn.

"I already have plans for you, Samantha," Cowle stood, placed hands on his hips, studying his captives. "But what do I do with your friends?" Was the question he posed.

The reply came from Sterner. "Maybe the Arab will take them off our hands. He might pay us extra, like he did for her," he pointed at Samantha. "We might make out like bandits this time," he grinned, "get to enjoy our time off."

Amanda strained against the ropes, cried past the gag, eyes bulging with confused fright, feared the possible implications and none of them good. *Samantha, who is this 'Arab'? What is this delivery they're talking about? What's going on here!* Samantha shook her head, didn't want Amanda or her friends to learn the appalling truth.

"Then I'd better shoot more video," Cowle picked up his smartphone, activated the camera, filming futile struggles from his recent captures. "Put on a nice show, ladies," he encouraged his indisposed subjects, prompting, "I want my generous friend to see what you have to offer. Your lives might depend upon it." He swooped in on his prisoners, camera documenting each of his immobilized hostages, starting with Amanda, then moving over to Lauryn and Ashleigh, recording close-ups of their terrified faces, pleased with pathetic sounds emitted from muffled mouths. Once done Cowle dialed the number for his client. "I do hope he has room for all of you. The flight might be a little...cramped."

In the Conrad Hilton Suite of the Chicago Hilton and Towers on Michigan Avenue, occupied by Sheik Abdullah al-Aziz Rahim of Daharan and his sizeable entourage, the phone on the dresser vibrated and chimed. From across the room where he prepared for an extravagant dinner held in his honor by the Cockrell brothers, Rahim spied the number on the screen. He glanced at the clock. *About time he contacted me about the delivery.* Saleh took the phone from the dresser, brought it to his master. "It is good to hear from you," Rahim answered cordially. "I was expecting your call regarding the arrangements for tonight."

"I'll get to that," Cowle replied curtly, Rahim sensed irritation in the voice, understood a more pressing reason for the call. "We have another complication," a pause followed, "like I said before, one we wouldn't have experienced if we kept to past procedure."

"What sort of 'complication'?" Rahim noted in a nonplussed tone. "Is this one you cannot handle on your own?"

"I'm sending you the details now," Cowle said, moments later a snippet of video played on the screen, the details in question three young women bound and made powerless. The video shot from inside of Marcus Cowle's 'front' business, a photography studio luring his prey to their doom. "We wouldn't need to address this issue if the exchange occurred after I took possession of the last girl. But you wished to delay the handover to personally take ownership of this shipment."

Rahim ignored the prod, impassively examined the video playing on the phone. Cowle may be impertinent in this instance but far too valuable an asset to discard, needed his particular range of talents to satisfy the cravings for female flesh. He watched the video, the first hostage with long, midnight-black hair sat bound securely to a chair, a bandage gag wound about her head, then the angle shifted to the second captive, a redhead, body delicate and slender as a reed, lying tied and silenced on the floor. He caught a brief glimpse of the helpless Samantha Grayson beside the incapacitated girl, his heart starting to race at the true object of his desires. The video focused on a darker skinned woman, her body curvaceous and sensual, an angry snarl through the bandage gag, fighting desperately the ropes tightened around her.

"I wondered if you might be interested in several more items to go along with this consignment," Cowle inquired. "They're Samantha's friends, came looking for her. I'd prefer if you'd take them, as with Samantha, off of my hands."

In the studio Amanda McKinnon listened, realized with sudden clarity as if a fog had suddenly lifted, understood what Cowle discussed and the fate he meant for them. *This guy is selling us! That's what he's doing with you! What he's wants to do with us!* She whined at Samantha, who barely nodded in bleak response, eyes watering as her friend finally understood the terrible revelation.

Intriguing, for a moment Rahim briefly considered taking all of them, doing as Cowle wished, the dark-skinned woman caught his fancy. *Something out of the ordinary*. But Samantha more than enough to satiate his thirst for violence, along with the five Cowle already acquired. *Such a waste indeed*. "My friend, I am sorry. This time I cannot help you in this matter," Rahim said with a twinge of genuine disappointment, "I wouldn't have enough room on my jet for all of them and my security detail."

"Couldn't you have your people fly back commercial?" Cowle asked hopefully. The silence from the other end deafening, a sign the jest failed miserably. "I meant that as a joke, my friend," Cowle swiftly backpedalled from the comment.

"I understand your unique brand of humor," Rahim smiled at Cowle's discomfiture. "But I must decline your generosity. I trust you will eliminate this problem so it doesn't affect our future business dealings," he demanded in cold, direct fashion, understood the statement sealing the fate of the unfortunate trio.

"Of course, Sheik Rahim, I will see they are properly disposed." Cowle grimaced, forced to eliminate unwanted guests the hard way. *Not the first time*, Cowle mused, *but a damn waste anyway*. The three helpless friends-Amanda, Lauryn and Ashleigh-exchanged horrified glances, the simple reply from Cowle a sentence of doom. Samantha gazed sadly at her friends, tried not to break down in tears. *This is my fault*, she thought, *I have to do something to save them*. Even if it meant sacrificing her chances at survival.

"There is still the matter of the location for the exchange," Rahim reminded.

"I am sending you the address. It's an abandoned factory on the West Side," Cowle told Rahim, tapping the address on the virtual keyboard. As Cowle sent the text he didn't notice Amanda, from her vantage point bound to the chair next to him, able to see the screen. She spied the address, *3100 West Carroll Avenue*, and silently committed the detail to memory, wondered if she'd live to tell someone. "Don't worry, it's out of the way, we won't be disturbed. I'll have Samantha and the others ready for you at the designated time, two in the morning."

"That will work perfectly," Rahim showed the address to Saleh to enter the location into the GPS devices of the limousine and accompanying Audi sedans so they didn't lose their way in the city. "If there is any change in my scheduled arrival I will inform you. I will see you then, my friend. You have done a fine service and for that I am eternally grateful." Rahim ended the call, knowing he condemned to death the women in the video. *A shame, but it must be so.* The fact their blood stained his hands didn't trouble him. By now he was quite used to the shedding of innocent blood.

Cowle turned off the phone, exhaled, studied his defenseless guests with a mocking melancholy; Sterner offered a nonchalant shrug of the shoulders. "Easy come, easy go," his associate said matter-of-factly. "Win some, lose some."

"But in losing we have a problem," Cowle nodded in agreement. "Samantha will be departing on her trip with those already at the factory." He cast his eyes over four coeds helplessly bound and gagged in the middle of his studio as they traded nervous and frightened looks. Cowle placed his hands on his hips, studied three captives in particular, those his client had shown no interest. "For you three," pointing to Amanda, Lauryn and Ashleigh, "it does suck to be you right now."

Cowle waited a moment before asking. "So what am I going to with you?"

None of the four, vulnerable and at his mercy, wished to know the answer.

Aaron Dinehart, news editor for *The Daily Northern*, was all business the moment he stepped into the office, carrying in his hand the four-pack of Red Bull to get him through the night. "All right, let's get to work," he announced to staff milling about socializing or working at their desks, then rattled off a cliché straight from the script of a movie set in the newsroom of a great metropolitan newspaper. "We've got a paper to get out." A chorus of groans greeted his statement.

"Has anyone seen Sam?" Aaron slipped into his chair, switching on his laptop and logging into the main server to start editing the queue of articles for the next day's edition, wanted to go over with Samantha Grayson the stories covering the appearance and speech by Senator Benton Fielding at Cockrell Auditorium. *At least there weren't any riots.* "Don't everyone answer at once," he muttered under his breath when he didn't receive a response. Then he remembered, calling up her first story on the screen, a recap of the speech, Samantha out to dinner in Chicago with her friends, celebrating Amanda McKinnon's victory at the Great Northern Invitational. She'd return to the office later that evening, but she did say he could call on her cell phone before then if he had any questions.

Hate to interrupt your night out, Sam. Aaron dialed Samantha's number as he scanned the copy. He heard her voicemail message. *Hi, this is Samantha Grayson….* He waited until prompted to leave a message. "Hey Sam, its Aaron, I'm at the office checking your stories. Look good but I have a few questions. Give me a call or I'll see you later tonight." Aaron continued editing the stories when five minutes later he noticed something odd and totally out of character for his typically conscientious colleague.

No matter how busy she may be, Samantha always returned his phone calls right away. This time Samantha hadn't called back.

"Let's get the cell phone records pulled for Emma and Alexandra, see who they may have been talking to the past few days," Detective Devin Carson told his partners on their return to Chicago Police Headquarters on 31st Street. "Maybe who they've talked to will give us someone we'll want to have a discussion with as well. Find out what they know. If there's nothing there we can at least start tracking the towers the phones pinged, get a rough estimation of where they went."

"We're already past forty-eight hours since anyone last saw or heard from them," Dawson Hilliard added. "We're way behind the curve."

"Didn't find anything in their apartments telling us where they went?" Carson asked.

Nathanial Hampton shook his head. "Other than they took clothes with them. So wherever they were going and whomever they met with it appears they did so willingly."

"And Alexandra left him," Hilliard waved at Wrigley the golden retriever, found in the apartment of Alexandra Cole, standing beside Hilliard's desk noisily lapping water from a bowl, "alone for two days without food or water. Like I told my new partner here," motioning at Hampton, "I don't think Alexandra is the type who leaves her dog to fend for himself."

"So to assume somethin' happened to the two," Patrick Flannery piped in, "someone had to have driven their cars to those fine neighborhoods," poverty-stricken and crime-ridden Englewood and Lawndale, "where they were dumped."

"That's what I was thinking on the way back," Carson added. "We can see what we can find through Virtual Shield."

"I see great minds think alike," Hilliard agreed.

"What's that?" Flannery inquired.

"It's a system linking the surveillance and traffic cameras at major intersections throughout the city, It's operated out of the Office of Emergency Management and Communications but we can access the system remotely from here," Carson explained, didn't want to deal with the chaos currently besieging the city's 911 center with the dispatchers on strike and an overwhelmed skeleton staff swamped with calls. "Whoever dumped those cars had to have passed through a few intersections covered by the system on the way."

"We have a network like that in London," Hampton noted. "That's how we found out who carried out the 7/7 bombing attack." A terrorist attack rocking the British capital a day after the joy of learning London chosen to host the Summer Olympics.

Carson nodded, realizing every moment they talked another minute the two women remained unaccounted for and in danger. "From what I've heard they've finished installing high definition cameras and a new software program that's able to pick up the license plate on a vehicle like you're standing right beside it." He spied Captain Hardaway approaching; expression solemn, possessed news Carson suspected not good.

"Had to bring the dog here?" Hardaway asked Hilliard, motioning to the golden retriever by his desk now lying down, head resting on the floor.

"Sorry, boss," Hilliard apologized, "I've got a soft spot for dogs."

"Have the parents' of the two missing women arrived yet?" Carson asked.

Hardaway shook his head. "Both women's parents are still on the way here, we'll have detectives interview them once they arrive." Emma's parents from outside of Minneapolis, Alexandra's family lived in a small dot on the map in Kansas, both sets of parents distraught and panicked. "But from contacting them neither has heard from their daughters since Saturday at the latest. Emma sent a Facebook post to her younger brother that morning, he's a freshman at Syracuse University."

"Did she say where she was doing," Carson inquired, "who she might've been meeting?"

Hardaway shook his head. "No, sent the usual 'how's it going' question. He posted a reply later that afternoon, didn't get a response."

"What else?" Carson sensed there was more.

"We have two more missing women," Hardaway handed him a sheet of paper. "Isabella DiBenedetto and Gabriella Taylor, students at Saint Vincent University, both are roommates living off-campus. Last seen Sunday morning, had brunch with friends at Stanley's Kitchen and Tap in Lincoln Park. They haven't been seen or heard from since. The Taylor woman didn't show for work at the university's computer center Sunday night, like Alexandra she's never missed a shift. Should've had this earlier but Isabella's father had a hard time explaining the matter with the trainee operators filling in at the 911 Center for those walking the picket line."

"Absolutely wonderful," Flannery muttered.

"We should've had this hours ago." Carson sucked in a breath as if punched in the gut, cursing the delay caused by the strike, an unfortunate occurrence setting them further back.

"That's four women in the course of two days," Hilliard voiced Carson's darkest fears.

"This is how it happened elsewhere," Carson pointed out, "quick and sudden, in a cluster, not much left to follow. The women fit the victim profile." The disappearances not a random happenstance, but a deviously planned event of truly horrific proportions. *But for what?* He looked at Hardaway. "This has to be the same person, or persons, responsible for the other disappearances." Who those perpetrators were, and the reason for snatching so many young women in so short a period of time, remained unknown and Carson didn't wish to begin imagining the unspeakable reasons why.

"Which means you may have another missing woman out there we don't know about," Hardaway noted calmly. Five had disappeared in Los Angeles the year before, the number of victims increasing as the nameless predator continued to hunt, seemingly unstoppable, practically invisible except when time came to strike and unsuspecting victims vanished.

"Maybe more," Carson remarked grimly, glancing at Hilliard. *Escalation, that's what I'm afraid of.* The expression stating an obvious fear, this time dealing with more than five victims.

"I have a call in to the Chicago FBI office, we'll get all the information they have," Hardaway told the four. "We have an APB out for Isabella DiBenedetto's car. It's a silver Nissan Altima."

Carson checked the address on the sheet of paper for the women's residence, an address in Lincoln Park blocks away from the campus, turned it over to Hilliard and Hampton. "Check out their apartment, see what you find, if it looks like they packed to go somewhere like the other women. Then talk to their friends."

"What are you going to do?" Hilliard asked.

"I've got a hunch to play, see what we'll find through Virtual Shield," Carson stated. "It's a longshot but someone drove those cars to where we found them, they couldn't have driven themselves there. At least we'll narrow down where Emma and Alexandra were on Saturday."

As Hilliard and Hampton departed Carson glanced at the clock, whoever responsible for the disappearances of four women held a considerable head start, perhaps insurmountable, over those engaged in a desperate search. Carson had no idea if the women he sought still among the living or already dead and forever lost. Or if there were more than the four victims they already knew about.

"So how was practice?" Tyler McManaway asked, walking beside Connor Aanonsen, followed by D'Andre Watson and Albert 'Fiji' Fatuamala, towards his silver Nissan Xterra for the drive from the athletic campus back to McDonough Hall.

"I'm anxious for the season to start," Connor carrying several goalie sticks along with his duffel bag. "Christen that hockey arena Cal McIllhenny built for us." He lifted the three goalie sticks in his hand, taped together for easy handling. "Can I leave these in your truck? FedEx made a late delivery. Left them outside the equipment room, but it was locked up for the night." Connor had his goalie sticks shipped directly from the manufacturer.

"No problem." Tyler checked his phone for messages from Samantha, found nothing. An odd occurrence, Samantha usually sent him silly, heartfelt texts professing her love at some point every day.

"How was your practice?" Connor asked.

Tyler smiled; the workout followed by a sit-down interview with a reporter from the Big Ten Network putting together a feature on the undefeated start to the season, ESPN sending its own crew to campus later in the week for a similar piece. Rumors flying if Great Northern won their next games against conference lowlights Minnesota and Indiana the ESPN *College Football Gameday* show to visit the Evanslawn campus for the Homecoming game against now eighth-ranked Iowa. "Nice and loose following a big win."

"Can't wait to get my shots against that Gopher run defense," D'Andre stated matter-of-factly.

"How many yards you predicting this time?" Connor challenged.

D'Andre grinned. "If Coach leaves me in for the whole game I'll break every school and NCAA record. I'm amazed South Dakota State only hung thirty-four on them."

"Don't get too over-confident," Fiji cautioned. "This could be tougher than you expect."

"Minnesota couldn't beat a high school junior varsity team," D'Andre replied, tone cocky and disbelieving, as the quartet loaded their gear into the Xterra.

"Put up or shut up," Tyler reminded his friend.

"You know I'll put up big time against that sorry-ass run defense," D'Andre laughed.

"I got some music for the ride back," Connor handed Tyler a compact disc as they got into the SUV.

"Not that country music you listen to!" D'Andre titled his head back, groaned. "It's nothing but girlfriends leaving, trucks breaking down and dogs dying."

"Not this time." Connor replied. "You'll like this. It's these two rappers who play a lot down in St. Louis and Kansas City, Brevin Tate," a teammate who hailed from the area, "gave me a CD to check out."

"Good," D'Andre mood changed. "No wailing about cow manure on your cowboy boots."

"Brett Gretzky?" Tyler read the name from the cover. "It figures you'd like this."

"As a hockey guy I dig the significance. Brett Hull, Wayne Gretzky, both played for the Blues and these guys are from St. Louis," Connor confessed as Tyler slid the disc into the CD player. "It's the same reason I like Five for Fighting. It's a hockey thing."

"Well, back to campus for training table and some studying," D'Andre, in the front seat with Tyler, announced as Connor and Fiji sat in back. "You have a hot date later," he reminded Tyler.

"That I do," Tyler eased the Xterra from the parking space, unable to dispel an uneasy feeling at the absence of messages from Samantha. *Maybe she hasn't had time;* Tyler quelled his misgivings. *She has been busy today.*

Chapter 31

"What to do with the three of you," Marcus Cowle directed his gaze on the bound and gagged forms of Amanda McKinnon, Lauryn Callahan and Ashleigh Morgan, smiled as the helpless trio traded fearful, apprehensive stares, deathly afraid of what their captor planned next. "Quite a quandary I'm faced with here," Cowle noted impassively, "what will I do with the three of you?"

Sterner shrugged. "I'll leave that up to you," he noted calmly, an uninterested observer. "You're calling the shots." He carried out the orders. "You know I'll clean up any mess you leave."

With a deep groan starting deep in her lungs, and a herculean effort made taxing by the rope painfully tight about her, Samantha Grayson heaved her bound body from the floor into a kneeling position. With a growl she vigorously shook her head, flowing auburn hair whipping wildly about her face. The noise, as Samantha had hoped, caught the attention of Marcus Cowle. A conceited smirk crossed the shallow face, peering over at her. "You have something to say on the matter, my dear?" Samantha moaned in confirmation through the wadding filling her mouth, wide cloth wedged between her lips. Cowle looked at Sterner. "Should we listen to what Miss Grayson has to offer?"

"Why not?" Sterner answered. "Not like they're going anywhere."

Cowle crouched next to Samantha, hands reaching for the cloth knotted behind her neck, stopped. "I want to make sure you don't do anything unadvisable." He motioned to Sterner, who knelt down on one knee, yanking the immobilized Lauryn from the floor, resting the tied body against his leg, a surprised whine from her defenseless friend at the rough handling. A thick hand enveloped her throat, emerald eyes widening in terror, sensed constricting pressure, gasping for breath. "If you do something stupid," Cowle cautioned Samantha, "my associate Sterner will snap the pretty little neck of your adorable friend. Do you understand?"

Samantha nodded meekly; Cowle undid the gag, Samantha using her tongue to expel packing sodden with saliva, sucking in several deep breaths. "Well, what do want to tell us, Samantha?" Cowle demanded. "I don't have a lot of time, on a tight schedule."

Summoning every grain of courage remaining in her soul, Samantha stiffened her back, brown eyes locking on the cruel gray eyes of Marcus Cowle as they pierced her defenses. She took a final deep breath, prayed the gambit worked, convincing him not to commit an act meaning a certain, terrible end for her friends. *I have to save them,* Samantha thought, *it's all I can do for them now.* "You don't have to hurt my friends," Samantha said with simple, straightforward conviction, avoided using the word *kill.*

"Really?" The statement intrigued Cowle, fascinated by the pluck of his captive in the face of overpowering peril. "Why is that?"

"You have me," Samantha continued, speaking evenly, masking the terror rumbling inside. "That's what Sheik Rahim wants, he wants me."

"That's correct," Cowle agreed. "Sheik Rahim wants you. Wants you very badly, in fact. He's paying good money to take you off of my hands." Cowle propped his chin in hand. "Go on, I'm listening."

Samantha took another deep breath. *Stay calm; don't show him you're afraid.* "You're handing me over to him in a few hours. Then you'll go wherever you're headed with your money."

"Somewhere warm with lots of liquor and women to spend it on," Sterner, the grin on his face spreading, added expectantly of a prodigious payout he hadn't foreseen.

"You only need to keep my friends out of the way until you've handed me over to Sheik Rahim and left Chicago," Samantha prayed the brutal human trafficker saw wisdom in her argument, spared the precious lives of her friends. *At least something good can come out of this; at least they can go on living.* "I'm sure you'll change your identity after you leave."

"You're right about that," Cowle nodded as Amanda, Lauryn and Ashleigh watched, listened silently to the conversation, Samantha bargaining with her life to save them from a hideous outcome, gags reducing the trio mute witnesses powerless to influence the discussion.

"I don't think anyone at Great Northern knows they're here," Samantha pointed out, lying. Someone did know, Riley Bradford, Samantha praying the freshman alerted somebody soon to their situation. "It might be days before anyone finds them." Amanda whined at the likelihood of days bound to the chair, body wracked with surges of pain from the tight webbing of rope. Then she realized the prospect far more palatable than the alternative. *I think I can handle a few days tied to a chair over dying right now.*

"Yes, I think you're correct," Cowle pondered what Samantha proposed, glanced at Sterner. "I don't think anyone would find them for days."

"By the time they're found you'll be far from here and I'll be…" Samantha swallowed, felt tears wet her eyes, let the sentence trail off. Accepted the fact while her friends lived, Samantha taken to a place far worse than ever imagined, faced terror known only in the bleakest of nightmares. *Gone forever…*

"Leave them here…won't be found for a few days," Cowle rubbed his chin, considering the offer, deep in though, then said abruptly. "Sorry, Samantha, I can't do that. What you're offering is impossible."

The three friends squealed in shock, statement a pin bursting the bubble of survival. "No!" Samantha cried out, horrified at the sudden decision, brief glowing ember of hope quickly doused, understanding the death warrant for her friends signed. "You don't have to hurt them! You can leave them here!"

Cowle lifted his hand, palm facing outward, quieting her protests. "Let me explain something, little lady," Samantha glared at him, insulted by the condescending tone. "You're right, I could leave your friends here. They likely won't be discovered for days, by then the three of us," meaning Cowle and Sterner and the captive Samantha, "will be very far away. But I can't possibly do that."

"But why…" Samantha began to say.

Cowle again cut her off. "Your friends, as we in this line of work say, possess inside information regarding my operation. There are, to be more specific, loose ends. I take care of such details prior to departing where I've been." The three bound captives, the object of the observation, cried in dismay realizing they didn't have long to live. "They know who I and my friend Sterner are, even if we alter our identities going forward, the police can use the information from your friends to track us. Besides, and most importantly, they heard the phone call to my client. They have an idea of who he is. My client, and those who employ me to fulfill his requests, wouldn't look kindly if I displayed a sliver of mercy to your friends, let them live to see another day. Such pangs of conscience are frowned on in my profession." Cowle smiled, the expression reminded Samantha of a grinning skull, devoid of emotion or mercy. "The most successful businessmen, the ones who make all the money, are never bothered by their conscience."

"You can't hurt them!" Samantha begged, straining against rope wound about her, wanting to wrap her hands around his throat, choke the smug expression off his face.

"I can, Samantha, and I will. If I want my business to remain profitable your friends have to die," Cowle retorted. "All successful businessmen have to deal with losses at some point." Cowle looked around at the room. "I have to eliminate this later tonight, there's as much evidence in this building as there would be if I let your friends live. I intended for the property to be vacant when it goes into...foreclosure," for her imprisoned friends Samantha feared the meaning of the innocuous euphemism. "Now it appears there will be several occupants still on the premises when the process goes through," he noted dourly.

Samantha shuddered in her bonds, the situation spiraling out of control. *As if I had any control in the first place*, now aware the efforts to save her friends futile.

"Hey boss," Sterner interrupted Cowle, "I got an idea you might like. Instead of offing them, why don't we take these pretty little things with us on vacation?" He smiled at Amanda bound to her chair, down at Lauryn in his arms, over at Ashleigh lying on the floor. The three girls moaned at the proposal, no desire to envision the sick designs upon them lurking in the deepest corners of his imagination. "Be a damn shame to waste this sort of talent. I'm sure they'd provide us with some entertainment." Samantha cringed at the remark, knew what this thug meant, despicable harm inflicted on her friends prior to inevitable and ugly deaths.

"Why didn't I think of that?" Cowle face lit up at the suggestion, impressed with his associate's recommendation. "I'll remember that for your next performance review, deserve a raise for initiative. But with the gear here and at the warehouse we have room in the trunk of my car for one lucky..."

"Or unlucky," Sterner kidded.

"Lady to join us on our little getaway," Cowle completed the sentence, looked over the three captives. "So which one of you will it be?"

Cowle stood, strode to the chair where Amanda struggled feebly against her bonds, amethyst eyes large over the thick gag quieting desperate protests as he approached, gray eyes appraising her body as if she a new car on the lot, deciding whether to take her for a test drive. His hand brushed her taut midsection and Amanda flinched, hand then trailing down her thigh. "You're very fit, Amanda, you must work out every day." Amanda found no pride in the compliment, only a malicious taunt in the midst of terror, a reminder she had no say over her eventual fate. Cowle trailed his fingers through the long dark locks, at the silken sensation against his skin smiled in erotic pleasure, caught a whiff of honeysuckle in the strands. His hand reached down, with lustful glee groped her breasts. "Nice set of personalities you have, Amanda." Amanda blushed, shamed by his touch, stared up at Cowle, murmuring through the gag, a mournful plea she knew this monster apt to ignore. *Please, don't hurt us, just let us go.* She jerked uselessly at the bonds keeping her immobile, muscles aching from ropes lacerating her skin, unable to relieve the pain pulsating numbly through her joints.

"I'm sure you'd put up a good fight, seeing how fit you are, you'd be fun to play with," Cowle sighed, "but you're too much like the girls we nab for Sheik Rahim. I want something different, something out of the ordinary." Amanda groaned, slumped in defeat, understood Cowle determined to extinguish her life, along with dreams and aspirations, before the flame of possibilities burned bright. "Sorry, you lose, Amanda."

Cowle turned, left Amanda to sob quietly over a decided fate, moved to Lauryn. As he neared she trembled like a timid, tiny field mouse cornered by a barnyard cat, mesmerized by the hungry, leering gaze, her petite, willowy form all but swallowed in the massive grasp of Cowle's hired help. "As for you, Lauryn, you're an adorable girl. You're the type who loves animals, right?" Cowle purred contemptuously as Lauryn uttered a piteous moan. "You're pretty in a wholesome sort of way, and so vulnerable too." His hand reached out for her cheek and Lauryn mewled, shrinking from his touch but finding no escape, the constricting embrace of Sterner holding her inert. "I like vulnerable."

"Don't touch her!" Samantha shouted, wanted to protect Lauryn from the deviant, sexual urges of this maniac, bonds preventing her from taking action.

"And you're going to stop me how?" Cowle found sadistic gratification reminding Samantha of her now powerless condition; the hopelessness of their situation, no matter how hard she tried Samantha could do nothing to change the inevitable outcome. "You're in no position to prevent me from doing whatever I want." Cowle resumed the assessment interrupted by Samantha's fruitless outburst "You're not as physically blessed as your friend Amanda," his voice hushed, breathing heavy, aroused, "but one can't have everything." Cowle gently stroked Lauryn's cheek, hand dropping down to her breasts as she closed her eyes, shivered against his touch, wished she could, like Dorothy from her favorite childhood story, tap ruby red slippers together and be any place other than where she was now. *There's no place like home, there's no place like home.* "You're scared, aren't you, little one? You're scared of what I want to do with you? What I want to take from you? I like it when girls are scared. I get a thrill when I take what I want." Lauryn opened her eyes, chest heaving with every breath, wondering if the next one her last or a nightmare of unspeakable indignities about to commence and continue indefinitely.

"Thing is, little one," Cowle noted dryly, his decision abrupt and Samantha knew Lauryn, as Amanda learned moments earlier, condemned to die. "You wouldn't last long in our company. I think our appetites might far outweigh your ability to bear them."

"Yeah, this one's too fragile," Sterner added, hand firmly pressed against Lauryn's throat. "Too bad, you're a cute one," Lauryn shuddered at the remark. "No fun if they end up only lasting a day or two."

"Which leaves you," Sterner focused a laser-beam of attention to the last of Samantha's companions. Ashleigh glared at him, breath exploding through nostrils in snorting bursts, a snarling, defiant growl passing through the silencing gag. "Winner, winner, chicken dinner. You'll have the pleasure of accompanying us once we're through with our work here." Behind her back Ashleigh clenched her bound fists, body shaking violently. "Too bad you won't be returning any time soon."

Cowle knelt down behind Ashleigh, wrapped his arm around her midsection. Roughly wrenched her towards him, hands fondling Ashleigh in places she didn't wish to be touched. "I'm surprised you didn't figure out by now you'd be the one all along." Ashleigh fought against the lewd grasp, bucking and twisting against his clutches, loud protests muffled. "My companions and I will make you regret how you treated me during our first meeting Saturday night."

The revelation shocked Samantha. "What do you mean?" How did Cowle know Ashleigh?

"Oh, I have history, however brief, with your delectable chocolate-skinned friend here." Cowle smiled evilly at Samantha. "I was in Evanslawn Saturday night enjoying the town's community festival, doing a last bit of shopping for Sheik Rahim," Cowle explained the encounter, hands rubbing Ashleigh's breasts as he spoke, forced from her an indignant grunt of rage. "Searching for the final piece of merchandise for this order and lovely Miss Morgan caught my eye, thought she might offer something exotic to my client. I approached her with a proposition."

Overcome with disbelief, Samantha stared at Ashleigh, her friend unknowingly crossing paths with the beast before Presley Harding succumbed to his beguiling charm. Cowle entwined his fingers into flowing brown sugar hair, yanked her head back, Ashleigh screaming as her eyes, wide and filled with fear, met his.

"Let's say she refused the offer and not in a polite fashion. Called me a 'man with a camera.' I think you understand now I'm much more than that. You'll regret mouthing off. College is about learning. You're going to learn one final lesson and that's respect." He tugged Ashleigh's hair once more, brought forth a groan of distress, hissed into her ear. "I'll warn you, uppity little bitch, I'm a tough grader."

Ashleigh yelled at Cowle through the gag; Samantha could tell it a stream of furious curses. "Good thing that's keeping you quiet," Cowle deciphered the garbled swearing. "Have a dirty mouth for such a beautiful thing." He pulled her hair again. "By the way, I don't like being called an 'm-fer'."

"Good choice, I like chocolate." Sterner appreciated the spectacle of the struggling Ashleigh. "She's a handful, but a bundle of fun."

"Fight all you want, Ashleigh," Cowle released her hair, Ashleigh whipped her head around, muted screams of wrath filling the room. "I own you, you're my piece of property. I can do whatever I wish with you for as long as I want," he taunted, "That's something your ancestors were familiar with, so you'll share the experience." The comment infuriated Ashleigh, struggles against his hold resuming with ferocious intensity.

"You bastard!" Samantha shouted, unsure anyone outside able to hear her cry. Ashleigh glowered at Cowle, continued cursing through the gag, Samantha understood the words despite the bandage wrapping about her head. *Fuck you, asshole.*

"Of course I'll have to do something with you when I and my associates have to go back to work," Cowle tightened his grip on Ashleigh, cupped her chin, stimulated by the heat of her breath against his skin. "I have clients in South America and Africa who'd enjoy your beauty." He stared callously into the chocolate brown eyes. "I do have one client who might wish to make your acquaintance. He produces videos for his clientele of women in extreme forms of distress," his tone calculated, chilling. "Unfortunately it's a one-shot deal, the leading ladies don't survive for a sequel." Ashleigh moaned, grasping the grim fate Cowle meant for her.

"You bastard! You fucking bastard!" Samantha shouted at Cowle, anger finally boiling over, praying someone outside might hear and come to their rescue.

Cowle released Ashleigh, shoved her to the floor, landing with a thud and a cry of vanquished agony. "If you're going to talk to me in that fashion I believe we no longer need to hear your contribution on this matter," Cowle sneered at Samantha, motioning to Sterner who eased Lauryn to the floor, moved to the duffel bag to fetch another cloth pad and strip of white cotton cloth.

"No! You can't do this! You can't hurt them! It's murder!" Samantha protested, about to be silenced again, Sterner clutching her by the shoulders, hands like a vise gripping her arms, Samantha huffing in pain. She twisted her head away, Sterner responded quickly, grabbing her chin, keeping her still, forced to look at Cowle as he methodically approached. "Please, don't," Samantha pleaded, voice finally cracking from emotional strain, "don't kill them."

Cowle loomed over Samantha, voice lowering, threatening. "At times murder is a business strategy. Not the first time I've dealt with unwanted merchandise." Samantha now understood Cowle and his associate capable of acts far more heinous and cold-blooded than kidnapping and selling young women into slavery. How much innocent blood stained their hands? Did they even care? "It's really too bad. I could've made excellent profit from your friends." Cowle glanced over at Amanda, bound to the chair and Lauryn, tied tight lying at Amanda's feet, the pair staring with eyes glistening and damp with terror at their captor and soon to be executioner. Lauryn cowed into petrified silence while Amanda whined through the gag sealing her lips. "But its business Samantha, have to cut my losses. I'm sure the analysts on Wall Street would understand what I'm doing. Good businessmen do it all the time; lay off workers, close factories, in business everything is expendable." Samantha gasped; to Cowle, since he couldn't sell or take them as prizes for ravishment Amanda and Lauryn reduced to inanimate objects designated for elimination. "Of course I need to sample merchandise once in a while." Cowle smiled at Ashleigh, despite the bonds and gag dark eyes glowed with seething fury. She screamed through the wrapping over her mouth, the only avenue of outrage directed towards her captor.

"You're a monster," Samantha said weakly, the pressure of Sterner's fingers on her cheeks unbearable.

"No Samantha, as I've been trying to tell you, I'm a businessman." Cowle nodded his head slightly and Sterner forced her mouth open, Samantha's gasp silenced as Cowle jammed the cloth ball past her lips. With a swift movement, before Samantha could force out the offending wad, Cowle wrapped the cloth strip several times around her head, knotted strictly behind her neck, stuffing secured in her mouth, once more left mute, an object seen and not heard. Samantha bit down on the fabric as Cowle proudly examined his handiwork. "The sound of silence, that's what I like from a woman." Sterner pushed Samantha to the floor, body landing with a thump against the hard surface, an intense blossom of newfound pain exploding in her shoulder. As the ache faded Samantha, body wracked with sobs of failure, looked up at Amanda staring down with sad eyes resigned to a terrible end, then to Lauryn and Ashleigh. *I'm sorry,* she told them.

Amanda moaned through the gag, an expression of sympathy. *It's okay, you tried.* Amanda understood Samantha never stood a chance to alter the ultimate plans of this beast.

Cowle checked his watch. "How long will it take to load the rest of our things?"

Sterner scratched his goatee, considering the request. "I figure about two hours, maybe more since I'm doing the heavy lifting now. That surveillance equipment upstairs isn't cheap." Neither was the arsenal of weapons in the third floor apartment.

"Fine," Cowle not satisfied with the estimate, but accepted the fact. "I'll keep an eye on our guests. Make sure they don't get loose." From his captives the observation met with a Greek chorus of hopeless moaning, arriving long ago at a conclusion the ropes holding them inescapable.

"Have fun," Sterner noted dryly.

"Oh, I will," Cowle smiled at his hostages, "When you're done loading the van bring the package here instead of leaving it in the basement. It'll be more effective eliminating our unwelcome guests," Amanda and Lauryn groaned, fearing the instrument of their demise.

"Will do, boss," Sterner exited the room, leaving Cowle with the bound and silenced quartet.

Cowle walked to the table, casually picked up his camera, scratched and dented from where Samantha hit him in the head in the failed attempt to escape. "I do hope you don't mind," he offered with mock graciousness, lifting the camera. "I wish to have mementos of our time together. Not every day I can gather four lovely young creatures in one place and in this unique circumstance." He clicked off exposure after exposure of his defenseless prey, visibly aroused by their situation. "I don't think I need to worry about you signing any releases for your cooperation."

Ashleigh's smartphone on the table began to vibrate then chime the Great Northern fight song. Cowle interrupted taking pictures of his unwilling subjects, Sterner probably disconnecting the cell phone signal jammer, checked the screen and number, read the text message. "Toscana," he said casually, "I've heard favorable reviews, not easy to get a reservation there. I assume you were headed to dinner?" He asked his silenced prisoners, Ashleigh's growl provided the answer. "Seems they're letting you know you're quite overdue." His grin now turned wicked. "I don't think you'll be making your reservations tonight."

We're not getting out of this, are we? Lauryn stared into Samantha's eyes; a pitiful whimper through the gag, emerald eyes glazed with terror made the guilt Samantha experienced even more agonizing.

No. Samantha shook her head, wished the answer she offered different. Cowle continued taking pictures of his helpless prizes, moving about them with the effortless grace of hawk far up in the sky circling his quarry, swooping down on each of his targets, the camera like talons extended to strike. "I think that will do," Cowle announced, casually packed his photography equipment into the camera bag, sat down on the couch, silently observed the four strain and struggle against the bindings limiting their movements, muffled sobs and gagged cries a symphony for his sole enjoyment. The air conditioning in the building shut off, the atmosphere quickly turned stifling and stale, a suffocating thick blanket dropped over them, adding to the interminable miserable suffering as their final hours together dragged out.

Marcus Cowle watched in silence, and smiled, thrilled with arousal, as the minutes passed with the grinding slowness of a glacier retreating up a prehistoric valley.

"How many intersections are we lookin' at and how many hours of video, fella?" Detective Patrick Flannery asked, on loan from the Dublin Police Department to oversee security arrangements at a global summit in Chicago and never imagining to be in the thick of a missing persons case of a deadly serious nature, the sort he never worked back in his native land. He and Detective Devin Carson sat at their desks, waiting to log onto the server connecting them to Operation Virtual Shield-the network of surveillance cameras throughout the city.

"A lot of intersections and a lot of video," Carson admitted, understood the task a proverbial needle, in this case two or three, in a citywide haystack. Carson checked his watch. "Where the hell is this IT guy from OEMC?"

"He's right here," a thickset man with a bushy salt-and-pepper mustache called out, approaching where they sat, "don't get your shorts in a bunch."

"Sorry, no offense," Carson offered his hand. "We don't have much time to find what we're looking for."

"I understand, Captain Hardaway filled me in," the man shook Carson's hand, spoke with the distinct accent heard on the city's South Side, accepting the unnecessary apology. "Pete Dobbins."

238

"You'll show us how this new software works?" Carson asked.

"You bet your ass I will," Dobbins replied, sat in front of the computer. As he did Carson spotted Dawson Hilliard and Nathanial Hampton enter the squad room, returning from their search of the apartment of the missing students from Saint Vincent University and interviewing their friends. Dobbins noticed the look. "It'll take me a few minutes to get everything up and running. The software program is new and new means it usually has a few bugs in the system. And we've been dealing all day with cyber attacks from hackers, those freaks from Also Known As, trying to crash the system in solidarity with the people walking the picket line."

"How bad?" Carson dreaded the answer.

"The systems running slow, might take time to sort through the video to find what you are looking for," Dobbins warned. "But the image will be clear as day. You'll be able to count the insects splattered on the windshield."

"Let's hope it doesn't take too much time, that's something we don't have," Carson muttered as he and Flannery walked to the returning detectives while Dobbins logged on to the server. "What did you find out?"

"Same as the other two," Hilliard replied, "they packed clothes to go somewhere. We had Isabella's brother, the family lives in Little Italy, with us while we searched the apartment. He pointed out what seemed to be missing, said it was outfits Isabella typically wore when she went out."

"So it appears, as with Emma and Alexandra, wherever they went they did so willingly," Hampton added, "and like them they haven't returned and no one's heard from them since yesterday afternoon. Dead silence."

"Where were they going and who were they meeting with? Why take the clothes with them?" Carson puzzled. "Anything else?"

"This is the interesting piece," Hilliard said. "A friend of Gabriella recalls she posted on Twitter Sunday morning about heading off to become 'America's next top model.' When she checked the feed Sunday night the post was deleted."

"So they might've been meeting a photographer?" Carson stated, or meeting someone posing as a photographer and taking deadly advantage of them.

Hilliard nodded. "The friend remembered Isabella mentioned the name of a photographer in an email. Isabella's password for her Gmail account was on a post-it note by her computer so we logged into the account."

"Mighty helpful of the lass," Flannery noted.

"Yeah, don't have to bother with a search warrant. I do the same thing at home," Hilliard grunted. "I have so many account names and passwords I can't keep them straight."

"What did you find?" Carson asked. Hilliard shook his head. "Deleted?"

"Looks like it," Hilliard added, Carson's apprehension increased exponentially at the revelation, faced with a predator cunning enough, and with the capability, to access the social media of his victims, erase the mere mention of his name. "I'm sure it exists on a server at Google, but we'll have to get a warrant for that to ask them to find it for us."

"That'll take time," Carson said. Time a commodity they sorely lacked.

"Are we looking for a bona-fide photographer or some homicidal maniac with a camera that's playing the game to find his victims," Hilliard added.

239

"And what he, or they," a possibility dealing with more than a single predator, perhaps a team of serial killers, a likelihood Carson didn't wish to contemplate, confronting a formidable foe, "are doing with them." *Or have done with them.* An image he didn't dwell on, continuing with the assumption the missing still alive. *For now.*

Dobbins called over from the computer. "I got you all set up."

Carson glanced at his companions, his hunch a long shot but they might be able to place where in Chicago their missing subjects had gone that weekend. "Ready to look at some video?"

Chapter 32

"Keep up the performance, Amanda, you're quite fetching putting up such a struggle," Marcus Cowle derided Amanda McKinnon with mocking clapping as she tugged and pulled against the ropes melding her to the chair, searching for a knot to loosen, rivulets of perspiration dampening her forehead, trickling in streams down her torso, soaking her clothes. She lifted her head, amethyst eyes boring a hole through a captor seemingly unaffected by the stuffy, oppressive conditions in the studio, unmoved by their horrid plight. No matter how hard she battled against the ropes this a contest Amanda feared she destined to lose and defeat meant the end of her life.

Samantha Grayson snorted at Cowle, brown eyes glistening with defiance and surrender at the same time. "I want to thank you for making this business transaction more profitable than I ever imagined, Samantha," Cowle taunted. "Couldn't have done it without your unannounced visit."

Cowle looked at Lauryn Callahan, curled up in a ball, crying softly. "Yes Lauryn, you happen to be an innocent bystander in all of this." Held a trace of pity for the petite woman, but for Cowle to succeed with his transaction and continue the lucrative operation Lauryn needed to die, silenced forever. *Besides, pity is for suckers.* His gaze shifted to the stubborn, headstrong Ashleigh Morgan, despite the ropes making her immobile relentlessly resisting the hopeless situation. *That attitude will soon change.* "I have plans for you, Ashleigh," Cowle coolly informed the ebony beauty. "I don't think you'll like them, but you aren't in a position to disagree."

"We're ready to go," Sterner grunted, panting heavily with exertion. Samantha heard the ping of metal against metal as he entered the studio, carrying something of prodigious heft. "Got the package right here."

"Bring it in," Cowle told him, "let Amanda and Lauryn see the gift we're leaving them." Samantha's eyes bulged in horror at the bulky apparatus the muscular goon lugged in his hands. Amanda squealed at the sight as she and Samantha realized at the same instant how terrible the method of execution.

Sterner set the unwieldy bundle of four propane tanks between the bound women, thick cable and chains joined the tanks together at the handles, bands of heavy-duty duct tape wrapped about the middle of the tanks, secured them as a single unit. On the front of one tank taped a brick-sized block of gray material with the familiar consistency of clay Samantha played with in grade school, a timing device attached to the block with more duct tape, a rainbow spectrum of colored wires leading from the timer into the clay-like substance. Samantha knew what a plastic explosive looked like; repulsed at the diabolical manner Cowle intended to finish off Amanda and Lauryn. Samantha shuddered at the discovery, an appallingly horrible demise by explosion and fire, in the process destroying the flat and the Potemkin photography studio within.

"This is what we call in my line of work an Improvised Explosive Device," Sterner informed the captives, the term arising from the Iraq War to describe bombs deployed by insurgents against American forces. "If the blast wave and shrapnel from the tanks doesn't finish you off," Sterner wiped sweat from his forehead, relished the frightened reaction from Amanda at the device resting inches from her feet, as a runner had reason to fear such a device, recalling a horrible terrorist incident at the most famous of marathons, squirming against the ropes sealing her to the chair growing more frantic, "the fireball will take care of what's left."

"You're right, Samantha," Cowle said impassively, "they won't find your friends for a few days." He paused. "It'll take them that long to identify what little they find of them." Lauryn whimpered, closed her eyes, didn't look at the device deviously engineered to snuff her life. Samantha growled at her tormentor. *You sick, cold-hearted bastard*, then gazed at Amanda and Lauryn, sentenced to a fiery, ugly death, sadness overwhelming the anger. *I never meant for this to happen.*

"So what do we do now?" Cowle asked the helpless Amanda and Lauryn. "Should I be merciful, finish the two of you off now so you don't feel the blast?" Cowle stalked behind the chair where Amanda sat bound, grinning as she trembled uncontrollably; feared her life now measured in minutes all too fleeting. "All I'd have to do is slap a piece of tape over your noses," Lauryn cried out, curling into a tighter ball on the floor, not wanting to die, having so much to live for, realizing all she loved and cherished about to be snatched away. "Only take a minute or two for you to suffocate. We'd have an audience for your final performance," he smirked devilishly at Samantha and Ashleigh, likewise doomed, though the time of their end not yet determined. "Wouldn't it be terrible, Samantha," Cowle said, "watching your friends take their last breaths, fighting to live, while you lie there unable to save them?" Cowle rested his hand on Amanda's shoulder and she stilled her struggles, wondering if the next instant tape pressed over her nostrils, sealing off her lungs, initiating a final descent towards eternal darkness. "Knowing you're responsible for their deaths?" Samantha screamed at Cowle through her gag, an agonized plea of mercy, didn't wish the ordeal of bearing witness to the execution of her friends.

"But I don't like getting my hands dirty," Cowle acknowledged, Samantha snarling back at him. Toying with her emotions, torturing Samantha to the brink of insanity, engaging in psychological warfare, finding perverse pleasure in the mental damage inflicted on his helpless victims. "I'd rather let our package here," he motioned to the bomb sitting amongst them, "to do the work for me."

Cowle strode to the device. Dual readouts on the timer, programmed the current time on the top readout. "How long should I give your friends?" Cowle asked of Samantha, "one hour, perhaps two." Cowle held up his index finger, an expression of pleased surprise on his face, struck by a heavenly revelation. "I've always had a flair for the dramatic," Cowle programmed a time on the second readout.

12:00 AM. *Midnight.* "Executions always take place either at the break of dawn or at midnight. Either way this will be your last day alive, ladies," he informed the doomed pair. "You won't be around to see another day." Cowle stood up, laughed, Samantha found no mirth in his action. "I do think this will wake the neighbors."

"No shit," Sterner added a brief opinion.

"See that Lauryn isn't able to move after we depart," Cowle ordered his associate, pointing at the cowering form of Lauryn Callahan on the floor. Sterner said nothing as he pulled a length of rope from the duffel bag, straddled the shaking girl, flipped her over on her stomach, a pitiful moan all Lauryn managed to utter in resistance. Sterner looped one end of the rope through the binding on her ankles, wrenched feet back to the hands until they almost touched, attaching the other end to the bonds about her wrists. Sterner yanked the rope taut, tied it off, Lauryn crying at being placed in an agonizingly arched position.

"Sorry to hurt you, little lady," Sterner patted Lauryn on the shoulder, Samantha unable to tell if the display one of genuine sympathy or a spiteful ruse. Cowle reached into the duffel, removed two more rolls of the white elastic bandage material, tossed one to Sterner who remained crouched over the hogtied Lauryn. Cowle walked back to the chair where Amanda sat motionless, wrapped in countless feet of rope, barely able to move an inch.

"So you have less than three hours left to live," Cowle callously informed Amanda and Lauryn, condemned prisoners sitting on Death Row awaiting execution but having committed no crime save for being in the wrong place at the wrong time, witnesses to be eliminated, no last-second reprieve to spare them the awful fate. "Doesn't that scare you? Knowing you only have so much time left on this Earth? Each passing minute bringing you closer to the end?" Amanda's murmured whimper the only reply, staring at the dual timers, one minute already ticking off, one minute closer to death. "Do you know what's more frightening than knowing you only have hours left to live?" Cowle asked his captive. Amanda offered a tiny shake of her head, not knowing what possibly worse than knowing the remainder of her life measured by minutes on a timer, impotent to stop the march of time towards a horrible demise.

Cowle leaned close to Amanda, whispered in her ear. "It's not knowing when your time is up," he informed her, ice coating his voice. Cowle began wrapping the bandage material over Amanda's eyes, blindfolding her, Sterner doing the same to Lauryn. Amanda whined anxiously, each pass of the stretchy fabric blotted out her vision until sealed in an impenetrable blackness. Amanda dropped her head towards her chest once Cowle finished, breathing heavily, resigned to a death she now wouldn't see coming.

Samantha slumped against the floor, watching as her friends blindfolded, their sight taken away. *This is all because of me*; the overwhelming tidal wave of guilt surged within her. *They're going to die because of me.* "Don't worry Samantha," Cowle said cheerfully, impressed with his work, no chance of either girl getting loose and escaping, in a matter of hours the explosive device taking care of the complication. "When we get to the warehouse I'll make sure you know when it's midnight, when your friends meet their eternal reward." Samantha glared at Cowle, her defeat total and crushing, as Amanda and Lauryn whimpered in horror. "I told you I had a flair for the dramatic."

"Let us take our leave," Cowle told Sterner, slinging the bag with his camera and laptop over his shoulder. "I'm sure Lang is wondering what's taking so long." He stooped down, lifted Ashleigh into a kneeling position, heaved her up from the floor and over his shoulder. "Time to start your vacation, Ashleigh," Cowle said, patted her hip. *You do have a nice piece of ass, baby.* "I'm sorry if the quarters are confined for a few hours."

Sterner stepped over to Samantha, grabbed underneath her shoulders, hauled up to a standing position, draped her bound body over his shoulder. Heard plaintive cries from her remaining friends, head lifting for a final glimpse at the terrible tableau burned forever in memory-Amanda bound to the chair, Lauryn tied and lying at her feet, both gagged and blindfolded, helpless, left with the powerful bomb ready to end their existence. Sterner followed Cowle from the room and down the hall. *Goodbye.* Samantha sobbed, forced to live with the searing, tragic image until her own life came to a violent end. Sterner hit the lights on his way out, the room plunged into darkness. *I'm sorry, forgive me...*

Moments later Samantha and Ashleigh hauled into the attached garage where a black cargo van and white Ford Lexus parked. "Take Samantha in the van," Cowle told Sterner as his hand rubbed Ashleigh on the bottom, eliciting an indignant squeal Cowle found endearing. *I'm going to have such fun with you.* "Ashleigh is riding with me."

Sterner opened the side door to the van, forcibly tossed Samantha on the metal floor in the narrow space between the partition separating the driver's compartment and the boxes and duffel bags piled towards the rear of the cargo hold. Samantha curled up instinctively, knees pulled to her chest, brown eyes brimming with fear as the door to the van shut and locked her inside. She'd been tied and gagged for hours, body brutalized and exhausted by the inescapable bondage; spirit crushed, now tormented with remorse, responsible for the terrible fate of her friends. Now alone again Samantha cried, wanted to be strong, fight back and resist these monsters and the man who'd soon purchase her life to do terrible things, but her strength drained and sapped. And the ordeal, already many hours old, was only beginning.

Cowle carried Ashleigh to the rear of the Lexus, popped the trunk, the lid lifting upward. The dark, cramped space awaiting Ashleigh ignited a furious struggle against his grasp, eyes growing wide seeing where Cowle meant to keep her prisoner on the first leg of a journey to a lonely doom. She started to scream, pleading through the gag, begging. *Do not put me in there!*

"Hope you don't mind," Cowle swung her off his shoulder, dropping her into the trunk, Ashleigh fighting all the way, forced to lie down. "Can't have you riding in the back seat. Don't worry, it'll only be for a few hours," he calmly reassured his hostage. The lid slammed shut and Ashleigh whimpered as an inky darkness wrapped about her.

Ashleigh shivered, remained motionless as the fight swiftly leached from her muscles, paralyzed with dread, hearing first the engine of the van and then of the Lexus start up, sensed movement as the Lexus backed out of the garage. Her eyes darted about the confined space, breathing rapidly, desperately trying not to panic. *Don't lose it, Ashleigh! Don't lose it!* A single fear Ashleigh kept hidden from everyone she knew, thought it irrational and unbecoming for her outgoing personality, didn't admit to the secret weakness concealed in her soul. Bound, gagged and kidnapped the most horrific of situations, but being imprisoned in the trunk of the car now something far worse.

Ashleigh Morgan was claustrophobic.

As he drove the white Lexus through the shadow-cast streets of Chicago, fingers drumming against the steering wheel Marcus Cowle, a man used to decisive action, found himself plagued with second thoughts.

I should've done those two girls back at the studio, he thought grimly. *Finished them off right then, let Samantha and Ashleigh watch them die.* Why he spared Amanda McKinnon and Lauryn Callahan's lives, even for the few hours left until the device detonated and leveled in an apocalyptic fireball the brownstone once home to Marcus Evans Photography and consumed the bound and helpless coeds left behind, puzzled him. Did he feel sympathy for Samantha Grayson, taking pity on her unfortunate soul; giving in to better angels to exhibit a minute morsel of mercy to the woman soon the sixth parcel of

Sheik Rahim's consignment? Was is that he was tired and irritated, angry at his client, not thinking straight under the strain of the situation? Whatever the compulsion allowing Amanda and Lauryn to live a few hours more Cowle now cursed the display of compassion for the beautiful victim. He understood one wild card yet remained this night, one beyond his reach, the person directing Samantha to the studio in search of the missing freshman from Great Northern University: Presley Harding's roommate, Riley Bradford. How long until she realized, as hours ticked away without hearing from the student reporter, that Samantha shared the same perilous situation as Presley and she sought assistance, perhaps this time from the police, to find them? With Amanda and Lauryn still alive, even for the brief time remaining, there posed a likelihood ever so slim they'd be discovered, a result threatening not only his business dealings with Sheik Rahim but the entire operation of The Trading Society. He needed Riley to hesitate in taking action, continue to wait for word from the now subdued Samantha, for a few more hours until the device did its grim work, eliminated the only witnesses to his undertaking, as he transferred the merchandise to Rahim and claim his substantial reward. The complicated affair only existed because Sheik Rahim, arrogant with omnipotence and wealth, wanted to personally oversee delivery of his new property. In hindsight a risky proposition Cowle should've advised his lucrative client against, the delay exposing their transaction to undue risk of discovery.

He heard Ashleigh crying from the trunk. "Not so uppity now, are we Ashleigh?" He called to his captive. "Hope you're enjoying the trip, too bad you can't enjoy the scenery." The crying continued as he drove south on Sacramento Avenue through Humboldt Park, glanced in the rearview mirror, the black van driven by Sterner with Samantha Grayson inside following behind. The sobbing from the trunk began grating on his nerves, Cowle switched on the radio always tuned to the classical station wherever he briefly called home. The notes of Wagner's *Ring of the Nibelungen* emerged from the speakers, turning up the volume to drown out pitiful cries from his prisoner. Cowle found the opera recounting the downfall of the gods of Valhalla befitting his current circumstance. If everything did go wrong and his venture uncovered The Trading Society employing precautions to insure he and his associates didn't live long enough to disclose their secrets to the authorities.

He turned onto Carroll Avenue, the black van following, drove to the abandoned factory where five unlucky women already waited inside for departure on a final journey, about to be joined by a sixth unfortunate victim. Night draped a soft cloak over the street lined with shuttered warehouses and factories, a depressing remnant of more vibrant economic times, the pale orange glow of streetlights barely denting the encompassing darkness. Cowle activated the remote to open the gate of their urban fortress, trundling back to allow the van and Lexus entrance to the enclosure. Cowle pressed a second button, the door to the loading bay rose from the ground, the van slipping inside the bay. They needed to load the last of their equipment into the van, then parking it outside to leave room inside the bay for the limousine and escort vehicles of Sheik Rahim and his security detail when they arrived.

Cowle parked the Lexus outside the building, towards the rear of the complex away from the street, switched off the engine, again heard sorrowful sobbing from the hostage in the trunk. No need to bring her inside, Ashleigh not about to go anywhere tied, silenced, and locked in the trunk. Cowle stepped from the vehicle, walked around the rear of the car, couldn't resist tapping the lid. "Hope you don't mind waiting out here?" He asked mockingly. *As if you have any choice, bitch.* The panicked scream he received brought a smile to his face.

Cowle entered the building, winding his way through darkened corridors to the loading bay where Sterner parked the van, already out and opened the side door. Lang joining his partner, emerging from where he stood watch over the other captives. Cowle strode up, peered inside the van, the fear-filled brown eyes of Samantha Grayson staring at him, wedged back against the corner warily observing her captors.

"I guess this why you're running late?" Lang jerked a thumb at Samantha.

Cowle smirked at the defenseless Samantha, shaking in her bonds. "And the friends who came looking for her."

"What's the deal with this chick?" Lang scrutinized the auburn-haired young woman glaring at him with apprehensive eyes. *Not bad*, he judged the shapely body, arrived at his conclusion. *I'd do her.*

"Her name is Samantha Grayson, she's a college reporter from Great Northern University, came looking for Presley who's already experiencing our fine hospitality," Cowle explained to his associate. "Let's say I couldn't have her leaving the premises. Her friends happened to get in the way."

"So what are we doing with them?" Lang, like his employer, not fond of complications, anything preventing his hefty payday, said to Sterner. "You off them like we had to do that guy down in Atlanta?"

"Samantha will be an additional parcel for tonight's consignment. Sheik Rahim is paying handsomely for her inclusion." Cowle continued grinning at his precious captive, watched her shudder, pleased by the whines of distress. "We left two of her friends at the studio with the device that in a few hours will eliminate that problem. The third is in the trunk of my car. She'll be joining us on our off time to provide some amusement."

Sterner nudged him. "I know you like chocolate." Lang nodded, understood the meaning.

"How are the other guests holding up?" Cowle inquired.

"All nice and pretty for their new owner," Lang noted, the five hostages again bound and separated into different cells.

"Good," Cowle turned to Sterner, "why don't you see Samantha to her room for the time being, I think there's someone she's very interested in meeting. Then pack the rest of our equipment, load it in the van and leave it outside next to the Lexus. Our client will need room to park inside upon his arrival."

"Our work is never done," Lang joked, then inquired in a serious tone. "You sure those two you left at the studio won't be a problem?"

Cowle checked his watch, didn't express his silent doubts. "They won't be after midnight," Samantha moaned at the callous comment. "Gentlemen, time's a-wasting. You have work to do."

"No rest for the wicked," Sterner replied.

"You're such a slave driver," Lang muttered as Sterner leaned into the cargo hold, dragged out the defenseless Samantha, struggling against the iron grip, heaved her over his shoulder. No way for Samantha to resist, only groan at her predicament.

"Let's go, little lady," Sterner said. Hanging over his shoulder like a sack of meal delivered to market for sale, Samantha saw the gray concrete floor below as Sterner carried her from the loading bay. She managed to lift her head slightly, strain on her back and shoulders incredible, pain flaring at the base of her neck, eyes taking in where they brought her. The interior of the loading bay cavernous, even with discarded pieces of machinery shoved to the rear and sides of the bay, the sound of her captor's voices echoed through the vast space. The building once provided livelihood to hard-working laborers, now abandoned and utilized by evil men to implement an equally vile plan of enslavement, Samantha among the victims sold into sexual slavery, facing an eventual death. Cowle followed behind Sterner, observed her pitiful squirming with barely concealed delight. *You're enjoying this, you damned bastard*, Samantha snarled. To Cowle Samantha nothing more than an object with a price attached, sold for his profit at the ultimate loss of her life.

"Stop moving about up there," Sterner warned, "you don't want me to drop you." During the ride to the hidden destination Samantha secretly wished with fatalistic resignation the boxes and cases loaded in the van toppled over, crushed her to put an end to her misery.

"Wouldn't want to damage the merchandise," Cowle drolly noted, entering a hallway off from the loading bay. Samantha saw Cowle reach for a clock hanging on the wall, lift it from the hook, carrying it in his hand. "Sheik Rahim wouldn't appreciate damaged goods, especially considering what he's paying for you." Samantha growled, exhibited her fearful displeasure.

They turned, headed down a second hallway, Samantha swiveled her head from side to side, peering inside rooms lining the corridor. The doors open, inside each a young woman securely restrained sat or lay on a mattress; Samantha understood the purpose of the rooms. *Cells to isolate the prisoners.* Samantha lugged past so quickly had no time to look closely at her fellow captives, only noting they shared expressions of resignation at a shared, imperiled jeopardy.

"Here's your accommodation for the next few hours," Cowle announced, following Sterner into the third room on their left. With a deft movement Sterner swung Samantha from his shoulder; the soft surface of a mattress cushioned the impact, Samantha shifting into a sitting position. "Hope you find the lodging to your liking." Samantha moaned, she didn't like them at all. "We brought you company to pass the time," Cowle informed the other occupant of the cell, Samantha's eyes darting to the form huddled in the corner as Sterner reached behind her head, undid the gag. The girl dressed in a purple floral-print long-sleeve top and black miniskirt, wore thigh-high gray suede boots. An eye-catching outfit if not for the rope bound about her upper body, fusing legs together as one.

"I think you have matters to discuss before the arrival of our honored guest," Cowle said, the tone condescending, as Samantha spat out the sodden wad of cloth and sucked stale, musty air of the vacant factory into her lungs. Cowle propped the clock taken from hallway in the corner opposite Samantha, offered a devious smile. "I want you to know what time it is, Samantha." The image of Amanda and Lauryn left helpless at the abandoned studio, with the explosive device set to end their lives in less than three hours, haunted Samantha. "I want you to know when it's midnight."

"No trying to free each other," he cautioned the duo, directing his words to the forlorn figure cowering in the corner, "your friend here was foolish enough to try. She found out what happens to disobedient girls who don't do as they're told. She didn't find the experience pleasant." Samantha shivered, didn't want to ponder what they'd done to the young woman for her transgression.

Cowle and Sterner departed, Samantha turned to the bound girl sitting beside her, recalled the picture Riley Bradford showed of a happily smiling Presley Harding back at the *Daily Northern* office, a time that seemed ages ago, immediately recognized the missing roommate after Sterner set her down. The long caramel hair hanging down over her face, soft brown eyes empty and void of emotion, hauntingly beautiful angelic face now disfigured by an expression of terrified defeat. Samantha wanted to be sure of her discovery. "Are you Presley Harding?" Samantha whispered, shifting her body closer to the girl with her head dropped in despair, the lengthy ordeal shattering the will to resist, a tragic tribulation having days, perhaps weeks and months, to run its horrible course.

The girl lifted her head. "Yes, I'm Presley." Shocked at the sound of her name, surprise sparking in her eyes. "How do you know who I am?" She wondered in amazement.

"I'm Samantha Grayson, I'm reporter at *The Daily Northern*," Samantha explained, talking might ease collective fears of a shared and terrible destiny relentlessly approaching. Ignoring the clock Cowle pitilessly left in the room, torturing her with the fleeting time Amanda and Lauryn had left to live, trapped with the bomb in the studio on Campbell Street.

Presley nodded, in her eyes a glint of recognition at the name. "I know who you are," she said, now confused. "I read your stories in the newspaper. Why are you here? What's going on? Does anyone know we're here? Is someone coming to save us?" The questions flowed quickly from Presley's lips.

"Your roommate, Riley, she came to see me this afternoon," Samantha continued, shifting her body to keep ropes from cutting into her skin. "She told me you hadn't been in your room since yesterday afternoon, she was worried about you. Came to see me because the police said they couldn't take a missing persons report until later."

"Riley?" Presley asked, eyes glistening with moisture. "Riley came to see you?" Samantha saw Presley swallow, emotions welling up. "Riley was worried about me?"

Samantha nodded sympathetically. "She's concerned about you. She gave me the business card for Marcus Evans Photography. Thought you might've gone there," Samantha paused. "She wanted to go to see if you'd been there." Samantha sighed, wanted to cry with her companion. "I told her I would check into it for her." A decision Samantha to forever regret, caught in a slavery ring with her friends condemned to their own brutal deaths.

"That's why you're here." Presley bit her trembling lip, shaking her head, tears starting to bubble in her eyes, voice cracking on the edge of hysteria. "He's not a photographer! He's kidnapped us! He's selling us to some sheik from the Middle East! There are five of us here!" Presley rested her head back against the wall, stared up at the gray ceiling. "Oh God, if Riley had gone there, she'd have never had a chance! She'd be here instead of you!" Presley stared at Samantha, a glimmer of hope casting aside the darkness of her impending, terrible fate, repeated her questions. "Is someone looking for us? Is someone coming to save us?" Waiting for an answer she so desperately wished to hear.

"I don't know," Samantha tried not to give Presley false hope, saw the expression of fearful doubt again crease the captivating face, bound body slumping in despair. Samantha didn't want to tell Presley of her friends, falling into the same trap and sentenced to a far different, yet just as cruel, fate. *My friends are going to die because of me.*

"Maybe Riley is going to the police right now." Samantha prayed for the possibility, with each passing hour since meeting at *The Daily Northern* and not hearing from her that Riley either returned to the paper or went to the police or campus security, alerted them to the imminent danger. *Maybe they'll listen to her this time.* This slim reed of hope the final, tenuous strand of salvation for Samantha and Presley, for Amanda and Lauryn left to a fiery doom at the studio, for Ashleigh locked in the trunk of Marcus Cowle's car, to cling to like a log amid a torrential flood. But time running out with each passing of the second hand on the clock in the corner.

"Riley...was worried about me, she cared about me." Presley started shaking uncontrollably, tiny body wracked with sobs, regretted the distant treatment towards her roommate in the brief time they'd been together. "She was worried...about me...and I ignored her." *She wanted to be my friend, and I pushed her away, I wanted to go out every night and party. If I had told her where I was going Sunday, I wouldn't be here now. She wanted to go to the studio to find me. She was a friend, but I thought only of myself, I didn't want to be her friend.* The sobbing intensified, echoing off the walls of the cell as Presley Harding realized then if the roles reversed, she wouldn't have done the same for Riley Bradford and a devastating guilt obliterated what was left of her spirit. *I'm going to die because I was so selfish...*

Samantha let Presley cry, releasing sorrow and angst bottled up inside. She glanced at the clock Cowle left behind, watched another minute tick off closer to midnight, Amanda McKinnon and Lauryn Callahan brought one minute closer to the precipice of death.

Chapter 33

"So we have Emma Hayden's car at the intersection of Milwaukee, Damen and North around eleven-thirty on Saturday," Devin Carson studied the video capture on the screen, the sunshine yellow Chevrolet Impala turning north onto Milwaukee Avenue, as the four detectives scrolled through hours of video culled from the network of cameras installed at major intersections throughout Chicago and linked to Virtual Shield.

"Makes sense," Nathanial Hampton added. "The last transaction on any of her credit cards is a charge of fifty dollars to her Citibank Visa at the Starbucks on that corner right around then."

"Loaded up her Starbucks card," was Dawson Hilliard's comment, "that'll buy a lot of decaf vanilla lattes."

"So we place her in the area of Wicker Park that morning," Carson said, then shook his head. "After that her car doesn't show up on any other cameras throughout the city." Carson typed in another command into the dialog box, called up as second image, this one of the blue Ford Fusion owned by Alexandra Cole. "Same thing, the last time Alexandra's car is recorded on video is at Fullerton and the Kennedy Expressway shortly before four," Carson stared at the image, "then nothing after that."

"Where did you find the two cars?" Pete Dobbins asked, the technician staying around to handle any software issues that might arise.

"Englewood for the Hayden car, North Lawndale for the Cole vehicle," Carson told him.

Dobbins growled in disbelief. "No way in hell you can drive from the Northwest Side to either the South Side or the West Side without going through at least one intersection covered by this network."

"Thinking they found a way to conceal the tag numbers?" Hilliard assumed.

An idea, a longshot at that, came forth in Carson's mind. *Worth a try.* "Is there a way to capture the manufacturer and model of a vehicle using this software? Sort results by the color of the vehicle?"

"Guess great minds think alike," Dobbins grinned. "I was about to suggest that. This upgraded software has vehicle recognition features built in. Designate the make and model and it'll find all of the possible matches." Dobbins sighed right after that statement.

"What?" Carson caught the hint of exasperation.

"It'll take time for the software to search through thousands of images." Dobbins let the other shoe drop. "You'll wind up with a lot of potential matches to wade through before you find what you're looking for."

"Don't have a choice," Carson said tersely. "Do it." With that Pete Dobbins typed into the dialog box on the search mode for a yellow Chevy Impala and a blue Ford Fusion.

*   *   *   *   *

"Dude, what the hell is with you tonight?" D'Andre Watson asked Tyler McManaway as his friend reached for his Android phone, tapped out another text message to Samantha Grayson as the roommates sat studying in their McDonough Hall suite, fulfilling the 'student' part in the term 'student-athlete.' "How many times are you going to text or call Samantha?" This the ninth text in the last ninety minutes, along with five phone calls immediately sent to her voicemail. With each missive unanswered Tyler approached a conclusion both disturbing and troubling.

"You're not the least worried you haven't heard from Ashleigh tonight?" Tyler didn't look at D'Andre, thumbs typing out a terse message. *Samantha where are u? Text me ASAP!*

"It's their 'Girls Night Out," D'Andre shrugged nonchalantly. "They're probably gabbing it up, telling each other their little stories about us."

"When they go out don't you usually get a blow-by-blow account from Ashleigh?" Tyler said, sending the message. He waited a minute for a response, Samantha typically swift with her reply. Like the eight messages he'd sent previously the text unanswered. *Samantha isn't like this*, Tyler thought, holding back a growing unease. *She'd answer at least one text. Let me know she's okay.*

D'Andre thought for a moment, Ashleigh prolific with her texts, firing them off with the rapid machine-gun pace of a stand-up comedian. D'Andre once joked Ashleigh possessed the fastest thumbs south of the Mason-Dixon Line. "Come to think of it."

"I haven't heard from Amanda all evening," Connor Aanonsen lifted his head from his book, thought nothing of it until then, when Tyler expressed his deepening anxiety. "She said she would post a picture of her dinner on Facebook. Call me when they're back on campus, we were going to do a little studying." *And a few other things.* He grabbed his phone, went to his Facebook page, no evidence of the victory dinner posted. "That's not like her," Connor added under his breath.

"When they go out don't they post pictures of them having a good time?" Tyler asked. Connor nodded at the observation, agreed something odd here. "Fiji?" Tyler turned to his massive friend. "Heard anything from Lauryn?"

"No, I haven't." Albert 'Fiji' Fatuamala quietly stated, sensed the depth of his friend's agitation, understood the reason for his apprehension.

"Samantha said she'd let me know when they were coming back to campus." Tyler glanced at the clock, time closing in on ten-thirty; fighting the urge to panic, stay in control of the circumstances. "They should've returned by now." Tyler the starting quarterback for a Big Ten football team, everyone looked to him to be the leader, have the situation in hand. "Samantha was going to finish working on the stories from this morning before we met up for..." His voice trailed off.

"Maybe she's at the office," D'Andre offered, confused by Tyler's restlessness. "The girls hanging with her until she's done."

"They're back and they didn't let us know?" Tyler answered, unconvinced, turned to D'Andre. "What's the name of the restaurant they were going to?" Had forgotten in the midst of his anxiety, mind buffeted by dark thoughts, knew the name sounded Italian.

"Toscana," D'Andre said as Tyler used the Google app on his phone to find the number. "Tyler, what the hell has you wound up?"

Tyler ignored the question, dialed the number, asked one of his own. "What time were the reservations for and who made them?"

"Ashleigh made them for seven, to avoid the three-month wait for reservations she dropped her Mom's name," D'Andre replied, glancing at Connor and Fiji, hands raised in exasperation, expression on his face saying *what's going on here?* "Can you tell me why...?"

"Hello, I'm hoping you can help me," Tyler raised a hand, cut D'Andre off as he reached the hostess station at Toscana. "I'm checking to see if my friends are there. They had reservations at seven for a party of four, under the name Ashleigh Morgan. Sure, I'll wait." The pause brief and the answer Tyler received not at all reassuring. "They never showed up?" D'Andre stiffened, a realization his friend might be on mark with his misgivings, something terribly amiss. "Did they call to cancel the reservation?" Another pause as Tyler listened. "No? And you called and sent a text message to Ashleigh's number and no one replied?" Tyler looked at D'Andre as he spoke, concern clouding his sky blue eyes. "Okay, thanks. Wait, if they do show up please have Samantha, she'll be in the party, call Tyler as soon as possible. She knows my number. Thanks for your help."

Tyler turned off the phone, lifted his head, sucking in a deep breath as his worst nightmare rose to life like Frankenstein's monster. "They never made their reservation, they didn't call to cancel and the restaurant contacted Ashleigh's phone when they didn't show. They didn't get an answer."

"Maybe they decided to go somewhere else for dinner?" Connor offered, though he didn't believe the words coming from his mouth.

"Ashleigh goes through the trouble to make reservations and they go someplace else at the last minute?" The retort from Tyler direct and sharp, though his friend didn't deserve the tart reply, his nerves fraying at the edges. "Then decided not to tell anyone what they're doing?"

"This isn't like them," Fiji added a certain fact, "they would've let us know if their plans changed."

"Tyler, what's going on?" D'Andre asked again, concerned with his friend's behavior and the news their girlfriends never reached the restaurant. "What the hell is up with you tonight?"

"He's right, you've been squirrely the past few days," Connor added, puzzled. "Something's eating at you, and if it involves Amanda, I want to know what it's about."

"I think I know," Fiji noted simply, Tyler looking at him.

"I've got a bad feeling about this," Tyler stated forcefully.

"Then enlighten us about this bad feeling!" D'Andre shot back, frustrated by the response.

"Damn it, you should know!" Tyler shouted. "You're from Los Angeles! It happened there around this time last year!"

"Know what?" D'Andre asked, thoroughly confused and increasingly irritated with Tyler's unaccustomed high-strung emotional state. "I'm not a Vulcan, can't do the mind meld to find out what's going on in your head!"

"You don't remember those five women who went missing?" Tyler rolled his eyes. "Never found a trace of them?"

"Wait a minute," now D'Andre remembered, raised his hands, what Tyler told him a bolt from the blue. "What does that have to do with us not hearing from our ladies tonight?"

"I know what you're talking about," Connor leaned forward. "One of the girls who went missing was from Minneapolis, went to UCLA. She and her roommate disappeared, police never found them."

"Did make my little sister's social life a little less social for a few months," D'Andre couldn't believe what Tyler suggesting. "Are you saying what happened there has happened to Ashleigh and the girls?"

"That is a hell of a reach," Connor added.

"Why don't you explain why you feel this way," Fiji told Tyler in a tone quiet and calm, tempered the simmering tension brewing in the room.

Tyler glanced at Fiji. *You know what's going on.*

Fiji nodded stoically. *Yes, I do.*

Tyler took a deep breath. "Remember Friday at lunch, when Samantha seemed a little distant?" Both D'Andre and Connor nodded in affirmation. "When we went into the city Saturday night to watch the fireworks at Navy Pier I asked her about it."

"What's up?" D'Andre asked. "There isn't trouble in paradise between you two?"

"No, nothing like that." Tyler wished that the case, something he could handle. "She saw an article in the *Chicago Tribune* last week about those missing women in California." Tyler took another deep breath, describing his fears for Samantha calming him, allowed him to focus. "Thought she might do a story on it, find an angle here at Great Northern. She did some digging on the background, found out this has happened over the past couple of years across the country: Boston, Denver, Atlanta and then in Los Angeles. Three, four, five women disappearing over the span of a few days, never heard from again. She found out how all these missing women might be linked."

"So that's why Samantha was out of it," Connor assumed.

"Yeah," Tyler acknowledged. "Researching this story reminded Samantha of her friends."

"And of herself too," D'Andre saw Tyler's point.

"She asked me what I'd do if she were gone, if she went missing." Tyler lowered his head, stared at the floor, continued somberly. "I told her I'd never let anyone hurt her, I'd do everything to find her."

"So that's why you've been off your game the past few days," D'Andre realized. "You're not worried about that Minnesota pass rush."

"Hardly," Tyler noted with a dry laugh. Every minute he didn't hear from Samantha burgeoning fears for the one he loved ratcheted another notch, deathly afraid someone had harmed, or was hurting, his Samantha. *And I'm not there to stop it.* "Two women went missing down at Texas Tech last week."

"I heard about that," a light of recognition glimmered in D'Andre's eyes, "one of my high school teammates plays at Texas. It's in the news down there." He stared at Tyler. "You still think what happened in Cali might've happened to Ashleigh and the girls?" D'Andre let out a long whistle. "Connor's right, that's a stretch."

"I'm not saying that's what happened," Tyler answered, "but I have a bad feeling something's not right. I don't like it when things don't feel right."

"He's got a point," Connor felt a hard knot of doubt forming in his gut. "It's not like Amanda, or any of them, not to let us know where they are."

"I don't know, man," D'Andre said, "I still think you're overreacting. Has to be a reason why we haven't heard from them."

"And that reason is?" Tyler demanded. D'Andre remained silent, didn't respond.

"So something might be wrong," Connor finally admitted. "What do we do about it?"

"Where's the most logical place I'd find Samantha?" Tyler asked.

Fiji immediately knew the answer. "At *The Daily Northern* office."

"That's where I'm headed," Tyler grabbed a moss green half-zip sweater from a nearby chair, tugging it over his head. "If Samantha isn't there somebody might know where she went," he told them. "The girls were supposed to meet Samantha there before heading into Chicago for dinner."

Fiji stood, unspoken concerns for Lauryn Callahan deepening. "I'm coming with you."

"I'm not sitting here on my ass," Connor grabbed a Great Northern Hockey sweatshirt to wear in the cool evening air, on his head jamming down the well-worn, sweat-stained Minnesota Wild cap.

D'Andre weighed the anxiety of his best friend, still couldn't fathom the notion his Ashleigh and her friends missing. But he hadn't heard from Ashleigh all evening. *That's unusual for Ashleigh.* "I guess this can wait," he said, closing the book. "If they're at *The Daily Northern* chattering away and didn't tell anyone, they're getting the lecture Dad gives me when I screw up." D'Andre rarely received such dressing-down, his father a decorated colonel in the United States Marine Corps; the reason why D'Andre didn't stray far from a straight-arrow path. Those stern admonitions delivered in an authoritative tone convinced D'Andre to never deviate from the high moral standards the father set for his youngest son.

"If that's all it is," Tyler said as they left the room, striding down the hall with single-minded purpose, heading across campus to Howell Student Commons and the offices of *The Daily Northern*, "I can deal with that." All Tyler McManaway desired was to know Samantha Grayson alive and safe, hold her in his arms and tell her how much he loved her. The continuing veil of silence told him otherwise, suspected his darkest fears for the well-being of Samantha and her friends might transform into an unsettling reality.

From a deep sleep she only intended to last several minutes Riley Bradford finally awoke. The darkness the first thing she noticed, reached up for the lamp beside the couch.

The pale light illuminated the room. Bleary eyes focused on the clock and she froze in horror.

Ten-forty? I was asleep that long? She wanted to rest for a moment, instead been out senseless to the world for hours. She glanced around the empty room, no sign her roommate Presley Harding returned during her slumber. Riley reached for her phone to see if either Samantha Grayson, or Presley, called during the time she slept.

Nothing. No indication of a missed call from Samantha or a left voicemail, not even a text message. Even if she found nothing amiss at Marcus Evans Photography Riley knew Samantha considerate enough to contact her with what she found. Riley dialed Samantha's cell phone number. After two rings she reached her voicemail and heard the message the voicemail was full.

Riley arrived at an immediate, and terrifying, conclusion. *Samantha is in trouble.*

An overwhelming dread shook Riley to the core, fearing whatever happened to Presley now claimed Samantha. *I'm the one who sent her there.* Riley shot up from the couch, running for the door, throwing it open, sprinting down the hallway of Cockrell Hall. Ignored fellow residents calling out to her, asking where she headed in such a hurry.

She needed to reach the offices of the *Daily Northern*. Tell them Samantha Grayson, like her roommate Presley, faced a grave danger.

The connection to both disappearances appeared to be Marcus Evans Photography.

Chapter 34

How little do you stupid Americans realize what I will leave your country with tomorrow, Sheik Abdullah al-Aziz Rahim thought, politely shaking the hands and engaging in mindless small talk with yet another batch of pandering, self-serving businessmen and elected officials at the dinner held in his honor by the billionaire Cockrell brothers. All the Americans sought from his people was black gold found underneath the sands of the Arabian Peninsula or off the coast of his land to prolong the final spasms of this feeble, aging giant, a superpower long grown frail and suffering the same slow, decadent decline experienced by the once mighty Roman Empire, enemies nibbling away at the periphery in preparation of striking for the heart. From these brash, egotistical Americans Sheik Rahim wanted more than money; these presumptuous Americans providing him what he truly desired as payment for the coveted dark treasure powering their rotted society, the sacrifice of six more young women to quench a violent bloodlust. Their lives added to the many other helpless victims taken away and breathing their last gasps in his presence, paying the ultimate price for the proud superiority of their homeland.

Rahim considered the exchange fair. He knew the Americans, understood their sense of arrogance, the hubris. To keep their economy churning and the profits flowing they speculated in a grim calculus, sacrificing whatever required to maintain the status quo. Be it the lives of the defenseless women Marcus Cowle delivered to him to satisfy the thirst for personal vengeance or the thousands killed as cannon fodder on the battlefields of Iraq and Afghanistan. *Now they wish to start yet another war*, Rahim thought, *with another country in the Middle East*. He assumed the Americans would've learned by now, remembered the bromide of history repeating itself, yet these pathetically proud people so blind to the obvious. The Americans hadn't learned the lesson, held a misguided faith in their superiority, the vaunted 'exceptionalism' bragged about at every opportunity, believing this time the outcome different, their morality far superior, prepared to squander more treasure and lives to conduct another endless war with the same, sorry result as all those in the past.

Such hypocrites. Rahim barely contained his disdain, gazing about the Grand Ballroom at those attending the gala. Knew only the privileged affording the price of admission to the narcissistic extravaganza where the pompous and vain rubbed shoulders, basked in the glow of their self-importance, isolation from the masses made complete, only present in the almost invisible wraiths serving them opulent meals, bussing leftover scraps from the tables, enough food thrown away to feed hungry families for days on end. *Someday the masses will rise up against you*; Rahim recognized reality, already signs in the streets of simmering unrest, boiling anger focused at the economic and governmental elite. One day the multitudes revolting and those holding power and capital resorting to the same brutal methods of repression his country utilized to keep cowed and controlled the unwashed multitudes. They'd quickly learn self-preservation of their lofty status a motivation far more persuasive than preserving high-minded concepts of freedom to which they offered meager, empty platitudes.

They're all hypocrites. The lords of the business world championed the principles of the free market, heralded free markets as the cornerstone of their great society, yet spent billions to purchase politicians willing to do their bidding with a simple aim of quashing competition the vaunted system of free enterprise brought forth to challenge their hegemony. Rahim shook his head. *Hypocrites.* Yet that made dealing with them, and taking what he truly desired from them, so simple and effortless.

The Trading Society

Does it not gall you that your President is a woman? Rahim silently asked the milling crowd of executives and politicians of conservative mindset, deep in their souls lay a festering sore of true, unvarnished emotions. Didn't bother to conceal their disdainful insults, derided her as a socialist, a communist, a radical, at every chance heaving slurs and smears against her character. Even with a woman occupying the office of greatest power in the land, these politicians and mercantilists engaged in deliberate and blatant warfare against her very gender, seeking to exercise dominion over the most intimate decisions concerning their bodies. Their hearts only satisfied if women once again nothing more than chattel, only purpose of existence as property to serve the desires of men, to propagate the bloodline. Rahim smiled self-knowingly, arrived at an ironic conclusion. *Something on which we both happen to agree.* But on this subject Rahim carried out his particular beliefs to a violent extreme.

Rahim regarded the occupants of the ballroom, grew tired of the revelry, bored with the insipid conversation; he wished to depart this city with his possessions. He glanced at Saleh, nodded ever so slightly. *We must leave this place.* Saleh acknowledged the gesture, motioned to the other members of Rahim's security detail stationed about the Grand Ballroom, departing the gala within minutes. *Have to say farewell to my gracious hosts.* Rahim strode across the ballroom floor towards the Cockrell brothers, couldn't be rude to treasured business partners, slipping away without taking his leave. He eased up to the brothers, in discussion with the head of an influential K Street lobbying group advocating lower taxes for the well-off, one adept at twisting arms and issuing threats of retribution to politicians insuring docile compliance to an oath not to country, but of fechly to his egotistical whims. "Excuse me Thomas, Edward," Rahim interrupted, extending his hand in friendship, "I must take my leave slightly earlier than expected to commence my journey home," he informed them, pleasant tone masking true intention for the premature departure.

Thomas shook his hand. "I hope there's nothing amiss?" he asked, aware of ongoing unrest in Daharan.

"Nothing of the sort," Rahim smiled, erased any suspicions, "There are matters in my country requiring my attention. I feel it better if I started my trip tonight rather than waiting for tomorrow morning."

"I hope you enjoyed your time here in Chicago and at Great Northern University," Edward chimed in.

You have no idea. "I found my time in Chicago, and at your beloved alma mater, most pleasurable and profitable," Rahim nodded, the brothers to never understand the gist of his innocuous statement. "I am in gratitude of your kind hospitality. When you travel to Daharan to discuss the business proposals you presented I will gladly return the generosity."

"We look forward to that, your Excellency." Thomas replied, pleased the discussions earlier that afternoon to expand the global reach of Cockrell Enterprises bearing fruit. "I wish you a safe journey home."

"Thank you for your concern, the flight does tend to be quite long." *At least I will have companionship for so lengthy a flight.* His new possessions blindfolded once forced into the limousine, the remainder of their journey in darkness, reveling in their terror while they were loaded on the jet, strapped into their seats, unable to see yet cognizant of approaching doom as the jet lifted from the tarmac. *Only a little while longer and they will be mine,* he thought with the glee of a child waiting to open a present. *Perhaps I will take pleasure with one of them during the flight.* "Again I thank you for your hospitality." Rahim spun on his heel, walked from the ballroom with his security detail following in his wake. Once out of earshot of the guests Saleh removed the smartphone from his jacket, handed the device to his charge. Rahim quickly dialed the number for Marcus Cowle.

"Yes?" The voice of the human trafficker calmly answered.

"I have good news for you, my friend," Rahim informed Cowle in a hushed voice. "I have decided to move up the time of my departure."

"I'm pleased to hear that," Cowle replied evenly, though Rahim sensed relief in his answer. "What time may I expect you?"

Rahim glanced at his watch. "About twelve-thirty." Ninety minutes earlier than originally planned. "My people have to take care of affairs here at the hotel."

"Excellent," Cowle said. "The product will be ready upon your arrival. Please text me when you're near the location."

"I look forward to seeing you, my friend, and take measure of the remainder of the consignment." Rahim ended the call, though only one piece of merchandise truly deserved his undivided interest, the stunning auburn-haired young woman spied during the speech at Great Northern University that morning and through fate delivered into his hands: Samantha Grayson.

Rahim took Saleh aside, whispered in his ear. "Contact the pilots, tell them we will be departing ahead of schedule," he commanded his assistant, the pilots already at the private hanger at O'Hare International, the Gulfstream jet fueled and waiting. "Have the guards bring my luggage down from the suite." His security detail-a dozen strong-to accompany him to the exchange. He didn't expect any trouble at the meeting; Cowle a trusted business partner, though seemed uneasy with arrangements for the transfer of this consignment, of Rahim's presence at the hand-over.

He worries too much, Rahim concluded. Understood Cowle's nature to be cautious, involved in the criminal enterprise of human trafficking for the omnipotent. Rahim had no such qualms.

"Where are you from?" Samantha Grayson asked a simple question once Presley Harding cried her eyes dry of tears, realizing the roommate she practically ignored the only one suspecting the danger she faced, the only person, except for Samantha, trying to rescue her from the insidious peril. As she spoke, Samantha warily watched the shorter of Cowle's hired thugs peer into the cell, checking that neither attempted to loosen the bonds securing them.

"New York," Presley sniffed, brown eyes red and raw from sobbing, "Upper East Side." She turned to Samantha, shifting her body, searching for relief from the confinement.

"I'm from upstate New York, you know, north of the Washington Bridge." A common joke for New York residents. There was New York City, then everything else north of the metropolitan area, explaining the fact many times freshman year when introducing herself to others. "I grew up in the Finger Lakes."

Presley thought for a moment, a detail emerged in her muddled mind. "Are you related to the owners of Grayson Farms Winery?"

Oh, God... The innocent question tore at her soul. At the mention of home, of safety and the love of her parents, Samantha almost lost control of her emotions. With the barest sliver of determination she maintained her composure, gave Presley a sad smile. No need to further trouble a young woman already terrified of her dangerous situation. "I should, they're my parents," Samantha explained calmly as memories of Garrett and Melanie Grayson filled her mind, prayed she saw them again, expressed to them her love and savor the warmth of their embrace. "I grew up there."

"I'm sorry," Presley swallowed; face falling, ashamed to have asked the question to begin with. "I shouldn't have..."

"It's okay, you didn't know." Samantha shook her head; the melancholy smile remained. She glanced out to the hallway, the second of Cowle's minions disinterested in their conversation, moved down the corridor with the authority of a guard walking his beat on a prison block. "When were you there?"

"This past summer," Presley sank back against the cold concrete wall, remembering better times, seeking to banish, if only for a few minutes, the dire implications of her impending fate. "My Dad works on Wall Street. I don't know if you've heard of Graceland Capital, he owns it. We have a private lake house on Keuka Lake." Samantha knew of where she spoke, one of the ten slender bodies of water comprising the Finger Lakes, carved from the land by retreating glaciers, Keuka Lake left with the peculiar shape of a crooked tuning fork. The north end of the east fork at Penn Yan a few miles removed from her home at Grayson Farms Winery. "We go there every summer for a few days, either there or out to the Hamptons, get out of the city when it's hot. We spent a day going to the wineries along Seneca Lake. Since I'm not legal," her face blushed, remembered using the fake ID to gain entry to the clubs in Chicago, setting in motion a chain of events condemning her to enslavement and a certain death, "I was the designated driver."

"Go on," Samantha gently told Presley, didn't recall seeing her, Presley and her parents visiting the tasting room and not dining at the café where Samantha worked as hostess during summer break.

"Your winery is very pretty," Presley continued. "Must've been interesting growing up there."

'It was.' A brief recollection of playing amongst the vines during childhood floated lazily through her head, running after her father as he checked on the grapes, of bright sunshine warm on her face, then a memory of baking cookies in the kitchen with her mother. Pondered everything she now poised to lose, never again experience: her friends, the wind on her cheek, a moonlit night, Tyler and his devoted love for her in which she basked. *Oh God, we've never...* Samantha never to know that cherished intimacy with Tyler, her innocence soon ravaged by brutal men. *Funny what goes through your mind when you know you're going to die.* Samantha focused on what she said next to rein in her emotions. "I think I know more about making wine than most people my age."

"I met your father, he was pouring wine for my parents. He's from Australia?" Presley asked.

"He is, so I'm part Aussie." Samantha closed her eyes at the image of her father, a man of quiet strength and formidable resilience, a wise counsel and thoughtful listener when Samantha needed advice, a shoulder to lean on when times tough. Certain he'd do anything possible; move the very heavens to save her if aware of the life threatening situation his daughter now faced alone, helpless in the presence of evil, seemingly without hope of rescue. *But he doesn't know*, Samantha closed her eyes, didn't want to cry. *By the time Dad and Mom find out I'm missing, I'll be on the other side of the world.*

"He must be a great father," Presley tried not to think of her parents, of the heart-rending anguish soon visited on them, of the tremendous loss and how she the cause of her own doom.

Samantha felt the tear form in the corner of her eye, with wrists bound behind her back impossible to wipe away. "He is," Samantha said simply.

"I liked the dogs," Presley said next. "They're greyhounds, right?"

"Mom loves them," Samantha tired not to cry. "We rescue them after they're through racing."

"There was one greyhound there. She was small, had a beautiful black coat," Samantha knew instantly the one Presley spoke of, heart ripping in two at the mention of 'her' greyhound. "She came up and leaned against my leg. I spent the whole time petting her. She was the sweetest thing."

"That's my Stormy." Samantha leaned her head against the hard wall, pictured her wonderful greyhound girl in her mind. Cal's Little Stormcloud her racing name, fitting for the small frame and coat of glistening midnight. Stormy never raced, the people at the rescue kennel saying she failed training, though Samantha knew better. *You saw how lovely you were, knew you were meant for something other than chasing a lure.* Stormy, her little princess, bowed with regal grace when Samantha sang out her name. She thought of home, not trapped in this horrible cell, walking into the kitchen, sitting down cross-legged on the floor. Stormy trotting up to her, toenails clicking on the floor, sniffing at her auburn hair, giggling at the sensation. Then Stormy dropped her head down, allowing Samantha to scratch her neck, rub the rose petal ears soft as velvet to the touch, pawing at Samantha the moment she stopped petting her. While other greys tended to be shy Stormy a confident girl, stared Samantha straight in the eye, a self-assurance born of magnificent bearing. Stormy a reminder of the warmth and security of her family sanctuary. Now a home as distant as the moon in the night sky, one she may never see again. Samantha reluctantly stepped back from the memory, change the subject or lose control. "What are you majoring in?"

"Business," Presley frowned, "at least that's what my parents' want me to study. They want me to work on Wall Street," for a moment she was silent, then added softly, "just like them."

"You don't want to do that?" Samantha's reply more an observation than question.

"It's boring. It doesn't interest me," Presley confessed, something she'd never honestly tell her parents, no matter how understanding they might be otherwise. "I wanted to study fine arts, maybe writing." Presley turned to Samantha. "Are you an only child?"

Samantha sighed. "I'm their only daughter."

"The doctors told Mom she'd never have children," Presley silent for a moment. "Mom and Dad call me their miracle baby." Presley closed her eyes, regret returning in a sudden rush. "Why did I have to go out to the nightclub? Why did I have to use that fake ID?" Presley stared with empty eyes at the opposite wall, tortured by answers she already knew. Even now, the instincts of journalism rose up within Samantha, wanted to ask Presley who provided her the false identification, understood this wasn't the time or place for such prying, Presley far too distraught to reply. *What would I do with that information?* Samantha thought darkly, unless rescue arrived soon her final stories written, but her obituary left for someone else to write.

"I'm never going to see my parents again," Presley started crying, the emotions too overpowering to keep at bay for long. "They won't know what happened to me! Won't know I'm missing for days! They're over in Switzerland for some stupid business conference!" Presley lowered her head, voice quieting, acknowledging a situation caused by naïve carelessness and blithe innocence, about to lose everything, pay a terrible price, facing a suddenly tenuous mortality. "I'm going to die."

I have to protect her, Samantha listened to Presley sob uncontrollably, already surrendering to her fate, uttered the silent oath. *With my last breath, with all my strength I have to protect Presley from what might come.* "Presley, listen to me," Samantha leaned close as Presley cried herself to exhaustion. "We're going to get out of this," Samantha whispered as Presley turned her head, didn't want Cowle's henchman overhearing what she told the terrified freshman. "We're going to be rescued. You have to

257

trust me. You aren't going to die, we're going to live. We're going to go home. We're going to see our families and our friends again." Samantha flinched, a pang of regret settling in her stomach, even if she survived this trial, escaped the clutches of Marcus Cowle and Sheik Rahim, never to see the friends she considered closest in her life. *I'm responsible for their deaths*; Samantha trembled, a burden of guilt forever resting on her shoulders.

"We can't fight back against them! Or this man they're selling us to!" Presley stared at Samantha, voice betraying raw passions, wished to believe in miraculous salvation but after her experience at the hands of Cowle and his thugs, resistance crushed by the long night of torture, expected no mercy from the man soon to own her as his sex slave.

"I don't know how, but we're getting out of this," the pendulum inside of Samantha swinging between utter despair and fleeting optimism veering back towards hope, though she knew it might pivot back at any time. "If we have an opportunity to escape these people you have to be ready to act, do you understand?"

"Okay." Presley nodded slightly, believed there no chance any of them imprisoned within the factory, awaiting the arrival of a man paying millions to make them his property to abuse at his whim and eventually destroy, surviving this madness. Presley leaned over, head resting on Samantha's shoulder, closing her eyes, desiring she was somewhere, anywhere, else in the world other than sitting bound on a mattress in the small room with bare concrete walls, powerless to prevent a horrendous reality. "I'm scared," she confessed, then added in a forlorn whisper, "I don't want to die."

Samantha couldn't lie. "I'm scared too," sensed the tiny body shudder against her, "and I don't want to die either." Samantha glanced at the clock Cowle left to torment her, saw the time. Amanda McKinnon and Lauryn Callahan, left incapacitated back at the empty studio in Logan Square, had a little more than an hour left to live.

Her body shivering Ashleigh Morgan curled up, knees close to her chest, trying to stay warm in the trunk of the Lexus. The coolness of the deepening night seeping through the metal frame of the luxury sedan into the confined space Ashleigh, bound hand and foot, couldn't escape. If the rope binding her not enough of an ordeal, locked in the trunk amplified rampaging fears. She hated small spaces, never comfortable in a crowd though never exhibited or gave voice to her discomfort. The darkness enveloped her, dispelled by the eerie phosphorescent glow of the escape handle to allow one trapped in the trunk to open the lid from inside and escape, taunting Ashleigh with its proximity. With her hands bound behind her, welded against her waist, she couldn't shift her body to trigger it, and even if she could unable to go anywhere tied to immobility.

This is what happened to those girls in Atlanta a few years ago; Ashleigh contemplated the horrible twist of fate she now shared with those unfortunate victims. Remembered her mother's concern during those terrible weeks following the abrupt slew of disappearances, had grown up during the terror of the Atlanta Child Murders. The lingering fear from that tragic time compelled her mother to keep close watch on Ashleigh, about to enter her senior year of high school, wanting to know where her only daughter was at all times when not at home. The uncertainty of the fate of four missing young women, quickly dubbed 'The Atlanta Four,' filled the newspapers and lead the local nightly newscasts for months, but as time passed without resolution fading into the mist as an unsolved mystery haunting Atlanta for years to come. Ashleigh never expected to learn the truth behind the disappearances, not years later and far from home, those unfortunate women falling prey to a band of vicious human traffickers. Through unforeseen circumstances, a cruel trick of bad luck made Ashleigh and her friends victims of the vicious kidnappers who inflicted such fear and terror upon Atlanta.

Ashleigh shuddered against the ropes, body slowly growing numb from the cold and the pressure of ropes tight against her limbs, tried to calm her ragged breathing, eyes peering about the cramped quarters. No one, not her family or D'Andre, ever to know what had become of her. *Just like those girls in Atlanta...*

No one out in the Logan Square neighborhood at the late hour of the evening-taking their dog for a walk, coming home from work or heading out to meet friends at a local drinking establishment-aware of the grim drama unfolding within the three-story brownstone on North Campbell Street. In the first floor studio of Marcus Evans Photography, concealed from view of those passing by, two young women waited for their death sentence to be implemented. The instrument of fiery destruction resting between the pair, clock ticking off the minutes until the moment of execution at the stroke of midnight, lives instantly snuffed out in a massive explosion and conflagration.

The condemned powerless to prevent their impending demise. Amanda McKinnon sitting on a chair; Lauryn Callahan lying on the floor, both secured so viciously they could scarcely move. The bonds didn't budge as they struggled for an elusive freedom, useless fight for survival relentlessly draining them of dwindling strength. The cloth bandages wrapped about their heads rendered the pair blind and mute, unable to alert those outside to an ever-approaching doom.

The building stood silent in the pale amber glow of sodium-vapor streetlights, a slumbering volcano ready to erupt when midnight struck.

Tyler McManaway bounded up the stairs to the third floor office of *The Daily Northern*, effortlessly taking the steps two at a time as his friends trailed in his hustling wake. Tyler knew if Samantha Grayson, the love of his life, might be anywhere in this world the newspaper offices where she spent most of her hours outside of class or with him was where he'd find her.

He pushed the door open, striding through the reception area and into the newsroom, busy at the late hour as the staff rushed to ready the next day's edition. In the middle of barely controlled chaos Aaron Dinehart, the News Editor of *The Daily Northern* and Samantha's friend and mentor, sat at his desk.

Aaron glanced up as Tyler entered his domain, the look on his face wasn't pleasant. "So what have you done with my star reporter?"

The flippant statement, though offered in frustration, the last thing Tyler wanted to hear.

Chapter 35

"You're telling me Samantha's not here?" Tyler McManaway's stomach rolled as if receiving a sharp blow to the gut.

"What part of my statement did you not understand?" Aaron Dinehart shot him a quizzical look, surprised by the distraught reaction. Tyler the first person who should know where Samantha was. "I haven't seen her all day. Got a few questions on her story about Senator Fielding's speech. I know she's out to dinner with her friends but I've been trying to reach her all evening. I haven't heard back and I'm staring at a deadline for tomorrow's paper."

"You haven't heard from her?" A sick sensation filled Tyler as in a moment his worst fears confirmed, confronting a disturbing reality.

"What did I just tell you?" Aaron weighed the expression on Tyler's face, realizing whatever reason behind Samantha's absence no longer a joke to laugh off. *Something isn't right here.* Aaron grew serious, the time for kidding past. "What's going on?"

"I haven't heard from Samantha tonight," Tyler explained, concluding right then something horrible indeed had happened to Samantha, suddenly feared for her life and that of her friends. He motioned to his companions. "We haven't heard from her friends either. They were going to dinner at Toscana in the city," Aaron aware of that fact, "but they never made it for their reservation. Never answered when the restaurant called and texted Ashleigh's number when they didn't show."

"I called her voicemail all evening, she never got back to me." The color from Aaron's face drained away, reached a similar assumption. "That's not like Sam. She always gets in touch with me if I have a question." Aaron shook his head. "She never returned to go over the stories."

"Now I've got a bad feeling about this," Connor Aanonsen added.

"Do you think..." Aaron started to say, thought of the other story Samantha working on.

Tyler placed his hands on his hips. "I don't know what to think," he admitted, none of the possibilities he considered reassuring. "All I know is that none of us have heard from Samantha and her friends this evening. We don't have any idea where they might be."

Aaron turned to his newsroom. "Hey, I need everyone's attention here for a moment!" He shouted, activity in the room subsiding, reporters and staff quieting, turning attention to their editor. "Did anyone here see Samantha Grayson in the office today?" Many of those gathered shook their heads. "Did anyone see her roommates?"

One reporter raised his hand. "I did, they came in around five, asked if Samantha was here. Told them I hadn't seen her. They stood there talking for a few minutes before they left."

At least that was something, Samantha's friends had come to the office. "Did you happen to find out where they were going?" Aaron asked.

"No," the reporter answered, shrugged his shoulders. "When I looked up they were gone."

"You didn't ask them where they were going." Aaron demanded.

"Should I have?" Was the reporter's reply.

"Start doing that if you want to work in this business." Aaron gazed out at his newsroom. "No one knows where they went?" He asked, received a blanket of blank stares in return. "Wonderful," Aaron grunted, disappointed.

"Stopped before we get started," Connor muttered, tried to keep from thinking where Amanda McKinnon might be and the bad things happening to her, didn't want emotions flying out of control. Wasn't the best at keeping his anger controlled once unleashed.

Ali Fahrajani, the lead beat writer for the football program at *The Daily Northern*, entered the office after an evening at the library, returning to finish his column for the next day's edition. Eyes looking down as he walked into the office, head bouncing to the beat thrumming through the ear buds of his iPod, didn't see the threesome of Tyler McManaway, D'Andre Watson and Albert 'Fiji' Fatuamala, the emerging stars of Great Northern's football team, until he lifted his head, spotted them surrounding Aaron Dinehart's desk. *I didn't think today's column was **that** critical.* Ali slowed his pace, walked past the trio, removing the earbuds while noting their intent gaze on him. He stopped, pointed nonchalantly at them, cocking his head with a puzzled expression. "Was it something I wrote?"

Tyler shook off his entreaty. "No, it isn't that."

"Well I know you can't be angry at me," Ali motioned to Connor, "because I don't cover hockey and your season hasn't started."

"Ali, have you…" Tyler tried interrupting him.

"You stared down Bailey on that interception," Ali informed Tyler. "You have to watch…"

"Ali!" Tyler cut him off. "Have you seen Samantha today?" Got to the reason for their presence.

"Yeah, early this afternoon," the strident request caught Ali off-guard. "I was working on my column for tomorrow. Don't worry I'm saying good things about you. She was working on the stuff from that speech by Senator Fielding."

"Was there anything out of the ordinary?" Tyler continued. "Anything wrong?"

"Not really," Ali replied, recalling their conversation. "She made a comment how politicians all sound the same, thought more of themselves rather than for the best of the country, how it was more about winning. I compared politics to the Michigan-Ohio State rivalry."

"Instead of Great Northern-Illinois?" D'Andre Watson asked.

"Our rivalry doesn't inspire the same level of passion," Fiji noted.

"That's what I told Samantha," Ali added.

"So Samantha was here when you left?" Aaron asked.

Ali glanced between the stern, solemn faces staring at him, confused by this sudden inquisition regarding Samantha Grayson. "Samantha was working away like she always is," then he remembered. "But before I left she was talking to this girl, a freshman."

D'Andre raised an eyebrow. "How did you know she was a freshman?"

"She had that 'what am I doing here' look on her face, the one every freshman has during their first few weeks on campus," Ali pointed out.

"Did you get this girl's name?" Tyler probed.

Ali held up his hands. "Time out for a moment." His head swirling in bewilderment from the barrage of questioning. "What's going on here? Has something happened to Samantha?"

"No one has seen or heard from Samantha since this afternoon," Tyler told Ali, anxiety rising to fever pitch with each passing second. Who was this girl with Samantha? Did she have anything to do with Samantha and her friends disappearing? "No one has heard from her friends either, they never showed up at the restaurant where they had reservations for dinner."

"Really?" Ali pursed his lips, eyes filled with surprise.

"Yeah, really," Connor emphasized, "so we've got four reasons to be concerned."

"We thought they might be here," D'Andre starting to share the disquieting sentiment the suspicions of Tyler McManaway on target and Ashleigh, along with her friends, facing dangers unknown. *And we're nowhere close to helping them…*

"What did this girl look like?" Tyler didn't wish to waste any more time.

Ali exhaled, lowering his head, thinking. "She was a small thing, appeared to be a little timid, like she wasn't sure about being here in the first place, reddish-blonde hair, pretty cute." Ali raised his head, glanced past those gathered around him, pointed back towards the entrance. 'Kind of like her."

The four turned to where Ali pointed. In the doorway to *The Daily Northern* stood a young woman matching closely the description he provided, chest heaving as if finishing a taxing wind sprint, her expression distressed. The blue eyes wide, damp and glimmering as she stared around the newsroom, searching for someone. Her panicked gaze locked on the group gathered around the desk of Aaron Dinehart.

"Is Samantha Grayson here?" The young woman asked, voice quivering with uncertainty, afraid of the answer to her question.

"No, Samantha isn't here," Aaron replied, warily eyeing the girl.

"We're trying to figure out where she is," Tyler added tersely.

"Oh my God," the girl cried out, hand covering her mouth, a gurgling sound from deep in her throat as if about to be sick. Her head began to spin and her legs buckled.

"What is it? Where's Samantha?" Tyler demanded; saw the girl swoon, taking a cautionary step forward, catch her in his arms if she passed out.

The girl steadied herself, a terrified look in her eyes, stared directly at Tyler. "I think Samantha is in danger."

"I didn't know there were so many yellow Chevrolet Impalas in the city of Chicago," Detective Dawson 'Dawes' Hilliard stared at the computer screen, scrolling through video collected the past Saturday from cameras positioned throughout the city.

"Or blue Ford Fusions," Detective Devin Carson added. Patrick Flannery and Nathanial Hampton, their colleagues from Europe in Chicago to coordinate for the international summits the next spring but recruited in this endeavor, sat before computer monitors scanning videotape culled from the Virtual Shield network. "There has to be something here," his frustration at the fruitless search starting to show. "They couldn't have driven those cars to where we found them without going through at least one intersection covered by a camera!"

"This could be a dead end, bloke," Hampton offered.

"God, I hope not," Carson wondering if they were wasting time, if his hunch indeed nothing but folly. *Have to pursue every angle*, Carson reminded himself, *no matter how tenuous*.

Hilliard stared at his screen. "I think I got something."

Carson shot up from his seat, looked at the computer monitor in front of Hilliard. On the screen an image of a yellow Chevrolet Impala. "What is it?"

"There's a Pacifica College parking sticker on the windshield," Hilliard pointed at the decal on the upper left hand corner of the windshield, impressed with the definition of the new cameras in the network. "Emma Hayden attends Pacifica College in the Loop."

Carson glanced at the license plate, noticed the Illinois tag. "But it's an Illinois plate. Emma is from Minnesota, the car we found in Englewood had Minnesota plates."

"I ran the tag number through the Secretary of State's database," Hilliard replied. "It doesn't exist."

"Doesn't exist?" Flannery asked.

Pete Dobbins, the computer technician, piped up. "You got to be kidding me."

"There's no record of it," Hilliard added. "Leads me to believe it's a fake."

Carson whistled, examined the image. "If it's fake it's a damn good one." *So this is how they got from Point A to Point B.* They knew where Point B was, the location of Point A still a mystery and likely the source of answers in their search for the missing women.

Hampton stood from his desk, came up behind them, joined by Flannery. He studied the image of the driver. "That's sure doesn't look like Emma Hayden."

"I kind of noticed that too." Hilliard nodded, studied the broad shouldered, bald man with a goatee sitting in the driver's seat.

"Look what's behind it, fella," Flannery pointed to the black Ford Econoline van trailing the Chevy Impala. "The witness down in Englewood said she saw a black van with two white fellas in it on Saturday afternoon before she noticed the Impala parked on her street."

"Here's the question," Hilliard said, "is Emma inside that van?" He advanced the video a few more frames to get a clearer view of the license plate on the front of the van, frowned at the result. "Can't read the number," Hilliard noted sourly, "there's a dark film over the plate."

"Yeah, that shit's illegal. It hides the plate number from cameras. You have people who drive on the Illinois Tollway using it to go through the I-Pass lanes and get out of paying the tolls, the cameras don't pick up the tag number," Dobbins called out from his computer. "I can run a filter, see if I can get you a clearer image."

"Do it." Then Carson had a different idea. "Wait! Run the plate number from the Impala, see if we get any other hits."

Dobbins grinned. "Have it for you in a few seconds, I'll put them up on your screen there," Dobbins fingers danced across the keyboard. A second later three images popped up on the computer monitor before Hilliard.

"There's Alexandra Cole's Ford Fusion," Flannery said.

"And the Nissan Altima of Isabella DiBenedetto," Hampton added. In the front seat of each car sat the same man caught driving Emma Hayden's Impala. In each image a black Ford van followed.

Carson pointed to the third image, a cobalt blue Lexus sedan. He knew what this meant. "We have another missing woman we don't know about yet."

"Or women," Flannery added, a possibility none of them wanted.

Carson looked at Hilliard. "Can you get a closer look at the car?"

Hilliard zoomed in the image. "Wait a minute," Hilliard focused on a sticker in the lower left hand corner of the front windshield, shifted the cursor arrow over it, enlarged the sticker.

Carson recognized the decal immediately, his heart sinking. "That's a Great Northern University student parking permit."

"Wonderful," Hilliard muttered.

"Danny!" Carson called across the squad room to Detective Danny Bryant, compact of stature yet a rock-hard package of muscle, a former college wrestler keeping trim his physique with a vegan diet. "Contact Public Safety at Great Northern University and the Evanslawn police, see if they've had any reports of missing students in the last twenty-four hours."

"Got it," Bryant replied, getting on the phone. "By the way, a patrol car found the Nissan Altima near the Sanitary and Ship Channel."

"Southwest Side," Hilliard noted, the victim's cars dumped across the city. *They want us chasing ghosts.* "These guys have their angles covered. Want us running all over the place."

"But why?" Flannery added. "What do these fellas want with these women?"

Carson turned to Dobbins. "Whatever they're using to hide the tag number on the van is good. I can't get the filters to penetrate it."

"Keep working on it," Carson encouraged, had another idea. "Can you give us the first location where those cars with the fake tags were picked up by Virtual Shield?"

"I can do that," Dobbins agreed, "I'll put it up on a map for you with the times as well." Dobbins typed in a few commands, seconds later a map of the Northwest Side of Chicago appeared on Hilliard's screen with four dots.

Carson pointed to the first dot. "Emma's car is here on a camera at Western and North," then to the second pin mark, "and Alexandra's car is picked up here at North and Kedzie."

"Here's Isabella's car, again at Western and North, on Sunday evening," Hilliard jabbed a finger to the third pin, then the last pin mark for the unknown victim, "and for who might be missing from Great Northern University, the blue Lexus is captured on video at the intersection of Damen, Diversey and Clybourn a few hours later that night."

"The last place Emma Hayden used her credit card was the Starbucks at North and Damen," Hampton added. "That's the Wicker Park area, isn't it?"

"So we can narrow where these women were to an area roughly around Wicker Park, Bucktown and Logan Square," Hilliard snorted, added derisively. "We've gone from a big haystack to one that's a little more manageable." *But not by much.*

"We'd have a better idea if we had the cell phone records," Carson added, "at least find the towers their phones pinged." He called over to another detective working the phones, Mychael Mustafa. "Anything from the cell phone service providers yet?"

Mustafa, Bryant's partner, shook his head, delivered bad news. "Tomorrow morning is the earliest they can get us the information on the tower pings."

"Tomorrow?" Carson was incredulous. "We need those records now!"

"I don't think that information will be any good then," Hilliard said. "They're probably busy figuring how to jack up my bill."

Carson's attention returned to the map, staring at the red dots where the vehicles in question with the false tag number first appeared on the city's traffic video network, forming a strategy. "We do have an idea where each of those women might have been on Saturday and Sunday."

"The tweet from Gabriella implied they were seeing a photographer," Flannery offered.

"Do you know how many professional photographers live in that area?" Hilliard asked. "I do, it's a good number. Some of them have studios and some don't, work out of their apartments or lofts."

"Let's get a list of who does," Carson said. "You and Hampton can work that angle."

"Won't make people happy banging on doors in the middle of the night," Hilliard observed.

"I don't care about disturbing people's sleep right now. I care about finding these women before something bad happens." Praying something bad hadn't already occurred, dealing with murder victims instead of those only missing. "I don't really give a damn who I piss off right now."

Hilliard got up from the computer, whistled at Wrigley the golden retriever, the cherished companion of Alexandra Cole, lying by the window. The dog raised his head, brown eyes looking expectantly at Hilliard. "We're going to look for your Mommy." Wrigley trotted over to Hilliard who reached for the leash on his desk, attaching it to the collar.

"You're bringing the dog with us?" Hampton couldn't believe this development.

"If all else fails we can turn him loose, maybe he'll pick up a scent," Hilliard explained, Hampton shot him a look the statement not convincing. "I'm willing to try anything right now."

"So am I," Carson added, sensing their options, and time to act on them, rapidly dwindling.

"What about us," Flannery asked his temporary partner. "We stay here or are we off somewhere?"

"We're going to the last place anyone saw Emma Hayden," Carson told him, the Starbucks at the six-way intersection of Damen, North and Milwaukee avenues after he briefed Captain Hardaway on their progress. "Maybe she met our photographer there. It's as good a place to start."

"Boss, take a look at this," Sterner stood by the laptop on the table, the last piece of their equipment left inside the factory.

Cowle walked over to see what caught Sterner's attention. The monitors from the closed-circuit surveillance system dismantled and packed away, loaded in the van now parked outside the abandoned factory. They were effectively blind, a feeling Cowle didn't find comforting, but they had about an hour until Sheik Rahim arrived to take charge of his consignment. Sterner had the Breaking News section of the *Chicago Tribune* website up on the screen, Cowle glanced at the title of the article.

Police Search For Two Missing Women.

Cowle scanned the brief article, smiling pictures of Emma Hayden and Alexandra Cole accompanying the text, a request for anyone with information to contact Area Central detectives. News of their initial captives released for public consumption far too soon for his liking. From previous shipments there existed a lag time of days before details of the vanished disseminated to the populace. By that time the shipment long delivered to Rahim's people, Cowle and his associates off to a far-off locale indulging in carnal pleasures, recuperating before heading to a new city to prepare for the next order of women waiting to be harvested for their most lucrative client.

In the past the delay worked to their advantage, but now that delay rested at their end with Sheik Rahim insisting on overseeing the exchange instead of his lackeys taking delivery after procurement of the final item. The lag between acquisition and delivery of the product left them vulnerable, exposed to unforeseen complications like Samantha Grayson and her unfortunate friends. The terse article evidence the police knew something afoot in their city, encroaching far too close on Cowle's desired zone for comfort.

At least his client on his way to the warehouse, thankful Rahim possessed a modicum of wisdom to push up his departure. *We'll get by this time*, Cowle thought bitterly, *by the skin of our damned teeth.* Cowle continued reading the article as he spoke. "We should prepare to depart the premises as soon as we've completed the transaction with Sheik Rahim."

Sterner checked his watch. "Couldn't agree with you more."

"I want our pretty maidens quiet until our guests arrives." Cowle pointed back at the screen. "I must discuss this matter with Sheik Rahim. We need to do things differently in the future." Hoped his lucrative client understood the reasons why and that he was the cause of the required change in operation.

Chapter 36

"What do you mean Samantha is in danger?" Tyler McManaway demanded. "What's going on? Who are you?" The girl shrunk back, cringing, didn't expect so harsh a response.

"Take it easy, Tyler." Albert 'Fiji' Fatuamala gently placed a hand on Tyler's shoulder, a calming touch. "Ease up. She's here to help us find Samantha and the others."

Tyler realized the girl didn't deserve his brusque manner, felt like a jerk for being so inconsiderate. "I'm sorry," he apologized, the girl relaxed, "it's that Samantha's missing and I'm really worried right now."

"I know. So am I," the nameless girl said.

"It appears her friends have gone missing too," Aaron Dinehart added.

"What!" The freshman gasped, at the implication eyes grew big with shock. "Oh my God..."

"Can you tell us what's going? Why you think Samantha might be in danger?" Fiji asked mildly, recognizing this unsure, frightened freshman the only tangible link they had to their missing friends.

"I think I can." The girl nodding as she spoke. "My name's Riley Bradford..."

"Hey, Riley Bannister is your mentor," Connor Aanonsen interrupted, earning a surreptitious glare from Tyler. *Not now...*

Riley nodded. "I came here earlier today to see if Samantha could help me find my roommate. Her name's Presley Harding. The last time I saw her was yesterday afternoon. I thought she might've gone into Chicago, she's been hanging out with these upperclassmen that go out to the clubs and I know Presley has a fake ID." Tyler noticed Aaron lift an eyebrow at the statement. "She didn't come back to the dorm last night."

"Why didn't you call the police?" Tyler wondered. "Campus security?"

"I did," was Riley's plaintive answer, "I tried to tell them, explain this wasn't like Presley. But they said I had to wait twenty-four hours to file a report. The officer from the Evanslawn police told me she probably ran off with a boyfriend."

"Figures that's the case," Aaron snorted. "They only care about students if they can cite them for underage drinking."

"But you think something happened to Presley?" D'Andre Watson asked.

"When I got back from my classes this morning and saw she still wasn't there I looked around the room. Saw her overnight bag and some of her clothes, the things she'd wear to go out, were missing," Riley pulled a business card from her pocket. "I found this on her dresser after I called the police. Since they wouldn't do anything I came here to see if Samantha could help. I see her stories all the time in the paper."

"Everyone reads her stories." Tyler said absently, took the card, studied the name of the business. *Marcus Evans Photography*, the address in the Logan Square neighborhood, handed the card to D'Andre and the others gathered around.

"Samantha said she'd go, see if Presley might've been there. If the owner knew her," Riley continued, anxiety building in her stomach, making her sick. "I don't have a car on campus, I couldn't drive there. Samantha said she'd call when she found something, but I haven't heard from her."

"Why didn't you get here sooner?" Tyler gritted his teeth, in attempting to be of assistance to Riley had Samantha unknowingly blundered into danger? "Why did you wait so long? Let Aaron know Samantha might be in trouble?"

"I fell asleep, I'm sorry," Riley confessed, body shaking, the strain taking a toll. "I had a big organic chemistry exam this afternoon and with worrying where Presley was I screwed up on the test. I was so upset," as she spoke the memory pushed Riley to the verge of tears. "I went back to my room to lay down for a minute and I fell asleep. I woke up a little while ago. When I saw Samantha hadn't contacted me I called her number but the voicemail was full. I knew something was wrong, that's why I came over here." Then the tears started as she apologized. "I'm sorry, I never meant for this to happen!"

"I know you're upset but you did the right thing." Tyler took Riley, as worried for Presley as he was for Samantha, by the shoulders to comfort her, atoning for his earlier insensitivity.

"I don't want anything to happen to Presley," Riley choked up, crying. "Now Samantha and her friends are missing and it's my fault…"

"We'll find them." Now Fiji soothed her misgivings. "Everything will work out." Tyler amazed at his friend's calm demeanor, placid and even-tempered when his own nerves already burned raw by Samantha's disappearance. *He's got to be worried about Lauryn.*

Aaron rushed to his computer, typed in the web address from the business card. A screen explaining Internet Explorer could not display the page appeared, a foreboding dread twisted his stomach. "The website's not there."

"Now my Spidey sense is tingling," D'Andre wanted to take action, not continue to stand and talk in the offices of *The Daily Northern*. "We have to do something."

"We've got an address. We know this might be where Presley went. It's where Samantha went to look for her and didn't come back from," Tyler mind worked furiously connecting the dots, painted a disturbing image. "We can assume the girls somehow found out Samantha went there."

Connor took off his Minnesota Wild hat, ran a hand through blond hair, completed the troubling picture. "Whatever happened to Presley and Samantha happened to them too." He prayed Amanda McKinnon and the others still alive, that they arrived in time to prevent any harm inflicted on them. *We might already be too late.* Connor closed his eyes to dispel the disquieting notion.

"I can only think of one thing to do." Tyler regarded his friends, *time to be the leader*, made his decision. Received quiet nods of agreement from each, understood they had the same idea. "Let's pay a visit to Marcus Evans Photography."

"Go kick some ass and chew bubble gum and I'm all out of Bubblicious." D'Andre concurred, the four started moving to the door.

"I'm going with you." Riley spoke, standing up straight, a sudden resolve displayed

"I don't think that's a good idea." Tyler stopped, turned to face Riley. "This could get dicey. We don't know what we'll find there." Or who there might not want Tyler and his companions to learn the seemingly dark secret of Marcus Evans Photography. "I don't want you getting hurt."

"I'm going with you," Riley adamant, ignoring his misgivings. "Presley is my friend," up until that very moment she never used the word to describe her roommate. "I'm responsible for getting Samantha into this. I'm coming with you."

"I don't think she's taking no for an answer," Connor impressed with the pluck shown by the petite freshman.

Tyler sighed in surrender, didn't have time to argue. "You can come with us," hoped he wasn't putting another innocent life in danger. "But you stay in the truck. Let us handle what we find there."

"Okay," Riley relieved, wanting only to find Presley and know she was alive.

"You guys get out of here," Aaron ordered, "and get my favorite reporter out of whatever it is she's gotten herself into. I'll contact the police, hopefully they'll beat you there and have this resolved by the time you show up."

"Samantha's my favorite too," Tyler headed for the door, "and I'm fond of her friends."

"Aren't we fond of all of them?" D'Andre asked as the four men, with the freshman girl in tow, hurriedly exited the office.

Aaron watched them depart, attention shifting back to a newsroom silent and paralyzed with shock. "All right everybody, listen up!" He announced, rallying his troops to an urgent new objective, a personal crusade for each of them. "Whatever you're doing drop it right now! Samantha is our friend and she, and she might not be the only one, is in trouble. We have to do what we can to help Samantha."

Aaron looked directly at Lily Rosenberg sitting wide-eyed at her desk, working on a story about that evening's Student Board of Governance meeting. *That can wait*, Aaron thought. With her vivacious eagerness and limitless talent, Lily reminded Aaron far too much of Samantha. "Lily, I need you to contact newspapers at the colleges in Chicago, see if they have any reports of women going missing."

"I've got it," Lily replied, didn't question further, reaching for the phone.

"Someone check the *Tribune* and *Sun-Times* websites, see if they have any reports up about missing women. I need people to find out who Presley was going into the city with to hit these clubs," Aaron shoved aside suspicion he already knew, and quite intimately, one of those companions. "Maybe they know or saw Presley with this Marcus Evans. Tomorrow's paper is going to have to wait." The coverage of the visit and speech by Senator Benton Fielding placed on the back burner as issues of a more imperative nature addressed.

Aaron whispered a quick prayer, hoped the front page of the next edition of *The Daily Northern* didn't feature solemn obituaries of five of her students, one the talented reporter Aaron considered the sister he never had. He picked up the phone, couldn't dial the Chicago 911 center directly, had to place the call through the Evanslawn center, expected an immediate connection with a dispatcher to explain the dire situation.

The other end rang...and rang...and rang.

What the hell? Aaron thought.

If Aaron expected prompt action he was to be sorely disappointed, unaware the walkout by the emergency center operators in Chicago creating a perfect storm of circumstance he unwittingly sailed directly into. The Chicago center, staffed by the inexperienced and inundated by calls both real and fake, computer system under siege from hackers, forced to funnel calls to 911 centers in the surrounding immediate suburbs, including Evanslawn, and in turn initiating a tremendous backlog where Aaron's call for assistance found itself trapped like a cork in a whirlpool.

Samantha Grayson glanced at the clock resting in the corner, watched the minute hand on the clock move closer to midnight, a relentless march of time she held no power to stop. Back at what was Marcus Evans Photography, the brownstone on North Campbell Avenue, Amanda McKinnon and Lauryn Callahan waited helplessly for the cruel implementation of their death sentence. *Thirty minutes*. The scarce amount of time left for her friends to live, trapped with an explosive set to obliterate the building and end their lives.

Samantha and Presley Harding heard noise down the hallway, from the cells where the other hostages waited bound for their miserable fate in an overseas land. Cries and pleas for mercy quickly stifled, Samantha understood the captives being gagged, within moments her own freedom to speak, to express her defiance, suppressed. *Can't let our new owner know we don't wish to be his playthings*, Samantha thought morosely. Heard one of the women curse, call her captors 'fucking bastards" before her voice silenced, raging protests quieted.

"That's Emma," Presley said, wanting to cry. "I don't think she'll last long where we're going."

At least she wants to fight. "Remember what I told you," Samantha whispered to Presley, who nodded meekly, as the heavy footfalls neared, "we're getting out of this. Someone will find us. If we get a chance to escape we have to take it. I promise I won't let anyone hurt you. We will see our families again." *I hope to see Tyler, I hope to see him again. I love him, it can't end like this.* Wondered if Presley believed anything she told her; Samantha found difficulty believing her own hopeful words.

Cowle entered the cell, Sterner following behind. "Sorry ladies, time for small talk is over," he informed them in a jovial manner. "Your departure has been moved up. You'll be meeting your new owner, and I do say he is looking forward to meeting you, within the hour." His smile cold and empty, the expression of a man absent of conscience. "Hope you're rested. It's a long flight to your new home." Samantha's heart sank, suppressed the queasy uneasiness sloshing deep in her stomach, time drastically shortened for someone to discover their plight, come to their aid. Samantha understood a simple, dire fact, once loaded on the jet and in the air they were doomed. "It's time for conversation to cease," Cowle and Sterner held strips of cloth in their hands. "Your new owner wants to see, not hear, you."

Samantha turned her head, offered Presley a sorrowful smile, her companion emotionally shattered, teetering on the verge of breaking down. "Everything is going to work out," Samantha reassured.

"How touching," Cowle sneered, "I think that possibility is quite unlikely."

Samantha glared at him, summoned her courage. "Go to hell," she said evenly.

"I plan on stealing the key to Satan's wet bar when I get there, Samantha," Cowle replied in heartless jest, crouched down, wrapped his arm around Samantha's bound shoulders, roughly pulling her towards him, in his other hand a thick wad of cloth; Samantha understood where that would go.

"Open wide, don't make this difficult for either of you." Sterner snaked his burly forearm about Presley's midsection, the girl trembling in his grasp, brown eyes glistening in terror, the big man smelling her fear. Without hesitation Samantha opened her mouth, Cowle stuffing the cloth deep behind her teeth as Sterner did the same with a compliant Presley, wound long strips of white cloth around their heads several times, wadding held in place, quieting any protest the pair might utter.

Samantha growled through her gag as Presley moaned softly. "Peace and quiet at last," Cowle admired the duo, pleased with his handiwork. He peered at the clock in the corner. "Your friends don't have much time left, Samantha," Cowle taunted the powerless Samantha, reminding her of Amanda and Lauryn and the Sword of Damocles dangling above their heads with the thin wire of time holding it aloft and about to be cut, her soul submerged in a flood of pervasive guilt.

"They're going to die soon. There's nothing you can do to help them, nothing you can do to save them. Nothing at all." As they left the cell Samantha felt her chest heave in despair. Cowle correct in his estimation, she could do nothing to save Amanda McKinnon and Lauryn Callahan from a death looming minutes away.

Chapter 37

"It won't help the girls if we don't get there in one piece," Connor Aanonsen remarked as Tyler McManaway recklessly wove his Nissan Xterra through traffic on the Kennedy Expressway, completing the trip from Evanslawn in record time considering the breakneck speed, and the number of stoplights he'd blown through, Tyler drove the SUV.

"Sorry." Tyler kept his eyes on the road as he answered. "But if we don't get there soon it might not help Samantha or Amanda." *Or Lauryn and Ashleigh*, he didn't need to add those names for the benefit of D'Andre Watson and Albert 'Fiji' Fatuamala. Spotted the exit for Fullerton Avenue, twisting the steering wheel hard to the right, bolting across three lanes in rapid succession to make the exit.

"Cutting it close there," D'Andre estimated the inches separating them from the eighteen-wheeler they cut in front of, the trucker blowing his horn in anger.

"Sorry about that," Tyler muttered past clenched teeth.

"I should've gone with Samantha," Riley Bradford, sitting in the back seat between D'Andre and Connor, moaned. "I shouldn't have let Samantha go alone."

"Then you'd be in trouble too," Connor soothed her uncertainty. "Nobody would've known."

"It's my fault," Riley insisted, tears filling her eyes. "Samantha's in danger because of me! All of them are in danger and it's my fault! Why did I have to fall asleep?"

Again Tyler reassured her. "Riley, this isn't your fault." Even with Samantha and her friends facing unknown jeopardy Tyler unwilling to let Riley take blame for the situation. No sin in caring for the welfare of a friend. "You did what you thought was right." *Let's hope this all works out.*

"Don't worry. We'll get there in time," Fiji added softly, "everything will turn out fine." How Fiji remained so calm with the newfound knowledge Lauryn possibly faced a life threatening situation beyond Tyler. Heard the placid serenity in the deep voice, without a doubt Fiji expecting all destined to end well.

Tyler only wished he could be as certain as his friend.

11:55

The darkened interior of Marcus Evans Photography deathly quiet save for the muffled whimpers of Amanda McKinnon and Lauryn Callahan from behind tight bandage gags wrapped about their heads. Blindfolded with the same material neither aware five minutes all that remained in their lives, the bomb consisting of four propane tanks with a block of plastic explosive taped onto it resting between the bound pair. Five minutes separating them from a horrible death by a fiery oblivion. An electronic signal at the stroke of midnight the trigger their instrument of their execution patiently waited for to unleash an all-consuming inferno upon the defenseless duo.

Through the long hours of the night Amanda fought against her hopeless predicament, tugged and pulled against the tight confining wrappings sealing her to the chair, searching for a hint of slack or a knot to loosen, release her from taut bonds like bands of tempered steel holding her immobile. Her battle came in waves; a burst of focused exertion lasting several minutes until her stamina expended, slumping in exhaustion as if finishing a long sprint, resting to recoup her ebbing resolve for the next unwinnable battle with the implacable foe.

Bastard must've learned his knots in the Boy Scouts, Amanda grudgingly admitted the skill Marcus Cowle exhibited in binding her. Strained again against the rope, listened to the chair creak from the restrained movement. A rivulet of perspiration trickled down her forehead, the lone reward for her exertions, limbs throbbing from bonds slicing into soft flesh. She flexed her hands, trying to get sensation into numb fingers. *Before they kicked him out for tying up all the Girl Scouts.*

The gallows humor on the precipice of imminent death provided no comfort to Amanda. *Why did you have to be so damn impatient! Why couldn't you have listened to Ashleigh!* At times Amanda brash and fearless, impetuous traits serving her well on the cross-country course or the track when she surged on a steep incline, increased the tempo and caught competitors off-guard, pushing the advantage to victory. Now those same qualities failed her miserably and at a terrible time. Instead of being cautious and wary, listening to the reservations of Ashleigh Morgan and her suspicions of the peculiar circumstances, Amanda blithely rushed headlong into the situation without thinking it through, anxious to get to dinner and celebrate her victory, didn't realize things not what they seemed and Samantha Grayson in grave danger, needing far more assistance than the trio could ever hope to offer. *Amanda McKinnon, you have royally screwed up this time,* a defeated sob escaped her lips, with her life paying for the miscalculation. What hurt more came knowledge one of her best friends in the world, gentle and innocent Lauryn Callahan, condemned to share this horrible execution by fire.

You should have listened to Ashleigh. She knew what we were getting into. Amanda flayed by her guilt-ridden conscience. Where was Ashleigh now? Was she a prisoner with Samantha or held captive alone, as Cowle and his thug planned to take Ashleigh with them once Samantha and the other women sold, in another location? The fact didn't matter, Ashleigh as doomed as they were to a cruel death but one to take far longer, and be far more violent, than their own impending, sudden end. Amanda didn't listen to Ashleigh, plunging ahead into the unknown, blind to the implications of her actions. Now the outcome inevitable, at any moment the timer on the bomb to strike midnight and a thunderous, fiery explosion instantly enveloping Amanda and Lauryn, and the building housing Marcus Evans Photography, in a fireball of destruction.

No! I'm not going to die! With a low grunt from behind the cloth filling her mouth and the duct tape and bandage sealing it shut, Amanda made one final, tremendous effort, marshaling remaining strength for a final dash across the finish line, free herself from the ropes bound about her, chair squeaking from the furious struggle. Her fingers frantically groped for the elusive knot to loosen, after a minute understood this last attempt in vain. Amanda trussed up as a goose ready for Christmas dinner. *And I'm about to be cooked.* She cried out an animalistic wail of agony and frustration, head dropping against her chest. She thought of the dreams now denied her: an NCAA championship; the honor of representing her homeland in the Olympics; the absolute, fulfilling joy found in each mile she ran; the tranquility of running along the shore of Lake Ontario as the sun rose above the horizon. Thought of her family in Toronto, the mother and father both noted archeologists she wished to emulate, younger sisters worshipping Amanda as their courageous champion, and of Connor Aanonsen, strong and passionate, to whom she gave her heart and love during the brief time at Great Northern, likely days until they learned the terrible truth of her passing, mourning the unfortunate, violent end. All of the dreams and hopes soon stolen away. *It's not fair*, she railed, *it's not fair, I have so much to live for.*

From across the room Amanda heard a barely audible moan from her friend, Lauryn brutally bound on the floor, she too left mute and blind by the gag and blindfold, not knowing when Death to arrive and take her away to the Hereafter. No longer did Amanda feel sorry for her approaching doom. *Lauryn is going to die because of you.* Because of her stupidity, because of impulsive recklessness the pair sentenced to die in the throes of a flaming conflagration. Lauryn sharing her fate, a horrible end her gentle friend didn't deserve. *All because of me.*

As Amanda McKinnon continued the struggle for freedom from the cocoon of ropes sealing her to the chair, in the end a futile, useless fight, Lauryn Callahan already capitulated to her stringent captivity, surrendering to the heartbreaking awareness at any moment she might die, life snuffed out as a candle in a strong gust of wind even before she reached the full potential of possibilities life presented. Denied the chance to say goodbye to adoring parents, prominent doctors in Denver, her mother a pediatrician, father a heart surgeon, supporting the decision to pursue a different sort of medical study, to save and nurture the lives of the animals she cherished so deeply. Never would she ever truly know the love and affection of the man she adored named Albert Fatuamala.

Lauryn cursed herself for being slight of stature, easily cowed by the bulk of Cowle's hired goon, threatened with harm, bound into a painful package from which she quickly realized there no escape after a single, feeble squirming attempt, only succeeding in rolling over on her side, the pressure on her shoulders unbearable. *I didn't fight back, I didn't resist, I let them do this to me.* Resigned to die lying next to the crude, but massive, explosive device, petite body confined in painful rigidity, every sound unintelligible, robbed of vision and sense of time by thick layers of bandages wrapped about her head. No idea if her next moment, next breath, next thought, to be the very last she'd ever known.

What might be Lauryn's final thoughts centered upon her friends, family and Albert. She could hear Amanda grunting, groaning through her gag, chair creaking as she strained against the prison of ropes holding her prisoner, sighing moans of disgust as Amanda gave up her latest battle for freedom, resting to restore her strength before resuming the fruitless endeavor. Lauryn knew Amanda raged with guilt for getting her and Ashleigh into the hopeless predicament, falling for the ploy from the human trafficker Marcus Cowle. *How could she have known*, Lauryn mused, *I didn't suspect anything either.* Only Ashleigh sensed the danger, the knowledge something not right inside the studio, a suspicion Samantha might be in danger. But Amanda hadn't heeded the warning; fell into the insidious trap Cowle set, friends overpowered and subdued before the horrible fate for them revealed. Despite her careless actions Lauryn forgave Amanda, no reason to hold her responsible when both of them condemned to, and about to share, a terrible end.

She mourned for Ashleigh and Samantha, considered close friends and sharing with them intimate feelings, remembering good times and laughter enjoyed in the fleeting, yet exuberant, time since they met as freshmen in Cockrell Hall. At least the end for Amanda and Lauryn to arrive in an instant, the suffering lasting but a millisecond. Their two friends not so fortunate, doomed to days, perhaps months and years, of suffering and vicious torture at the hands of monsters and maniacs, their dignity shredded. Lauryn prayed to a merciful God for their salvation from the horrible fate, found before it was too late, though time for Lauryn and Amanda about to run out, doomed to die helpless and alone.

She thought of Albert Fatuamala, one poignant memory lodged in her mind. Every night after they finished studying at the Starbucks in Howell Student Commons the pair walked across campus to spend time in Philosopher's Grove, a secluded copse of maples and elms surrounding a small fountain of bronze adorned with fawns and birds, a circle of marble benches arranged about the humble monument. A memorial to a beloved philosophy student who departed Great Northern to fight in France during the First World War, losing his life in the bloody struggle for Belleau Wood, Philosopher's Grove a peaceful hideaway where the bustle of a lively college campus faded away in a tranquil silence, offered a soothing haven from the pressures of student life, of deadlines for papers and cramming for exams.

On a cool night the previous spring, under a starry sky and bathed by the glow of a full moon, they discussed life after death, if there was a Heaven, what happened to the essence of the soul when the physical vessel took its final breath and the last heartbeat pulsed. Albert, the philosophy major who every day pondered such profound musings, told her there had to be something, exactly what left to much debate, after one departed this mortal world. He contended, as they sat luxuriating in a glorious quiet broken only by the trickle of water in the fountain, the soul moved to another plane of existence, noted every culture and religion in the world taught a concept of paradise, nirvana and heaven, where the soul experienced a state of peace. He even thoughtfully offered a fanciful conjecture the soul moved on to the person's physical body in a parallel universe where the course of life played in an infinite loop, though with different outcomes.

Lauryn didn't care what the afterlife involved, or the vision of paradise presented by the myriad of the world's religions. She held a solitary concern regarding life after death, a condition for wherever her spirit ended up when her days on Earth done. *I'll be happy as long as there are dogs in heaven.* She sniffed back a tear. *I'll soon find out.* Lauryn wasn't afraid of death, understood the natural course of life, always a beginning and an end. Learned the lesson early in life, owned dogs since childhood, suffered the sorrow of their loss, forced to say good-bye to a pair of faithful companions as their days reached a final sunset. It wasn't the fact she was about to die ripping at Lauryn's soul, it was the manner of leaving this world, a sudden and violent end, denied a chance to say goodbye to those she loved, the last memory of her the horrible way in which she was taken away from them.

A single regret burned a gaping hole in her mourning heart waiting for the inevitable, powerless to prevent her death from occurring. *I'll never be able to tell Albert that I love him.*

11:57.

Three minutes remained in the lives of Amanda McKinnon and Lauryn Callahan.

"I don't like the looks of this," Connor Aanonsen commented as Tyler turned onto North Campbell Street.

"Now there's an understatement," Tyler McManaway grumbled, pointed at the blue Ford Mustang parked on the west side of the street. "There's Samantha's car." Samantha going in search of the missing Presley Harding, now Samantha had vanished as well. The Mustang on the same street as the studio for Marcus Evans Photography signified a dark omen.

Connor motioned down the street. "There's Amanda's car." The red Hyundai Sonata with the white and blue Ontario provincial license plate proclaiming *Yours To Discover* sitting on the same side of the quiet street as Samantha's car.

"You still think I'm overreacting?" Tyler asked of D'Andre Watson. *Samantha, what have you gotten yourself into?* Tyler wondered for the thousandth time since leaving the Great Northern campus, now sick to his stomach. He prayed the search ended here, and in time to stop a tragedy.

"My apologies for not believing you in the first place, my Spidey Sense just kicked into hyper-drive," D'Andre muttered as Tyler double-parked the Xterra in front of Marcus Evans Photography. "I hate to say this, but you were right about that bad feeling."

"Where are the police?" Connor glanced about. "If Aaron called them after we left they should be here by now."

"Don't have time to wait for them to show up." Tyler shook his head, noticed the street deserted, studied the three-story brownstone at 2371 North Campbell Street, the building eerily dark.

"Let's be cool," Albert 'Fiji' Fatuamala cautioned, voice even, betraying not a hint of anxiety. "Let's keep our heads here." Couldn't blindly rush into a threatening situation, no matter how much they desired to save their loved ones. Deep inside where none of his companions could see he feared for Lauryn Callahan and her friends. If any harm inflicted upon the willowy, gentle redhead he so dearly cherished, there to be Hell to pay and Fiji prepared to collect payment with full interest.

"Oh my God, they're in trouble," Riley Bradford gasped, hand covering her mouth, the quest to find her missing roommate leading Samantha, and it appeared her friends, into peril. A crushing weight of responsibility crashed down on her shoulders. "What've I done?"

"Riley, stay here," Tyler ordered as the four young men stepped from the Xterra, left her in the SUV. Tyler stepped up to Samantha's Mustang, peered through the driver's side window. Saw nothing inside to clarify the situation, provide answers to countless disconcerting questions. "Come on," he motioned, running to the front of the darkened photography studio.

Tyler pulled out his Samsung smartphone, touched the screen and the surface flashed to life, directing the powerful light through the blinds to illuminate the reception area. "See anything?" Connor asked.

"Nothing." Tyler started to say before noticing a dark brown lump resting on the couch. A familiar object Tyler saw every day slung over the arm of Samantha Grayson. His heart started racing, breaking from the line like a top-fuel dragster, bile gushing up in his throat. "It's Samantha's messenger bag!" Tyler tugged on the locked doorknob, banged an open palm against the glass pane. "She has to be inside! Samantha! Samantha!"

What is that? At the sound Amanda McKinnon lifted her head, squealed through her gag, heard banging on the front door. Lauryn whined, she too heard the commotion. Concealed in the studio from sight of those out front, unable to see their bound forms and the terrible device in their midst. Amanda strained to hear a voice calling out "Samantha!" and recognized it immediately. *Tyler!* Was Connor with him? *How did Tyler find out we were here?* Amanda had no idea and didn't much care, explanations to wait until after they were free, still hope for salvation. If only there was enough time and Amanda didn't know how many minutes or seconds separated her from life and death.

Amanda and Lauryn resumed frantic struggles against the bondage securing them, screaming into the fabric silencing them, making whatever noise to gain the attention of Tyler and whoever else stood outside Marcus Evans Photography.

Amanda and Lauryn didn't know the two-minute warning had already passed.

*   *   *   *   *

"I think I hear something," Connor cocked an ear.

The statement enough justification for Tyler. "We have to get inside! They could be in danger!" Tyler reared back, ready to thrust his shoulder into the heavy door, break it down and barge inside the building.

Fiji grasped Tyler gently by the arm, moved him aside. "You screw up your shoulder and our plans for a bowl game at the end of the season are done," he politely informed Tyler. "Allow me." Tyler expected a display of tremendous, brute force from his friend to bust down the door. Instead, to his surprise, Fiji balled up his massive fist, picked a spot inches above the lock, gently rapping against the door. They heard a click. Fiji turned the knob and the door opened easily, allowing them entry inside the studio.

In astonishment Tyler, D'Andre and Connor stared at Fiji. "How did you do that?" D'Andre questioned.

"Ancient Samoan secret," Fiji noted simply.

"Can you teach me that sometime?" Connor asked.

"Then it wouldn't be a secret," Fiji replied as the quartet entered the building, charging into the deserted reception area shouting the names of missing loved ones. "Samantha! Lauryn! Amanda! Ashleigh!" Muffled screams from the next room alerted them to danger very near, rushed towards frightened, desperate sounds. The room pitch-black like a devil's soul, but Tyler able to discern two forms, one sitting in a chair, a second lying on the floor as Connor groped along the wall for the light switch, flicked it on.

"Oh God!" Tyler exclaimed, stopped dead, abrupt illumination revealed a horrifying sight. In the chair sat Amanda McKinnon, at her feet on the floor lay Lauryn Callahan, what appeared to be hundreds of feet of white rope bound and knotted tightly into an inescapable webbing immobilizing the helpless pair. Gagged and blindfolded with white elastic material wound about their heads.

Samantha Grayson and Ashleigh Morgan, or Presley Harding, nowhere to be found. Something else though sat on the floor inside the studio.

Between the helpless women rested four propane tanks held together by chain and heavy wire around the handles. The block of gray clay-like substance taped to the side of one tank caught the undivided attention of the four hurrying to the rescue. A spectrum of colored wires lead from the block of explosive to a timer, two panels with red LED digits on the device. The number on top read 12:00 AM, the number below read 11:59 PM.

Tyler McManaway knew what a bomb looked like.

"I don't think we want to be here when that timer hits midnight," D'Andre said, felt the inadequacy of a now suddenly fragile mortality.

"And we've got a minute until that happens," Connor added as Amanda squealed through her gag, horrified by the statement.

Tyler stared at the timer. Now was the time for the mother of all Hail Mary's.

At the abandoned factory Samantha Grayson stared numbly at the clock resting in the corner, watched the second hand sweeping around the face, counting down the final seconds until midnight and the imminent execution of two of her friends.

Thirty seconds….

Samantha tried banishing from her mind the image of Amanda McKinnon and Lauryn Callahan trapped in the studio, engaged in futile struggle against the ropes binding them. The bomb sitting between them set to explode. Silenced by thick gags, no one hearing their cries for help. About to die a terrible death alone.

Fifteen seconds….

Soon Samantha she too bound and gagged and helpless as a newborn, handed over to a ruthless buyer in exchange for cold, hard cash. Taken away from parents never to learn the horrible truth surrounding her disappearance, never to experience the safe harbor of home and their love. Never to see Tyler McManaway again except in tortured memories. Never to feel his strong arms about her or his gentle touch against her cheek, never to savor his devotion for her, never to feel his love.

Ten seconds….

Samantha glanced at Presley Harding sitting beside her, petite body wrapped in rope and gagged. Ordained for the same heart-rending fate as Samantha, life cut viciously short as it was beginning.

Five seconds….

As Amanda and Lauryn met their end in an explosion and fire, Ashleigh Morgan carried off to suffer a slow death as a prize of her captors, her friends murdered because Samantha sent a text to Lauryn telling where she'd gone. They came to the studio for her, unaware of the peril until too late. Amanda and Lauryn doomed, knew too much to live, and Marcus Cowle seeing to their elimination with utterly ruthless efficiency.

Midnight.

Samantha wailed in anguish, tears streaming down her cheeks, spirit conquered by guilt. She tried dispelling the final, horrific image of the death of her friends, prayed the moment sudden for their sake, so quick they felt no pain.

You killed them, Samantha agonized, the remorse overwhelming. *You killed Amanda and Lauryn.* Overcome with sorrow, it no longer mattered to Samantha what Sheik Rahim planned for her.

Samantha had no idea a difference of twenty-four seconds existed between the clock in the abandoned factory where she was prisoner and the clock attached to the bomb resting between Amanda McKinnon and Lauryn Callahan.

Chapter 38

Tyler McManaway stared at the timer on the explosive device, understood something very bad to happen when the second timer hit midnight, something *KA-BOOM* bad, of that simple fact Tyler very certain. Tyler, along with his roommates and the helpless Amanda McKinnon and Lauryn Callahan, stood at the epicenter where the *KA-BOOM* set to occur, in the space of a millisecond sent sky-high to Kingdom Come, bodies torn asunder, ripped to bits and pieces of bloody flesh and bone. *Not the way I want to leave this world.* He crouched next to the device, Albert 'Fiji' Fatuamala beside him, Connor Aanonsen and D'Andre Watson leaning over them. A rainbow of wires-red, blue, green and yellow-lead from the timer to the detonator attached to the chunk of plastic explosive taped to one of the four propane tanks. Was there a way to disarm the explosive? Could they carry Lauryn and Amanda, one tied to the chair and difficult to maneuver through the doorway, out of the building before the explosion? Which wire did he need to pull? Tyler wondered how much time he had left to act. A full minute? Only a handful of seconds? Time, whatever remained, dwindling rapidly, trickling like water down a drain and Tyler hadn't even begun considering his options. This not a football game where he could signal a time-out to the referee, walk over to the sidelines to compose his nerves, consult with the coaching staff to decide the next play.

"What do I do?" Tyler asked out loud, wondered then if he'd conceded defeat, which in this instance meant death. For Amanda and Lauryn the pained statement the last thing they, bound, gagged and blindfolded next to an explosive device ready to detonate at any moment, wished to hear. *What do you do?* Amanda screamed frantically through the gag, swinging her head about, perspiration streaming down her face. *Do something! Anything! Like, right now!*

Tyler swallowed hard, taking what might be a final breath of life, making his decision, focused on the wire of the color he absolutely certain he needed to pull, trembling hand reaching forward, hoping this not the last action of his existence. Before Tyler able to yank the wire he grasped at Fiji reached over him and, with an almost casual, detached nonchalance, snapped the blue wire out from the timer.

A second later the second readout flashed to 12:00 AM.

A buzzer wailed.

Everyone in the room but Fiji jumped, startled by the high-pitched buzz rattling the room. As his friends remained frozen, shocked how close the brittle grip of death brushed against them, Fiji switched off the alarm with the same unperturbed coolness used to tug the blue wire and silence, except for heavy breathing of relief mixed with an equal measure of incredulity, once more filled the room. D'Andre first to break the stillness, his voice shaky, the bravado absent. "Now that was a shot going in at the buzzer..."

Connor let out a deep breath, one held for the past minute, eyes transfixed on the inert device, then looked at Fiji in disbelief. "Is the ability to disarm a bomb another Ancient Samoan Secret you haven't told us about?"

Fiji shrugged. "Maybe." Tyler turned, stared dumbfounded at his broad-shouldered friend. "It's always the blue wire," Fiji informed him in a matter-of-fact tone as if stating *it's raining outside.*

A gasp escaped Tyler's lips, mouthing the words *always the blue wire.* "I always thought it was the red wire," he told Fiji in shock.

"If it was up to me we'd be dead." D'Andre rolled his eyes. "I was thinking the green wire. You know, my Green Lantern fetish."

"Yellow was my favorite color as a kid," Connor added.

"It's always the blue wire," Fiji returned unbelieving stares from his companions, repeating his statement with unquestioning certainty.

"How did you know it was the blue wire?" Tyler astonished by the degree of certitude Fiji exhibited and at this moment that display of self-assurance drove him absolutely crazy.

Again Fiji shrugged his massive shoulders with nonplussed, inscrutable calm. "I just know."

"Good thing you did or we'd be singing spirituals with the angels now." D'Andre said.

Amanda moaned pitifully through the gag keeping her silent, interrupting the discussion, pulling weakly with what little strength left in her limbs against the ropes melding her to the chair. *Guys, a little help here?* Lauryn cried meekly, joining Amanda in agreement.

Fiji motioned to Amanda and Lauryn. "Isn't this is why we came here in the first place," focusing the attention of his friends back to the helpless young women. Examined with alarm the intricate lattice of ropes and multitude of Gordian Knots binding the cords about their bodies, fixing them immobile as trees rooted firmly into the ground.

"Christ," D'Andre gasped, "they," whoever 'they' were, "wanted to make sure you didn't go anywhere."

You think? Amanda snorted, aching body yearning for release from the agonizing bondage, wished for the stifling gag removed from her mouth and her sight restored.

"Where do we start?" Tyler shook his head. Was Samantha suffering a similar predicament, crying out for freedom? Amanda moaned again. *I think anywhere will work just fine!*

"That's why a good craftsman," Connor dug into the pocket of his jeans, removed a Swiss Army knife, extracted the sharp knife blade from the handle, "always has the proper tools with him."

"Always carry that around?" The first time Tyler had seen Connor display the versatile implement.

"You do when you're from Minnesota. Never know when you're going to filet a trout or fight off a bear," Connor stepped behind the chair to which Amanda tied. "Don't worry, babe, I'll have you out of this in a minute." Amanda gave a relieved whimper as Connor quickly sliced through the ropes. Fiji not waiting for Connor to finish cutting away Amanda's bonds, kneeling next to Lauryn, fingers working on the knot connecting the rope pulling ankles up to her wrists, knew the position causing terrible strain, soul aching quietly seeing Lauryn in such pain. Fiji undid the knot, Lauryn whined as her legs, for hours frozen in place, moved and straightened out in a symphony of agony, each throbbing ache in her limbs a different note of pain. Fiji gently lifted Lauryn, cradling her against him to start working on loosening the bonds about her. Tyler and D'Andre stood by, letting their friends release the ones they loved.

Amanda felt the intense pressure from tight ropes ease then disappear as Connor continued hacking through cords fastening her upper body to the chair. Sensed her hands become free, blood flooding numb fingers with a flush of tingling warmth; arms released from secure confinement. Wanted to reach up, tear away the gag and blindfold, but found she could barely lift her arms, joints and muscles flaring hot like a wildfire raging through a wilderness. *Oh God, this hurts so much!* She groaned as each minuscule movement brought an avalanche of misery, tortured body feeling as if she'd run not one, but a dozen marathons in the time she'd been left bound and helpless to her fate.

"Here, cut Lauryn loose." Connor finished with the bonds around Amanda's upper body, handing the knife to Fiji, about to peel away the bandages from Lauryn's eyes. Decided the blindfold and gag could wait, first releasing the petite redhead from the bondage punishing her tiny body.

"It's okay," Fiji reassured Lauryn, doing swift work on the rope prison. "You'll be free in a minute." Lauryn sighed in reply, willing to wait that minute more with the knowledge she was safe in the arms of the one she loved.

"What's going on?" The subdued voice of Riley Bradford asked as she stepped into the studio, eyes gazing in surprise at the sight of Amanda and Lauryn liberated from captivity, the bomb inert, sitting harmlessly in the center of the room. The implication now clear, her friend Presley in terrible danger. If Riley had come here, surrendering to her initial instincts, a mortal peril she too may well have faced. "Where's Presley?"

"I'm hoping we find out soon enough," Tyler told her, waiting for Connor to remove the gag from Amanda for her to explain what happened and where whoever did this to them had taken Samantha Grayson and Ashleigh Morgan.

While Fiji used the Swiss Army knife to cut Lauryn's bonds, Connor removed the thick bandage wrapped around Amanda's head and over her eyes, emerging into the light like a resurrected Lazarus from a tomb of darkness she thought to be eternal. The light grew brighter with each layer stripped away, Amanda blinking as it jabbed her eyes with the sharpness of a thousand tiny needles. She turned towards a familiar face blurry and out of focus. After a few seconds her vision cleared, regained clarity, beheld blue eyes brimming with concern, the blond hair and hardy Nordic features that, Amanda joked in lighter moments, made Connor Aanonsen 'her Norse thunder god.' She sighed, chest heaving as she gazed longingly at him, tears filling her eyes. *You're the best thing I've seen in all of my life.* An image of her love Amanda thought denied to cast sight on ever again. Connor pulled the bandaging from around her jaw, revealing layers of silver tape sealing her lips, hesitated as fingers hovered over the strips plastered across her mouth. "Babe, this is going to hurt," he cautioned.

Tell me something I don't already know, in a mournful whimper came Amanda's answer, forlorn amethyst eyes beseeching. *Just get this crap off my face.*

"Don't say I didn't warn you," Connor took a deep breath, peeling back the thick gag of heavy silver tape. Amanda grimaced as adhesive grudgingly surrendered a sticky embrace against tender skin; she closed her eyes, gave a pitiful moan as Connor gingerly stripped away the tape with delicate care. Once removed Amanda coughed, spitting out from her mouth the sodden wad of cloth, watched it plop wetly into her lap. "Ow," the first tortured word she spoke, greedily sucking air into aching lungs, each inhalation gulped down like a large glass of water. She raised her arms, the simple action induced a screaming surge of pain racing through the back and arms, yet ignored those harsh aches to wrap her arms around the shoulders of her boyfriend.

"Never thought I'd ever do this again," she whispered, voice hoarse, hugging Connor tightly, not wanting to let go, nostrils sniffling, wiped at trickling tears. "I love you, Connor Bear."

"I'm here, Gazelle, I love you too." Connor brushed away raven hair, kissed Amanda on the forehead, then softly on the lips, tasting gummy residue left from the tape. "You're safe now. Nothing's going to happen to you." *That was way too close.* He glanced at the inactive explosive, whispered a silent oath he'd never again allow something this horrendous to happen to his Amanda. *If I find the people who did this to you, the people who tried to hurt you,* dark thoughts filled his head, temper starting to flare, *I will kill them.*

"Who did this to you? Where's Samantha?" Tyler demanded.

"And Ashleigh, where is she?" D'Andre followed with his own question.

Connor whirled about, a momentary flash of anger reddening his face, usually cool and reserved Scandinavian demeanor evaporating. That Amanda suffered this dreadful ordeal, came within seconds of dying, and he hadn't been there to protect her filled him with rage. The recrimination weighed heavily on his conscience, wanted to lash out, exact revenge on those placing Amanda in deathly peril. "Christ! She almost died here! Give her a few seconds!"

"We don't have a few seconds!" Tyler shot back.

Amanda grabbed Connor's shoulder. "Tyler's right. We don't have time." In a mirror on the far side of the room spotted her reflection staring back with empty and haunted eyes, shuddering at the rat's nest of tousled dark hair about her head, smeared make-up and disheveled clothes soaked with sweat, the result of being tightly bound, gagged and blindfolded for hours. *I look like hell*, she observed. *But it's better than the alternative.* "Samantha and Ashleigh don't have much time left, they're in terrible danger! They need our help!"

"What's going on? Who did this to you?" Tyler repeated again. "Where are Samantha and Ashleigh?"

"This studio, it's all a set up. This guy isn't a photographer, his name's not Marcus Evans, its Marcus Cowle." As Amanda began explaining Fiji cut away the last bonds from Lauryn's ankles, handed the knife back to Connor who hurriedly went to work on the remaining ropes holding Amanda to the chair.

"Who is this Marcus Cowle? What does he want with Samantha?" Tyler insisted, afraid of what this meant for Samantha. *I promised I would protect her,* not doing a good job of that now. "Has this bastard hurt her?"

"Not yet." Amanda sucked in a breath before continuing. "He's a human trafficker. A very nasty human trafficker. He's selling Samantha to some Middle Eastern sheik in a few hours, I think his name is Rahim or something."

For long seconds silence fell over the room as a startled shock took hold. "Someone is going to sell Samantha?" Tyler finally spoke words he thought utterly impossible, staggered by the revelation, brain refusing to compute the facts presented, staring in disbelief at a grim possibility never expected.

"White slavery," Fiji grunted, unwinding the bandages about Lauryn's eyes, the redhead blinking as vision restored, eyes focused on the bronzed face of the Samoan, a most beautiful thing to see.

"My people have a history with slavery, bad history," D'Andre snarled at the mention of a terrible chapter in the history of mankind, of ancestors brought unwillingly to the New World. "No one's selling my lady."

Amanda closed her eyes, shuddered. "They don't plan on selling Ashleigh," Amanda replied. *I got her into this! It's all my fault this has happened!.* "After they sell Samantha and the other women they're holding hostage," she paused, eyes tearing up, "they're leaving the country and taking Ashleigh with them." She opened her eyes, using the sleeve of her sweater to wipe at the tears. "D'Andre, I'm sorry! She thought something was wrong, but I didn't listen to her!"

D'Andre's face turned hard, eyes narrowing. "No one is taking my lady away from me." He understood the implication, a cold fury seeping into his response. "No one is going to lay a hand on her."

Fiji about to strip away the duct tape sealing Lauryn's mouth shut, apologized in advance. "I'm sorry, this will hurt a little." Lauryn looked at him sympathetically, *I understand*, emerald eyes reassured him, whimpering slightly in discomfort as tape peeled from her cheeks, coughed out the cloth wadding inside her mouth. She cried softly, collapsing into the protective arms of Albert Fatuamala.

"Presley?" Riley Bradford asked. "Are they holding Presley too?"

Who is this? Amanda glanced at Tyler, confused, never seeing the girl with them before.

"This is Riley Bradford, she's a freshman. Her roommate Presley has been missing since Sunday afternoon. She went to Samantha for help when she didn't get any from the police," Tyler explained quickly, all the puzzle pieces falling into place, creating a sickening picture. "Her roommate had a business card from our photographer friend."

"So that's why Samantha came here," Amanda groaned as the last ropes securing her legs to the chair cut away, a shooting pain like the point of a knife plunged into her hips. Had being bound for so

280

long caused an injury, had she pulled a muscle or strained a ligament, in the course of her struggling? For a moment Amanda feared what this meant for the remainder of her cross-country season, the hopes for a national championship. The concern for her own well-being replaced by a sudden flush of guilt at so selfish a thought when her friends remained in perilous danger. "She wasn't here to get sexy pictures for you," Amanda blushed, embarrassed by the notion discussed on the drive from Evanslawn.

"What was that?" Tyler perplexed by the statement.

"Nothing, it's nothing," Amanda waved her hand, looked at D'Andre. "Ashleigh had a close encounter with this Marcus Cowle at Summer's End Fest Saturday night. He wanted Ashleigh to be an item on his shopping list, told him to get lost."

"That's my girl," D'Andre replied. Now he had to save his Ashleigh. *If I knew where they took her.*

"So wherever they took Samantha and Ashleigh is where they have Presley," Connor told Riley.

"That brings us back to where we started," Tyler said somberly, defeat in his voice. "We don't know where this Cowle has them."

"You do now," Amanda glanced at the bomb, running a hand through tangled tresses. *You thought we'd never be able to tell*, she grinned wickedly, *that we'd be dead and your secret safe. The joke's on you, asshole.* "When he was on the phone discussing what to do with us with his friend," she motioned to Lauryn, resting silently in Fiji's sheltering embrace, "he texted the address of where they're making the exchange. That's where they took Samantha and Ashleigh. Didn't realize I could see his message."

Tyler knew what she meant. "Amanda McKinnon, I love you." The distraught expression of a moment earlier replaced by nascent hope.

"Hey, back off," Connor said, reminding Tyler, "I'm the one who loves her." Connor kissed Amanda.

"Where did they take them?" Tyler asked the question he wanted an answer to more than anything in his life now.

"3100 West Carroll Avenue," Amanda triumphantly offered the information. "The exchange is taking place at two."

Tyler checked his watch, exhaled in relief. "We've got time."

D'Andre typed the address into his iPhone. "And I've got directions. It's less than four miles from here. At this time of night and with the way you drive we can be there in no time."

Tyler nodded, only one course of action to follow, wasn't about to back down now. Samantha and Ashleigh remained in mortal danger, their lives, and those of Presley and any other captives these traffickers might have, resting in his hands. "Let's go."

Fiji gazed down at the petite form of Lauryn Callahan cradled in his arms. "Are you okay?" He asked in a placid, soothing tone unbecoming of one so imposing in stature.

Lauryn nodded, wiped away the tears. "It's tomorrow right, and tomorrow is now today. Marcus Cowle said we wouldn't live to see tomorrow, which is now today," the words tumbled from her mouth, a jumble of thoughts expressed all at once, the sentiment rambling. "So he left us with that," her head motioned to the now lifeless explosive, "and set the timer for midnight because he didn't want us to live to see tomorrow, which is now today. But you came and you knew you had to pull the blue wire, so that thing didn't go off and so it's now tomorrow, or today. And because it's now today and I'm still alive, that means I'm okay."

"You're fine." Fiji smiled at Lauryn, understood perfectly what she meant, leaning over, hand sweeping dark cinnamon-red bangs from her eyes, lovingly placed a gentle kiss on the forehead. "You're safe now."

Lauryn stared at Fiji, emerald eyes moist and glistening. Her silent expression spoke volumes. *I came within a second of dying, of losing you and my friends and everything I cherish in life and all I'm going to get is a little kiss on the forehead?* Lauryn threw herself at Fiji, arms flung around the thick neck and broad shoulders, soft lips meeting his with an unrestrained passion none of her friends ever before witnessed, kissing the young man who at this moment meant everything in the world to her. Lauryn's abrupt, impromptu reaction startled the Samoan, dark eyes widening with surprise, then slowly closed, almost dreamily, as his strapping arms wrapped about the waist of the willowy redhead, the tender act a sign he accepted Lauryn as the absolute center around which his life revolved.

The others observed the pair hopelessly lost in a private moment. "If I'd have known it would take *this* to get them together we should've been kidnapped months ago," Amanda sighed with the ironic observation.

The fervent kiss lasted thirty seconds when Connor noted, as he held Amanda and massaged arms sore from the bondage. "That sure isn't an imaginary online kiss there, Fiji."

Amanda shook her head. "They have to come up for air sometime."

"Fiji." Tyler said, received no response from his friend. He leaned in closer. "*Fiji!*" Shouting to gain his attention, breaking at last the bewitching spell Lauryn cast over him. Lauryn grudgingly ended the kiss, yearned for it to last forever so he'd understand how much she loved him. Fiji leaned back, placed his hand over his heart and the massive Samoan, so stalwart and ferocious on the football field, a Rock of Gibraltar on the defensive line, swooned with the vacant, love-struck astonishment of a smitten schoolboy after the first innocent kiss on the playground from the girl of his dreams.

"You can share a bowl of poi later," Tyler informed Fiji, staring back at him starry-eyed. *God, you are so owned now.* "We have to save Samantha before they ship her to God knows where."

"Don't forget Ashleigh," D'Andre reminded. "These bastards aren't hurting my lady."

"Poi is overrated," Fiji answered absently, eyes glazed over, peering down at Lauryn with devoted adoration. "Actually," he reconsidered, "poi doesn't taste very good at all."

"We have to go," Tyler insisted, "we're not done yet."

"I'm coming with you," Amanda tried to stand up from the chair when a wave of pain so intense, as a runner dealing with grueling workouts and thousands of miles Amanda able to bear all sorts of excruciating pain, flared through her hips with the fury of a blast furnace, stopping her dead. She whined in anguish, sinking back down on the seat, every muscle in her legs and back protesting vehemently the failed effort. 'On second thought…"

"You and Lauryn are staying here," Connor put his arms on Amanda's shoulders, easing her back on the chair.

Riley about to say something and Tyler knew exactly what it was, cutting her off before she could utter a word. "No Riley, you're not coming with us this time," Tyler said forcefully. "Where we're going is way too dangerous. We have no idea what we'll face there. I don't want anything happening to you."

"But Presley…" Riley implored, tears brimming in her eyes at the unspeakable truth of Presley's peril, feared for her friend's life and of the courageous student reporter unknowingly sent to share her predicament.

"We'll get Presley out of this," Tyler reassured Riley, understood the desire to accompany them. "We need you to stay here, take care of Amanda and Lauryn."

"I might be able to stand up sometime tonight," Amanda muttered in disgust, despite freedom from the bindings her body weakened, remained helpless as a baby.

Tyler glanced at Amanda's handbag on the table, reached inside for her smartphone. "Have enough strength to call 911 and tell them where we're going?"

"Maybe the cops will beat us there this time," D'Andre added, "and they can take care of these punks." Wondered, with Aaron Dinehart calling from the office of *The Daily Northern*, why the police hadn't arrived at the studio before them. *What's up with that?*

"I can do that," Amanda turned to Connor. "You be safe," she told him as the embraced, "I want you back."

Connor kissed her, caressed her cheek, hoped the farewell wasn't forever. "Don't worry, I don't plan on leaving you anytime soon."

Lauryn hesitated in letting go of Fiji, filled with a sense of comfort from the strong arms circled about her, curled under a heavy blanket on a cold winter day. "I don't want to lose you after I realize what you mean to me." She inched up to kiss her newfound love. "I love you, Albert Fatuamala."

"She called him by his first name." Amanda rubbed her temples. "Now it's serious."

Fiji smiled, only his family used his given name. "I love you too, Lauryn Callahan." With reluctance Fiji released Lauryn, stood up to join his friends at the door.

"Get Samantha and Ashleigh..." Amanda started to say.

"And Presley," Riley added.

"...out of this mess," Amanda continued. "You have to save them."

"That's the idea," Tyler reassured the trio. "We're not letting anyone take them away."

"Get out of here, we'll be okay," Amanda waved, encouraging them. "Go."

With the simple urging the four departed the brownstone, headed to Tyler's Xterra. "Let's roll," D'Andre said as they got in, Tyler firing up the engine. "Don't hear no fat lady singing yet."

Tyler allowed himself to smile at his friend's braggadocio as they drove off, tires squealing against the pavement. "Neither do I."

Samantha strained to listen; sounds of activity from the rooms where her fellow captives held. Fearful cries muffled by the gags, a coarse comment about one putting up a fight, had to be Emma, another lewd remark The Arab having his fun with this consignment. A terse order from Cowle to one called Lang, the second assistant, to take them to the loading bay. Samantha looked over at Presley, the pair trading nervous, frightened glances. Footsteps approached, growing louder as Samantha and Presley sat motionless against the cold concrete wall, unwilling to accept their fate yet resigned to what now seemed inevitable.

We'll get out of this, Samantha's eyes implored of Presley. *I won't let them hurt you.*

Presley stared at Samantha, brown eyes wet with terror. *I'm scared.*

So am I. Samantha acknowledged the fact.

Cowle entered the cell, a broad smile on his face, followed by Sterner and Lang. "Your new owner is on his way," he announced grandly, "time for you to join the others. I know prior to payment he'll wish to inspect his new property upon arrival."

Sterner stepped up and grabbed Samantha about the waist, heaving her from the floor with a single fluid motion, again effortlessly tossed over his shoulder like a sack of flour. Lang gathered Presley, squealing behind her gag, into his arms.

"Time you meet your new friends, Samantha," Cowle lead his accomplices from the cell, carrying human burdens down the corridor. "You'll be spending time together." Samantha watched the gray concrete of the floor passing underneath, lifted her head, peered back at Presley struggling in Lang's arms. With her eyes tried reassuring Presley, but her own hopes for a miracle to spare their lives ebbing away with each second. *Even if I'm saved*, Samantha thought of a possibility quickly diminishing, shuddered as guilt flowed through her, *there won't be any rescue for Amanda and Lauryn, or Ashleigh*.

They brought Samantha and Presley into the loading bay, Samantha heard moaning cries from the other hostages. Sterner stopped, swung Samantha down from his shoulder, forced her to kneel against the cold cement floor, a fiery pain instantly ignited in her knees. Tried shifting her weight to make bearable the torturous position, found it nearly impossible with her legs securely bound. Turned to see Lang place Presley beside her, to her left the other four women kneeling, helpless, arranged in a row like goods offered for sale in a village market. *That's what we are to him and this Sheik Rahim, we're not people, we're merchandise*, Samantha realized, swallowing in fear.

"Please remain kneeling, I want no movement at all," Cowle ordered, pacing before the six captives. He checked his phone, nodded in satisfaction. "Your new owner will be here shortly to take delivery."

Samantha stared at the loading bay door, waiting in horrified dread for it to open and a terrifying nightmare vision of flesh and blood filled with the heinous desire to inflict violent and cruel degradations upon Samantha and her helpless companions revealed.

Chapter 39

"What the hell is this?" Aaron Dinehart slammed the phone into the cradle. "Amateur night?" He spent most of the last hour listening to either a dial tone or a busy signal when trying to call the Evanslawn 911 Center. He resorted to using a phone operator to connect with the Chicago center, only to plow headlong into a brick wall of a dispatcher under the assumption Aaron playing some sort of joke, hanging up in the middle of Aaron's attempt to explain Samantha Grayson and her friends, along with the freshman Presley Harding, faced an unknown, yet life-threatening, danger. "What the hell is going on here!"

"This wouldn't be the time to tell you the dispatchers at Chicago's 911 center went on strike?" This morsel of unwanted information from Kaitlyn Ross, the Assistant News Editor for the evening. "They're using supervisors and trainees until the strike is resolved. They're transferring calls to the emergency centers in the suburbs and everything is overloaded." Information gleaned from the *Chicago Tribune* website. "There are people make prank calls too, making the situation worse."

And the Mayor of Chicago wants to have both the WTO and G-20 summits in the city next year? On the same damn weekend? Aaron thought with detached amazement. "So you're saying everything is all fucked up right now?" Uttering the unusual profanity a sign Aaron stressed. "Anything else you want to tell me to improve my sunny disposition?" Sarcasm dripped from each word.

Lily Rosenberg spoke up. "Chicago Police are already looking for two missing women. I spoke with the editor at *The Vincentian*," that was the student newspaper at Saint Vincent University in Chicago's Lincoln Park. "They have missing students there as well."

"How many?"

"Two," Lily replied shakily. "One of the other missing women is from Pacifica College. The police are already looking for her." That news also found on the *Chicago Tribune* website.

"The two from Saint Vincent's are women, right?" Aaron asked the sixty-four thousand dollar question.

Lily nodded. *Jackpot,* Aaron thought. "That's four women who've gone missing in two days." Lily nodded, Aaron saw her eyes misting, taking it hard, lived in Cockrell Hall where Presley Harding was a resident. "You think this has something to do with what happened in California last year?"

"Some other places at other times too. Christ," Aaron muttered, "Samantha might've been onto something here." A something meaning Samantha's life in danger.

"I think I can help." Ali Fahrajani ran over from his desk after rummaging through his notes. He handed a slip of paper to Aaron. "He's a detective with the Chicago Police Department. If someone will understand what's going on, I think it'll be him."

Aaron looked at name on the paper, Devin Carson. Hadn't he played tight end for Great Northern back in the nineties, projected as the next big star at that position in the NFL? Then remembered an important detail, an incident forever altering his life, a professional career never realized. *Damn*. Ali was right. If anyone in Chicago able to help Samantha and her friends at this dire time, and the rescue effort heading to Marcus Evans Photography, it had to be Devin Carson.

"All right, let's see what we can find out," Detective Devin Carson told Detective Patrick Flannery, the pair exiting the unmarked sedan stopped in front of the Starbucks at Milwaukee, Damen and North Avenues, one of the city's notorious six-way intersections, coming here after updating Captain Hardaway on the status of the investigation. "Emma Hayden bought a double latte here, maybe she met our photographer friend inside too." He pointed to the shop on the southwest corner, their last solid trace of the first missing woman. "Maybe someone there or in these bars might've seen something, knows a photographer who likes sweet-talking young women with dreams of stardom."

"She got the coffee Saturday morning," Flannery pointed out. "I think most of the people in these bars were rollin' out of bed with their heads throbbin' from hangovers then. We should be askin' the natives around here in the mornin'."

"It's a start," Carson insisted, gave him a look. *We're running out of time.* "If we wait until tomorrow it could be too late."

"Didn't mean it that way," Flannery apologized; he the visitor from Dublin, not his place to question Carson's methods. "I understand how you feel. But we're clutchin' at straws."

"It's something," Carson turned, headed towards the Starbucks, felt his phone vibrating in the holster on his belt. Pulled it out, saw the area code for Chicago's northern suburbs, a number on the screen he didn't recognize. "Hello?"

'Is this Detective Devin Carson?" The voice asking possessed a distinctly Southern drawl.

"Who is this?" Carson demanded.

"I'm Aaron Dinehart, I'm the News Editor of *The Daily Northern* at Great Northern University," he replied in a terse tone.

Why was someone from the student newspaper of his alma mater calling him now? Had contacted the campus police to see if there were any reports of a missing student possibly matching their fifth victim, said they'd 'get back to him' if they had any information. Did they instead notify the student newspaper before contacting him? With his reply Carson controlled a simmering anger. "Listen, I really don't have the time…"

Aaron cut him off. "Are you searching for four missing women right now?"

"I am." The directness of the comment surprised Carson. Details of the two women missing from Saint Vincent University not yet released to the media. "What's this about?"

"You have five more missing women to worry about." The statement struck with the force of a nuclear device detonating at Ground Zero.

"What!" *Five more*? What was going on? "What do you mean?" Carson shouted into the phone.

"Earlier today the roommate of a freshman here at Great Northern, Presley Harding, came to our campus office. The roommate hadn't seen or heard from Presley since the previous day. Public Safety and the Evanslawn police told her they couldn't file a missing persons report at that time. She spoke to my top reporter, Samantha Grayson, and gave her information where Presley may have gone. I suspect Samantha went to check the information. No one here has heard from Samantha since early this afternoon."

Presley Harding. Had a name to go with the blue Lexus with the Great Northern parking sticker. Samantha Grayson heading off to investigate and now missing as well. "That's two. You said there were five."

"We think Samantha's roommates may have gone to the same address to find her," Aaron continued. "No one has heard from them either," Aaron paused, "they might be in the same heap of trouble as Samantha and Presley."

"Shit," Carson cursed under his breath. "I hope you can tell me where they went?"

"That I can, sir," Aaron replied immediately. "It's Marcus Evans Photography at 2371 North Campbell Street."

He shoots and scores, Carson thought. Now everything made sense, their subject posing as a photographer, perfect cover to hunt his prey. What he intended with his victims, and Carson fearing what those designs might entail, the sick, twisted violence he wished to inflict, very much in question. "Thank you very much!"

"You get Samantha and her friends out of whatever trouble they're in," Aaron told him, voice deeply concerned for a close acquaintance. "I think rather highly of that little lady, don't want anything to happen to her or her friends."

"We'll take care of it," Carson reassured him, ready to hang up.

"One other thing," Aaron interrupted him, "you might run into some people coming down from here. Samantha's boyfriend, Tyler McManaway, and his roommates are headed there."

He knew who Aaron spoke of, everyone who followed sports in Chicago did. *Touchdown Tyler*. "Don't worry. We'll take care of this." Now Carson possessed an idea of the situation confronting him and it wasn't good for all involved. Carson ended the call; hit the speed-dial for Dawson Hilliard's cell phone.

"Hope you've got something for me, just got bitched out by a photographer whose sexual adventure Hampton and I interrupted with our midnight knock on his door." Hilliard answered. "All I'll say is it involved the largest vibrator I have ever seen in my life. I'll have disturbing dreams about it for quite some time."

That story will have to wait, as intriguing as it may seem. "Where are you?" Carson asked.

"We're at California and Logan Boulevard," only a few streets away from the location on North Campbell Avenue, "about to hit the third name on our list," Hilliard said. "Marcus Evans."

"That's our guy!" Carson shouted, motioning for Flannery to get back in the squad car. "Get over there now!"

"Mind telling me what Magic Eight-Ball told you that?" Hilliard asked, in the background Carson heard the acceleration of a car engine, sirens switched on and screaming.

"Let's say I got an assist from old alma mater," Carson could only explain, "rest will have to wait. You might find someone already there to help us out."

"Got it," Hilliard said, "on our way." The phone call ended as Carson and Flannery got into their vehicle, hitting the sirens, pulling into traffic. They wouldn't be far behind Hilliard and Hampton arriving at the address for Marcus Evans Photography, discovered the dark secrets locked within the building. Carson prayed there still time to save the victims, a number doubling in the course of seconds, from the unknown terror they faced.

"Anyone have an idea how we do this?" Tyler McManaway asked, parked the Nissan Xterra on the corner of Whipple Street and Carroll Avenue a hundred yards to the east of the darkened factory inside which Samantha Grayson, Ashleigh Morgan and five other women held hostage, shut off the engine to the SUV, dousing the headlights. The Xterra positioned between two warehouses on each corner, shielding the truck from view of those in the factory. He exhaled, fought down the urge to bolt from the truck, charge the industrial complex with the single-minded intention of rescuing Samantha from the clutches of her abductors.

"I think walking up to the front door and ringing the bell is out of the question," Connor Aanonsen commented dryly.

Tyler sighed, shook his head; no playbook he knew offered a solution to this quandary. "We can look for another entrance to get inside, find where they have Samantha, Ashleigh and the others. Maybe we get the drop on these punks." *Maybe* was the operative word. Tyler never let his gaze stray far from the vacant factory, fingers drumming on the steering wheel. "Or we sit tight, keep an eye on this place, wait for the police to get here. This Rahim isn't supposed to show for another hour, I think by then Chicago's finest will get here to put an end to this." *And Samantha and Ashleigh will be safe*, Tyler tried convincing himself. *I hope.*

"Dude, I'm ready to go in and knock heads together, get Ashleigh out of there before she's hurt anymore by these goons," D'Andre Watson quietly seethed at the knowledge Marcus Cowle wanted to use his girlfriend as a sexual plaything to satisfy twisted desires. *Not my Ashleigh*, D'Andre promised, *no way I'll let that happen to my lady*. Tyler glanced over at him; saw D'Andre clenching his fists, muscles tense, spoiling for a fight. "Thought you wanted to go in and start down taking names?"

"We don't know how many of them," meaning the kidnappers, "are in there and we have no idea where inside they have Samantha and others," Tyler pointed out, attempting to formulate a plan to carry out, efforts coming up disappointingly empty. He didn't like that fact, used to being in control, calling the shots, taking risks and reaping big rewards. "We could blunder into a trap." The urge to act back at the studio now darkly shaded by clouds of doubt, hampered by questionable logistics of entering an abandoned factory complex, finding seven helpless women held hostage within the Minotaur's maze and confronting an unknown number of adversaries in the process. *This isn't a video game or television show, this is real life.* Their attempt to rescue Samantha, Ashleigh and the other captives might end in disaster, harm those they sought to save, too much a risk to consider. *And game over here means just that.*

"I don't have a problem being in harm's way, I'll do anything to save my lady," D'Andre told a friend now uncharacteristically hesitant. *It is Samantha he's worried about,* D'Andre understood the concern, *doesn't want her to get hurt.* D'Andre had the same worries for Ashleigh but willing to act, take matters into his own hands, rather than wait for the professionals to show up and do the job.

"That's a great movie, *In Harm's Way,*" Connor piped up from in back, eased the crackling tension. "John Wayne, Kirk Douglas, Burgess Meredith."

"My Dad likes that movie," D'Andre replied. "But he likes Marines in his war movies. His favorite John Wayne movie is *Sands of Iwo Jima.*" D'Andre hoped he remembered the lessons his father, a decorated Marine Corps colonel, taught about the art of defense, schooling him on the sweet science. *Hope I was a good student.* D'Andre laughed. "As much as Dad liked *Flags of Our Fathers* he thought *Letters from Iwo Jima* was the better movie."

"John Wayne's character dies at the end of *Sands of Iwo Jima,*" Tyler informed D'Andre.

"I know," D'Andre quietly conceded. "Hey, Tyler."

Tyler looked over at him. "What?"

"That wisecrack I made at lunch, you moping about Samantha going overseas," D'Andre told him. "My bad."

"No harm, no foul," Tyler replied, smiled at D'Andre. "None of us knew this was going to happen."

"Hate to bring this up but," Connor said, "if Amanda called 911, shouldn't the police have beaten us here or about to show up? We got to the studio before them and Aaron Dinehart was about to call 911 when we left *The Daily Northern* office."

"I've got the same vibe too," D'Andre agreed. *The cops should be here by now.*

Tyler about to answer when interrupted. "Guys, heads up," Albert 'Fiji' Fatuamala whispered sharply, the others turning to spot three sets of headlights approaching slowly down the street to their right. The vehicles didn't have lights flashing a bright blue through the night. *Bad people,* Tyler instantly realized who the new arrivals were, *very bad people.* One in particular named Rahim intended despicable things for Samantha and the other captives held prisoner inside 3100 West Carroll Avenue. "Get down," Fiji warned.

The four slid down in their seats, concealing their presence from the black limousine with an escort of two sleek, shark-nosed black Audi S8 sedans, one in front and one trailing behind the limo, as the vehicles passed the Xterra, continued down the street to the factory. As the cars reached the address Tyler saw the automatic gate to the property open and the loading bay door on the side of the building begin to rise.

"As Lee Corso is fond of saying 'not so fast, my friends,'" D'Andre sat up in his seat, quoted the host of ESPN's *College Football Gameday*. In the course of a single minute the nature of the ballgame changing dramatically.

"Son of a bitch," Tyler hissed, watched the limo and two Audi sedans pull inside the factory, the door closing. "The damn bastard's early!"

"So he's a punctual bastard." Connor grunted. "So much for our idea of waiting for the police."

"What do we do now?" D'Andre asked. "Fish or cut bait?"

"Fish. We don't have a choice," as he answered Tyler continued staring at the warehouse. Samantha a prisoner inside the building, Tyler tried eradicating the image festering in his mind of her alone and afraid, helpless and fearfully waiting her fate, crying out to him for rescue. Now the danger she faced reaching an extreme apex with the premature arrival of the man seeking to purchase her like a piece of meat, spirit her to a place faraway where Tyler unable to reach her, couldn't protect her. "We can't wait for the police any longer."

"Looks like we're the cavalry," D'Andre said evenly.

"Let's hope we don't end up reenacting the Battle of Little Big Horn," Connor pointed out, *with us in the role of Custer and the Seventh Calvary*. "They're going to outnumber us. I'd lay odds these punks are armed."

"Don't have a choice. Let's go." Fiji put an end to the discussion, opening the door, stepping out on the street. "We're wasting time."

"We still don't have an idea how we're doing this," Connor replied.

"We can improvise," Fiji answered as calm as ever, smiled at Tyler, "quarterbacks are good at improvising." Tyler offered him an uncertain glance, only wished he so confident facing the long odds of this situation.

"My social calendar is empty now," Connor made the lame joke, joining Fiji outside the SUV.

"Let's do this," D'Andre told Tyler. "Get our women out of there and kick some ass in the process, you dig?" His voice tinged with cocky bravado; same confidence exhibited charging through an opponent's defensive line for a big gain.

"My thoughts exactly." Tyler answered simply. They stepped from the Xterra, joining Fiji and Connor on the desolate side street, surrounded by empty buildings and factories. *There's no one else around to stop this. It's just us.*

Connor walked to the back of the Xterra, opened the hatch, reached inside the rear cargo hold. "Too bad you don't have a bullwhip, Doctor Jones," D'Andre tried lightening the grim mood.

"Don't need it," Connor removed the taped bundle of goalie sticks left in the Xterra earlier that evening. An effective weapon if needed. "Bullwhips are overrated."

Tyler removed a crow bar from the truck's emergency kit, the only other weapon available, gazed at the abandoned factory looming in the darkness like a monster in a horror movie lying in wait for its next victim. Somewhere inside the forbidding structure, endangered by an awful peril, was Samantha Grayson, Tyler remembered the promise made to her the previous Saturday evening. *I will never let anything happen to you. I will never let anyone hurt you.* "Let's go see if these punks want to dance."

Now the time had come for Tyler to keep that promise to Samantha. Or die trying.

Chapter 40

The Crown Victoria skidded to an abrupt stop before 2371 North Campbell Street, the address for Marcus Evans Photography. As Nathanial Hampton exited from the passenger side of the vehicle, Detective Dawson Hilliard turned to the rear of the car, behind the Plexiglas partition a golden retriever named Wrigley, owned by the missing Alexandra Cole, sat with a nonplussed expression as if riding in the back of a police car speeding through the streets of Chicago in the middle of the night an everyday occurrence.

"Make sure we don't get a ticket," Hilliard told the retriever, received a hearty bark in reply, stepping out to join Hampton. With guns drawn the pair moved to the front of the brownstone. Hilliard noticed the door already ajar, pushed it open and slipped into the reception area, saw light coming from the next room.

Whoever was there heard the sirens approaching and the detectives enter, a female voice calling out. "It's about time you got here!" The voice not the least bit happy. Hilliard and Hampton stepped into the room, guns held at waist level to use if needed, but Hilliard suspected the threat no longer present. A young, college-age woman with long dark hair sat on a chair in the middle of the room, a petite woman of the same age with fiery red hair and green eyes sitting on the floor next to her. Both dressed as if they had planned on going out somewhere, clothes now disheveled, hair tousled. Strands of rope strewn around them on the floor, signs of being cut away, resting next to lengths of bandages and crumpled up strips of duct tape. A third young woman, about the same height as the redhead but with strawberry blonde hair, wearing blue jeans and a t-shirt, stood above the pair. Showed no signs of the sort of distress the other two obviously suffered.

There was one other object in the room garnering the attention of the detectives, Hampton moving to examine closely the device. The cluster of four propane tanks connected with thick cables wound through the handles, a block of gray material with the consistency of children's clay taped to tanks with a timing device attached. *Now that's something you don't find every day...*

"The police are here, so I don't have to waste any more of my time explaining to you what's going on, goodbye," the dark-haired woman spoke into the phone with a sarcastic lilt. Hilliard moved closer, noted whitish residue of adhesive about her lips and jaw and red, raw rope marks about the slender wrist. That detail, added to the rope and tape scattered across the floor and their unkempt appearance, allowed Hilliard to guess what happened to two of the three young women: *someone left them bound and gagged with that bomb.*

This, Hilliard thought with a self-knowing smirk, *this going to be one hell of a story.*

The raven-haired woman took a deep breath. "Are you here to help us or arrest us, eh?" She demanded, anger swiftly rising to a boil. "Because your 911 operators think I'm involved in some sort of crazy sorority initiation stunt and don't consider this a matter of life or death. Which it happens to be! I'm ready to call the Royal Canadian Mounted Police, I'm from Canada, you see, and maybe they'll send some Mounties to help because I sure wasn't getting any from the people on the other end of this damn phone!" She snorted, waving her smartphone at Hilliard.

"Watch out," the tiny redhead warned Hilliard, emerald eyes apologetic, nodding at her frustrated friend. "She's about to go Canuck on you."

"God, what I wouldn't give for a Mountie right now!" the raven-haired woman snarled, amethyst eyes flashing angrily after an unfortunate interaction at the wrong time with the city's stand-in 911 dispatchers.

"Sorry, they're holding amateur night," Hilliard commented, matching the woman's sarcasm, then turned serious. "I'm Detective Dawson Hilliard. We're here to help you. Tell me what happened."

"Thank God," the young woman exhaled, realizing the detectives there to assist, not arrest, them. "Okay, I'm a college student so here's the Cliff Notes version. I'm Amanda McKinnon, this is Lauryn Callahan," she pointed to the petite redhead, "we go to Great Northern University and our friend Samantha Grayson is a reporter at *The Daily Northern*. Riley here," Amanda motioned at the petite strawberry blonde nervously glancing between Amanda and the two detectives, "went to see Samantha because she hadn't seen her roommate since yesterday, suspected something happened to her and campus security and Evanslawn police proved to be pretty much worthless, kind of like your 911 operators."

"I think Presley came here, I found a business card in our room," Riley said. "I think they have Presley." Hilliard wondered who 'they' were, but kept quiet, knew he'd learn soon enough.

"We were supposed to meet Samantha at the office and go into the city for dinner," Amanda spoke rapidly, understood every second counted if her friends to be saved, and that included her boyfriend Connor Aanonsen off to rescue Samantha and Ashleigh Morgan. "She wasn't there but Samantha sent Lauryn a text message earlier in the afternoon saying she'd be here. So we came here on our way to dinner and were greeted by a...welcoming committee, found out they were holding Samantha captive. They took her and our friend Ashleigh, left us tied up here with," Amanda pointed to the propane tanks with the block of plastic explosive, "that."

Now came time to ask. "Who's 'they?'" Hilliard wondered as Hampton crouched beside the bomb, studied it closely, heard him emit a low whistle under his breath. "Why did they take your friends, leave you here with that?" He jerked a thumb at the device.

"They're human traffickers," Amanda explained, a hand nervously running through the tangle of raven hair, revelation catching the detectives off guard, the last thing they, or anyone working the case, considered the motive behind the disappearances. "They're took Samantha to sell her to some Sheik Rahim. I think that's what they plan for Riley's roommate too. It sounds like they're holding more women than just them." Amanda closed her eyes, fighting to ignore the throbbing in her head. "They have other plans, bad plans, for our friend Ashleigh, taking her wherever they're going next. This guy tried convincing this Rahim to take us too but he declined, so they left us here with that...thing."

"He didn't want us to live to see tomorrow," Lauryn added helpfully.

Hampton studied the inert explosive device, grunted in grim amazement. "Whoever built this device was a professional, knew what they were doing. Who disarmed this?"

"Fiji did." Lauryn said, straightened up, a measure of pride in the soft voice.

Hampton raised an eyebrow, confused by the response. "The island of Fiji?"

"No, that isn't what she means." Hilliard familiar with Great Northern football, knew whom Lauryn spoke about. "Albert Fatuamala, he plays for Great Northern, Fiji is his nickname," the Samoan defensive end terrorizing opposing quarterbacks, made their Saturday afternoons miserable affairs. "That's who disarmed the device?" Hilliard asked incredulously.

"He did," Lauryn confirmed. "He knew it was the blue wire so he pulled the blue wire and nothing happened and we're still here." Then she noted dreamily, emerald eyes glowing. "That's why I love him."

Amanda nodded in agreement. "Our boyfriends got worried when they didn't hear from us, went to the newspaper office, that's where they ran into Riley."

"I would've been there sooner but I fell asleep in my room," Riley apologized, tears wetting her eyes. If she hadn't fallen asleep, gone to the office of *The Daily Northern* earlier the situation already resolved, Samantha and Presley safe. "I told them how Samantha was helping me find Presley, said she'd come down here and check..." Riley started crying, the strain from stressful events finally overwhelming her. Lauryn stood on shaky legs, gathered Riley in her arms to offer comfort.

"They got here and Fiji pulled the wire right before that thing would've gone off," Amanda concluded the story.

"Good thing he did." Hampton stood up. "If he'd pulled any other wire we wouldn't be having this pleasant conversation."

Amanda put her chin in her hand. "You don't think I'm not aware of that fact?"

"Crap, human traffickers, FBI always assumed it was a serial killer," Hilliard grunted at Hampton. If these suspects responsible for the other disappearances across the country they confronted a band of human traffickers with a high degree of sophistication. "Do you know where your friends were taken? Where they're holding the other women?"

Amanda smiled, licked cracked lips. "It's some warehouse or factory at 3100 West Carroll Avenue." She laughed self-consciously. "The bastard had to text this Rahim the address, saw it from where I was tied to this damn chair. Our guys are on the way there." Amanda thought of Connor, prayed fervently he didn't get hurt or worse doing something heroic to rescue Samantha and Ashleigh. *And that's exactly what he's going to do. If I had listened to Ashleigh, hadn't been so dammed stubborn none of this would be happening!* "They're supposed to hand over Samantha and Presley and the others at two."

"Let's go," Hilliard told Hampton, "the action has moved on from here."

"We're coming with you," Amanda announced, a semblance of tenuous strength returning to a tormented body, standing on legs still rubbery from the lengthy ordeal bound to the chair, ignoring pain with the searing intensity of a blowtorch flaring through her hips.

"Are you okay?" Lauryn moved to Amanda on wobbly legs, reaching out to steady her friend.

Amanda took a deep breath, felt light-headed, dizzy, realized how terribly dehydrated she was, could drink a bottle of Gatorade in a single gulp right then. "Honest answer, probably not," she accepted Lauryn's hand, took a tiny step forward, then another, quickly found her footing, hobbling on weakened legs as if she'd crossed the finish line of a marathon. "But I'm not hanging around here."

"I'd suggest you stay here and wait for an ambulance," Hilliard proposed, "looks like you," directing the comment at Amanda and Lauryn, "have had a hell of a night already. Might be better to go to the hospital and get checked out."

"Where we're going might not be the safest place for you," Hampton added.

"Oh no, you're not getting rid of us that easily," Amanda shook her head, replied adamantly. "You're going where our boyfriends are, and where they're holding our friends. So we're going with you whether you like it or not."

"I'm going too," Lauryn offered a united front, "and so is Riley." Riley nodded in agreement.

Hilliard glanced at Hampton; to argue only wasting time. "Okay, but you're sharing the back seat with someone."

"Fine, we can squeeze in and get acquainted." Amanda's face twisted in anguish as she staggered towards the door, appreciative of the assistance from Lauryn even if her movements just as unsteady, shambling along like wounded soldiers heading for a battlefield aid station. *I'd probably fall flat on my face without her help*, Amanda thought ruefully.

Hilliard pulled his smartphone from his bulletproof vest; hit the speed-dial for Devin Carson. His partner answered instantly, phone on speaker so he could drive. "We're about a minute out!" Carson shouted over the wailing siren.

"Head to 3100 West Carroll Avenue," Hilliard informed him as the party moved through the front reception area. "Get everything you can there now!"

To Carson his partner's estimation of the situation ominous. "What are we dealing with?"

"You won't believe this," Hilliard said, "human traffickers."

"What?" The revelation caught Carson by surprise.

"In two hours they're selling our missing women to what sounds like a big money man from the Middle East," Hilliard explained.

"Son of a bitch!" Carson cursed loudly, this possibility didn't register on his radar as a motive behind the abductions.

"These traffickers are heavy hitters, professionals," Hilliard said as they exited the brownstone, Amanda helped along by Lauryn and Riley but with each step her movements grew less hesitant and jerky. "They left two women at the studio with a bomb, didn't want them telling anyone what they knew. Fortunately for them someone got there in time to disarm the device."

Carson knew instantly who; *Tyler McManaway and his roommates*. "How did they do that?"

"Wouldn't believe me if I told you," Hilliard answered. "Might put the Bomb Squad out of business."

"Where are they now?" Carson suspected he already knew the answer.

"Headed to the West Carroll address," Hilliard crossed the street, his party in tow.

"Damn," Carson hissed, "I hope they don't get themselves killed trying something heroic." An outcome ruining Great Northern's fantastic start to the college football season.

"Then get over there and make sure it doesn't happen," Hilliard insisted. "We'll be right behind you."

"On our way." With that the call ended.

They reached the car, Hilliard opening the back door for the three young women as Hampton trotted to the other side and got in. "Like I said, hope you don't mind sharing the back seat."

The three women peered in, saw a four-legged form of golden fur already occupying the rear compartment, heard a friendly bark of greeting. "Well, then…" Amanda said, the last thing at this critical moment she expected to find sitting in the rear seat of a police car.

"Breaking in a new partner," Hilliard said matter-of-factly.

Hampton rolled his eyes. "You're an interesting one, bloke," But he found the dry humor a brief respite from the severe circumstances.

"You're a pretty boy!" Lauryn brightened as she slid inside, face glowing with happiness at the ecstatic smile of the golden retriever, rubbed the dog behind the ears, checked the tag on the collar. "Hi

Wrigley, that's a pretty name for a pretty boy!" The comment, and affectionate scratches on his neck, earned Lauryn a wet, sloppy kiss on the cheek from the grateful canine.

"We're helping him look for Mommy," Hilliard deadpanned as Riley slid in next to Lauryn.

"I'll assume Mommy's missing too," Amanda said, *and she's probably with Samantha and Ashleigh.* Sitting down she scowled in discomfort, the seat hard and unyielding. *This will do wonders for my legs,* she frowned, a new serving of pain added to a menu of already aching muscles.

Hilliard slid in the front seat, started the engine, hit the sirens. "Hold on, this is an E-ticket ride."

"Thanks for the warning," Amanda secured the seatbelt around her lap. Didn't care how fast or reckless the detective drove to where Connor and the others had gone to rescue Samantha and Ashleigh, as long as they got there in one piece.

"Is there an Ancient Samoan Secret for this?" Tyler McManaway whispered as they neared the locked gate along the fence surrounding the factory.

"Yeah, 'cause I don't think we're getting in that way." D'Andre Watson pointed to spirals of concertina on top of the fence, made entry by that route highly unlikely or extremely painful.

"Do this the old-fashioned way," Albert 'Fiji' Fatuamala grasped the heavy, industrial strength chain, a Masterlock joining the ends together. Fiji braced himself and with a low grunt, steely muscles of his arms flexing, he pulled on the chain until the lock snapped with the feeble resistance of a dry twig.

"You are strong like bull," Connor Aanonsen affected an Eastern European accent, complimenting Fiji as he grabbed the gate, swung it open, the quartet entering the compound, one step closer to the women held hostage, Samantha and Ashleigh among them, within the vacant building. They needed Fiji to be as wild and strong as a bull in the china shop dealing with the unknown number of enemies waiting inside. They ran towards the nearest door, beyond a white Lexus parked beside a black Ford van outside of the building.

What's that? Ashleigh Morgan, trapped inside the trunk of Marcus Cowle's white Lexus, heard running feet near where she laid a helpless captive, sounded like more than one person. Was it Cowle returning to check on her? Or was it someone, maybe the police, coming to save her from the utterly hopeless predicament bound, gagged and locked in a car trunk without hope of escape? If it was a rescuer, a final slim chance of deliverance, Ashleigh had to alert them to her plight, let them know of her imprisonment in the back of the vehicle.

Ashleigh closed her eyes, crying through the gag, lifted bound feet up towards the trunk lid, banging them against the metal interior. A desperate bid to gain the attention of those outside the confined space where she lay powerless and vulnerable.

"Hold it!" D'Andre hissed as they neared the white Lexus and the black van, raised his hand, stopped his friends. "Amanda said these fools taking Ashleigh with them once they were done with their business here, right?"

"That's what she said," Connor acknowledged.

"I place even money Ashleigh isn't even inside," D'Andre jerked a thumb to the Lexus and Ford van parked outside the building.

The four stood silent, listened, heard a muted banging from the trunk of the Lexus. "I think you're right on the money," Tyler smiled, the four moving swiftly to the luxury vehicle. Samantha inside with the other captives, but Amanda told them of Cowle's sick intention to use Ashleigh for 'entertainment,' Tyler didn't wish to ponder what that term meant, after the exchange.

D'Andre turned to Fiji, hopes rising on encouraging tides. *Hang on, Ash. Your man is coming to the rescue.* "Does this Ancient Samoan Secret of yours work on car trunks?"

"I think it does." Fiji stepped up to the Lexus, balled his fist, tapped lightly against the metal. The trunk popped open, Fiji lifting the lid, sliding aside to allow D'Andre the first to discover the contents inside.

Ashleigh heard sounds of hushed discussion near the Lexus, whimpering as she listened, praying for it to be someone there to help her and not Cowle or his hired thug checking on their prize. She heard a muted thump, interior of the compartment shaking with the impact. The lock clicked and the trunk lid opened slightly, saw fingers grasp underneath, lifting it up. Ashleigh held her breath, waiting forever for seconds to pass and her fate determined.

That eternity passed and she exhaled, even in the darkness able to make out the familiar faces looking down at her, tears pouring from her dark eyes the moment she saw D'Andre Watson in the moonlight, expression at her condition both shocked and relieved. *I'm safe,* her desperate prayers answered, *I'm not going to end up like those girls in Atlanta. I'm not going to disappear. I'm not going to die. My man is here to save the day.*

"I've got you, babe, I've got you," D'Andre comforted Ashleigh, easing her from the floor of the trunk, cradling the bound, trembling body in his arms as if afraid to drop a fragile parcel entrusted him. "It's all over, Ashleigh. No one will ever hurt my lady." Those who hurt his Ashleigh, placed her in this terrible position, yet to pay the price for their brutality and D'Andre expected to collect full payment. Connor pulled out his Swiss Army knife, flipped out the knife blade, hastily slicing at the ropes binding Ashleigh's wrists and upper body.

"You okay?" Tyler asked, Ashleigh nodded, body continued to quake from the cold and fear, tears streaming down her cheeks from wide brown eyes as D'Andre unwound the bandage around her head until he reached the strips of duct tape underneath.

"Sorry babe, this going to hurt," D'Andre cautioned as Ashleigh moaned, replying with sad eyes. *I know it is,* willing to exchange fleeting pain for freedom of speech, *just get it off me.* D'Andre lifted a corner of the tape, peeled it from her mocha skin, Ashleigh squealed as adhesive grudgingly released its grip. Once D'Andre removed the tape, at the same time Connor finished cutting away the ropes around her chest, Ashleigh spat out the thick cloth wadding, jaw sore from hours suffering the offending stuffing jammed in her mouth, coughing and gasping for air, arms thrown around D'Andre's shoulders, face buried into his solid chest, crying as a torrential flood of distraught emotions released.

"I thought nobody was going to find me," Ashleigh whispered in D'Andre's ear. "I was so afraid I'd never see you again."

"I'm here, babe. You're seeing me, you're holding me." D'Andre rubbed her shoulders, kissed her forehead. "You're safe now."

Ashleigh raised her head, a sudden panic clouding the dark eyes. "Amanda and Lauryn?" She feared the worst.

"We got there in time, they're okay," Tyler explained as a wave of relief swept over Ashleigh. *The proverbial nick of time*, he reflected.

"Thank God," Ashleigh sighed under her breath. The argument with Amanda outside the studio, when her friend ignored warnings of danger, now forgotten. Wanted to hug still absent friends, tell them how much she cared for them.

"Took care of that little gift with help from Big Guy here." D'Andre jerked a thumb at Fiji.

"You okay?" Fiji asked.

"I'm all right…scared…but I'm okay." Ashleigh answered as Connor cut the bonds from her legs and ankles, D'Andre lifted her from the trunk where she spent the long night captive, cradling her in his arms. Then her tone turned frantic, thought of one more friend in unspeakable danger, in desperate need of immediate rescue or her life forfeit. "You have to get Samantha! They're going to sell her! If they do we'll never see her again!"

"That's the next item on our agenda for this evening," Tyler said, "no one is selling my Samantha." *No one is going to hurt Samantha*. Handed D'Andre the keys to his Xterra. "Take Ashleigh to the truck," then said to Ashleigh, "lock the doors once you're inside, don't open them for anyone unless they're wearing a Chicago Police uniform or flashing a badge, got it?"

"If I don't see a badge I'm not getting out," Ashleigh replied.

"Make sure she's safe, then get your ass back here as quick as you can," Tyler told D'Andre. "We're going to need you."

"I'll be back like The Flash." D'Andre's eyes filled with steely resolve. "Don't worry, Touchdown, I got issues to settle with the punks who did this to Ashleigh." Issues best decided through the use of flying fists. D'Andre hurried off into the night with Ashleigh in his arms.

Tyler watched them disappear into the darkness. *Three saved, one left to save*, he thought, *the most important life of all*. Had to rescue Samantha Grayson from the slavers holding her hostage, about to sell her into a life of endless captivity or his efforts this horrendous night proving for naught, failing in his promise to Samantha two nights earlier.

I won't let anyone hurt you. He turned to Connor and Fiji. "Let's go get Samantha."

"'Once more unto the breach, good friends,'" Connor recited an appropriate quote.

"I'm right with you, Brother," Fiji told him. The three moved to the closest door at the rear of the factory. Tyler turned the knob, found it locked.

Tyler stepped aside, motioning to Fiji. "I'll let you do the honors."

Fiji stepped to the door, balled his fist, picked a spot a few inches above the handle, struck the door solidly as Tyler and Connor stood witness with bemused wonderment.

"Like I told you, Ancient Samoan Secret." He jerked the door open and they were inside.

Chapter 41

The stinging pain in her legs as she knelt on the concrete floor, with all her weight borne on her knees, proved unbearable for Samantha Grayson. Yet she didn't dare relax, remained rigid and unmoving as a statue of marble as ordered by her captors. One of the other women, a statuesque brunette kneeling second in the line, sunk back slightly on her legs, roughly hauled back up on her knees by Lang, the shorter and thinner, but no less imposing, of Cowle's two thugs.

"On your knees," Lang sneered at woman, the brunette whimpering, cringing at the brutal treatment. "You have to learn to do as you're told. Might remain alive a little longer where you're going. Life as you know it is about to change," Cowle checked his smartphone. "They're here," he announced to his associates and six unwilling captives. Sterner pressed a button on the remote in his hand, the overhead door to the loading bay rumbled, moved upward, a pair of headlights beaming brightly into the space, Samantha blinked, squinting as the light shined directly into her eyes.

A black Audi sedan entered first, followed by a black limousine, a second black Audi sedan in the wake of the limousine. The limo came to a stop ten yards from where Samantha and her helpless companions knelt in stupefied terror, the one who sought their purchase inside the vehicle, revealing soon his identity. The lead Audi parking ahead of the limo, the second Audi pulling up alongside the luxury vehicle, the doors to each sedan opened and from each four men in dark suits exited, the security detail for their employer. A sick sensation of familiarity swept over Samantha as seven of the eight took positions around Cowle and the hostages, had seen them before and quite recently. *No, it can't be!* A security guard stepped to the limo as another two exited from the driver's compartment, took positions with the other seven, expressions on the tanned faces stern and emotionless. One security guard, thickly built and bald, opened the door to the rear compartment of the limo and out stepped two more men, additional security for their new master. Samantha surmised Cowle's client held some position of importance given the layers of protection surrounding him.

The bald, bullheaded security man, obviously the leader, motioned to four of the guards, no words spoken, only made a sweeping gesture with his arm and the men broke off in different directions throughout the loading bay, methodically and meticulously checking the premises, peering behind and around the machinery and debris shoved up along the walls and edges of the vast space, examining every corner and nook, Samantha noticed Cowle impatiently tapping his foot on the floor as they carried out the inspection. For twelve insufferably long minutes the survey lasted before the men returned, nodded satisfaction to their superior.

The bald security man stepped to the rear of the limo, leaned down, nodded to a figure within. A man exited the limo, stood up, adjusted the perfectly tailored jacket of his suit.

Oh my God! Samantha froze, stunned at the identity of the buyer, recognized the face, the dark eyes locked on her and the other hostages. *He was at Senator Fielding's speech this morning!* Recalled the man in conversation with the Cockrell brothers at the event to Samantha now seemed to have occurred on another planet. *He was looking at me!* Remembered how uncomfortable she felt under his intent gaze. *Is this why he wants to possess me? That he found me attractive?* Was this sick desire to possess her the reason Amanda and Lauryn now dead, Ashleigh doomed to a similar fate?

"Sheik Rahim, it is good to see you again," Cowle cordially welcomed his guest, stepping forward with hand extended as the remainder of Rahim's security detail arrayed themselves around Cowle and his associates and the defenseless women awaiting sale to this cruel and brutal master. Samantha saw Presley's eyes dart about nervously at the men surrounding them, a hitching sob of resignation escaping her chancing a look at Samantha. *We're not getting out of this.* For the first time Samantha, as brown eyes scanned about at the security men of Sheik Rahim and Cowle's hired associates, constructing an impenetrable wall around them, realized Presley might be right, dreams of somehow escaping this predicament nothing but wishful fantasies unrealized.

"Marcus, my friend, a pleasure to see you," Sheik Rahim accepted Cowle's hand, shook it warmly, turned his attention to the row of bound, subdued young women kneeling motionless, the grin on his face reminding Samantha of a lion ready to devour his fallen prey. The eyes betrayed erotic pleasure at what he perused, Samantha realizing how vulnerable she felt under the penetrating gaze. "I see you have done quite well this time."

"Thank you for the gracious compliment. I do my best to provide you with the finest product," Cowle smiled in agreement, then his face grew serious. "However, there are serious issues we must discuss regarding how we proceed with our future consignments."

Rahim cocked his head, hadn't expected discussion of the topic so soon. "How so?"

"The delay between the acquisition of this merchandise," he motioned to the six women, "and delivery has given the police an opportunity to gain an understanding of my operation." He paused. "They will collect intelligence on my methods, no doubt disseminate those details to other entities. Might make setting up operations in a new city after this problematic."

"So what is it you suggest?" Rahim crossed his arms, Samantha sensed the man perturbed discussing the matter; wanted to take possession of his slaves, depart for a place far from Chicago where they'd be horribly abused in methods Samantha didn't wish to conceive, eventually murdered when he tired of them. "You must understand I don't wish to revert to the previous form of procurement, having the product secured on an individual basis," Samantha sickened at the reference of the living as nothing but goods to be sold and bartered, disposed as trash once used up. "I have grown, as you say, quite accustomed to the deliveries in bulk."

"I don't intend to skimp on the size of the consignments," Cowle replied, the men deep in conversation while their hired men took silent measure of each other. "I no longer think it advisable to be rooted in one city for an extended period of time. I think this method has outlived its usefulness."

"What are you proposing?" Rahim asked, his interest piqued.

"Mobility, operating over a greater geographical area, quick strikes after selecting desired merchandise," Cowle offered his plan in general terms, details hashed out at a later date. "An area such as Texas, fertile territory with many large metropolitan areas. In close proximity to a safe haven provided by another of my clients."

"Ah, Commander Omega," Rahim smiled, knew of the ruthless drug lord. "So you need an additional outlay of funding to oversee this new method of procurement?"

Samantha slightly shifted her legs, attempting to ease the pain burning in her knees from kneeling on the cement, as the two continued their dialogue. "I'd appreciate an additional infusion of capital to fund this venture." Cowle smiled. "May have to hire on additional associates. We will need to compensate Commander Omega for his hospitality and support."

Rahim closed his eyes, his right hand rubbing his chin. "I will consider this for the next consignment." A time when Samantha and the other unfortunate captives long dead and buried. Rahim turned his attention to the row of women, waiting their fate in fear, terrified by the hungry stare. "I see you've gone through the trouble to offer a proper presentation of the merchandise."

The pleasant smile returned to Cowle's face, reminded Samantha of a snake-oil salesman hoodwinking the gullible townsfolk of their hard-earned money with a cure-all potion. "Of course, since you were coming to take personal possession of this consignment," in the past Rahim's trusted right-hand assistant Saleh served as go-between, Cowle handing over the captives to him for transport to Daharan. Those instances he hadn't cared about the appearance of his victims or what they wore, if anything at all. "I wished to ensure the items met your approval." Cowle motioned with his hand. "Shall I make the acquaintance of your six fair maidens, Your Excellency? Forgive them if they do seem a bit...distressed at the present time."

As they should be. Rahim nodded. "I'd be most pleased." Introductions a mere formality, Rahim understood Cowle playing to his ego. After this night the women no longer having any identities, their names forgotten, only objects for his to use and abuse, their brief time left alive on this Earth satisfying his violent desires. *Like all those before them*, he thought, eyed his strictly restrained prizes as a starving man does a sumptuous feast laid before him on a banquet table.

Cowle and Rahim walked to the women kneeling before them, observing in wary fear the man there to procure their lives, soon to hold over them the capricious power of life and death. Cowle stood in front of the first woman in line. "This is Emma Hayden," Cowle informed his benefactor, "she wanted to be an actress." The turquoise eyes of the petite mahogany-haired girl, wearing a denim miniskirt and black knee-high boots, leather jacket over a tight-fitting white top, flared with burning hatred for Sheik Rahim. Cowle sighed witnessing her reaction. "Unfortunately, she has a stubborn streak, somewhat feisty." Cowle smirked at Emma, then said to Rahim. "I'm sure you have ways of dealing with such intractability?"

"There are ways," Rahim stared at Emma, cringed as dark eyes pierced through her, caused the tenacious façade to crumble like a sand castle deluged with waves from the ocean, "to break the spirit of one so obstinate." Rahim shook his head, thought silently as he studied Emma. *You will not last long, little one. You will be the first to die.*

They moved to the next hostage, the tallest of the captives, dressed in a gunmetal gray pinstripe pantsuit and simple white blouse. She whimpered into the cloth gag between her teeth as Rahim examined her with the trained eye of one bidding on a prized show horse up for auction. "This is Alexandra Cole," Cowle made the introduction, her body trembling as Rahim ran his fingers through long brunette hair with reddish-brown highlights, nodding his approval. Her brown eyes showed no sign of resistance, only surrender to the inevitable. "She hoped to start a new career," Alexandra whined at the comment, recalled the trust she mistakenly placed in him, for the error paying with her life. "I don't think she expected this sort of change in occupation."

"It appears she did not." Rahim tilted his head, pleased with the offering, Cowle a fine judge of beauty, knew well the type of victims quenching his bloodlust. Rahim knew this captive believed, as did so many American women, in her independence and the ability to do anything, be anything, say anything. In his domain far from America their place far different, rights enjoyed in this decadent land nonexistent, little more than property and Rahim soon taking untold pleasure in shattering the illusion of freedom for this young woman.

The pair moved to the third captive in line. "This is Isabella DiBenedetto, I did a photo session with her before our final session," Cowle noted of the young woman with flawless olive-skin, attired in a long-sleeved floral print minidress, the plunging neckline allowing full view of ample cleavage, black platform pumps on her feet. Isabella kept her head bowed, crying softly, tortured with thoughts of a family she'd never see again. Cowle motioned to Sterner, who stepped behind Isabella, grabbed a handful of raven hair, yanking her head back. Isabella screamed, mouth-filling gag barely preventing the sound from echoing through the loading bay, forcing the dark eyes to look directly at her soon to be master.

Again Rahim indicated his satisfaction with the slightest of nods. "At least she already knows her place," he commented impassively. *She's compliant, might live a little longer than the others.*

They moved to the fourth hostage. The girl with honey-blonde hair and hazel-green eyes shivered under Rahim's cold, unfeeling gaze. "This is Gabriella Taylor," Cowle smoothly made the introduction, a master of ceremonies at a social function, hostages the debutantes entering high society. Gabriella dressed in a sleeveless, tight-fitting baby blue dress; a subtle and comely shade Cowle thought becoming, wearing black platform sandals. "She and Isabella are roommates," at the statement Samantha heard Isabella cry in despair, flush with guilt she responsible for her friend's fate. "She recommended Gabriella do some modeling for me, never knew what I intended for them." Cowle chuckled; thrilled with the scent of shared terror as they stared fearfully at each other, doomed to die together. "Friends until the end."

Rahim smiled. "Yes, they'll be together until the end." The simple statement chilled Samantha, understood what he meant. *You sick bastard.*

The two stepped up to Presley, whimpering softly, every muscle in her body trembling against the ropes holding her motionless. "This is Presley Harding," Cowle waved at her. "She was supposed to be that 'special' one for you. The innocent, naïve waif who never expected something like this to happen to her."

Rahim studied Presley's quaking body, tearful brown eyes pleading for mercy, seemed pleased with this sacrificial offering from Marcus Cowle, reveling in her cowering terror. He imperceptibly licked his lips, the action disgusting Samantha. *God, he's turned on by this!* Could smell his arousal at their fear, the helplessness of their situation. This wasn't some fictional dilettante millionaire playboy dabbling in erotic adventures with willing participants. Before the line of kneeling, helpless captives stood a cunning sexual sadist and cold-blooded predator, ordering the abduction of Samantha and the other women to satisfy deviant pleasures, inflict on them violence most unspeakable.

His eyes caught sight of the silver crucifix hanging around Presley's neck, reached for the religious icon, jerk it from her throat. Presley squealed, edged away from his grasp, wanting to keep from him the holy relic, a gift from a beloved and departed grandmother, a final fragile remnant of a former, carefree life now slipping away with the relentless flow of sand through an hourglass. At her action Rahim's eyes flashed with anger as this sign of resistance, however meek, couldn't be tolerated, lifting his hand back, preparing to strike the defenseless young girl cringing in terror before him.

Samantha finally had enough of the arrogance of Sheik Rahim and Marcus Cowle. *Get away from her! Don't touch her!* Samantha screamed through her gag, gained the attention of Sheik Rahim, diverting his violent focus away from a vulnerable Presley. Rahim halted his hand in mid-air, never delivering the intended blow on the hapless girl, turning to face Samantha glaring at him, breath snorting hotly through her nostrils.

Samantha growled once more, sworn to protect Presley from harm, time now as good as any to start regardless of the consequences. *Get away from her!*

"You already made the acquaintance of Samantha Grayson earlier today," Cowle noted coolly as Rahim moved to her, loomed threateningly. "You took quite an interest to her."

Samantha didn't break her gaze from Sheik Rahim, courageously stiffening her body ramrod straight, ignoring pain shooting through her limbs. *You're the bastard who condemned Amanda and Lauryn to death. I hate you. I'm not afraid of you.* But her soul quivered with dread, very much afraid of this man and what he might do to her. Something in the way Rahim stared at her, ravenous glances directed at the other women more of a buyer pleased with items offered for sale, revealed a deep, unsettling hatred towards Samantha as he casually studied her helpless form. He smiled at Samantha, but she sensed a dark, sinister evil hidden behind the seemingly pleasant expression.

"I do have an interest." Samantha shuddered as a cold fear bloomed inside her, shivered as it swept through her. The back of his hand caressed her cheek. "You, my pretty Samantha, have made my trip worthwhile," he said in a low voice, reaching up to stroke silky strands of auburn hair. "I never thought I'd find a woman who so resembled one from my past, someone who caused me great discomfort," Samantha grunted, puzzled by the statement. *What is he talking about?* "That is until I saw you this morning, Samantha. If you hadn't so fortuitously fallen into Marcus Cowle's hands I'd have directed him to return at a later date to acquire you for me."

Suddenly Samantha understood the dire meaning of his words, a fear bubbling beneath the surface exploding with the force of a geyser, threatened to overcome her fragile bravery. *I remind him of someone, a woman who wronged him.* Samantha assumed whoever this woman she the first sacrifice to a mad, misguided thirst for violence. *Because of what this woman did to him, he wants to do bad things to me, to all of us.* "You shall be my Scheherazade. You will far outlive your companions here, they will be dead long before I decide it is time to end your pathetic misery," the cruel statement incited a chorus of agonized cries from the other prisoners, "and each day you live will be filled with endless pain and suffering." Rahim put his hand under Samantha's chin, lifted her head, stared into her brown eyes, revealing with frigid impassivity a fate she already suspected. "I will find the utmost joy in breaking you."

I will not go quietly into this night! I will not be a lamb led to the slaughter! Samantha jerked her head away from his touch, growling past the cloth between her lips, wadding forced into her mouth. *Go to hell, bastard!*

Rahim stepped back, gestured with a casual motion of his wrist at two of his security detail, then to Samantha and Presley. With the silent command the burly pair jumped forward, rushed the helpless pair, stout arms encircling defenseless targets, lifted roughly from their kneeling position and dragging them, struggling and fighting, towards the waiting limousine. Samantha grunted indignantly at the treatment as Presley, despite the gag meant to silence her, emitted a shrill cry at the top of her lungs as first she, then Samantha, pushed into the passenger compartment of the limo. The remaining captives knelt in petrified horror, knowing they'd soon join the pair to begin a journey to a horrible destination and a terribly bleak end.

Cowle cleared his throat, caught Rahim's attention after Samantha and Presley shoved inside the limousine. "I typically don't allow the merchandise to be handled until payment for product delivered and services rendered has been secured."

Rahim adjusted his jacket, fixed the cuffs, regained his composure. "Of course, please forgive me," he apologized, brief rage subsiding, nodding politely. "I meant you no disrespect. In the heat of the moment I acted out of hast." He motioned to Saleh, his trusted assistant. Saleh spun on his heel, walked to the Audi parked in front of the limo, from the trunk removed a briefcase, brought the attaché case to a table beside Cowle. Saleh placed the briefcase on the table, opened the case and removed a laptop computer, set it on the surface and powered up the device.

"I'm sure this transfer of funds into your accounts won't take long," Rahim smiled, satisfied with the bounty Cowle provided him, the singular prize of Samantha Grayson more than worth what he'd pay for the entire shipment. Hoped the transaction processed swiftly, through the wonder of wireless technology and satellite uplinks, to take ownership of the remainder of his order, load them into the limo with Samantha and Presley, depart for the private hanger at O'Hare International Airport and the Gulfstream jet whisking him and his newly purchased chattel back to his homeland.

The empty factory proved a maze of cluttered spaces and darkened corridors for Tyler McManaway, Connor Aanonsen and Albert 'Fiji' Fatuamala to navigate, strewn with rusted-out remains of machinery and piles of debris left by whatever company last occupied the building, noticing plastic barrels with labels warning of dangerous contents flammable and corrosive. They honed in on the sound of voices from the front of the complex as a beacon towards their goal, a combination of male voices and muffled cries of women one of them Tyler could tell, with sinking heart, was Samantha Grayson. *They're hurting her*, he raged, deep shame of failure forming in his stomach. *I'm not there to protect her!* Tyler carried the crowbar from the emergency kit of the Xterra, expecting long odds, exactly how long he didn't yet know. Connor had his goalie sticks; Tyler knew the sporting equipment, the only other weapon available, could inflict serious damage in a close-contact, face-to-face fight. *If we can get close*, Tyler thought sourly. Had to surprise their adversaries, of which they didn't have an accurate count, get the drop on them to even the odds and have an underdog's chance of saving Samantha, Presley and the other women Marcus Cowle about to hand over to Sheik Rahim. *How are we going to do that?*

The voices grew louder as the three approached their destination, Tyler fought down waves of bile surging through his gut, wanting to see Samantha to know she was alive, but at the same moment dreading the sight of his love in the condition they found Amanda, Lauryn and Ashleigh: bound, gagged, helpless, in desperate need of rescue. One Samantha uncertain might arrive in time.

The trio entered the rear of a large loading bay, voices originating from here. Only the front of the bay illuminated, darkness cloaking the remainder of the immense, cathedral-like space, thankful for the discarded machinery and containers lining the walls providing concealment for their movements. As Fiji slipped behind one piece of machinery, Tyler and Connor eased behind another, peered around the apparatus hiding them from sight of those at the front of the bay. Tyler took measure of a situation as seemingly hopeless as facing a fourth-and-twenty-five from deep in their own territory and down by five with seconds remaining on the clock, only a touchdown winning the game.

The black limousine and two black Audi S8 sedans they saw drive up to the abandoned factory sat parked in the bay, occupants standing outside the vehicles. Tyler noted the men had Arabic features, dressed in identical black suits, eyes hard and alert, exuded the stern and severe manner of highly-trained security operatives. Stood arrayed in a semi-circle shielding a man in his mid to late forties with dark-hair and ruggedly handsome face, attired in an impeccably tailored suit, an air of subtle arrogant authority to the countenance. *Has to be Sheik Rahim*, Tyler assumed, blood boiling at the sight of the man who meant to take Samantha from him, noting the thin, wiry-built, blond-haired man standing beside him, gesturing with his hands, *and that has to be Marcus Cowle*. Tyler felt his left fist clench, fingernails dig into his palm, wished then to strangle both men with his bare hands. *If I could even get close to them.*

He caught a glimpse of six female figures kneeling on the floor before the pair, the captives Cowle offered for sale to Rahim, trembling in the imposing presence of the men and Rahim's retinue of guards. Tyler spotted two additional men standing directly behind the six prisoners, dressed in dark military fatigue-style clothing. One as large and broad in stature as Fiji, the second a black man compact with a solid, sinewy build, demeanor forbidding and hostile, capable of vicious acts. Had to be Cowle's hired thugs, likely one or both assisting Cowle in subduing Amanda, Lauryn and Ashleigh back at the studio.

Tyler remained as calm as possible, eyes trailing down the line of vulnerable captives kneeling in the middle of the bay, surrounded by evil men with equally insidious intentions, awaiting a terrible fate they desperately feared. Tyler scowled, Cowle the trafficker taking great lengths to insure his unwilling wares presentable for the man ready to purchase their lives. His stomach rumbled with unease at the sinister implication these young women nothing more than items for sale to Cowle and Rahim. Then Tyler saw her, at the end of the row of hapless hostages, heart crying out in agony at the heart-rending sight.

Samantha.

Tyler thought he was prepared for the moment he'd find her, nerves steeled in expectation. But the sight of Samantha so defenseless reignited a silent rage, delivering a heart-wrenching blow of guilt to a tortured ego, stark reminder of the failure to keep his promise. *I wasn't there to protect her.* Like the other women sharing her predicament Samantha knelt before her captors, securely bound and gagged with a thick white strip of cloth wedged between her lips. Unlike the other hostages, forced by their captors to make themselves attractive for their new master, the stylish outfit Samantha wore for the speech by Senator Fielding that morning disheveled, in disarray, white silk blouse torn to expose the black floral print satin bra underneath, auburn hair a tousled tangle about her head. Tyler knew Samantha hadn't submitted to Marcus Cowle without a struggle, put up a tremendous fight for freedom as her father taught her, yet in the end overpowered by an enemy far more cunning. Despite her dismal circumstance Tyler could see a glimmer of defiance in the brown eyes, but in those eyes he also saw Samantha scared and alone, hiding raw fear gnawing beneath the surface. Samantha totally helpless and Tyler, crouched behind a piece of machinery only yards from her, felt as helpless as the woman he loved enmeshed in the rope imprisoning her, minutes removed from being sold to a dangerous man who intended nothing for her but harm and eventual death.

Cowle and Rahim walked up to the row of waiting captives, Tyler tormented by pitiful moaning and whimpering from muffled mouths, the distressing sound of those realizing lives soon forfeit. Cowle went down the line, stopping before each bound and gagged hostage, gesturing, offering a remark about each to their new owner, displaying the arrogance of a big game hunter exhibiting mounted trophy heads of his conquests to an appreciative admirer. But these trophies Cowle proudly flaunted lived and breathed, dreamed of the future, brutally snatched from their daily existence and those who loved them to wait alone, defenseless and fearing for their lives, surrounded by cruel, heartless men in the middle of a dark, abandoned factory.

We're their only hope. Tyler realized the burden resting on his shoulders, more than any lofty expectations from rabid fans to lead their team to the spoils of victory. He remembered words from his father about the weight of responsibility. *It's not always about you. Sometimes it has to be about others.* At this moment Tyler and his companions the final, fleeting hope not only for Samantha, but for all the women kneeling helpless in the midst of uncompromising malevolence. *We can't fail.* Then he reached a sobering conclusion. *If we fail, they will die. Samantha will die. We will die.*

Connor counted the number of men surrounding the hostages, eyes betraying his shock. He flashed fingers at Tyler and Fiji-five, five, five and one-then pointed at his friends and flashed three fingers, then Connor held up five fingers followed by one solitary finger. Tyler understood what Connor attempting to address. *There are sixteen of them and three of us, that's five to one odds against.* Connor shook his head despondently, wondered how long he had left to live, if he'd ever see Amanda McKinnon again. *I don't like those odds.*

Fiji jerked a thumb towards the outside of the factory, expression nonplussed. *D'Andre should be on his way.*

That makes it four to one. Connor rolled his eyes. *Talk about short-handed situations.*

Cowle moved down the line, reached the girl next to Samantha, a petite young woman with long caramel hair, an angelic face pretty if not clouded by terror. Tyler assumed this was Presley Harding, Riley Bradford's roommate. She cowered underneath Rahim's penetrating gaze. Rahim reached for something around Presley's neck and the girl shrank from him, whining in terror. The reaction not sitting well with the man, raising his hand to strike, inflict punishment for this show of insolence. A muffled, yet ferociously angry, cry stopped him, attention shifted from the shivering Presley to, even in her helpless state, a brave and resolute Samantha.

Oh God, no! Tyler forced himself to remain still, not burst out from his hiding place, as Rahim stepped up Samantha, glared at her. Even from where Tyler crouched he spied a coldly murderous cast in his gaze, wished to hurt Samantha, end her life right there in the middle of the loading bay. The cruel expression of suppressed violence and restrained brutality scared the daylights out of Tyler McManaway, one typically fearless in the face of adversity, able to stand his ground and take the hit. Tyler knew he needed to act, and soon, to spare Samantha from the man's vicious rage.

Rahim made a sudden motion, two of his guards snapped into action at the wordless call, striding over to Samantha and Presley, grabbing them with strong hands, hauling the struggling pair to the waiting limousine. Samantha screamed in protest, bound legs kicking out, black high heel pumps falling from her feet, clattering on the concrete floor. Presley squirmed against the hold of the guard, pushed first into the rear of the limo, quickly followed by Samantha brutally shoved inside and disappearing from view.

I have to do something! Tyler panicked at the sight of Samantha thrust into the limo, came within a second of losing control, started to rise from his hiding place, move into the open to rescue the woman he loved from captors who meant her harm. Felt the large, steadying hand on his shoulder stopping him, swung about to the calm face of Albert Fatuamala, saw him shake his head.

No, my Brother, not yet, dark, tranquil eyes told him. Tyler realized then he came close to violating the cardinal rule about using the element of surprise to their advantage, surprise didn't work if you let your opponents know you were there. Tyler eased back behind his hiding place, wondered if they could do anything to save Samantha and the other captives from their predicament.

Cowle spoke to Rahim; his words calming the man. Rahim motioned to one of his people, a thickly built, bald man who strode to one of the Audi sedans, retrieved an attaché case from the trunk, setting it down on a table next to Cowle, removing a laptop from the bag. Tyler understood what was happening and he grimaced angrily; *Rahim has to pay before he can play with his new toys.* The transaction buying them a few minutes to think of some way to keep Samantha, and those young women, from becoming the property of Sheik Rahim.

Tyler turned to Fiji. *What do we do?*

Fiji scratched his chin, studied the surroundings, an idea quickly formulating in his mind. *Use the element of surprise to neutralize their numbers.* He nodded at Tyler. *I have a plan.*

I'm the quarterback; Tyler gave him a quizzical look. *Shouldn't I be calling the play?*

Not this time, Fiji shook his head, smiled with the mystical serenity of the Cheshire Cat. *Trust me.*

Connor rolled his eyes again. *What the hell, you only live once.*

Fiji leaned forward; pointing to a dumpster a few feet ahead of them, on the edge of the clutter of machinery crowding the rear of the loading bay, presented a clear shot at Rahim's retinue of guards. *I'm going to get behind there.*

This time Tyler nodded, knew the force Fiji able to generate through his massive legs and powerful arms transforming the metal dumpster into a barreling cannonball. *What about us?* He pointed to Connor.

Fiji reached down, from the floor picked up two heavy bolts lying next to them, noticed the objects as he hid behind the machinery, handed them to his friend. Tyler tested the heft of the bolts, heavy, but not too heavy, could throw them, and far, if needed, trying to fathom the plan Fiji conceived out of thin air. *What do I do with these?*

Pointing at Connor and Tyler, Fiji moved his finger along the outer wall of the loading bay to a spot along the adjoining wall where additional equipment rested unused, concealing their presence. He noted a spot placing Tyler and Connor at a ninety-degree angle from where Fiji would be positioned. *I want you over there.*

Tyler exhaled. *What do we do when we get there?*

Motioning to the bolts Tyler held, Fiji made a throwing motion, pointed to opposite corners on the far side of the loading bay, past where the limousine and black sedans parked. *Throw them there and there in quick succession, that will distract their attention.*

Tyler closed his eyes, visualized the action, thought of what Fiji wanted in football terms. *Play action fake, get them focused on the misdirection.* Flying by the seat of their pants with the strategy, Tyler wondered if they had a gambler's longshot chance of pulling it off. *Got it. What then?*

Fiji motioned at the dumpster he'd be hiding behind, mimicked a shoving movement with his hands. *Once they're distracted*, a pantomime of the guards looking where Fiji wanted Tyler to toss the bolts, *I'm going to push that*, the dumpster, *at them*. Fiji made a motion, spreading his hands out. *I'll knock a few over like bowling pins.*

Even the odds, get them off balance; hit them from where they aren't looking. Tyler smiled, understood the crux of the plan. *This might work.* He glanced at Connor. *Or we might get killed doing it.* Tyler nodded, didn't have any other option, no hole card to play. *Love it when a plan comes together.*

Conner pointed at Tyler. *What do we do?*

As soon as I start moving, you attack from that side. Fiji swept his hand from where he wanted them hidden out to the middle of the bay where the remaining hostages knelt, fist striking an open palm, the message clear. *Hit them from two sides at once.* Fiji touched the goalie sticks Connor cradled in his arms, the crowbar Tyler clutched. *Put those to good use. Hit them hard.*

Connor grinned wickedly. *I'll rack up the penalty minutes.* He peered over his shoulder. *Hope D'Andre gets back soon. Going to miss the fun.*

He'll be back to help. Fiji checked his watch, held up one finger. *You've got a minute to get over there.*

Tyler gave his friend a thumbs-up. *Good luck.*

Connor patted Fiji on the shoulder, then glanced at Tyler. *We're going to need it.*

Fiji gave an imperceptible nod of his head. *Get going.* With the final gesture, Tyler and Connor slipped away through the maze of discarded machinery, moving silently in the darkness to where Fiji wanted them. With a deep breath, Fiji eased out from behind his hiding place, with catlike grace unusual for one so imposing quickly covering the few feet up to the dumpster, none of the hired muscle crowded around Marcus Cowle, Sheik Rahim and the four remaining captives without hope of salvation aware of his presence.

Fiji crouched behind the dumpster, placed his hands on the cool metallic surface, waiting for the sound to signal the start of their desperate onslaught. If their impromptu plan succeeded, six young women to survive this harrowing ordeal of kidnapping and possible slavery to continue with their lives. If they failed, they would all be dead.

Samantha Grayson growled with furious indignation, forced into the rear compartment of the limousine, shoved on the seat beside a terrified Presley Harding. She snarled angrily at the security man who dragged her, resisting the entire way, across the floor of the bay and tossing her into the vehicle like a limp rag doll. The minion's face void of emotion, cast out of stone, more of an automaton than a human being, mindlessly doing the bidding of his master. Samantha glanced down, realized her high heel pumps slipping off in the struggle, feet sheathed in black microfiber tights. *That's the least of my worries now.* Samantha thought frantically, gears in her mind clicking, grinding despite the overwhelming fear and exhaustion, searching for a way to escape what now seemed inevitable. *There has to be a way out of this!* She shoved aside rising panic to clearly assess the situation. Her brown eyes scrutinized the interior of the limousine, nothing special or unusual about it, the type Samantha and her friends might rent when heading to an off-campus formal. She continued to scan the surroundings, glancing around Presley towards the rear seat, vision shifting back to the front of the compartment, saw the empty ice bucket in the carriage alongside the seat. *Not as if he's one to drink alcohol,* Samantha surmised, aware of the tenets of Islamic faith, likely there to entertain guests more willing than her and Presley. Beside the bucket she spotted a shiny object familiar for one growing up on the grounds of a small estate winery in Upstate New York. An object Samantha able to utilize with deft skill. *A wine key.* Samantha closed her eyes, prayed and hoped. *Please let there be a blade on this one.*

Samantha edged along the leather seat, slowly sliding her body towards the objective, attention of the guards outside focused on the transaction between Sheik Rahim and Marcus Cowle. *Okay, now comes the hard part,* Samantha mused, taking a deep breath as she braced her body against the carriage. Lifted her body up, weight placed on her toes, back arching like a cat sunning in a window. She gasped for air, breathing heavily with the exertion, leaned and twisted her torso to maneuver bound wrists to reach for the wine key, fingers numb and tingling stretching out, grasping at the utensil.

Harder than I thought it was going to be, Samantha grunted, never expected to attempt this tightly bound with wrists tied behind her. Couldn't feel with deadened fingers, peering back over her shoulder to see she had hold of the object. The cold metal of the tool, shaped like a folded barber's blade, a shock to the skin as Samantha palmed the utensil in her hand, exhaling in relief as she sank back on the seat.

Samantha glanced at Presley, a confused expression on the frightened freshman's face trying to figure what she was doing. Samantha trailed her fingers over the wine key, searched for the notch in the blade used to cut away the foil around the neck of the bottle. *Found it*, she smiled through her gag, a sense of accomplishment surging within, felt a dribble of sweat on her forehead, looked over her shoulder as she wedged a long fingernail in the notch, a simple action made difficult with wrists secured, eased the blade out from the utensil.

The blade small, almost pathetically insignificant, yet sharp enough to cut through the rope if she had enough time. *This will have to do*, Samantha concentrating her effort through fingers throbbing as if asleep to position the tool so the blade rested against the bindings. With tiny, methodically even movements Samantha started sawing at the rope. She noticed one difference in her bondage from that securing the other hostages, her elbows not bound together. If she could slice through the ropes about her wrists, she'd easily shrug off the bindings restraining her upper body.

Samantha closed her eyes, a single-minded focus on the task; free herself from the ropes holding her prisoner. What she'd do when, and if, she found release from the bonds to escape the security detail of Sheik Rahim, or save Presley and her fellow captives from a shared, and likely horrid, fate matters Samantha didn't possess anything closely resembling a solution. *I'll deal with that when I get there...*

"You heard what Tyler said," D'Andre Watson helped Ashleigh Morgan, physically spent and emotionally drained, reeling in shock from her ordeal in the trunk of the Lexus, into the front seat of Tyler McManaway's Xterra. "Lock the door. Don't open it for anyone unless they're wearing a uniform or flashing a badge. You got that, Ash?"

"Loud and clear, Honey Bear," Ashleigh used her nickname for D'Andre spoken only when the pair alone, head spinning at the sudden turn of events. One minute alone and defenseless in the trunk, surrendering every last shred of hope of ever seeing D'Andre or her family, resigned to a frightful fate suffering the violent whims of Marcus Cowle and his thugs. Then her D'Andre appearing out from the darkness like one of his comic book heroes to spirit her to safety. Her desperate prayers to God answered and she quietly thanked Him.

"You have to get Samantha!" Ashleigh pleaded, dark eyes brimming with frantic concern.

"Don't worry. We'll get Samantha and the others they have out of there." The grin on his face that confident, world-beating smile flashed whenever D'Andre knew the moment arrived for the big play, break the long dash downfield for the touchdown. "It's time to play the hero."

Ashleigh smiled weakly through tears running down her face, D'Andre her hero, now and always. "Be safe, be careful, I love you." She grabbed D'Andre by the shoulders, drew him close, passionately kissed him hoping this wasn't for the last time, whispered a prayer. *Bring him back to me, please.*

"Hold that thought," the confident, some of his detractors derided him as unbearably cocky, grin never left D'Andre's face as he exclaimed a favorite line from an animated movie, exactly what Ashleigh expected him to proclaim in this situation. "Honey, where's my super suit? The public is in danger!" With the display of exuberant courage, D'Andre ran off into the night, heading back into the maw of peril.

As D'Andre hurried to rejoin his friends, engage in the fight to rescue Samantha Grayson and five other unfortunate victims, Ashleigh shut the door and hit the automatic door lock sealing the interior of the Xterra. In the silence Ashleigh offered another prayer to God.

Keep D'Andre safe. Let him save Samantha from these monsters. Bring him back to me.
Ashleigh Morgan didn't feel she was asking very much.

Marcus Cowle and Sheik Rahim stared at the screen of the laptop, watching the status bar showing the process of the financial transaction creep ever slowly forward. Rahim turned to Cowle, the glare he gave his business associate none too agreeable.

Cowle smiled, unperturbed. "You might need to update your wireless card."

Rahim's expression remained unchanged; Cowle suspected he wasn't the least bit amused by the jest. *Screw you, I'm the one doing your dirty work.* A few minutes more and the relationship between seller and buyer properly mended with the successful transfer of the consignment.

Chapter 42

The minute it took for Tyler McManaway and Connor Aanonsen to reach the point in the loading bay where he wanted them for the attack on the minions of Marcus Cowle and Sheik Rahim the longest minute in the life of Albert 'Fiji' Fatuamala, each second dragging interminably, allowing him time to prepare for action and far too much time to think. Fiji prayed the plan, one drawn up with all the elegance of a play scrawled in the dirt during a rowdy sandlot football game, worked and all ended well. *If it doesn't work…* Like a dog shaking water from his coat after swimming in a pond, Fiji brushed away nagging doubts. The plan was going to work. The three of them, four when D'Andre Watson returned from insuring Ashleigh Morgan safely in Tyler's Nissan Xterra remained, barring the sudden arrival of the police to the factory in the next few minutes, the best, last and only hope for the hostages in the clutches of the human traffickers and the man purchasing their lives. If they failed Samantha Grayson, along with five other precious lives, doomed to a horrible end.

I can't let this happen. I will not fail Tyler. I will not fail my Brother. I won't let harm come to Samantha. I will not let this evil take place. Fiji lowered his head, dispelled lingering misgivings from his mind. *Failure isn't an option.* There wasn't a game the following week to make amends for mistakes, and miscues here proving fatal. *Hit them fast and hard, don't give them a chance to strike back.*

Is this why I am here? Fiji mused philosophically, attempting to answer a question asked by family and friends why he chose Great Northern over schools on the West Coast closer to home in climates far more hospitable for one growing to manhood on an tiny island in the middle of the vast expanse of the Pacific Ocean. Never able to articulate a specific, suitable answer, falling back on the renown of their Chandler School of Philosophy, the chance to start immediately for an up-and-coming football program loaded with young stars. His wizened grandfather, like Albert tranquil of soul, mystically told doubters far more to Albert's decision than superficial considerations of study and sport, the reason for choosing Great Northern only Albert to discover in time and on his own terms.

So this is why. Now Fiji accepted his destiny, why he came to Great Northern, the reason far more than playing football and earning a degree. There to save the life of Lauryn Callahan and find the love of his life, to rescue Samantha Grayson and the women held prisoner by Marcus Cowle, about to be sold as slaves to the imperious Sheik Rahim. Here now the reason for his existence, acknowledged unquestioningly the same way he understood his peculiar 'gift.' For the first time this terrible night exhibiting the skill to his friends, able to open doors with a slight tap of his fist, a trick discovered to the amazement of his parents when a child. The ability to know, without doubt or second thought, the correct wire to pull to disarm the bomb at the studio. Fiji didn't try understanding this incredible insight, accepting the wondrous talent of prescience for what it was, a gift bestowed on him by a just and righteous Creator to save the lives of those in dire need.

Fiji studied the strong and broad-shouldered associates of Marcus Cowle and Sheik Rahim surrounding like the walls of an impregnable fortress the four women who remained kneeling in the center of the bay. The black limo inside which Samantha and Presley imprisoned as Cowle and Rahim finished their transaction, an exchange once completed dooming six treasured, delicate lives to an unspeakable fate Fiji must prevent from taking place even if it cost him his life. The men exuded the callous arrogance of those exercising brutal power over those unable to resist their cruelty, exacting terror and pain upon the weak and defenseless.

They're bullies, Fiji told himself, *that's all they are*, the young Samoan familiar with the dregs of humanity preying on those who couldn't fight back, found perverse pleasure bordering on the erotic in agony inflicted on the powerless. He knew Sheik Rahim's thugs far worse than the two in the employ of Marcus Cowle, only engaged in the endeavor for the money. The guards had the authority of their government granted on them, acting with brazen impunity to terrorize the populace, immune from any punishment for their heartless deeds.

A memory flashed into Fiji's mind, a time in high school, visiting relatives in Hawaii, came across a group of bullies tormenting one much younger and smaller, gleefully tormenting the unfortunate target through strength in numbers. By then Fiji already grown into his body, towering tall and strong as a grizzly bear, walked up to the group and in an even, yet forceful, voice demanded the bullies cease their actions, leave the victim alone. The bullies didn't relent, despite his imposing frame thought they held the advantage, a wolf pack outnumbering him five to one. The leader of the cadre a pitiless, sneering teen with a flabby gut, face ugly and acne-scarred, derisively asked Fiji how he was going to stop them.

Much to his dismay the sneering teen discovered exactly how. With a swift move, Fiji grabbed the bully by the collar, grabbing his leg as he hoisted him into the air. Fiji lifted the body over his head, easily managed the weight, standing defiantly before the others as if he were Superman on the cover of the first issue of *Action Comics,* effortlessly holding a car over his head by dint of super strength, ready to heave the object at villains fleeing his righteous might. The sneering teen whimpered in protest, his façade of cruel bravado shattered, fearing at any moment tossed through the air like a doll. His compatriots, unprepared by the show of incredible strength, cowered in fear at the vision of Herculean prowess. Fiji glanced up at the bully and again demanded in the same even, yet forceful, voice for them to stop bullying the young boy they preyed on.

The sneering teen, false courage shredded, ready to bawl his eyes out, nodded wildly, his companions frozen in shocked awe, none challenging the mighty Samoan. Convinced the bully learned his lesson Fiji placed him gently down on terra firma, said not a word watching in satisfaction as they hurried away with the honor of rats scurrying down a back-alley sewer pipe never to bother anyone again.

Fiji gazed out at the bay, to the men gathered around four helpless young women and the limo containing another pair of hostages, one the cherished love of his closest friend, of the man he considered a brother.

Albert Fatuamala understood what he needed to do. *They're bullies, nothing more and nothing less.* He knew how to handle bullies.

"You ready?" Tyler McManaway quietly asked Connor Aanonsen once they reached the spot where Fiji directed them with moments to spare.

Connor closed his eyes. *Either this works or we're dead men fighting.* "I'm as ready as the Light Brigade before that charge in the Crimea," the observation from Connor, with his double major in history, appropriate. "Half a league, half a league, into the Valley of Death rode the six-hundred," he recited under his breath. *We could use those six hundred right now.*

"Don't worry," Tyler whispered, about to stand, toss the first of the two bolts across the loading bay, instantly followed by the second, a diversion distracting the attention of the phalanx of burly men surrounding the limousine with Samantha and Presley inside and the four hostages left in the middle of the bay. "We've got this," Tyler added, echoing the same confidence he did on the field when he stepped into the huddle to call the play, hiding doubts over what might end up a heroic deed or a fool's errand.

"That's what King Leonidas told those three hundred Spartans before Thermopylae," Connor hissed back. Took his Swiss Army knife, with the blade cutting the bands of tape holding the three goalie sticks together. He folded the blade back into the handle, stuffing it in his pocket. *This might come in handy in a pinch,* Connor assumed. Then he again quoted Shakespeare. "Cry havoc, and let slip loose the dogs of war."

"Let's do this," Tyler coolly remarked, "let them know these dogs bite." With newly discovered poise standing up yet shielded from view by the discarded machinery, a sensation he was back on the turf of Warren Field sitting deep in the pocket, protected by the girth of his offensive line against the rush of the opposing defense. His arm cocked back, positioned to heave the bolt in a high arc to gain distance, landing on the far side of the space as Fiji wanted. His arm fired forward, launching the bolt, about six inches long and two inches in diameter, in a perfect spiral high above the unsuspecting henchmen of Marcus Cowle and Sheik Rahim. In a fluid motion, as the first bolt soared in mid-flight, Tyler shifted the second bolt into his right hand, adjusted his feet to heave the bolt so it landed further left of the first one. His arm eased back, bringing the bolt up parallel to his ear, powerful throw sending the second bolt on its journey. His job done Tyler ducked down next to Connor, picked up the crowbar, waiting for the reaction from the thugs guarding the hostages, hoping they did as Fiji predicted, waiting for the massive Samoan to initiate the second part of their spur-of-the-moment, seat-of-the-pants plan, praying the effect what they expected.

If not, none of them had a chance of surviving this battle.

"What was that?" Marcus Cowle's head shot up at the sound of metal against concrete, attention jerked from the computer screen. A second noise followed the first, this one metal on metal, echoing through the expanse of the loading bay. The sound from the far side of the loading bay broke the desperate silence as Cowle and Sheik Rahim waited for the satellite uplink to complete the transaction for the sale of six young women into a short, brutal and inhumane existence of sexual slavery ending with inevitable death.

The associates of Sheik Rahim, along with the four vulnerable hostages kneeling in the center of the bay, swung their heads about at the sounds, eyes and senses alert, guards searching for a hidden threat, hostages praying for unseen salvation.

Lang shrugged his shoulders, nonplussed by the noise. "There've been rats running around this place all day."

"Been getting into our trash," Sterner added in agreement, heard rats scurrying about the empty factory, spotted the rodents rummaging amongst the discarded bags containing leftover scraps from fast food meals consumed by their prisoners. "I'm sure they were after what she," Sterner pointed at the shivering Isabella DiBenedetto, "didn't eat during her stay."

"Let's make sure it's only Mickey Mouse and nothing bigger." Cowle motioned to Sterner and Lang, the pair moving around the four bound captives, strode across the bay. Rahim made a similar silent motion, four of his guards joining Sterner and Lang. Nothing to worry about, Rahim convinced of that, structure appeared unused for years, but neither he nor Cowle wished to leave anything to chance so close to completion of the business transaction, so close to returning home with the prize of Samantha Grayson in his possession.

None of the six henchmen noticed they walked directly into the path of the dumpster which Albert 'Fiji' Fatuamala used to conceal his massive frame, seconds away from being run over as so much road-kill on a lonely country highway.

Fiji waited until the guards, two of them Cowle's associates, the other four from Rahim's cohort, lined up with the dumpster, a set of six pins set for a spare. He glanced at the remaining guards, their focus locked on where the noise originated, backs turned away from where Tyler and Connor crouched hidden, ready to burst forth and make known their presence. The time had come. *Give me strength, Lord, give me courage.* Even though he studied philosophy Fiji believed in the Almighty, swiftly intoned a prayer not for his well-being but for those he sought to save from evil's grip. *Give me strength to see through this trial. Give me strength to help those who need protection.*

With a war cry emerging deep in his lungs, shattering the eerie stillness of the loading bay, Fiji thrust the dumpster forward, colossal arms and mighty legs propelling the object forward like a tackling sled on the practice field or an opposing offensive guard across the line of scrimmage. With each step the dumpster gaining speed, instantly transformed into a dangerous weapon with every ounce of force his biceps heaved into the side of the refuse container, offering a shield if any of the guards decided to shoot at him. Fiji taking a calculated gamble the close quarters of combat, where his adversaries might hit each other or the women Rahim intended to procure, keeping his adversaries from taking this deadly action.

The heads of Rahim's guards and Cowle's henchmen whipped about in surprise, at the last moment caught sight of the imposing green metallic form hurtling towards them, given no time to react, unable to evade the onrushing container. With a final massive shove, Fiji sent the dumpster careening into the six minions directed by their masters to investigate the diversion created by Tyler McManaway. The container, rolling wildly, collided into the gathered group, taking them out like ducks on a pond hit by a double-barreled round of buckshot. Two absorbed the full brunt of impact, sent sprawling against the concrete floor, knocked senseless, others diving out of the way, vulnerable to the attack of Fiji Fatuamala as he leapt out from behind the dumpster used as weapon and shield, commencing his onslaught on the men.

Rahim's other bodyguards, those left to watch over the hostages, started to move to their comrades' aid, overwhelm the huge, bronze-skinned Samoan by sheer weight of numbers. A shout from behind, their rear left unprotected with attention focused on Fiji's frontal assault with the dumpster, caught them off-guard, unprepared to counter the attack striking from a different direction.

"GET DOWN!" Tyler shouted at the quartet of women kneeling bound and gagged in the midst of a gladiatorial arena, sprinting from his hiding place with crowbar raised, charging the guards standing nearest them. Connor Aanonsen running in full stride by his side, dropping two of the goalie sticks to the floor, wood clattering loudly against cement, third carried by his side like a Viking battle-axe, ferociously wielding the weapon to hack down the enemy as a scythe slices through wheat ready for harvest.

At the sound of Tyler's strident command the women swung their heads from where Fiji drove the dumpster into the six unsuspecting guards, saw two men approaching, unknown liberators coming to their rescue. The young woman with mahogany hair on the far end, wearing a denim mini-skirt and leather jacket, grunted loudly through her gag, understood what Tyler wanted, get out of harm's way with the battle for their lives about to rage around them. With a muffled groan the girl leaned against the next woman in line, the tall one wearing a gray pantsuit, and one by one the four toppled over, a line of dominos tipped over by an invisible finger.

Tyler headed at the closest guard, the nearest target of opportunity, the action like going through progressions on a passing play to find the open receiver. The henchman lunged at him, throwing an ill-aimed punch, Tyler deftly ducked under the errant blow, crowbar held tight in his fists swinging upward, propelled by momentum, the iron curve of the tool connecting with the man's midsection, heard ribs cracking from impact. The man doubled over and Tyler, a blind rage washing over him, brought the crowbar down across his back, hard into the spine, dropping his adversary to the floor, didn't care if he caused serious injury. *Screw him…*

A second henchman rushed at Connor, executed a spinning kick with his right leg, expecting to take Connor down with the martial arts maneuver. The foot flying through space found nothing, connecting with empty air as Connor utilized the lightning-quick dexterity and flexibility of a top-flight goalie to drop down to his knees in a butterfly position. Closing his legs as if blocking the five-hole to prevent a puck from trickling through for the score, his right hand with the goalie stick sweeping in a wide arc, the blade striking the left ankle supporting the man's weight. His opponent yelped in surprise, robbed of his balance and falling backwards, shoulders hitting hard against the concrete. As swiftly as he dropped to the floor Connor leapt to his feet, no time for the guard to react as Connor took the stick in both hands. Twirling the stick so the blade flat, he brought it high over his head and thrust the flat edge down with incredible force on the skull of his fallen foe, stunning him.

"Two minutes for roughing!" Tyler shouted at Connor as another of Rahim's thugs rushed him, the attacks uncoordinated, coming at them piecemeal as Fiji expected. *Divide and conquer.* One objective central in Tyler's mind, reach the limousine across from him in the loading bay with Samantha Grayson helpless inside. Nothing to prevent him from reaching the high ground, the goal he sought, freeing Samantha from this unthinkable horror. For Tyler McManaway the limousine yards away from him now the other team's end zone, Omaha Beach, Little Round Top, San Juan Hill, no opposing force no matter how numerous or formidable stopping him from reaching the objective and saving Samantha Grayson.

I made her a promise; I'm going to keep that promise. Tyler either rescuing Samantha from this ordeal or die trying. He understood there could be no middle ground in this fight.

I'm going to do this. I'm going to do this. I'm going to do this. In her head Samantha Grayson repeated a single-minded mantra, eyes closed tight, will focused on the blade of the wine key, slowly sawing through the ropes restraining her wrists. She leaned forward slightly; panting through her gag with each stroke of the blade against the bindings. Presley Harding watched the desperate work with hopeful eyes, praying Samantha succeeded in the endeavor, their only chance to avoid the deadly fate as possessions of Sheik Rahim.

The banging noise of metal against concrete followed a few seconds later by the ringing sound of metal on metal halted Samantha in the middle of a stroke, interrupting her efforts, frozen in place. She opened her eyes, swiveled about to look at Presley in puzzlement.

What was that? Presley asked, brown eyes glistening with panic.

I don't know. Samantha shook her head, peered out the open door of the limousine; saw Cowle and Rahim directing their people to investigate the noise. Heard a shout, deep-throated and full of righteous fury in a voice she thought familiar, sudden outburst made Samantha jump in her seat. In quick succession heard sounds of something rolling, then the deep thudding of a solid object impacting on human flesh, shouts of surprise from the associates of her abductor and would-be purchaser, a clattering of wood against concrete. The darkened interior windows of the limo obscured Samantha's view of what was occurring, seeing only shapes moving frantically about, couldn't tell why chaos had erupted out of thin air.

Then Samantha heard another voice above the chorus of grunts and exclamations.

"GET DOWN!"

Samantha knew the voice, loved to hear it whisper in her ear during quiet moments, now urgent and strident, heart leaping from the depths of despair spotting his figure through the open door. *Tyler?* Lunging at one of Rahim's guards, Connor Aanonsen by his side wielding a goalie stick. For a brief moment Samantha wondered if trapped in a wishful hallucination brought by stress of the situation before she realized the vision real, a torrent of thoughts and questions released by Tyler's appearance. *How did he find me? Riley, it had to be Riley! Did he find Amanda and Lauryn before the bomb went off? That's the only way he could have found us! Did they save Ashleigh?* The answers to wait, Samantha swung her head to Presley, managed a smile despite the gag in her mouth, a whimper of optimism emerging past her lips. *Help is here! We're going to be saved! Everything is going to work out.* For the first time in hours Presley's eyes glimmered with newfound hope.

You told me you'd never let anyone hurt me, you promised to do anything to protect me, Samantha wanted to cry out in joy at Tyler's presence, so near to her, prayed he and his roommates overcame this force of evil attempting to carry her away to enslavement and death. Samantha kept churning emotions in check, attention returned to the ropes around her hands, cutting at them with the blade. Even with salvation outside the limousine, hoping her captivity lasted only a few moments more, Samantha not about to sit and wait passively for rescue to arrive, a damsel princess trapped in a medieval tower. She wanted dearly to join the fight, had issues of her own to settle, in personal and painful fashion if possible, with both Marcus Cowle and Sheik Rahim.

D'Andre Watson was at full sprint, arms and legs churning in breakneck rhythm, as he hit the door at the rear of the vacant factory, the access he'd been ready to enter with his friends when interrupted by the discovery and rescue of Ashleigh Morgan from the trunk of the Lexus parked outside the abandoned complex. D'Andre paused for a second after stepping into the building, listened, sounds of a desperate fight towards the front of the structure.

Looks like they started the party without me, D'Andre concluded, cocking his head, *time to join in the fun before it's over.* He resumed his sprint, winding his way through darkened corridors, homing in on the sounds of battle growing closer with every step. *It's go time, it's show time, it's time to save the day.* Though now he wasn't on the gridiron on a sunny Saturday afternoon, streaking down the sideline with the ball, defenders in hot pursuit, taking it across the goal line for a score. Ten seconds elapsed from when D'Andre burst into the rear of the building, navigating the maze of darkened corridors and hallways, to the moment he emerged into the light of the loading bay, saw his companions already engaged in a frenzied struggle against the hired thugs of Marcus Cowle and Sheik Rahim.

In brightest day. Four hostages, bound and gagged, huddled in a heap on the floor watching the fight flow and ebb around them, unable to affect the outcome, impotent witnesses to the fray. Samantha not among them, was she in the limousine parked in the bay? He spotted Tyler McManaway, the closest one to him, swinging the crowbar at one of the Arabic-looking men, the blow connecting with his target, doubling the man over in pain. Tyler didn't see a second man coming up behind him, charging headlong like a blitzing linebacker attacking from the blindside, the thug clutching a two-by-four in his hands, raised above his head to strike down his friend.

In blackest night. D'Andre not about to allow harm to befall Tyler. *You always have your teammate's back.* Lunging ahead with elbow raised, aiming for the man's head, hurtled forward with vigorous velocity. Took the man unaware, not expecting an assault from behind, D'Andre's elbow connecting with the base of the skull. The man staggered forward, regained his balance, attention distracted from Tyler, now directed at this new opponent. Tyler heard the man grunt, swung about to see D'Andre standing there, protecting his back, evening up dire odds and ready for action. "Nice of you to show up!"

Despite the fact he found himself in the middle of chaos D'Andre grinned broadly at Tyler, his reply bordering on ecstatic. "You think I was going to miss the chance of opening a six-pack of whoop-ass on these jokers?"

No evil shall escape my sight. The minion he struck regained his senses, anger flushing his face, circling about D'Andre holding the two-by-four in both hands like a Louisville Slugger, stepping into the batter's box to hit a home run, but D'Andre presumed the man unfamiliar with the national pastime. As his father, once middleweight boxing champion of the United States Marine Corps and competed for gold in the Olympics, coached D'Andre when his youngest son briefly flirted with the sweet science, excelling in Golden Gloves competition before finding glory on the gridiron, he assumed the classic boxer's stance, feet apart and moving, shuffling, fists up, ready to attack or defend, eyes alert, head bobbing left and right, searching for an opening. D'Andre willing to let the opponent commit the first move.

314

Let those who worship evil's might. The man before him big, not the imposing bulk of a defensive lineman but more the hard, yet tapered frame of a strong safety. *I know how to get around guys like you*, D'Andre smiled at the man, knew the casual, almost flippant expression infuriated his adversary, in return received a glaring sneer. *It's all about speed and quickness.* The man sprung forward, with the lumber taking a full swing at D'Andre's head in a wild, twisting swipe he easily ducked, action leaving the thug's midsection vulnerable. Offered the opening D'Andre sought and he attacked, stepping in to fire a quick as lightning left-right combination under the rib cage where the kidney, the organ closest to the skin, should be. The man bent over in pain from the successive blows, struggling to suck air into his lungs, as D'Andre bounced backwards, then like a cat hunting a mouse he pounced again.

Beware my power. D'Andre pitched a roundhouse right into the jaw, sent the head of his enemy snapping violently, stepped in to launch a brutal uppercut landing square on his chin, watched in satisfaction as a glaze of bewilderment found residence in his eyes, the bodyguard losing his grip on the board, fingers going limp, dropping the weapon to the floor. *Time to finish you off, sucker, goodnight and sweet dreams…*

He fired a haymaker left into the jaw, head snapping but now in the other direction as the sharp blow staggered the thug, D'Andre saw the legs buckle underneath his body. Then came delivery of the business end of a right jab to the face, powerful and succinct, landing on the bridge of the nose, D'Andre grinned as the light in wide-open, staring eyes extinguished, the man twisting to the ground with the suddenness of a pine tree felled by a lumberjack. *One down, more than a few more to go.* Had to fight until the end to help Tyler save Samantha as he helped rescue Ashleigh. *Anything for a friend.* Sensing someone coming up behind him, D'Andre whirled about, confronted another member of Sheik Rahim's goon squad charging at him. D'Andre adopted the trained stance of the boxer, bouncing up and down on his toes like Muhammad Ali, the bell in his head ringing for the next round, coming out to the center of the ring to face another opponent.

You're next…

Chapter 43

As henchmen rushed one by one to challenge Albert 'Fiji' Fatuamala, and as quickly as the sound of fingers snapping together, a change in demeanor never before experienced swept over the young Samoan. No longer was he a 'gentle giant,' the quiet, introspective philosophy major spending placid evenings in the tranquil setting of Philosopher's Grove with the caring and compassionate Lauryn Callahan. His aggressiveness, and a tempered, measured ferocity at that, only exhibited on the football field, fighting through an offensive line to sack the quarterback or bring down a fleet-footed running back. Now the spirits of his ancestors, a race of warriors brave and fierce, feared among the islands of the Pacific for their skill at physical combat and tireless tenacity, fueled the taut, chiseled body and transformed him into a furious force of nature unleashed on numerous foes who had yet to understand they stood no chance against him.

Though outnumbered, facing attack from every direction, any hint of fear absent within the soul of the Samoan, focused totally on the urge to fight, conquer and avenge, obliterate those who sought to harm the love of his life, threatened the one his best friend dearly loved and imperiled the lives of five other innocent women. His dark eyes no longer concentrating on the facial features of his enemies, vision narrowing to absorb the outlines of bodies rushing him. Senses heightened to razor sharpness where Fiji could *hear* the labored breathing as they charged at him, *feel* the shifting movement of the air as his adversaries attacked, brought awareness of onslaught from every quarter, effortlessly countering their assaults, striking back with violence unrestrained.

The first man to feel Fiji's angry wrath one of Rahim's men scrambling up from the floor, his only misfortune being the one closest to him. Fiji firing forward a tree-trunk thick forearm, bicep graced with tribal body art signifying to all he matured to manhood, propelled into the man's throat, sent the thug spinning about in mid-air like a child's toy pinwheel before the body crashed to the concrete.

A second form came at him, one of Cowle's thugs, the shorter of the two, a man physically less commanding than his partner but no less dangerous. A dizzying flurry of punches and jabs thrown at Fiji, realized the man well trained in physical combat, versed in martial arts, but he blocked each blow, hands flashing with blurring swiftness in reply. Fiji flattened out his right hand, tips of his fingers formed like the sharp tip of a spear, found the slightest of openings in the blitzkrieg of his adversary, rammed the hand home with terrific force into his throat underneath the jaw. The man gurgled for breath, clutching at his throat, dropping to his knees.

A third attack, another of Rahim's men, running at him from his left, Fiji sensing the approach, aware of the shifting air around him as if noting a subtle change in the direction of the wind. Fiji caught him with an elbow in the jaw, halting him cold in his tracks. Grabbing his shirt collar Fiji heaved the body, easily judging from hours spent in the weight room at Great Northern the man weighed exactly two hundred and sixty-four pounds, over his head in an impressive press. Tossed him through the air with the casual ease of a beanbag thrown in the game popular at a pre-game tailgate, instead of aiming for a hole in a board launched the unlucky attacker at another of Rahim's men running at him. The flying body slammed into his compatriot, both men toppling to the ground.

The second of Cowle's hired men, light reflecting off his baldhead, a scraggly goatee on his chin, a physical equal to Fiji in every way, charged at him, threw a quick series of punches. Fiji's hands responded, moving in a blur to block every attempted blow, blunting the attack. The big man's cold blue eyes colored with surprise but also a touch of admiration facing so skilled an adversary, a respect Fiji in his unrestrained fury unaware. The Samoan switched to the offensive, unleashed a swift flurry of sharp jabs and mighty blows to the man's chest staggering him backwards, left dazed by the Samoan's combination of sheer power and elusive quickness. The adversary rallied, shook his head of the haze clouding his vision, throwing a punch at the Samoan's head. Fiji caught the man's fist in his huge hand, gripped tight, twisted the wrist violently until there was a loud snap, the big man grimacing in agony, knees locking, knew then the joint shattered. Only given a moment to realize the fact before an elbow from the giant Samoan crashed into the side of his head, sent him sprawling.

The man's compatriot recovered, engaged in a second attack short-lived and ill-advised, Fiji deftly sidestepping him, grabbing the back of his shirt, with a potent heave flinging him into the dumpster, head smacking hard against the steel surface, skull cracking like an eggshell, collapsed to the ground with brains scrambled into a jelly of clouded, muddled confusion.

Sterner, cradling the broken wrist with his other hand, crawled to his partner as the Samoan fended off renewed attacks from Rahim's retinue. He checked Lang's eyes, glazed and unfocused. *Nobody's home, he's out of it.* Sterner saw Cowle motioning to him, understood what he wanted, grabbed Lang under the shoulder, lifting the slack body and dragging the dead weight of his lifeless partner towards the door where Cowle stood. Sterner glanced back at Albert 'Fiji' Fatuamala, muttering under his breath as he lugged his dazed comrade to safety.

"The kid's a beast."

Can I be a hero?

As Connor Aanonsen swung the second of his three goalie sticks with the unbridled fury of a berserker raging on a frozen Nordic battlefield, the first of his sticks broken in two after slamming the flat blade of the stick hard against the head of one assailant, a question asked on many occasions echoed through his mind. The heroism he considered not the type found on the field of competition, Connor familiar with this known quantity, the cheap, easy valor of athletic accomplishment. The heroism he pondered the sort where life and limb, and everything held close and dear to the heart, risked to do that which was right and just, protect those in danger even if such action meant the ultimate sacrifice.

There was a simple reason why, in the midst of a desperate battle, he asked this question of himself, why he studied archeology and history to one day dig up old battlefield sites, to search for the remains of those declared missing in action and lay them to peaceful, honored rest. During World War II a great-uncle piloted a P-47 Thunderbolt fighter, a fearsome aluminum bird-of-prey swooping down from the heavens to eat for breakfast the dreaded Panzer tanks of the vaunted German Wehrmacht, risked life and future doing what he considered right and just, fighting the tyrannical terror of Nazi Germany. He fought for country and family, suffered loss of close friends, did his part like millions of other brave men and women to vanquish the most vile, inhuman evil ever to visit the face of the planet. Once his days as a valiant warrior of the skies complete he returned home, resumed a life placed on pause and pursued his future, married and raised a family. Connor admired the quiet feats of courage his brave great-uncle performed, the wrinkled and wizened face he knew once a fresh-faced, clever farm boy raised on the wide-open prairie of western Minnesota. Young life, the same age as Connor now, interrupted by circumstances half a world away, thrust into the cauldron of the greatest war ever known to man, in the process forging a tempered maturity through the crucible of battle. Connor pried stories from his uncle, modest and reserved regarding his exploits during those terrible years, never once thought his actions special or noteworthy but to Connor the man a hero bigger than life. The tales fired in Connor a healthy desire for history, searched for a way to honor the sacrifice of those who served and paid with their lives. On the back of his goalie mask, the front adorned with an artist depiction of Siberian Huskies howling at a winter moon, a depiction of the proud Republic P-47 Thunderbolt his great-uncle guided through the battle-scarred skies of Europe, a simple sign of honor to his dauntless relative. Connor wondered how he'd have acted, if by some chance of fate born in that time of war and called to serve his country, if he too able to perform acts of courage, willing to sacrifice his life doing what was right and just.

The fact he came so close to losing his precious Amanda, vivacious and sensual, athletic and quick-witted, so full of life, to the evil men who held Samantha Grayson along with five other women prisoner for reasons inhumane, fueled a rage burning hot as the scorching surface of the sun. The women couldn't defend themselves, thought their lives and futures forfeit, no one hearing anguished pleas for help, alone to face their fate. His uncle once fought for the helpless, protected the defenseless as Connor did now, swinging the stick in a wide sweep to catch another of Sheik Rahim's hoodlums in the ribs, inflicting a dose of well-deserved pain. His teammates called the goalie stick he wielded in the crease 'The Hammer of Thor.' Now the imagery fitting, equipment originally intended to knock aside pucks fired on goal swung about as a lethal weapon, cutting down any who dared challenge him in combat.

As Connor Aanonsen fought on with urgent frenzy, calling on spirits of ancestors long dead and once the most fearsome of marauders on the European continent, for the lives of Samantha and the other hostages he thought again of the question and realized he at last had an answer.

Yes, I can be a hero.

I am so sick of this.

Emma Hayden, tied and gagged, lying on the floor of the loading bay, witness to the mêlée whirling madly about her, a passive spectator to a brutal contest deciding her possible destiny, raged at her impotence to affect the outcome as frantic, individual fights swirled and eddied around her fellow captives. Emma knew in minutes if she'd be lucky to live to see another dawn or condemned to die a brutal death.

Once the shock of her kidnapping on Saturday, and the sudden, insidious betrayal at the hands of Marcus Cowle, faded and she suppressed with every ounce of emotional strength the terror of her plight, of the despicable fate Cowle planned for her, Emma seethed with unbridled anger at a situation of her own making. *God, how could I be so stupid to trust him!* Cursed how gullible she'd been accepting Cowle in his wolf's clothing as the photographer Marcus Evans, willing to go to his studio alone without an escort, taken down without a fight and bound into an unresisting, silent package. Brought to this God-forsaken hell-hole, kept bound and gagged for most of the time in this dank, creepy place, a grim portent of her future once sold to her new master. Enduring endless hours mercilessly terrorized by Cowle's hired thugs amused by her struggles, feasting on her fear, Emma enraged at how powerless she was. Even when briefly free of the ropes still manipulated by her abductors, felt shamed humiliation knowing they watched from the shadows as she relieved and cleaned herself in the dingy bathroom.

She wanted to fight back, to strike out at her captors, do something to stop the horrible conclusion, spirited off to what Emma certain an end most violent. She wanted to resist, escape from the first moment of captivity, but such a chance never arose. Shown an example what happened to one who did fight back, tried to flee this horror, tormented by the muffled screams of Presley Harding as Cowle and his goons tortured her through the night, haunted by the faraway, glassy shock in the brown eyes when they dragged her into the cell the following morning, dumping the lifeless body on the floor. Emma and the others delivered a concise message, resistance in any form foolish and ill advised, for defiance paying a brutal price, yet the urge to fight back, to survive, still burned in Emma Hayden. The way Sheik Rahim gazed at her with chilling, cruel desire glowing in his eyes told Emma she wouldn't last long where he took her, for the first time since her abduction truly terrified at her situation and resigned to face an appalling outcome.

Then the sudden attack from the darkness when it seemed everything lost, four young men strong and brave, assaulting the guards of Marcus Cowle and Sheik Rahim, taking them by surprise, rescuers of an unknown identity fighting to save them from certain doom. Emma looked closely at one of men, about her age, wielding the goalie stick through the air, felling his attackers with the ease of Paul Bunyan chopping down mighty pine trees in the Northwoods of Minnesota. *God, I know him from somewhere!*

Emma surprised at the familiarity of shaggy mane of blonde hair and beard, sparkling blue eyes flashing with righteous anger, watched the fluid way he avoided the attacks from Rahim's men. The hat he wore on his head falling off and lying beside her, Emma recognizing on the peak of the cap the logo of her beloved hometown hockey team, the Minnesota Wild.

Emma rolled on her side, glanced over her shoulder at Alexandra Cole, head motioned to the ropes pinning hands behind her. *We have to do something!* Alexandra understood what Emma wanted, shifting her body so they lay back-to-back, numb fingers working on the other's bonds. Within moments, after fumbling with unyielding knots, tugging futilely at the cords Emma realized with sinking heart she couldn't get loose, helpless and ineffective. *At this rate we'll never get free,* Emma moaned, resigned to relegation as a spectator to the unfolding drama.

From across the room Emma spotted one of Rahim's guards regain his footing, head shaking to clear his senses, with horror in her turquoise eyes saw him grasp a discarded metal pipe from the floor, running at the young man with the goalie stick. His back to the guard, attention fixated on his battle with another of Rahim's men, unaware of the surprise attack approaching from behind. With a groan deep in her lungs Emma heaved herself up from the floor and into a kneeling position, every muscle protesting as the thug came near, eyes locked on the back of her savior, didn't see Emma rising from the ground. *Here goes nothing.* Emma waited until the assailant about to run past, tightly closing her eyes, flinging her body across his path, screaming in agony as his foot slammed into her side as he tripped over her. A sensation of satisfaction swept over Emma as she opened her eyes, smiling through the gag, ignored the throbbing ache in her ribs as the man toppled over, dropping his weapon, face smacking against the concrete surface. *Not as helpless as you think, asshole!*

The momentary glee of triumph faded, swiftly replaced by a tsunami wave of terror as the thug turned to Emma, blood from a broken nose trickling down over his lips, eyes flaring with rage at her interference, leaping on top of her bound body. *This is not good,* Emma quickly regretted the impetuous act as thick fingers wrapped around her slender throat, immediately blocked oxygen from reaching her lungs, cutting off the flow of blood to her brain. *I might have made a little mistake here.* Emma shrieked through the gag, realized she suddenly faced a deadly peril.

It can't end like this! It can't! Not this close! She railed hopelessly as in seconds the room swirled about her, dark spots danced before her eyes as Emma Hayden, paying the price for her act of defiance, starting to drift off slowly into a dark void, wondering if she'd ever escape the black veil dropping down to smother a life so tantalizingly close to salvation.

Out of the corner of his eye Connor Aanonsen caught sight of the mahogany-haired girl in the leather jacket and denim mini-skirt toss her body in the path of one of Rahim's guards rushing at him, causing the thug to trip, stumble to the ground, planting his face hard on the cement surface, preventing an assault on an undefended rear. *Thanks for the assist.* He smiled at the girl, shifted his attention back to his opponent, bringing the goalie stick up across his face, knocking the man out cold, in the process shattering the stick in two. Connor dropped the handle of the mangled stick, swiveled about to pick up the final goalie stick in his arsenal, stopped in his tracks by what filled his vision.

The thug the girl in the leather jacket tripped up now straddled the helplessly bound form, blood from a broken nose dripping down on to her white top, droplets staining the pristine fabric a vivid ruby-red, wrathful eyes filled with homicidal rage, beefy hands wrapped around the throat slowly squeezing the life from her, the girl's breathing ragged and labored, gasping for air, eyelids fluttering. The tall brunette in the gray pantsuit on her knees, though bound trying to shove the guard off the woman he attempted to suffocate. The thug shouted angrily at her in Arabic, roughly pushed the brunette away and she tumbled to the floor, turned back to resume his grisly work as the other two captives screamed in terror, unable to help their defenseless friend.

That's no way to treat a lady. Connor ran towards the man, not enough time to grab his last goalie stick, but had a weapon in reserve, fishing in the pocket of his jeans for the Swiss Army knife, pulling out the blade on the all-purpose tool.

The guard so focused on his terrible deed he never saw Connor come up from behind, only knew of his presence when a solid forearm enveloped his neck. Connor heaved him off the defenseless young woman, at the same time hand holding the knife swinging down, blade plunging deep into the soft flesh of the man's thigh. With a piercing shriek of agony, like a small child falling off a bicycle and skinned his knee, the guard clutched uselessly at the knife handle protruding from his leg. From his throat breath exploded in gurgling bursts as Connor yanked him to his feet, twirled the man about, grabbing the back of his jacket and tugging the garment over his head like a hockey jersey, facing off in a bare-knuckle brawl at center ice. *Let me demonstrate how we fight in hockey, bastard. First lesson, I kick the living shit out of you. Enjoy.* The opponent couldn't fight back, arms tangled uselessly in the sleeves of his jacket, left exposed by the maneuver. Connor landed three haymaker uppercuts in succession on his chin, the body sagging heavily in his grip, released his hold on the jacket collar and the guard crumpled whining to the floor, hands grabbing feebly at the knife sticking from his upper leg.

Connor, stepping over his fallen opponent, knelt down to check on the girl who saved his life. "Thanks for watching my back," he thanked her. The girl gazed at Connor through hazy vision, thankful to be alive, coughing as air flowed back into her lungs, glimmer of life restored to turquoise blue eyes.

You're welcome, same here. The girl moaned, attempted a meek smile. *I'll just stay out of the way while you take care of this.*

D'Andre witnessed Connor's quick-thinking action. "Dude, that was nasty!" He shouted, firing a sharp blow below the belt of his latest adversary, the hard punch landed squarely on a sensitive area of the human anatomy between the legs, the man crying out, hands clutching at a wounded manhood, sinking to his knees in pain. D'Andre took advantage of his vulnerability, delivered a left to the temple, knocked the man down.

"Look who's talking!" Connor shouted back, sprinting to where his last goalie stick lay on the floor, picking it up to rejoin the fray.

"They can't fight if they're holding on to the family jewels!" D'Andre yelled, having the time of his life. "Damn, ain't this a blast!" Experiencing a vicarious thrill through each thrown punch and every blow landed, searching for another attacker upon whom to unleash his wrath.

"I can take him!" Lang insisted, shouting, blood streaming from the ugly purple welt creasing his forehead as Sterner and Marcus Cowle dragged the staggering, disoriented associate away from a loading bay erupting into unexpected pandemonium. "I can fucking take him!"

"Dude, you couldn't take your grandmother now," Sterner informed his comrade, brain scrambled into mush when slammed head first into the dumpster by the massive Samoan defensive end from Great Northern University. Sterner nursed his own wound from the battle, right arm with a broken wrist dangling limply at his side. He glanced over his shoulder at the ferocious whirlwind named Albert Fatuamala, laying a path of frightful destruction through Sheik Rahim's men. *The kid is a beast*, Sterner observed with a twinge of admiration. *You got the best of me...this time.*

"Fuck! We can't leave! We can take them!" Lang screamed again, legs giving out, about to collapse.

"No, we're leaving." The bitter taste of defeat filling his mouth, Marcus Cowle watched the wild fight between the four young men, had to be friends of Samantha Grayson and her companions, and the guards of Sheik Rahim's security detail. *They found the two I left back at the studio before the bomb went off*; Cowle now realized his miscalculation. But how had they found the factory? Then Cowle remembered where he stood when he sent the text to Sheik Rahim, next to Amanda tied to the chair. *She saw the text, the address.* He shook his head, engaged in Monday morning quarterbacking, cursed his momentary weakness, a mistake costing him dearly. *Should've offed them before we left, then they wouldn't have been alive to tell anyone.*

"We can take them!" Lang asserted through a concussion-fogged mind. "We can't leave!"

"Must I remind you," Cowle pointed out, "if we are apprehended The Trading Society will take the necessary steps to insure we don't live out the day?"

That fact, the organization they worked for ordaining ultimate sanction to protect their secrets finally quieted Lang's protestations. They hauled him from the factory and into the night, headed towards the Lexus and black cargo van. *At least we can take out our frustrations on poor little Ashleigh*, Cowle thought sourly. The bitch not so fortunate, paying dearly for the interference of her friends. As he approached the Lexus, Cowle noticed the trunk lid popped open. He shoved Lang to Sterner, guiding his partner to the van. Cowle lifted the lid, peered inside the trunk, found it empty. "Shit," was all he could say with the discovery his last remaining prize gone.

"Some days just suck more than others," Sterner noted philosophically, bundling his dazed partner into the passenger seat.

"I have a way of evening things out," Cowle replied, hit the remote to open the front gate of the complex, slipping into the Lexus as Sterner hopped into the van, ignoring the pain in his wrist to grip the steering wheel. A moment later the two vehicles turning right onto Carroll Avenue and heading west, speeding from the factory and a payday gone horribly awry before the police arrived to complicate matters further.

Not the first time I've liquidated inventory. Cowle fingered the remote device. "Enjoy your triumph while it lasts, gentlemen," he muttered coldly, hitting the button to activate the timers on the explosive devices, the propane tank bombs, left in the factory to obliterate any evidence of their presence. Now the devices given a new purpose, in twelve minutes killing both the rescuers and the rescued.

Perhaps Marcus was correct. Sheik Rahim evaluated the situation swirling about in the bay with the unrestrained havoc of a devastating hurricane, laying waste to everything in its path, his security detail engaged in chaotic mêlée against four young men who seemed to appear from the darkness like ethereal apparitions. *I shouldn't have delayed delivery of the consignment.* A grievous misjudgment Rahim never admitting to Cowle.

Rahim crouched by the limo, shocked to observe his guards, skilled in hand-to-hand combat, exhibiting ruthless brutality in action, bested in battle. The element of surprise with the attackers, diversion distracting their attention and the attack dividing them, negated their strength in numbers. He assumed the rescuers companions of Samantha Grayson, saw one wearing a sweatshirt with the name of the school on the front. *If I had accepted the offer from Marcus of the three women,* Rahim realized, *my people could have flown back commercial.*

Rahim glanced at Saleh, his trusted associate not yet engaged in combat, watching with pursed lips and a narrow stare of disgust as men he selected and trained mauled and manhandled, waiting for the moment to interject his formidable presence into the fray. Saleh turned to his master. *You must leave now. I will handle things here.* Rahim understood the gesture, imperative he flee the factory. Make his way to the hanger at O'Hare where the jet awaited, get into the air. *The Americans won't force my plane down*, he conjectured, *not at the risk of losing the precious military base in my homeland.* The other women no longer mattered, in the limousine sat Samantha Grayson, the lone prize desired from this consignment, along with the other unfortunate young woman from Great Northern University.

Beads of sweat formed on Samantha's forehead, trickling down the bridge of her nose. She leaned forward, concentration centered on the wine key grasped between palms slick with perspiration, moving the blade against the ropes restraining her wrists. *Come on, hurry up!* She willed fingers to work faster to slice through the rope, blocking out manic sounds of violent confrontation raging outside the limo, a situation deciding her fate and of her defenseless companions, a life-and-death contest Samantha unable to offer the slightest bit of influence at the moment. The sound of a car door slamming startled Samantha, action halting in mid-stroke. Samantha raised her head, peering through the opening in the partition dividing the compartments. Saw Sheik Rahim slide behind the steering wheel; he turned the ignition, engine roaring to life. *What's he doing?* A bubble of uneasiness in her stomach, a surge of horror overwhelming Samantha as she realized what was happening.

He's trying to get away...

The limo lurched backward; abrupt movement threw Samantha against Presley, squealing in surprise as Samantha fell heavily into her. Tires shrieked, the limo pirouetting around in a tight circle. The maneuver caught Samantha unprepared, tossing her from the seat, bound body hitting the floor, dazed by the impact. Saw the door to the passenger compartment remained open as the limo accelerated; the next sound heard over the screaming engine the grinding crunch of metal against metal, limo crashing into the paper-thin aluminum skin of the loading bay door. The bolts holding the door to the building yielding under the tremendous force, but before surrendering to its destruction the bay door inflicting damage on the limo, tearing away the open door to the passenger compartment, denting the front fenders, buckling the hood. The bay open to the outside world, though not by conventional means, providing Rahim a route of escape. Samantha felt the limo turn tightly to the left, thrown hard against the base of the seat, scrambling her senses. The fog clouding her head cleared swiftly, an electric surge of terror recognizing her hands were empty.

No! As she was thrown from the seat to the floor Samantha lost her hold on the wine key, the only chance to free her body of the imprisoning bondage and save her life.

What the hell?

The rumbling of an engine coming to life caught Tyler off-guard, head jerking towards the sound. He stood a stunned observer as the limo, with Samantha and Presley trapped inside, wheeled around in the confined space, smoke pouring from the tires, speeding towards the closed door of the bay. *No! I was so close to reaching her!* Tyler rooted in place, gaze fixed on the fleeing limo as the driver, it had to be Sheik Rahim, aimed the vehicle like a spear at the bay door, used the front end as a battering ram. With a horrendous metallic shriek the limo slammed into the thin aluminum barrier, tearing the door from its moorings, forcing an opening to the outside. The passenger side door, wide open as the vehicle slammed into the gate, ripped from the body as the limo scraped against the frame.

What the hell do I do now? His attention shifted from the front of the loading bay where the limo collided with the overhead door to the frenzied battle his friends still engaged in and the four women lying on the floor bound and gagged, anarchy swirling about them as a tornado ravages the prairie landscape. Tyler rested his eyes on the two sleek black Audi S8 sedans parked in the bay, the only way for Tyler to pursue Sheik Rahim, escaping with his hostages imprisoned in the back of the limo. *I can't leave the guys here*, Tyler's mind shifted into overdrive, pulled in different directions by conflicting purposes. *They're outnumbered and the women are still in danger. But Rahim is getting away with Samantha and Presley! I have to go after them. But I can't go chasing them through Chicago, I might hit someone, get someone killed! What the hell do I do?*

D'Andre Watson realized the struggle raging within Tyler McManaway as he stood motionless, the hesitation uncharacteristic. Had to get him to move before one of Rahim's goon squad got lucky and took him out. "Tyler! Go after them!" D'Andre shouted, ducked under the wild swing of his latest adversary, landed a blow to an unguarded midsection in response.

"We've got this, Tyler!" Connor yelled, saw Tyler pause, standing like a statue, this not the time or place for uncertainty. "We'll take care of them!"

D'Andre landed a hard right jab on his attacker's nose, staggered him, pointing at the limo exiting the loading bay. "Dude! Go! You have to save Samantha!"

Samantha. Her name broke Tyler from the haze of indecision as one of Rahim's men charged at him. Tyler's eyes flashed back to life, swinging the crowbar in time, striking the assailant flush in the jaw, body crashing to the ground. *I promised her I wouldn't let anyone hurt her.* The decision made, setting his course of action. *I can't let him hurt Samantha; I have to go after him.*

Tyler ran to the closest Audi, opened the driver's door, slid into the seat. *I hope the keys are in the ignition.* The ignition a push-button on the dashboard, a fortuitous sign. He punched the button, shutting the door, buckling the seatbelt. *Might want to wear this.* The full-throated roar of unbridled horsepower echoed through the cavernous space, roar of a lion staking claim to his territory on African grassland. One of Rahim's men sprinted towards the car to stop him. Tyler snarled at the man, shifting the sedan into drive, barely touching the accelerator, jerking the steering wheel to bring the car about. The Audi sprung to life, guard couldn't jump out of the way of the speeding vehicle in time, the right rear fender clipped his thigh, twirling him through the air with the gyration of a windmill. *At least I took care of one on the way out*, Tyler grinned with pride, pressing the accelerator, aiming the sleek, black missile at the gaping hole where the loading bay door stood seconds earlier, zooming through the space and into the waiting night. On the street, Tyler twisted the wheel to the left. The limo, with Samantha and Presley as unwilling passengers, ahead of him and turning left onto Sacramento Boulevard, heading north. Tyler jammed the accelerator to the floorboard, tachometer bolting to the right, halogen headlights piercing the darkness, Audi responding effortlessly to his command with a subdued purr of power, springing ahead like a racehorse bursting from the gate at Churchill Downs in search of a win at the Kentucky Derby.

Stopping the limo, and rescuing Samantha and Presley without getting both of them killed, Tyler realized might prove far more problematic than chasing it down.

Chapter 44

This isn't good.

Samantha Grayson thought as the limo with Sheik Rahim behind the wheel sped away from the abandoned factory, fingers frantically groping about the floor for the wine key jarred from her grasp when the limo plowed through the loading bay door, Samantha thrown hard against the bound Presley Harding then tossed on to the floor. *And that isn't much better.* She stared at the yawning void where the door to the passenger compartment of limo had been, torn from its hinges in the escape. An empty space beckoned like the open maw of a Great White Shark through which either she or Presley, trussed and helpless, ejected to a certain death if Sheik Rahim took one corner too fast.

Samantha struggled to her knees, peered out the back window; saw the sleek silhouette of an Audi S8 sedan shoot out of the factory, a black bullet fired from the barrel of a gun, headlights turning towards them, accelerating to close the distance. Tyler behind the wheel of the pursuing vehicle, Samantha knew he'd never let Rahim take her, never let this monster hurt her. *I will never let anything happen to you. I will never let anyone hurt you.* The soothing words of reassurance from Saturday night as he held her by Buckingham Fountain echoed in her mind.

I believe you. Samantha closed her eyes. *You won't let anything happen to me. You are going to save me.* But Samantha still needed to save herself and Presley from this new and immediate threat. *Where is it? Where's that damn wine key?* Samantha fought the temptation to panic, focused on her task. She slumped back down to the floor, numb fingers furiously groping along the carpeted floor, head swiveling about, eyes searching to locate the lost tool. Samantha knew her course of action. Had to find the wine key, use the blade to cut the ropes binding her wrists, to have even the slimmest chance of surviving this reluctant ride. Get free of the ropes confining her movements before considering how to stop Sheik Rahim, madly careening the limo with his powerless passengers through the streets of Chicago in an insane effort to escape with his his spoils.

The bald henchman stood imperious as a colossus, an even match for Albert 'Fiji' Fatuamala in height and bulk, muscles thick as rope and hard as granite. The three friends understood this was the right-hand man of Sheik Rahim, an expressionless witness standing patiently aside while his fellow minions staged futile attacks, fell before the onslaught of the trio, Fiji inflicting the greatest damage, a one-man wrecking crew. He glared impassively at Albert Fatuamala, gray eyes cold and aloof, face breaking into an inscrutable smile directed at his opponent, casually removing his jacket as if finally deciding to settle personally a situation his comrades unable to resolve. His head nodded slightly in salute to the fighting skill of the towering Samoan, an off-handed compliment fending off the frenetic assaults of his associates, yet at the same moment the action condescending, informing Fiji he considered the Samoan no match for him.

"It's down to you and Oddjob," D'Andre Watson invoked the name of the infamous James Bond nemesis from *Goldfinger*. D'Andre up on his toes, fists at the ready, guarding his friend's flank as the two squared off. One henchman struggled to his feet, eyes hazy, body present but the mind lost in some faraway place. D'Andre dealt a blurring overhand right to the jaw, sent him sinking down to the floor.

"Own him Fiji!" Connor Aanonsen, holding the broken handle of his last goalie stick in both hands as a knight of medieval times wielded a sword, weaving around one of the few thugs of Sheik Rahim's entourage left standing, shouted at his friend. "Show this bastard how we do business in Chicago!" The enemy lunged at Connor, who deftly stepped aside and brought the butt-end of the stick clenched in his fists down solidly on the base of the attacker's skull, the guard reeling, collapsing to the ground. "If, by chance," Connor looked over to D'Andre, lowered his voice, "this guy does go through Fiji you think we can take him?"

"Not a chance, Doctor Jones," D'Andre grinned knowingly. "He'll kick our asses and have a big smile on his face while he does it."

"Wonderful," Connor muttered, found the assessment hardly reassuring.

How much blood of the innocent is on your hands? Fiji silently asked the bald man as they circled about, taking measure of the other, searching for an opening to strike their adversary. *How many have you tortured? How many women like Samantha have you killed?* Would Oddjob and his minions been allowed by their Master to inflict merciless, unspeakable violence on Samantha and the other captives? His foe a ruthless henchman with a heart of stone, deaf to the cries of his victims while undertaking the bidding of his overlord. Oddjob the lowest form of humanity Fiji ever confronted, a personification of darkest malevolence void of emotion, experienced nary a qualm of remorse unleashing pain and indignity on helpless victims unable to resist his brutality until their spirit crushed or lives snuffed. *I'm not helpless, I'm not defenseless, I can fight back*, Fiji's dark eyes stated his intent, quiet oath uttered. *I will defeat you. I will avenge those you have tortured, those you have killed.*

Oddjob struck first, a right thrown at Fiji's head, a punch parried with ease. The retaliation following quick, Fiji landing a solid left into Oddjob's chest, staggering him, the man absorbing the blow, eyes narrowing at the discovery his adversary far stronger and quicker than any he ever faced. Oddjob came at Fiji again, his movements aggressive, a flurry of punches thrown in rapid succession, Fiji deflecting some, others landing on the body. Not one of the blows, dropping a lesser man to his knees, having any effect on the Samoan, standing resolute and unyielding as a thousand-year redwood.

Fiji struck back, took the offensive, a guttural war cry from his lungs as he flattened his right hand, fingers forming a knife-like point, attacking in the same destructive manner used on the security men lying motionless or barely stirring on the floor. One tried to rise, come to the aid of his leader, but D'Andre delivered a knee to the side of the man's head at the same time a second operative attempted to gain his footing, Connor ramming the jagged end of his goalie stick into his eye, deaf to his scream of agony, uncaring of the pain he caused, wanting this battle to end and once more take Amanda McKinnon into his arms.

The flat hand, a lethal weapon, struck home underneath Oddjob's jaw above the larynx, a choking sound coming from his throat as he struggled for air, staggering backwards. Oddjob composed himself quickly, shaking off the attack, his stamina plentiful, charged again at Fiji, throwing a right at his head. Fiji caught the blow in his left hand, held it tight, wouldn't let go. Oddjob flung his left fist; with his right hand Fiji caught it as well, grip possessing the crushing power of a steel vise. In startled shock Oddjob stared at Fiji, for the first time in his life fear crept into his belly, never before had an opponent shown such brute strength, never facing one his equal. Fiji reared his head back, shot it forward, forehead colliding with terrific force on the crown of Oddjob's skull, releasing his hold on his fists at the same moment as the man reeled backward.

Oddjob stood woozily, shook his head, clearing away cobwebs rapidly collecting in the corners of his mind. He charged at Fiji again, threw a right cross, connected with Fiji's jaw, snapping it to the side. Oddjob stood smiling, waiting for Fiji to topple over as proof he the superior combatant, no man able to defeat him. Fiji whipped his head back, glaring back at his attacker, exhibiting no sign of pain, displayed no indication the solid punch, one knocking senseless a weaker opponent, had the slightest effect on him. Oddjob stared at Fiji, astonished the man still stood, shrugging off his punch. He whirled his body about, swung his right leg up into the air, aiming to land his heel on the side of Fiji's head.

Fiji stood his ground, didn't flinch a muscle, no effort to dodge the kick. At the last second his left arm shot up with lightning speed, Fiji grabbing the leg in mid-air as the foot arched towards his temple, hand grasping tight the ankle and not letting go. Oddjob stared in stunned amazement at him, surprised by the swiftness of the response, struggling to maintain balance teetering on his left foot.

Fiji glowered at the man. *This ends now.* Oddjob, used to producing terror in the hearts of others, now felt that very sensation fill him with dread.

In a blur of movement Fiji raised his right elbow, brought it down on the vulnerable right knee of his adversary with tremendous force, the sound of cracking bone like the blast from a double-barreled shotgun. Oddjob shrieked, the cry filling the space, as Fiji released his hold on the leg and the man collapsed to the floor, lower part of his right leg dangling loose, bent away from the thigh at an grotesque angle. D'Andre and Connor cringed at the piercing scream and the appearance of the shattered leg, understood the horrendous magnitude of the damage inflicted.

"Damn, I know a busted kneecap when I hear it," D'Andre grunted under his breath, watched Oddjob clutch the obliterated joint, "with a torn ACL and MCL thrown in for good measure."

As quickly as the fury of combat swept over Albert Fatuamala, the rage evaporated as a fall mist dissipating in the warmth of morning sunshine. He gazed down at the man, realized the wound inflicted destructive in nature, wished he never forced to take such violent action, yet conscious the situation left him no other recourse. "I am sorry, brother," Fiji whispered softly, remorse in his voice.

Connor bent over, hands on his knees, breathing heavily from exertion, glanced up at Fiji standing in the middle of the bay, staring with wonderment upon the vanquished foes arrayed about him, the last gladiator left standing after a contest to the death on the floor of the Roman Coliseum.

"We did it," was all Connor needed to say.

None of them yet aware of the explosive devices, of the same design as the one Fiji disarmed at the studio, hidden in the catwalks above their heads and placed throughout the abandoned factory, now activated, the timers counting down. Only minutes remained until their celebration of victory came to an abrupt, and fiery, end.

"What's that?" Detective Patrick Flannery asked as he and Detective Devin Carson, speeding south on Sacramento towards where human traffickers about to hand their victims over to a buyer, saw two pairs of headlights hurtling towards them.

"We're about to find out," Carson said as the first vehicle, a limousine with one of the back passenger doors missing, shot past them heading north. A black Audi S8 sedan trailed seconds behind in close pursuit. Carson made an instantaneous decision, slamming on the brakes, twisting the steering wheel hard, Flannery bracing his body against the dashboard. The unmarked squad car swung about, tires and brakes squealing with the sudden deceleration and change in direction. Once the car pointed the opposite way Carson hit the accelerator, set off after the limo and the Audi.

"Playin' a hunch here, fella?" Flannery asked.

"That I am," Carson replied, speeding to catch up to the fleeing vehicles, passing the train of marked and unmarked police cars, blue lights flashing through the night, heading towards whatever awaited them at the factory on Carroll Avenue.

"Now that's what I'm talking about!" D'Andre Watson surveyed the results of the carnage unleashed by the trio, pleased at the tableau of a fallen enemy, listened with unrestrained glee at the low moans of pain from vanquished foes. *That's what you fools get for messing with us!* D'Andre stared down at the closest of Rahim's security detail sprawled at his feet, leaned over and pointed a defiant finger in his face, shouted a braying victory cry at the prostrate foe. "Welcome to Chicago, bitch! We own your ass!"

"Real men don't taunt," Connor Aanonsen remained bent over, panting, adrenaline flooding his body dissipating in a blink-of-the-eye, leaving him tired and sore.

"This one does," D'Andre said. "Believe me, this one does."

Connor looked over at Albert 'Fiji' Fatuamala; the Samoan gazing at the physical wreckage he exacted on the underlings of Sheik Rahim with a wondering expression of *did I really do all of this?* "Remind me never to make you angry." Connor told him as he brought his body erect, extending out his arm, dropping the broken handle of the last goalie stick on the floor with the audacity of a rapper concluding a show before a raucous audience. "I never want you angry at me."

"We don't want to see you angry," D'Andre added. "I don't think we'd like to see you when you're angry."

Fiji cocked his head. "Why are you worried about me being angry with either of you?"

D'Andre swept his hand across the human debris field of moaning, barely moving forms of Rahim's men lying around them. "This is why we never want you angry at us."

"Guys, we're forgetting why we came here," Fiji pointed out. A nagging notion nibbled at his thoughts, couldn't place the reason for the trepidation. *This is too easy.*

"What are we forgetting?" D'Andre wondered as Fiji motioned at the four women huddled, still bound and gagged, on the floor, faces relieved at their salvation, yet apprehensive. *You came here to rescue us.* The one in the leather jacket with tousled mahogany hair gave out a pitiful whimper. *Could you please get us free now?*

"Oh yeah, that's why we came here," D'Andre smiled sheepishly at hostages anxiously awaiting freedom. "Sorry, I tend to run my mouth sometimes."

"Yes, you do tend to run your mouth," Fiji chastened D'Andre as they moved to the captives gazing up at unknown rescuers, desiring release from the torturous ropes and thankful for this most unexpected deliverance.

D'Andre studied the webbing of cords binding tight their limbs. "These guys go to town with the Boy Scout knot-tying skills," he sighed, glanced at one of Rahim's fallen cohort. The man writhing in agony on the concrete, clutching at the distinctive red handle of the Swiss Army knife protruding from his thigh, blood soaking his trousers. "Be a lot quicker cutting these ladies loose if we had your knife," D'Andre told Connor, jerked a thumb. "But that guy's using it right now."

"Hold that thought." Connor, a hard glint to the blue eyes, walked over to the wounded man, placed a hand on the man's leg, other hand grasped the knife handle. "Excuse me, I need this." With a sudden yank jerked the knife from the flesh, the man squirming, howling with a banshee shriek of anguish. Connor grabbed the thug's hand, shoved it on top of the bleeding gash. "Direct pressure on a wound helps stop bleeding," he advised the henchman in an icy, impersonal tone.

"Dude, that is stone *cold!*" D'Andre exclaimed as Connor wiped blood staining the blade across the leg of his jeans, leaving a dark streak on the denim.

"About as cold as that bastard Cowle leaving Amanda and Lauryn with that bomb?" Connor shot him a quick, merciless retort, cool Nordic reserve replaced by Viking blood boiling hot, still spoiling for a fight, as he leaned over to work on the rope tied around the brown-haired young woman in the leather jacket and denim miniskirt who saved his life during the fight. "Or this Rahim wanting to buy these women so he could abuse them? Kill them when he's done getting his jollies with them?" Connor cut the ropes around her wrists and arms, breathing hard as he toiled, removed the gag around the girl's head. "I'm in no mood for sympathy now. These punks are kidnapping, murdering bastards. None of us should be holding hands singing a chorus of Kumbaya after what they tried to do. And this isn't over, not until Samantha and Presley are safe." Somewhere out in the city the limo with two remaining captives, driven by a murderous maniac, pursued by Tyler McManaway.

"We understand how you feel, Connor," Fiji nodded as he undid the gags silencing the other three hostages, tone placid as ever, understood the ferocity of his friend's rage though not about to condone the callous disregard for the vanquished. He turned his attention to the captives; spoke in a voice calm and reassuring. "It's okay, it's all over, you're safe now. I'm Albert," he used his first name as introduction, didn't want to bother explaining his peculiar nickname, put the women at ease, let them know they no longer had anything to fear. "Are you all right?"

"We are now. I'm Alexandra," the woman in the gunmetal gray pinstripe business suit said after spitting cloth from her mouth, jaws achingly sore from the gag. Alexandra sniffed back tears welling in her eyes, didn't want to break down. The four young men, whoever they were, a lifeline thrown at the last possible second to Alexandra sinking slowly in a quagmire of terror about to swallow her, pulled to safety. "Thank God you came when you did," she gasped, the identities of the quartet, or how they discovered where they held captive, still a mystery. The only hint the Great Northern Hockey sweatshirt the blond-haired one wore. Were they friends of Presley Harding or the other young woman, Samantha Grayson, who fell into the hands of Marcus Cowle? What mattered was they spared Alexandra and her companions from a brutally short future of painful suffering and a violent death, forever grateful for life and freedom, never again taking another minute of either for granted. "I thought it was over, they were going to take us..." Alexandra couldn't finish the statement, didn't want to envision the horrible reality if Sheik Rahim accomplished his goal, spirited to his homeland as his possessions and never to return, left rotting in some unmarked grave.

"I think I'm okay," the woman with long raven hair and dark eyes added, her reply subdued and hesitant, on her face the stunned expression of one pulled from the path of a speeding train at the last instant. "I'm Isabella."

"Thank you for finding us," the woman with dark honey blonde hair answered. The lingering residue of fear causing her to shiver against the ropes still wound tight about her slender body. "I'm Gabriella."

The sound of sirens in the distance broke the tense mood. "Now they're on their way after we've done all the heavy lifting!" D'Andre spread his arms wide in disbelief.

"Sometimes things work out that way," Fiji told him.

Connor sliced through the last ropes imprisoning the girl in the leather jacket, handing the knife to Fiji, who quickly worked on the ropes binding Alexandra. The young woman he released rubbed her sore, aching arms as she sat on the floor. "Thanks for the assist there," Connor said as she massaged throbbing, raw wrists, circulation returning to her fingers, "I'm Connor Aanonsen."

"Thank you for finding us, I'm Emma Hayden." She stared at him, heard the name before, studied the Great Northern Hockey sweatshirt, in her mind shaved the beard and trimmed the blond hair, thought of the Minnesota Wild hat he'd been wearing and finally made the connection, a glimmer of recognition flashed in her damp eyes. "God, I thought you looked familiar! I went to Edina! You beat us in the state hockey finals my senior year in high school!"

"Now ain't it a small world?" D'Andre noted, took the knife from Fiji to cut the ropes binding Isabella, once she free D'Andre moved over to Gabriella, did quick work on the rope about her body. "Those goalie sticks he was swinging about should've been a dead give-away."

Once free of their bondage Isabella leaned over to tightly embrace Gabriella, the pair in tears as the danger finally faded, their expressions that of shocked relief, the last two passengers slipping into lifeboats from the sinking *Titanic*. "Briella, I'm sorry I got you into this," Isabella offered an apology she thought never able to give between hitching, painful sobs. "I trusted him. I thought he was my friend." Isabella swallowed, closing her eyes. "I almost got you..."

"It's all right, Bella," Gabriella consoled her friend, "we're safe now, it's over."

"I remember that game," Connor smiled at Emma, a bright and shining recollection of his greatest achievement from high school cooling his anger, "no one gave us a chance of winning."

"You were standing on your head making those of saves," Emma told him, recalled happier times, asked with a twinge of disappointment, "You're taken already, aren't you?"

"Yeah," Connor smiled self-consciously, "saved my princess on the way here." Connor grimaced at the observation, didn't know if his actions at the studio in any way heroic, stood in stupefied confusion while Fiji disarmed the device to save their collective skins.

"Just my luck," Emma sighed. "When I think I've found my knight in shining armor..." Connor studied the young woman with mahogany hair and turquoise blue eyes, a brave soul who saved his life in the heat of battle, an unusual notion entered his mind. *I wonder if I can introduce her to Sean Mittersley...I think Emma's just the type for Han Solo.*

The sound of approaching sirens outside of the complex grew louder as two of the fallen guards regained enough of their senses to stagger to their feet and stand uneasily, staring at the three men and the captives they freed, trying to decide their next course of action. As they did a third stirred from his stupor, struggled to rise, unsteady on his legs like a punch-drunk boxer beating a ten count.

D'Andre nudged Fiji. "Looks like these chumps want to take the kick-off for the second half."

The three women braced their bodies against the Plexiglas partition separating the back seat from the front of the police squad car, Lauryn Callahan wrapping an arm about Wrigley the golden retriever sharing the compartment with them, as the Crown Victoria screeched to a stop near the abandoned factory complex on West Carroll Avenue.

"Do I need to remind you to stay here and out of trouble?" Dawson Hilliard asked as a convoy of marked and unmarked cars pulled up alongside, officers both uniformed and in plainclothes emerging from the vehicles.

Amanda McKinnon smiled, not about to argue as the detectives departed, had more than her fill of excitement for the night. "This is your show," she replied, praying Connor Aanonsen had survived whatever took place inside the factory and Samantha Grayson and Ashleigh Morgan, along with the others held prisoner, safe and the terrifying ordeal finally over.

"What I want to hear," Hilliard said, sprinting towards the complex with Nathanial Hampton beside him.

Silence filled the car until Lauryn spoke, breaking the stillness while she clutched the leash of the golden retriever. "These seats are pretty uncomfortable." Wrigley barked in agreement.

D'Andre Watson stood up with a confident swagger, stepped forward to confront the three guards rising from their stupor to pose one final challenge. "Now boys, I know what you're thinking," he informed them in a casual, cocky manner telling them he didn't feel threatened by their unsteady rejuvenation. "But if you do that my friend here," D'Andre pointing at Albert 'Fiji' Fatuamala standing next to him, hands on his hips, dark eyes staring down the men, "will turn all green again and shout 'Hulk smash' while he cleans the floor with you. My other friend here," D'Andre motioned to Connor Aanonsen, grabbing from the floor the broken handle of one of his goalie sticks, stood on the other side of D'Andre, presenting a united front to shield from harm the women they freed, "he's got Scandinavian blood in his veins, ice-cold like a blizzard. You saw what he did to your friend. He'll go all crazy Viking on you." Connor saw Emma get to her knees, grab a length of pipe lying on the floor, clutching it in her hands, noticed the hatred in her eyes, wanted to be part of the action *Yeah, she's Han Solo's type,* Connor smiled.

D'Andre gave the three a knowing smile. "Me? I'll be floating around you like a butterfly, stinging like a bee. Do I need to remind you what happened during the first half of this game, you couldn't stop our offense and our defense went to town on you. Looking at the scoreboard I'd say you're way behind and on top of that we took out your quarterback." D'Andre pointed at Oddjob grabbing at the knee Fiji shattered with his elbow, shook his head in sympathy. "It's your call, but I really don't think a second spin on the dance floor will turn out any differently."

The guards weighed their options, glaring at the three young men standing resolute in opposition, recalling a thrashing fresh in their minds, routed despite overwhelming odds in their favor at the onset of the fray. From outside the building came sounds of sirens, cars screeching to a stop, running feet approaching the factory as urgent shouts filled the air. The three guards of Sheik Rahim's detail made their decision, figuring the odds far better to face this new threat instead of a second confrontation with three adversaries who delivered so complete and devastating defeat upon them minutes earlier.

Dawson Hilliard and Nathanial Hampton raced into the abandoned factory, steps ahead of the vanguard of officers with guns drawn, Hilliard noticing the overhead door to the loading bay torn from its anchor, something ramming its way through from inside with terrific force. The two detectives at the point of the assault, the tip of the spear and the first to learn the result, the success or failure, of the rescue attempt by four intrepid young men from Great Northern University.

"Oh shit," Hilliard hissed under his breath, spotting three men in business suits, Arabic in appearance, coming at them, didn't have time to order them to halt, only time to react. The first one lunged at Hilliard, threw a wild punch at his head. Hilliard grabbed him behind the neck, leaping from his feet to deliver a blow with his right knee directly on the chin of the attacker, knocking him out instantly. Hilliard released the guard, light in his eyes blotted out as the limp body crumpled in a inert heap, without hesitation turned to the second suspect bearing down on him. Hilliard came in low this time with a double-fisted axe-handle blow, hands still gripped around his nine-millimeter automatic, finding the mark on the man's exposed midsection, doubling him over, gave Hilliard a clear shot at the back of the head, unleashed a second axe-handle blow to the base of the skull. Without uttering a sound the man fell face-first to the ground. Hampton ducked under the swing of the third guard, delivered a forceful clothesline across the man's throat, sending the man tumbling backwards, body twisting and screwing around like a top from the force, landing on the concrete with a thud. The detectives stood over the three prostrate guards, wary of attack from a different quarter.

"I don't think they taught you that particular maneuver in your police training academy," Hampton observed succinctly to Hilliard.

Hilliard stepped over his fallen suspect. "Wicker Park School of Hard Knocks," he told his new partner. "I don't think you learned that little move at Scotland Yard either."

Hampton smiled. 'Of course not," he answered diplomatically, adjusted his tie.

"You have the right to remain silent," Hilliard informed the three motionless figures, "and you're doing an excellent job." The two detectives approached three young men standing with steadfast bravado in the middle of the loading bay, proud bearing of those accomplishing a heroic deed facing daunting odds, formed a protective buffer in front of the four women who minutes earlier faced the dreadful prospect of being sold into slavery. The bay quickly swarmed with police officers handcuffing the adversaries who experienced, and fallen victim to, their relentless onslaught.

The young black man in the middle of the three, the shortest of the trio yet still six feet tall, tilted his head as the detectives neared, a hint of disappointment creased his face as if Hilliard and Hampton late for an appointment. "About time you showed up." He grinned with satisfaction, waved at bodies barely moving lying on the floor. "Missed out on all the fun."

"Had to pick up your friends at the studio," the detective explained, then apologized, "got lot of newbies working the 911 center tonight. Looks like you had a handle on this. By the way, nice game Saturday, D'Andre," the detective said, offering his hand to D'Andre Watson, then to Albert Fatuamala. "You too."

"Never know where you'll run into an adoring public," D'Andre smiled broadly as the detectives, along with Connor and Fiji, turned their attention back to the quartet of women sitting close together, comforting each other after a shared and terrible ordeal. Hilliard immediately recognized one of the women huddled on the floor, crouched beside her. "Alexandra Cole?" He asked, touching her shoulder, saw she'd been crying.

"Yes?" Alexandra nodded her head, wiped at tears with the sleeve of her gray blazer.

"Detective Dawson Hilliard," he introduced himself, Alexandra thought him attractive in a rough around the edges but with a good heart underneath the scruffy exterior sort of way. "There's someone outside for you. Wants to know you're okay."

Alexandra nodded reflexively. *Is my family already here?* Making the trip to Chicago from her small hometown in Kansas after learning she was missing. *God, I hope it isn't my ex.* Over the wailing of sirens and shouts of police officers she heard a familiar barking. *Wrigley, oh my God.* Remembered her beloved dog, loyal friend and companion, a shining light in her life, always there for her, left alone in the apartment on Saturday afternoon with the promise of only being gone for a few hours, Alexandra never knowing what terror waited for her at the studio. *He was alone for so long!* Her reserve cracked, started sobbing uncontrollably. "Wrigley..." The only word she able to utter, collapsing into Hilliard's arms.

"Found him when we searched your apartment," Hilliard smiled as Alexandra buried her head into his shoulder. "Helped us look for you. I might have a new partner," Hilliard rubbed the trembling shoulders, let her release distraught emotions locked inside.

"Are you the one they call Fiji?" The second detective approached Albert Fatuamala; spoke in a British accent out of place in an abandoned factory complex where a human trafficking ring established their heinous operation. The detective a large man, broad in the shoulders though shorter, by three or four inches, than the Samoan.

"I am," Fiji looked closely at the detective; he appeared familiar, then recalled he'd seen the man before, at the women's soccer game on Sunday, embracing an astonished Caitlin Hampton prior to the contest. Fiji made a logical conclusion. "You're related to Caitlin Hampton."

"She's my niece," the detective offered a hand, then an introduction, "Detective Nathanial Hampton, Scotland Yard." Fiji didn't bother asking why a member of Scotland Yard present at the scene. Wasn't his place to ask right then.

Fiji shook his hand, the man's grip strong, still unable to dispel the uneasy rumbling in his stomach. "Caitlin's a fantastic soccer player, you should be proud."

"I am," Hampton smiled, turned serious. "That device back at the studio, how did you know the blue wire would disarm it?"

"I knew it was the blue wire," Fiji shrugged his massive shoulders. "Don't ask me how, but I just knew that was the wire I had to pull."

"If you pulled any other wire..." Hampton started to say.

"I know," Fiji acknowledged, "bad things."

"Smashing job," Hampton complimented, moving away, "no matter how you managed to do it."

As the detective from Scotland Yard walked away the discussion of the explosive device set off a peculiar awareness sweeping over Fiji, as if it was winter and someone left a window wide open, allowing a freezing wind to rush in and chill the skin. *This is too easy,* Fiji realized, suspicion ramped up by unknown apprehension. The sense of foreboding compelled Fiji to search for the source of his uneasiness.

His eyes trailed upward, found what unsettled his soul. *That's not good.*

Along the catwalk lining ceiling of the loading bay he spotted devices similar to the one found at Marcus Evans Photography, left behind to kill Lauryn Callahan and Amanda McKinnon, started counting, stopped when he reached six. Didn't matter if he made a full accounting, one of the insidious contraptions more than enough trouble. *We're sitting ducks here.* His keen eyesight spotted the time remaining on one of the timers. "Excuse me," Fiji cleared his throat, staring up at the catwalk, said in a voice loud enough to gain everyone's attention. "But I believe we should leave here as soon as possible," announced calmly despite his frightening discovery. "I don't think I'll be able to reach all those blue wires in time."

Hilliard glanced up to the catwalk where Fiji fixed his gaze, froze in horror as everyone else looked to where the giant Samoan trained his vision, an instant conclusion the loading bay wasn't a place to remain much longer. "Make like sheep, people!" Hilliard shouted, gathering Alexandra in his arms, running for the exit.

"I hope you don't mind," Fiji apologized graciously, hoisting Isabella and Gabriella in his huge arms, carrying them to safety. *I hope Lauryn won't be jealous*, he thought, looked over to see Connor sprinting next to him with Emma in his arms.

"Can't we leave these jokers here?" D'Andre asked flippantly of an officer, grabbing one of the insensate guards under the arms, dragged him towards the front of the factory.

"That wouldn't be good for public relations," the officer told him matter-of-factly as others hustled Rahim's security men, now securely in custody, from the building.

For a moment D'Andre considered the notion. *Might look bad when I'm up on the stage accepting my Heisman trophy.* "Guess you're right." Even the bad guys didn't deserve to be blown up to kingdom come.

"I don't care what Detective Hilliard said," Amanda McKinnon muttered, groaning as she stepped out from the rear of the squad car, "I have to get out, that seat is hard as a rock." Followed out of the vehicle by Lauryn Callahan, holding the leash of Wrigley the golden retriever, and Riley Bradford, the roommate of the missing Presley Harding. Amanda stared at the abandoned building bathed in flashing blue lights from the police cruisers, arms reflexively wrapped around her midsection, shuddered at the evil, forbidding aura radiating through the night air, seemed the sort of deserted locale where a vicious white slaver should hold kidnapped women hostage, two of them their friends, Samantha Grayson and Ashleigh Morgan. Despite the order to stay in the car for their own safety Amanda needed to stretch her legs, muscles cramping from sitting on the unyielding surface.

"There's Tyler's truck," Lauryn Callahan pointed to the silver Nissan Xterra parked at the next corner, Wrigley agitated by the police cars screeching to a halt, sirens blaring in the air. *She is here! My Mommy is here!* Wrigley whined nervously, barking loudly, straining on the leash Lauryn struggled to hold on to, knew the dog sensed his missing owner inside the factory, wanted to find her. Riley said nothing, staring wide-eyed at everything swirling around her, then at the factory the officers rushed towards, praying Presley soon released from captivity and reunited with her friend.

The three ran up to the truck, spotted a figure crouched down in the front seat. As Amanda approached, ignoring the pulsing, steady drumbeat of dull, aching soreness vibrating through her legs with every step, she realized who sat inside the Xterra and breathed a sigh of relief.

"Ashleigh! Ashleigh!" Amanda reached the door and cried out, banging the palm of her hand against the window to gain her friend's attention.

Ashleigh Morgan turned, dark eyes glazed from her ordeal. Warned by Tyler and D'Andre not to get out unless police officers on the other side, but these were the best friends, Amanda McKinnon and Lauryn Callahan, she feared killed in a terrible explosion and consuming fire. Their presence reason enough to unlock the door, stumbling down from the front seat into welcoming arms and given living, breathing proof her friends alive and spared from harm, tears flowing freely with the reunion.

"Oh my God, you're safe!" Ashleigh whispered.

"We're still here, for better or worse." Amanda told Ashleigh, the trio hugging tightly, thankful to be together once more. "God, Ashleigh, I'm so sorry for all of this! All because I was being such an insufferable little bitch back at the studio, not listening to you. This is my fault, I got us into this crap because I was being stubborn," Amanda said, running a nervous hand through dark hair stringy and unkempt, offered a sincere apology not pulling any punches.

"Bygones be bygones, Gazelle, water under the bridge, girlfriend. I'm happy both of you are safe!" Any anger Ashleigh fostered towards Amanda following the argument outside the studio erased, replaced with thankful relief expressed in tears streaming down her face, knowledge her friends survived what Ashleigh feared a certain doom. "The two of you are alive, that's all that matters."

"Where's Presley?" Riley Bradford asked Ashleigh, hoped for an answer.

Ashleigh glanced at Amanda with a questioning look. "Riley is the roommate of a girl, Presley Harding, Samantha went to the studio looking for," Amanda explained, filled in blanks. "Samantha was working on a story, she wasn't there getting racy pictures for Tyler."

"More importantly, where's Samantha?" Lauryn added, shaky uncertainty in her voice.

Ashleigh about to answer when the air filled with frantic, urgent shouts from the abandoned factory. People pouring out the front of the building, waving wildly at others approaching, shouts to get back from the complex. "What the hell is going...?" Amanda started to ask, heard a thundering crescendo of explosions rumbling within the structure. The four stared transfixed as a fireball expanded from the mouth of the open bay, a dragon of lore emitting a fiery breath incinerating with flame the huts and townspeople of a medieval village. A staccato drumroll of additional explosions, windows blown out by percussive force, shook the building, tongues of red-orange fire spitting skyward in blooming tendrils from openings rendered by the cataclysm.

Amanda took a deep breath, stared in horror as the factory suffered the throes of death by conflagration, realized the absolutely horrific death she avoided by seconds at the studio. "Thank God Fiji pulled that blue wire..." her voice trailed away. Wrigley barked furiously, whining, the canine's supple body heaving against the leash until his strength overcame the resistance Lauryn managed to offer, leash jerking out of her hands.

"Wrigley!" Lauryn cried out, ready to chase after the dog.

Amanda stopped Lauryn. "I think Wrigley knows where he's going." Watched Wrigley head for Detective Hilliard, in his arms carrying a woman with dark brown hair wearing a gray pantsuit, setting her down in the back of a waiting ambulance.

A puzzled expression crossed the face of the paramedic attending to Alexandra Cole as Wrigley the golden retriever wedged his body between them, knocking the paramedic out of the way, tail wildly swinging back and forth like a metronome, pawing at Alexandra as a deluge of wet, sloppy kisses rained upon her face. *I found you! I am here! I found you!* Wrigley seemed to tell her.

Alexandra clutched the dog tightly and buried her face into his neck, never wanting to let go, sobbing uncontrollably in joy as her companion displayed undying devotion, rubbed the gleaming golden coat. "Mommy's here," Alexandra whispered hoarsely, scratching behind Wrigley's ears, the dog a life preserver she now grabbed. The retriever's rear leg twitched in contentment as she scratched, kept licking her face. "Your Mommy's here, Wrigley, she's here. She's not going to leave you again."

"Nice job, partner," Hilliard rubbed the back of the retriever, patted his head. Wrigley turned, mouth open in a smile. *Thank you for finding my Mommy!* Hilliard then turned to a thoroughly perplexed paramedic. "Good luck getting them separated," he informed him as Fiji gingerly set Isabella DiBenedetto and Gabriella Taylor in the rear of a second ambulance, Connor taking Emma Hayden to the third ambulance in line.

"Where's Samantha?" A sick sensation washed over Amanda, didn't see Samantha Grayson among the saved, now feared the worst.

"I don't see Presley!" Riley cried out in anguish, no sign of Presley Harding among those around the ambulances. "Oh my God!" Riley screamed, fearing what might've happened. "Is she still in the factory?"

"I was about to tell you," Ashleigh started to say as Connor, D'Andre and Fiji approached, weaving their way through a mass of first responders now multiplied exponentially with the arrival of firefighters to combat the fiery blaze consuming the factory. "A limo crashed through the door of the building and took off. Another car went after it. Tyler was driving the other car."

Amanda knew what that meant. *This isn't over.* "Samantha had to be in that limo."

"You're safe!" Lauryn threw herself into Fiji's arms, the giant Samoan lifting her from the ground, kissing his newfound love. "Too many blue wires this time?"

"And out of reach too," Fiji kissed her a second time, felt his heart flutter, enjoyed the new phase to their relationship, asked himself an honest question. *What took me so long?*

"Thank God!" All Amanda said as she embraced Connor, relieved her love unharmed, brave in heart and courageous in deed. D'Andre and Ashleigh hugged, reunited again, Ashleigh quietly thanking God for bringing her man back to her. "Where are Samantha and Presley?" Amanda suspected she already knew the answer.

"That Rahim bastard got away," was the to-the-point comment from D'Andre. "Unfortunately he's got passengers along for the ride." Saw Hilliard and Hampton run to their unmarked squad car, get in and the vehicle peeled off, blue lights set in the grill flashing, siren wailing into the night, followed by a train of marked squad cars. "Tyler's off after him."

"Let's hope he isn't getting away for long," Connor said, rubbed the top of his head, peered over his shoulder at the factory slowly consumed by a cauldron of flame.

"What is it?" Amanda asked in confusion, hoped he wasn't hurt.

Connor frowned, pointed back at the factory. "My Minnesota Wild hat is in there."

Amanda kissed him, stroked his cheek. "I'll buy you a new one." A new hat the least she could do for her hero.

D'Andre pointed at the multitude of police cars and officers milling about on the street. "Think we can find someone who'll give us a ride." To where the limo, with Samantha Grayson and Presley Harding inside, and the Audi with Tyler McManaway in pursuit, had ended up.

Chapter 45

Tyler pressed his foot down on the accelerator of the Audi S8 sedan, the engine thrummed smoothly with the incremental, and imperceptible, increase in horsepower. If he wasn't chasing a limousine with his kidnapped girlfriend imprisoned inside through the streets of Chicago, trying to save her and the unfortunate freshman trapped with her without getting either of them hurt or killed, Tyler might've thrilled at the heart-stopping experience of driving an example of precise, finely tuned automotive craftsmanship. Instead Tyler tightly gripped the steering wheel, anxious beads of sweat dampening his brow, panting rapidly, heart hammering against his ribcage ready to burst from his chest. His eyes locked on the rear bumper of the limousine, mirroring every move his quarry made, winding a helter-skelter route through darkened streets of Chicago at breakneck speed. *At least it's late*, Tyler thought thankfully, not much traffic on the streets, but there were still cars, trucks, and CTA buses travelling the thoroughfares at this early hour to avoid. The limo wove and dodged crazily around other vehicles, narrowly missing shattering collisions by the barest of razor-thin margins, only inches separating them from disaster.

The limo blew another red light, screaming through the intersection, almost broadsided by a pickup truck, jamming on the brakes at the last second as the limo flew past. Tyler shot through the intersection seconds later, heard the blaring horn as he sped around the halted pickup. Glanced up in his rearview mirror, caught a quick glimpse of the unmarked police car trailing behind, following since somewhere on Sacramento Boulevard, blue lights set in the grill flashing in darkness, spotted a second police car, this one a marked white and blue squadrol, behind the unmarked squad car.

Tyler switched his attention out the front windshield, eyes again focused on the limo, pulse matching the rapid humming of the powerful engine. *How am I going to stop this maniac?* Tyler watched in horror as the limo swerved around a car ahead of them, ducked back into the lane to avoid by inches a head-on crash with a car in the opposite lane. Tyler waited for the other car to pass, sawed on the wheel to the left, threaded the Audi around the car ahead of him, pressing down the accelerator to pick up the chase.

I have to save Samantha, the mantra burned like a cattle brand into his mind; the promise he made to Samantha and intended to keep. Tried to keep from picturing Samantha Grayson helpless in the rear of the limo, spied the gaping maw open to the outside created when Rahim drove through the loading bay door, tearing away the passenger compartment door in his escape. Feared the possibility, if Rahim took one corner too fast or too sharp, Samantha or Presley ejected through the opening, thrown to a certain death. *I have to save Samantha.* Nothing else mattered to Tyler McManaway now, not football, not his scholarship, not his studies or his life, every ounce of willpower and concentration centered on the single purpose of saving Samantha from this nightmare ordeal. He ignored the instrumentation on the dashboard noting the speed the same number as a noontime temperature on a blistering hot summer day in Chicago.

The question was how he would save Samantha, and that answer still eluded him.

The twisting and turning of the limo as Sheik Rahim drove recklessly through the streets of Chicago to shake the relentless pursuit of Tyler McManaway and the Chicago police rocked the rear of the vehicle like a lifeboat caught in the middle of a typhoon. Tossing the helpless Samantha Grayson about on the floor, slamming her bound body hard against the base of the seats in the passenger compartment as she struggled to locate the missing wine key, the small blade on the utensil her only hope of salvation, of gaining freedom from the ropes holding her prisoner.

Where is it! Samantha battled to keep a tide of rising panic from overwhelming her, head whipping frantically about the interior. Being kidnapped, bound and gagged, terrifying enough. Now trapped in the back of a limousine driven at dizzying speed through city streets, no matter the late hour, by a man with nothing to lose made for a situation all the more fraught with peril. As her brown eyes searched for the wine key, Samantha at the same time watched how close she lay to the gaping hole in the side of the vehicle where the door should've been. *And if I didn't have enough to keep me occupied right now,* Samantha kept an eye on Presley Harding, her unfortunate companion and, like Samantha, a bound and helpless passenger on this wild ride through Chicago. With all of the waning might in her tiny body Presley clutched a seat belt strap to keep from falling out of the seat, pitched through the hole to a terrible doom. Presley whined, straining to hold on, brown eyes frightened, imploring Samantha to do something to end this nightmare.

There it is! Samantha spotted the wine key at the base of the seat, inching across the floor towards where it lay tantalizing close, beckoning her with the promise of liberation if she could reach it, use the blade to hack away her bonds. Samantha about to wrap her fingers around the utensil when the limo hit a deep pothole, sending her body bouncing in the air, slamming back down on the floor with a hard thud, screaming through the gag as her shoulder absorbed the impact. The wine key skipped away from her grasp as the limo took a tight right turn, skidded across the floor, winding up towards the rear of the passenger compartment. *This night really sucks.* Samantha growled, aggravated by how close she'd come to snaring the tool only to be denied at the last moment, started again to nudge her body across the floor towards the beckoning object.

This is going to be a lot harder than I thought. Samantha had no other choice.

"Getting a little dicey here, isn't it, fella?" Patrick Flannery commented drolly at Devin Carson, maintaining a close distance to the limousine and the pursuing Audi sedan as the three car convoy sped north on Central Park Avenue, the latest roadway traversed on their haphazard high-velocity excursion on side streets and thoroughfares wending through Humboldt Park and Logan Square. A squad car joined the pursuit as the unmarked squad car snaked around cars travelling the highways at the early morning hour.

"That's a bit of an understatement," Carson grumbled, kept his concentration fixed on the rear of the two vehicles weaving and darting in and around other vehicles, mimicking the pulse-pounding computer generated graphics of a car chase video game, hoping this pursuit didn't end badly, thankful this wasn't earlier in the evening when the volume of traffic much heavier, the chances of calamity greater. "At least you're getting a tour of the city."

"I'd like to see what I'm passin' by," Flannery gasped, bracing himself with the door handle. "That fella in the limo doesn't want to get caught," he observed as the limo came within inches of sideswiping a car traveling in the opposite direction, the Audi braking slightly to let the car pass, then accelerating after the limo. "Wonder who this fella is?"

"Someone with the money," and the requisite arrogance to believe himself above the law, "to have someone kidnap women for him," Carson replied as the limo, followed by the Audi, turned left onto Milwaukee Avenue. Carson slowed as a marked squadrol heading north on Milwaukee joined the chase, got in position ahead of him, settling in behind the two speeding vehicles. Carson guessed the driver of the Audi one of the four student-athletes from Great Northern who'd gone to rescue their friends from the human traffickers, wondering if it Tyler McManaway piloting the Audi and Samantha Grayson a hostage within the limo he chased.

I hope he doesn't get himself killed doing this.

Tyler maintained his pursuit of the limo, heading northwest on one of Chicago's diagonal streets, didn't know if he was on Milwaukee or Elston, saw a marked patrol car take the place of the unmarked Crown Victoria following behind. *Do I pull aside and let them take over*? Tyler considered for a second, decided against the idea. *No, I made a promise to Samantha. I wouldn't let anyone hurt her.* He was going to save Samantha, free her from the grasp of her captor, do whatever it took, pay whatever price to fulfill the promise he made. *Hang on, Samantha, I'm coming for you.* Tyler clutched the wheel, a smooth vibration of uninhibited mechanical power generated by the V8 engine massaged his body through the driver's seat. *I'm going to save you.* Nothing else mattered but getting Samantha away from this madman.

The limo approached the next intersection, the light turning red as the luxury vehicle barreled through. Tyler kept pace, eyes on the limo, speeding into the intersection, glancing to his left. *Oh, shit...* His stomach twisted in a sudden spasm of horror.

He spotted the boxy form of a CTA bus looming to his left, lighted sign atop reading 77N BELMONT, moving at him as an elephant charges a sportsman hunter on the African plain, ivory tusks poised to gore him, blaring horn the animal's cry. A second all Tyler given to respond to the imminent threat, reacting instantaneously as he did on the football field with the defense bearing down on him. Jammed his foot on the accelerator, powerful engine producing an instantaneous burst of horsepower, emitting a banshee scream of acceleration, the sedan shooting out of the intersection, avoiding a devastating crash by a hair's breath. Tyler exhaled as he sped away, for the second time this night experiencing a narrow escape with fragile mortality intact. Didn't need to find out if he, like a feline, had nine lives, suspecting he might use up a few more before the next dawn broke.

He glanced in the rearview mirror, grimaced at what he saw. The Chicago Police squadrol following behind wasn't as quick, or as lucky, as Tyler was getting through the intersection.

"Shit! Hang on!"

Devin Carson saw the CTA bus entering the intersection of Belmont and Milwaukee, the Audi barely skimming across the front of the bus, accelerating away like a ghostly wraith into the night. The rear taillights of the marked squad car ahead of them glowed cherry red as the driver slammed on the brakes. The effort in vain, the squadrol unable to stop in time, skidding into the intersection. The front of the bus slammed into the left front fender of the squad car with the force of a wrecking ball against the side of a condemned building. The momentum and impact of the collision lifting the car from the pavement, sending it spinning around in the air, shards of metal and glass spraying through the air as water streams from a fountain in a park.

Carson jammed his foot on the brake, grimaced at the sound of tires squealing in protest, smelled an odor of burning rubber. The rear of the Crown Victoria lifted slightly in the air, vehicle screeching to a halt less than a foot from the stopped CTA bus blocking the intersection, the squad car following behind coming to a stop at the last second, keep from crashing into the rear of Carson's unmarked car.

"Christ!" Patrick Flannery exclaimed, removed his hands from the dashboard bracing his body for the expected collision. "Hey fella, I'd like to return to Dublin in one piece next bloody spring when this stupid summit business in your city is done with!"

A bitingly sarcastic answer about being glad to send him back to Ireland poised on Carson's lips when he saw the screen of the laptop set below the dashboard flash with an instant message from Captain Hardaway. *Now what?* Carson wondered, saw additional squad cars coming up Milwaukee Avenue behind him. They could handle the accident scene and any injuries, Carson hoped they were minor, suffered by those involved. Carson looked at the screen. *You have got to be kidding me.* "Son of a bitch." Carson muttered, digesting the message, backing away from the CTA bus and the demolished squadrol, threaded the sedan around the wreckage to pick up the chase. 'Wonderful," he scowled, shaking his head in disbelief, "absolutely fucking wonderful."

"What is it?" Flannery asked.

"We know who this trafficker was about to sell those women to. This thing just got a lot more complicated," all Carson said as he hit the accelerator, let Flannery read the message and the reason for his unease.

"Christ, puts a wrench into things," Flannery remarked as the car sped north on Milwaukee Avenue to close the gap with the fleeing limo and pursuing Audi.

"Let's hope we don't start a war tonight." The last thing Devin Carson expected when given the case of two missing women earlier that afternoon was an international incident with ramifications far beyond what Carson, or the Chicago Police Department, ever anticipated.

Come on, Samantha, you're running out of time! Do it...now!

In one final, desperate movement after several failed attempts Samantha Grayson timed the moment she rolled across the floor as Sheik Rahim took another sharp turn and the wine key skidding across the floor of the limo towards her, trapped the utensil underneath her body. *I did it!* Samantha grunted in satisfaction, quest to free herself far from completed. Forced fingers tingling with soreness to grasp the tool, position the blade to resume the interrupted task, knowing every second mattered as she sawed frantically at the rope about her wrists. Presley Harding clutching the seatbelt strap with her bound hands, Samantha could see the girl weakening, struggling to hold on as her strength ebbed. *Hurry up, please, hurry up!* The brown eyes of the freshman, saucer-wide with terror, pleaded.

Believe me, I'm working on it. Samantha closed her eyes, centering a diminishing reservoir of energy on moving the blade against bindings pinning her wrists behind her back, each frantic stroke cutting away a few more strands of cord. She arched her back, screaming in frustration, couldn't give in, unwilling to surrender with rescue so close. Suddenly she sensed slack in the bondage, constriction no longer biting against the skin, at last able to move her wrists. Samantha opened her eyes, a quiet sigh of victory passing her lips.

I'm free.

A rush of gratifying relief, one never so satisfying experienced in her life, swept over Samantha as she sat up, commanding numb fingers to shake the ropes from her wrists, watched in triumph as they dropped to the floor. A warm tidal-wave of blood flooded her hands once released from the bonds imprisoning her for hours. Samantha worked automatically, no time to celebrate the accomplishment, not yet completely free of her bondage and still a reluctant passenger on Sheik Rahim's crazy joyride through Chicago.

Samantha shifted her hands from behind her back, in doing so loosened ropes looped around her upper body, shrugging easily the bands up and over her head. She reached behind her head, groaned lifting her arms as an aching pain flared in her shoulders, fingers picking at the knot in the cloth tied behind her neck. Within moments Samantha undid the hated gag, tongue ejecting the damp wadding crammed in her mouth, breathed deeply. "Don't worry, Presley, I'll get you free in a second," Samantha told her powerless companion, Presley's soulful brown eyes exuding faith, answering with a plaintive but hopeful whimper she might survive this terrible ordeal.

With single-minded focus Samantha cut the rope tied around her legs with the wine key blade, with her hands free an easy task. Sawed through bindings encircling her thighs and knees, precious seconds expended hacking at the ropes and ripping them from her legs, then sliced through the binding around her ankles. *Now I'm free!* For the first time in hours Samantha smiled, free to move without restriction though her entire body pulsated with a dull soreness, unending waves of discomfort in joints and muscles restrained and immobile for so long. Had to ignore the pain, couldn't rest, not now with work yet to be done. Samantha scrambled to her knees, crawling towards Presley, ignoring the throbbing aches tormenting every nerve. "It's okay, Presley, I'm going to..."

The limo swerved, cutting Samantha off in mid-sentence, taking a turn to the left so severe Samantha caught off-guard, body thrown against the opposite side of the compartment, shrieking in agony as a supernova burst of pain exploded at the base of her spine. Presley screamed, momentum of the turn pitching her forward, hands torn from the seat belt she held onto. The small, bound body flung violently across the compartment, hitting the floor, Presley's eyes widened as she rolled towards the hole in the side of the limo, unable to stop her movement, about to be helplessly ejected from the vehicle travelling at a high rate of speed, hurtling to a certain oblivion awaiting outside. Presley tightly closed her eyes expecting, at any second, to experience a brief, devastating pain then nothingness as her life came to a sudden end.

Presley felt something grab her legs, wrapping around her calves and ankles, halting the seemingly unstoppable momentum out the opening to an inevitable death. She opened her eyes; peered through the yawning opening inches from her head, gazing out at buildings and houses, and the parked cars her body would've been thrown into, speeding past in a seamless blur, whimpered with the realization how close she'd come to dying. Lifted her head to find Samantha holding her legs, gasping for air. Samantha dazed by the impact against the seat, but recovering enough of her senses in time to lunge for Presley as she tumbled towards the gap, catching the girl by the legs at the last possible moment, saving her from a horrible demise.

Presley whined at Samantha. *That was too close*, face frozen in terror at the close brush with mortality. Samantha offered a silent reply with her brown eyes. *I know.*

"I've got you," Samantha reassured the terrified freshman, lifting her into a sitting position, dragging her body back to the seat. Had to keep Presley from being thrown from the limo while she dealt with Sheik Rahim, finding some way to stop the limo in its flight from Tyler and the police. She positioned an arm underneath Presley's legs, groaned in pained exertion heaving the petite girl back on the seat. Samantha untied the gag, pulled it from her lips.

"Are you okay?" Samantha asked as Presley gasped for air.

"I'm really scared," Presley admitted in a shaky voice, anxiously biting her lip, eyes glistening with tears.

"That makes two of us," Samantha grabbed the seat belts, winding them across the tiny form, locking them down to secure her.

"What are you doing?" Presley asked, confused by Samantha's actions.

Samantha stroked Presley's silky caramel hair to reassure her. "I don't want you going out that way again," she said, pointing to the yawning opening Presley came within inches of being thrown through seconds earlier. The limo took a sharp right turn; Samantha clinging with diminishing strength to the straps holding Presley to the seat. She felt the limo accelerate, going up an incline, no idea where in Chicago they might be now.

"What are you going to do?" Presley asked in desperation, wondering if there was any way of surviving this terror.

Samantha panted heavily, already exhausted, what little stamina remained in her battered body rapidly draining. "I'm going to figure out how to stop him and this thing," she paused for a breath, "in a way that doesn't get us both killed."

Samantha didn't believe a single word she told the frightened girl.

Where the Hell are we? Tyler McManaway thought, continuing his pursuit of the black limo through Chicago, his focus on the lumbering vehicle with Samantha Grayson and Presley Harding imprisoned within. The speed of the chase so blinding, the twisting and turning route along narrow side streets dizzying and confusing, eyes fastened on the rear of the limo ahead only allowing the briefest of moments to orient him to his location. He chanced a quick glance in the rearview mirror, saw the bright blue lights on the Chicago Police cars flashing behind him, trailing the racing tandem but off in the distance and trying to catch up, delayed in the aftermath of the crash.

They turned onto a wider thoroughfare, heading east, that much Tyler able to gauge, heading towards the lake, an overpass ahead of them. Tyler spotted cars travelling atop the bridge, realized this was the Kennedy Expressway running on its northwest axis between downtown and O'Hare Airport. Which major east-west artery were they on? Diversey? Fullerton? At least he now possessed a general idea of where they were in Chicago.

The limo took a sharp right turn, accelerating up the ramp. Tyler followed close behind as they sped onto the expressway, realized the signs facing the other way. *Oh, crap.* His eyes bulged in unaccustomed horror, hands clenching the steering wheel in a death-grip, sweat breaking out on his forehead at the realization of the direction of traffic.

We're going the wrong way...

Chapter 46

Rising unsteadily to her feet on legs composed of jelly, Samantha Grayson crouched in the confined space of the passenger compartment after strapping Presley Harding to the seat. She struggled to maintain her balance, the limo weaving and bucking from side-to-side like a car traversing the tracks of a roller-coaster ride. She peered through the opening into the driver's compartment, Sheik Rahim sawing wildly on the wheel, attention focused on the road ahead and the Audi driven by Tyler behind him, trying to shake his pursuer. Samantha heard the loud blaring of car horns, noticed they were on an expressway heading towards downtown Chicago, familiar glittering outline of the skyline growing larger with each passing second. Then Samantha realized she was looking at bright white headlights of the cars ahead instead of red taillights, cars and trucks on the four-lane expressway coming *towards them*.

The frightening revelation froze her soul into a solid block of ice. *We're in the wrong lanes!* They were heading inbound on the outbound Kennedy. *He's going to get us killed!*

The limo took a sudden, sharp swerve to the right and Samantha, caught unaware by the unexpected maneuver, pitched across the rear compartment of the limo, a sailor on a boat tossed by a tempest sea. A scream escaped her lungs as her back and shoulder slammed into the edge of the seat, a new explosion of hot pain blossoming in her ribs, shooting up the spine absorbing the impact. Samantha slumped to the floor in a daze, sick to her stomach, head spinning with confusion. *I have to stop him*, Samantha fought off the surge of nausea, incessant ringing in her ears, shaking her head to put scrambled senses back in some semblance of order to figure out the situation. *Before he gets us, and somebody else, killed.*

The answer she sought appeared elusive. *But how?*

Samantha propped her body up on her hands and knees as the limo swerved, eyes darting around the compartment, searching for a weapon to wield against her captor. She had to act, couldn't sit in the limo hoping for a miraculous resolution. Had to take a longshot chance and attack Rahim, force him to stop the limo, or relinquish control of the vehicle without causing a massive collision killing both her and Presley so close to deliverance.

I'm not asking a lot of myself right now, am I? Samantha thought hazily, nothing in the interior but the ropes that until moments earlier held her captive and the wine key with the blade Samantha used to gain her freedom. The wine key slid up to the front of the compartment, Samantha scrambled over to pick it up. *Anything can be a weapon.* The advice from her father echoed in her muddled mind as she studied the utensil. The blade used to cut the ropes small but honed to razor-sharpness, able to inflict damage. Was it alone enough to force Rahim to surrender the steering wheel?

Samantha pulled out the corkscrew, the point on the tip of the metal worm sharp enough to pierce through cork or the man-made polymers used to seal wine bottles. *Sharp enough to stab through skin; cause some serious pain,* Samantha smiled wickedly, *make the bastard hurt.* She could rest the key in the palm of her hand as if a set of brass knuckles, fist closed around the utensil, the corkscrew protruding from between her fingers, generate significant force driving home the point of the screw into skin and bone. Samantha flipped out the bottle opener on the end opposite of the blade, the stainless steel points as finely honed as the blade, use it to tear and gouge at the flesh. *This might work.* With the wine key Samantha provided a ready arsenal of implements with which to assault her captor.

So I attack him, I fight back, Samantha concentrated, formulating a plan. *What then? How do I stop this thing,* the limousine weaving through oncoming traffic on the Kennedy Expressway, *without getting Presley and me killed?* There were options, none of them perfect, each once carried a degree of deadly risk. She could grab the gearshift; pop the limo out of drive and into neutral, causing the transmission to lose power, the vehicle moving but slowing, Samantha gaining control of the steering, guide the limo to the shoulder. Could try to pull the keys from the ignition, disabling the vehicle, or wrestle control of the steering wheel from Rahim after disabling him, pilot the limo out of oncoming traffic. Maybe get the vehicle to spin out, then pray whatever action she took didn't trigger a massive pile-up with Samantha and Presley, trapped in the limo, at the horrendous epicenter.

She couldn't wait any longer, accepting the possible danger and somehow stop the limo. Rahim not about to end this insanity of his own volition, driven mad by the notion of escaping with Samantha, committing terrible acts upon her. *I have to stop him,* Samantha decided, *before this gets any worse, before it gets any further out of control.* A second thought quickly followed on the heels of the first in a jumbled mind. *As if it isn't already out of control.*

Samantha swallowed, mouth as dry as a barren desert, shifted the wine key in her hand so the corkscrew protruded from between her fingers. Prayed she'd have enough strength to gain control of the careening limo, bringing to a conclusion the heart-stopping drama. The wind rushing into the compartment from the shattered opening blew auburn hair crazily about her head, chilled the skin, causing Samantha to shake uncontrollably, then realized the trembling more a result of outright fear. She closed her eyes, banished the paralyzing terror from her soul to focus her energy, summoning every last reserve of depleted stamina to attack Sheik Rahim, overpower him and end the suicidal chase through Chicago.

Samantha glanced through the rear window of the limo, at the Audi with Tyler at the wheel following behind, matching every move of the limo. Samantha willed herself not to cry, knew she might fail in the desperate assault, in doing so sacrifice her young life. *I love you, Tyler;* she quietly called out to him, so close to her yet so distant, desired only to rest in his sheltering embrace, to feel his love for her. Didn't want to take the action she planned but no longer left any choice, had to stop this madness before calamity ensued.

God, give me strength, Samantha prayed, holding onto the seat as the limo swerved from side to side. Samantha didn't want to die, wanted only to be safe in the company of cherished friends and beloved family. Then she thought of sixteen young women, and likely many more than that horrible number, like Samantha on the cusp of their futures with glimmering hopes and bright dreams. Kidnapped by Marcus Cowle, kept helpless and terrified until sold into slavery, tortured and abused to the very last moment of life, never having the chance to fight back. Precious lives callously snuffed by the man in the front seat driving the limo careening wildly down the Kennedy Expressway, not caring if he killed Samantha and Presley, or anyone else, in the crazed attempt to escape. *I will stop him.* A cold rage took root deep within Samantha, able to fight back where other victims of this monster never given that opportunity.

I can do this. Samantha breathed deeply, steeling her nerves, hauling her body up, ignoring the pain vibrating through every muscle. She grasped the inside edge of the opening separating the compartments, lunging forward, forcing her head and torso through the space, letting go with an animalistic scream, giving voice to the suffering and agony of sixteen lost lives.

I can do this. Rahim swung his head about, startled by the sight of Samantha, shocked at the sudden appearance of his prized captive free of her bonds, so intent on fleeing the pursuing Audi thought her subdued in the back of the limo.

I can do this. Samantha flung her right hand at Rahim's face; the diplomat wondering what insanity possessed his hostage, felt the tip of the corkscrew dig into his cheek and draw blood, shouting in anguish, realized the girl found a weapon to attack him.

I can do this. Rahim let go of the steering wheel and Samantha, switching the wine key to the left hand, grabbed for the wheel with her right hand. Trying to stabilize the vehicle, keep it under control, while she continued her frantic, ferocious attack with the wine key.

I can do this. Her position ungainly, body half inside the front compartment, leaning over the partition, awkwardly using her left hand to assault her captor, stabbing and slashing his face. Despite the handicap Samantha fought, imbued with rage, jabbed at Rahim with the pointed opener on the one end, slashed with the blade on the other, gouged with the corkscrew to inflict damage on her tormentor, tearing at his skin, gashing the deceptively handsome face that concealed a horrible beast underneath.

I will do this. A perverse pleasure filled Samantha hearing Rahim cry in pain, deserved every wound, yet never matching the suffering he inflicted on countless victims. *I will do this.* Rahim slumped against the window, hands clutching at his bleeding face, rubbing at the litany of cuts and slashes Samantha dealt with her weapon, blood red as merlot streaming from the wounds. *I will do this.* She took advantage of his confusion, reaching for the gearshift to shift the vehicle into neutral, kill the power of the engine to the wheels, steer the limo off to the shoulder and out of harm's way. *I will do this.* Samantha smiled, victory within reach, dropping the wine key to grasp the shifter.

The explosion of pain in her temple took Samantha by surprise, unprepared for a counter-strike from her captor, Rahim rallying from her onslaught, elbow reared back and rammed violently into her skull. A brief, passing darkness enveloped Samantha, forced to release the steering wheel, limo slewing out of control. She slumped over the partition, dazed and reeling. Rahim shoved her limp form back into the passenger compartment, heard the body hit the floor. He grabbed the wheel, wiping at the blood clouding his vision, fought to regain control, saw the huge tanker truck skidding towards him, horn blaring like the call of a thousand trumpets heralding the entrance to Paradise. Twisted the wheel wildly to avoid a collision, hit the brakes to slow the hurtling vehicle rocketing towards the outer wall of the tunnel the limo had now entered, a gray wall of concrete looming before him the last thing Sheik Rahim saw before impact.

I have to do something before this maniac kills Samantha and Presley!
Tyler weaved the sleek black Audi sedan through oncoming traffic with the skilled dexterity of Luke Skywalker piloting his X-wing fighter down the trench of the Death Star heading for the two-meter wide exhaust port, dodging vehicles swerving and twisting to get out of the way as if they were the Imperial TIE fighters of the Galactic Empire. *I have to do something to stop this*, mind working furiously as it did when stepping up to the line of scrimmage, checking the defense arrayed against him, weighing the options available.

I don't have a lot of options. Tyler realized darkly, jerking the Audi hard to the right to avoid a blue Toyota Corolla in his lane, missing a collision by inches. The shrieking horn wailed a cursing oath at him, driver of the Corolla wondering what lunatics sat behind the wheels of the limo and the sedan speeding down the wrong lanes of the Kennedy at this early morning hour. *I don't have **any** options!* Tyler almost panicked, a sinking sensation of scrambling around in a collapsing pocket, all of his receivers covered, about to be taken down for a huge loss, then reconsidered his alternatives. *Except one.* Tyler unsure he possessed the skill to complete the contemplated maneuver. *Don't think I have much of a choice.* Tyler veered the Audi out of the path of a U-Haul van, another crash missed at the last possible second by less than a foot.

Here it goes, Tyler gritted his teeth, clutched the wheel as he edged the Audi up to the back bumper of the limo, planning the next move, perhaps the last he'd ever take in his life. Made his decision, didn't back away despite immense risk, determined to carry through. *Either this works or it doesn't*, Tyler didn't ponder the implications of failure. *That can't be an option here.* The police referred to it as a pit move, brushing the front fender against the rear bumper of a fleeing vehicle with enough force to cause it to spin out, in auto racing the move more direct and straight-forward, taking the other car out, compelling it to spin to make the pass. Tyler didn't have half of the driving skills of either a trained police officer or top NASCAR racers like Dylan Dinehart or Tony Stewart, but he had no other choice, could wait no longer to act. The longer the chase continued the chances increased the pursuit ending in a terrible crash and the limo, with Samantha and Presley helpless inside, destroyed.

The limo and Audi approached Hubbard's Cave, the tunnel through which the Kennedy Expressway passed underneath the maze of train tracks taking Amtrak and Metra trains to the north and northwest suburbs and beyond. *Have to do it, now or never.* As the speeding tandem wove through oncoming traffic Tyler held the steering wheel tight in his sweating palms, lined the front bumper of the Audi on the rear of the limo, whispered a short prayer. *Please God, for Samantha and Presley, don't let me screw this up.* Pressed the accelerator ever so slightly, engine responding with a subdued roar, nudged the steering wheel ever slightly to the left to initiate contact.

Before Tyler could tap the rear of the limo with the front bumper, his intended target veered sharply to the left, crazily slewing out of control. *What the Hell?* Tyler reacted a split-second later as the limo swerved back towards him, jerking the wheel quickly to the left, getting distance from the limo. Then his focus switched away from the wildly skidding limo to not getting himself killed. Tyler twisted the wheel of the Audi hard to the right, barely missing a van veering out of his way in the next lane; saw the inner wall of Hubbard's Cave looming in the windshield like the face of a steep cliff, certain his heart rate maxed out at the terrifying sight. Yanked the wheel back to the left, swinging away at the last possible instant from what seemed certain impact, slamming his foot on the brake, the shriek of tires gripping the pavement. The Audi rocked to a sudden halt, immediate loss of momentum throwing Tyler against the shoulder restraint and he closed his eyes, bracing his body against the steering wheel. Expected oncoming traffic to smash into the sedan, turn precision engineered automotive machinery with him inside into a jumbled tangle of metal. *Looks like this is the end.* Heard the high-pitched squeal of tires, a cacophony of car and tractor-trailer horns playing a chaotic symphony, wondered if this might be the notes to his own funeral dirge.

Nothing.

Tyler opened his eyes; peered out the windshield at the silver Toyota Camry resting inches from the front end of the Audi, sighed in relief. Other cars spun out and stopped around him, a tractor-trailer jack-knifed in the middle of the six-lane expressway, clogging up traffic approaching from the south. Tyler searched for the limo with Samantha inside, glanced through the space underneath the carriage of eighteen-wheeler, spotted the vehicle wedged against the other wall, front end crumpled like an empty beer can from the collision. Tyler sank down in his seat, exhaled deeply, *that was a bit too close,* body shaking from the incredibly close call, heart hammering against his chest, pried his hands off the steering wheel he continued to hold in a death's grip. *That's three lives used tonight,* Tyler exhaled, struggled to collect rattled senses, *I still have six lives left to use,* he mused. *They make it look easy in the movies.* He quickly composed his nerves, had to get to Samantha. He exited the Audi, ignored the driver of the Camry screaming obscenities at him making a sailor blush beet red as he ran across the highway towards the wrecked limo. Weaving his way between the stopped traffic, Tyler McManaway driven forward by a singular thought.

Is Samantha alive?

The impact threw Samantha Grayson hard against the wall separating the compartments, right shoulder striking the partition, igniting her nerves with an explosion of blistering pain, heard a sickening metallic crunching sound as aluminum struck concrete, instantly transforming the front end of the limo into scrap. A high-pitched scream of terror from Presley filled her ears, the unwilling passenger on this amusement park thrill ride coming to a very abrupt conclusion. Samantha heard brakes screeching, horns shrieking, instinct taking over and curling up her body, at any moment anticipating a second impact, expected a car or tractor-trailer to plow into the limo, obliterate the compartment with them still inside. Samantha closed her eyes, hoped a benevolent God heard her plea, allowed a miracle to occur. *Let me get out of this alive, let me see Tyler again. Let me see my friends, my family again...Please.*

Nothing.

Samantha slowly opened her eyes, every muscle protesting vociferously as she tried to move, an incessant buzz filling her ears as if attacked by a swarm of maddened hornets. She peered up at Presley Harding, with wide eyes the girl staring back at Samantha, quaking against the ropes and seatbelts holding her in place, appeared unharmed, yet shaken in spirit, from the crash.

"Is it over?" Presley asked tenuously. "Are we safe?"

"I...think it is." Samantha swallowed, tasted the salty tang of blood in her mouth, jaw aching where Sheik Rahim struck her with his elbow. "I think we're safe now." She smiled to comfort Presley, joints throbbing as she rose from the floor, knelt by the freshman. "I'll have you out of this in a minute, okay?" She reached to undo the seatbelts, free her companion this frightful night from the imprisoning bonds.

"*Samantha!*" Presley's eyes swelled in terror, alerted Samantha too late of danger from behind. Felt the powerful arm wrap around her throat, pressing against her larynx. Samantha coughed, choking, wheezing for air, hands reflexively shooting upward, grasping at the arm strangling her, dragged away from the shocked Presley. Samantha sensed something cold and metallic pressed against her temple, eyes darting to her right, caught a glimpse of the gun jammed against her head. Over her shoulder saw Sheik Rahim, froze in fear seeing his eyes filled with icy rage, face twisted in malevolent anger as blood flowed freely from a deep gash Samantha tore open on his forehead with the wine key. Samantha hurt her tormentor, but she also enraged him to the brink of irrational action. Rahim hauled the struggling Samantha through the gap in the limo where the door had been, rush of cool night air stinging her face, wheeling about to use her a human shield.

Samantha heard the distant wail of sirens, with each second getting closer to Hubbard's Cave; noticed blue flashing lights approaching as Rahim dragged her, legs kicking in resistance, across the hard pavement, stocking feet dragged against the rough surface. Help on the way, but would it arrive in time? How might Rahim react when confronted by the police? Samantha took in the chaotic scene in the confines of the tunnel. Cars spun out, a tanker truck jack-knifed feet from where the limo rested against the outside wall of the tunnel with front end smashed in, all lanes blocked and traffic backing up even at this early hour. Horns blaring, people exiting their cars, shouting and pointing, confusion everywhere she looked. Her eyes frantically searched for the one person who swore with all his heart to protect her from harm. *Where's Tyler? Where is he?* Had his car crashed? Was he grievously injured and unable to help her?

"Hey! What the hell are you doing?" A deep, booming baritone voice, but not that of Tyler McManaway, shattered the train of frenetic thoughts. The voice came from the tanker truck, a large eighteen-wheel rig, red placards on the side warning of flammable contents inside. Samantha stared dumbly at the tanker truck, realized how close they'd all come to a disastrous, fiery catastrophe. The driver of the rig, a towering black man with huge shoulders, stepping down from the cab, jumping to the pavement, approaching Rahim and Samantha. "What the hell are you doing?" The driver shouted at Rahim, furious after seeing potential disaster, and his life, flash before his eyes. The limousine speeding towards him, swerving out of control in front of his rig containing the lethal cargo, a calamity in Hubbard's Cave averted by a matter of inches and seconds. "Trying to get us all killed? You damn drunk or something? You almost got a lot of people killed here!"

"Stay away from me," Rahim ordered the driver, his voice even, yet threatening.

The driver noticed the gun pointed at Samantha's head, the panicked expression on her face, fear in her eyes. The driver stopped, raised his hands, understood the man unhinged. "Hey, take it easy," he wondered what crazy situation he happened upon by chance, "why don't you let the young lady go. Don't hurt her."

Rahim swung the gun away from Samantha, pointed it at the driver. "Stay away from me," Rahim warned again, his tone calm yet chilling.

"Easy man, let the lady go..." The driver stepped forward. Rahim fired the weapon at the man.

Samantha screamed, deafened by the thunderous gunshot, watched in horror as the driver tumbled to the pavement, clutching his midsection, blood staining his white T-shirt. The sound of gunfire sent people, stepping from their cars to check the commotion, scurrying back inside for safety. A sickening wave of revulsion swept over Samantha at the sight of someone, a total stranger coming to her aid, gunned down before her eyes. Rahim rammed the muzzle against the side of her head, dragging Samantha from the crashed limousine through the maze of stopped cars and trucks clogging Hubbard's Cave. Samantha whispered a silent prayer for the driver, now dreading Rahim's reaction when cornered by the police with no route of escape. With sinking heart, and so desperately close to freedom, Samantha understood he would kill her in cold blood rather than allow her to live.

Chapter 47

Tyler McManaway moved around the back of the jack-knifed tractor-trailer, the limo he pursued coming to a rest on the other side of the monstrous eighteen-wheeler. From what he could see it appeared the vehicle mostly intact, except for the front end crumpled upon striking the concrete wall, passenger compartment where Samantha and Presley held captive miraculously untouched except for the door torn off in the escape from the factory. In seconds Tyler reaching the limo, free Samantha and Presley from the maniac who sought to spirit them to a distant land and a deadly fate. Noticed the driver of the eighteen-wheeler, a black man built solid like an oak tree, had stepped down from the cab of his rig, walking towards the limo. Then Tyler spotted, and his heart dropped in horror, Samantha already out of the limo but not of her own will. Sheik Rahim, blood trickling from a deep, ugly gash on his forehead, standing behind Samantha, his arm around her throat. In his other hand held a gun pointed at the truck driver, warning him off. The driver stepped forward, ordered Rahim to release Samantha, struggling against the confining hold, brown eyes filled with panic.

Tyler flinched as the gunshot echoed through the confines of Hubbard's Cave, saw the driver hit in the stomach, spinning down to the pavement. Samantha screamed in horrified shock as Rahim violently dragged her deeper into Hubbard's Cave, wending a path though the jumbled tangle of halted traffic clogging the roadway. Tyler swung out from behind the tanker, ran to the fallen driver writhing on the pavement, moaning and clutching his midsection. Tyler bent over the man; saw he was still conscious. "You okay?"

The man grimaced in pain, pulling a hand stained with blood from his belly. "Does this look like I'm okay, man?" He turned to Tyler, shook his head. "I'll live, I'm too damn stubborn to die." The man motioned into the tunnel where Rahim had taken Samantha. "The goddamn bastard shot me! He shot me! What the hell is going on?"

Tyler patted the man on the shoulder, another motorist with face blanched white as a bed sheet after observing the shooting, approached the pair in apprehension. "Long story," Tyler said, "love to tell you everything but I've got things to do." Tyler turned to the man standing off to the side. "Can you take care of him?" Tyler didn't wait for an answer, stood up, sprinting in pursuit of Rahim and Samantha. Crouching down and weaving through the halted cars, Tyler mirrored his quarry's every move, stopped traffic behind the jackknifed tanker shielding his movements, eyes locked on captor and hostage, searching for an opening to strike, get Samantha away from this homicidal maniac. An unaccustomed rage burned deep inside him, under pressure Tyler usually poised and self-assured, flared with the white-hot intensity of a steel foundry furnace, a final weight added to the emotional burden and a final straw finally breaking his reserve. Enough was enough and in the course of this night Tyler suffered more than enough of Sheik Rahim and the human traffickers who tried to sell Samantha to him. Tyler whispered a silent promise as he stalked Rahim, waiting for the moment to attack and save an imperiled Samantha, willing to cross a moral Rubicon and take an unthinkable action he thought himself incapable of hours earlier.

If this is what it takes to save Samantha...I am going to kill you...even if I have to do it with my bare hands.

Devin Carson wondered if the drivers and passengers of the cars spun out and stopped in Hubbard's Cave ever realizing their fortune not to have died this night. How there wasn't a massive, fiery pileup behind the jack-knifed tanker in the confined space of the tunnel on a freeway still busy this late at night a feat only accomplished by dint of benevolent fate or divine providence. He brought the unmarked squad car to a screeching halt ahead of the scene as additional squad cars with blue lights flashing, part of the pursuit speeding inbound on the outbound Kennedy, stopped alongside.

Carson stepped from the car, pistol out and ready, Patrick Flannery emerging from the other side of the vehicle as they headed towards the jumble of halted cars and trucks jammed inside Hubbard's Cave, a ragged melody of car horns echoing through the night added to the tumultuous song filling the air. "Every night like this in Chicago?" Flannery asked lightheartedly to ease the tension.

"This isn't every night," came Carson's rebuttal, turned to the officers rushing from behind. "Do not use force against this suspect!" He ordered, shouting. "Do not use force!" *Unless we want to be stuck cleaning up an international incident.*

"How do we handle this, fella?" Flannery proposed as the line of officers entered the tunnel, spreading out among the mass of vehicles, officers ordering drivers to remain in their vehicles.

"I hope he's willing to listen to reason." Carson moved around the tanker truck, spotted a large black man lying on the pavement, driver's side door to the cab open, assumed the prostrate figure the driver of the rig. Another motorist, an older man with salt and pepper hair, bending over him, pressing a shirt or towel on his midsection, blood staining the white fabric a dark red and blackened the asphalt underneath. The driver was conscious. "We have help on the way for you, sir!" Carson told him.

"I'll be all right," the driver replied, grimacing. "The crazy-ass punk went that way," he pointed down into the tunnel at the stopped cars plugging the roadway as effectively as a stopper in a sink, the honking of horns reaching a crescendo. "He's got a girl with him! Some young guy went after them."

"We're aware of that, sir," Carson surveyed the tunnel, appraised the situation; observed the limo resting against the wall of the tunnel, front end crushed by impact, motioned for Flannery and two uniformed officers to check the interior of the damaged vehicle. More police cars approached, stopping at the entrance, from one emerged his partner Dawson Hilliard and Nathaniel Hampton.

"The two our friend took in the limo are Samantha Grayson and Presley Harding. The other hostages are safe." Hilliard came up beside Carson. "Have any bright ideas?"

"Block the other end," Carson explained, units already directed to the southern entrance of Hubbard's Cave, sealing off the only other possible escape route, "and hope he'll be reasonable when he sees there's no way out."

Hampton snorted. "I don't think he's the 'reasonable' type of chap," he remarked as they cautiously moved deeper into Hubbard's Cave, pursing their subject and his hostage.

Is it over?

For Presley Harding the few minutes lying alone within the wrecked limousine, tightly bound and strapped to the seat, seemed never-ending. She floated listlessly in a hazy state of shock after witnessing Samantha, as both believed the nightmare vanquished, overpowered by Sheik Rahim, brutally forced from the limo, heard someone challenge Rahim and the gunshot that followed. The sounds of sirens getting louder, more urgent voices nearby. Presley remained quiet, so uncertain of what taking place outside she didn't call out for help, trembling in her bonds, fingers fumbling to undo the knots around her wrists yet found the bindings secure. Presley heard footsteps approaching the limo and she closed her eyes. *Please let this be over. I want to go home.*

The sight of a head with a shock of bright red hair and beard poking inside the passenger compartment greeted her opened eyes, bulletproof vest over his shirt and tie, the automatic pistol in one hand he now holstered as he stepped inside, a welcome sign to Presley the horrendous trial of abduction and captivity finally over and she at last safe. "Don't worry, little lady, we'll have you out of here right away." The sound of his Irish brogue, living in Manhattan she heard the accent often, so out of place but akin to hearing a chorus of angels singing from the heavens. He squeezed his large frame into the compartment, bending over to fit, inched over to where Presley lay, undoing the seat belts shielding her from harm in the crash ending her captor's flight. "What's your name, little one?" He asked in a gentle voice so unbecoming of one so imposing in stature.

"Presley," she answered in a voice as soft as his, "Presley Harding."

"That's a lovely name, lassie," his smile put her at ease. "I'm Patrick Flannery, as you can tell I'm not from around here, just helpin' your police department out tonight."

"Thank you," all Presley managed to say as Flannery lifted her bound body from the seat, carried out of the limo Presley thought might be her tomb during the chase through the city. Cradling the precious load in his strong arms, Flannery trotted to an ambulance parked outside of Hubbard's Cave, away from the action occurring deep inside the tunnel.

"We'll get you free of this in a minute," Flannery told Presley, motioning to the web of rope around her body. Presley didn't mind the delay, however brief, in being freed from the ropes. The ordeal over, like Sleeping Beauty awakened from the terrible nightmare, soon reunited with her parents and her roommate Riley Bradford, the only one who realized she was in danger. *My friend.* Then she thought of Samantha, final fleeting glimpse of her yanked from the limo, Rahim pressing the gun to her head. Presley started to pray, lucky to be alive and safe from harm. But had the price of her freedom been paid in full with the life of Samantha Grayson?

They will not stop me, Sheik Rahim swore silently, enraged by the unforeseen turn of events, dragging Samantha Grayson, resisting ferociously with every step, into the deepest part of Hubbard's Cave, threading a route through the clutter of stopped cars, waved his weapon menacingly at anyone who toyed with the slightest notion of confronting him. *They cannot do anything to stop me. They cannot hurt me. They cannot harm me. They will do as I will tell them.* He glanced down at the face of his hostage, his property, the one he must possess, brown eyes staring at him seething with terror and rage, fighting mightily against his hold, hands gripping the arm pressed across her throat. *I will escape with my prize.*

He turned his head to the south end of the tunnel, spotted flashing blue lights in the distance, men in uniform moving towards him through halted traffic. His head swiveled back to the north end, more police officers approaching from that direction, boxed in with no way out. "There's nowhere to go," Samantha glared, snarling in defiance. "You can't get away."

Rahim pressed his forearm harder against her throat; Samantha choked, gasped for breath. "Do you think for a moment," he whispered into her ear, jammed the pistol into her temple, let her understand with rescue so close there no hope for her, "that this will compel me to allow you to live?"

Now comes the tricky part. Devin Carson cautiously approached Sheik Rahim, arm wrapped around the throat of Samantha Grayson, hand pressing a gun to the side of her head, his route of escape out of the south end of Hubbard's Cave sealed. Rahim turned with his hostage to face Carson and the officers nearing from the north end of the tunnel, backing up against a car skidding to a stop at an angle to avoid a rear-end collision. The driver wanted no part of the developing confrontation, scrambling to exit through the passenger side door, running towards the line of police approaching from the south. Off to his right Carson spotted a blond head crouched down, moving about the stopped cars, recognized Tyler McManaway working his way closer to Samantha and her tormentor, Rahim not yet aware of his presence. *I hope you have an idea what you're going to do, Touchdown,* Carson inhaled deeply, stepped ahead of the line, nine-millimeter automatic pistol held at the ready, trained on Rahim to let him understand the gravity of the situation. *Have to buy Touchdown Tyler some time.*

"Let her go," Carson commanded of Sheik Rahim, couldn't risk a shot even if allowed, a chance he might hit Samantha. *Not to mention set off an international incident.* "Let Samantha go. We can take care of this without any trouble." Carson feared the diplomat not so amenable to the request.

Scylla and Charybdis, between a rock and a hard place the perilous place Samantha now found herself trapped.

Sheik Rahim the rock, his forearm pressing against her throat as Samantha fought for every gasp of air into her lungs, using her body as his shield, gun jammed to her temple. An ounce of pressure from the finger twitching against the trigger, an insignificant amount, ending her young life in a sudden flash. At such close range the bullet shattering her skull, transforming instantly a mind full of memories and hopes and dreams of the future into a bloody mush.

The long line of Chicago police officers facing Samantha and her captor, both uniformed and in plainclothes, weapons trained on the pair, the hard place. Here to rescue Samantha, but now as powerless with Rahim using her as a human barrier, unable to acquire good enough aim on their subject without risk of hitting her. Samantha trapped between forces of good and evil, neither prepared to yield, if she lived or died depended on who won this contest of wills.

One of the detectives, tall with a fit build reminding Samantha of Tyler, stepped ahead of the line of police facing Sheik Rahim from the north. A second line of police barred escape through the south end of Hubbard's Cave. "Let her go, let Samantha go and we can take care of this without any trouble." The detective spoke calmly, even with his weapon trained on Rahim, eyes searching for an opportunity, an opening however slight, to take down her kidnapper without harming Samantha.

"Really, Detective, you believe I am that naïve?" Rahim laughed. The taunting lilt of his voice and crooked smile on his face chilled Samantha, revealed a man of unstable mental state with nothing to lose, executing her in cold-blood if he didn't soon have his way. "You will allow me safe passage back to my country with my...companion here," Samantha shuddered as he tightened the hold on her throat.

The detective shook his head, eyes fixed on Rahim and Samantha. "You understand I can't let you do that," he explained. "Let Samantha go and we can discuss this matter."

"There is nothing to discuss," Rahim replied evenly, though Samantha realized the man growing increasingly agitated. "Either you allow me to leave or my beautiful companion here," he shoved the muzzle into her temple; Samantha closed her eyes, brutal action forcing her head slightly to the left, "will die."

Samantha opened her eyes, saw a figure crouched between two cars, vision focusing on the form. She gasped once she realized who it was, yet made no other reaction to raise the suspicions of her captor.

Tyler. Attention centered on the phalanx of Chicago police arrayed before them, neither Samantha nor Rahim had seen Tyler quietly working his way through the labyrinth of halted traffic. With the cover and distraction Tyler able to reach a position about forty yards to the left of where Rahim stood with Samantha as his shield, gained a clear view and unimpeded path to them.

I'm here, Tyler's blue eyes calmed her, *everything will be all right*. Samantha swallowed, briefly comforted by his presence, so close she wished to reach out to touch him, have him hold her in his muscular, yet gentle, arms. At the same moment agonized he was so far away, the distance between them an unbridgeable chasm, a witness to her suffering, life hanging in the balance and powerless to save her.

Tyler mouthed a single word. *Sunday.*

For a second confusion swirled and eddied in her muddled mind, unsure what he meant, before she remembered the demonstration that afternoon, a time so recent yet seemed so long ago, of self-defense skills learned from her father. In that instant she understood what Tyler wanted.

I can handle myself. Samantha, with confidence in her voice, told Tyler. *I'm not some delicate defenseless girl.* Never, when she made the assertion to ease her boyfriend's fears, did she imagine this circumstance of a gun pressed to the side of her head, body shielding a lunatic who wished to brutalize her. *Time to put up.* Closing her eyes, Samantha slowed her breathing, thinking through the situation. Disabling Rahim long enough to flee towards the protection of the line of police the answer to escaping this peril, breaking the hold of the forearm wedged against her throat, not giving him the opportunity to shoot her. *Fight, then flight.* Samantha understood Tyler not about to be a bystander, springing from his concealed spot to attack her kidnapper as she broke from his grasp, sprinted to safety. Samantha knew she had to act, couldn't wait any longer, with each passing second Rahim growing increasingly erratic and willing, at the slightest whim, to finish her life with a bullet to the head.

Samantha opened her eyes, an imperceptible nod to Tyler her answer. *I hope this works.*

It will. Tyler smiled, belief in her abilities unwavering. *Trust me. You can do this.*

I trust you. Samantha never let her eyes leave Tyler, observed his body tense, coiled as a mongoose hiding in the brush ready to strike at a deadly cobra, wanted the image of him burned into memory if this to be the last thing her eyes gazed upon. *I love you…*

"Sir, let Samantha go and we will let you return to your country," the detective called out, trying one final time to reason with Rahim.

The cruel and evil grin, Samantha reminded then of The Joker, Batman's insane nemesis, never left Rahim's face. "You do think me a fool," he replied callously. "Either you allow me to leave with her now or I will kill her."

The cold, lifeless statement told Samantha time had run out. Any moment he might fire the bullet into her temple to end her life. *I have to do this, now or never.* Samantha closed her eyes, sighed as if faint. Released her hold on his arm tight to her throat, arms dropping weakly to her sides; let her body go limp as she slumped against her captor, seemingly ready to collapse towards the ground.

Rahim cursed as he felt Samantha's body go slack, sinking in his grasp. *She's fainted.* He growled in frustration, eyes never leaving the cordon of police. *Not as courageous as I was lead to believe.* He shifted his feet, locking his knees to hold up the dead weight serving as his shield, pistol moving slightly away from the side of her head. Even unconscious her body remained an effective impediment against the police officers he faced.

You have to time this perfectly. Tyler focused on captor and hostage standing ahead of him, never let his eyes leave the pair, vision locked on the gun jammed up to Samantha's temple. *You get this wrong and Samantha is dead.*

Tyler crouched down, waiting for Samantha to act, catch Rahim unaware, strike out at him. Breaking away from her assailant's grasp as Tyler raced towards them, ready to unleashing unholy retribution on this maniac. Timing his move as if taking the snap from center and dropping back into the pocket with the defense unleashing a jailbreak blitz, everyone coming at him, holding onto the ball until the last second as the pocket collapsed around him, waiting for his primary receiver to break into the open, full in the knowledge the rush obliterating him once he released the ball. *Come on, Samantha, you can do this!* Tyler silently coaxed her. *Be brave and take this bastard down!* He estimated the distance between him and his target about forty yards, able to cover the gap in less than five seconds. But was that enough time to save Samantha?

Tyler saw Samantha close her eyes, body sagging against the chest of Sheik Rahim, the diplomat adjusting his grip on her suddenly deadweight, forcing him ever so slightly off-balance, the gun eased slightly away from her head as he kept his eyes glued firmly on the line of police officers assembled before him.

Go time.

Tyler sprung from his crouch, within two steps at full sprint, bearing down on Samantha and her kidnapper with the unerring accuracy of an arrow launched in flight, praying he hit his target.

Samantha sensed Rahim adjust his grasp on her lifeless form, keeping her upright while his focus remained on the threat posed by the line of police, falling for the ruse as Tyler expected.

Let him have it.

Samantha released a feral scream, eyes flashing open, left elbow shooting back, connecting solidly with Rahim's rib cage. Heard the gasp of surprise, body doubling up behind her, pressure on her throat easing, loosening. But as Samantha lifted her right heel up towards the vulnerable part of the male anatomy between his legs she realized with horror how the long ordeal of her kidnapping and imprisonment exhausted her, joints and muscles tired and feeble being bound immobile for hours, unable to muster enough striking power to debilitate her antagonist. Her leg heavy like a lead weight mustering what little strength remained in her fatigued body to swing it upward, at least hurting Rahim, compel him to release his grasp from around her throat so she could run towards the police, away from the gun in his hand.

Samantha missed her target. Either from weakness or the fact Rahim moved the back of her heel didn't slam into vulnerable testicles, not delivering the incapacitating blow she intended. Her heel struck the soft flesh of his thigh, inflicting pain but not the devastating impact Samantha hoped to deliver. But the strike forced Rahim to release his hold on her neck, gave her a chance for freedom, Samantha twisting her body to break free, stumbling as feet became tangled. *Run, run, run!* She pleaded silently of legs leaden as stone, stocking feet tripping on the pavement. Her right foot landed atop a small stone on the roadway, a shooting sensation like a dagger jammed deep into her arch almost causing her to fall.

Samantha regained her balance, tears streaming down her face from the pain, running at the cordon of police twenty yards from her, a distance seeming like twenty miles, a gulf she couldn't breach, every step taking an eternity to complete. At any moment, because she'd been unable to cripple Sheik Rahim with her attack, Samantha expected to die only feet removed from deliverance.

You little bitch. Two seconds elapsed before Sheik Rahim regained his composure from the painful blow dealt by Samantha Grayson. Lifted his head, saw her running away from him, towards the line of police where she believed safety lay. *No, you will not escape me, Samantha.* He stood erect, ignored the hot flame of pain flaring in his leg, pointing the gun at her back. Aiming for the spot where he knew the bullet would tear through her heart, cease its beating, instantly killing the young woman so close to freedom.

If I cannot have you, if I cannot possess you, Samantha, a blind rage clouded his vision red, *I will kill you. You will not live to see another dawn.*

Rahim pressed his finger on the trigger.

Chapter 48

With legs deadened by numbing fatigue and muscles transformed to the consistency of rubber, Samantha Grayson ran towards the line of police officers ahead of her, away from Sheik Rahim and the gun she knew trained on her back with a bullet primed in the chamber aimed at her fleeing form. She wasn't running, more of a drunken stumbling, Samantha willing weakened limbs to move faster. Safety so close, so near, saw police moving towards her, yet with every clumsy, ungainly step seemed so far in the distance. Samantha heard the gunshot, a loud report like cannon fire, sensed a gush of hot air brush past her ear, for a moment wondering if she'd been shot, then flushed with relief realizing she hadn't been hit. Her legs became entangled, last vapor of strength evaporating, tripping over her feet, this time losing her balance and tumbling to the pavement. As she fell her left knee struck hard on the roadway, Samantha screaming in pain as blue clad forms surrounded her, arms grabbing under her shoulders, hauling her to her feet.

Then she heard a second gunshot.

She moved forward, but not under her own diminished power, pulled and tugged along by a phalanx of Chicago police officers forming around her a protective cordon, their bodies a shield against further attack. In seconds hustling Samantha past stopped traffic crammed together in Hubbard's Cave like miniature cars in a young child's toy-box to reach the first line of police cars stationed outside the tunnel, didn't offer resistance as they guided her towards a waiting ambulance. Everything about her disintegrated into a swirl of noise and lights confusing and disorienting, overwhelming her frayed senses: insistent shouts from police officers; the high-pitched wail of sirens; the peculiar chopping sound of helicopter blades cutting through the air, spotlights beaming down from darkened heavens playing and dancing on the highway below. As she was half-dragged, half-carried to the ambulance Samantha Grayson turned her head back to where she stood moments earlier a hostage of Sheik Rahim, straining to see what was taking place there as a single thought embedded in her mind, filled her with anxious apprehension.

What about Tyler?

The urgency of the officers whisking her from danger subsided as they reached the ambulance, easing Samantha down on the back fender. Samantha saw a face before her, brown eyes glazed over with fatigue struggling to focus on a fierce countenance with pale alabaster skin and eyes the icy blue of a cold winter sky, hair and beard a bright, fiery red Samantha thought closer to orange.

"Are you all right, little lady?" The accent Irish, unmistakable and to Samantha seemed so out of place right then. She swallowed, adrenaline draining from every pore and she grew lightheaded, exhaustion quickly settling into every fiber of her devastated body. A paramedic moved in, flashed a light into her eyes.

"I think...I am," a sob caused her voice to hitch, couldn't say more. Her head throbbed; arms and legs ached, never known such devastating pain. *But I'm alive.* "I'm...okay," she finally managed. *But what about Tyler?* Samantha's body started shaking as if emerging from immersion in the waters of a frigid mountain lake, hands trembling and spent muscles quivering. Someone draped a blanket over her shoulders; Samantha clutched at the edges, tugging the fabric close for warmth. Shivering not because she was cold, but from the unmistakable knowledge how close, in the short space of hours, she'd come to losing everything in her life held dear and have death close a cold, unrelenting grip around her.

"You stay right here," the officer, Samantha noticed he was in plainclothes, wore a bulletproof vest, told her. Samantha noticed, reporter's instincts working despite the terrible ordeal, the badge he wore not the distinctive five-pointed star of the Chicago Police Department. She nodded, too weak and disoriented to answer. "Everythin' is goin' to be all right."

"Okay," Samantha wrapped the blanket closer around shuddering shoulders. Safe and alive, no longer faced threat from Sheik Rahim or Marcus Cowle. *But what about Tyler?* Tears trickled from her eyes, moistening her cheeks as Samantha stared down at her wrists, studied purplish indentations bonds left tattooed on her skin. In a single-minded effort to eradicate the bruises Samantha rubbed at the offending marks with the mindless passion of Lady Macbeth attempting to wash imagined blood from her hands. *Out, out damned spot!* The physical scars slowly fading over the coming hours, but Samantha unsure if her spirit, ravaged by this horrific trauma, ever again made whole. Feared unseen wounds never healing, from now on always afraid of what lurked in the shadows, boundless confidence and courage forever suppressed.

Maybe she had lost everything. *I can't live without him, I don't want to live without him.* Samantha lowered her head, sobbing quietly. Had Tyler McManaway sacrificed his life for her?

She again asked a question that didn't have an answer.

What about Tyler?

As Sheik Rahim's finger pressed on the trigger the solid frame of Tyler McManaway slammed into him with the irresistible force of a runaway freight train, left hand extended, shoving the gun away from the back of the young woman as Rahim fired. The bullet screamed through the air, whizzing harmlessly past the ear of the woman he swore to protect with his life. Samantha Grayson living to see another day, the bullet Sheik Rahim intended to end her life never finding its mark.

Tyler slammed Rahim up against the car behind them, locking a firm grip on the hand holding the gun, thrusting the barrel skyward away from Samantha fleeing in a shambling, awkward run towards the blue line of police. Rahim squeezed the trigger again, a second report echoed through the tunnel, bullet ricocheting off the steel girders above. A primitive rage flamed bright in the eyes of Tyler McManaway, staring with a hard, icy hatred at the man who sought to take Samantha from him, gun her down as she fled to safety. Rahim stared back at Tyler as shock, not anger, filled his eyes, face blanching white as if confronted by an apparition rising from the grave.

Only a coward shoots people in the back, Tyler rationalized, breath exploding in hot, infuriated bursts. A depraved coward with deluded belief of omnipotence, above the law, kidnapping innocent women to fulfill vile pleasures, horribly violate them, commit unspeakable, inhuman acts upon them, slaughtering them once he no longer had use for them. *You're a coward, you bastard. I'm the hero here, and the hero always wins;* Tyler's eyes told his nemesis with quiet, unrelenting fury. A notion not heroic but born of bloodthirsty wrath seeing the woman he loved abducted and terrorized, almost murdered in cold blood before his eyes, found root deep in his mind and wouldn't leave no matter how hard he attempted to dispel the thought.

I am going to kill you.

With a shout of rage releasing pent-up rage fostered during the long night when he thought the woman he cherished so dearly forever lost, Tyler brought Rahim's arm down against the hood of the car, slamming the limb off the metal, Rahim crying out as pain shot through his wrist. Despite the blow he didn't release the pistol, Tyler again yanked the arm high into the air, once more rammed it down on the hood, bouncing off the aluminum surface. This time Rahim did yield, relinquishing his grip on the weapon, gun clattering to the pavement.

Rahim broke away from Tyler, staggering back a few steps, Tyler charging at him when Rahim lunged, fist swinging wildly through the air in desperation. Tyler ducked under the errant blow, crouching down, fired a punch into an unprotected midsection under the rib cage, heard Rahim yelp in pain. Tyler moved in, ready for a quick finish to this fight, going for a first-round knockout. Rahim's elbow shot upward, took Tyler off-guard, caught him flush in the chin. *Crap, left myself open for that,* Tyler cursed, pushed the advantage too far, a detonation of pain in his jaw, dazed for a moment. The blow sent Tyler stumbling backwards, put on the defensive, back striking against a car. Rahim shouted, sensing an opportunity to attack, running at Tyler with fist raised, poised to strike.

Tyler let him get close before twisting away. *Caught you, sucker.* Rolling alongside the surface of the car, dodging the onrushing Rahim, letting his fist find nothing but empty air until it made contact with the window, shattered the pane into a thousand jeweled fragments. Rahim screamed, stepped back staring horrified at a hand hooked and stiff as a lobster claw, blood streaming from a multitude of cuts and gashes scarring the skin.

Let's see how tough you are now that you aren't hurting a woman, Tyler taunted silently, going for the midsection with his right, landing a heavy blow on the sternum, Rahim gasping for air. A left jab below the rib cage followed, whatever air left in the lungs of his adversary escaping with a weak wheeze. *Here comes the Sunday punch,* Tyler fired his right fist up from below his waist, *I'm about to own you.* The punch arced in a perfect trajectory towards Rahim's unprotected chin, found its mark, violently snapping his head back. Tyler didn't let up, *anger makes you strong,* left fist flying next, striking Rahim solidly in the jaw, knees buckling and eyes rolling back into his head, disoriented and woozy from swift, successive blows. Tyler slammed into Rahim, shoving the man to the pavement, falling on top of him. With his left hand, Tyler grabbed a fistful of white linen shirt now speckled bright red with splotches of blood, right hand striking mercilessly at his foe, rearing back to fire blow after blow into the face of his nemesis with the rapidity of a machine gun. Every blow retribution for the pain this man inflicted on his Samantha.

I am going to kill you.

Tyler pummeled away, intoxicated by wrathful, righteous anger pouring from his soul, punch after punch landing solidly. Rahim unable to defend himself against the furious onslaught, hands up to his face in a useless defense like an overmatched fighter in a mixed martial arts contest going turtle, trying to fend off the unceasing torrent of blows. Tyler kept hitting him, couldn't stop, driven to exact revenge, fist landing impact after impact on his face. Heard the crack of breaking cartilage as Rahim's nose gave way under Tyler's vicious assault, blood spurting from his nostrils, a gurgling sound deep in the man's throat, choking on warm blood. *Good. I want you to die, bastard! I want you to fear me!* A flush of grim satisfaction washed over Tyler as he hauled back, ready to strike one final time to finish off this monster, end his reign of evil and Samantha's suffering. Somebody grabbed his arm, prevented him from delivering the deathblow, trying to pull him off the prostrate foe. Tyler strained against the restraint, eyes wild with animalistic ferocity, wanted to administer an old-fashioned brand of personal justice for the terror he inflicted on so many helpless and innocent souls.

"Touchdown! Touchdown!" Tyler heard the shout; part of the nickname 'Touchdown Tyler' the Chicago sports media coined embellishing his high school athletic endeavors. His fist clenched, fingernails digging deep into the flesh of his palms, drawing blood, body quaking as a boiling point of fury attained. Tyler turned to face who held him back, prevented him from dispensing the blow ridding the world of the beast now cowering beneath him. *Let me finish him...please let me finish him!*

"Touchdown, it's over! It's over! Let it go!" The man, Tyler saw the gold star of a Chicago Police detective clipped to his belt, shouted in his ear, attempting to break the spell of vengeful bloodlust. "We've got him! Don't stoop to his level! You're a better man than he is! We'll take care of him from here."

Tyler unrelenting, face contorted in hatred, fist balled tight, ready to land the killing strike. *One more to finish him off.* The detective had a tight end's build, a good downfield target, said the one thing wrenching Tyler away from the abyss of single-minded retribution, stopping him from taking a life, even one as despicably evil as Sheik Rahim. "Tyler! Samantha needs you!"

Samantha? Her name shattered the madness blinding him, transforming his blood into molten lava. Tyler relaxed as the spell of vengeance broken, hand easing from around Rahim's neck, fist opening, tension in his body dissipating. "Tyler, go to Samantha. She's safe, she's all right, but she needs you. It's over, we're taking him into custody," the detective explained as Tyler sank back on his knees, breathing ragged as hate drained slowly from his eyes. "Samantha needs you," the detective said.

Samantha needs me. Tyler stumbled to his feet, staring down at the prone figure of Sheik Rahim, blood pouring from the shattered nose, gasping for air. *I'm a better man than you.* The detective, assisted by a second detective with body art inked on thick forearms, rolled Rahim over on his stomach, without hesitation yanking arms behind his back, wrists secured with handcuffs. The detective looked up at Tyler as other officers crowded in on the prostrate Sheik Rahim, now the defenseless one and under arrest. "You did good," he told him, then repeated, "go, Samantha needs you."

Samantha needs me. Tyler stood there for a few seconds, frozen in place, in a daze impassively studied the blood on his knuckles. The moment for retaliation finally passed and Tyler McManaway regained control of his humanity. He turned away, running back through the throng of police, weaving between the jumbled mass of vehicles blocking the inside of Hubbard's Cave.

I'm coming, Samantha, I'm coming.

"Samantha."

At the sound of her name spoken softly in a voice tired and hesitant yet so beautiful, Samantha Grayson lifted her head, gazing with eyes clouded by tears at the man who swore fervently to protect her, keep her safe from harm. A welcome warmth of relief washed over Samantha as she realized Tyler

McManaway not a ghostly vision but alive and unharmed. Saw blood staining his knuckles, knew he exacted his fair measure of retribution on Sheik Rahim. Without saying a word Tyler sat down beside Samantha, eased his arms about her trembling body. In his presence Samantha found comfort; during the terrible hours of captivity never thought she'd again look into the captivating blue eyes, experience the gentle touch, never know his love. Samantha buried her head into Tyler's chest, sobbing uncontrollably, racked with quaking tremors, shoulders shaking as emotions blocked for hours fighting for survival finally broke free of containment, flowing freely until fully spent.

"It's okay, I'm here," Tyler reassured Samantha, rubbing her arms, stroking the soft auburn hair, smelled a lingering scent of lilac, providing solace with the soothing embrace. "You're safe now, it's all over. Let it out, just let it out." Tyler didn't say much, didn't need to, let emotions run their course as Samantha nestled deep in his arms, body heaving with every breath. "It's all over, you're safe, it's all over," he repeated, with his thumb tenderly brushed away tears trickling down her face.

"Marcus Cowle, he called me Lois Lane," Samantha finally spoke after a few minutes, after she was all cried out, sniffing back lingering tears, wiping at damp eyes with the sleeve of her jacket, recalling what Cowle told her at the studio when she first awakened to her dire predicament. "Said I had a big story." Samantha rested her head against the muscular chest; let Tyler caress her hair, simple action calming her. Tyler there when she needed him the most and in the strong, protective arms Samantha found safety, everything once more right in her world. "He told me Superman wasn't coming to my rescue this time."

"Your Superman got there just in time." Tyler pushed back wayward strands of auburn hair, kissed Samantha on the forehead, then ever so gently on the lips. "Hope you weren't expecting blue tights and a red cape."

Through dissipating tears Samantha at last managed a smile, a self-conscious laugh. "Blue jeans and a sweater work for me." Could never imagine Tyler in a red cape. "You're not the type for blue tights. Blue football pants, yes, but blue tights, not so much."

Tyler smiled at the lighthearted remark, a hopeful sign, leaned in close. "I'm sorry," he whispered, holding her tight, never wishing to leave her side, bruises and tears a brutal reminder of his failure. "I didn't keep my promise. I let someone hurt you. I wasn't there to protect you."

Samantha raised her head, eyes glistening. "You kept your promise," gave a shake of her head, affectionately stroked his cheek. "You found me when I thought no one would. You protected me from him, saved me from what he wanted to do to me."

Tyler placed a lingering kiss on her lips, held Samantha close, sensed the reassuring beat of her heart. "I promise I will never let this happen again."

"You were here when I needed you," Samantha sighed, "that's what matters. You saved my life." Samantha looked at Tyler, brown eyes troubled, needed to know. "Amanda? Lauryn? Ashleigh? Are they safe?" If she spared a despicable fate, but any of her friends harmed or lost, relief brought by her salvation a hollow, meaningless victory.

Samantha suspected good news as Tyler smiled, about to answer when a familiar voice shouted over the wailing sirens. "Samantha!" The voice that of Amanda McKinnon, threading a path through gathered police officers and paramedics to the ambulance where Tyler and Samantha huddled together, leading Lauryn Callahan and Ashleigh Morgan. Tyler released Samantha, sharing his love with her cherished close friends. Amanda rushed up, threw her arms around Samantha's shoulders, hugging her tight.

Lauryn and Ashleigh followed steps behind Amanda, the trio embracing a friend they feared never to see again as tears, this time of joy, streamed down their faces.

"Are you okay?" Amanda wiped at her eyes as she studied her friend as if not believing she looked upon Samantha, cringed at the dark bruise above her left eye. "You're not hurt? On the way here, on the police radio they said the limo crashed and there were shots fired and we thought…"

"I'm all right." Samantha smiled to soothe their anxieties, saw Connor Aanonsen, D'Andre Watson and Albert 'Fiji' Fatuamala approach, waved weakly at Tyler's roommates, intimate coterie of friends together, at times that evening a reunion Samantha doubted ever to take place. "Have some bumps and bruises, that's all. I'm tired, pretty sore too." *I probably look like hell.* Samantha ran a hand through tangled auburn hair. *Now I know how Tyler feels after a game.*

"Join the club," Amanda remarked, "rode hard and put away wet." Samantha smiled at the off-color statement, only Amanda capable of uttering so amusing a comment in the wake of a terrifying experience. "I didn't know my body could hurt so much. I'll need some heavy duty massage to feel right again."

Ashleigh hugged Samantha. "Girlfriend, I thought I'd never see you again."

"The feeling was kind of mutual," Samantha thankful her best friends in the world safe, accepting a hug from little Lauryn.

"It's good to know you're here," Lauryn said, vision blurred with tears. "And not there, because there, where that man wanted to take you, would've been been bad."

"Here is good," Samantha admitted. From the corner of her eye Samantha watched Riley Bradford sprint past, heading to the ambulance with Presley Harding inside, sitting on a stretcher, petite body wrapped in a blanket. Riley ran to her roommate, thought forever lost but now found and spared an unspeakable fate, threw her arms around Presley who stared at Riley in startled disbelief before breaking down, sobbing in each other's arms.

Tyler leaned over to Samantha, whispered. "You did good, babe." Samantha observed the happy reunion. *Presley is alive because of what you did. Riley will never know the pain of losing a friend.* There were four other young women rescued from a horrific destiny because of her actions, families and countless friends never to suffer the loss of those dear to them. Samantha understood something good had come from this awful ordeal. *You stopped a terrible evil from ever hurting anyone ever again.* Riley and Presley looked over at Samantha, their eyes silently telling her the same thing. *Thank you.*

"Riley? She told you where I was?" Samantha turned to Tyler and asked. "Is that how you found Lauryn and Amanda?"

"If she hadn't shown up at the *Daily Northern* offices when we were there, after not hearing from you all night and realizing something was wrong, we'd have been off on a wild goose chase searching for you," Tyler explained. "We had no idea where to start looking."

"She might be a small thing," Connor gave a jaunty salute to Riley. "But the little lady's got guts. Insisted on coming with us, wasn't about to wait back at campus."

"We got to the studio, found Amanda and Lauryn," Tyler continued. "Along with the little present your friends left behind."

Samantha knew what he meant, a serious question now posed of Tyler. "How…close?"

"Let's say a little too close." Amanda nervously bit her lip. "A few more seconds and this joyous get-together isn't happening."

Samantha stared at Tyler. "But how...?"

"Fiji pulled out the blue wire." Lauryn stated matter-of-factly, moving to stand beside the giant Samoan, wrapped her arms around his waist, face glowing with a contented smile.

"I was about to pull the red wire," Tyler said. "Which would've been bad."

Samantha observed the way Fiji held Lauryn close, a blissful expression on Lauryn's face, loving gleam in their eyes as they looked at each other, how Fiji smiled warmly at the adorable redhead with an intimacy the pair never before exhibited. The realization struck Samantha. "Are you two...?" She started to ask.

Lauryn, enchanting emerald eyes glimmering with heartfelt affection for Albert Fatuamala, replied with a question of her own, which in itself was an answer. "Are you asking if we're a couple?"

"I'd say we are." Fiji agreed, stroking Lauryn's cinnamon red hair.

"It's about time," Ashleigh said under her breath.

"Never thought it would take something like this to get them together," Amanda added.

Samantha smiled at Lauryn, who came over to hug Samantha again. "I'm happy for both of you. I'm sorry I got all of you into this mess. That it had to happen this way," she apologized.

"Maybe that's how it was supposed to be." Lauryn shook her head, moved back to Fiji's side; let him gather her up in his protective arms. "When I was lying there, waiting for everything to end I realized what Albert meant to me, how much I cared for him and he cared for me." Lauryn paused, gazing into the placid dark eyes of the Samoan. "I realized I never told him how much I loved him."

Fiji leaned over, kissed Lauryn, this time on the lips. "I thought the same thing on the way to the studio. I never let you know how much you meant to me." What his friends told him true. He did love Lauryn Callahan, wondered why it had taken so long to admit an attraction so obvious to everyone else around them in the first place.

A commotion from the direction of Hubbard's Cave caught their attention. A mass of police officers moving their way, at the center Sheik Rahim, posture stiff and bearing proud even with hands cuffed behind his back. Imperious manner exhibiting barely a hint of concern at his situation, seeming to suffer as a brief nuisance being hauled away in the custody of the Chicago Police Department. The calm, yet superior attitude of a man with the blood of sixteen, and perhaps many more, young women staining his hands troubled Samantha, acting as if he had nothing to fear. Rahim turned towards Samantha and her friends, dark eyes locking on her, flaring with unfettered hatred.

"So that's him," Amanda glared at the source of their shared ordeal. "Arrogant prick."

"Looks like you did a number on him, Tyler," Connor observed the blood trickling from Rahim's shattered nose. "I think our friend is about to experience the fine hospitality from the permanent residents of Cook County Jail. Maybe they'll finish what you started." If so...*good riddance.*

Tyler nodded coldly. "Samantha got in a few licks of her own," he pointed out the bleeding wounds on Rahim's face. "Nicely done, babe," Tyler kissed her on the cheek, "no one messes around with my girl."

"Never thought a wine key could be such an effective weapon," Samantha's voice trembled, remembering the desperation of her attack, "does more than open bottles." Samantha stared at Rahim as he was hustled past, body shaking from his proximity, Tyler easing his arms around her to soothe resurgent fears.

"Looks like it opens up a big can a whoop-ass too," D'Andre remarked, holding Ashleigh tight.

"He'll never hurt you again," Tyler calmed Samantha. "As long as I'm here I'll keep you safe from that animal. He will never hurt you again."

"I know you'll protect me." Samantha gazed into the disarming blue eyes, stroked Tyler's cheek with her hand. She kissed him and for the first time this night her soul at peace.

Amanda watched the phalanx of officers guide Rahim to one of the squad cars, forcing him into the back seat, pushing his head down as he slid inside. "He would've gotten away with it too if it hadn't been for those meddling kids and their dog," she joked.

"When will you stop with the wisecracks, Gazelle?" Ashleigh amazed by her friend's pluck.

"Using humor as a defense mechanism to deal with a highly stressful situation," Amanda explained. "The moment I stop to think about what I went through or how I'm going to tell my parents about this I'll turn into a quivering blob of sobbing emotion and..." Suddenly her voice trailed off, amethyst eyes grew wet, tears trickling down her cheek, lips trembling, hands fluttering up to her mouth.

"And what did we think about?" Connor asked and Amanda nodded, fighting to hold back the tears. Connor accepted a blanket from a paramedic, draped it over shuddering shoulders, wrapped his arms about Amanda to draw close the shaking form. "Time to tell you everything will be alright because Connor Bear is here?"

"Just hit the emotional wall," Amanda buried herself deep in Connor's arms, tears trailing down her face, protective shell finally fractured, pent up anxieties pouring out from between the cracks, "don't let go until I say so, Connor Bear." Connor didn't have any problem complying with the request.

"So who makes the four in the morning phone call to Coach Carl?" D'Andre wondered.

"What about the four in the morning phone calls to our parents?" Samantha dreaded that call, telling them details of a nightmare all too real yet at the same time wanting to hear their voices and know their love for her.

The friends grew quiet as the Chicago Police detective who prevented Tyler from killing Sheik Rahim with his bare hands approached, accompanied by the second detective with the tattooed arms and a scraggly beard. "How are we doing?" He politely asked of the group.

"Being alive is a good start," Amanda the first to speak, voice remained shaky and unsteady.

"I'm okay," Samantha offered heartfelt appreciation. "Thank you for all you did."

The detective offered his hand to Tyler. "Devin Carson," Tyler shook his hand, noticed the Great Northern class ring, as Carson motioned to his companion. "This is my partner, Dawson Hilliard." Carson's name sounded familiar, Tyler reflected for a moment. Wasn't there a Devin Carson who played tight end for Great Northern back in the nineties? Left the program because...*oh my God.* Tyler grasped the significance, felt terribly selfish allowed a reunion with Samantha where Carson denied to ever know the fate of the woman he loved.

"What is it?" Samantha noted with puzzlement Tyler's sober expression.

"I'll tell you later when we're alone," Tyler whispered, now wasn't the time to relate the tale.

"I'd like to say this is over and you can return to campus," Carson explained, "but we need statements from each you. We have a lot of questions that still need answers."

"That's okay," Amanda sniffed back tears. "Sleep is for the weak."

"We'll get you to a hospital first, have them check you out, make sure you're okay," Carson nodded at the four young women. "I know you've," he looked at Samantha, "had a pretty long night."

"Tell me about it." Samantha snuggled into Tyler's arms, rested her head on his shoulder. "Pretty long day too," she laughed self-consciously. *I hope I never again have such a long day.*

"When can we call our parents?" This question came from Lauryn. "Let them know we're safe before they see this on the news and freak out?" The last way any of them wanted families to learn of the dreadful experience.

"After we get you checked out at the hospital," Great Northern Medical Center the closest facility, "you can make the calls. I'd like to have our detectives first tell your parents what happened."

Amanda rubbed the bridge of her nose, blinked eyes raw from crying. "This will make for a pleasant early morning conversation."

"What are you doing with Laughing Boy," D'Andre referred to Sheik Rahim, "and his playmates?"

"They'll be spending the night at Area Six lockup," Hilliard told them, "we'll hand them over to the Feds in the morning, transfer them to the Metropolitan Correction Center," the fortress-like tower in the Loop where prisoners awaiting trail in federal cases held in custody.

"I'm sure the Feds will have fun with this sick bastard." In his head, Connor added up the possible years in a federal penitentiary the man to face, giving up after reaching triple digits.

Tyler cleared his throat. "I think I violated...a few traffic regulations tonight," he confessed. "If you want to take away my driver's license..."

"Don't worry," Carson waved him off, grinned slyly. "You were in the process of making a citizen's arrest."

Samantha looked at Carson, asked simply. "Have you found Marcus Cowle?"

"Not yet," Carson shook his head. "But we've got bulletins already out across the Midwest for him and his partners." He paused, next statement meant to reassure Samantha and her friends. "They won't get far, we'll find them."

Samantha tightly squeezed Tyler's hand, gazed into comforting blue eyes. *I'm not safe until Cowle is caught.*

I know. Tyler silently nodded. *I'll protect you from him. I won't let him hurt you.*

"I think we need to get you to the hospital now," Carson told them.

"See you there," Amanda waved weakly at Samantha as paramedics guided them to waiting ambulances. Tyler and the attending EMT helped Samantha into the back of the ambulance where she'd been sitting. "I'm from Canada, my national health insurance will cover this," Samantha heard Amanda say as she walked away.

"You okay?" Tyler asked Samantha, voice tender with concern, eased her on the stretcher as the doors to the ambulance slammed shut. A moment later the vehicle lurched forward, sirens blaring, high-pitched wail shattering the quiet of deserted streets.

Samantha leaned her head on Tyler's shoulder. "I'm fine," she told him, her voice distant, knew how far from the truth her statement. "As long as you're with me."

Tyler kissed her cheek. "I'm not going anywhere," he comforted her. "No one is going to hurt you. You're safe."

"So much for our quiet evening together." Samantha closed her eyes, exhaled deeply, body depleted of every ounce of energy. A curtain of numbing exhaustion, Samantha found it useless to resist the sensation, fell over her like curling up next to a fire roaring in the fireplace of her home at Grayson Farms Winery. With the peaceful vision of the tranquility firmly lodged in her mind Samantha quickly slipped into a slumber filled with thoughts of home, of her parents and cherished greyhounds, of the hero sitting beside her, handsome and bold, rescuing her from frightful harm. She drifted off despite the screeching sirens, lovingly cradled in the protective embrace of Tyler McManaway.

Samantha Grayson knew she was safe.

For now.

Chapter 49

Garrett Grayson understood, as the father of a daughter away at college, receiving a phone call at four in the morning never a pleasant occurrence. Such phone calls in the dead of night a portent of distressing news, of things gone wrong. Especially when the first voice on the other end a detective from the Chicago Police Department explaining the dire reason for the call, followed by the voice, exhausted and drained, of his precious daughter and only child.

"I'm okay, Daddy," Samantha Grayson said, tone subdued, usual bubbly exuberance absent. "I'm...just tired." He realized the statement a well-meaning lie, an honest effort not to worry her parents. Garrett knew better, glanced at Melanie listening on the other line, eyes filled with horrified disbelief, hand clasped over her mouth, body trembling as frightening memories she wished forever suppressed escaped from the deepest recesses of her mind where she stored them under lock and key. Both husband and wife confronted a similar, and desperate, situation years earlier when all seemed lost and hopeless, almost at the cost of their lives overcoming that insidious evil. From the wreckage of that dreadful time falling in love, bringing into the world a precious daughter. Now their Samantha, lovely and vibrant, the center of their lives, falling prey to an almost identical nightmare, enduring what seemed the same hellish ordeal.

"You're safe," Garrett reassured her, "that's what matters." *Is it?* He thought. *Will it ever be?*

He heard the sigh from the other end, so far off and distant in Chicago, wanted to reach through the phone and put his arms around his daughter to comfort her. "I'm sorry, Daddy," Samantha apologized. "I shouldn't have gone there alone. I should've known better." She paused. "I'm sorry for getting into trouble."

"There's no need to apologize," Garrett replied. "You did what you thought you needed to do. It's not your fault what happened. It's the fault of evil people doing evil things." Evil actions Garrett Grayson all too familiar with. "Because of you those women they held captive are safe. They're alive because of what you did." He stayed quiet for a moment; allowed his courageous daughter to absorb the fact. *It runs in the family*, he thought, proud of his daughter. *It's in the bold blood of bravery from the Australian side of the family.* From her mother's side she inherited lissome beauty and a compassionate soul. "You made a difference, Samantha."

"Okay, Daddy," Samantha said drowsily, sounded ready to fall asleep.

Melanie finally spoke, quiet through most of the phone call, biting her lip, fist clenching tightly during the account from Detective Devin Carson of the traumatic peril Samantha suffered, unspeakable memories awakened from their slumber deep in her subconscious to terrorize her again. "We're just...worried about you. We're relieved that you're safe." All Melanie managed to say, teetering on the edge of hysteria, emotions shredded, wanting to lash out at forces unseen and shadowy, criminal forces once unleashing upon her the same waking nightmare, a terror almost destroying her life now visited unfairly on their only lovely child.

"I love you, I love both of you. Thought I'd never see you again." Samantha answered; Garrett knew Samantha at the brittle end of endurance. "Never hear the sound of your voices."

"Is Tyler there?" Garrett asked quietly.

"Yes, he is."

"Can I speak with him for a moment?"

"Okay." There was a pause, then another familiar voice not as tired as his daughter, but tone strained from a very long and trying night. "Yes sir?" Tyler McManaway said.

"Melanie and I want to thank you for saving Samantha from these people," Garrett offered a sentiment heart-felt and genuine. "She's alive, and we have her back safe, because of what you did. From what Detective Carson told us you risked a great deal to rescue Samantha from them."

"Thank you, sir," Tyler answered. "I'd have done anything to get her away from those fucking bastards." Realized he uttered a swear word to Samantha's father. "Sorry, I didn't mean that."

"That's what they are." Garrett grinned, had heard salty language far worse. "You don't have to call me 'sir.' I haven't been called that since I was an officer in the Australian Navy years ago. It's Garrett."

"Okay, sir," Tyler returned, Garrett shaking his head. *I guess we're going to have to work on that*, he thought, a trait changing only after a day in the future when Tyler requested his daughter's hand in marriage. *He's already proved himself worthy of Samantha to me...*

"Can you give me back to Samantha," Garrett asked, followed by another brief silence, the voice of Samantha once more in his ear.

"Daddy?"

"Your mother and I will be out there as soon as we can," Garrett putting her at ease with the knowledge they'd be there for her during this difficult time. "We have to make sure the winery and the hounds are taken care of then we'll be out there. Spend time with you, make sure you're alright."

"I'd really like that, Daddy," Samantha said, voice tiny like a child afraid of the storm, seeking reassurance from the fearful sound of approaching thunder. "I really want to see both of you right now."

"You will," Garrett said. "Let Tyler take care of you until then."

"He already is." Garrett could picture the Samantha smiling. "I love both of you so much."

"We love you too," Melanie tried to remain calm, fighting back emotions attempting to get the better of her. "We'll see you later today. We'll get out there as soon as we can."

"Love you too, Samantha, we'll be there soon." With great reluctance Garrett switched off the phone, turned to his wife who put down the other phone, body shaking from a potent concoction of terror and rage.

"It was them, wasn't it?" She couldn't bring herself to use the name, sounding so banal and ordinary yet terrifying in its evil meaning. "They're the ones who did this to Samantha. Did they find out she was our daughter? Did they do this out of revenge?"

Garrett set the phone down, walked to his wife, placed his hands on her shoulders to still her trembling, shook his head slightly, sought to soothe rampaging fears. "We don't know for sure," Detective Carson vague on that point, but in his heart Garrett already knew, "but I'm calling someone," a good man Garrett worked with years earlier, "who'll have the information I need to know who was responsible."

"I don't want Samantha to suffer like I did. I don't want her to be hurt the way I was." Melanie collapsed into her husband's arms, crying softly, sharing Samantha's agony as if in the same room with her daughter. A pain she understood all too well, a horror experienced when she was Melanie Barrett, a college student from Cornell University studying in London, a terrible ordeal thought left in her past, days of horror she hoped never to tell her daughter.

"She's safe, she's with her friends." Garrett rubbed her shoulders, shuddering in his embrace. "She has someone protecting her." A brave young man named Tyler McManaway. Around them in the living room mementos and pictures of Samantha from the stages of her life: as an infant new to the world; through childhood as her inquisitive nature blossomed; maturing through high school into a beautiful, intelligent and caring young woman with a bright future; off to college at Great Northern, pursuing a dream of fighting for what was right and just. If not for the actions of Tyler McManaway this night pictures and memories the only things left to remember their daughter, vanished into a despicable hell. He let his wife cry, only sound in the house save for the ticking of the antique grandfather clock standing a solid sentinel in the room, Garrett waiting patiently until the tears ran dry before he spoke. "We have to be strong for Samantha. We can't tell her the truth yet. Not now, but when she's able to handle it."

Melanie eased her head from Garrett's chest. "We have to tell her sometime." Had to tell Samantha the truth of those frightful days one autumn in Europe, the abominable reality behind the falsehood of how Melanie Barrett and Garrett Grayson came together, a story seemingly coming full circle decades later to lay claim of their treasured daughter.

Garrett wiped at the tear on Melanie's cheek. "Trust me, we will, but not now. This isn't the time. She isn't strong enough. It's much too soon." He continued to rub her shoulders. "One day she will be ready, and we'll tell her." Garrett motioned with his head. "I want you to go upstairs, get our things ready to go to Chicago. I have to make a few phone calls to make sure everything is taken care of while we're gone."

Melanie didn't speak, broke the embrace, given a task to occupy her fretful mind, hurrying upstairs as Garrett turned back to the phone. The odd activity at the early morning hour roused their six greyhounds from nighttime dreams of chasing squirrels, keen eyes observing Garrett and recognizing something not right. Stormy, the favorite of Samantha, the small female with black coat shining in the light, stood up from her bed, head cocking to the side, ears perked picking up the distress of Melanie Grayson. Garrett glanced at the clock. France, specifically the city of Lyon, six hours ahead of Grayson Farms in Upstate New York. *He should be there now*, Garrett reached for the phone, dialing a number not called for years, thought he'd never again in his life need to call the number for matters such as this.

The female voice answering polite and professional, efficiency personified. "Interpol, may I be of assistance?"

"Inspector Drulliard please," Garrett said simply.

"Inspector Drulliard is in an important conference right now," the female voice informed him.

"Tell him Commander Garrett Grayson, Royal Australian Navy, is on the line," Garrett replied. "I think he'll take my call."

"Commander Grayson," the name, and a title well-known, immediately garnered the operator's attention, "I will let him know you are on the line." Garrett heard a click, followed by silence as the call placed on hold. As he waited Stormy trotted to his side, toenails clicking on the wooden floor, resting her body against his leg, a 'greyhound lean' Samantha called it, Garrett absently reaching down to scratch the hound behind the front leg. With every motion the hound leaned harder on his knee, expressing comfort and contentment. She raised her head, the shape reminding Garrett of a triangle, the look in her dark eyes asking a question. *Is Samantha okay?*

"Samantha's fine." Garrett told the hound, amazed by the hidden power of sleek canine as she pressed harder against his leg. "Christ, you might be little, but you're strong," Garrett observed under his breath.

A voice came on the line. "Garrett," the voice spoke in heavily-accented English, "it is good to hear from you, my friend." Inspector Henri Auguste Drulliard sighed. "It has been a long time, but I do wish the circumstances were far more pleasant than this."

"Can't help the reason why," Garrett noted, got to the point, reminiscing of better days coming later. "This was The Trading Society?"

"I am sorry to say. One of their best, a Collector by the name of Marcus Cowle." Drulliard gave substance to Garrett's suspicions. "Only an organization as The Trading Society has the resources to engage in an operation of this magnitude. A man such as Sheik Rahim doesn't deal with...amateurs."

Garrett moved to the next question, one far more personal. "Did The Trading Society, this Marcus Cowle, know Samantha was our daughter?"

"It appears Samantha's involvement was through unfortunate circumstance," Drulliard explained. "The roommate of the missing girl from Great Northern enlisted her assistance to locate her friend that lead Samantha to Cowle and his operation." He paused. "She was merely a victim of chance."

Garrett exhaled, relieved to discover Samantha hadn't been a target, yet sobered by the thought The Trading Society likely aware Samantha Grayson the daughter of a dogged nemesis from their past. "Samantha was fortunate her friends found where they were holding her and the others in time," Drulliard continued. "From what my police sources in Chicago tell me they overcame tremendous odds to free her and the other hostages. I presume this Tyler McManaway is close to Samantha?"

"Good thing he is," Garrett acknowledged. "If not for him we aren't having this discussion."

"He is a brave man, as are his companions," Drulliard acknowledged, then politely inquired. "How is Melanie taking this?"

"As you'd expect," Garrett said, "not well, she's upset. Brought back bad memories." Recollections of days of terror and violence, when her conception of innocence shattered and learned a lesson the world a cruel and dangerous place. Melanie thought the disturbing memories repressed, only to find them reanimated through the unexpected ordeal of their daughter.

"I am sorry," Drulliard offered, "let her know my thoughts are with her."

"I will." Garrett continued rubbing the greyhound leaning against his leg.

Silence before Inspector Drulliard spoke. "Does this mean you are back in the game, as they might say?"

Garrett understood the veiled remark. "Perhaps, on a part-time basis when needed." He laughed self-consciously. "I have other matters keeping me occupied these days. I'm a businessman now. Have a winery to run. I'm opening a distillery in a few weeks."

"Thank you for the shipment of merlot and cabernet sauvignon, it was very good." The Inspector a connoisseur of fine wine, the quality of product from the Finger Lakes in Upstate New York proved a satisfying surprise.

"You're welcome," Garrett replied. "You have something in the works?"

"This situation might finally provide impetus for direct action against The Trading Society," Garrett understood the clandestine human-trafficking organization enjoyed protection from those in lofty stations of power, a dirty secret little known to the public at large. "We're in the planning stages, but this incident will likely accelerate the unit's activation. The designation will be CONSTELLATION." Drulliard paused as the significance of the name sunk in for Garrett, a fitting name for the fledgling unit, sharing the name of a sailing frigate of the United States Navy, a bold ship with courageous crew hunting slave traders on the high seas in the years preceding the Civil War. "Your brother Jackson will be an integral part of this unit. I was in a meeting concerning this matter when you called. He sends his regards."

Little brother Jack, Garrett grinned. "I guess this will be a family affair," he told Drulliard. "Someone's got to keep an eye on him, make sure he's doing things right. Show him how it's done."

"Very well, my friend," Drulliard said. "I will be in touch."

Garrett hung up the phone, glanced about the living room, out the window to what he and Melanie built from scratch to become Grayson Farms Winery: the ramshackle barn converted into the tasting room and housing wine production; the café; the bed and breakfast; new construction to house the latest business venture, Grayson Manor Distillery. Up until a few minutes ago this was the nexus of his life: a loving wife, precious daughter and a successful winery in a bucolic countryside, dangerous activities of the past left to memory.

Until they tried to take Samantha from us, Garrett darkly mused, understood this changed his situation. Garrett took a deep breath, came to grips with a new reality. Couldn't escape his past, walk away from the pain and suffering caused by the wicked, not with The Trading Society out there as a threat to Samantha. "I thought I was out and they pulled me back in." Garrett absently quoted the line of movie dialog, realized he never should've walked away in the first place, not until the evil vanquished and The Trading Society no longer existed.

Garrett gazed down at Stormy, greyhound leaning hard against his leg, staring up at him with sympathetic eyes. "I hope you don't mind taking a trip, you're coming with us to Chicago," he said, rubbing the hound behind her ear. Samantha needed the affection of her beloved greyhound as much as she did the love of her parents.

"We had absolutely no idea this was the reason for Sheik Rahim being in the country?" Thomas Cockrell asked his top executive assistant. He and his brother Edward returning to Manhattan after a flight at the break of dawn on their private Gulfstream jet, eating a late breakfast in the private penthouse dining room of the Midtown skyscraper bearing the family name, headquarters for the international conglomerate. The magnificent vista of the city skyline the penthouse offered and the breakfast served on plates of expensive china the furthest thing in the brothers' minds. "This was why he accepted our invitation to attend the speech given by Senator Fielding?"

The functionary, Whittington by name, shook his head, appropriately dismayed by troubling events continuing to unfold in Chicago. Though not directly involved or affected by the situation Cockrell Enterprises fully engaged in damage control. Sheik Rahim the guest of the Cockrell brothers at the speech by Senator Fielding, feted at a reception that afternoon and a dinner that evening, no doubt the media soon making queries of the Cockrells questioning knowledge of Rahim's true motives. "It appears attending the speech by Senator Fielding at Great Northern University served as a cover for his intentions. Offering him the opportunity to come and, it seems, take personal possession of those kidnapped women."

"How are Senator Fielding's people handling this?" Edward Cockrell asked in a voice hardly perturbed by the course of events, casually sipped his coffee waiting for the answer.

"They were as surprised by this as we were," Thomas and Edward might contest their assistant's assessment, but only in private as they knew far more than Whittington. "They've already released a statement stating as much." Both Cockrell brothers certain the proclamation from Senator Fielding's staff nothing but necessary boilerplate to limit possible damage to his future aspirations. "Expressing concern for how this event will impact relations between our countries and for the women who were victims of this ordeal, praising the police and the four student-athletes from Great Northern who uncovered this human trafficking ring and rescued the women."

"And Sheik Rahim?" Thomas said.

"A demand he faces justice for these kidnappings and for the other sixteen disappearances he's been linked to," the assistant explained, "but I think we all know that is highly unlikely."

Thomas looked at Edward, gave him the slightest nod. *Very unlikely*, the message conveyed. "Release a similar statement," Thomas informed the assistant, "note, but mildly, that our government should pursue whatever legal action necessary against Sheik Rahim." No need to antagonize an important asset such as Daharan to their global business empire, though Rahim exhibited a streak of recklessness requiring circumspect consideration. "That will be all for now," Thomas dismissed the man, scurrying from the penthouse dining room to carry out their bidding.

Edward Cockrell waited until the Whittington departed, the brothers alone. "This situation struck very close to the heart of our affairs," he observed. "It appears we were quite fortunate."

Thomas nodded in agreement, glanced at his brother from across the table. "We need to take measures to monitor Samantha Grayson," Thomas said, biting a forkful of eggs, chewing slowly.

The brusque statement caught Edward by surprise. "What do you mean?"

"She's a threat to us. A threat to our preparations implementing the vision our mentor Professor Mittersley sought for America, change the destiny of this country before it descends into decadent socialism. Before it falls to the Others, before they steal it from the True Americans." Thomas lowered the fork to the plate. "She might learn of our plans for Madame President, and for the summits in Chicago next spring she is dependent upon to lift her political standing."

"What? She's only a girl." The expression on Edward's face incredulous. "You truly believe Samantha Grayson poses a danger to The Creators? A danger to what he have planned?"

"This isn't the first time we've been affected by this 'girl,'" Thomas Cockrell pointed out with derision. "Her interference, poking around and asking questions, forced President Russell from the presidency at Great Northern." Thomas pointed a finger at his brother. "Now this occurrence, even if purely through happenstance, is troubling. She bears circumspect observation. She's a reporter. She'll press further on this, it's in her nature to do so. If she presses hard enough she might uncover the plans of The Creators."

"We've taken precautions, no one, the media, the government, has the slightest hint of our intentions," Edward dumbfounded by his brother's admonition. "We've managed the risk effectively. We've concealed too well our dealings with the parties involved to be discovered. And you think a mere intrusive college girl who works at a student newspaper will find this out?" Edward shook his head. "That is completely absurd."

Thomas lowered his voice, the tone sinister. "She may learn of our connections with The Trading Society." His eyes narrowed to deliver the succinct message. "This must not be discovered at all hazards. They're a crucial component in our designs, the most dangerous weapon we unleash when the time is ripe to strike and take back America from the Others."

Edward quieted, chastened by his brother's rebuke, understood his meaning. "You are correct. We must watch her. There is too much at stake." He pondered his words carefully. "If she does happen to stumble upon our operation for the future of this nation, she will need to be dealt with accordingly."

"If only we'd only known of our friend's particular predilections." Thomas lifted his coffee cup, sipped the hot liquid. "We could've given him free use of The Compound to do whatever he desired in private. Disposed of the trash when he was finished." If they'd been aware of Rahim's intent, taken precautions to control the situation, the murderous secret of Sheik Rahim still shrouded in the shadows along with those of the brothers Cockrell. If Samantha Grayson did uncover their plans for the rebirth of America under the rule of an elite capitalist class, starving and crushing the leeches feeding greedily on the industrious enterprise of enlightened white men, then she too might find herself a permanent visitor of The Compound.

"That sick bastard wanted to know why we don't do business in his country!" Caleb McIllhenny muttered under his breath, sitting in his Dallas office watching coverage on MSNBC of the startling events involving his alma mater back in Chicago. "I knew the bastard was hiding something, but I had no idea it was something this sick." He snorted in anger, thoughts flashing to the day before. "I shook that bastard's hand."

"That's the third time this morning you've called him a bastard," Miles Warfield, his head of security and confidential assistant, keeping count.

"The description suits him fine," McIllhenny snarled. "Damn Cockrell brothers can have all the business they want in Daharan." Men lacking common decency and morals, and McIllhenny had a checkered, contentious past with the brothers. The Cockrells, in their relentless pursuit of profits at the expense of honest, hard-working Americans, deserved to deal with one so coldly bloodthirsty as Sheik Abdullah al-Aziz Rahim. "I will never do a dollar of business with that damn country for as long as I run McIllhenny Energy."

Warfield allowed McIllhenny to vent, understood the reason residing in his soul for deeply ingrained rancor following the revelation Rahim behind the apparent abduction of sixteen, perhaps more than that terrible number, young women to satisfy deviant, murderous pleasures. "There are times when I wish the story of The Garden of Eden was true and dinosaurs never existed," the oilman shook his head, "then we wouldn't have to deal with bastards like Rahim."

"Grand slam, fourth time you've called him a bastard," Warfield added. "What would we use to power this economy of ours?"

"Pixie dust sounds right fine by me," McIllhenny growled, bidding to find humor in a somber moment. "Why do you think I've spent billions developing alternative energy sources? So we don't have to deal with people like him or have the Cockrell brothers trying to run things from top to bottom." McIllhenny slumped in his chair, resigned to what he said next. "Have our people in the region start asking questions. Find out what happened to those other women Rahim had taken." Deep in his heart McIllhenny knew their fate, didn't give voice to uncomfortable truths. "Their families deserve to know what happened," no matter how repulsive the end for their loved ones might have been.

"I'll get on it right away," Warfield replied. McIllhenny nodded in agreement, rubbed his chin. Warfield a good man, trustworthy, honest, a former Marine who bravely served in both Iraq wars, yet another wayward folly foisted by proud, arrogant men who believed they knew better than those wisely advising caution, a war in the name of protecting America's interests in the Middle East. *When will we ever learn?* McIllhenny shared a kinship with his assistant having served in a different, but no less quixotic, conflict in the steamy jungles of Southeast Asia long ago, left behind a close friend on that battlefield whose name now graced the new hockey arena at Great Northern University in his memory.

"Can you give me some time alone?" McIllhenny asked Warfield. "I need to make a phone call."

"Yes sir," Warfield said, bearing ramrod straight. *Once a Marine, always a Marine,* McIllhenny surmised with a subtle smile. Warfield turned smartly, exited the office, leaving him to silent musings.

Cal McIllhenny sat behind his desk, hands folded on his chest, thinking. *I have to call him.* He reached for the phone, dialed the number, probably couldn't take his call, already headed to Chicago and Great Northern University. *"You've reached Garrett Grayson of Grayson Farms Winery. I'm not available to take your call."* Caleb let the message to play, estimating where in the trip between Upstate New York and Chicago Garrett and Melanie might be waiting for the prompt from a female voice.

It took a moment for McIllhenny to collect his thoughts. "Garrett, it's Cal McIllhenny," he sighed, "I heard the news about Samantha," a young and talented woman to which he was a godfather, though a fact kept secret from Samantha, an agreement with Garrett Grayson unless circumstance dictated revelation. "I know you're on your way to see her. I'm praying she comes through this ordeal well and safe." He paused. "I met her after the football game Saturday, and she interviewed me yesterday after the speech by Senator Fielding." No need to tell Garrett he'd also spoken with Sheik Rahim, no matter how brief and curt, standing accused of ordering others to kidnap Samantha and five other young women, transport them to his homeland and inflict unthinkable indignities in the name of fulfilling twisted, violent fantasies. "You and Melanie should be proud of her. She's a lovely, smart and brave young lady. I think I know where she gets those qualities."

Caleb remembered the dreadful autumn decades earlier, events beyond his control and a terrible personal loss averted due to the heroic actions of the man to whom he left the message. "Garrett, I have my daughter because of your actions. You never gave up. You saved my daughter from those same animals," criminal predators of a vicious, shadowy criminal enterprise known only as The Trading Society, "that hurt Samantha. You let me know if you need any assistance. I have resources. I'll do whatever I can to help. If it means using my people to protect Samantha from The Trading Society I won't hesitate to do that."

McIllhenny rubbed his eyes. "Samantha was with Tyler McManaway when I saw her Saturday. He's a good young man, cares for Samantha, that's why he did what he had to do to save her. He'll make a fine son-in-law." Caleb knew he was rambling, didn't care, emotions usually controlled and measured now jumbled and raw after the startling incident in Chicago. "You don't have to call back, you know how to reach me," Caleb said finally. "Spend all the time you can with Samantha." As he hung up Caleb McIllhenny shifted his eyes to the framed picture on the desk of his own beautiful daughter and her family, a daughter whose life he owed to the actions of Commander Garrett Grayson, Royal Australian

Navy. After her rescue wounds physical and psychological from her ordeal at the hands of The Trading Society mended over time with help from the best in the field. Once the scars healed she returned to college, received a degree at the University of Texas, went to law school where she met and fell in love with a fellow law student, whip-smart yet considerate and kind, a solid man with good heart like Garrett Grayson and Tyler McManaway. They married, gave to him and his wife two beautiful granddaughters: Tara, now a junior at the University of Texas and Lily, weeks earlier commencing her freshman year at Great Northern University, excited out on her own and spreading her wings, joining the student newspaper, *The Daily Northern*. The same newspaper where Samantha Grayson worked as a reporter. He stared at the smiling face of his granddaughter, so young and innocent, and a chilling thought lanced his soul. *It could've been Lily.*

Caleb McIllhenny swiveled around in his chair, gazed out the window at the panorama of the Dallas skyline. A squall line of thunderstorms bearing down on the Metroplex from the northwest, birthed by the first blockbuster Canadian cold front of the fall and poised to shatter the oppressive, blast furnace heat of a Texas summer. The solid wall of towering dark clouds black as a bottomless pit of evil, arcs of lighting dancing across the face of the wall cloud an ominous harbinger.

Caleb knew there existed many storms in the world, some the work of nature, others created by the hubris of men inebriated with power, angry tempests unleashing harm on those caught in the relentless path. At times one received ample warning of the approaching storm, able to take cover in time, prepare for the squall before it struck. The storm one didn't see coming and had no warning of, caught out in the open and completely unaware, caused the most grievous of damage.

Such a storm struck Samantha Grayson and she was fortunate to have survived.

Cal McIllhenny knew she might not be so lucky the next time.

"Let's do this, gentlemen," Detective Devin Carson announced to his fellow detectives, two of them from parts far beyond the city, working a long day and longer night to topple a vile sex trafficking ring. *We did have unexpected assistance*, Carson thought, couldn't take all the credit for success. Entered the lockup at Area Six Police Headquarters at Belmont and Western to take custody of the disgraced sheik of a Persian Gulf emirate, along with his security detail, who hours earlier came perilously close to snatching six young women against their will, taking helpless victims overseas to face a deadly destiny. Carson and his colleagues transporting the prisoners to the monolithic Metropolitan Correction Center in Chicago's Loop where they would wait for the Feds to decide their fate in the American justice system.

Carson strode to the nearest cell, Sheik Abdullah al-Aziz Rahim sitting on the cot inside, despite confronting an uncertain situation impudent and haughty, arrogant to the last. "Time to take a trip downtown, Your Excellency," Carson announced, voice dripping with sarcasm, reveled in the irony of the moment. The man who intended to abduct six defenseless women, take them back to his homeland, make them his slaves and commit unspeakable acts upon them, now a prisoner in a cell in a Chicago police station. Yet he showed not a shred of unease at his condition. A uniformed sergeant unlocked the cell for Carson.

Carson stepped inside, stood before him. "Please stand up, sir," he ordered. Rahim glanced up at Carson, seemed slightly perturbed at the inconvenience of his custody, irritated by Carson's presence, wounds inflicted on him by Samantha Grayson in her courageous struggle to stop his flight in the

371

limousine and Tyler McManaway during the final fight in the confines of Hubbard's Cave bandaged. Carson unsure, after considering the magnitude of his crimes and the number of possible victims who disappeared and perished at the hands of this beast, if he'd have been so merciful treating his wounds. *That's why we're Americans*, Carson surmised, *we know the measure of mercy*. Rahim remained silent, as if Carson didn't deserve the dignity of a simple response, the detective beneath his lofty station. Finally he stood, faced the detective without compunction or resistance. The diplomat held out his hands, Carson locking handcuffs around his wrists, reminding himself he was dealing with a monster with innocent blood on those hands.

"This way," Carson noted curtly, taking Rahim by the arm, guiding him into the corridor to join the other members of his security detail in custody, seven in all, another five under police guard at Cook County Hospital receiving treatment for injuries suffered in the thrashing delivered by four courageous college athletes. The pilots waiting at O'Hare International Airport with the Gulfstream jet to whisk the diplomat and his helpless cargo to the other side of the world taken into custody by Cook County Sherriff's deputies and the Illinois State Police, held at Cook County Jail at 26th and California awaiting transport downtown.

Hilliard nodded at Carson. "We're set, let's go."

"I apologize for the transportation in advance," Carson said, leading Rahim and the remainder of his entourage down the hallway, Rahim not familiar with the back of a Chicago Police paddy wagon.

The party entered the front foyer of Area Six, Carson taking note of men in business suits waiting there. *Weren't they going to meet us downtown?* Recognized FBI Special Agent William Ryland, worked him with in the past, standing at the front of the group. *What's going on?* A bad feeling festered in his gut, spying the pained expression on Ryland's face of one chosen to fulfill a duty he found distasteful. Hilliard shook his head, a look of loathing on his face expecting what was about to happen.

"What's up?" Carson fought down percolating suspicion. "I thought we'd be handing them over at the MCC?"

Ryland put his hands on his hips, head shaking in disgust. "Change of plans," Ryland motioned to a man by his side, short and bespectacled, emitting the familiar officious air of a bureaucrat. "Detective Carson this is Lee Colson from the State Department."

Colson cleared his throat. "Detective, if you and your people would remove the restraints from Sheik Rahim and his party."

Shock, then anger, darkened the face of Devin Carson. *You have to be fuckin' kidding.* "What are you talking about?"

"As a member of the diplomatic mission of the nation of Daharan," Colson cleared his throat, didn't mention Rahim a member of the powerful ruling family of the Persian Gulf nation, "Sheik Rahim has diplomatic immunity. He is being returned to his home country immediately."

"WHAT!" Carson stepped up to Colson, wanted to throttle him on the spot. "You have to be joking, right? This can't be happening!" Carson pointed to Rahim, rage venting like magma from a volcano, temper made more incendiary by lack of sleep. "He hired human traffickers to kidnap women for him! You want to know where those women who disappeared in Los Angeles, in Atlanta and everywhere else are! You know, American citizens! Why don't you ask him? He's the one who ordered it done for him!"

Colson cleared his throat again; an insignificant paper pusher tapped to deliver unwelcome news, uncomfortable with his selection as messenger, but knew Carson wouldn't kill him. "The government of

Daharan has made assurances Sheik Rahim will face justice on his return." The smug expression on Rahim's face, displaying not a trace of fear at the declaration, told Carson the assurance nothing but an empty lie.

"They have now?" Nathanial Hampton commented sarcastically. "That's so sporting of them."

"As of this moment Sheik Rahim is considered persona non gratia," Colson hoped this tamped down Carson's temper, "if he sets foot in the United States again he will be dealt with accordingly."

It didn't. "Fat lot of good that does us now," Carson snorted, not convinced.

"If you refuse to release Sheik Rahim and his associates," Colson once more cleared his throat, the mannerism driving Carson mad, "I will order the agents accompanying me carry out this directive."

Carson slipped aside. "Be my guest," said to Ryland, "they're all yours, guys."

"This isn't my idea, Devin," Ryland shared his displeasure with Carson. "I don't like it either, if I had my way..." He let the statement trail off, Carson guessing what pleasantries his FBI colleague wished to visit on the conceited diplomat.

"I'm not angry at you," Carson replied, anger smoldering. "I'm angry at people sitting on their asses in Washington right now." Bureaucrats and politicians viewing the world in terms of alliances and policy statements. The FBI agents, through half-hearted actions removing restraints from Sheik Rahim and his entourage, obvious held no enthusiasm for the duty assigned them. Once free of the handcuffs Rahim made a show of rubbing his wrists, adjusted a rumpled jacket and tightened a loosened tie, glared with simmering hatred at Devin Carson.

Hilliard shook his head and started laughing, reaction filled with irony instead of humor. "What's so damn funny?" Carson demanded.

"I could see this freight train coming down the track a mile away," Hilliard explained. "Not only does our friend have diplomatic immunity, he's a member of the ruling family of Daharan. Now where's Daharan? Smack dab in the middle of the Persian Gulf with big, bad Iran sitting up to the north, you know, the country building a few nukes, flexing a little geopolitical muscle. Do you know what else is in Daharan? The headquarters for the Fifth Fleet of the United States Navy."

"Absolutely friggin' wonderful," Hampton muttered under his breath.

"So I'll connect the dots so you'll see the picture," Hilliard continued, filling in blanks Carson already able to guess. "I'm sure the ruler of Daharan contacted our government and let them know, in no uncertain terms, if the United States moved to prosecute our friend here for his actions," Hilliard jerked a thumb at the conceited Rahim, "the United States Navy is looking for a new home for the Fifth Fleet. With Iran rattling the sabers I think the Defense Department doesn't want to have that on their 'to do' list right now, tramping around the Persian Gulf pricing property and negotiating a new lease for our naval forces." Hilliard paused. "We saw how the Dow responded this morning to the news, down two hundred points at the opening bell, oil shooting up five dollars a barrel. Put it all together, it's not about lives here, it's about money and power."

"Son of a bitch," Danny Bryant cursed as the last of Rahim's security detail released.

"No matter how much the United States wants to bring this bastard to justice, we can't afford to lose that naval base or our access to oil at the moment. So we're forced to play ball with our 'ally,'" Hilliard wiggled his fingers, placing the word in quotation marks, "and send our friend back home free and clear." Hilliard, a shrewd smirk on his face, peered at the State Department official. "Please tell me I'm right on all counts."

Colson cleared his throat again. "I can neither confirm nor deny the reasons for Sheik Rahim being returned to his homeland."

Hilliard smiled. "That's all the answer I need."

"And why this scumbag is heading home," Mychal Mustafa growled.

Carson stepped up to Rahim, stood eye to eye, stared at him with a cold gaze. "I should've let Tyler McManaway finish you off. Then we wouldn't have this little problem," he told the diplomat, blood boiling at the turnabout. "I'll tell you this," Carson thrust his finger in his face, "if you ever set foot in this city again, if you ever threaten Samantha Grayson or any of her friends, you won't have to worry about Tyler McManaway taking you out. You'll have to worry about me, because I will finish the job for him."

"Is that a threat, Detective?" Rahim nonchalant in the wake of the tirade.

Carson nodded. "What do you think?"

Rahim snorted, with an exaggerated shrug of his shoulders and a proud flourish spun about without reply. Devin Carson watched in disgust as Sheik Rahim and his bodyguards escorted outside Area Six to a black limousine and three town cars waiting to take them to freedom. *What about the freedom of those sixteen other women? What about their lives?* Carson thought bitterly. *Do their lives even matter? Or is sixteen young women an acceptable price for national security? For the flow of oil?* Somewhere, in an office in Washington or on Wall Street, someone likely thought that price was acceptable.

"With friends like that," Hampton snorted, "who needs enemies?"

"Friends, enemies, who can tell anymore? They're all alike now." Patrick Flannery spit on the floor, glaring ruefully as Sheik Rahim and his party stepped into the vehicles. "You're goin' to have to tell that Tyler McManaway fella about this," he paused, 'don't think he's goin' to be too happy."

"I will," Carson knew it too soon for either Tyler or Samantha Grayson to learn the man who terrorized her free once more. Had to make the call before they discovered the unsettling development from the media. *I don't want that messenger delivering this message.* "Not too happy about this either."

"You figure there any drinkin' establishments open this time of the mornin'?" Flannery asked. "Have to get this bad taste out of my mouth."

"I'm sure we can find one," this from Hilliard. "First round is on me. And I'm having a pint of strawberry milk."

Chapter 50

"How are you doing today?" Tyler McManaway asked.

Samantha Grayson expected the question, Tyler offered this simplest of queries every day since the terrifying nightmare at the hands of Marcus Cowle and Sheik Rahim and this Saturday morning, three weeks removed from that awful day, no different. Samantha guessed the question, even with the passage of time, might never go a day unspoken.

"Doing better," Samantha sipped her Starbucks Pike Place coffee, paper cup warm against her palms, as they sat on the promenade of Howell Student Commons watching the sun rise over the glass-smooth waters of Lake Michigan. Great Northern remained undefeated after two impressive victories on the road, routs over out-matched Minnesota and Indiana earning them the number eleven spot in both polls, Tyler enjoying a well-deserved weekend off before the schedule grew daunting. Visits from ranked rivals Iowa, Michigan, Nebraska and a trip to Ohio State, the conference slate broken up by a home game against SEC powerhouse Georgia, loomed large in the coming weeks, Tyler suggesting the day to themselves, spending quiet time together before heading into Chicago.

Tyler smiled. "Good," all he said.

"A little step each day," Samantha nestled against Tyler. The morning crisp and bracing, the first bite of autumn pervading the air, trees painted with brilliant reds, yellows and gold like brushstrokes from an impressionist's palette, a crystalline frost dusting the grass, Samantha wearing a wool coat, scarf and finger-less knit gloves to ward off the chill. A day earlier Samantha took one such little step returning to familiar surroundings, the offices of *The Daily Northern,* filing her first news story after the first person account of her abduction by the insidious human trafficking ring and fight for survival, an event forever casting a troubling shadow looming over her life. That her first story after the extended absence, on the advice of Aaron Dinehart, concerned the banality of new parking restrictions around Warren Field for Homecoming Weekend against sixth-ranked Iowa, a story typically assigned to the greenest of freshman reporters, didn't bother Samantha. Had to start somewhere, climbing back on the bicycle after falling off, disregarding fear and uncertainty to move on with life, facing challenges both new and unknown. *Returning to normal, that's all I can do.* But her 'new normal' altered and ambiguous since the moment she stepped inside a supposed photography studio, the sinister instrument of an international abduction scheme, a vicious trap snaring unsuspecting young women. A discovery Samantha almost paid for with her life.

"Little steps are good," Tyler reassured, pulled Samantha close, hoped she didn't feel he being overprotective in the wake of her arduous trial. Samantha didn't mind the attention, no need to say otherwise, comforted by the tender touch, always safe in his embrace. "How are the roomies?" Tyler asked, concerned for the well-being of Samantha's best friends-Amanda McKinnon, Lauryn Callahan and Ashleigh Morgan-as he was for Samantha.

"I think we're all managing in our own ways." Samantha sipped her coffee, since that terrible night each meeting with crisis counselors to navigate troubled emotions and newfound anxieties, yet traveling their own roads towards healing. After taking a week off to rest and heal a tortured body following the ordeal imprisoned inside the photography studio by the white slaver Marcus Cowle Amanda back in pursuit of an individual NCAA cross-country title, off with her teammates competing in an invitational at the University of Wisconsin in Madison, finding solace and redemption in running. Lauryn Callahan and Albert 'Fiji' Fatuamala, having discovered heartfelt devotion for each other that night, now inseparable, the blossoming relationship between the pair, a coupling a long time in coming, one of the few good things to emerge from the harrowing event. Ashleigh Morgan spending the weekend with D'Andre Watson at the Notre Dame-Stanford game in South Bend, watching a high school teammate of D'Andre's play for the Fightin' Irish, a rising powerhouse Great Northern might face in a post-season bowl game, perhaps even in the National Championship game. Ashleigh no longer afraid of small, confined spaces, but Samantha wondered if that phobia only exchanged for one far darker, a fear of men who kidnapped women for sale to the highest bidder.

Samantha remained silent until Tyler broke the morning stillness, knew something on her mind. "What did you want to tell me?"

Samantha bit her lip, sat up and turned to Tyler. "I think I've found my destiny." Her eyes flashed with a fire of determination. "I think I know why God put me on this world. What He wants me to do."

"I think I know too," Tyler answered without hesitation.

"Human trafficking is more than this organization Marcus Cowle was involved with. They're only the worst incarnation of an evil that's everywhere in this world, the predators at the top of the food chain," Samantha began. "We don't want to open our eyes to the evil, don't want to admit slavery has never gone away. There are so many victims of despicable people like Cowle, women and children who're walking beside us, living in our towns, imprisoned in the house next door, and we have no idea of the terror they live with every day. How these brutal animals control them, hurt them, abuse them, take away their dignity and freedom, their hope for a better life." Samantha stared into the sunrise, letting warm light bathe her face. "Someone has to expose the evil, fight for those who can't fight back, speak for those who have no voice. They need someone brave to stand by their side when they think they're alone, think that no one cares for their plight." Tyler sat quietly as Samantha gave voice to her feelings. "I have to be that person, I have to be their voice. I don't know where this will take me, where that road leads, but I need to be the one who takes up this cause. I have to fight the battle for them." Samantha paused, looked directly at Tyler. "If you feel I'll be putting myself in too much danger…"

Tyler held her hand; let his undying love flow through the touch. "I can't keep you from your destiny. I can't prevent you from fighting for what you believe in. That would be selfish of me." Tyler sighed. "Just be careful, let me know what you're doing whenever you can." With his other hand Tyler stroked her cheek. "Remember what I promised. I will never let anyone hurt you. I will never let anything happen to you. That's my promise. I will keep it for as long as we're together." Tyler hoped he kept the promise for the rest of their lives. "I will always be here for you no matter what."

Samantha leaned over and kissed Tyler, understood his devotion strong and heart true. "I love you, Tyler Ian McManaway," she told him softly, almost in a whisper.

"I love you, Samantha Elise Grayson." Then Tyler started to say. "Unto every generation there is born…"

Samantha smiled, recognized the line from a favorite television show of her childhood, wished to be as fearless and intrepid as that heroine. "If it were only as simple as staking a vampire through the heart."

"You can take up archery, be like Katniss Everdeen," Tyler deadpanned, invoking another dauntless heroine, this one from *The Hunger Games*.

Samantha tilted her head back, laughed at the image conjured by the comment. "I think the university would frown on me walking around campus with a bow and arrows."

"I think a girl with a bow and arrows is hot," Tyler remarked casually.

"I'm sure you do," Samantha smiled, fingers trailing gently down his cheek. "How are you doing?" Now Samantha asked Tyler.

Tyler caressed the back of Samantha's hand. "When I signed my Letter of Intent," before a packed auditorium at Wheaton-Warrenville South High School, in front of a slew of television cameras from ESPN, CNN and every local television station recording the momentous, yet at its very core a personal decision, "I never thought I'd be at the center of an international incident."

"Neither did I when Great Northern accepted me," Samantha admitted. The repercussions from the revelation of human traffickers abducting and selling young American women to a high-ranking diplomat of a lynchpin ally in the Persian Gulf, a country home to the United States Navy's Fifth Fleet guarding vital economic interests from a possibly nuclear-armed Iran, continued to reverberate in Washington and overseas. The American public, egged on through fervent demagoguery from strident pundits standing on personal soapboxes, righteously outraged by the actions of Sheik Abdullah al-Aziz Rahim and the fact sixteen young women, and perhaps unknown others, kidnapped to satisfy cravings for violence and likely paid with their lives. Infuriated further with the invocation of diplomatic immunity allowing Rahim to evade prosecution and what should've been a certain death sentence. Both political parties lobbing partisan hand grenades of accusations and blame as the administration danced and dodged to deflect criticism and establish balance in a situation where no one stood to gain.

As politicians argued and pointed fingers Tyler, Samantha and their friends stood at the center of the maelstrom, the human face to the story. In the weeks following the events of that longest day sitting down for interviews with each major television network along with those from CNN, ESPN, Fox News and MSNBC. Reliving the night their paths crossed with the insidious ring of professional kidnappers and the Middle Eastern diplomat with dark, vicious secrets employing their services for the heavy lifting, providing living material to act out his twisted fantasies in the security of his compound on the other side of the world. Only now, three weeks after that night, the glare of media attention starting to subside, but to peak again this week with the first home game for Great Northern since that terrible night. Tyler, D'Andre and Fiji honored for their actions before kickoff against Iowa while Connor Aanonsen honored later that night prior to the first varsity hockey game played at the new Thomas C. Travener Ice Arena. ESPN deciding to bestow the nickname 'The Fantastic Four' on the four heroic friends, though Tyler kept to himself the thought such moniker distasteful, trivialized the fact of victims whose fates never fully known.

For Tyler the moments in front of the camera proved surreal more at ease talking about football and fielding questions regarding an upcoming opponent, instead of being asked his opinion what his government should to do in response to the crimes, and seemingly impervious invulnerability, of Sheik Rahim. Tyler grunted. His opinion how to address his nemesis a closely guarded secret, what he should've done in Hubbard's Cave. "I'm wondering when we're," meaning the United States, "sending Seal Team Six to Daharan. Have one of our guys put a bullet between that bastard's eyes."

"I don't think that's happening anytime soon," Samantha replied regretfully. "Not with our Navy based in Daharan or Iran on the other side of the Persian Gulf building nuclear weapons." Rahim secure in his homeland far from Evanslawn and Great Northern University, under warning his life forfeit if setting foot on American soil, yet Samantha unsure if the dire threat of deadly retribution enough to prevent Rahim from seeking revenge on them. *He has nothing to lose.*

Tyler looked into Samantha's dark brown eyes, knew what she was thinking. "I will never let that monster hurt you, I'll kill that bastard if he ever tries," he reaffirmed with uncharacteristic coldness.

"I know," Samantha replied softly.

For a minute they sat silent, watched the sun continue its ascent into the sapphire blue October sky. "I've been thinking about something," Samantha changed the subject to matters more light-hearted. "I read Nancy Drew mysteries when I was in grade school."

Tyler cocked his head. "Really?" Samantha never revealed this detail of her childhood.

"Well, she was smart and brave and pretty," Samantha started to explain. "There were times when I wanted to be like her, solving mysteries, helping people who were in trouble."

"I think I see the resemblance," Tyler pointed out, Samantha sharing all those attributes. "But wrong hair color," he added. Nancy Drew a blonde while Samantha blessed with gorgeous copper-red auburn hair.

"But there was one thing I never figured out reading all of those books." Samantha paused. "Did Nancy Drew ever go to therapy to deal with all the dangerous situations and close calls with death she faced in every book?"

Tyler dropped his head, laughing at the observation. "I wouldn't have wanted to see those medical bills." He shook his head. "Wonder if insurance covered it."

"Really!" Samantha exclaimed, happy that Tyler saw her point. "She comes within moments of dying in some deathtrap and the next book starts and she's ready to investigate the next mystery as if nothing bad ever happened in the past! Forgetting in the last book how she was locked in a trunk and dumped in a lake and almost drowned or trapped in a house that's burning down around her! I couldn't decide if Nancy Drew was resilient and courageous or a walking basket-case on the verge of a nervous breakdown," Samantha concluded, then sobered. "I don't know if I'm resilient and brave or if I'm that potential mental train-wreck waiting to go off the tracks."

Tyler stilled his laughter. "I always wondered why Superman didn't tell Lois Lane to work in the sports department at *The Daily Planet*. Less risky covering sports. Not too many super-villains out to capture you when you're trying to find out who's starting at quarterback." Samantha leaned over to kiss Tyler, able to do this simple act of affection all day if she so desired. "I think you're a resilient, brave soul who wants to help people in trouble," Tyler told her. "And you have someone there to play the hero if his damsel in distress ever needs to be rescued." Though Tyler prayed his role as dashing hero, rescuing his love from a life-threatening dilemma, proved a one-time engagement.

"What's the plan for today?" Samantha asked.

Tyler gazed over the calm waters of Lake Michigan, then at Samantha, the center of his universe around which his life revolved, reaching out to sweep away auburn hair from her forehead. "It's pretty simple. You, me, an afternoon in the city, a quiet place for dinner, a carriage ride this evening along Michigan Avenue," he proposed, hoping she approved. "I don't think we need much more than that."

"Sounds wonderful." Samantha smiled, brown eyes gleaming brightly, a day to enjoy being alive. Though spending time with Tyler was wonderful in itself.

Tyler stood, offered his hand, Samantha took it and Tyler eased her up from the bench, arm wrapping around her waist, pulling her close, kissed her again. "Remember what I told you last year, on our first date?"

"Look up." Samantha found the advice as relevant now as it had been then.

"Let's live for today." Tyler grinned with the knowledge he'd never know a life without Samantha Grayson.

The same sun rising into the morning sky above Lake Michigan and casting its light on two young, fortunate lovers approached its zenith above southern France, rays warming the balcony of the isolated chateau as Marcus Cowle continued to stew in the juices of defeat, drinking yet another glass of fine Bordeaux wine to drown petulant anger. After a week spent dodging and evading the best efforts of law enforcement tracking them, he and his associates reached the haven offered by his mentor, nursing wounds to his pride still fresh inflicted by the student reporter and star football player, along with their companions, from Great Northern University.

"Cheer up, my friend," Marcel Portier, his Patron in The Trading Society, consoled, sipping from his glass. "Even the best of us suffer the occasional setback."

"Wait until next year." From his chair Sterner, one of Cowle's apprentices, echoed a familiar refrain, drinking a Belgian white ale, not a wine person like Cowle and Portier. The glass held in his left hand, right hand encased in a cast mending the broken wrist incurred during battle with Albert 'Fiji' Fatuamala in the abandoned complex on Carroll Avenue. He shook his head, possessed grudging respect and a healthy admiration for his nemesis. *The kid's a beast.* Lang, Cowle's other assistant, plagued by the aftereffects of the severe concussion delivered by the mighty Samoan, confined inside the chateau as bright sunlight exacerbated his delicate condition, played havoc with his senses.

Cowle didn't acknowledge his Patron, understood he meant well, soothing a damaged ego, stared down into the glass of vintage Bordeaux. "I don't like to lose," Cowle replied coolly. "You should know that after all these years." Missing a payout beyond his imagination, a jackpot establishing him as the preeminent Collector, the best in the organization, a force everyone both admired and feared. Now his status within The Trading Society tenuous, marred by the events in Chicago, fellow Collectors sensing vulnerability in a once ironclad reputation, smelled blood in the water. *My blood.* Cowle seethed, after three weeks barely containing the rage towards the objects of his hatred. *Samantha Grayson and Tyler McManaway, you will pay for what you have done.* Cowle suspected he wasn't the only one wishing violent retribution upon the pair.

"You must have faith, my friend. Events will turn for you." Marcel Portier a short man with a round, balding head and an even rounder midsection, as if his upper body composed of a small ball resting on top a larger one. The physique brought about by the opulent luxury of his position as a Patron in the hierarchy of The Trading Society, his days as a Collector, and the far leaner build during those years active as a professional kidnapper, far in the past. His plump cheeks and chin graced by a pencil-thin moustache and beard, dark eyes gleaming with charm and a devious intelligence, Portier the cat who ate the canary and proud of the fact. "The Curators agree with us regarding what took place in Chicago." The Curators controlled The Trading Society, descendants of the mercantilists who worked the African slave trade and never left that brand of commerce behind, serving as an executive council found in any business enterprise addressing essential operational issues, establishing the blueprint towards ever greater profits. They also dealt with crises, such as the incident in Chicago ending Cowle's lucrative venture. If the Curators didn't find in your favor one as good as dead and the Adjustors, the Praetorian Guard of The Trading Society, designated to clean up the mess and rectify matters in brutally efficient fashion. *At least they'll let me live,* Cowle thought sourly, though his ego bruised by the unforeseen setback. "If Sheik Rahim hadn't decided to go to Chicago to personally take possession of the consignment, if you'd been allowed to follow procedure as with past consignments, it is highly unlikely your undertaking would've been discovered."

"I tried telling him that," Cowle noted matter-of-factly.

"Sheik Rahim understands that now. The Curators had their own...discussion with him," Portier added, the Curators not hesitant to deal with, and in a similarly lethal fashion, intractable clients and unreasonable demands posing a threat to their enterprise. "In fact he accepted responsibility for that oversight."

"Nice of him," Cowle sipped his wine, "does he want his money back?"

"Not quite." Portier ignored the snide comment. "Because his visit to Chicago and Great Northern University brought him into contact with Samantha Grayson, he now has an object he wishes to possess at any cost, pay any price to own." Portier drank from his glass. "Not only does Samantha remain a target, but it also appears Miss Grayson's friends," Amanda McKinnon, Lauryn Callahan and Ashleigh Morgan, "have generated interest from Sheik Rahim and other clients of The Trading Society." Portier dragged his finger along the lip of his glass. "This situation might prove quite profitable for all involved."

"Really?" Cowle heartened by the news. Perhaps salvaging his loss, and exacting revenge in the process, on Samantha Grayson.

"You may still be able to make amends with the good sheik," Portier offered. "There are many American students studying in Europe. You could make good on at least part of your lost consignment."

"Yes, there are." Cowle never considered the possibility. *Lemons into lemonade.*

"There is one detail regarding the Grayson girl and her companions of which I must inform you," Portier cleared his throat, delivered discomforting news. "You'll have competition acquiring the prize." Cowle stared at Portier in disbelief. "The Curators have declared Miss Grayson and her companions an open order." The banal terminology meant any Patron could direct their Collectors to capture Samantha and her friends, sell them to Sheik Rahim or other interested parties and reap the substantial reward.

"Samantha Grayson is mine!" Cowle quickly grew indignant, temper flaring. "I'll be the one handing her pretty little body to Sheik Rahim!"

Portier shook his head. "That isn't what the Curators think," he informed. "Whoever is able to acquire and deliver her to Sheik Rahim wins the reward." A crooked smile blossomed on his round face. "That doesn't mean you cannot...interfere in the plans of your fellow Collectors. Insure they aren't successful in their endeavors."

"A fly in their ointment," Cowle smirked, understood the jealousy his success engendered among other Collectors, lesser men desiring to best his efforts. *Good luck with that.* In the Trading Society there existed no honor among thieves.

"Be patient, my friend," Portier cautioned Cowle. "Do not rush, wait for the proper time, strike when they least expect it."

"Oh, I'll wait," Cowle sneered, "but I'll make sure no one takes what's rightfully mine."

"That's the spirit, Boss," Sterner sipped his beer, pondered a second encounter with Albert Fatuamala, grinned broadly. *I'll make sure the outcome turns out differently next time.* Off in the distance a white van approached, heading up the winding drive leading to the chateau. The cargo vans in Europe smaller, more compact and boxier in design, than those Cowle utilized for his operations back in the States, designed to navigate narrow streets and thoroughfares found on the continent. Yet the vans here as efficient transporting the same amount of restrained human cargo.

"He's right on time, always punctual," Portier glanced at his watch, a satisfied smile at the impending delivery of living merchandise. He turned to Cowle. "You've never met him, Johann Gaulten, the Collector who handles my European affairs, have you?"

Cowle shook his head. "I haven't had pleasure of making his acquaintance." Cowle didn't feel inclined to be sociable right then.

"I know you don't like competition," Portier purred as the van eased to a stop in front of the chateau, the three peering down from the veranda at the new arrivals. Portier sensed a proud streak in his protégé, a stubbornness to prove his downfall if he continued exhibiting an unwillingness to walk away. Portier once faced a similar situation, an obsession with another young woman and her protector, gained the wisdom to let be in the end, thriving from the lesson learned. "I believe he and his apprentices may be of assistance in whatever plan of vengeance you may have for Samantha Grayson."

Cowle watched as a man of confident, almost imperious, bearing emerged from the passenger side on the right side of the van, much younger than Cowle, perhaps in his late twenties to early thirties. Cowle estimated his height around six feet with a head of dark, wavy hair impeccably styled. Aviator-style sunglasses shielding his eyes from the bright sun did nothing to conceal striking features of one able to earn a substantial income as a professional model instead of abducting unsuspecting women for sale on the open market for human flesh. He exuded a dangerous and provocative sensuality luring women to his presence as the scent of a flower attracts a honeybee. *Looks like a party boy, frequents the clubs and the discos, finds the merchandise for his clients there*, Cowle quickly guessed Gaulten's preferred method of securing his product.

From the driver's side on the left side of the van, in Europe the positions switched as they drove on the opposite side of the road, the second man, a bald, hulking figure who somehow managed to squeeze his immense bulk into the cramped seat, emerged. Sterner whistled in admiration of the imposing associate. "That is Bludo," Portier pointed out. "He isn't the most agreeable fellow."

"No shit. Big dude," Sterner complimented simply. If Albert Fatuamala a beast and a match for Sterner, maybe he needed a beast of his own by his side to even the odds the next time their paths crossed.

"Johann is quite adept at what he does," Portier motioned at Gaulten, who with Bludo moved to the rear of the van, "very much like you, Marcus. He's a fixture on the party circuit." Portier confirmed Cowle's assessment of his approach. "Young women cannot resist, very much to their detriment, his particular charms." Portier rubbed his chin and smiled, though his chateau nestled in the mountains on the Franco-Swiss border, within close distance of Lyon and the headquarters of Interpol, sworn enemy of the human trafficking enterprise, Portier ran his operations with flagrant impunity. *What one is able to do with the assistance of friends in very high places.*

"What goodies did he bring you today?" Sterner wondered in curiosity as Bludo opened the rear doors, bent his six-eight frame into the cargo compartment.

"Three girls from the Czech Republic, they'll be shipped to a profitable Asian client later this evening," Portier revealed. "The product found in the former Eastern Bloc countries is quite enticing, of the finest quality, like what you find in America." Portier's smile grew wide. "The economic distress America is experiencing at the present time is far more dire in Europe, the politicians don't yet see the threat of their inaction," the vaunted European Union teetered on the cusp of financial chaos, "the local authorities no longer have time and resources to hamper our trade. The austerity measures some countries have implemented play into our hands. Bribes are convincing persuasion to look the other way when it comes to our interests."

Cowle nodded appreciatively at the observation; perhaps a similar state of affairs soon entrenched in America, the slashing knife of budget cuts by cash-strapped governments at all levels blunting the effectiveness of law enforcement. *Make my job a little easier*, Cowle thought, *if I get a chance to return.*

Bludo tugged the first captive out from the van, a young woman with copper-red hair reminding Cowle of Samantha Grayson, wearing a black satin cocktail dress, upper body firmly bound, gagged and blindfolded with white cloth. He shoved the terrified girl, tripping and teetering precariously on platform high heels and almost falling, at Gaulten who deftly caught the girl by the arm before she toppled face-first to the ground. He checked the security of her bonds, a satisfied smile spread across his face examining his prize, from his hostage whiffed the intoxicating scent of fear. He glanced at Bludo, tilted his head to one side as if cautioning his associate. *Please be more careful with the merchandise. We don't want to break something this fragile.*

Bludo wordlessly acknowledged the rebuke, a second captive quickly followed the first, Cowle knew a second apprentice inside the rear of the van forcing unwilling prisoners into Bludo's grasp. A pretty, yet unfortunate creature with shimmering blonde hair, wearing a frilly sundress, attired for a night out at the clubs. An evening terribly interrupted and ending with her a bound, gagged and blindfolded package transported halfway across Europe to an unknown location. The girl squealed, yanked roughly from the van, forced to stand beside her luckless companion in the driveway, Bludo attempting to be gentle with the helpless girl but delicacy a trait the big man didn't seem to possess. From where he surveyed the scene Cowle listened to her muffled screams, observed the blonde's blindfolded and gagged head whipping about, trying to sense where she was, frightened at where she might be and terrified at the unknown fate intended for her.

The third victim emerged from the rear of the van, a brunette about the height of Presley Harding, even with the gag and blindfold obscuring her face Cowle perceived an achingly haunting attractiveness. "The client has particular tastes in his merchandise," Portier explained, "three women every time: a blonde, a redhead and a brunette." Cowle saw the brunette, like her companions wearing a short cocktail dress of shimmering blue satin for partying away the night at the discos. None of them expecting so horrifying a conclusion to their evening, disappearing into a nightmarish black hole of sexual slavery without any hope of rescue or salvation. Stepping from the van with the struggling hostage, hand gripped firmly on the girl's arm dragging the captive into the sunlight was the second of Gaulten's apprentices.

"What do we have here?" Cowle asked in amazement at the identity of the apprentice.

The dark-haired beauty, couldn't be any older than her early-twenties, same age as the captive she so roughly handled, cut a stunning figure of breathtaking exquisiteness, able to pass for a professional model in the same way as Johann Gaulten. *They work as a team*, Cowle assumed, *operate in tandem*. She stood tall in stature, towering over her tiny captive, body taut and fit, wearing skin-tight jeans and a leather jacket over a black top hugging supple breasts. Cowle smiled self-consciously, Gaulten's apprentice the type of target he might hunt and capture back in the States, selling to the highest bidder. But Cowle knew this woman dangerous, not the kind to meekly submit.

"She'll kick your ass," Sterner guessed what Cowle contemplated, comment delivered under his breath. Cowle closely observed the woman, moving effortlessly with the lithe grace of a cat prowling along a narrow ledge guiding the bound, blindfolded and gagged girl to join her imprisoned friends. "Her name is Daphne Talbert," Portier noted, caught Cowle's expression. "There's nothing that says an Apprentice or a Collector cannot be a woman." Portier smiled wickedly. "Besides the female can be the more lethal of the species."

"Indeed," Cowle locked his gaze on Gaulten's alluring assistant. Her luminescent face and blue eyes betrayed a smoldering sexual attraction for the elfin young woman defenseless in her grasp. She noticed Cowle's scrutiny from the balcony, smiled at him with burning, unbridled sensuality. Daphne leaned over her bound captive, blew gently into her ear, girl squirming at the sensation, whining in surprise quickly transformed into shock as Daphne dropped her head, tongue grazing across the soft skin of her prisoner's shoulder, inducing from the hostage a shudder, struggling in her grasp. Daphne tightened her hold on the girl, hand cupped under the resisting prisoner's chin, lifting the blindfolded and gagged face towards her. Mewling in panic, the girl felt the moistness of Daphne's lips brush against her gagged mouth, kiss an obscene gesture of wanton affection, wetness of a tongue flicking against her cheek. Daphne's other hand fondled firm breasts, then eased down to her thigh, stroking slowly upwards, pushing the hem of the girl's mini-dress towards her waist, seeking to pleasure a vulnerable spot on the young woman's defenseless anatomy.

Please, some decorum here, Gaulten cleared his throat, glanced at his assistant, expression one of exasperation. *Must you act so scandalously in front of a colleague?*

Daphne licked her lips as one does after a sumptuous meal. *Why not put on a show for our guests*, her manner mischievous, erotically teasing. *Let him know I enjoy the rewards of my profession.*

The unspoken, yet fraught with sexual excitement, exchange between the pair brought forth the germination of an idea in the mind of Marcus Cowle. *Daphne could pass for a college student at Great Northern...and Johann for a professor.* Cowle smiled. *The police are looking for me, but this way I can get close to Samantha without being there.* Wondered if his fellow Collector and his captivating assistant amenable to his proposal. *I'll have to give them a piece of the pie.* But Cowle expected the reward to be a very sizable pie and large enough to share.

Gaulten motioned to his associates, shoving reluctant captives towards the entrance of the chateau. He peered up as he led his hostage inside; Portier and Cowle an audience for his arrival with his enslaved prizes. Gaulten raised a hand to his brow and grinned, offered a jaunty salute to his collaborator from across the Atlantic. *Sorry about what happened in Chicago*, the gesture said. Gaulten nodded, seemed to understand what Cowle considered. *I'd like to discuss business later.*

Fine product you have there. Cowle raised his glass in admiration. *We'll talk.*

"They're taking them to the dungeon," Portier said of the dank, foreboding chamber in the cellar of the chateau Cowle familiar with from previous visits. "Gaulten and his associates will commence the orientation process for our guests before representatives of their new owner arrive later this evening for the exchange." Portier rose from his chair. "You're more than welcome to join us."

"Not in the mood now." Cowle stared into his glass of Bordeaux, swirled the blood red wine around the bottom. "Perhaps later," Cowle demurred politely. "I have things to think about."

Portier wordlessly extended a similar invitation to Sterner. "Hell, why not," Sterner shrugged, stood from his chair. "Should at least say hello, talk shop with them."

"I know you are impatient, my friend, and want to act. But please accept this counsel," Portier again said to Cowle. "There are events afoot and the instability of the world's economy presents an opportunity for The Trading Society not seen in more than a century. Plans are being laid by influential friends, great and wealthy men we have done much business with. If these machinations bear fruit the structure of the world will change forever and The Trading Society will be in position to take full advantage of such opportunity. We will emerge from the shadows, able to operate in the open, live as kings of the Earth."

"I'm intrigued, tell me more," Cowle prompted his mentor, sipping from his glass.

"Sorry, my dear friend, not at this time," Portier returned. "This is a closely guarded secret of The Trading Society. Only when the time comes will the plan be fully revealed." Portier gazed into the horizon, reminiscing of years earlier in London. "Samantha Grayson, she is as beautiful as her mother." The statement took Cowle by surprise, head swung about, staring at his Patron. "Oh yes, I know her mother intimately, years ago when her name was Melanie Barrett." He chuckled. "Let's say a client I dealt with had similar interest then in the mother that Sheik Rahim has now in the daughter." Portier sighed. "That is a story for another day, another time." Not ready to tell the tale, leaving Cowle with curiosity aroused of the connection between his Patron and the mother of Samantha Grayson.

"A pity," Cowle frowned, disappointed. "I do like stories."

"Remember what they say about revenge, my friend," Portier said, heading inside to examine the parcels Gaulten brought, judge their value to his client and set the price for sale, witness the start of their new existence as slaves for sexual pleasure. "For your enemies sitting down at the banquet you've prepared for them there is only one proper way to serve the feast."

On delivering the advice Portier and Sterner departed, left Cowle sitting in the chair watching the sun drop below the horizon of the French countryside. From deep inside the chateau heard muffled, anguished screams from the latest acquisitions of his Patron. In time he'd descend to the depths of the chateau to participate in the activities, make acquaintance of his European counterpart and his enthralling assistant, wished Samantha Grayson one of the helpless prisoners they tortured. As he slowly savored what remained of the Bordeaux, he turned over in his mind the advice Portier offered him. In silence he considered the angles, examined every perspective. The seed of an idea took root, a plan requiring time to grow and bear bitter fruit, required assistance from his fellow Collector Johann Gaulten and his charismatic apprentice Daphne Talbert to realize fulfillment. Now Cowle found wisdom in the sage guidance of his mentor. He did have time; there no need to rush the next act while interfering in the machinations of any other Collector so bold to claim the auburn-haired beauty as their own prize. He'd choose the proper moment to strike, when the defenses of Samantha Grayson lowered, exacting his vengeance on the girl from Great Northern University and her friends. His mentor correct in his appraisal of the nature of revenge.

Cowle spoke to the encroaching dusk, words only he heard in the cool air.

"Best served cold."

About the Author:

Eric Martin is the *nom de plume* of this 1988 graduate of The University of Notre Dame, where he worked as a news reporter on the staff of *The Observer*, the independent student newspaper. When not spending time writing, he puts his bachelor of arts degree in government use to excellent use selling running shoes and spreading the gospel of a healthy lifestyle at Fleet Feet Sports where he also writes and edits copy for the store's website. He does not have an advanced degree in fiction writing, wasn't a lawyer or police officer, didn't serve on some special military force, only has a fertile imagination that has been with him since childhood in Upstate New York. It is his wish to tell an enjoyable tale people might want to take time out of their busy day to read and escape the grind of reality for a few hours.

This is his debut novel under his pen name; expanding on a shorter work originally developed in a Yahoo story group in 1999. He lives in Homewood, Illinois, a suburb south of Chicago, with his rescue greyhound, and sometimes muse, Cubbie.

You can follow his musings on all things in the political and sporting world, along with other random thoughts, on twitter @ericmartinwriter

385